STEEPED IN TRADITIONS OF
THE PAST, PLUNGED INTO A WORLD
OF EXPLOSIVE CH⸻

SIR C⸻   patriarch,
famed   ⸻nizer, and
fiercely⸻   l son home
and m⸻

MICHAE⸻   ⸻pologist by training,
an adventurer by nature, a survivor by necessity.
Born in Hong Kong's slums, his need for respectability
was great—until his need for love became greater.

CATHERINE MORGAN—Young, brilliant, ambitious.
She was barely aware of her unique beauty, her passionate sensuality, until she embarked on the expedition
that entwined her life with Michael's forever.

KARA STANFORD—The pampered daughter of a
powerful Dutch colonial family, she wasn't prepared
for the hardships of war—or for sharing her husband
with another woman.

JULIENNE STANFORD—Possessive of her brother,
Michael, jealous of Catherine, she lived on the edge
of an explosive madness that only waited to be ignited.

PRINCE AHMAD AÇVAVARMAN—The handsome, charis-
matic son of Borneo's greatest sultan. His ambivalence
toward power and his love for Catherine would shape
Indonesia's destiny for years to come.

THEY NEVER DREAMED THEIR LIVES COULD
BE CHANGED BY . . .

THE SEEDS OF SINGING

THE SEEDS OF SINGING

Kay McGrath

A DELL BOOK

Published by
Dell Publishing Co., Inc.
1 Dag Hammarskjold Plaza
New York, New York 10017

To Maggie,
mole holes,
and old friendship

Dell ® TM 681510, Dell Publishing Co., Inc.

ISBN: 0-440-19120-3

Printed in the United States of America

First printing—February 1983

Acknowledgments
I want to thank my editor, Peter Guzzardi, whose skill,
support, patience, and encouragement were invaluable.

In the remote highlands of former Dutch New Guinea, undiscovered until the mid-twentieth century, the Dani people lived a Stone Age existence essentially unchanged from the dawn of man's tenure on earth. The Dani called man's soul his seeds of singing and gave these a physical presence near the heart. The essence of life itself, the seeds had to be carefully guarded against all harm. Unhappiness could wither the tender seeds as surely as a spear could injure them, and such was the link between all men that the death of the seeds of one member of the tribe would weaken the soul of all.

Prologue

Grand Valley, Dutch New Guinea Highlands: 1938

The early-morning mist shrouded snow-peaked Arolik and the surrounding mountains like a shimmering wet spider web, trapping the tall evergreen araucaria trees of the forest in great gray strands. Degewatek, whose name means "spear death" in the language of the Dugum Dani, stood shivering at the top of his fifty-foot-high *kalai*, or watchtower, which reared itself up on three spindly legs from the grassy slope. When the fog cleared, he would be able to see his gardens, and those of his neighbors, as well as keep watch over the no-man's-land which separated his village and its allies from the enemy villages beyond. He stood with his arms folded high around his neck in the characteristic manner of his people, the Dani, farmers and warriors of Dutch New Guinea's central highlands. Degewatek was naked, except for a crown of white egret feathers and the narrow eighteen-inch *horim* strapped around his waist which covered and protected his manhood. These, and a shiny coating of pig grease, were his only protection against the chilly, humid air, but they did little to warm him, and he continued to shiver.

The thin remains of the morning cooking fires rose from the compounds and mingled quickly with the mist. Occasionally the drifting fog parted enough to reveal the pale, sightless orb of the sun, as blinded by the fog as were Degewatek and the other warriors perched on their watchtowers throughout the forty-mile length of the valley. To the Dani, this was *huben sue-ane*, the "time of morning bird voices," but on this day the grasses and surrounding forest were strangely silent. As if confused by the delay of light, the birds watched and waited. Like Degewatek, they were uneasy.

Degewatek peered intently around him and listened for unfamiliar sounds or movements in the tall savanna grasses which might indicate the presence of enemies. Seeing and hearing nothing unusual, he blamed his nervousness on ghosts. He began to sing a song to pacify them, but the notes floated off and were absorbed into the surrounding mist as easily as the trees around him, still leaving him with the uneasy feeling that something was amiss.

He broke off singing. Now he no longer merely sensed the change, but he could hear it as well. It was a noise like distant thunder which approached swiftly, filling the valley with its urgency. It seemed the noise could not grow any louder, yet still it grew. Suddenly, out of the mist, a great gray bird flew directly over him, so low that Degewatek crouched down in the height of his watchtower. The sound it made was deafening, and it struck Degewatek with a terror he had never known. His fear immobilized him for an instant; then, as his years of training as a warrior took over, he grabbed his laurel bow and shot a flurry of arrows at the invading bird. Though still trembling, he felt his confidence return as it appeared he had frightened the intruder away.

He didn't know that the real danger would come later, that the coming of the great gray bird would bring the death of a way of life that had existed for thousands of years, since the first man, Nopu, had gathered up his women, children, bows, bamboo knives, stone adze, and a great bundle of living things and had come to live in the great valley of the Baliem, where his children founded the Dani clans. The descendants of Nopu had lived out their lives in the Stone Age culture which he had brought with him. Unchanged for countless centuries, they remained cut off from the world by the 16,000-foot mountains, perpetual clouds, and dense jungles of the second largest and least-known island in the world.

The Dani have a legend that the birds and snakes once had a race to see if men would die like birds or shed their skins like snakes and live forever. The birds won, so man became mortal, not eternal. When venturesome Dani traders first saw the white man in 1909, far to the south of their own mountains and valley, they had called him *waro*, a creature who was not a man at all but a serpent with the power to shed its mortal skin and live forever. The Dani traders, returning to their isolated valley, had concluded that there would be a new race in some future time. And who would win? The birds, who must die, or the snakes, who were immortal?

Part One

In the Morning
of the Earth

Still the world is wondrous large—
seven seas from marge to marge—
And it holds a vast of various kinds of man. . . .

Rudyard Kipling, "In the Neolithic Age," 1895

Chapter 1
Kalimantan, Borneo, 1939

The tiny white plane flew in low over the South China Sea, catching a first glimpse of the island of Borneo, its tropical rain forests stretching to the southeast in unbroken green splendor. Chartered by the Stanford-Columbia University anthropological expedition, the plane was currently en route from Singapore to the Stanford family plantation in Kalimantan, that vast area of southern Borneo that had been part of the Dutch East Indies since the 1600's. Aboard were an assistant professor of anthropology and two graduate students, arriving early to assist with plans and preparations for the expedition. In two months they would be followed by an extensive entourage including several prestigious academics. Once the group was assembled, its members planned to fly to the Asmat region of Dutch New Guinea, some 1,600 miles east of Borneo across the Makassar Strait and Celebes Sea.

Leaving the coastal swamps and marshes behind, the plane skimmed dizzily over the endless sea of trees that stretched from the forest floor to the sky in a chaotic competition for sunlight. The inevitable winners, the mengaris trees, often reached a height of 250 feet. Even the ocean had not given the plane's four occupants as much of a feeling of vastness as did the living emerald sea below them now. Underneath that impenetrable canopy of trees moved rhinos, elephants, leopards, deer, anteaters, orangutans, monkeys, bears, lemurs, rodents, 600 species of birds, and an endless variety of reptiles and insects, including cobras, deadly poisonous kraits, thirty-foot pythons, six-foot monitor lizards, and seven-inch centipedes. This remarkable diversification of living things was a vestige of the great Glacier Age, when the islands of the Indies were linked by land to the Asian continent.

Along the ribbons of river winding through the mountains and down to the coast, occasional small clearings appeared, marked by single longhouses in which lived entire villages of several hundred people. Resting on slender stilts, these thatched 150-foot dwellings resembled fat centipedes drinking at the water's edge. The Iban tribes, famous for their fierce headhunting way of life, lived here in remote regions which had little contact with Dutch government patrols.

Picking out the Barito River from among its central mountain tributaries, the pilot turned south, pursuing that winding artery to Maitreya, the Stanford rubber and copra plantation on the Barito banks north of the small city of Banjarmasin. After seven hours of flight the plane set down on the plantation airstrip. From it alighted Dr. Donald Seabaugh, Julienne Stanford, and Catherine Morgan, all three tired but elated. Julienne's joy was that of a traveler returning home; Seabaugh and Catherine's was that of explorers who had successfully left all that was familiar behind.

Julienne Stanford climbed out of the plane first and walked purposefully across the field. She stood alone for a moment at the end of the runway, waiting for the others. She was almost twenty-eight years old, small-boned and boyishly thin with her hair cut pixie-short so that she scarcely looked older than a child. Standing there in baggy khaki slacks rolled up above well-worn tennis shoes, she could see a broad sweep of immaculate lawn sloping down toward the road, which was out of sight. Surrounding the field and the road, the jungle edged as close as it could.

"Papa will be waiting for us at the house," Julienne said in a clipped British accent to the other young woman who had just climbed out of the plane. Like Julienne, Catherine wore slacks. Her dark hair was poked up beneath a long-brimmed cap which hid her face in its shade. For the past year the two women had been roommates in one of the boarding houses that accommodated many of the graduate women students at Columbia.

"I can't wait to meet him," Catherine said. Julienne's father, Sir Charles Stanford, was anthropology's most eminent figure.

14

His psychoanalytically based theories on the interaction of culture and personality and his use of psychological tests in his field research had revolutionized the entire discipline.

"No, I suppose not," Julienne replied with a tinge of regret often felt by the daughters of famous fathers. She had never liked sharing him with admiring colleagues, the general public, or even other members of her own family. The small shiver of an old jealousy passed through her. She shook it off.

A short distance to the east, purple mountain peaks, swirling with clouds and mists, rose high above the rain forest. To the south stretched the coastal plain in whose lateritic soil thrived over one hundred square miles of Pará rubber trees imported from the Amazon fifty years earlier by the Stanfords. They had been the first to introduce South American rubber to the Indies.

"I always hate leaving this place," Julienne said. "Each time I'm afraid it might not be here when I come back, that the jungle will have swallowed it." She smiled at the absurdity. "When I was a little girl, it was just the opposite. I was certain Maitreya would always be here but that I would disappear if I ever left it. Silly, wasn't I?"

Catherine didn't answer. Intrigued by a glimpse of the house through the trees, she had been drawn to the middle of the road for a better view. Seeing her curiosity, Julienne laughed. "It scandalized the Indies when it was built one hundred and twenty-five years ago. It's a native house."

Servants, barefooted and dressed in immaculate white pants and shirts with bright swaths of cloth tied about their foreheads, were hurrying down the road toward the airfield to help unload the plane. Without waiting for her colleagues, Catherine began to walk in the direction they had come, searching as she went for another look at the house. It was totally hidden by the thick canopy of trees that covered the road. As she rounded the bend, the forest abruptly ended. She stopped and caught her breath. Before her rose the most famous house in the Indies.

Some one-hundred-twenty-five feet in length, it was constructed in the Minangkabau style of Sumatra. The high, saddle-backed thatch roof soared to sixty feet and had jutting peaks at either end. Three miniature versions of the house rested on the ridge of the roof to house the family spirits. The shingled and wooden sides of the house were elaborately carved and brightly painted with geometrical and floral motifs. A low-walled stone terrace, open at intervals to accommodate steps, surrounded the structure. On one side of the house the lawn sloped down to the wide river. On the other the huge dark wall of the rain forest plunged in a chaotic tangle to the very edge of the neatly trimmed grass and abruptly stopped, held back by an invisible barrier of English orderliness and determination. In addition to warding off the jungle's advances, the house had survived a century of attacks by Iban headhunters who came down the river from the mountains attempting to reclaim the land from which the English had driven them. Only within the past fifteen years had an end been put to the raids.

As Catherine stood on the road, admiring Maitreya, the brilliant colors suddenly faded from the scene. One of the clouds racing across the sky had hidden the sun, but nothing could dim her first impression of this monument to English endurance that the first white rajahs of Kalimantan had built in the midst of this wild land. Maitreya, named for the Buddhist god of the future. Guide out of darkness to the source of all light.

Chapter 2

Catherine Morgan dressed early in order to enjoy the sunset and beauty of the estate grounds alone before dinner. Although tired from the flight from Singapore, she had been too excited to rest since arriving that afternoon. She now wore a black, halter-neck evening dress which flared gracefully from her slender form when she moved. The few large, dramatic rose hibiscuses printed on the dress were her only decoration. Her straight black hair hung simply down her back, and she wore no makeup. She needed none. She was dark and lovely in an exotic way that could hardly be improved.

At age twenty-five Catherine had never before left the United States, traveled by ship, lived outside a city, stayed in a hotel by herself, or even spent an entire day alone, for that matter. Now, about to embark on six months of fieldwork, gathering data for her doctoral dissertation in anthropology, she had done, or would soon do, all these things under what would be difficult—and possibly dangerous—circumstances. Whereas some women her age might have felt intimidated, Catherine did not. On the contrary, she enjoyed the prospect of adventure, a fact her family found difficult to accept. Catherine had often mused ruefully that if she had chosen to become a native witch doctor instead of an anthropologist they might have considered it less bizarre. Religion, at least, was something her family understood.

Catherine's father was a federal district judge and respected legal scholar who was known for the fairness of his rulings and the harshness of his sentences. He had been a successful trial lawyer before taking the bench. Her mother was the daughter of a wealthy Chicago clothing merchant. She was devoted to her social role as the wife of a leading citizen and patroness of the arts. In her mother's view, classical music, if not taken too seriously, was an appropriate pastime for a young woman until she could be successfully wed. Living in jungles, unchaperoned, decidedly was not. Her father did not share her mother's opinion that an academic education was wasted on well-bred young women but he did not approve of Catherine's choice of a career. "Savages should be left to missionaries," he told her. Unlike her mother, he was not religious, but he believed primitive societies exhibited aspects of man's nature better quickly modified than closely studied.

Throughout the afternoon, Catherine had heard other planes arriving, landing on the airstrip or on the nearby river. Tonight would be a special occasion to welcome Julienne home and to greet the first arrivals of the Stanford anthropological expedition. Because of the investment in time and effort necessary to attend social events in the vast river region, guests at Maitreya would come for dinner and stay for days.

Abandoning the path she had been following, Catherine moved into the fringes of the surrounding forest just as the sun began going down behind the towering mengaris trees. As if on cue, the crickets and cicadas began to tune up. Monkeys chattered and quarreled in the high branches out of sight. Birds came home to join them. As day began to turn into night, nature seemed full of expectation.

The sky now burned a brilliant orange and pink. Huge cumulus clouds, outsized like every other aspect of this island, drifted by like enchanted golden castles. The air of enchantment hung about her. It was humid, warm, breathless. Falling under the spell of the evening, Catherine stretched out her arms, returning the evening's embrace. The sweet scent of jasmine and frangipani and the pungent odor of fermenting fruit mingled with the sights and sounds to fill her senses.

Catherine moved deeper into the forest. Here the leafy canopy was so thick that there was little undergrowth. She could see that no light penetrated the heart of the forest at all during the day,

18

but at night the forest found magic ways to illuminate itself. Fireflies danced, glittering and twinkling through the trees. Glow-worms trailed light over fallen tree trunks. Mushrooms glowed yellow-green beneath their umbrella caps. A peculiar moss, resembling iridescent dust, was scattered about the decaying forest floor like fairy trails. The air here was even heavier, if possible, redolent of the musty odor of decay.

Almost reluctantly Catherine turned back toward the house, unaware of a man watching her with interest as she concentrated on the path before her. She was ten yards away when she looked up in surprise, startled to see him leaning against the wall of the house, gazing at her with cool gray eyes. He appeared to be about thirty, wearing boots and khaki work clothes. He wore no hat, but a bright red bandanna had been folded and tied around his forehead to absorb the perspiration of an afternoon's work in the intense heat. The sun had bleached his hair a bright reddish blond, and it tumbled over his headband in appealing dishevelment. As she neared him, she could see that he was very handsome.

She paused for a moment, overcome by an uncharacteristic shyness, followed by the slight resentment she always felt toward good-looking men—as if they had committed some offense by being born too attractive. Surprised by him, she had forgotten that she, too, had been born into that special group for whom heads would always turn, eyes would always follow.

From where he stood he could feel the young woman's reserve, and it puzzled him. He noted that in an age of bright lipstick, rouge, and permanent waves, she wore her beauty plainly, as though, he thought, in apology or penance. If that was her intent, she did not succeed. If anything, her disregard for her beauty only enhanced it. Seeing that she was not coming closer, he spoke, pushing himself away from the wall and moving toward her as he did. "You're Catherine, of course. I'm Julienne's brother, Michael." The warmth of his smile belied the cool gray of his eyes.

Catherine had time to observe that he had an American accent and did not in any way resemble Julienne before she smiled in return and extended her hand, feeling her own coolness disappear. After a brief exchange of pleasantries Michael excused himself to change for dinner. There was nothing extraordinary about the meeting, yet she found herself dwelling on it. No, on him. As she stood alone in the garden, she tried to recall what Julienne had told her about her brother. She remembered that he was married and had two young daughters. She also knew that Michael had gone to Harvard as an undergraduate and received his Ph.D. in anthropology from Oxford. Like generations of Stanfords before him, he had led extensive anthropological and archaeological explorations throughout Borneo, New Guinea, the Philippines, and the Solomon Islands. He would be acting as guide for the upcoming expedition to New Guinea.

Catherine came back into the main house through the study, a room filled with works of Oceanic art from throughout New Guinea and the South Seas: marvelous masks and carvings, fierce, feathered, and sometimes amusingly pornographic. She paused to view the family portraits and photographs which occupied the tables and desk. Strange, she thought. She found one formal portrait of Michael when he was about eight years old, dressed in a suit and looking very serious, but it wasn't until he was fourteen or so that he began to appear with the other children in the numerous informal family snapshots that filled the room. She was puzzled. The only explanation seemed to be that for some reason, he had been absent from the family until that point. Yet Julienne had never mentioned it. Catherine stared at the photos, then finally turned away to join the gathering guests for dinner.

Chapter 3

The time of kings was over. True kings, that is, the ones with divine and absolute power. But if the sultan of Matapura recognized that fact, he didn't show it. He continued to gaze upon the world with the same disdainful and proprietary air with which his ancestors had viewed it for the past six hundred years. He was seated in the Stanford dining room, next to Sir Charles. As a living god, it did not befit his position to mingle with the guests during the cocktail hour, so the moment of his arrival had marked the beginning of dinner. Since this was a celebration, a traditional Indonesian rice-table was being served. It had begun with a parade of servants bearing a large mound of rice on a tray followed by plates of spicy meatballs; numerous fowl dishes; wild boar; pickled, spice-boiled, fried, and dried fish; shrimp; sea turtle eggs; noodles; grated fried bananas; roasted nuts; shredded coconuts; cucumbers; hot chiles; hot bamboo shoots; and eight bowls of spices and curries.

The light of hundreds of candles reflected brightly off the highly polished table and sparkled in the crystal, silver, and china settings. Bouquets of tropical flowers filled the center of the table and scented the air. However exotic the setting, nothing in it equaled the presence of the sultan himself. He was a handsome man in his early fifties, with fine features and the heavy-lidded eyes of the Javanese Matarams from which ancient Hindu empire his own Açvavarman dynasty had descended. He was dressed in a short batik jacket and a long gold silk skirt or *kain*, slit up the middle. Beneath it were dark silk breeches. His blue turban was covered with flowers whose petals were made of clusters of precious stones and whose leaves were sculptured gold. A huge sapphire called Smile of Surprise was set in a simple ring on his first finger. He was barefoot, but his feet rested upon a gold silk cushion beneath the table. Beside him sat the Ratu, his favorite wife and queen. She was French and, at fifty, still beautiful. Her dark hair was pulled into a chignon and her hair was covered with a crown of tiny white flowers and diamonds. She wore a green silk sarong that matched her eyes and large diamond and emerald earrings.

Twice a year the sultan took the royal barge upriver on a trip of several weeks, visiting his subjects and making offerings in the ancient Hindu temples and monuments crumbling in the jungle. Like most of the Indonesian population, the sultan was Moslem, but it was a thin religious veneer through which the Hindu mysticism and the spirit beliefs of an earlier age shone strongly through. This time he had made the journey to coincide with Julienne's homecoming in order to show his high regard for the Stanfords. The sultan was ten years younger than Sir Charles. Unlike their sons, who were close friends, their ties were based on history and tradition rather than personal friendship. In the early nineteenth century Sir James Stanford, an English baronet and adventurer with command of his own fleet and small private army, had helped the sultan of Matapura rid his coast of Buginese pirates. As a reward, the sultan had made Sir James a *rajah*, a local king, and granted him land along the Barito for a British settlement. Soon a flourishing independent colony of English copra, sugar, and tea planters, Malay small farmers and village craftsmen, Arab merchants and traders, Chinese mine owners and entrepreneurs, and primitive Dyak tribesmen had developed in the only area of the Indies not controlled by the Dutch—at least not yet.

The Dutch conquest of the Indies had begun in the late sixteenth century when a group of Dutch burghers attempted to gain a monopoly on the spice trade. By 1858, having consolidated their hold on the rest of the Indies, the Dutch turned their attention to south Borneo. After a series of skirmishes, the British were defeated. Sir Charles's great-grandfather and the other English planters were allowed to retain the land they had already settled but the remainder of the English rajah's holdings was given over to the Dutch government, and the colony became a part of the Dutch Indies. The sultan of Matapura, who had fought on the side of the British, also fell under Dutch rule, though he still retained semi-autonomous authority over the more remote regions of his old kingdom.

Tonight there were no Dutch present among the guests dining at Maitreya, which was a relief to the sultan, who despised the Dutch as an unimaginative and uncultured people. Not that he had expected any Dutch officials to be here this evening. Sir Charles was quarreling with them again. Two Indonesian friends of Sir Charles had been among those recently arrested at Batavia in the middle of the night and sent to the notorious Boven Digul exile camp in New Guinea. They had been sentenced, without trial, for distributing literature advocating full equality for the Indonesian people and independence within a Dutch commonwealth. With a recessed world economy and the increasing threat of war in Europe, the Dutch had become even more oppressive toward those who challenged their authority in the Indies. Even the word *Indonesian* had been outlawed as a subversive precolonial term.

Sir Charles held a position of power in the Volksraad, the colonial advisory body, where he had vigorously protested the arrests but to no avail. Speaking out in the Volksraad supposedly carried immunity from prosecution but the government-controlled press had begun to attack Sir Charles with hints of treason and demanded he be removed from all positions of political influence. The hysteria would die down where he personally was concerned, but the danger to the fledging movement for Indonesian independence—which he supported—was great.

Except for the American anthropologists and a trade delegation from Japan, the Stanford guests were local English planters and Indonesian leaders, all well known to the sultan. The presence of the Japanese disturbed the sultan, especially the military contingent dressed in civilian clothes. They had probably come along to recruit spies from among the local population. Aware of the harsh treatment the Japanese army had meted out to Chinese civilians during the current war, the sultan saw no reason why he

23

should trust the Japanese or look to them as potential liberators, as did many of his countrymen.

Aware that Roosevelt had proposed a naval blockade of Japan to protest Japanese aggression in China, the Japanese had begun to intensify their effort to obtain oil and other raw materials from the Indies. Though British Prime Minister Chamberlain had refused to support Roosevelt's proposal, Sir Charles agreed with the American President that a policy of appeasement toward Japanese acts of aggression would inevitably lead to the war all parties hoped to avoid, so Sir Charles had instituted his own trade embargo. He had refused to renew his agreement to sell rubber to Japan and he had convinced other planters along the Barito to do the same. To save Japanese face and avoid confrontation, the reasons for the refusal were given as production problems. Tonight Sir Charles had seen to it that the Japanese were royally entertained. Although displeased by the refusal, they were appreciative of the grace with which it had been delivered, enabling dinner to proceed in social harmony.

Admiral Inoye, head of the Japanese delegation, sat opposite the Ratu. From here he had a clear view of Matapura's sultan, whose kingdom held some of Borneo's richest oil fields. Though devoted to his emperor, the admiral had no use for other Asian potentates, whom he viewed as weak, pampered, and effete. How else could they have been corrupt enough to surrender their people into colonial captivity and continue to endure it with so little resistance? The admiral had overcome a sickly and overprotected childhood to rise to great power. Despite his coldness he had an exceedingly polite and charming manner and thus was an excellent negotiator. He had spent years in the United States as a naval attaché, spoke excellent English, and knew America's strength. Like Admiral Yamamoto, he vehemently opposed war with the United States on the grounds it could not be won, yet he pursued Japanese expansion into Asia as a holy war to free it from colonialism and Communism. Their differences notwithstanding, he admired Sir Charles, who had a reputation among Japanese liberals as an unprejudiced man sympathetic to Asian aspirations for freedom. He perceived Sir Charles as a man like himself, an aristocrat with a socialist's heart. On the spur of the moment Inoye leaned across Julienne, seated next to her father, and delivered a warning. "In the spirit of friendship, I must tell you that you gain nothing by your refusal except Japanese ill will and financial loss. If we don't buy rubber from you, we will get it from your British countrymen in Malaya.''

Sir Charles was momentarily surprised by the directness of the remark, but he recovered to reply softly, ''Withdraw from China with a negotiated peace and you will get all the rubber you want from me. Otherwise, get it elsewhere as you can. We both know it will be neither equal to mine in quality nor enough to fully meet your needs.''

Catherine sat at the other end of the table, unaware of the tension elsewhere in the room. Fascinated by the presence of the sultan, she scarcely paid attention to the conversation around her. The royal gamelon orchestra had come with him. They sat on the floor in the corner of the room using gongs and drums and xylophonelike instruments to make a strangely muted music. The Stanford servants, also the sultan's subjects, crouched on the floor to serve him, scurrying about like agile crabs, none of them daring to raise themselves above the sultan's sacred head.

Michael Stanford arrived late for dinner. Fascinated by the sultan, Catherine had forgotten him. She looked up in surprise just as Michael passed her chair. Momentarily distracted, she almost spilled her glass of wine. Flushed with embarrassment at her reaction, she steadied her glass and raised her eyes only to find them rudely locked by a pair of unfamiliar eyes even darker than her own. They belonged to a man of Michael's age who had entered the room with him and taken a seat beside the Ratu. His handsome face was too dark to be entirely European, yet he was dressed in formal European evening clothes which he wore with a casual elegance that bespoke complete familiarity. His eyes held hers for a moment, studying her carefully and then abruptly dismissing her to turn their attention elsewhere. Catherine felt mildly annoyed that she had not been the one to end the encounter, but he was not a man from whom one could easily turn away.

''Who is he?'' she asked of the blond young woman with the short, fashionably curled hair who presided over this end of the table, opposite Sir Charles.

''Prince Ahmad Açvavarman,'' Kara Stanford replied. ''The sultan's heir.''

Kara was Michael's wife. Sir Charles had been a widower for fourteen years, so Kara, who would be mistress of Maitreya in her own right one day, had assumed the role of his hostess. Warm, gracious, and very beautiful in a fragile way, Kara had become like a daughter to him. The only member of the immediate Stanford family not present was Margit, Julienne's older sister. She had remained in the capital at Batavia. Margit's husband, a high-ranking and ambitious Dutch official, had found it advantageous to his career to absent himself from his father-in-law's home for the time being. Margit had not argued with him. She shared her father's preference for remaining in an unhappy marriage rather than seek a divorce. She had sent her regrets to Julienne with no explanations. None were needed.

Dinner was suddenly over. The sultan had risen to leave and the other guests were drifting outside to see him off. He was met by his escorts—tall, proud-looking men, naked to the waist and wearing patterned kains. One of them carried the gold-fringed parasol that was the mark of royalty. Each had a curved-blade *kris* stuck in the back of his wide belt. Their hair was tied in single pigtails which protruded from the bottom of their tall gold conical hats. The procession was met at the river by assorted courtiers, villagers, and children who had found room on the accompanying boats. Anyone was free to come, just as any one of the sultan's subjects could enter the palace, eat food, and bask in his reflected glory. The court was the center of Matapuran culture, the keeper of its theater and art. The sultan himself was a symbol of their identity.

The sultan never traveled except by palanquin or boat. Matapura owned limousines and airplanes and yachts, but they were luxuries purchased by the sultan's ministers. He never used them. As a young man he had traveled a great deal in the world. He had seen Paris in 1917 at the same time that he had visited the trenches at Verdun and on returning home to Borneo he had turned his back on the modern world. Civilization, he believed, was not measured by technological advances, but rather by how much a country loved its young, revered its old, honored its gods, and lived in harmony with its natural surroundings.

As the sultan reached the river, his subjects bent to touch their foreheads to the ground, rising, when he passed, to board the numerous escort boats. The Japanese had already departed, bound by plane for Banjarmasin and then to Batavia, where they hoped to persuade the Dutch governor-general to sell them oil. The

Sultan's son had also left, to attend a clandestine meeting of the Indonesian socialist party. The sultan did not share his son's political beliefs. The only utopia the sultan believed in was spiritual. Yet he knew something close to physical paradise existed in Matapura. Something fragile. And so he had closed his kingdom to outside influences in order to preserve it. As long as the Dutch had his permission to develop Matapura's rich oilfields, they were content to leave him alone.

He stepped onto his barge, an unimposing vessel, its only touch of opulence the gold stool that served as his throne. He sat down and looked back toward Maitreya. In the glow of the torchlight he could just barely make out the faces of the Europeans gathered on the riverbank. However pleasant the evening had been, the sultan was certain it had seemed to them a night no different from a hundred others. Yet even before he had arrived at Maitreya, he had known it would not be. He had seen it predicted in the hornbill's flight and heard it in the forest's voices. But even if he could persuade those present of his ability to foresee the future, it was unlikely his warnings would have been heeded. As a student of ancient history, the sultan knew the Rubicon had already been crossed: for all of them, including himself, the point of no return had been reached.

He closed his eyes, shutting out the faces, and gave the signal to depart, leaving the remaining guests to return to the house for drinks.

Chapter 4

Harriet Dunston, the Countess Tremont, sat in the living room after dinner, sipping cognac and studying the guests. She was in her early thirties, a pretty woman with dark brown hair pulled into a neat chignon on the top of her head. Her skin was fair and pleasantly covered with freckles. Harriet's mother had once promised her that they would go away when she grew up, but they never had. Now, however, they gave her a seductive air of wicked innocence. She was seated on the fringes of a heated discussion on the possibility of war in Europe, not paying the least bit of attention. Sizing up people at a party was Harriet's favorite pastime, and she was indulging it now. It was a talent greatly appreciated by her diplomat husband, John Dunston, Earl of Tremont, the current British ambassador to Japan, and a cousin of the king.

At one time, years ago, Harriet had secretly hoped that Michael Stanford might marry her. She had been the most eligible girl around: intelligent, attractive, and from one of Kalimantan's most prominent families. The age difference (he was two years younger) had never been important, as Michael had always seemed more mature than other boys his age. But all her dreams had come to nothing. Michael had never shown any romantic or sexual feelings toward her. At first this had baffled and angered her. She had felt humiliated—since her own feelings must have been so obvious. She had even wondered if he might be homosexual. Not one to forever pursue lost causes (she enjoyed herself too much), she had immersed herself in London's social life, ignoring but never quite forgetting Michael Stanford. She had already been married to John Dunston for three years when she heard of Michael's marriage in Batavia to Kara van Hooton, a niece of the governor-general designate. It had surprised and angered her at the time. She had never expected Michael would choose a Dutch wife, let alone one so close to the colonial establishment. After all, he opposed Dutch policies. Harriet had not been any more pleased when she had met Kara for the first time. She had found her blond, beautiful, and somewhat vacuous—content to run the house and care for her two young daughters, just the kind of woman Harriet would have expected Michael to be oblivious of. Even now, after five years, the reason for Michael's choice seemed no clearer to her. Harriet could only conclude that Michael had married Kara precisely because she was uninterested in everything he did, leaving him free to go about his business alone, as he preferred.

Tonight Harriet had to admit to herself that Kara could be charming in a girlish way, and she obviously adored Michael. He, in turn, appeared to be very fond of her. He was always thoughtful and attentive in her presence, even affectionate and relaxed, something Harriet had never seen in him before.

For the past few minutes Harriet had been observing Julienne, who now stood talking to Harriet's brother, Philip. Julienne had changed since the last time Harriet had seen her. She seemed more outgoing and animated, and yet there was a disturbing intensity about her gaiety. Julienne had always been so shy. Only Michael had ever really paid attention to her. Poor thing, Harriet thought. Michael had always been his father's favorite child.

From Julienne, Harriet's roving eye was drawn to the beautiful young American who sat in the chair to her right. While the woman seemed to be part of a heated discussion on Hitler, her thoughts, Harriet noted, appeared to be elsewhere. Her curiosity aroused, Harriet followed the woman's gaze across the room to where it rested steadily on Michael Stanford, intensely engaged in conversation with two neighboring planters. Upon discovering the source of the distraction, Harriet smiled to herself and turned back in time to see the woman anxiously look away from Michael, as if her thoughts had disturbed her. Her eyes, meeting Harriet's, seemed startled, and a slight flush of embarrassment crossed her face as she realized her preoccupation had been noticed—for the second time that evening.

Harriet leaned over to whisper in friendly conspiratorial tones, "Don't be embarrassed. People should never feel guilty for what they think. Only for what they do." Harriet swept her empty glass around the room. "Otherwise, where Michael Stanford is concerned, every woman in here would be in jail for obscenity." She turned back to the woman and cocked her head slightly with a lazy smile that never failed to put people at their ease. "I don't believe we've met. I'm Harriet Dunston. You're one of the Americans, aren't you?"

The woman's composure quickly returned. Eyes—frank, intelligent, and not without a hint of wariness—looked squarely at Harriet. "I'm Catherine Morgan."

"Catherine . . ." Harriet absorbed the name on her tongue as she might have done her last sip of cognac. "Do you mind a piece of advice?" She did not wait for an answer. "You can look, but don't try to touch. I know. I've pursued him myself." She gave a husky laugh. "Even after I was married."

Catherine felt annoyed—more with herself than with her new acquaintance. Her pride had been hurt by Harriet's advice, but she had to acknowledge the accuracy of the observation. Much as it bothered her, she was finding herself drawn to Michael Stanford, a fact her disciplined scholar's mind could not help rejecting like a wandering thought at exam time. She gave Harriet a controlled smile. "He's very attractive, I must admit, but I should add that I'm not in the market either. David, my fiancé, will be here in a few weeks. We're both part of the New Guinea expedition." With David she felt safe.

Harriet stood up with her empty glass of cognac. "I'm going to get another one of these. Why don't we go out on the terrace and talk? Neither of us seems terribly involved in what's going on here. All these men seem to be able to talk about is the coming war in Europe."

A few moments later Catherine picked up her unfinished glass of brandy and followed Harriet to some rattan chairs on the terrace. The tree frogs still serenaded. Harriet sipped her drink quietly for a moment, listening. Her white silk gown, wrapped like a sari, leaving one shoulder bare, seemed alive in the moonlight. Opposite her, Catherine ignored her drink and stared at the moon overhead. Under Harriet's scrutiny she felt some of her earlier embarrassment return.

Harriet broke the silence. "I hope you weren't too offended by what I said. He turns the head of any woman he meets, of course," Harriet continued. "He always has, ever since he came here."

"Since he came here?" Catherine seized the opportunity to divert attention from herself. "Wasn't he born here?"

"No. He's Charles Stanford's illegitimate son. You didn't know that?"

"No," Catherine acknowledged. "Julienne said only that Michael was her brother."

"Half brother," corrected Harriet. "He came here when he was fourteen, after his mother died. It caused quite a scandal, needless to say. Lady Stanford was still alive at the time. But people got used to it—though I doubt that Lady Stanford did." Harriet took a sip of her drink. "His mother was a student of Sir Charles's in one of his countless visiting seminars at some eastern university in America. He was, and still is, always guest lecturing somewhere. He likes playing God to students, and of course, many of his women students have fallen madly in love with him over the years. Michael's mother was no exception, although she distinguished herself by becoming Charles's mistress. She was only eighteen. He brought her here to Banjarmasin, the town on the river. When she became pregnant, Charles refused to divorce his wife. Michael's mother's family, strict Irish Catholics, had already disowned her for running off with Charles, so she ran away again. Charles was beside himself, I gather. He had detectives searching for her, but it took eight years before he finally found her in Hong Kong.

"I know very little of what happened in those years before Michael came to Maitreya. He has always refused to talk about it. I do know that Charles took Michael and his mother to San Francisco after he found them and bought them a house in Berkeley, near the university, where Charles had friends who could look out for her in his absence. She refused to come back to the Indies, so he visited them often there. When Michael's mother died, Charles brought Michael here, to Maitreya, over his wife's adamant oppositon. She had put up with his endless affairs

31

without so much as a word of protest, but bringing home his bastard son was too much to ask. Still, Charles did it in spite of her." Harriet paused, thinking over that last remark. "Michael has always been very special to him. Sometimes I think Michael's mother must have been the only woman Charles ever really loved." Harriet leaned back, lit a cigarette, and was suddenly silent.

"Then why," Catherine asked, "didn't he divorce his wife and marry her?"

"Supposedly his father, old Lawrence Stanford, threatened to disinherit him. He didn't approve of Charles's way of life. But who knows what really stopped him? English law did not easily permit divorce—it still doesn't. Dutch law either." Harriet's face glowed briefly as she paused to draw on her cigarette. "Anyway, he has given Michael the unconditional love he withheld from Michael's mother. Charles adopted Michael, and when Edward, Charles's elder son, was drowned, Michael became heir to Charles's title, the estates here, and those in England. Everything."

Harriet looked away to Maitreya's exotic jungle. "I suppose Stanford men have always been irresistible to women. Sir Charles accommodates them all while Michael accommodates none, except his wife, of course. He's a devoted family man as far as I or anyone else can tell. There's never been even a hint of scandal where he's concerned." She gave an exaggerated sigh. "Such a pity for us all, isn't it? So you see, I simply wanted to spare you the pain of discovering the hard way that Michael Stanford doesn't like women very much. Neither does his father. Michael is just more honest about it."

Harriet looked into the living room to where Kara had just gone up to stand beside Michael. His arm rested lightly and affectionately around her shoulders. "And that dislike includes that silly wife of his, though he probably doesn't know it." She finished her cognac and set it down emphatically upon a nearby table. "Oh, well, ignorance is bliss, or so it seems."

Catherine couldn't see Harriet's expression, but she knew Harriet wasn't joking this time. She heard the anger in her voice. She's still in love with him, Catherine thought in surprise, and for some reason the realization disturbed her.

Sir Charles joined them. He bent down to give Harriet an affectionate kiss.

"Charles," Harriet mildly chided him, "whatever has possessed you to put up all that money to send this poor girl—not to mention Michael, Julienne, and all the others—off to New Guinea with a war about to start?"

Sir Charles sat down on the chair arm beside Harriet. "If there is going to be war, then that is all the more reason to go now. This may be our last chance to study many of these primitive societies. Missionaries and the rising tide of Western culture have already destroyed the old ways of life in many areas before we had the chance to record them. All of us in anthropology have been feeling the pressure to do what we can before it's too late." Sir Charles paused to light a cigarette. "Of course, I'm not the one taking chances this time. I'm too old. Michael will look after this one, and Dr. Ryder, from Columbia, will be handling the research side of it."

They were silent for a moment before Harriet observed sadly, "Well, Catherine, the depressing talk of war seems to have followed us to the terrace. My fault. And I'm the one who said we should escape it."

The sweet smell of native mosquito repellent set out by the servants drifted across the terrace. Harriet tried to change the mood. "As a career diplomat's wife I've had to rough it as much as any anthropology fieldworker." She laughed. "You should have seen some of the consulate assignments John got when we were first married eight years ago!"

They talked lightly on, careful to avoid politics, but neither the languid tropical night nor the sound of laughter drifting from the living room could dispel the feeling that the mention of war had produced. Harriet broke the undeclared moratorium.

"I'm going home, Charles. I'm taking the children with me to England. I'm not going back to Tokyo." She ignored his surprise and continued with an urgency uncharacteristic of her. "John will stay in Japan, of course. But I think Philip and his family should consider leaving Borneo as soon as possible. You should leave, too, Charles. All of you here in the Indies have such an unrealistic view. I came here to try and persuade my brother to stay no more than another year, but Philip insists nothing will happen, or that it won't happen for at least five years. Haven't you all heard the rumors of Japanese atrocities against civilians in China? They say two hundred thousand people were slaughtered in Nanking. And there have been attacks on Westerners in the streets of Tokyo while the police stood by and did nothing. I'm afraid for you all!''

Harriet looked at her brother conversing amiably with Michael in the living room. ''Perhaps we ought to sell them whatever they want. John feels we should. If President Roosevelt cuts off their oil supply because of their war with China, then they'll surely try to take the Indies' oil and rubber by force.'' She shrugged and leaned forward, stabbing out her cigarette. ''Perhaps nothing will stop them. Maybe they will take it anyway.''

A chill moved through the warm night air. Catherine felt the sharp grip of fear for the first time since she had left America, but her ambition and strong will quickly overcame it. She wanted to finish her degree. She would rather face the possibility of death than the certainty of failure.

When Catherine reentered the living room sometime later, Michael Stanford was no longer there. With some alarm she noted that the evening suddenly seemed uninteresting, even empty, without him. She determined for the second time to force him from her thoughts and keep him there.

Chapter 5

The canopied boat sat very low in the water under the weight of its twelve passengers. The alien sound of its straining engine startled the river into watchful silence as the patrol boat made its slow but determined way toward the village of Wiat Kargas. A machine gun poked its hot metal nose over the bow. In the stern Dutch District Officer Voorhoeve was sweating profusely not only from the heat but from the fear he always felt on these patrols.

Voorhoeve took off his bush hat and wiped his face and neck with his handkerchief. He hated sweat. It was so untidy, the dark stains upon freshly laundered khaki, the damp wrinkles pressing into his khaki shorts whenever he sat. So now he stood, holding on to the canopy pole with a white-knuckled grip while sweat trickled down through the bleached hair on his bare legs to dampen the tops of his socks.

Ordinarily Voorhoeve avoided patrols, leaving them to the boat's other passengers: a young Dutch army lieutenant, five Dutch soldiers, and five Javanese recruits, who were part of the small military unit stationed at the Dutch district headquarters in Agats. Despite his twenty years with the colonial service, primitive cultures still frightened and offended Voorhoeve. In the year he had been at Agats, Voorhoeve had moved quickly to pacify the region, burning those villages that did not comply with the ban on taking heads. Some officials in the Dutch New Guinea capital of Hollandia said he had moved too fast, creating tension and increasing the danger of eventual confrontation between the Dutch outpost and the natives. Taking heads was the key part of Asmat ritual and ceremonial life. Without first taking a head, a boy couldn't become a man or marry. Such customs took time to change, but Voorhoeve had been anxious to pacify the area quickly so that exploitation of its resources might take place as rapidly as possible, earning him the approval of his superiors.

Since then Voorhoeve had come to his own conclusion that New Guinea was worthless real estate (aside from the interior, which was unknown), composed only of cannibals, unhealthy jungle swamps, and the world's largest and most vicious insects. He replaced his hat and suddenly felt his brow knit together in the beginnings of a headache. It was, he reminded himself, anthropologists who were the current cause of this patrol, specifically the American expedition which would soon be arriving in the Asmat. Voorhoeve swore under his breath at the thought—as if that Catholic missionary wasn't enough of a nuisance for him to put up with.

Wiat Kargas had supposedly been the victim of a headhunting raid only a week ago. With the expedition impending Voorhoeve had decided to investigate the report himself, taking along eight extra men on patrol as a show of force. So far he had turned up two suspicious skulls in the last village downriver, skulls with the telltale hole in the temple which indicated the brains had been emptied to be eaten. The villagers had claimed the two skulls were as old as the others scattered around the village, but they had lacked the patina that comes with frequent handling. As yet Voorhoeve couldn't prove a thing—unless the villagers at Wiat Kargas could be persuaded to identify their attackers. Most likely they would prefer to seek their own revenge, making matters worse. Voorhoeve gritted his teeth angrily at the thought and glanced over his shoulders at the soldiers behind him. He raised his voice to be heard above the droning motor.

"How much farther, Lieutenant?"

The young officer seated behind him nodded toward the peninsula which jutted into the river just ahead. "Around that bend."

"Good," Voorhoeve replied, and then added, with determination in his voice, "This time I want it made clear to these savages that I'm going to start lopping off the balls of any Asmat warriors who decide to enter manhood by going headhunting. They'll either prove their masculinity some other way or lose it altogether!"

The thought occurred to Voorhoeve, not for the first time, that he would like to be rid of the whole native population. They were worthless as a labor force anyway. There was nothing he or anyone else could offer to get them to work. They had no interest in material things, or if they did, they simply waited for the opportunity to steal whatever had taken their fancy, rather than earn it. Consequently all the labor at Agats had to be performed by Javanese workers brought in by the Dutch.

Voorhoeve's eyes scanned the jungle nervously for some sign of human life. There had been none for the past five miles—not even any boats on the river. That was unusual, and it made Voorhoeve uneasy. With relief he caught sight of an old woman, bent over as she hunted for crabs at the water's edge. Almost deaf, she did not hear the boat approach until it was before her. She rose, startled, and Voorhoeve saw that her nose and lips and earlobes had been eaten away by yaws. As she stared at the boat in fear and surprise, Voorhoeve stared back, so fascinated and repelled by this evidence of physical vulnerability that he failed to notice the sudden appearance of the village just beyond the bend until the lieutenant's hand gripped his arm in warning and forced his eyes ahead. At first Voorhoeve saw nothing unusual. The villagers had heard the approaching noise, and though modern machines were rare on this part of the river, they all had seen such boats before. Expectantly they had paused in the midst of their activities to await its arrival: The women, holding bamboo tongs, looked up from cookfires full of roasting sago balls and crabs while curious children had stopped their games to watch the river.

But it was not this normal village scene which had led the lieutenant to grip Voorhoeve's arm. In the shadows of the forest beyond the clearing stood as many as 100 warriors—far more than the small village usually contained. Motionless, they stared out at the river in stony silence through rings of white clay which encircled their eyes, making them look wild and dark. The boat slowed its progress to a crawl.

"My God," Vooorhoeve muttered at the sight of the spears and bows with which they were armed. "It must be a raid."

"No. I don't think so," the lieutenant replied. "But we'd better stay clear just the same." The boat had moved to less than 100 feet of shore.

"I don't understand," Voorhoeve said. "Why so many?"

If the lieutenant knew the answer, he had no chance to speak before a young warrior shattered the silence with a scream. Arm drawn threateningly back with his spear held high above his head, he raced toward the riverbank.

Hearing rifles cock behind him, the lieutenant attempted to calm his anxious men. "It's only a bluff!" he told them. "He's as scared as you are."

Voorhoeve's breath caught in his throat as the warrior reached the edge of the water and leaped high into the air. For a moment it seemed he might release the spear; but then his arm relaxed, and he backed off slightly, still making threatening gestures with his lowered spear as he retreated. Any relief the boat's occupants might have felt was quickly dispelled by a sudden surge from the other warriors which took them forward in a howling brown wave threatening to sweep out into the river itself and engulf the boat.

"Turn the boat around and withdraw at once, Sergeant," the lieutenant ordered.

"No!" Voorhoeve's shaking voice rose in sharp countermand. "I'll not be bullied into running away."

The warriors stopped at the river's edge and milled about as the boat lurched back to comply with Voorhoeve's orders. Suddenly several shots rang out as one of the inexperienced Javanese recruits fired wildly into the air. Instantly the sky filled with arrows and spears which miraculously collected into a cluster that splashed down a few feet in front of the slow-moving boat—all but one wayward spear, which landed with a dull thud in the thatch directly above Voorhoeve's headache. He felt a moment of pure terror.

"Order the men to fire!" he shouted at the lieutenant.

"No, sir," the lieutenant said grimly, knowing the price for his insubordination.

Voorhoeve looked down at the dumbfounded corporal who sat

manning the bow machine gun. "Fire, Corporal, or I'll have both you and your commanding officer court-martialed!"

"Into the air, Corporal—over their heads!" the lieutenant countered.

Voorhoeve grabbed the machine gun barrel to prevent the corporal from raising it. "Ahead. Fire ahead!"

Swallowing hard, the corporal hesitated, looking from Voorhoeve to the lieutenant for confirmation. At that moment another volley of arrows rained down around the boat. This time several struck the roof, but by now the corporal was more terrified of Voorhoeve than of the Asmat warriors. He closed his eyes and squeezed the trigger. A long, staccato burst of gunfire split the air. Within seconds the villagers had fled into the jungle, and all was quiet. The patrol craft cut its engines to idle and bobbed up and down in its own wake as its occupants stared at the riverbank. Nine bodies lay in the mud.

The lieutenant shook his head in stunned disbelief. "It shouldn't have happened. We were under standing orders from Hollandia to avoid confrontations whenever possible."

"You're mistaken, lieutenant," Voorhoeve replied with a steely calm which surprised even himself. "We were ambushed, and we defended ourselves."

The lieutenant turned away from the riverbank to look at Voorhoeve. "There will have to be a retribution payment to Wiat Kargas for the killings—a pig to the families of each victim."

"Nonsense!" Voorhoeve snorted. "That would be an admission of guilt—and we aren't guilty of anything. We were attacked."

"What about them?" the lieutenant nodded toward the bodies, some of which were possibly only injured.

Voorhoeve shrugged and sat down. He was no longer even sweating. The burst of violence seemed to have relieved his insecurity. "Leave them. The villagers will come back and take care of them. This is an isolated, unimportant village. No one will care what happened here. You, least of all. I hear you are due for a transfer to Batavia soon."

"Not for several months."

"Perhaps it can be sooner." Voorhoeve smiled. "Unless, of course, you want me to request an extension of your tour of duty here or a court-martial." He reached over and touched the lieutenant's shoulder, a gesture which caused the young officer to flinch. Voorhoeve laughed and withdrew his hand. "All right, Lieutenant. Let's head back home. A successful patrol. Taught them a lesson or two which will make them behave themselves, I should think."

Chapter 6
Maitreya

Daniel Forman and Carl Geller, two more graduate students from Columbia about to take part in the expedition, arrived at Maitreya in the small seaplane which delivered the weekly mail along the river. Forman and Geller had come to help arrange the transport of supplies to the base camp at Agats, New Guinea. In four weeks they would be joined by two other graduate students, along with David Carter, Catherine's fiancé, and Professors Ryder, Levine, and Wieder.

Catherine was especially happy to see Carl. When he caught sight of her on the landing dock, he greeted her with a hug, exclaiming, "Catherine, my lovely, I do believe you're blooming like a bloody orchid in this heat! You're going to drive all us men on this expedition mad. Women like you should stay properly locked up—and preferably pregnant."

She accepted his teasing good-naturedly. Though he might kid her, Carl, she knew, admired her for more than her good looks. Like Catherine, Carl was from the Midwest. He and his high school sweetheart, Ginny, were the only young married couple among the anthropology graduate students at Columbia, though Ginny herself was not a student. Ginny had taught school until she had become pregnant two years ago, and since the birth of their twins she and Carl had struggled along on his small research and teaching fellowships, which were barely enough to support one person.

Catherine had observed that most graduate students exhibited the social instincts of sharks in a feeding frenzy. Naturally competitive to begin with, they competed with one another for grades, scholarships, teaching positions, office space, sex, apartment vacancies, bridge scores, and even a place in the cafeteria line. Carl was different. Carl was like the brother she had never had. Without his friendship, she might not have been able to stick it out—and he felt the same way about her.

For Catherine, Carl's presence at Maitreya dispelled some of its exotic hold on her. She now found it easier to concentrate on the job of preparing for her research: reading related articles, attending meetings to discuss research methodology, studying the language, and listening to Michael's lectures on how to make the best of inevitable discomforts and inconveniences. Nevertheless, she still spent part of each day exploring the estate on horseback. Sometimes Julienne came with her—or Carl or Daniel—but mostly she went alone, enjoying the solitude. She always wore her bathing suit beneath her riding clothes and ended her ride with a late-afternoon swim at a limestone pool a mile from the house.

Even with Carl's sobering influence, there was still no denying that Catherine felt more at home at Maitreya than she had anywhere before. Except for her college education at Barnard and Columbia in New York, Catherine had spent her life in Chicago, where she was born. Here, in Borneo, her dark beauty seemed to fit into her surroundings. She loved the island's lush greenness, its abundance of life. Even its heat enchanted her. She especially loved Maitreya, where the wild profusion of tropical plants had been tamed into an orderliness that had lost none of its original beauty. Perhaps it was the dusky Malays with their warm dark skins that made her feel so comfortable. Catherine had been born a black-haired, dark-eyed, dark-skinned beauty in a family of fair-skinned Irish redheads. When she had been young, she had fantasized about having been adopted, but having been assured that this was not the case, she had decided she was descended from an Indian princess. In adolescent moments she had imagined that her mother had been seduced by the Filipino elevator boy in her grandmother's rich and dowdy old apartment building or by the Italian opera star who used to come to dinner often when she was young. Since she was aware of her mother's proper manners as well as her prejudices, these fantasies amused Catherine the most.

The question of her heritage had never really been resolved to her satisfaction, but more important differences had begun to emerge as she grew older. Catherine's mother had married when she was very young. She was a beautiful woman who had made a career out of being a gracious wife, and she expected a storybook child. Catherine, an only child, had definitely not been the kind of little girl her mother had wanted or expected.

Catherine remembered her mother trying to make waves of Catherine's stubborn straight hair, her elegant voice always slightly petulant. Mother with shiny red-gold curls around her own tiny, doll-like face, frowning at her only child. Mother with long black lashes like exclamation marks around her large china blue eyes. Mother looking anxiously at Catherine's thin, delicate frame as if it posed a threat to her own reputation. "You're so skinny, Catherine. Eat your dinner. Look at how your knees turn in. I think you must have had rickets as a baby." Dark and thin and ugly. Not at all what her mother had expected, or wanted. What could be worse?

The truth was she had always been pretty, even as that small, shy child. Only she hadn't known it then. And she really couldn't believe it now. That lovely reflection in the mirror and the shy child deep within her were forever strangers.

Though many boys had been attracted to her in high school, Catherine had had no boyfriends. In college, when she had finally accepted men into her life, she had chosen the men no other women wanted. She had, at the time, provided many rationalizations. They were, she told herself, the more intelligent, creative men most women couldn't appreciate. She had no lover because her dates were men with whom she would have only nice, safe, platonic relationships. It all had become clear to her when one of her undergraduate psychology professors at Barnard, himself a handsome, brilliant man, had told her bluntly that she deserved better from the men in her life and that she should ask herself why she wasn't getting it. Though he no doubt had himself in mind as a replacement, the remark, coming from someone she respected, had stunned her into realizing she had been depriving herself of the men she really wanted.

She began making up for lost time with attractive, successful men, but for all her new popularity, Catherine had never been emotionally attached enough to give herself fully to any man.

Before David, she had restlessly moved from one relationship to another. She seemed always to withhold something from her relationships, not just sexually but emotionally. David was no exception. She had agreed, finally, to marry him as a result of careful thought, not feeling. Despairing of ever really loving someone, she decided she had to settle for something else—an appropriate and agreeable partnership. David was the perfect choice. He was intelligent and handsome and shared her interests. Their friends all thought they were a perfect match. What looked perfect must be perfect, Catherine had concluded. Lacking other criteria, she had accepted his proposal. David had brought stability to her life. That is, he had until she had met Michael Stanford three weeks ago.

Today the rains had not stopped. Catherine sat alone at the desk in her room, trying to ignore the humidity. High on the wall in front of her, one of the small lizards that populate all households in the Indies suddenly pounced at a fly, then fell to the floor and quickly scurried out of sight. The ceiling fan hummed overhead, stirring air too moist to absorb the perspiration that collected on the tip of her nose and chin and had to be dabbed away. When it dripped upon her notes, blurring the ink, in exasperation she decided to quit working and go out for a ride, rain or not.

It had stopped by the time she reached the stable. She took Admiral, the big, surefooted hunter, and rode toward the pool, determined to go for a swim. Beyond the stables, the cooperatively worked field of sugarcane shared by the village and the Stanfords swept down to the river in neat rows. There were workers out cutting the cane, oblivious of the rain. Apart from the rubber crops and livestock, the Stanfords took no more than a villager's share of what Maitreya grew: rice and copra and fruit. But the rubber had made them rich.

When she rode by Michael's gray gelding tied to a tree, Catherine realized he must be among those working the fields. For the past few weeks she had had a chance to study Michael more closely. Though she carefully avoided any close personal contact with him, she had still seen a great deal of him in planning sessions, and what she saw impressed her more and more. Beneath the quiet seriousness was a man who was startlingly fierce, direct, caustic, creative, and brilliant. He was passionate about the things he believed in. The cool exterior hid a burning but controlled intensity—a degree of drive and energy which had produced remarkable accomplishments and discoveries in his brief thirty years. He was an idealist—a romantic who loved the primitive people he studied and respected the ways in which they lived. She sensed his interest in other lands, other cultures, was born, like her own, from a sense of alienation and isolation, a feeling of not quite belonging where he was.

The intensity with which Michael involved himself in everything he did might have overwhelmed those around him if it had not been tempered by an unfailing sense of humor, which was usually directed at himself. It served to soften the competitiveness and drive with which he was, perhaps, too strongly imbued. He was honest, sometimes painfully so, and he could not tolerate social games played at someone else's expense. Catherine remembered, with amusement, an incident with Donald Seabaugh in one of their earlier sessions. Seabaugh, a junior untenured faculty member at Columbia who was about Michael's age, had once hired Catherine as his graduate research assistant. (Valuing her independence, she had not accepted financial assistance from her family, preferring to support herself through graduate school.) She had made tactful but constructive criticisms of Seabaugh's work, which she was paid to do. However, Seabaugh, who never responded well to suggestions from anyone, let alone a beautiful woman whom he wanted to impress, had begun to develop academic impotence, and Catherine had recognized she would have to resign, although she badly needed the money. Seabaugh had never quite forgiven her for being more intelligent than he. No, it was more that he had not forgiven her for letting him realize she was more intelligent. Now he never passed up an opportunity to discredit her in any way, usually in the form of a joke at her expense. Jokes were particularly effective because they were hard to defend against without her seeming to be a poor sport. He had made just such a joke during a planning session. Almost everyone had laughed. Even Carl, who understood Seabaugh's motives, could not resist chuckling. Michael had not even cracked a smile.

Instead, he had appraised Seabaugh carefully and then said in that quiet, firm voice which so easily commanded attention, "You're angry with Catherine about something. You've been wearing that chip since you got here, and I seriously doubt that it has anything remotely to do with the value of her ideas, which I've always found to be exceptional.'' His eyes challenged Seabaugh, though the tone of his voice was mild. ''It's not a fair fight. You outrank her, and she can't fight back. So why don't you cut the crap and start asking yourself why you really do it? I'll bet you'll come up with an interesting answer.''

The group had sat in stunned silence. Seabaugh had held Michael's gaze silently for a moment and then dropped the challenge by changing the subject, but the incident had brought the real issue between Seabaugh and Catherine close enough to the surface so that he would not abuse his position again. Catherine had been grateful to Michael for his remark, but afterward he remained as aloof as ever, not just toward her but toward everyone. He wasn't shy. He was always polite, even cordial, and readily talked about almost anything. He just didn't talk about himself.

Catherine reached the pool and suddenly realized she had been thinking of him the whole ride. Rain was threatening again. She dismounted and stood by the edge of the pool, still holding the reins. At this point the limestone walls fell straight down, making diving easy. The sound of the growing wind in the trees made Admiral restless. She no longer felt like swimming. Without sunlight the pool seemed bottomless, dangerous.

She was afraid of Michael. Why? The pool, dark beneath the gathering clouds, stared blankly back at her. She looked beyond her image, deep into the water, as if the answer might lie there among the brightly colored pet koi, or fish, that inhabited the pool. Seeing none, she dispelled her image with a flick of a pebble, sending ripples across the pool's smooth surface, leaving only fragments of herself behind.

She mounted her horse and started for the stable. It had begun to rain, and she quickly became soaked in the downpour. She did not mind, having become used to the daily rains of Borneo. She began to gallop her horse along the trail toward home. As a child she had taken chances that had been the bane of her mother's existence, but as a woman she had become more conservative. Yet now she found herself racing down a muddy lane, her small English saddle slippery wet and precarious beneath her. One bad fall, and she would forfeit any immediate chance of gathering data for her doctoral dissertation. Still she pressed on, urging the

46

big thoroughbred jumper faster as her confidence in him and herself grew. As a young girl, when she preferred the company of horses to boys, she had been a skilled rider, but until these past three weeks at Maitreya she had not ridden for years.

Her mother had disliked horses. It was her father who had taken her riding each week with him in the park. As a child, that hour they spent alone each week had been the most important in her life. He was a handsome man, full of sharp wit and a charming manner. There was athletic grace in his every movement, and he dressed with style and unaffected elegance. A Brahmin by instinct rather than birth, he was drawn to whatever was finest and most beautiful in life, whether in art or horses or women. As a child, Catherine had adored him. He did not love her. She knew he wanted to but couldn't. In his eyes, love was a father's duty and it was a bitter experience to him to have failed in one of his responsibilities. His devotion to her mother seemed to have exhausted his limited capacity for love. It was likely he had never really wanted children.

He had always treated Catherine as if she were an adult—and a male adult, at that. He wasn't comfortable with either women or children, having had neither a childhood nor a mother himself. Orphaned almost at birth and self-supporting at an early age, he had risen to eminence in his profession—with its attendant financial rewards—through hard work and a brilliant mind. He had little sympathy for those who exhibited neither and held stern traditional views on morality. Catherine assumed these arose as much from the years spent in Catholic orphanages and the questionable circumstances of his own birth, something he would never discuss.

The realization that he didn't love her had come to Catherine at an early age, and since he appeared faultless to her at the time, she had blamed herself. Perfection, she had concluded then, might make her lovable to him, and so she had pursued it with considerable success in the academic areas he valued. By the time she recognized that she would never earn his acceptance any more than her mother's, her ambitions had found their own rewards.

Looking up as she neared the five-foot enclosure surrounding the stable, Catherine didn't bother to circle to the open gate. Instead, she turned straight into the fence and urged the big bay gelding on. He made his approach without hesitation, trusting her, sensing the skill in those firm hands upon the shortened reins.

47

She took the fence at a full gallop, and her heart rose to her throat as he left the ground. As he soared up and over the fence, she felt an exhilaration born of a freedom she had not experienced in a long time. Both horse and rider made a perfect landing in the sandy, well-drained soil of the stableyard. She trotted to the stable door and dismounted with a jump. Her face flushed with excitement, she led Admiral through the open door. Two of the stableboys applauded as she entered. Michael stood just inside the door, with his saddle over his arm, soaked from tousled head to the toes of his boots. He was grinning at her in admiration.

"That was one hell of a jump!" He turned and disappeared into the tack room before she could give more than a smile in return. When she finished unsaddling and entered the tack room, he was gone.

On her way to her room to change for dinner, she met Julienne coming down the hall.

"I've been looking for you," Julienne announced brightly in a way Catherine had come to distrust. "I'm going to Batavia for a few days with Kara tomorrow. You can come with us if you like. I want to see my sister, Margit, and I've got some shopping to do."

Catherine reacted with a tinge of disapproval. It seemed irresponsible of Julienne to be running off to Batavia with Kara when there was so much work to do preparing for the expedition. "No, I don't think so."

Clearly relieved, Julienne went on. "Then you'll be a dear and identify these Asmat markings for me, won't you?" She handed Catherine a stack of photographs showing spears with carvings on the shafts that signified village and clan memberships. "Dr. Seabaugh wants them in two days."

Catherine frowned. "Don't you think you ought to stay and do it yourself?"

"Now, don't be cross, Catherine," Julienne countered cheerfully. "You know I wouldn't be going if it weren't important. Besides, you always do a better job than I."

Without waiting for a response, she continued down the hall, leaving Catherine holding the photos. Annoyed, Catherine entered her room and tossed them on a table. It wasn't the first time she had found herself taking on Julienne's responsibilities. Julienne would have been dropped from the graduate program long ago for lack of commitment to her studies if she had not been Sir Charles Stanford's daughter.

Catherine wrapped her hair in a towel, filled the tub with cool water, and sat soaking up to her chin, staring at her knees, while her mood gradually puckered along with her skin. She glanced with irritation toward the bathroom door, where one of the laundresses had hung her two short dresses. Besides the long black evening dress she had worn the first night, these were the only dresses she had brought with her. She had selected them primarily because they were cool and comfortable and because Julienne had warned her it was the custom at Maitreya to dress for dinner each night: men in suits and ties; women in dresses. While these two dresses accommodated the rules, they no longer accommodated her mood. She was tired of them both. They certainly were not as stylish as what the fashionable Mrs. Stanford wore each night. Kara obviously bought her clothes in Paris. Catherine hadn't even brought lipstick with her. She seldom wore it at home, so she had scarcely expected to miss it here, and yet, awkwardly, her appearance had become important to her lately. She rose suddenly from the tub, shedding a lapful of water as she wrapped herself in a towel, splashed across the cool tile floor, and selected the flowered print sundress—for the simple reason that it was nearest. After quickly putting on her clothes, she twisted her long hair into a coil and pinned it to the top of her head without bothering to look in the mirror to check the results. Then, on impulse, she went out to the terrace, leaned over the stone wall, and plucked two gardenias, which she jammed carelessly into the top of her hair.

Entering the study, she found Carl alone, standing beside a library table, glancing through one of Sir Charles's old articles. Carl's tie dangled loosely about his neck like a noose. His shirt sleeves were rolled above his wrists, and his suit jacket was slung carelessly over his shoulder, where it hung damp and rumpled from the back of his tall, thin frame. Carl's grooming habits would have reduced the finest London tailoring to a baggy mess; but the white suit he now wore had been created by a back-alley Chinese tailor in Singapore on a few hours' notice, and it looked as shabby as he had secretly hoped it would. He considered the suit a political statement of his views on wealth and privilege—not to mention the idea of dressing for dinner every night.

"The only time we ever dressed for dinner was on Sunday afternoons," he had grumbled on his first night at the Stanfords. At dinner, after a few drinks, he had announced that on his last night at Maitreya he planned to burn his white suit, as a symbol of the dying British Empire. Sir Charles, used to the peculiar vanity of graduate student poverty, had merely laughed in approval.

"Ah—our class Beau Brummell, dressed to kill," Catherine said to him as she entered the room.

He looked up and, seeing the two gardenias atop the dark mass of her hair, smiled with one corner of his mouth.

"Feeling festive, I see," he commented sarcastically.

Her eyes fell to the whiskey decanter and the empty glass on the table beside him, and she realized he'd already had a few drinks. It wasn't like him. Sensing her disapproval, he nodded toward the decanter.

"I'd be a lush if I always had this good booze around, but I'll never be able to afford it, so don't worry. I'll be as sober as a judge when we reach New Guinea," he added, and slammed shut the stapled papers he had been reading with a theatrical gesture. He stared at her for a moment, recognizing the discontent he saw there as sister of his own.

"Let's play hooky tonight," he said suddenly. His hand went to his chin to tug automatically at the beard he had recently shaved off in order to escape the heat. The skin was still tender. Missing the beard, he spread his long fingers and combed through the wave of straight, fine dark hair which was forever stubbornly springing back to his forehead. With the infinite patience of a drunk, he reached up and carefully repeated the gesture. His expression beamed with enthusiasm.

"We'll send excuses, and I'll get Wong to give us a bite of whatever chef's delight he's preparing. Then I'll steal a bottle of expensive French wine, and we'll go to the river and get politely drunk—what do you say?"

She laughed and said, "Fine," relieved to feel she might escape the Stanfords and everyone else for one evening.

Carl went off to make his appeal to Maitreya's Cantonese cook. When he found Catherine, she was seated, barefoot, at the end of the dock, staring down at the brown water which eddied below. He stopped and watched her for a moment. She sensed his presence, looked up, and smiled, then leaned back on her hands, still dangling her feet in the river.

"Little piranhas will bite off your toes," he cheerfully chided her.

"Wrong river—that's the Amazon." She laughed.

"Oh," he said, pretending he didn't know. "Then the crocs will do it. They take even bigger bites."

She ignored his teasing, never having seen crocodiles around Maitreya's carefully maintained banks. He spread a lunch cloth and set down two wineglasses and some pieces of chicken and bread.

"Sorry there's not much to eat. Wong wasn't too keen for my plan. Seems it upset the quantity of all his ingredients. But I did get the wine." He dragged a bottle from under his coat, already opened, and poured. Raising his glass in a toast, he hit hers a trifle too hard.

"To discoveries"—he smiled enigmatically—"of all kinds." He drank and then added, "May we keep our heads"—he belched slightly and continued—"upon our shoulders in all ways, both physical and emotional." He raised his glass again, nearly tumbling off the pier, and both of them suddenly realized he was more sober than he pretended to be.

"I'm homesick," he said to the river as he steadied himself. "I've never been away from Ginny and the twins before."

"I know." Catherine touched his knee in sympathy.

Sensing her acceptance, he could let himself look at her without embarrassment. For a moment her flowered dress blurred in his vision and became part of the forest. Her tanned skin and lustrous eyes melted into the wild shadows of the river, and he realized she had always seemed a bit unworldly to him, as exotic as Maitreya itself. She belonged here while he did not. The thought made him uncomfortable. Behind them, in the growing dusk, the silhouette of Maitreya's main house loomed against the sky, its gables soaring like twin masts of a huge sailing ship, the roof billowing between, heading full tilt into some unseen storm. Even here, surrounded by jungle, the house dominated everything. Carl gave a slight shudder. He fumbled in his coat for his pipe, which he had forgotten, and found a cigarette instead.

They talked of school, and Carl entertained her with his imitation of eminent anthropologist Franz Boas, professor emeritus at

Columbia. The performance never failed to make her laugh. Here, with Carl, she felt a lovely peace, and the river breezes seemed to suck the heat from her body. She drew one knee up from the water so that her cheek might rest there against the flowers of the dress she had hated only an hour ago. She was aware that Carl, when he looked at people, really saw them, made them feel flattered by his attention. It was part of the secret of his charm. She let it wash over her, amuse her, take care of her.

For a moment they both fell silent, letting the river's calm motion envelop them, content as they watched the sky blaze orange with its last light. People have favorite moments in their lives, ones they will always remember, and knowing this would be one of his, Carl carefully took it all in: the smell of frangipani; the growing sounds of insects and frogs. He couldn't help noticing that Catherine was quieter, more remote than usual. Her eyes, even when fixed on his, seemed to be focused on some other horizon, so he tried even harder to amuse her, to steal her back from whatever was taking her away.

Finally he asked, "When do you think you and David will get married?"

She looked startled for a moment, as though the question were unrelated to her. "We still haven't decided," she answered.

She looked down at the river, but before she did, he saw panic briefly flash across her face.

"There's no reason to rush, of course," he said soothingly. He wondered why he had asked the question. He knew it would upset her—it always did. Perhaps he wanted to punish her for whatever made her quiet tonight. He changed the subject.

"I wonder if the Stanfords are really happy here," he mused, and then answered himself. "Why not? They've created their own little world, and they run it any way they like. Except, of course, for the lovely Mrs. Stanford. She doesn't fit in. I feel sorry for her somehow."

"You feel sorry for everyone," Catherine replied coolly, annoyed to find that Kara Stanford had a champion in Catherine's own corner.

Carl ignored her coolness, knowing he could cajole her out of whatever irritation she felt toward him. Besides, he liked Kara Stanford; perhaps she reminded him of Ginny, graciously playing den mother to graduate student gatherings, cooking to support conversations of which she could never really be a part. He and Catherine had disagreed about many things, but there were no differences between them that mattered. Through her he had discovered the secret which still eluded the members of the male faculty club—the knowledge that the deepest friendships were between men and women, not between men. Not that he was oblivious of Catherine's beauty. Quite the contrary, he reveled in it, but with the same detached pleasure with which he viewed a work of art.

As they talked again of school, Carl felt a certain sadness. After this field trip they all would converge briefly at Columbia to write their dissertations, then scatter to teaching posts around the country. Catherine and David would probably remain in New York. Carl himself would return to the Midwest, as he had promised Ginny he would when he finished. Afterward they would only see each other occasionally at those yearly class reunions known in academia as scholarly meetings.

"When this is over I'll miss you, Cat." His voice was serious enough to make her turn toward him.

"I'll miss you, too," she said softly.

In Carl's wine-filled vision she seemed to be fading away again in the twilight, becoming one with the river and jungle. For a moment he felt a strange sense of panic, as if he had lost her forever, then he found it equally strange that the thought should affect him so.

"I don't much care for this place," he said with irritation, as if Maitreya were to blame for the illusion. A lump rose to his throat, bringing with it a sour taste of digesting wine. He rose, a little dizzy, and offered her his hand. She took it and smiled, and the jungle which had swallowed her yielded her back to him. He slung the empty wine bottle as far as he could out over the river.

"Dead soldier," he cried, then paused to stare after it. "Maybe there will be lots of real ones soon. Maybe I'll even be one of them."

Fearing he was about to become maudlin, Catherine steered him toward the road. Ahead the lights of Maitreya spilled onto one side of the long terrace, indicating dinner was still going on. At the foot of the terrace steps stood a greenish bronze image of the god Maitreya, bearing in his mysterious smile the promise of a golden future, rich beyond men's dreams. Stolen from a Cambodian Buddhist temple by an earlier Stanford, he seemed serene in his adopted home. The palms of his four hands, turned upward, were filled with rainwater and thirsty insects and tiny flower petals—nature's offerings.

"I love this place," Catherine sighed softly.

"Do you?" Carl asked.

"Yes," she replied, then added a thought which had caught her fancy. "The Indonesians believe houses have spirits, just as people do."

Above them the carved gable of the house rose like the prow of some ancient Viking ship. Feeling Carl pause on the terrace behind her, Catherine turned back at the door.

"Coming?" she asked.

"I think I'll stay outside a minute for a smoke. I'm always afraid I'll burn this thatch-covered, wooden monstrosity down if I smoke inside it. Come to think of it, wouldn't be a bad idea."

He could just glimpse her smile in the fading light before the house swallowed her up, leaving him behind to find whatever warmth he could in the glowing tip of his cigarette.

Chapter 7
Casuarina Coastline, New Guinea

Father Kessel steered the small outboard motorboat toward the shoreline of the river. Here, near its mouth, the Eilenden was so wide that the opposite bank could not be seen. He raised his eyes and squinted at the blinding sun. He had forgotten his watch and was estimating the time. A floppy old hat protected his head from the scorching sun, and he held an unlit pipe between his teeth. Beneath his hat, his hair was cut to a short, practical stubble which blended perfectly into the length of his beard. Together they framed his features in a wreath of iron gray, yet it was not a cold face. Bright blue eyes and a deep ruddy tan gave it warmth. Father Kessel was a small man, lean and wiry and full of restless energy which led him to chew on the end of his pipe when he had no one to talk to, as was often the case. He did not resemble a priest, and when he was honest he admitted it was more his endless curiosity about the nature of men's minds and hearts than his concern for the condition of their souls which had led him to missionary work. It was a confession he made only to God— never to his bishop, who would not have understood.

Six months ago Father Kessel had come to Dutch New Guinea to start the first Catholic mission on the Eilenden River, near Agats. Before that he had been in the Solomon Islands and the Sepik River area of New Guinea.

He was fifty-two years old, and the primitive conditions he had endured for the past twenty-five years had begun to take their toll. He suffered from a variety of chronic parasites and diseases, including malaria. For the past week he had been laid up by one of the periodic infestations which tormented him. But that morning one of his native assistants had come to him with news so disturbing it caused him to leave his bed in spite of his illness. He had decided to investigate for himself the report that a week ago there had been an attack on a Dutch patrol craft upriver at Wiat Kargas.

The mangrove swamps he passed along the riverbank made foot travel impossible along the entire coast touched by the Arafura Sea. Huge crocodiles, up to thirty-five feet long, slept among the tangle of roots and trunks. Occasionally they could be seen floating in the muddy water, giant living logs, unchanged for millions of years. They mingled, often undetected, among the real trunks and limbs of fallen trees, which themselves posed a no less dangerous threat to the river traveler. Father Kessel carefully scanned the river for these underwater obstacles which could easily sink his small boat, leaving him at the mercy of the treacherous current or the steely-jawed reptiles. In spite of his efforts, the boat would sometimes hit a waterlogged limb hidden beneath the murky water.

Taking one of its numerous tributaries, he left the Eilenden and headed five miles upstream to the Asmat village of Wiat Kargas. When the village finally came into view, it appeared deserted, perplexing him. It was a small village, and one of the region's more isolated ones. Customarily the warriors of a village would greet visitors like a milling army, shouting and brandishing spears in order to frighten and intimidate their guests into behaving themselves. Since the Dutch had pacified the region, the bluff and blandishment of the welcoming committee usually came to nothing. That is, until a week ago. Perhaps the size of the patrol group had frightened them. Whatever the reason, things must have gone beyond the usual threats and gestures. If his report was to be believed, three warriors had been killed and six more injured before the patrol retreated down the river.

It had taken Father Kessel months to win even marginal acceptance from these former headhunters, whose social belief system was built on blame for all misfortunes that befall an individual. To the tribes of the Asmat, no death or illness is ever accidental or free of malevolence; enemies or the spirits of dead enemies are always to blame, and the dead must then be revenged by their relatives. Wars between individuals, clans, and villages traditionally raged over these issues of blame and revenge rather than the issue of territorial gain that characterized the wars of Western culture. Father Kessel now feared that the recent murders would inspire a ritual *biz* ceremony in which the tribe made public pledges of revenge, which would be followed by retaliatory attacks on the tiny and precariously situated white outposts, engulfing the entire region in war.

His alarm at the first report of shootings had not been based on his concern for his own life or the lives of the Dutch soldiers and officials at the outpost. He had reconciled himself to the inevitability of his own death, and he felt that soldiers had to accept the risks of their profession. Instead, he had been thinking of the Stanford-Columbia field expedition scheduled to arrive in the Asmat in just a few weeks. Father Kessel had met Sir Charles Stanford during one of the distinguished anthropologist's field trips to the Sepik River area in northeast New Guinea, and when the two men discovered they shared a mutual interest in Oceanic mythology, they had become lifelong friends. The Dutch priest had been pleased to be able to offer his assistance in arranging this latest expedition. It was to be the largest and most extensive field study ever done in New Guinea, and he looked forward to the stimulating company the eleven-member expedition would bring to his otherwise isolated and lonely life. It was his real fear for their safety, on the one hand, and his conflicting eagerness for their companionship, on the other, that made him decide to investigate the situation for himself. He knew the government could not make such an assessment. It had not yet earned even the minimal trust and acceptance he had managed to achieve. Now it might never attain it.

He cut off the outboard motor and raised it, letting the boat's momentum carry him to shore. Barefoot, he clambered out of the boat, pulling it behind him through ankle-deep mud. Dugouts sunned on the riverbank like fierce wooden crocodiles, with their richly stylistic animal carvings decorating bow and stern. Beside them his small craft seemed timid and afraid.

The early-morning cookfires lay spent but still warm, their wispy trails rising into the midday air. The village had obviously been recently occupied, but it appeared deserted now. No doubt, thought Father Kessel, the occupants had vanished at the sound of his boat, fearing another Dutch patrol. He had often come alone into the area and could count some of the villagers as his friends. He called out their names, then stood waiting in the hot sun. Flies buzzed about his face. He brushed them away and called out again. Not even the squawk of parrots could be heard. The silence began to sound its own alarm. He stood for anxious minutes of indecision that felt like hours. Still no sound; not even the air stirred about him.

Overcoming his uneasiness, he began to search the village for some clue to the meaning of its emptiness. Only lizards lurked in the ceremonial house. Then he saw a furtive scurrying in one of the longhouses on the edge of the village clearing.

Cautiously he entered the only opening in the dimly lit hut. A form like a brown crab scuttled sideways across the floor on all fours and crouched in a corner of the single room. It was a man, too old and sick to join the hasty retreat of the others. Father Kessel recognized him and spoke in the native language. "Don't be afraid, Otompi. I've come alone. I won't hurt you. The soldiers are not coming. Where are the rest of the people of the village?"

The crouched figure was silent. Father Kessel took some tobacco from his pouch and rolled it into some cigarette paper. He held it out before him. "Here, Otompi. For you."

A fragile claw shot out and clutched the gift. It disappeared within the huddled form, which unfolded a minute later with a burning cigarette. Otompi relaxed against the wall while Father Kessel sat down across from him and patiently waited. Then he probed again.

"About the killings last week, Otompi. Who were the warriors of your village who were killed by the soldiers?"

The old man sat in silence looking back at Kessel. His lips moved only to puff the cigarette. The priest felt frustrated. The answer to his question was crucial. If important warriors or members of powerful clans had been killed, then revenge would be inevitable. He tried a different approach.

"Otompi, if you will answer these questions for me, I will give you two more cigarettes. Now listen carefully. Were the men killed last week important men of your village?"

The old man shook his head in the negative.

"Were they relatives of important clans in your village?"

Again the old man shook his head no and then held out his hand for his reward. With relief, Father Kessel rolled two cigarettes and gave them to him. Then he rose and left the dark enclosure. It occurred to him as he walked to the river that Otompi was probably no older than he, a man in his early fifties. Men aged quickly here.

He stood on the bank of the river, looking about him at the empty village and attempting to assess the situation. On the basis of geographical considerations alone, the expedition would appear to be in no potential danger. While the Wiat Kargas village was only five miles from the mission, it was at least twenty-five miles southeast of the areas to be studied by the expedition. Then, too, the men killed had not been powerful men with powerful connections. He reasoned that the spirits of the murdered warriors who demanded to be revenged would seem less a threat to the villagers than would the spirits of the white men, dead or alive. The white man's weapons and what the natives believed to be his supernatural powers would probably make them reluctant to seek revenge, at least until some time when it might seem safe and easy. He decided that he would inform the pending expedition of the incident, but he would not advise it to cancel its plans.

He pushed the boat into the water and clambered onboard. Before starting the motor, he hesitated and let the current carry him out into the main stream unaided as he contemplated the mangrove and sago forest that surrounded him. He had never seen a *biz* ceremony of revenge. It had been banned by the government before he arrived in the Asmat. But he had once seen evidence of its existence in the form of a huge mangrove tree trunk with totemlike carvings he had found rotting among the sago trees of the forest. The pole had been expertly carved into a fierce representation of the deceased and erected at some previous ceremony. Afterward it had been discarded among sago trees so that its supernatural power would increase the productivity of that plant as a basic food source.

Remembering the feeling of power emanating from that angry image of the dead, Father Kessel experienced uneasiness. He forced it away. He was convinced the old man had not lied. He started the motor, and the reassuring roar dispelled his mood. He turned purposefully in the direction of home. What he had no way of knowing at the time was that he had misunderstood the old man, and, by so doing, had misled himself on both the extent and the source of the danger. It was a mistake that would prove fatal.

Chapter 8

Catherine was not sure how it had happened, but in looking back later, she was sure that it had been deliberate on her part. She had gone for a ride and then to the pool for a swim immediately after lunch instead of her usual late-afternoon time. Consciously she had not come seeking him, yet she had come at a time when he was almost sure to be there, a time she had deliberately avoided before. Looking back on it, she could not explain why she had done it.

As she rode up to the pool that afternoon, the dappled sunlight played peacefully and brightly across the water's quiet surface. She made no attempt to conceal her approach. His horse whinnied a brief greeting, but he lay motionless, naked upon his back on a rock across the pool, ignoring her presence. It was apparent from the evenness of his tan that he often sunned himself here in this manner. She stood for a moment, staring at him, waiting for him to acknowledge her presence. The fact that he did not made her want to challenge him, to force him out of his constant aloofness. Her heart began to pound in her ears. Since she had not planned to come to the pool until late afternoon, she had not yet put on her bathing suit. She began slowly to undress and fold her riding clothes on the rock beside her riding boots. When she finished, she stood beside the pool, exhilarated, yet trembling with fear of what she was about to do. She dived into the sparkling water.

He still gave no sign that he was aware of her, though he could not have missed the sounds of her presence. He was lying on his back, one arm cradling his head and the other over his eyes, shielding them from the sun. One leg was drawn up. She could see the quiet regularity of his breathing. His quietness calmed her fears, allowing her curiosity and excitement to overcome her shyness. As she swam toward him, her heart began to pound harder, and she felt as though some other person were acting for her.

She climbed out of the water and knelt on the rock beside him. He moved his arm from his face and cushioned it behind his head, squinting at her through the brightness of the sun. Without looking at his face or speaking, she began to explore his body with her eyes. She had never seen a man's body before. Her father's had remained carefully hidden from her. She looked with curiosity at the pink maleness nestled in the thatch of blond hair between his legs. It looked out of place, an imperfection in an otherwise perfect body, and she found herself amused. With a boldness that again surprised her she reached out and touched the hard brown surface of his body. Beginning with her fingers at his navel, she followed the blond, curly hair downward until she touched him lightly where it gathered like a decoration at the base of the mound. She watched in curiosity as that pinkish brown and somewhat undistinguished organ began to harden and extend itself at her touch. She could feel his body grow tense, but still he did not move, nor did he speak. She could sense that he continued to watch her, though she did not look into his face. She felt curiously clinical, as if she were conducting a lab experiment in anatomy. She was so absorbed in exploring his body that she was only half-aware of the changes her own body was undergoing, indications of a degree of excitement she had never experienced before. She touched his nipples and was surprised to find that they hardened and extended like her own. She ran her hands over the sun-bleached hair upon his chest and down the length of his body to his thighs. Her fingers and eyes explored between his legs, satisfying her curiosity with a freedom she had never dreamed possible. Whatever her original motives, anger or the wish to shock him out of his distant stance, her actions were now motivated by pleasure and excitement. She touched his upraised knee with her hand and then brushed it lightly with her lips. How beautifully strong and well shaped his leg is, she thought.

As she felt his leg tighten and press against the ground, she turned and looked into his face for the first time. His lips were pressed firmly together, and his jaw was set, reflecting the tension of his whole body. It gave him a grim appearance except for his eyes, which were filled with passion and a kind of softness. She turned back to his body, kissed his organ, and gently put her tongue upon it. With surprise she found herself taking it into her mouth, exploring it briefly. Then she stroked it with her hand while she kissed his thighs and his firm, hard stomach above it. He groaned softly, and unable to help himself, he began to thrust himself gently into her hand. After a gasp of relief he relaxed beneath her as his semen spilled over his stomach and her caressing hands. It was warm and sticky. She put her fingers on his glistening stomach, exploring the milky liquid. She found herself accepting it, loving it as she did every part of his body. She kissed his stomach, gently letting her tongue come into contact with the stickiness. She pulled back and looked at him again. Her eyes shone brightly with her own passion. He was watching her carefully. The tension in his face had been replaced by amusement and something else, a warmth. She felt herself blush self-consciously, acutely aware of what she had just done. The excitement of her own body was still with her. She chose to rise and take it away with her, giving it up to the coolness of the water. She was not ready yet for anything else. He turned his head and watched her as she swam back across the pool and quickly dressed.

The uninhibited freedom of the moment had vanished. She did not feel guilty. She felt flushed with a different kind of excitement from that she had washed away in the pool. A new part of her had been awakened, and she was not yet completely comfortable with it. She had trusted Michael completely with that part of her, and he, sensing that trust, had not betrayed it. As she mounted her horse and started to leave, she glanced back at him. He was lying beside the pool in essentially the same pose that she had found him, arms shielding his face from the sun. It was as if nothing had been disturbed, and yet everything had changed.

*　　*　　*

63

Catherine didn't see Michael until dinner that night. He seemed as remote and aloof as ever. It was impossible to tell what he thought about what had happened between them. She avoided looking at him, afraid of the rejection she might see in his eyes, and afraid of what her own expression might betray to anyone who saw her look at him. She could scarcely eat. After dinner they all adjourned to the library to look at pictures of New Guinea Sir Charles had received from explorer Richard Archbold. They were aerial photographs and a rough map of the unexplored interior some 100 miles inland from where their own expedition would take them. The photographs provided glimpses of a beautiful valley hidden from the world by thick layers of clouds and tall, forbidding mountain peaks capped with snow and glaciers. All were bird's-eye views of forests and rivers except for one remarkable picture taken as the clouds briefly opened up and the plane flew in low over the valley. It revealed a warrior in a white egret headdress standing atop a tall watchtower. His bow had been fired, and the frail shaft of an arrow hung forever suspended in its flight toward the retreating plane.

"Thought you might want to get a look at Shangri-la," the pilot who took the pictures had written to Sir Charles. On the map Dutch cartographers had given the area the more prosaic name of Grand Valley of the Baliem River. The younger members of the expedition seized upon the photographs with the eagerness of astronomers getting their first close-ups of Mars. With everyone's attention on the photographs being passed around, Catherine had a chance to study Michael. He must have sensed her gaze; he looked up, and for the first time since that afternoon his eyes met and held hers. She felt her heart catch in her throat, but she didn't look away. His expression was not cool but thoughtful. Fearful that in one more moment her eyes might begin to make love to him there, before everyone, as freely as her hands had done that afternoon, she turned from his gaze and struck up a conversation with Daniel Forman, who sat next to her, glancing briefly at the others to see if anyone had caught the exchange. They were almost all engrossed in conversation. Only Carl thoughtfully appraised both her and Michael and then turned his attention back to the pictures.

Sir Charles observed that his son's spirits seemed to have improved. During dinner Michael had seemed unusually quiet and preoccupied. He had decided that Michael was tense as a result of Kara's departure. It was unfortunate that she had been called away to Batavia so close to the time when Michael would have to leave. He had never talked to Michael about it, but he knew that these separations must be difficult for him as well as for Kara. It was too bad that Kara had never been able to interest herself in anthropology, but then, neither had his own wife.

Sir Charles began to study the only woman in the room. Catherine, he observed, was indeed an exquisite woman—a bit too dark for his tastes perhaps. Exotic-looking women made him feel uncomfortable, although he wasn't sure why. He had never had a Malay mistress for that reason. Still, Catherine was damnably attractive, and he briefly toyed with the possibility of having an affair with her. Then he realized regretfully she was too young to have any interest in an old codger like him. Twenty years ago he would have gleefully pursued it, taken up the chase; now he would have to leave it to the younger men. He looked at Michael thoughtfully and wondered if his son found Catherine attractive. Sir Charles shook his head. He could never really understand his son's indifference to women, but he was willing to bet that Catherine was completely safe from seduction where Michael was concerned. Besides, thought Sir Charles, Catherine, like Michael's mother, was probably not the kind of woman with whom you had a casual affair. He had learned to distinguish that difference the hard way.

As he thought of Michael's mother, he felt a stab of regret, as he always did. His eyes filled with tears, and the glass in which he held his brandy shook slightly as he set it on the table. Funny, he thought guiltily, memories of his wife's more recent death did not fill him with the same deep sense of loss. He blinked away the tears and turned purposefully back to join the conversation in the room.

Chapter 9

The next morning's planning session also proceeded as if nothing had happened between them. They worked together as colleagues. There was no hint in his manner that it was otherwise, nor in hers. Catherine avoided the pool that afternoon when she went riding. She told herself she needed time to absorb the changes that were taking place within her, but the real reason was her fear he would not be there. She was not yet ready to handle that possibility. As she returned to the stable from her ride late that afternoon, she saw Julienne, back from accompanying Kara to Batavia, seated with Michael, Philip Sanders, and the children on the terrace having tea. One of the girls perched on Michael's shoulders while the other played ball with the dog around his feet. Though she had seen it before, the sight of Michael with his children now caused her a moment of intense pain. Was it jealousy or guilt? Perhaps both. It was obvious that Michael was very fond of his two small daughters and enjoyed his role as their father. They clearly adored him. Catherine had noticed that when they were present, he always seemed to be touching them, as if needing physical contact to confirm their existence—or perhaps his own.

Julienne waved from the terrace, and Catherine waved back, but Michael had not glanced her way. She took her time unsaddling Admiral, preferring to do it herself rather than turn the horse over to one of the grooms. It had never been easy for her to let people wait on her. When she reached her room to change for dinner, she found Julienne there, lying on the bed, head propped upon an elbow. She was reading the notes that Catherine had been working on earlier.

"I can see you're aiming to get more than a dissertation out of this trip, Catherine. A book maybe? *Everything You've Always Wanted to Know About the Sex Life of Headhunters*, by Catherine Morgan, Ph.D. Or perhaps a nice cookbook, *Favorite Cannibal Recipes of New Guinea*!"

Amused, Catherine laughed. "Why not?" She realized that Julienne, three years older than she, was often uncomfortable with Catherine's single-minded pursuit of her degree. In the one year they had shared a room, Catherine had sensed a rivalry from Julienne which seemed odd, since Julienne had never taken her studies particularly seriously. Her academic history had been filled with starts and stops before she had entered the graduate program at Columbia four years ago. Now, like Catherine, she was in the final phase of her graduate work. Studies and exams behind her, she was about to begin field research for her doctoral dissertation.

Catherine crossed to the nearest armchair. "I didn't know you were coming back today." She sat down and began to tug at her riding boots.

"I caught a flight back with Philip a couple of days early." He had brought Harriet to Batavia to catch a ship.

"Oh?" Catherine's voice sounded casual, but her heart was pounding. "Did Kara come back with you?"

"No. She's staying on a few more days."

Hiding her relief, Catherine stepped into the dressing room to take off her jodhpurs and put on a robe. As the door closed behind her, the relaxed look Julienne had worn when Catherine entered the bedroom faded into a frown.

When Catherine reentered the room, Julienne's frown quickly disappeared. She yawned lazily, though her unblinking eyes didn't leave Catherine's face for an instant. "What have you been doing since I've been gone?"

In spite of herself, Catherine's cheeks flushed with an embarrassment she quickly hid. "Oh, the usual. Working. Exploring Maitreya." Relieved she could be sincere, she added, "It's beautiful, Julienne."

Julienne was pleased. "It would take years to explore all of

Maitreya, you know. We don't measure land here in the same way you do in America. Maitreya covers more than three hundred square miles, most of it unclaimed jungle. The house itself was built for Sir James more than one hundred years ago by Sumatran slaves. The site had previously been occupied by an Iban longhouse. In keeping with Iban tradition, the body of a young girl had been sacrificed and buried at the base of each of the six pillars which supported the longhouse. They say the bodies still lie beneath the foundation of the house. The Iban picked the most beautiful girls in the village to die. But then, if they had picked someone who looked like me instead of someone like you, it wouldn't have been a sacrifice, would it?''

Julienne laughed, but her voice contained no mirth. She rolled over onto her back on the bed and began to trace a finger around the lengthening shadows that played about the walls and ceiling. "When we were children, Michael and I, we used to hunt for relics of Maitreya's past around the grounds. We would find skulls buried in one spot, leg bones in another, left over from some feast or ritual." She stabbed at the shadows above her with a poke of her finger. "I should be the one to inherit Maitreya—it belongs to me more than the others. Michael would like to get rid of Maitreya after Papa dies."

Catherine looked at Julienne in surprised disbelief. It was obvious that Michael loved Maitreya. Sir Charles had already turned almost the entire responsibility for running it over to him. It would be his someday, although Margit and Julienne would certainly share in its profits.

"Michael told you that?" Catherine asked.

"He used to talk about it after Edward died. He'd like to return it to the native Malays and Dyaks he feels we took it from unfairly. Most of it anyway. He might want to keep the house and a small part of the land. But he knows Margit and I would oppose him—and Kara, too. Even though he will have title to it, he would still need our permission to dispose of it."

Catherine wondered why Michael would want to give most of his ancestral land away. She knew so little about him.

"I think Michael feels guilty about inheriting everything after Edward died. He doesn't feel he deserves it," Julienne continued. "Michael has suffered a great deal in the past. He isn't like the rest of the Stanfords, raised with silver spoons and a firm, comfortable identification with the rich and the powerful." Julienne propped herself back on her elbow and abruptly said, "You should have come with me to Batavia, Catherine."

Seeing that Julienne wanted to avoid discussing Michael any further, Catherine realized that Julienne had deliberately kept Michael's background a secret from her in the past, perhaps to protect her father's reputation but more likely in order not to lessen her blood relationship to her brother in anyone else's eyes. She was fiercely possessive of him.

Julienne was chatting on about Batavia. "I went to lots of parties. The governor-general was at two of them. His wife is American, did you know that? I've never danced so much in my life. The place was crawling with British and Dutch naval officers."

Lately Julienne had been more animated than Catherine had ever seen her. Something about Maitreya seemed to bring her out of her shell. But the image of Julienne gaily attending balls in Batavia was almost more than Catherine could imagine. Julienne had never shown much interest in men during the two years Catherine had known her well.

"Dutch men are good-looking, don't you think? But not half as good-looking as Michael." She talked on about Batavia's male population, her voice flat and mechanical, as if her thoughts were elsewhere.

Catherine was beginning to feel uneasy, yet she couldn't identify the source of her discomfort. She felt as though she were standing on the edge of a cliff that was about to give way. Sensing that Julienne's conversation was leading somewhere she didn't want to go, Catherine changed the subject, pointing to the pile of books on the desk near Julienne.

"I've decided not to take some of those along after all. I was wondering if I might leave them here and ask you to ship them back to the States with some of your things when you return."

"Sure. I'll be happy to send them back, but I probably won't be returning to Columbia after the expedition."

Catherine was surprised. "How come?"

Julienne shrugged. "There's no need. I'll finish my dissertation here at Maitreya."

Catherine looked doubtful. Long-distance dissertations often were never completed or took a long time at best. "That's a change of plans, isn't it?"

"Not really." Julienne volunteered nothing more.

Catherine studied her carefully, trying to read between those short, evasive lines. "You are planning to finish, aren't you?"

"Of course. But if I don't, it won't be the end of my life." She looked at Catherine's notes upon the bed and then added, "As it would be for you if you didn't finish."

There it was again. No mistaking it this time. An undercurrent of hostility, which bewildered Catherine. What was creating the tension? Julienne had been chatting amiably and openly about Batavia. A bit too openly. Catherine began to feel she was being drawn unwittingly into a game of cat and mouse.

"What do you think of my brother?" The question came out of nowhere, taking Catherine completely by surprise.

It seemed to Catherine now that the question had been planned all along and everything that had come before had been a mere diversion to throw her off guard. Or was she imagining it? Catherine flushed, but she attempted to conceal her reaction with studied indifference. Was Julienne eyeing her more sharply, carefully noting her reaction? For a moment Catherine thought guiltily that Julienne might know about what had happened yesterday at the pool with Michael. That was ridiculous, of course. Julienne hadn't even been here at the time, and certainly Michael would not have told her. She wondered what Julienne would think if she'd known. It was hard to guess. Julienne was not particularly close to Kara, so she would not feel angry out of loyalty to her sister-in-law. Still, Catherine sensed that Julienne would not approve.

Catherine attempted to sound casual and reassuring, looking at Julienne more calmly than she felt. "I really haven't had a chance to get to know him very well."

Apparently she was convincing because Julienne appeared to relax visibly. Catherine felt confident enough to add offhandedly, "He certainly is attractive." She knew Julienne would expect her to notice that. Not to do so would arouse her suspicions.

Julienne smiled with satisfaction. "Yes, isn't he? He looks like Papa, of course. He's the only one of us who does." Julienne yawned and stretched. She was still cramped and tired from the 500-mile flight from Batavia. "I suppose I should be honest and admit that I'm glad you weren't in Batavia at all those parties. This past month at Maitreya I've become aware again of how men pay so much attention to you."

"Your brother doesn't," Cathcrine said truthfully, and smiled.

"No. He wouldn't." Julienne rose from the bed. Her appearance led one to expect her to move like a nervous bird, but instead, her body unfolded in one graceful, single motion that implied something held back—a reserve of untapped energy waiting to spring, muscles which belied the pale skin and thin flesh.

Catherine took the hairbrush from the dresser and began slowly to brush her hair. She watched Julienne in the mirror as she came over to stand behind her. For a moment Julienne just stood looking at Catherine's reflection in the mirror; then she reached down, took the brush from her, and began to pull it through the long, silky strands of Catherine's hair.

Julienne smiled to herself. Catherine would never guess what she was thinking. Right now she was admiring Catherine's beautiful face and her body, revealed beneath the thin wrapper: the small high breasts; the slender waist and hips. She wanted to slip her hand down beneath that wrapper and touch those breasts, to bend over and kiss her lips. The thought of Catherine's reaction amused her and gave vent to her hostility. She observed that Catherine's eyes had assumed a kind of wariness. She suddenly laughed and handed the brush back to Catherine.

"Don't worry, Catherine. If men prefer your company to mine, I won't hold it against you . . . except for one man."

"Oh?" Catherine felt herself treading carefully again. "And which one is that?"

Julienne continued to smile, her eyes holding Catherine's gaze in the mirror. "You'll just have to guess."

Catherine's voice betrayed her annoyance. "My main interest right now isn't men—not even David. It's just getting my research and degree done as soon as possible." Her eyes dropped from Julienne's to confront her own in the mirror. Oh, God, she thought. Two days ago that had been comfortably true. Now she wasn't so sure.

Julienne touched Catherine's shoulder lightly with her hand. "I should go dress for dinner."

"Yes, see you later," Catherine remarked casually as Julienne left the room. Not until she heard the click of the door closing behind her did Catherine relax. Julienne's discussion of men had surprised her. Catherine had never known her to show any interest before, despite many opportunities: as Sir Charles's daughter, she had been something of a celebrity among the other graduate students.

Outside Philip Sanders had finished his whiskey on the terrace, and he and Michael were walking toward the airfield so that Philip might leave before dark. The two men had been discussing the news from Europe, where the situation had rapidly deteriorated these past two weeks. The Germans had stepped up their propaganda war against the Poles and were threatening an invasion. Britain and France had just vowed to defend Poland. Philip had urged his sister, Harriet, to remain in Borneo until the situation was resolved peacefully, but she had been determined to return to England despite the increasing tensions. "I'm far more certain to die here of boredom than I am from a bomb in Picadilly," she teasingly told him.

The men had just reached Maitreya's airfield when they heard a giggle and Caroline, Michael's older daughter, burst between them.

"I didn't want you to leave without my kiss, Uncle Philip!" she cried exuberantly as Philip bent to gather her up into his arms with a hug.

"I'm so glad you remembered." Philip smiled at her. "I shall give you an extra one to take back to Rachel for me."

"I shall keep it for myself, I think," she said.

Philip put her down, and she grabbed her father's hand. Caroline's pink sundress was dirty and rumpled from playing, and the bow in her hair had come untied, drooping like a torn battle pennant among the disarray of her golden curls.

Michael offered Philip his free hand. Philip shook it firmly and held it for a moment, aware that this time it would be longer than usual before they saw each other again, aware, too, that the times were beginning to add new meaning to good-byes. "Good luck, Michael. I'll help look after things while you're gone."

He released Michael's hand and reached down to touch Caroline's curls. "Good-bye, Caroline. I'll come back to see you and Rachel next week, and we'll have a picnic by the river." By then, Michael would be gone.

She nodded vaguely and stared up at him. Good-byes tore painfully at Caroline's heart. She had said so many to her father in the past, and this one reminded her that she would soon have to say another. She tightened her grip on Michael's hand while her other hand brought her thumb to her mouth and planted it there. Her eyes seemed to glaze over as she leaned her head against his arm and sucked on her thumb. Michael felt a sudden stab of guilt. It was always this way before he left. Caroline clung to him while Rachel, who was more honest with herself and him, grew cross and out of sorts. He was feeling guilty enough about other things without this, he thought wearily as he squeezed Caroline's hand in reassurance.

They watched together as Philip started his plane. Rachel caught up with them, her stubby two-and-one-half-year-old legs churning up the road to arrive just as the plane taxied down the runway. She stopped beside her father and Caroline, annoyed that events had just outrun her, her fingers curled into a tiny fist which she struck at the departing plane. Michael looked down at her and smiled. Delightful Rachel—so serious with every gesture as well as with the few words she possessed. Michael reached down and lifted both girls into his arms, giving them each a kiss. Each put her arms possessively around his neck as if to steal him from the other.

The plane had reached the end of the runway and was coming back, gathering speed. It took off just before it reached them, and Philip got only a glimpse of their three heads, close together, before he was gone.

Chapter 10

Her heart began to pound as her horse reached the final slope of the jungle trail that ended at the pool. The trail was heavily overgrown here, and huge vines hung about like fishing nets in wait for an unwary quarry. No whinny of greeting broke the silence of her approach this time. She was afraid of both finding him there and not finding him there as she broke free of the jungle curtain and saw the pool before her.

He was lying on his stomach in the sun on the smooth rocky ledge opposite her. His face was buried in the cradle of his arms. She paused and stared at him as the sunlight shimmered on the placid pool surface with a brightness which hurt her eyes. Forcing aside her doubts, she dismounted her horse and quickly shed her clothes. She entered the water quietly so as not to disturb the pool's lazy midday reverie. The tranquillity of the scene did not succeed in dispelling her anxiety. As she neared the place where he lay, her fears began to clamor noisily to be recognized. She did not stop to listen to them, knowing they would take from her what she most desired, as they had in the past.

Upon reaching the rock, she left the water as quietly as she had entered it and knelt beside him. His face was hidden from her, and he had not moved from the position in which she first saw him. The cool water that had clung momentarily to her shoulders and breasts now dripped onto his sun-warmed body—a shock which he did not acknowledge in any way. She gazed in admiration at his well-muscled brown back with its light covering of freckles. With a slight shock she noticed three tattoos which she recognized immediately as belonging to the Iban tribe, those fierce headhunting warriors of Borneo. The larger one, a stylized flower design denoting tribal membership, was located on his left shoulder blade. Another, which appeared to be an animal of some kind, was located near the small of his back and the third, whose design she could not decipher, was just beside it. She was filled with curiosity, which for the moment she put aside.

Hesitantly she reached out a trembling hand and traced a line from his firm, slender buttocks through the shallow curving small of his back to the blond hair at the nape of his neck. His muscles tensed beneath her touch. Without lifting his head, he reached up and grabbed her wrist, swiftly removing it from his body. She felt a shock of rejection. He slowly turned onto his side, still holding her wrist firmly in his grasp while his eyes held hers closely. His face betrayed no emotion except perhaps curiosity. Her own startled face flushed deeply. Still gripping her wrist, he gently forced her down upon her back, propping himself upon an elbow beside her. Her eyes opened wide in surprise. A slight smile now played at the corners of his mouth, and his eyes narrowed as he continued to study her face closely as if probing it for an answer to some question. Pressing her wrist firmly against the smooth stone beneath her, he leaned over and covered her mouth with a soft but thorough kiss that left her senses reeling. He pulled slightly away and began to scrutinize her body with the same thoroughness with which he had studied her face, caressing her with his eyes from head to toe, lingering where he willed. She flushed again. She felt a modesty that had not been present before, when it was his body that was being so closely explored. When he finished his scrutiny and looked at her again, his expression was frank and open with desire. He had let her have control that first time, but he clearly intended to keep it for himself today. This time it was her body, not his, they were going to explore.

Narrow rivulets of water ran off her glistening skin onto the rock beneath her. Releasing her wrist, he lazily traced their course with a finger. Her body tensed at his touch, and she briefly held her breath. He drew a slow circle around her navel with his finger and then lightly drew his hand to her breasts to stroke the nipples gently until they were rosy and hard. He leaned over and softly kissed them until she was filled with a spasm of pleasure. His hand drifted down her body to her legs, caressing her first and then slipping his hand into the warm pocket between her thighs. He drew himself up and knelt over her, raising her knees and kissing each of them before gently forcing them apart. His hands moved lightly down the inside of her thighs to the secret openings of her body. With his eyes and fingers he tenderly explored what she had never seen, had never touched, at least in pleasure, and he made her body burn with new sensations.

As she began gradually to relax under his slow and tender caress, her knees willingly moved farther apart, opening up and inviting his touch. Slowly, enticingly his fingers complied with her invitation to explore the entrance to her body. Finally he placed both hands on her knees, pushing them up as he leaned forward and covered her body with kisses and teasing traces of his tongue. She gave a little cry of agonized pleasure, and her whole awareness became focused on that throbbing area of her body that longed for release. She grabbed the back of his head and held it against her body. He smothered her with kisses and then raised his head to look at her. Veiled by his passion, his light gray eyes appeared dark, and like her own, his breath behind his parted lips was quick and shallow. He lay down again beside her and rested on an elbow while he looked deeply into her eyes. His hand was trembling as he began gently to stroke the tiny peak between her thighs until she felt a burst of pleasure, sharp and quick. She closed her eyes and shuddered, then relaxed and lay quiet and content beneath his touch. Her body where he had just caressed her was sore and tender, but still it throbbed with spent pleasure. He smiled down at her. His lips lightly brushed her own and then returned to linger. He leaned back and ran his fingers through her long black hair. With a grin he arranged it modestly over her breasts, carefully hiding all but the nipples, which he proceeded to kiss. He buried his face in the sweet scent of her hair and skin, and then he rose and kissed her mouth again, this time with a fiery warmth that rekindled her own fires. When he looked at her again, the strange light was back in his eyes. Suddenly he stood up, the evidence of his unreleased passion still hard and erect between his legs. He dived quickly into the pool and left her lying lazily and contentedly in the sun, just as she had done that first time. For a moment she lay there, puzzled by his quick departure. She sensed he knew, perhaps better than she, that she was not ready for more than the step they had just taken. As she was suddenly seized by a deep fear, her eyes flew open and sought him, but he had already dressed and gone. Suppose he took his unquenched desire for her to Kara for relief? The thought filled her with such distress that even her immediate realization that Kara was still away could not comfort her. The contentment of the previous moments had fled, and she could no longer languish in the sun, enjoying her memories and the tumultuous, confused new feelings within her. Now, even in the heat, she shivered as she rose to swim back to her clothes to return quickly to the house. With a pounding heart she realized that she now feared for herself. She felt possessed emotionally by a man she herself could not possess.

Michael knew that Catherine had been puzzled by his sudden departure. He didn't want to alarm her. No, that wasn't it. He didn't want to have to explain anything. Not yet, and maybe not ever. After he had dressed, he carefully searched the area around the pool. He was sure he had heard something. Just the faintest sound, but he was used to sorting out sounds that belonged from those that didn't. There they were. Fresh tracks belonging to neither his horse nor Catherine's. Leading to the pool. Pausing. Pausing for how long? Long enough. The rider had not dismounted. He had been right. Well, there was nothing he could do about it now. He paused and looked at Catherine still resting on the rock, and he felt a rush of warmth and tenderness. No, he would not tell her now. Let her rest with her illusions a little longer. He knew, of course, who the intruder was. He turned his horse quietly around and headed for Maitreya just before Catherine sat up with a start, full of her own fears and premonitions.

Julienne sat staring at the clean white walls of her room. Bare walls. That cable on which she hung suspended over the chasm had slipped a bit a few minutes before. She had felt it. No, it was more as if she had heard it, creaking with the strain, sagging with the weight of her insanity as it swung back and forth, almost but not quite ready to break with reality. Not quite yet. She sighed. No doubt about it, the weight was growing heavier. The scene she had just witnessed had added to it considerably. Catherine and Michael. Michael and Catherine.

She hated Catherine. She hated them both. Michael knew she hated him. Catherine didn't even suspect. What to do with them? Poison perhaps? She laughed to herself at the thought. Something painful. A slow death. Something to make them suffer as she had suffered, spending her life over an abyss. It had always been there. She had been born over it, had fallen right out of her mother's womb and there she was, hanging over it, held only by the placenta at first: dangling, screaming, terrified.

Only Michael really knew her, and not even Michael would think her capable of killing someone. She smiled to think what he might feel if he'd known she had killed their brother, Edward. Indirectly, that is. She had simply not saved him. Edward had found out about her and Michael and threatened to tell her father. He hadn't really found out. She had told him one day when she was angry with him and wanted to shatter his prim and proper calm. She had certainly done that. Shocked his socks off. She could see the hair stand up on the back of his neck. Goose bumps, too, like a frightened dog. She had made him listen to all the sexy details there, in the boat, where he couldn't get away. He had stood up as if to strike her and had fallen overboard. When he had bobbed to the surface, the swift current had carried him a little distance from the boat. She could have caught up with him; only she didn't. Instead, she watched him, smiling slightly at him as he bobbed about like a cork, up and down. Five times, not three. When he finally failed to come up, she took the boat to shore, got out, and turned it back into the river. No one ever knew that she was with him on the river that day when he drowned. His bloated body had been found downstream a week later.

She wondered if Michael ever suspected. She hoped he did because it would make him uncomfortable. Dear perfect Michael. Vulnerable Michael. She allowed her thoughts to drift to that time when Michael had first come to Maitreya and changed everything. Frightened, unwanted by everyone but her father. Fourteen. Even then he was blond, dazzling, perfect. Until then she had been her father's unquestioned favorite. More than Edward. Much more than Margit, who early on had allied herself with their mother. Julienne had been just like her father's son; she had ridden with him, explored with him, shared his interests. Until Michael. Blond image of their father.

Know thy enemy. She had been the only one other than her father who welcomed him at first, befriended him. They had become inseparable companions. It had pleased her father. It had pleased her. Then she had gone to his room one night to visit as she often did. Demons burning. He was lying on his bed, reading. She was flushed. Rising, concerned. "Julienne, what's the matter!" She put her fingers to his lips. Her robe slipped open. She had nothing on beneath it. Her lips upon his mouth. Urgent. Unbuttoning, unzipping, loosening his clothes. He was stunned, mortified, protesting. She had begged and cajoled and kissed and threatened and finally aroused him into making love to her.

Spoiling perfect things like Michael was so much fun. No longer perfect Michael. Too bad. Power. That is the key to everything. To safety. If you have power, you're safe. Sexual power, financial power, political power, blackmail power. The first and the last. That's what she had over him. In return she condescended to adore him more than anyone in her life, before or since. True, she hated and envied him, too, but she kept that to herself. He finally realized it, of course. To the world she had followed him around back then like a puppy dog. Only the two of them had known it was she who really held the chain.

Finally, when he wanted to end it, she had threatened to go to their father and tell him everything. He didn't care. He was even going to go himself and confess. Anything to end it. He had shut her out. That's when Edward had died, as a warning to Michael about what might happen to someone who made her unhappy. Only it was too late. Michael finally knew it was he who had the power. Papa loved him. Would forgive him anything, everything. Even this. Slip, strain, swing. Dangerously close to falling. After Edward's death Michael did not touch her again. Nothing to do but accept it. He did not turn against her. He became her good brother: considerate; concerned; even affectionate. Only not in the way she wanted. She was lying on her back now, looking at the ceiling, projecting images onto the white screen above her. Michael, that first night and all the other nights. Her hand moved down beneath her dress. Her lips parted.

79

Secret, dear little mound. "Julienne, you mustn't do that! Don't touch! You naughty girl. What's the matter with you?" Can't help it, Mother. Demons burning. Always. Never stops. Except like this, for a little while. Like the way Michael made them stop. He made them stop the best, Mother.

Chapter 11

Michael sat across the desk from his father. In the late afternoon it was Sir Charles's habit to take tea privately in the study adjoining his bedroom while he worked upon his various projects, articles, and books. At Sir Charles's request, Michael had joined his father today, although at the moment Michael was having a difficult time concentrating on the conversation. After that afternoon's encounter with Catherine at the pool he didn't feel like being with anyone, especially anyone in his family. He still carried a disturbing ache in his groin which tormented him whenever he thought about that meeting, which was often. And then there was the evidence they had been watched, which deeply concerned him.

Sir Charles had been making preliminary small talk while tea was served, aware that Michael seemed preoccupied—not for the first time these last few days. When they were finally alone, Sir Charles made no further effort to hide his concern. "I'm afraid there's been a bit of bad news. I got it on the wireless coming from Batavia an hour ago when I radioed Bernard. The Japanese have taken Hainan Island."

He immediately succeeded in getting Michael's undivided attention. "That gives them a base to launch an attack against Malaya and Borneo."

"I'm afraid it does."

Silence, broken finally by Michael. "Perhaps I shouldn't leave Maitreya now."

"On the contrary," Sir Charles responded quickly. "It's more important now than ever. You'll be gone for only six months. Nothing will happen before that time. We'll be all right here at Maitreya. Percival assures me that Singapore will prove impregnable, and of course, Bernard is convinced the Dutch and British naval forces can thwart any Japanese attack on the Indies or Malaya."

Michael felt a twinge of distaste at the mention of his brother-in-law. "Well, we both know Bernard tends to exaggerate things. Especially," he added ruefully, "where the health and safety of his favorite in-laws are concerned."

Sir Charles smiled. "But we know that where the safety of Margit's fortune is concerned, Bernard will be most cautious." His expression became immediately serious again. "I want you to go, Michael. Any threat of war should not stop you now. If you decide to call it off, it should be for another reason."

Michael looked at his father in mild surprise and felt a stab of guilt. Good God, did he know?

"I've received a cable from Father Kessel."

Michael felt a warm surge of relief.

"Bernard relayed it from Batavia. It seems there's been some trouble in the Asmat between a village some twenty-five miles from the expedition sites and the Dutch authorities. Here. You'd better read the report." He handed Michael the news he had received from Father Kessel. "Seems the Dutch have gotten themselves into a bloody mess that could force us to cancel.

"What do you think?" he asked when Michael had finished reading the report. "Nobody knows that area better than you."

Michael shrugged uneasily. "There's no way to assess the situation from here. We have to rely on these reports. You know I don't like to do that; there's too much chance for error."

"Father Kessel seems to think that the expedition would not be in any immediate danger from retaliatory moves, even if they occurred."

Michael made only a noncommittal noise that indicated he was not satisfied. He respected the priest, who was an old family friend, but he did not trust the Dutch authorities. "Do you want me to leave now, ahead of everyone else, so I can take a look into the situation?''

"No. There's no time. Ryder is in Batavia now. He's going to be arriving early—tomorrow, in fact. Wieder and the others are with him.'' Dr. Wieder was a curator of primitive art from the Koninklijk Instituut voor de Tropen. He was coming with the expedition to collect wood carvings from the Asmat people, considered the finest carvers of Oceanic art.

"Well''—Michael shrugged—"then all we can do is take precautions when we get there.'' He rose to go.

Sir Charles looked at his son with affection and concern. Why did it seem harder to see him go this time than ever before? Sentimental nonsense! He shook off the melancholy with annoyance. Old age must be creeping up on him, he thought.

Michael reached over and put his hand on his father's shoulder in a warm gesture of farewell, and Sir Charles again felt a pang of unexplained anxiety. Perhaps, he told himself, anxiety was natural, in view of the times. He suddenly brightened, for he had been saving some good news for last.

"There's one more thing.'' He smiled. "Kara will be coming home tomorrow with Ryder. She sent a message through Bernard that she would be able to leave earlier than she had expected.''

"Good,'' Michael mumbled. His expression was a mixture of relief and regret. It confused Sir Charles as well as himself.

Confound it! Sir Charles thought. What's the matter with him lately? Why wasn't he exuberant? In fact, his son's behavior for the past several days seemed a mystery to him. Quiet and preoccupied. Moody even. Not like Michael's usual equanimity at all.

On that unsettling note, they parted.

Michael went to his room. It was too early to dress for dinner, but he wanted some time to himself. He took off his boots and crossed to the shuttered doors that stood open to the terrace along one entire wall of his bedroom, pulling his khaki shirt out from his belt and unbuttoning it. It made him somewhat cooler, but not much.

He heard a sound in the room behind him, a polite clearing of the throat. It was Damal, the Malay head houseman, discreetly announcing his presence. Michael turned and greeted him in Bahasa. Damal ran the household, under Kara's direction, and acted as valet to Sir Charles. Michael had no personal servant.

He did not want one, but when Kara was away, Damal seemed to feel Michael became his responsibility. He saw to it that Michael's bath was drawn, his clothes laid out and ready for dinner, boots polished and ready for the next day's work. It both amused and annoyed Michael. Since Kara never did those things for him (he would never have allowed it), he had always failed to understand why Damal insisted on doing them in Kara's absence.

He said nothing of this to Damal. He knew Damal would not understand his objections and would only feel hurt. Damal's family had served the Stanfords for generations. As a result, Damal adhered more to the customs of the British Empire than did even Sir Charles. He was very loyal to the Stanford family, especially the Stanford men. He had accepted Michael into the household as Sir Charles's son when Michael first came to Maitreya, showing him much attention and kindness. He had taught Michael to speak Bahasa Indonesian and had helped feed Michael's insatiable curiosity about the customs of native Borneo in those early years. Now Michael returned Damal's kindness by accepting his attention, even though it made him uncomfortable.

"It seems empty here with Njonja Stanford gone," Damal remarked in his soft, impeccable British accent. It was often the case between them that Michael spoke Bahasa Malay and Damal spoke English.

"Yes—yes, it does," Michael replied absentmindedly.

Damal disappeared into the bathroom, emerging a few minutes later to announce the bath was ready. Michael sighed.

"Is there anything you might like before dinner?"

"No. Thank you, Damal."

The servant left the room, and Michael returned to his thoughts. He still could not quite comprehend what had happened to him the past few days—since that first day at the pool when Catherine had come to him. Actually it had begun that first evening he had seen her coming out of the forest, her slender form clad in that black dress with the tropical flowers and her long black hair falling loosely about her shoulders. He had felt stunned by that first sight of her, as if he were dreaming or, most likely, enchanted. She was hauntingly beautiful. But it was more than her beauty which startled him that evening. It was the shock of recognition which swept over him—as if, without realizing it, he had been waiting all these years for her to walk out of this dark forest and change his life. That was why he had so carefully avoided her since. He was determined to ignore the feelings she had roused in him that first meeting. And if she hadn't come to the pool that day, he would have succeeded. But she had, and now he could ignore her no longer.

After he had showered and dressed for dinner in a white suit, white shirt, no tie, Michael decided he would seek out Julienne and confront her. No point in putting it off.

He found her in the library, curled up in an oversize chair, reading. He leaned back against a table directly in front of her, gripping the edges firmly.

"You were at the pool this afternoon."

She looked up at him, eyes cool. She appeared much younger than her twenty-eight years. Even when she was seated quietly in a chair, there was a kind of restless energy about her that filled and charged the room.

"Whatever are you talking about?"

"You were riding Shiva, and you were at the pool today," he replied evenly.

Her eyes glinted sharply. "I don't know what you're talking about. I was riding Shiva today, but I was nowhere near the pool. We took the path along the river. Ask Damal. He saw me."

The muscles in his jaw knotted as he clenched his teeth.

"I don't have to ask Damal," he said quietly. "Shiva's tracks were by the pool this afternoon."

She closed her book with a snap. A cold smile played across her face, and her eyes were staring intently into his.

"Perhaps you should tell me, Michael, just what happened at the pool today that makes my whereabouts of such concern to you."

"You know what happened." He struggled to control his anger.

She rose and slowly crossed the few feet until she stood before him. Her face burned briefly with hate. Gazing intently at him, she said, "You know I would have liked to have been there, don't you, Michael? Lying on that rock in the sun with you to touch me." She reached up and brushed his cheek lightly with her hand.

"But you'll never guess something else I would have liked, Michael." She was examining him closely for his reaction. "I would have liked to have been in your place. Touching, playing with her body. Kissing those high little breasts." She saw the surprise she expected.

"Can I still shock you, brother dear? I thought you were the only one I could no longer surprise. How disappointed I am in you. I thought you understood me!"

She stood smiling before him, eyes glittering with such brightness that it shocked him, he who knew her better than anyone. It was not her bisexuality that stunned him; it was her lack of identity as a woman, as a person. He stared incredulously into her eyes, gazing beyond them into her mind, seeing dazzling splinters that could never be put together, fractured parts that had never made a whole. He had nothing to say.

She was still smiling into his stunned face. "Yes. I'd like to make love to her. Almost but not quite as much as I'd like to make love to you."

She reached her hand down toward the soft bulge between his legs. Without taking his eyes from hers, he caught her hand and pulled it away. She laughed.

"Now don't be selfish, Michael. Don't act as if there's not enough to go around."

He let her go, and she made no further attempts to touch him. Instead, she tucked her book under her arm and headed for the library door. Before she left, she turned and said, "Don't worry, Michael. Your little secret isn't exactly safe with me, but you can be sure that I'll tell no one else about it. At least you don't have to be afraid of *that*."

She left. A chill went through him. He had a strong feeling that, provoked, she was capable of anything.

Chapter 12

Catherine lay awake. Laden with its own moisture, the night air was able to absorb little from Catherine's body. Her gown clung to her. Even the flimsy mosquito netting seemed to make the heat more oppressive. Although she blamed the heat, Catherine knew that the real source of her torment came from within her. A fire had consumed her, and now she was sifting through the ashes, trying to find something of value left. Her engagement to David? She could no longer marry him. She wanted more from a relationship than appearance and convenience. Her self-esteem? Badly burned, too. She was no longer able to concentrate upon her work. Michael's presence in a room could now define her mood. Constantly surrounded by colleagues, family, servants, they could respond to each other only in the most impersonal way. Unable to touch him or talk to him in the way she would like to, she now found herself with surprisingly little to say. Yet while his presence disturbed and distracted her, his absence left her with a disquieting sense of loss.

She reached out and drew the mosquito netting back. Books had always been more satisfying, more fulfilling to her than the men in her life; achievements, degrees had always been most important. She had always been determined to define her own status, her own worth, rather than to marry it or to love it in someone else. Now to find her thoughts and feelings so possessed by someone frightened her. The personal values that had always supported her were in shambles. Yet her life was not desolate. Her feelings about herself as a woman gleamed triumphantly through the ruins. Passionate. Glowing. Alive in a way she had never dreamed of. A shiver of delight passed through her. In her mind she pulled him to her and felt his body pressing against hers. She could see his face clearly. Gray eyes, always so serious, even when he smiled.

She tried to force her thoughts away from him. Time was running out. Tomorrow the remainder of the expedition members would arrive and Kara was returning from Java. Tomorrow David would be here. She recalled the image of Michael standing alone that first night on the terrace, staring curiously at her as she emerged from the forest. In the month she had been at Maitreya they had been alone only three times. Two of those three times alone they had made love without speaking a word. Two people who were so skilled with language letting their bodies talk for them. The notion was strange now, yet it had seemed so natural then. What would she have said to him if that first day at the pool had been different? Desperate small talk, perhaps. Never would she have volunteered, "Michael, I want to make love to you." Not Catherine, who always proudly spoke her mind in every other situation: in class discussions; in seminars; in doctoral orals.

Now she struggled to give words to what she felt for Michael. Liking, admiring, wanting, loving. Loving? She didn't know. She knew only that she was obsessed by thoughts of him. Restless now, her senses rummaged through her memories of him, searching for something to ease her hunger. Tender morsels of memory to fill the emptiness of a sleepless night. Eyes, hands, lips, bodies, thoughts . . . all touching. The food of that fantasy made her hunger only more. She tried to imagine transferring her longings to David. It was no use. She could not obtain relief from David for feelings that belonged specifically to someone else; that could come from Michael or not at all.

Without putting on a robe or finding her slippers, Catherine rose and went out onto the terrace. Tiny neon fireflies blinked in the trees like glittering diamond tiaras. On-off, on-off, miraculously in unison. The night danced about her, dressed in firefly jewels and perfumed with the sweet, rich scent of jasmine. She followed the terrace around toward the other side of the house, the stones smooth and cool beneath her feet.

The shuttered doors of Michael's room lay open to the night. She stood for a moment in the darkness outside, gathering courage. The light beside his bed was on, its faint orange glow barely illuminating the walls of the room. He was reading, a book resting on his bare chest. He had not yet lowered the mosquito netting, and a sheet lay loosely across his body. The walls were covered with weapons, masks, and other ceremonial and ritual objects of Oceanic cultures. This wild display of primitive energy was broken in one spot by a portrait of a beautiful woman with blond curls and a sad face that hung on the wall across the room. In the dim light the woman resembled Kara, but her clothing indicated an earlier time. Strange, Catherine thought, as she looked at the journals and papers stacked about the desk, this didn't look like a room he shared with anyone. There was nothing of Kara in evidence anywhere in the room, yet Catherine knew that Kara slept here.

Catherine was shaking as she stepped from the darkness of the terrace into the shadows just beyond the glowing light of the room. She stood without speaking as she had done before. He looked up at her, slowly closed his book, and placed it on the table beside his bed. His eyes, clear, steady, and questioning, never left hers. But something else was in the look he gave her. Something reflected in her own. She was trembling visibly now. She didn't try to hide it from him. Instead, she crossed slowly into the glow of the lamp and knelt beside him at the bed. "Michael . . ." His name caught in her throat. The quiver in her voice matched the trembling of her hands as she hesitantly touched his chest. He drew his breath in sharply at her touch. It escaped reluctantly a moment later in a soft sound halfway between a sigh and a groan.

His own hands shook as he touched her cheeks gently with his fingers. Then, holding her face between his two hands, he pulled her down to him. His mouth covered hers with a tender kiss that soon became more urgent. Catherine returned it fully, eagerly. He broke away from her long enough to cast the sheet aside and lift her gown over her head. He pulled her onto the bed, on top of him, where he resumed kissing her hair, her neck, her face, and finally her mouth. The sensation of his body against hers for the first time—sent spasms of pleasure through her. He slowly ran his hands down her back, caressing, lingering, teasing her body as he explored it.

She savored the contrasting softness and hardness of his body against hers, acutely aware of every inch where his flesh touched hers. She moved her body slowly against his, and Michael pressed up against her in response. He seemed to hold nothing back, and yet he made no move to enter her. Puzzled, she braced herself upon her elbows and looked down into his face. It was transformed with passion.

"Please, Michael," she begged him softly. "I want you inside me this time."

He didn't respond. Instead, he took her hands and covered her mouth with his. With his knees, he drew her legs apart so that the swollen mound between her legs lay against the hardness of his own body. She gasped. Slowly he moved against her, and she felt herself caught up and pulled along against her will. "Not this way," she heard herself protest before she felt herself helplessly carried off in a sharp burst of pleasure and relief. At that same moment the semen flowed from his body and lay warm and wet between them.

He gently hugged her close to him. She rested her head upon his chest as he lightly brushed her neck and eyes and shoulders with kisses. When he raised his head to search her face, she lay quietly in his arms, her eyes closed. He relaxed against the pillow and stared at the ceiling for a few moments before he closed his eyes and drifted off to sleep.

She lay quietly against him, listening to the regular rhythm of his breathing. Her passion spent, she still felt mildly troubled. Her thoughts threatened to keep her awake; but her body finally triumphed, and she gradually drifted off to sleep, content to feel his arms about her. The lamp still burned, and the soft glow reflected off their entwined bodies, shiny and wet from their passion and the humid night air.

Sometime later Michael woke suddenly. The room, the night appeared to be just as they had been before. Catherine still lay sleeping in his arms. Yet something had alarmed him. Catherine must have passed Julienne's room on her way to his. Suppose Julienne had seen her? He had been worried earlier, when Catherine first appeared in his room tonight, but his desire for her had caused him to ignore all else. Now he could avoid his concern no longer. He gently moved from beneath her, trying not to disturb her. Relieved, he noted that she stirred but did not waken.

He rose and crossed the room toward the terrace. The framed photograph of his brother, Edward, which had suddenly appeared upon his desk the evening after the second afternoon with Catherine at the pool, caught his eye as he passed and increased his fears. He paused beside it, knowing that Julienne had placed it there as a warning to him. He had never been sure whether Julienne had really killed Edward or merely wanted Michael to think so in order to torment him. He suspected the former. He knew that Julienne would not harm him; the warning was directed toward Catherine. It meant that something might happen to Catherine as it had to Edward if Michael allowed their afternoon meetings to continue. He picked up the photograph and studied Edward's smiling face a moment. Then, with a slight shudder, he placed it facedown upon the desk and stepped cautiously out onto the terrace. As he did so, he felt a sharp stab of old familiar guilt. If it had not been for his relationship with Julienne, Edward might still be alive.

He stood quietly in the darkness and carefully studied the night, testing it with all his senses alert, straining for any sign of human presence. Years of exploration and constant exposure to danger had made him expert in sorting out stimuli instantly so that the soft scurry of a lizard on the terrace wall behind him just now was dismissed as irrelevant before it ever registered on his awareness. Sensing nothing unusual, he moved down to Julienne's room. The shuttered doors were partly drawn. He slipped between them. She lay facedown upon her bed. The hum of the overhead fan drowned out the jungle sounds. Carefully he moved toward the bed and stood over her. Her breathing was deep and regular. With relief he noted the open bottle of sleeping pills beside her bed. She must have taken the pills early in the evening, and that meant she would not have seen or heard Catherine pass her room.

Sure now that they had been unobserved, Michael left Julienne's room and returned to his own. Catherine was still sleeping, just as he had left her. He went into the bath and sponged himself with Maitreya's water, drawn cool and clear from the same underground spring that fed the pool. He returned to the room with wet cloth and towel and hesitated for a moment, taking in Catherine's slender, well-shaped form, before he began to wash away the heat and signs of his lovemaking. The cool water against her skin woke her. She looked startled for a moment. Seeing Michael's smiling face above her, she let herself relax again, smiling, closing her eyes while he bathed and dried her. When he finished, he began to rub her skin with oil, beginning with her face and neck, slowly working along her arms and hands and fingers, then to her breasts, gently rubbing until her nipples were taut and her skin glowed, tenderly massaging her stomach, hips, thighs, legs, and feet until her body glistened. She resembled an exotic beauty from a Gauguin painting, her black hair spread about her on the pillow. She opened her eyes to watch him, observing that his eyes as well as his fingers were tender. She tingled with satisfaction and a returning sense of desire. Touching her had roused his own passion; when he finished and put the bottle of oil down, he looked directly at her, his gray eyes burning fiercely. Yet he did not touch her again. Instead, he rose and went out onto the terrace to return in a moment with a white orchid, which he placed upon her black hair. Then he lay down on his back beside her, one leg bent, arms crossed behind his head, staring at the ceiling.

She picked up the wild orchid and held it before her. White with red veins, delicate. She turned her head to look at him. The troubled thoughts that had followed her to sleep returned. He continued to stare at the ceiling. She hesitated, feeling shy, but the need to know compelled her to take the risk. "You've made love to me, Michael, but not inside me. Why? Haven't you wanted to?"

He turned his head slightly to look at her. His voice was low and barely audible. "Of course I want to. I could hardly stand being near you these past few weeks. There were so many nights I've wanted to make love to you . . . completely." He turned the turmoil on his face back to the ceiling.

She turned on her side, leaning on an elbow so that she could clearly see his face. "Then why haven't you, Michael? Even now you seem to hold back from me. It's driving me crazy. I can't think about anything else. Don't you know it's what I want, too?" She reached out and touched his hard brown stomach. The muscles tightened beneath her touch.

"I know it's what you want. And you're right, I have held back from you." Eyes still firmly on the ceiling. "I've tried to resist you completely—but I can't. And each time it gets harder. Each time we go further." He got up from the bed without looking at her and walked to the open terrace doors.

She admired the perfection of his body and the way he carried it, naturally and proudly, completely sure of himself. Oh, God, Catherine cried out inside. I want this man! "Why have you held back, Michael?" She barely managed to get the words out before a flood of fear seized her.

He leaned against the shuttered doors. Now he was looking at her, and there was torment on his face. "Because it can go nowhere. It can only hurt both of us."

"But I haven't asked that it go anywhere, Michael."

"I know, Catherine. But you're not the kind of person to take love affairs lightly. I don't want to hurt you. You've never really made love before, have you?"

Catherine was seized with an anger that concealed from her the fact that she felt vaguely threatened by the question. It aroused her old doubts; it implied a criticism of her engagement to David. Her feelings too painful to explore now, she turned them against Michael.

"The arrogance of it all! Poor little Catherine. Michael must protect poor little Catherine's virginity. As if you have to decide what's best for me. How noble! Why can't you be honest, Michael? I'm not the one you're trying to protect!"

The steady gaze came back, patiently. "I know that. I'm protecting myself, too. I don't want anyone or anything complicating my nice, secure life."

"But you're willing to go just so far and no further, to make love to me up to a point. Just what *is* your definition of 'complicating,' Michael?" Catherine was becoming angrier by the moment. "A little heavy petting and some mutual masturbation isn't complicating, but intercourse is!"

"Having a baby is complicating," Michael replied angrily, feeling attacked and defensive now. "I have no intention of populating the world with bastards, as my father did, and hurting women like you, Catherine, in the process. My father ruined my mother's life by putting his own pleasure before anyone else's needs or feelings: before my mother's, his wife's, mine!" Michael

93

was shaking with anger now, and Catherine was taken by surprise at the depth of his feelings. She chose to ignore them.

"Come now, Michael. There must have been other women who have complicated your life."

"Since my marriage, none," he said simply. Calmer now, he turned his back to her and stood looking at the night, one shoulder lightly resting against the shuttered doors. He thought of telling her about Julienne but decided against it. There was no need now. Not that he underestimated the danger. He was sure that Julienne would never accept his relationship with Catherine, whom she already envied for her beauty and her academic success. He knew that under the present circumstances Julienne would destroy Catherine if she could. However, if he ended his relationship with Catherine now, she would no longer be in danger. And if Catherine remained ignorant of his sexual history with his half sister, Catherine's friendship with Julienne, or at least some semblance of it, would continue. In view of the upcoming expedition, that would be best for all concerned.

"And before your marriage?"

Lost in his own thoughts, he failed to hear the question until she repeated it. He didn't answer. Instead, he turned around to face her and asked, "Why haven't you made love to David, Catherine?"

There it was. She couldn't avoid it now. She felt cornered. It must have shown, for he said softly, "I'm not accusing you, Catherine."

Of course not. She was her own judge and jury. Always. "I've never wanted to," she said. And then, softly; "I've never wanted any man before you."

He did not move from where he stood across the room. A silence fell between them which she finally broke.

"You're ending it then." It was stated simply, as a fact.

He stood, eyes haunted. "I can't hurt them, Catherine. My family, Kara, the children." He sighed. "What more can I say? I want this thing between us to go no further. I have no intention of leaving Kara. I love her. We have had a good life together. But I wouldn't leave her and my children even if we hadn't," he added. Inside he felt desperate, afraid. He wanted her to understand, but he would not try to make her. To make her understand would mean to draw her closer to him. He had already shared

94

more of himself with her than he was willing to—emotionally, physically.

He stood looking at her. She said nothing. His last remarks made her feel at first defeated, then angry. Angry that she loved him and could not have him.

"You can hurt *me*, though. Right, Michael? That seems easy enough for you to do."

"You're strong, Catherine. You'll survive without any scars."

"I'm not so sure, Michael," she said bitterly. What had she wanted? What had she really expected from him? Surely not more than this. Wasn't this inevitable?

Is this what it felt like to go to war? Swept into it helplessly, unable to stop marching forward while all the time you wondered why you were there? What were the stakes of battle? Pride, honor, power, territory? Territory. Yes. That was it. She had invaded his territory. Now he was accusing her of wanting to occupy it. That wasn't true. She was only marching through on her way to—to where? To David? Michael had been right. In that brief rest upon her journey she had begun to covet what was his: his body; his feelings; his thoughts. She had begun to want to stay and make it her own.

"You were right," she said finally. "I do want more. I want all of you. Not just a night together."

He gave a sigh of resignation, and then he said quietly, "You deserve more than just a night from a man—from me. I think you should know that I've never admired anyone more or liked anyone as much as I like you, and"—his voice caught slightly—"I've never wanted a woman physically as much as I've wanted, and still want, you. This has been as difficult for me as it has for you—maybe more so. I sometimes think my feelings may run even deeper than yours, Catherine. You meet needs of mine that Kara never will. Besides," he added ruefully, "I'm not so sure that part of your attraction to me may not be the fact that you can't have me. You must have known that before we even started."

Catherine didn't reply. She was not completely sure of what she did feel toward him, except an overwhelming physical passion, a yearning without end that could not be satisfied by any other man. What now? Turn back? Retreat? Rebuffed, her pride, not her passion, was now her stake in battle. With Catherine, pride was no small matter; wounded, it must be avenged. She lay back against the pillow, staring at him as he stood across the room. Right at the moment she hated him, but even that failed to remove the longing. She wanted to hurt him as he was hurting her. Humiliate him as he had humiliated her. Anything to alleviate this feeling of helplessness, of powerlessness that panicked her.

She rose from the bed and crossed the room to where he stood. He had given her sexual power. Just a moment ago he had told her that she had it. All right. If it was all she had, she would use it against him. She put her arms around his neck and pulled his mouth down to hers. He didn't resist her, but his arms remained at his sides, and he didn't return her kiss. This angered her even more, and she kissed him harder, forcing her body into his. With a feeling of triumph she felt his body harden as she pressed against him, in spite of his wish to resist. He was a prisoner of his anatomy in that respect.

He tried to pull away from her, freeing his mouth long enough to whisper, "Don't, Catherine, please." She ignored him and sought his mouth again, insistently, biting his lip, probing with her tongue, pushing her body against his. She forced her hand down between their bodies to touch the mound where his hardness grew. He knew fully well that without being aware of it, she was trying to provoke him into an act of violence, not of love, but he felt helpless to stop what was happening. Driven now by his own aroused sexual desires, he could no longer hide his feelings behind a mask of indifference. Now he must battle himself as well as her. Gently he loosened her grip from around his neck and pulled her hand up from his body. "Respect what I feel, Catherine. Don't do this to us."

She sank to her knees, embraced him, and took him into her mouth.

"Stop it! I—" he cried hoarsely, choking on the last word. Beads of perspiration stood upon his forehead and upper lip. The torment in his eyes reflected the conflict that was tearing him apart. He pulled her roughly to her feet, gripping her tightly by the shoulder. His eyes were bright with anger. "Stop it, I said!" He wanted to shake her, but instead, he tightened his grip upon her shoulders until she flinched and he could see tears welling in her eyes. He saw defiance in her look.

"No. You'll have to throw me out." He knew she meant it.

At that moment he surrendered. He wanted her, and he could no longer defend himself—or her—against that desire. Angry now that he was giving in, he would take that anger out on her. For a moment he looked as if he might strike her. Instead, he again increased the pressure of his hands on her shoulders until she cried out in pain. She began to feel afraid that she had started something she could not control.

Forcing one arm behind her until she gasped in pain, he pulled her roughly to him and kissed her throat and her shoulders. Burying one hand in her hair, he pulled it, slowly forcing her head back until her back arched, forcing her breasts up to him. He kissed them until they hurt.

"Stop it, Michael, you're hurting me," she choked. Pushing her free hand against his chest, she attempted to wrench free. His grip tightened.

"Always on your terms, right, Catherine?" he said sharply as he half pushed and half carried her to the bed. She continued to struggle to free herself.

"You should have picked a verbal battlefield, Catherine. I'm much stronger than you are physically."

"Not like this, Michael, please."

"You play a dangerous game, Catherine," he whispered angrily. "I think you want me to hurt you so that it will be easy for you to hate me. Okay. I'm willing to comply." His eyes were hard and dark. She had never seen him look like that. "I didn't want it this way, but if the only way we can part is to hate each other first, then so be it."

He pushed her onto the bed, pinning her body down with his own so that she could no longer struggle. He forcefully turned her head to his and kissed her again, harshly, forcing her legs apart with his knees. He entered her abruptly, and she felt a stab of pain. A cry escaped her throat, only to be smothered into silence by his mouth covering hers. He began to thrust himself inside her, roughly, deeply. She was filled with spasms of pain. He came quickly and immediately rolled off her.

His hands clasped beneath his head, he lay staring at the ceiling while she turned her back to him and sobbed softly. She groped for her gown beside the bed and slipped it on with difficulty. Her shoulder had been wrenched, and her body was bruised and aching. She rose and left without looking at him. Ignoring her departure, he continued to stare at the ceiling long after she had gone. Finally he glanced down at the spots of blood on the sheets. Tomorrow he would tell Damal to burn them. He began to tremble and felt as if he might cry. Instead, he went into the bathroom and threw up. There was no doubt, now, that he had ended it. Having vented his anger, he was left with an unexpectedly strong feeling of loss.

Chapter 13

Michael came awake with a start, gasping for air like a drowning man, drenched in his own perspiration and trembling with fear. The dreams again; festering memories had erupted into nightmares.

He reached over to turn on the light, got up, and began to pace the room. How many times before had he awakened, shaken by his dreams, and quietly paced a darkened room so as not to awaken Kara? He could not run forever. One day he would have to turn and face what was back there. But not now. Not tonight. He had already lost too much tonight.

His mother had been very young, beautiful, frightened, depressed. Not ready to be a mother, especially not alone. Disowned by her family, rejected by her lover, she had fled to Singapore and then to Hong Kong, determined to destroy herself and, indirectly, her son, whom she saw as an extension of his father. It had been Michael's misfortune to be cast in the same image as his father, and that resemblance had heightened his mother's ambivalence toward him. She alternately smothered him with love and abandoned him, disappearing for days, leaving him alone, terrified, and often without food. By the age of four he had learned to beg on the streets of Hong Kong in order to survive those times. Things were not much better when she returned. She supported them haphazardly on the "donations" she obtained from endless men she met in the streets and bars: armies of them, in and out of her life. He never even knew their names. They treated him as if he hadn't existed, as if he weren't in the room when they . . . Most of the time he could effectively shut those scenes out. But there were nights when his memories bubbled up in dreams.

The dream tonight. He had had it before. This one was no fantasy. He had been seven years old at the time. Alone. His mother gone again. A man, drunk, looking for his mother. Nothing unusual about that. Forcing entry into the room. Different. Michael knowing right away something was wrong. Something glinting and mean about those eyes. No drunker but angrier than the others. Angry and frustrated. Going to take it out on him. Threatening him with a knife, forcing him to undress, exploring his frail, frightened child's body. Please don't. Shrinking from the man in shame and terror, his childish distress only feeding whatever monster lived in there. Feeling so helpless. Dear God. Promising himself he would never again let himself feel so trapped and helpless; only strong, always in control. The sour smell of stale, cheap liquor, the sound of the man's heavy breathing. Overwhelming. They came to him now over the distance of twenty-three years as clearly as if they were just happening.

He was still trapped, unable to run as he stood transfixed there on Maitreya's terrace in the darkness, staring inward, unable to take his eyes from the scene or switch it off. The man was sitting down, unbuckling his belt. Going to beat him perhaps. Unzipping his pants. No. He isn't going to make him do that. Pushing Michael to his knees, grabbing him by his hair, pushing his head to . . . sticking it in his face . . . trying to force him to . . . No! Gagging, choking. Finally vomiting what little food he had eaten all over himself and the man. Refusing to submit, hitting with his tiny fists. The man jumping up, enraged, starting to beat and kick him. Curling into a ball, covering his head with his arms. Desperately trying to protect his vulnerable parts. He stood watching the reel of memory flicker to its closing scene. No happy ending. No one to the rescue. Feeling his ribs cracking, head bursting. Feeling it all over again. Finally, mercifully, darkness.

He had not regained consciousness for almost a day. Bruised and bloody, ribs cracked, he had struggled to his feet and bathed himself as best he could. He did not go for help. He cried. Hard. Perhaps for the last time in his life. When his mother returned two days later, hung over and sick, she had not even noticed his swollen face, the bruises on his body, the pain in his eyes. He hated her then, although it was frightening to hate her. She was all he had. She had gone immediately to bed, and he had taken care of her as best he could. As he always did. She had never been there, physically or emotionally, when he needed her. It was nothing new. But this time had been the worst. This time he would never forgive her as he had in the past.

Now, standing on the terrace, he took a deep breath as if he were letting go of something and turned to go back to his room. He knew there were other experiences, perhaps worse ones, that were not conscious memories. He had no direct access to them, but in his dreams he caught glimpses of them, disguised, fleeting, frightening. He had never shared any of those with anyone. Even his father did not know what had happened during those eight years before he had found Michael and his mother, though Michael knew he suspected some of it from the reports of the private detectives who had found them.

He left his light on and stretched out on his bed, remembering that first time he had met his father. His mother hurriedly scrubbing him for some reason, something she never did. Not telling him why. Turning him around to face a tall, well-dressed man standing in the doorway. The man staring at him intently for a long moment with eyes brimming over with tears, then coming quickly forward, kneeling and swooping him up, gathering him into his arms, almost crushing him in that embrace. Michael thinking as he gasped for air that this was a wonderful way to die. He knew without being told this man was his father. Michael's eyes had opened wide; then he had closed them in relief, letting himself be taken over by this warm, clean, delightful-smelling man. Knowing he would be safe now. Letting himself believe for a moment in happy endings.

The bond of love between Michael and his father had been strongly sealed in those three months they had been alone together. His father had sent his mother to a sanitarium to recover from her drug addiction while he stayed with his son. Sir Charles had been especially tender with Michael, as if almost losing him had made him dearer. Sir Charles had been touched by Michael's obvious need for him and had opened himself up to him in ways he had not to his other children. It was still that way today.

Those who knew Sir Charles but did not know the circumstances thought Sir Charles's preference for his illegitimate son to be one of simple narcissism since Michael bore such an astonishing resemblance to his father and Sir Charles was known to be a vain man. Those who knew the truth realized that the real bond had been established during those early months by their mutual need for love and acceptance.

His mother had not wished to remain in the Indies, so his father had bought them a lovely house in Berkeley near San Francisco. There was no discussion about divorce this time; that was a battle she had already fought and lost. She would now settle for what she could get, security and a good home for herself and Michael. Sir Charles supplied her with a Japanese housekeeper and a generous income. She returned to school and obtained a degree in art. His father visited them at least twice a year, staying several weeks at a time and taking Michael with him to visit his academic friends at the University of California at Berkeley. With his father Michael was finally free to vent his natural good humor and high spirits, his enthusiasm for life and adventure.

His mother was good company, too, in those days. Stimulating, fun to be with, but rather more like a sister than a mother. There were darker moments. His mother made few friends and still relied too much on him for emotional support. At times she would grow depressed and frightened, and then she would cling to him. "Don't ever leave me, Michael. Promise me. Don't leave me the way your father did." And he would promise with a little cringing pit of rage in his stomach. At those moments he felt anger toward his father, too, for leaving him with the sole emotional responsibility for his mother. She was frightened and childlike; but she was also talented, witty, and charming, and she had successfully endeared herself to these two men who shared that part of her life. Her own paintings and photographs had become a permanent part of Sir Charles's room after his wife had died.

There was also one of her paintings in Michael's room. It was his favorite, a self-portrait of a serious young woman with blond curls about her face and a wistful smile showing only slightly at the corners of her mouth. The eyes, however, were sad. Michael still felt tenderness when he looked at that lovely face. Poor little

Mother. As much as he hated her insecurity, her selfishness, he had always loved her. He still did.

She had been only thirty-three and he fourteen when she had left him for good. She was just beginning to achieve success and recognition as an artist when she developed pneumonia. It had been so sudden. He had cabled his father that she was seriously ill, and even though Sir Charles had come immediately, she was dead by the time he arrived.

Michael had felt numb, bewildered, disbelieving. His father had been devastated with grief, a reaction that surprised Michael. He had never really completely understood his parents' relationship. He did not to this day. His father had taken care of all the arrangements, including the funeral service. Just the two of them in attendance. His father had wept openly, but Michael had not cried. His feelings were a puzzling mixture of grief and relief. He felt anger, too. She had always made him promise never to leave her, and now she had gone off and left him first. Just like her to do that. But how could you feel angry toward someone who was dead?

It was certainly not Michael's first or his last experience of guilt. He had been bound by guilt to all of them: Kara; his mother; his father; even Julienne. Feeling responsible. Trying to make up to his mother for the loss of his father and her self-respect. Making up to his father for the death of his mother and for the loss of Edward, his elder son and heir. He had coped with his guilt by finally becoming the perfect son, brother, husband. Restraint and self-denial were now deeply ingrained characteristics in Michael, and he had applied them diligently throughout his marriage. Until Catherine.

He forced his thoughts to his wife: Kara with her curly blond hair and blue eyes, looking, smiling like his mother. He had recognized the similarity at once. He had married her anyway. Another doll to care for. Perhaps he needed that to feel important. But Kara was all the good parts of his mother: adoring, charming, bright, if childlike. She let him have his independence. She never troubled him about intimacy or demanded a closer relationship. Or an equal one. Indeed, she probably hadn't the slightest notion of what real intimacy with him would mean. He shared few of his thoughts and feelings with her, communicating mainly about practical or superficial things. He knew he probably sold short her ability to understand him. But he preferred it that way. It was safer. He was less likely to be hurt. She was not lover, friend, companion, partner rolled into one. She was not, nor could she ever be, Catherine.

The lightplane circled the small group waiting near the airfield below and then began its approach for a landing. The early-morning downpour was only now, at midday, beginning to lighten to drizzle. Kara was the first one off the plane. She threw her arms around Michael, who gathered her close to him. He was glad to see her. She was safety, security, familiarity. In relief, he buried his face in the curls of her blond hair. Then he found himself greeting the new arrivals he had already met: Professor Ryder, Professor Levine, and Dr. Wieder. He shook hands with the other new members, among them David Carter, Catherine's fiancé.

It was only when Catherine was safely beside David, with David's arm protectively around her, that Michael allowed himself to look closely at her. She wore navy blue slacks and a simple white blouse. The tan she had obtained these past few weeks glowed healthily above the white open neck of her collar. There was a very slight swelling around her eyes that anyone but Michael would take as a sign she had overslept, a hypothesis supported by the fact that she was late and had only just arrived at the airstrip.

Michael found himself studying David closely as well. He was a handsome man, perhaps twenty-four or twenty-five years old, tall, with brown curly hair and brown eyes. His smile was appealing, friendly: perhaps too friendly, ingratiating. Stop it, Michael warned himself. Whether David deserves her or not is none of your affair. Stay out of it. He noted that Catherine looked right through him as if he weren't there. Just as well.

He wondered if he could as successfully block her out of his existence. Certainly self-deprivation was not new to him. Soon, he told himself, he would be able to shut himself off from his feelings so that he could be around Catherine and not want her. But standing there now, close enough to touch her, he realized with a stab of pain that the time had not yet come. Taking Kara by the hand and walking away, toward the house, he vowed it would come soon.

*   *   *

The huge twin-engine Consolidated 28 seaplane sat beside the dock on the wide Barito River, rocking gently, resembling some giant prehistoric flying reptile dozing in the early-morning clouds and drizzle. Its enormous wingspan reached well past the dock beyond the riverbank and into the clearing. Like the extinct creature it resembled, it was ungainly and awkward on the ground, gaining grace only in flight. It dwarfed the Stanford seaplane tied nearby which Michael flew on his own solitary expeditions.

The Dyak dockworkers at Maitreya had just finished loading the personal luggage of the expedition members aboard the plane, and the three-man crew of the chartered craft was now in the final phases of the preflight checkout. The expedition party stood on the dock, ready to board. Sir Charles was bidding each of them a personal farewell. He stood by the bobbing door as they filed past, shaking hands, like the host at a reception.

When Catherine reached him, he took both her hands into his own. "I hope we have not seen the last of you at Maitreya, Catherine. You've brightened my life considerably in the past few weeks."

Catherine smiled and expressed her thanks. The truth was that she both fascinated and puzzled him. As he leaned forward now to kiss her good-bye, he realized that he had still not reached a successful compromise between treating her as a beautiful woman and as a professional colleague. He wanted her to return so that he could continue to try.

He went on with his good-byes until only Julienne and Michael remained. Sir Charles put his arms around Julienne and kissed her on the cheek.

"I slipped a book in your valise for you to give to Father Kessel for me. It's a copy of Kroeber's latest book on Northwest American Indian myths. He'll enjoy it. He's collecting Asmat myths now."

Business aside, he studied her face. It suddenly occurred to him for the first time that he knew her hardly at all. How had that happened? He brushed the unpleasant thought aside.

"For the first time, little Julie, you're going on an expedition without me." He gave her arm a squeeze. "Keep me well supplied with news. I know your brother will be traipsing off into the wilderness first chance he gets and won't be able to keep me posted. And don't forget to work hard: I expect a splendid piece of work from you."

Did he? Hardly likely, Julienne thought. She murmured a compliant "I'll try not to disappoint you, Papa." What did she want him to say? That he was proud of her no matter what she did? That he loved her best, always? That he loved her, even though she was not beautiful like Catherine? She turned to her sister-in-law, who stood with her head resting lightly against Michael's shoulder, her arms about his waist.

"Good-bye, Kara. I know you'll take good care of Papa." One last blank smile at the three of them, and she turned and entered the plane.

Sir Charles smiled affectionately at his son as he extended his hand to him. "Good-bye, son."

"Good-bye, Dad. I'll try to contact you by radio as soon as we arrive."

Sir Charles moved a discreet distance away, giving Michael a chance to say his final good-bye to Kara in private. When Michael finished embracing her, Sir Charles stepped forward and gave his son a hug and a pat on the shoulder. Michael boarded the plane with one last glance at Kara.

The door closed behind him as the big engines sputtered, then started with a roar that sent gusts of air over the dock. Sir Charles freed the plane from its moorings, and it began to drift with the current, away from the shore. The wind from the propellers whipped at the two figures on the dock as the plane started to taxi out into the river. Sir Charles put his arm about Kara as they stood watching it go. Her eyes were filled with tears. Suddenly Sir Charles found himself overcome with apprehension. He had parted from his son and daughter many times before, but this time was different. Yesterday news had come by shortwave radio that Hitler had invaded Poland. By treaty, Britain and France would now be forced to declare war on Germany. It was possible, even likely, that the Germans would launch an attack on Belgium and the Netherlands as well as on France. England itself might not survive. If Europe, particularly Holland, were to fall to German troops, the Indies would provide a tempting and vulnerable target to the Japanese.

The plane had turned downriver with the current and, gathering speed now, was passing before the dock once more as it lifted off. Inside, the passengers were chatting animatedly, excited by the prospect of being under way. Only Michael, seated in the cockpit of the plane next to the pilot, and Catherine, curled up by a window in the passenger section, watched Maitreya and the two tiny spectators on the dock disappear.

He loved Kara. Catherine could see it clearly now that she was no longer trying to hide it from herself. She wondered, as she followed the river's course below, what he had felt for her—if he could love more than one woman at a time. Catherine, who had had so much difficulty in loving even one man, found it strange to imagine loving two.

Chapter 14
The Asmat, Dutch New Guinea, September 1939

Throughout its history New Guinea had been a divided island. The eastern half was currently controlled by Australia, which had taken over from the Germans and the British. The western portion had been annexed by the Dutch in 1828. Both were largely unexplored. The few white inhabitants lived mostly in scattered, isolated outposts along the coast. Some 200 miles inland from the southern Casuarina Coast, the Snow Mountains rose to divide the Dutch area of the island down its length like the spines of a monitor lizard. The Carstensz Glacier crowned the peak of that name, soaring more than 16,500 feet in the northwest part of the range, perpetually dressed in white clouds and snow. Mount Wilhelmina, 15,585 feet, jutted seventy-five miles to the southeast of Mount Carstensz. Rivers poured from the mountain highlands and ran like veins beneath the lush green jungle surface. Tributaries carried their loads of silt and mud until they spilled into the Arafura Sea, bleeding rich brown soil into the ocean like an erupting artery, the lifeblood of the land eroding inevitably away.

Nearing the Asmat coast, the rivers split again into numerous streams. Mangrove trees left the beach to walk through saline water on upraised roots like bathers testing the water. The tangled roots of these trees made the entire coastline as well as the riverbanks impassable on foot. The rivers themselves were the only thoroughfares.

The thatch-canopied boat, loaded with supplies, rode low in

the water. Its twin outboard engines buzzed like Mixmasters churning up the river bottom. The boat was piloted by Captain De Jong, commanding officer of the small Dutch army unit at Agats, and his Javanese assistant. Near them, Michael sat barely listening to the conversation of the four graduate students he was accompanying upriver to see settled at their field assignments. They were joking and laughing, but he knew there was anxiety as well as excitement beneath their high-spirited banter. Leaning back against a canopy pole, hands folded behind his head and feet outstretched, Michael appeared relaxed. He was anything but. He was angry and worried, still smarting from his unsuccessful confrontation with District Officer Jan Voorhoeve. That arrogant bastard had flatly refused Michael's request to visit Wiat Kargas. Michael had wanted to investigate for himself the circumstances surrounding the attack on the Dutch patrol several weeks earlier. Since arriving at Agats a few days ago, he had become increasingly suspicious that the Dutch were engaged in a cover-up and that the truth might pose a far greater threat to the expedition than he had been led to believe.

Father Kessel and two of his Asmat assistants sat across from Michael in the boat. The priest had been visiting converts in Agats and was on his way to attempt to make some more in Septj. Michael usually had little use for missionaries. He generally found them too obsessed with exposed genitals and too ignorant of the cultures they came to alter. Father Kessel was an exception. He had been trained as an anthropologist. In the five years since they had met on the Sepik River in Australian New Guinea, Michael and Father Kessel had formed a real friendship. Of the ten people on board the boat, the priest was the only one who knew of Michael's confrontation with Voorhoeve and shared his concern.

David Carter sat on Michael's right. When Michael cared to admit it to himself, he didn't much like David. True, he probably wouldn't have liked any man who was going to marry Catherine, but that was not the only reason for his reservations. David was pleasant enough. Michael might have even found him a tolerable companion in most situations, but where Catherine was concerned Michael sensed in David an underlying current of rivalry and professional jealousy carefully hidden beneath his apparent devotion, an undercurrent of which Catherine seemed oblivious.

Michael suspected that David was the kind of graduate student who used school as a shelter to hide from adult responsibilities. Whenever such thoughts about David occurred to Michael, as they did now, he tried to shut them out. After all, he reminded himself grimly, David's personality was none of his business.

At that moment Michael wasn't the only passenger on board who was having trouble concentrating on the conversation. Catherine sat at the boat's bow, between Carl and Daniel Forman, her face turned aside from the others, watching the river. From the corner of her eye she had just briefly glimpsed Michael, casually stretched out near the stern. To keep sweat and his unruly hair out of his eyes, he had tied a red bandanna around his forehead, just as he had on that first day she had seen him. Her feelings sank to the pit of her stomach. Whenever she looked at him now, she felt a humiliation that could be made bearable only by maintaining an attitude of icy loathing. She quickly brought her thoughts back to the river, drowning them in its peaceful expanse. Sudden showers of orange butterflies burst forth among the trees, and chains of bright red flowers hung over the water. Occasionally they passed villages, with their distinctive forty-foot-long dwellings, built on ten-foot stilts to escape the ocean tides which often surged as far as forty miles inland on the rivers. The height of the houses was protection from another danger as well—headhunting raids.

"Did you ever eat anybody, Kio?" Daniel Forman asked the oldest of Father Kessel's assistants.

"Once." Kio nodded. "An old woman. No good. Too tough." He grinned.

Michael's attention was finally captured by that lie. He knew Kio to be a converted Asmat warrior who had taken as many as 100 heads. "Don't spare them, Kio. Tell the truth. Tell them how it's really done."

Kio glanced uneasily at Father Kessel, but seeing no objection, he smiled broadly. "First we go to capture the enemy and cut off their heads on the way home in the boats. The women are waiting, singing and shouting and shooting arrows to greet us. We cut the bodies like this." He drew a line with his thumb from his anus up under his armpit to his neck and back down the other side. "Take off the arms and legs and cook them with the upper body and eat. Save the lower part." He gestured toward his genitals. "Mix it with sago to eat later at ceremonies." His voice had a singsong quality, as if he were instructing the young boys in the men's house. "Bake the skull slowly—high above the fire—all night. The next day scalp it. Take off nose and jaw. With a sharp shell, cut line from the nose to the neck and peel off the skin. Then knock hole in the temple and put brains in a sago bowl to be eaten." He shrugged. "Save the skull. That is all."

"And what would you do with the skull, Kio?" Catherine asked him.

"That depends," he said slowly, his eyes brightening. "Yes, that depends." As he spoke, civilization seemed to fall away from his dreaming eyes as easily as he might have discarded the old khaki pants he wore. Catherine could almost see the ceremonial stick covered with lime tracing white circles around his face, his nipples, his navel, preparing him for battle.

"When I was to become a man," he continued, "I went on my first raid to capture an enemy and kill him. I sat afterward in the men's house, and my father placed the skull of the man I had killed tight against my penis." Kio placed his hands between his legs and cupped his groin. "The power from my enemy flowed into me through my penis, to make it grow big like a man's. I sat with legs drawn up and the skull between them. For days I did not move. I did not eat. I grew weak and died." As he spoke, he seemed in a trance. "They put me in a boat, the skull with me, and set it adrift on the river. When it came to shore, I was born again . . . a man."

Michael, seeing that Kio had finished, looked at Father Kessel with a smile and a glint of challenge. "Now you must tell us, Father, how you were able to convince warriors with extensive dietary experience like Kio that by eating stale crackers and grape juice, they are partaking of the body and blood of Christ."

"Only symbols," the priest protested good-naturedly. "They understand that."

"Now I eat God," Kio interrupted proudly. "It's more powerful to eat God every day than a man once a month."

Michael was amused. "Less nutritious, though. Right, Father?"

Father Kessel laughed affectionately. "I've been putting up with your kidding and irreverence for years, Michael, and it has taken a sense of humor to survive, believe me. You're an incorrigible heathen. Worse than any out there." He nodded toward the riverbanks. "I've long since given up any hope of formally saving your soul. Your only chance for heaven will be if God makes allowances for good men as well as pious ones. I, for one, happen to think He will."

"Who says God has to be a 'he'?" protested Catherine.

Father Kessel laughed. "A good point, Catherine. Well, if God is a woman, then Michael will be welcomed to heaven with open arms for sure."

The others laughed, too, except for Catherine, who turned away to face the river again before they could see her blush. It annoyed her to see herself as merely one member of an army of women to whom Michael Stanford had proved irresistible.

A short while later they reached Septj. De Jong slowed the engines and headed toward the river landing. There they deposited the three men who had come to deliver the truth, leaving those who had come seeking it to continue their journey upriver.

Another boat, a dugout, drifted by on the wide expanse of river. A woman stood fishing in it, a basket lowered in the water, her brown bare body glistening in the warm sun. It was at once a peaceful yet dramatic sight.

"Straight out of *National Geographic*," mused Carl, watching her. "That was my first sex manual. I used to look through it for every bare breast I could find. Long and swinging, high and round. I loved them all. My parents were prudes. The whole damned town were prudes. So I used to go to the library and sneak looks at a *National Geographic* I hid behind a copy of *Wee Wisdom* or *Jack and Jill*. For twenty-one years," he said jokingly, "I thought only brown and black women had breasts. White women had lace and ruffles attached to their skin."

He squinted off into the sun at the disappearing woman. "Anyway, that was the source of my early interest in anthropology. By the time I got to college those sexual feelings were channeled into a love of primitive cultures. Now when I look at that woman, all I think about is whether she is part of a matriarchal or patriarchal system of kinship. That's what psychological development does for you. All that beautiful early lust turned into academic bullshit."

He gave an exaggerated sigh and leaned over to give Catherine a light kiss on the lips.

"Now I can see this beautiful woman only as a friend and colleague. How's that for a sad state of affairs?"

Catherine smiled and rested her forehead affectionately against Carl's shoulder, closing her eyes. Since she had known him, he had been her port in an emotional storm.

"How did you get interested in anthropology, Catherine?" Daniel asked.

"Trying to get as far away from Chicago as possible," she replied without elaborating.

The ocean breeze had died down and sunset was turning the river into a flat sheet of gold when they left Carl and Daniel at Omadesep an hour later. In the five-mile ride to Fos, where David and Catherine would be staying, the river had turned pink and orange and the trees and riverbanks were becoming silhouettes. The remaining occupants of the boat fell silent, each lost in the drama of the changing sky.

As they rounded a river bend near Fos, they met an astonishing sight. A twenty-vessel escort regatta of warriors in ceremonial dress with feathers and plumes in splendid display was paddling toward them with a vehemence that was frightening. The long, narrow dugouts each contained ten to fifteen standing warriors with ten-foot paddles moving in unison, clacking rhythmically against the sides of the boats. These boats were so shallow and narrow that unskilled Westerners would immediately overturn them while sitting, let alone standing. The warriors tossed up clouds of magical lime while chanting war songs, screeching and blowing bamboo horns. At the end of each song they uttered grunts and high-pitched yelps. Their splendid headdresses were made of pigeon plumes and cockatoo feathers, with some bands made of highly prized fur from the cuscus, a monkeylike marsupial. Carved nose bones and shells pierced the septums of their noses. Loops of woven leaves pierced their ears, and carved bamboo and shells formed necklaces of status and wealth. The bamboo sticks were indications of the number of heads taken. Some of the warriors had painted black charcoal masks about their eyes and stripes upon their bodies. White lines of clay and sago starch added contrast. Human vertebrae pendants hung on chains of shells and seeds. Many of the men wore whole skulls around their necks, burnished gold from constant handling. The skulls were even slept upon, like pillows.

113

As they reached the patrol boat, the dugouts swung around to accompany it on the final half mile to Fos. Catherine felt both excitement and fear at the spectacle of paint, feathers, naked bodies, and churning water. To her relief she saw that the warriors carried no weapons except small bone knives stuck in their woven grass armbands.

"It's incredible how fast they can move those boats," said David. The women, children, and older men of the village waited on the riverbank just now coming into view. Though some of the women also had white and black stripes painted on their bodies and ropes of shells around their necks, they were not as fancifully dressed as the men. Most women wore grass G-strings while the men and children went naked.

Catherine found herself overwhelmed by the the activity whirling around her on the riverbank until she felt Michael take her firmly by the elbow and steer her through the curious crowd that, having never before seen a white woman, touched and poked and pulled at her.

Somehow they finally reached the guesthouse perched on its ten-foot stilts. A notched log was the only means of entry, which Michael nimbly negotiated. Catherine grumbled as she shakily followed.

"I can see it now. The headlines will read, FEMALE ANTHROPOLOGIST DIES FALLING OFF A LOG IN NEW GUINEA. They won't mention it was ten feet off the ground. All journalists hate women."

Michael laughed but offered her no assistance. He knew better than to try. Since their arrival in Agats, every time he had been around Catherine she had picked a fight over something—procedures, supplies, even the weather. To the sensitive observer, like Carl, it was obvious that they fought not like the acquaintances they appeared to be, but like intimates. She would accept nothing from Michael—not even an opinion, let alone assistance. The quarrels left Michael depressed, even though he understood them. He knew she needed to lash out at him; she had to hate in order not to feel the anguish of her love. To protect himself, he had become as wary and defensive as she. And he avoided her as much as possible.

She stood now in the doorway of the guesthouse, looking out onto the river and the village, listening to the sounds of the jungle in the twilight. Michael had prevented the villagers from following them into the guesthouse, and they had gradually wandered away to more interesting diversions. She rested her head against the doorpost. He stood quietly watching her. A faint pink glow was all that remained in the sky, but even in the darkness he could sense that she had softened and her guard was down.

"Oh, Michael, it's so beautiful! I've dreamed of it—imagined it for so long. I can hardly believe I'm here." She gave a laugh of pleasure.

He was oddly touched by her delight. She was always beautiful but never so much as when she laughed.

"Far enough from Chicago?" he asked quietly.

"Chicago?" She smiled.

De Jong and David arrived with the luggage and supplies, carried by curious villagers who would gladly have traded their payment of shells for a look at what was in the boxes. That evening the four members of the expedition feasted with the villagers on shellfish and bread made from the white starchy pith of the sago palm. Baked into hard little cakes, the bread was filling but had little nutritional value. Nevertheless, it was the staple of the coastal areas of New Guinea.

After eating, they entered the ceremonial *yeu* house where Catherine and David were to be initiated into the village. It was a sign of acceptance that had not been offered to expedition members whose villages lay nearer Agats, since hostility toward whites increased among those villages having close contact with the Dutch.

Skulls decorated the walls and hung from the ceiling beams of the 100-foot-long room. A single torch lit the center of the ceremonial house, leaving the rest in darkness. The heat from the night and the crush of unseen people around her made Catherine dizzy as she stood with David in the center of the room. The poles supporting the longhouse were rich in carvings. With no pottery and no stone available for tools except stone axes which came by way of mysterious trade with the interior, wood provided everything to the Asmat tribesmen, from shelter and transportation to utensils and weapons.

Now, to the beat of a snakeskin drum, naked warriors danced across the floor, feet slightly apart, advancing in small steps from one side of the room to the other. As the chanting of the onlookers gradually intensified, punctuated by shouts and howls from the excited dancers, the steps did not change but they began to take on a wild and convulsive rhythm. Penises jiggled and bounced and rubbed against one another with increasing sensuality. With bare hands the dancers wiped the sweat from each other's buttocks and thighs and smeared it over their naked bodies as if it were a magic ointment.

In the midst of the mounting excitement, an old woman, one of the chief's wives, took Catherine by the hand and led her to the center of the crowded room, where ten warriors lay outstretched on bare stomachs less than a foot apart. A woman stood between each of them, bent over, legs outspread as if giving birth. At the old woman's directions, Catherine lowered herself onto that outstretched floor of flesh and began to pull herself through each pair of legs, her hands gripping the firm thighs and buttocks of the men as her body wiggled and slid over bare flesh. Above her the women groaned and writhed in the pain of childbirth. What had begun as a slight repulsion at first contact with the prone unclothed bodies of the men became an experience both sexual and primal. When she had passed through the last twisting pair of legs and was symbolically reborn from that brown womb as a new member of the village, her face was flushed with a mixture of excitement and embarrassment.

As she rose, an old woman, her face a shapeless mass of wrinkles, offered Catherine a withered breast to suckle, as to a newborn. The woman held up the shriveled tip, urging Catherine to take it. Another, younger woman beside her made the same offer. Catherine closed her eyes and shook her head, unable to complete the ritual and upset with herself for failing.

A shout went up, and her failure was quickly forgotten as David emerged smiling from the village womb, eyes bright with an excitement which looked intense enough to be a drug. Near him, a young woman put aside her own newborn infant and stepped shyly forward to offer herself for David's nourishment. Evidently her baby had a poor appetite, for her breasts looked swollen enough to burst. David cupped one of the tight breasts with both hands and bent to suckle it. The woman smiled with pleasure at the eagerness with which his mouth took hold. She closed her eyes and raised her hands to crush his face against her breast. Around them the men yelped and screamed, and the dancing continued. David gorged himself like a starving man, enjoying it to the point that the laughing men finally pulled him away and the woman's nipple popped from his mouth, shiny from her milk and his greedy tongue.

The woman laughed and offered him her other breast. The other women laughed, too, and urged him to take it while they remarked in admiration about his appetite. "Make it look happy like the first one," they cried to him, pointing at the swollen nipple he had just released.

David laughed but refused good-naturedly, rubbing his stomach as if it were full. When he looked at Catherine, she turned away from him with a little shudder of disgust, a gesture he seemed not to notice as someone placed a fried sago ball and a piece of cracked crab into his mouth.

She felt suddenly sick from the heat and the feeling that David's actions had been meant deliberately to humiliate her. The dancers pressed around her until she could not move and there seemed no air to breathe. With a rising sense of panic she realized she was in danger of losing consciousness, and if she did, she might slip to the floor and be crushed beneath oblivious, pounding feet. She fought off her dizziness and looked for the exit, but she could not have pushed her way through to it even if she had known where it was. She glanced anxiously at David for help, but his glazed eyes seemed incapable of registering her fear or even her existence.

Suddenly a strong hand gripped her forearm. She looked up to see Michael's cool gray eyes in the midst of all that chaos, and then she was being pulled firmly through the crowd. He kept his grip on her until he got her to the door and then released her. She leaned against the doorframe and gulped fresh air and fought back her nausea. He said nothing, and no expression betrayed his thoughts or feelings.

Catherine felt ungratefully annoyed that he had rescued her and even more annoyed with herself for needing it. She hated David for humiliating her and hated Michael even more for witnessing it. She realized she was probably being too hard on David. Perhaps he had only meant to make her jealous. Or more likely, he had intended nothing at all and been merely carried away by the situation. He had at least been able to do what was expected of him, if a bit too enthusiastically. Perhaps what really bothered her was the sense that she had failed and he had not.

By the time she recovered and looked around for Michael he was gone. He had stayed only long enough to make sure she would be all right. After the constant strain between them of the past few weeks, this was the last she would see of him for a while. Though she was up early the next morning, he and Captain De Jong had already left. She told herself she was relieved as she went about her work, but the relief was short-lived. Without realizing it, she had already begun to miss him.

Chapter 15

Sweat ran down from Catherine's forehead, down her cheeks, down her nose, dripping onto her upper lip. She tasted its saltiness with annoyance. Her clothes were already soaked with perspiration generated by the heat and humidity, and it was only midmorning. Her energy ran out of her body in those rivulets of water, leaving only apathy and anger. She watched David cross the clearing and enter the men's hut. The swarm of tiny flies called *agas* which buzzed about her further increased her irritation. She was annoyed that David was working while she, most determinedly, was not.

She had, in fact, been irritated with David since they had arrived in the Asmat the month before. David had initially been bewildered, and then he had finally resigned himself to Catherine's peevishness, though he failed to understand it in the least. There appeared to be nothing he could do about it either, though he had tried. She appeared to find fault with everything he did. He gave up the hope he had once nurtured that he might get closer to her during their six months of work together. Actually he had hoped to sleep with her, imagining this trip as a romantic time when work and mutual need would throw them closer together. Instead, it had seemed to isolate them not only from the familiar world but from each other.

They had divided the labor along lines which would accommodate the subjects of the research, David spending time in the

119

men's house and Catherine accompanying the women on their chores. Days passed without their speaking, each returning at night to their separate shelters and preparing separate meals. It had been a lonely time for David, far from what he had anticipated and further still from what he had hoped.

The night before David couldn't sleep. At first he was tormented by the heat, which gave him time to dwell on Catherine and his frustrations. He decided to make one last effort to overcome their state of armed neutrality. He could not understand what had come over her. She had always been so gay and charming in college. There, in the dark, alone, he determined to get to the bottom of it. He would confront her, make her tell him what was the matter. Having decided to act, he no longer felt so helpless and uncomfortable. He realized vaguely that not only did he not understand her, but she frightened him. He finally fell fitfully asleep.

That morning his resolve was still with him, stronger than ever. After he had paid his usual visit to the men's hut, he took some of his rations to the guesthouse with the intention of offering to prepare breakfast for them both. He found Catherine hadn't dressed yet, though it was late in the morning. She accepted his offer, if not with enthusiasm, then at least with more cordiality than he had seen of late. Heartened, he set out preparing a cookfire and fixing coffee, canned ham, and rice, which were as close as he was able to come to bacon and eggs.

When he finished and reentered the guesthouse, he found her sitting on her sleeping mat with a light robe over her pajamas. She accepted the food with what might have been a small smile and began to drink the coffee. She watched him carefully but did not speak. He had the distinct impression that his presence was a matter of profound indifference to her. She would tolerate it, but his absence was equally tolerable. He would have been surprised to know that Catherine herself was taken aback by her indifference toward him. It was not what she wanted, yet she appeared unable to change it. She constantly found fault with him, often when she did not wish it. She had told herself at first that all she needed was a little time. Now she sat staring at David, realizing that her feelings hadn't changed and blaming him for her indifference. Why couldn't he make her feel something? Arouse her, make her want him.

David was wavering under her cool stare. Some of his newfound assurance was in danger of leaving him. He looked at her, sitting cross-legged and barefoot, her black hair tumbling in disarray about her shoulders. He knew that glorious hair must be hot—but she would never cut it. If she was vain about anything, it was her hair. He had finished his own coffee and was trying to decide how to begin. His rehearsals of the previous night now seemed foolish in the steamy light of morning. Last night he had prepared answers to everything she might say. But he had not anticipated having to break her silence.

He was about to speak when a commotion erupted outside. The Asmat greeting cry broke out, accompanied by barking dogs and general confusion. David went to the door. Michael, Father Kessel, and Carl Geller were coming toward them. Catherine joined David at the entrance of the guesthouse, surprised to see them. She and David weren't due for a delivery of supplies for another week.

Father Kessel appeared somewhat embarrassed as he approached. Carl seemed amused. Puzzled by their reaction at first, Catherine realized that the good father must have misunderstood when he saw her in her robe and David emerging from the guesthouse, plate and cup in hand. It must have appeared to be a domestic scene. She wondered if Michael had the same impression. It was impossible to tell. No clue flickered in those gray eyes.

Michael wiped the sweat from his forehead with the back of his hand and sat down in the shade. He absentmindedly ran his fingers through his hair, brushing it aside.

"I could use a cup of coffee," he said. There were shadows around his eyes, and he closed them briefly as he leaned back against the post. Catherine was startled to see how weary he looked. For a moment she felt a surge of tenderness for him. It confused her, but it quickly passed when those cold, reflective gray eyes were once again open and looking into hers.

She handed him the coffee and offered some to Father Kessel and Carl. Father Kessel shook his head.

"No, thank you, Catherine. Too hot for coffee." He opened his canteen and offered it to the others.

"Tea." He smiled, giving it a pat. "Not iced the way you Americans like it, but still refreshing."

Since her initial stay at Agats, Catherine had found herself liking this congenial man. He smiled and laughed easily and appeared to take hardships in his stride. Most of all, he had an appreciation of the customs and life-styles of others.

David squatted on his heels and poured himself a second cup of coffee while Catherine sat down next to Carl. She drew her knees up and encircled them with her arms, as if to comfort herself.

"How are things going at at Omadesep, Carl?" David blew into his coffee to cool it.

Carl smiled. "About as well as could be expected, I guess. Being the largest and most powerful village on the river only seems to make them paranoid. They're very reluctant to let Daniel and me intrude in their lives, even as observers. They hate the Dutch, and we've had to suffer the results of it."

"Most belligerent group in the area," Father Kessel added. "No doubt about it. I've never been able to make one convert there. They were the last local village to give up headhunting. There are rumors that they still do it, and I don't doubt it a bit. That's probably why they're so secretive around Carl and Daniel."

"So why are all of you here?" David asked abruptly. "I'm sure this isn't purely a social call. Or are we a rest stop on your way somewhere?"

"It's really both a social call and a rest stop," Father Kessel said, not offended by David's abrupt change of topic. "With one other purpose. The main one, actually." He shifted into a comfortable position before continuing. "Michael has been doing some surreptitious investigation of the Wiat Kargas area in spite of Voorhoeve's threats to have him arrested."

"And?" David asked impatiently.

"And," interjected Michael, who up to that point had appeared to be totally removed from what was going on around him, "I couldn't find out a thing—which in itself told me something. The people of that village know and trust me, but something is frightening them. They're afraid to talk, and I don't think it's the Dutch that are scaring them."

"Then what is?" demanded Catherine, feeling some growing alarm.

"I don't know. But I think there is going to be trouble."

"What does it have to do with us?" David asked, sipping the hot coffee to avoid burning his tongue. "The natives here have

122

never killed a white man that we know of. They take heads only from each other.''

"We haven't killed any natives in the past, so they've had no cause to seek revenge.''

"But it's the Dutch they have the quarrel with, not us," David protested.

"They won't make such fine distinctions, I'm afraid. They're very democratic that way. Besides, all white men look alike to them," Michael added wryly. "I've advised Ryder that we should get out immediately.''

"What did he say?" David asked.

"He disagreed. He accepts Voorhoeve's reassurances because he wants to, not because they have any real basis in fact. Of course, I can't order him out—or any of you, for that matter. I can only tell you that it's my best judgment that we should go. It's up to you whether you want to accept it or not.''

"What have the others said?"

Michael leaned back again and looked up at the sky. It was almost always overcast. Only now it depressed him. "They've all decided to stay," he said quietly.

"Even Julienne?" asked Catherine.

Michael looked at her closely. "Even Julienne," he replied, adding nothing more. Even Julienne, who knew him best, would not take his advice. It was insanity to stay. He knew it. He felt angry with them all.

"What if only some of us want to go?" Catherine asked.

"I'll make immediate arrangements for anyone who wants out to go to Cook's Bay. They can catch the first boat out.''

"You're staying?" she asked.

He nodded.

Of course, she thought. He would have no other choice now.

"And you, Carl?" She turned to where he sat beside her.

"Staying." He looked at her seriously and added. "But I think you should go, Cat. That's why I came along—to persuade you."

Catherine rose nervously and walked a few feet away to where she could look out over the river and have time to think. She was in a dilemma created by her fears, on the one hand, and her ambition, on the other. To stay would be to risk her life. She did not doubt Michael's judgment. But to go would risk her career

123

and everything for which she had been working for the past four years.

"How about you, Carter?" Michael addressed David.

David sat silently trying to sort out the turmoil he was feeling. He was not one to risk his life for a career he had never pursued wholeheartedly to begin with. On the other hand, the others were staying and he did not want to appear a coward.

"David," said Carl, who knew David well, "no one is going to think you're any less of a man if you want to go."

"In fact," added Michael in support, "I'll credit you as the only one with any sense. Believe me"—the gray eyes held David's firmly—"if I had your choice, I'd go."

David was wavering. "I couldn't leave Catherine. It's up to her." He turned to where she was standing.

Catherine had been feeling a rising panic. She turned back from the river to face the little group.

"There will be no more anthropology expeditions if war breaks out," she said.

"That's no reason to risk your life," Michael said sharply. "You can do fieldwork among the American Indians—safe and at home."

"But I don't want to study American Indian cultures!" she said fiercely. "They've been too altered by Western culture to supply data for my theories. Besides, they've been overresearched already. I want to study cultures which haven't!"

"A career will do you no damned good unless you're alive to pursue it!"

"It's a matter of priorities," Carl interceded gently, seeing that Michael's opposition was only making Catherine more determined. "Your life should come first, but that doesn't mean you have to give up your career. Michael's right. You could study American Indians."

"But it would take months to prepare to study a different cultural group. All my preparation since I began graduate school has been for New Guinea fieldwork. It would be like starting over."

"Priorities, Cat, remember?" Carl interjected. "You'd be starting over, and that's a pain in the ass; but you can do it."

"But you're not willing to do it, Carl."

"It would be harder for me, Catherine. I have family responsibilities. Ginny has already had to sacrifice too much to help support me through school. Financially I can't afford to start over, but you can," he said urgently.

"Ginny and the kids are exactly the reason that you, of all people, should be going home!" Her voice was raised.

"Either way the risks are high for me. Yours are high only if you stay here. I'm doing what I feel I must," he added sadly.

Catherine sat down next to him again and took his hand in hers. "I'm going to have to take the risks of staying here, too, Carl. Right now I can't bear the thought of waiting or starting over again. It's been too long already." And she leaned over and kissed him on the forehead. Tears brightened both their eyes as they looked at each other.

"Well, David," Father Kessel said with a sigh, "that leaves you the only one still to make a decision."

David struggled with himself. Damn Catherine, he thought. He wanted to go, but if she stayed, how could he? It would look like he had less ambition and courage than she.

"Don't stay on my account, David. Please. I'll be all right . . . really," Catherine said.

David knew there was no way she could stay in the isolated area alone. Either she would have to move or, more likely, Stanford would have to stay with her. Somehow that thought did not appeal to him, although he didn't know why. With that in mind, he swallowed hard and overcame his indecision.

"I'll stay, too," he said simply.

Michael sighed. Well, he told himself, he had done everything he could. The Dutch government was too concerned with covering things up to order foreigners out of the area, and he had no power to do it for them.

"I hope you know that the bed you've just made is a hammock swinging by a thread over a five-hundred-foot chasm," he said, and took a piece of paper from the pocket of his khaki shirt.

"You should each prepare an emergency backpack with enough food, clothing, and medical supplies to last for three weeks. Here's a list of what you'll need. You should also have a boat located where you can reach it quickly to escape. It's completely impossible to cross these swamps on foot. I've made a map of areas along the river where it will be safe to hide if your escape route down the river is cut off. I've stored additional supplies there. If you can make it to the coast, the Dutch ocean patrol boat will be standing by to pick you up between the mouth of the Eilenden and Agats. In case of trouble they'll constantly patrol that area, but they won't come upriver. They couldn't save you if they did. They'd make too good a target, even protected by their guns, especially where the river gets narrow. If you need to escape, try it at night. The river's more dangerous at night, but the tribes are more dangerous in the day.'' He spoke quickly, efficiently, without emotion. Then he added, ''Any questions?''

No one spoke. Catherine felt a growing fear brought on by the realization that for all her education, she had not learned how to defend herself or how to survive under such conditions as Michael was now describing. The people of the Asmat were cannibals— or had been, although she didn't know why that should bother her. Once she was dead, it would hardly matter to her how her remains were disposed of.

Catherine did not express her concern to the men sitting with her. She was aware that Michael was watching her intently. She was determined not to let him see her fear. She knew it was ridiculous, but still, to be afraid was to need him. He was so strong, so sure of himself, so smug, she thought with annoyance.

They all continued to sit in silence, lost in their own thoughts. Finally, when no one spoke, Michael rose. ''Since there aren't any questions, at least for now, I'm going up the river a bit. I'll be back later.''

Catherine rose, too, and went into the guesthouse to dress. When she returned, he had gone. Father Kessel had excused himself to take a short nap. Only David and Carl remained.

''Well,'' said David with forced cheeriness, ''I don't think anything is going to happen here. I feel we have established some trust and respect with the people of Fos.''

''Then you're a fool,'' Catherine said lightly as she stepped over his outstretched legs and strode away toward the river, her notebook tucked neatly under one arm, her camera around her neck.

Carl sat quietly, watching the exchange. After a moment he got up and followed Catherine. Catching up with her, he said amiably, ''You were a little hard on David just then.''

''I know, and I'm sorry. It's this heat,'' she said exasperatedly, wiping her forehead with the sleeve of her shirt. ''And all the pressure of what we were just talking about.''

"Are you sure, Cat?" He took out a pipe from his shirt pocket and began to fill it with tobacco as they walked along. He raised a quizzical eyebrow at her. "It seems to me that it's been going on since before we left Borneo."

"Of course I'm sure. What else do you think it is?" she asked defensively.

"Nothing that I'm willing to talk about if you're not." He lit his pipe and took several quick draws to get it started. "But I'm always available for a talk or a shoulder to cry on if you should want it." He paused to give her time to reply.

She had become preoccupied with focusing her camera on some playing children. He realized she was deliberately ignoring him and took a different tack.

"Stanford bagged a big croc yesterday off Biwar. A thirty-five footer that had killed fifty-four people in the past three years. Caught it sunning on the riverbank. Shot it right between the eyes at a distance of about two hundred yards. One hell of a shot."

"Hmmmm." Catherine made a noncommittal noise and continued with her work. It was clear she wasn't about to be drawn into a conversation concerning Michael Stanford. He changed the subject again.

"Got a letter from Ginny yesterday. Steamer came from Diney, dropped off the mail at Agats. She said to tell you hello. She's going to take a teaching job this fall, and meantime, she has taken the kids to Cape Cod to visit her mother. She said Tom has just been assigned to teach at the Naval Academy at Annapolis for two years beginning this fall term. He's already left Pearl."

Tom was Ginny's twin brother. Career Navy, Lieutenant JG, an Annapolis graduate. Catherine had gotten to know him well when he had been stationed in Norfolk, Virginia, before he left for Pearl Harbor two years ago. He had been just setting out on his naval career at the same time she and Carl had started graduate school, and Tom had been a frequent houseguest at the Gellers. He and Catherine had taken to each other immediately; but neither had been remotely ready for a serious relationship, and it had come to nothing.

"It's nice for Ginny that Tom will be around while you're gone." Relieved to be away from the subject of her own feelings, she began to talk and laugh freely with him.

Carl spent the rest of the morning helping Catherine take

127

photographs and notes. He made no further mention of what might be bothering her, and he knew better than to press her. She had confided in him in the past. He knew she would again when she was ready.

That evening Catherine and David prepared dinner for their guests. Father Kessel appeared rested and relaxed. Michael did not return for dinner, and David expressed some concern, which Father Kessel put to rest.

"Michael Stanford will be fine. Left to his own resources, he manages better in these situations than any man I've ever known."

"Will you stay here, Father?" Catherine asked. "I mean, if war spreads throughout Europe, what will you do?"

"What else can I do but stay?" he replied. Then he added with a sigh, "If it spreads in Europe, it will come here eventually, too. No place will be safe, not even the Asmat. No"—he took out his pipe and lit it—"I'll wait here if the world goes mad. I'd rather be with the headhunters of the Asmat than the Nazis of Europe. I've been reading about what Hitler is up to." He puffed vigorously on his pipe as the conversation turned to Holland, the Philippines, and the Sepik River area of Australian New Guinea, where he had lived before his assignment to the Phillipines.

It was beginning to get dark. Catherine rose and left the three men talking by the cookfire. She walked down toward the river as the frogs and cicadas started up their song. She was filled with sadness and she didn't know why. Tomorrow she would bury herself in research and forget about everything else. It had worked in the past, and with luck it would work again now.

Chapter 16

Father Kessel sat in front of his hut, smoking his pipe and enjoying his view of the river. Here at Atsj, where the Eilenden neared the Arafura Sea, the river was about one mile wide. This was his favorite time of day. The sky had cleared in late afternoon, leaving him the warm red-orange colors of a sunset to watch from his porch. Out on the river, a lone fisherman standing in a dugout boat was silhouetted against the deepening red sky. The sun was going down as a wall of clouds lay waiting along the ocean horizon to put an early ending to the day.

Father Kessel often felt a little twinge of sadness at the death of a day. Perhaps it was part of growing older, he thought, and realizing that the days are not limitless. This had been an especially satisfying one. He had conducted a christening that morning in one of the villages where he had made a number of converts to Catholicism, then had celebrated the christening with a feast. Earlier that evening he had dined with Donald Seabaugh and Julienne in Biwar before coming home. Now he was content to sit by himself, watching the day end. He rose, stretched, and began to prepare for bed. He had no way of knowing this day would be his last. None of them did.

Carl Geller was the first to see it coming, but by then it was too late for him to warn the others. He had gone for a walk in the twilight, in Omadesep, the village where he and Daniel had been gathering the data, and when he returned, there it was, rising some thirty-five feet into the twilight sky. Three glaring ten-foot warrior figures rose one upon the other, totem fashion. A six-foot lacework of intricately carved wood protruded from between the legs of each figure, like an erect winged penis. It had been carved in secret in the *yeu* house with primitive tools—stone ax, boar-tusk chisel, and oystershell scraper—and its effect, in the last red glow of the sunlit day, was an awesome evocation of savage energy. The village was quiet, empty. The jungle was still. Only the *biz* pole itself seemed to be alive.

Carl Geller was not superstitious, but the fear evoked in him at that sight was a fear of the supernatural. The faces staring from the *biz* pole were like medieval gargoyles, powerful symbols of the evil spirit world, of things almost but not quite human, of which man has little understanding and over which he has no control. Carl had seen *biz* poles in the museum in Amsterdam, and for a moment he could not believe his senses. But there was no time now, he knew, to sort out his confusion. Daniel was not in Omadesep. He had gone to Agats that morning. Carl knew that he must get out immediately, even though it was nearing dark.

He turned and headed for the river, abandoning his notes, supplies, everything. He knew he had time to save nothing but his life. He arrived at the river and started to push the nearest boat off the bank. His terror caused his blood to pound in his ears as he struggled with shaking hands to get the boat into the water. He did not succeed. The warriors fell upon him just as the boat slipped free, and he knew they had been toying with him, waiting to take him when they knew his terror would be at its height.

Shouting and brandishing spears, they dragged him back to the clearing beside the *yeu* house, beneath the angry pole. A fire had been made. He was pinned to the ground, his clothes were stripped from him, and he was vaguely aware of laughter among those who were attempting to put them on. For them it was a comical scene as trousers went on over heads and shirts were pulled on backward. A celebration. Bizarre, the anthropologist in him noted, the contrast between his feelings and theirs.

Accepting death, he felt almost detached from the scene

about him. He saw the ax poised directly over his head and was relieved that he would die quickly. He had only a brief second to wonder, as the ax came down, why his last thoughts were of Catherine, not Ginny. He was forever spared the answer.

Death had come quickly and mercifully to Father Kessel in his sleep. Jan Voorhoeve was not so lucky. He had been working late, and from his office window he had glimpsed the flames in the evening sky toward Atsj and the mission villages to the southeast. He rushed out, heading for the radio shack, shouting for the operator and any of the army contingent he could rouse. Unable to find anyone, he sat down and sent a message to the nearest Dutch naval vessel, some thirty miles off the coast, asking it to stand by for a possible rescue operation.

Before he completed the message, the door burst open, and he was surrounded by angry warriors shouting at him and threatening him with spears. Voorhoeve could hardly believe it. He sat speechless, his mouth open. Then he stood up, took off the earphones, and tried to sound authoritative, but he was hampered by the fact that he had never really learned the language. Where was De Jong or that damned sergeant anyhow? he thought angrily. These animals could smell fear, but they could also be intimidated by confidence. That was what he would show them now.

The warriors hesitated only momentarily before they grabbed him, tied him, and carried him out into the night. Their frustration had been building for the past year. It was about to be released in a primitive ferocity that was extreme even for their culture. Voorhoeve was the symbol of their oppression. It would take powerful magic to destroy him and the forces he represented. He was about to become the object of the most sadistic and destructive ritual acts they knew.

At a nearby village they stripped him of his clothes, tore out the nails of his fingers and toes, then cut off the three fingers used for drawing a bow and holding a spear, thus symbolically protecting themselves from retaliation. His skull was denuded of its blond scalp, and rocks and hot ash were heaped upon his bleeding head while the women beat him with sticks. When they finally tired, a great war chief, brother to one of the warriors slain at Wiat Kargas stepped forward with a knife he had taken from the barracks kitchen raided earlier. He stood staring at Voorhoeve's eyes and bloodied face while two other warriors held Voorhoeve immobilized between them. Then the warrior suddenly thrust the knife into the center of Voorhoeve's stomach and opened it toward the right. While Voorhoeve gasped in shock and horror at the blinding pain, the warrior reached into the wound and pulled out Voorhoeve's liver and intestines and tossed them to cook in the nearby fire.

They let go of Voorhoeve, who sank slowly to the ground. He did not die. He remained half-conscious while the chants and dancing went on around him. Still alive one hour later, he was hoisted up and slowly roasted over the fire. He believed even then that the navy would still come to his rescue, though he was beyond saving. No one was there to appreciate the irony that he left the world he had mistrusted all his life trusting it to save him when it could not.

It was almost ten o'clock when Michael turned the boat toward the riverbank near Omadesep. The motor buzzed noisily, and he was weary of the sound and the vibration. Today Michael had accompanied Dr. Wieder on his collecting trip, along with Captain De Jong and three Dutch enlisted men. The darkness had slowed their speed considerably. They were supposed to have been in Omadesep in time to have dinner with Carl, and Michael felt annoyed with the lateness of the hour. He had missed both dinner and the pleasure of Carl's company for the evening, all because Dr. Wieder was unable to resist carefully studying every piece of carving he could find.

Because it was late, he did not pull the boat up on the riverbank. Instead, he tied it to one of the other boats, letting it swing free. The villagers would not use the boats in the night, and he would move it early in the morning before some indignant fisherman had time to complain. A few minutes earlier, in the beam of light he had flashed along the shore, something had caught his eye that hadn't been there before, a flash of color, a piece of paper perhaps, or a cloth hanging from a tree branch. Rather than follow the others as they left the boat and headed for the village, he had decided to investigate before heading for the guesthouse and bed. Tracking back along the muddy riverbank on foot, he caught it in his light again, maybe fifty yards farther down. As he drew closer, it appeared to be a piece of cloth. But the villagers had no cloth. It was draped over something. A signal perhaps? Suddenly he wished he had not left his rifle in the boat. He considered going back for it, but now he was nearing the spot where the cloth was hanging.

As he parted the ferns and grasses which partially blocked the view, his breath escaped him like a blow to the stomach. A *biz* pole was lying there in the grass among the sago trees. The white cloth that had first caught his eye was a pair of bloody Jockey shorts draped over the tip on one of the penislike protrusions of one of the *biz* figures. Running his flashlight up the pole, he saw a khaki shirt tied around another one of the *biz* figures. What he saw next made him gag. Stuck in the mouth of the last figure on the pole were the genitals of a man.

Instantly he turned off the flashlight and stood listening intently to the night. Nothing stirred around him. No sounds came from the village. He turned and swiftly made his way back to the boat and grabbed his rifle. Alarm pounded like bells in his ears as he headed for the village. Just then he heard shouts followed by screams. The bedlam that had been hiding there in wait had broken loose. When he came upon the scene a few moments later, it had become a rampage. Bodies were being literally torn apart. A pole with Captain De Jong's head on it was hoisted into the air.

It was too late to save them. He stood paralyzed by the scene before him. "God! Oh, God!" he murmured over and over. He found himself sobbing in both anguish and fear as he began cautiously to withdraw into the darkness toward the river. The natives had not seen him, so preoccupied had they been with the others. He jumped lightly into the boat at the same time that he lifted clear the rope that tied it. He let the boat drift silently into the current of the river before starting the motor. As he turned the bow upriver, he glanced briefly over his shoulder toward the ocean to the west. The sky was pink with what appeared to be the sun's last rays, but it was two hours past sunset. He knew that the glow came from Agats and that it was burning. There was no going back to the coast now. He could also see the glow of other fires, in the villages Father Kessel counted among his converts. The whole area was in rebellion.

As he thought about it, the puzzle of the last few weeks became clear. The warriors that the Dutch had shot must have been the powerful Omadesep, rather than members of the village of Wiat Kargas, where the killings had occurred. They might have been a trading party or a group visiting relatives. It didn't matter. All that mattered was that they were Omadesep and they had frightened all the other villages into silence so they could plan their revenge without suspicion. By tomorrow morning there would be no foreigners left alive. There was no helping any of the others. He only hoped he could reach Catherine and David in time.

Julienne stood up in the dugout, balancing against the rolling action of the ocean waves. In the weeks she had been at the coastal village of Biwar she had managed to master the perilous dugouts. It had not been difficult for her because of her childhood experience with the Dyak praos of Borneo. Recently it had become Julienne's habit to go for a swim at sunset each day. She usually paddled out far enough to sea to avoid the small native fishing boats in the area. Tonight, to her surprise, there were none.

Julienne took off her clothes and dived into the warm, dark, twilit ocean water. She was a good strong swimmer, but she did not go far from the boat. There were few sharks in the area, and Michael had killed the only reported man-eating crocodile; but the ocean currents were treacherous here near the river mouth.

She dived deep into the water, touching sand and rock in the shadowy darkness. When she rose to the surface, she saw the sky glow pink and then red to the northwest, near Atsj. For a moment she was puzzled, and then she realized what it meant. A few minutes later a smaller glow began farther east, and then another, and finally another, in the north near Agats.

Julienne slowly treaded water, holding on to the bobbing boat. Watching the fires, she was aware at the same time of the waves beneath her and the sun's last rays upon the surface of the water, lending the scene its own last fiery light. She thought of what she must do now. Michael had indicated that a Dutch naval boat would patrol the area if there was trouble. If someone had had a chance to get off a radio message, the patrol boat would be along in due time. She knew that she would be safe here until it could reach her.

She thought of being pulled naked from the boat by earnest young Dutch naval officers, and she ran her tongue lightly over her lips. She reached in and took her clothes one by one from the boat and discarded them into the water. She smiled and rested her head against the side of the dugout as she watched them slowly float away.

She lay back, floating, watching the red sky above her as she thought of her colleagues dying in the villages. She was alive. Caressed. Rocked. Teased. Her nipples grew hard, and she moaned softly as she felt the swollen ache between her legs that begged for release. God! She couldn't stand it. She thrust her pelvis slowly out of the water. One time and then again and again until the rhythm of her movement and the caress of the water brought her relief; she arched a final time, then lay back, a smile on her lips.

She and Michael had often gone swimming together in the nude those many years ago when they were lovers. Making love in the water, in the boat, on the sand, in her bed, in his. Once she had even tormented him into doing it in her father's bed. She liked the dangerous times best—the times they almost got caught. While they were making love, she used to imagine people watching. Her mother. Her father. Edward. All horrified. She had even tried to get them caught a few times, but Michael had successfully avoided it.

She rolled over and looked toward shore again. Even more fires were burning now, Biwar among them. Golden, tan, beautiful Michael. He might die in all that. She imagined some horrible, screaming death for him as she watched the fires. Unexpectedly she was filled with panic, and a dry sob excaped her throat. As much as she hated him she could not imagine living in a world without him.

Catherine sat on the ground in the shadows, huddled against one of the poles that supported the guesthouse. Wearily she closed her eyes and rested her forehead on her updrawn knees—

not that she could sleep. David had been gone about fifteen minutes. The moon had slipped behind the clouds, and it was too dark to see her watch. It must be midnight by now. It seemed as though hours had passed since he had left.

In the darkness she strained her ears against the jungle noises, trying to pick up some unusual sound, trying to differentiate safety from danger, salvation from destruction, David from—from what? She didn't know. She knew only that she had gone for a walk after dinner and found the village empty. That was hours ago. She had sought David in his house, and he had gone out to investigate. He had returned without any explanation. The dugouts were gone as well, including, ominously, the one they had carefully hidden in the grass down the river. They had no means of escape now.

As the hours went by, they became increasingly alarmed. Finally they decided that they would try to get away, even though there was no clear evidence that they were in danger. They decided to go some distance down the river, wading and swimming where they had to, taking their chances with crocodiles. David had gone back for his backpack and his papers and notes. He should have returned by now. Catherine was about to go look for him when she heard a noise near her. Her body stiffened in apprehension. The moon had reappeared, and she searched the darkness with her eyes but saw nothing. Then she heard a fainter sound coming from a different direction, and her heart leaped to her throat. She was about to cry out to David when she felt an arm reach around from behind her and a hand was planted firmly over her mouth. She struggled in terror to free herself until Michael's familiar voice whispered in her ear.

"It's all right. I didn't mean to frighten you, but I was afraid you might cry out before you recognized me. The area is being watched. I just knocked one of them unconscious."

Catherine felt the hard butt of the rifle brush against her as he released her and sat down.

"We have to get out of here—now," he said softly.

"What's happening?"

"There's no time to go into it now. The moon will be completely behind those clouds in a minute, and then we'll try for the river. Stay close behind me. We'll stick to the shadows of the buildings. I have a boat tied downriver."

"But David—"

"I've already found David. He'll be waiting for us at the boat."

"Why haven't they stopped David? Or hurt me?"

"They know you can't escape without a boat. They're probably enjoying your fear for a while."

The last bit of moonlight had disappeared.

"There. We'll have to move quickly."

They headed cautiously toward the river. Catherine felt comforted by the simple act of placing one foot before the other, having something to do. Anything but the waiting of the previous hours. The outlines of the village were faintly visible. Nothing had changed, yet seen through her growing terror, the familiar had become unrecognizable. They came to the river and turned downstream. They followed the path until it ended and then waded out into the shallow water. Now they had to watch for crocodiles.

When they reached the boat, David wasn't there. Michael swore quietly. "Evidently he's more concerned about saving his notes than his life," he whispered angrily as he climbed into the boat. "He'd better hurry because I'm not waiting much longer."

Catherine climbed into the bow. The boat had been hewn from a log and seemed little wider than the native dugouts. It rocked precariously but did not tip over. Michael wrapped the cord around the outboard motor and prepared to pull it to a start. He uttered a nonbeliever's prayer that it would start the first time. There might not be time for a second try.

They sat in tense silence as the minutes passed. Suddenly a splash upriver startled them. It was either David or the Fos villagers. Michael did not wait to see. He pulled the starter cord. The motor sputtered and caught, and the boat rocked with the sudden turbulence. The sound of splashing upstream was lost in the noise of the idling motor. Agonizing seconds passed before they glimpsed David running toward them through the shallow water. He was pursued by a number of warriors, who were gaining on him.

Catherine reached out and helped pull David aboard as Michael shifted the motor into forward and swung the bow around, pointing it downstream, away from their pursuers. Something brushed by Catherine's ear, and she realized suddenly that the warriors were firing arrows. One caught David in the thigh as he pulled himself over the side of the boat. They headed out into the river as their pursuers were joined by more warriors carrying spears and torches.

"Sorry," David panted apologetically. "I met them in the clearing. I guess they had finally decided to come after us. Or maybe someone saw you leave."

As he lay in the bottom of the boat, he pulled the arrow from his leg. Fortunately it was not a deep wound.

"There's a first-aid kit on board," Michael shouted over the motor. "We'll fix the leg as soon as we can stop."

He headed for the river's opposite bank, about half a mile away, and then swung the boat's bow around again and headed back upstream, past the Fos village, now a safe distance across the river.

"Why are you going back upstream?" Catherine shouted over the motor.

"It's not safe below. We'll stop and rest upstream until daybreak." He could not bring himself to tell them now that there was no going back.

An hour later he pulled into shore and tied up. The full moon had emerged from the clouds, making it easy for Michael to see as he opened the first-aid kit and began to clean David's wound.

"What's happening anyway?" David asked.

"The whole area is in rebellion. Apparently the people killed at Wiat Kargas were from this area, and they've been planning revenge for weeks."

Catherine felt her throat constrict. "And the others? What's happened to everyone?"

Michael shook his head and answered with a partial truth, "I don't know." He wanted her to leave it at that, but he knew she would not.

"Then we must go back!" Catherine cried. "Carl, Julienne—maybe we can help them."

"We can't help the others. Our only chance is up the river, over and across the mountains and down to Hollandia on the opposite coast."

"That's impossible!" Catherine exclaimed. "Besides, the army will probably have order restored in a few days, a week at the most."

"That's only in American movies, Catherine," Michael said

wearily as he finished bandaging David's leg. "There won't be any cavalry to the rescue this time."

Catherine persisted. "But Carl and Julienne and the others may need us. We can't just leave them." Catherine was shaking with anger and something else she did not want to recognize.

"We're not going back, Catherine." His mouth was tight and angry, and his eyes locked fiercely onto hers. He was still in shock from what he had seen and what he could all too easily imagine. He was tired, afraid, and grief-stricken, and he did not want any arguments from her right now.

"Greater love hath no man than to give up his friends for his life, right, Michael?" She immediately regretted her comment as she saw the anguish on his face.

"Carl is dead, Catherine," he said softly. "And so are the others by now if they're lucky. There will be no survivors—except us maybe. And I'll be truthful. It's going to be rough. One hundred miles of unknown river and more than two hundred miles of unknown jungle and mountains. The only thing I know of the area is what I remember from the rough map Archbold sketched and sent to my father with the photographs of the Grand Valley. I took several paddles from the dugouts at Omadesep. We have enough gas only for emergencies. We'll have to go on foot once we reach the mountains anyway."

"But what if we just hid out for a while and then tried to get to the coast farther south, using some of the other rivers?" David asked, not yet willing to accept the overwhelming task that faced them.

"As whites we won't be safe anywhere along the Casuarina Coast. It will be years before the Dutch are able to get in here again. Our only chance lies over the mountains."

David was silent, in no position to argue. Michael had been right before when no one had listened. Now they were left with the consequences. Catherine was numb with grief and barely heard the discussion.

Michael returned to the stern of the boat, leaving David resting on his pack and Catherine in the bow.

"Let's try to get a few hours of rest," he said.

It was almost daybreak before Catherine finally fell asleep, only to be tormented by dreams that jarred her awake in panic. She realized that she was about to scream. She firmly closed her mouth and groggily shut her eyes as well. It had begun to drizzle, and damp white clouds of mist and fog rose from the river and drifted across the occupants of the boat, concealing them from one another.

Chapter 17

David sat paddling in the canoe's stern during the heat of the afternoon. He felt angry and frustrated, feelings which he considered an improvement over the terror he had experienced the night before. He did not altogether trust Michael Stanford. Not that he didn't trust his knowledge or ability. It was something else. He could see, too, that Catherine did not like Michael. He sensed the tension between them whenever Stanford was around, and it puzzled him since he had never seen anything happen between them which revealed a clue to what had produced it. He finally concluded it was based on what he himself felt, a dislike of the man's personality.

David had never felt altogether comfortable with men who easily assumed authority. They reminded him of his father, an aggressive, successful railroad developer with whom David had never felt he could successfully compete. Even Catherine frightened him sometimes, although he had convinced himself that he loved her. Her drive to succeed put him off at the same time that the admiration she received for it stroked his own ego: This successful woman was going to be his wife and mother to his children.

He was jarred from his reverie as the boat's bow struck something, throwing him forward, almost causing him to lose his paddle. He heard Michael cursing and an awful scraping sound as the bottom of the bow, lodged between the limbs of a sunken tree, strained to accommodate the swing of the stern. David sucked in his breath sharply. It felt as if the boat would snap in two.

"Damn it! Swing the stern around!" Michael shouted as he pushed to free the bow. The violent swinging of the boat's stern had wedged the bow more firmly into the waterlogged vise. David recovered and, with Catherine's help, paddled to halt the boat's wide arc.

"Use the pole," Michael shouted.

The pole sank into mud some three feet deep before it reached a foundation solid enough to give some support to their efforts. Slowly David and Catherine swung the stern back into position.

The boat appeared to have suffered no serious damage, but the incident had badly shaken at least two of its occupants. David noticed that Catherine's face was white as the boat finally slipped free and they paddled a detour around the fallen tree. His own hands were shaking. He could not see Stanford's reaction. It was hidden by Michael's back, which was all he showed the boat's other occupants for most of the day.

The rain began later in the afternoon. Catherine caught a glimpse of Michael's profile from time to time as he scanned the river and its banks with a gaze which was intense but not perturbed. He was used to danger and reacted quickly and rationally in a crisis. The incident with the boat that afternoon made Catherine realize more than ever that neither she nor David could survive this without him. They were totally dependent upon his knowledge and skills. That being the case, she knew they could not be in better hands. Tears pressed her eyes, and she didn't know why. Then she realized this was one more reminder of what she had lost. She lifted her face and let the rain mix with her tears. She grieved not only for Michael but for the loss of Carl and her friends and colleagues. She looked down at the river passing beneath her, thinking that it would soon reach the scene of that carnage.

As the rain began to drum down harder, Michael told David to steer closer to shore. Lashing at the overhanging jungle with his machete, Michael cut pandanus palm leaves and fashioned them into rain hats. As usual, the rain did nothing to relieve the heat; instead, the river became swollen and the current grew stronger, making it harder for them to make their way upstream. Gradually the river narrowed as they continued, becoming deeper and swifter as the miles went by.

Recognizing the effect of the long hours of struggle against the current, Michael decided to search for a spot to spend the night. He decided they would have to sleep in the boat again since it was useless to search for a spot onshore high enough to be safe from the rising waters. The land was still flat swamp and marshland, a tangle of roots and grasses and vines which was impassable except by boat.

After tying up to a tree along the shoreline, Michael set out fishing lines. Catherine sat, feeling miserable, under her palm-leaf hat. It was hot, and she was drenched from the downpour. Her clothes stuck to her. Finally fighting her condition no longer, she took off her hat, loosened her hair, and let the rain wash it. If she had been alone, she would have stripped off her clothes as well. Since the river was muddy and unpleasant either to drink or to bathe in, they put out containers to catch rainwater for their needs.

When the rain stopped, Michael took their dwindling supply of hardwood sticks and charcoal and built a fire on the back platform of the boat, Dyak-Borneo style, cooked some rice, and baked some fish wrapped in damp leaves. In a few days they would have to find fuel. While the meal was cooking, he left the boat and returned shortly with tender nibong-palm hearts, which he added to the boiling rice. No meal had ever tasted better to Catherine. The leaves gave a delightful flavor and aroma to the fish. Using sticks, they ate the rice Chinese style, not bothering to take utensils from their packs. They had little to say to one another. Each of them was lost in the immensity of what faced them and the deaths of friends and colleagues. They needed to give vent to their feelings, but the tensions among them kept them from being of help or comfort to one another.

That night the water level dropped, and when Catherine woke, the boat was moored to a different tree and Michael had already set out the fishing lines. This time they were not so fortunate. No fish were caught. Saving their canned food for a time when neither fish nor other food might be available, they ate the rest of the rice and palm hearts for breakfast.

The river had become wide and shallow again. Poling as well as paddling now, they made good progress, using the motor only when the current became too difficult or they were too tired.

After the first day they passed no further villages. In seven days they reached a river fork where the Catalina River joined the Eilenden. They took the left fork, the Catalina, and found that river to be somewhat narrower than the Eilenden but still surrounded by mangrove trees, sago palms, and taller trees as the marsh and swamplands merged into the jungle rain forests.

Fish remained plentiful enough so that their diet gave them the strength they needed for their ordeal against the river. The soreness in their muscles hardened into new endurance. The heavy currents and swollen water walls from the daily rains still threatened, at times, to swamp them. Huge reptilian logs lay sunning on the shore and half-submerged among the fallen tree trunks drifting with the current, demanding constant watchfulness and providing yet another reason to sleep in the boat at night.

Following what he remembered of Archbold's rough map, Michael decided to leave the Catalina before it was joined by the Baliem farther inland and to follow the Somneg tributary until that connected with the Baliem. They could save about fifteen miles by this shortcut. However, this route would mean abandoning the boat sooner and proceeding on foot. The mountains lay before them, an impassable barrier into the unknown heart of New Guinea, close enough now that even the high jungle wall could not conceal them. Catherine gazed in awe at the purple-shadowed pyramids rising before her, topped with ice and snow. Only the Himalayas and the Andes were taller. She could not believe they were about to try to cross them.

After its violent descent from the mountains, the Somneg River disgorged onto the plain peacefully, dividing into four branches which extended into the Catalina River. Michael picked a clear, sandy beach on one of the finger tributaries for the site of their first night onshore. It had taken them exactly two weeks to reach the Somneg. With considerable trepidation they prepared to abandon their boat, packing supplies into backpacks, strapping on machetes and axes.

As if to celebrate the end of the first part of their journey the sun began to put on a spectacular sunset. The water from the Somneg being clearer than the Catalina, they decided to bathe. Catherine took a towel and some antiseptic soap and went upstream some distance from the men. The rocky riverbank was not a favorite hiding place for crocodiles, but she made enough noise to frighten them off just in case. She bathed while the gentle current soothed her tired muscles, washed her hair, then left the river reluctantly. After putting on clean underclothes, khaki pants, and shirt, and combing out her hair, she drew on her boots, set her wide-brimmed palm-leaf hat jauntily on her head, and strode back to camp, feeling better than she had in the past two weeks. She found that the men had shaved and bathed and Michael had put out the fishing lines.

"Let's hope we catch some fish tonight," he said. "There may not be any more where we're going."

"No fish?" questioned David. "I thought we were staying near the river."

"We are," Michael replied. "But the mountains are steep, and chances are that fish will have never made it that far up the stream. From now on we'll have to ration our supplies and eat whatever we can find along the way."

Catherine looked at him. He was resting on his heels near the fire he was building. He did not look up. She felt he was trying to prepare them—gently—without alarming them too much.

"You're telling us that we're going to get very hungry before this is over," she said simply.

His gray eyes looked steadily up at her. "It's possible. That's all that I'm saying."

Catherine took off her hat and ran her fingers through her hair. Even in this heat it did not dry quickly. The two men stared at her and did not speak. She felt self-conscious, and for the first time in the two weeks of isolation with them, she became aware of her appeal as a woman. She looked at David, and she saw him swallow hard, then avert his eyes. She knew what he was thinking, and she flushed. She sat down in the sand and looked at Michael, who did not look away. His face betrayed nothing of what he thought, and this time it was Catherine who looked quickly to the ground. She folded her arms on her bended knees, resting her forehead on them so that her face was shielded from both men. She did not look up until she heard Michael rise and disappear into the jungle. When she raised her head, she saw that David, too, had gone.

Relieved, she rose and walked down to the river's edge and sat upon a rock. She felt bewildered and a little frightened by the feelings she had seen stirring, at least in David. Yet she found it

145

peculiar that she had not anticipated them or been aware of them before. No doubt David, isolated with her at times these past weeks, had developed a healthy desire to sleep with her, and she had only just now become aware of it. She realized that she had used him in the past to gratify her ego. That he loved her had made her feel lovable. That he desired her had made her feel desirable. Those needs taken care of, she could then pursue her intellectual and career goals free of doubts about her femininity.

He had asked her to marry him, and she had accepted without any real consideration. She accepted because it pacified him and kept him there. There had been other times, before the expedition, when she had ignored him, immersed in some more gratifying pursuit. But he was always there for her to turn to, and eventually she always did. Today, for the first time, she felt ashamed of her selfishness. She ought to have admired him for his devotion, she told herself. But she didn't. She despised him for it. He allowed her to use him. Perhaps he believed she would give her body to him out of guilt, if not out of love.

She recognized that it might have been a good possibility. She doubted now that she would ever have married him, though she probably would have slept with him if she had not met Michael. Now, even though she hated Michael, she could not bear the thought of sex with any other man. She wondered if Michael had recognized the true nature of her relationship with David. She knew he would hold her in contempt for using David, just as she held David in contempt for being willing to settle for so little.

She heard the shuffle of loose rocks behind her and turned to see David sit down on a rock next to her and look out on the river and the sun's last faint pink glow. As he gazed out at the great, slow-moving river they were leaving behind, David said sadly, "It seems the last contact with everything we know. I'll hate to leave it behind."

"Yes. It seems so final, doesn't it? As if there's really no going back."

Catherine looked at him in the fading light. His brown hair curled becomingly about his head. He was deeply tanned from the journey. His large dark brown eyes were framed in long black lashes. We must look enough alike to be taken for siblings, she mused. And that was exactly how she felt about him: like a brother. She enjoyed that feeling. At least it had some warmth and tenderness in it instead of the indifference and impatience she had felt in recent weeks. She knew that she could not yet tell David that she could not marry him. Chances were good that they would not survive their present journey. Injury, disease, starvation, hostile villagers—too many threats lay between here and safety. No, she could not tell him now. If they were not going to survive, there was no point in hurting him.

David was surprised and pleased to see Catherine smiling warmly at him. It was the first smile he had seen since they had reached Fos, and he felt a surge of pleasure and hope. Large annulary birds, named after the age rings on their beaks, circled overhead, getting ready to roost. Catherine studied them.

"Perhaps we ought to try shooting one for dinner."

David smiled and shook his head. "Too tough. Even the natives don't eat them."

David considered approaching Catherine now about their relationship, but he discarded the notion. Better let the thaw continue awhile before saying anything, he told himself. He looked at her and confirmed that what he saw before him was the most beautiful woman he had ever known. Her black, silky hair and the tanned glow of her complexion gave her an exotic beauty that his romantic imagination found irresistible. Aloof, impenetrable, promising much and giving little—to him she was like the jungle around her, lush but unable to provide sustenance.

It had always been remarkable to him that Catherine had never appeared to be aware of her beauty or was indifferent toward it. She had never used it, as did so many women, to manipulate men. He admired her for that. But now the sight of her face, her slender, delicate body filled him with longings he could barely contain, and he felt himself swell against his khaki trousers. With the intensity of the longings came anger that she should have treated him with such indifference over the past six weeks. After all, he was a handsome man and a talented scholar. From time to time he had vague, uncomfortable suspicions that Catherine might be more brilliant than he, but he quickly rejected them. She certainly worked harder than he did, and he used that explanation to hide his doubts. Still, she awed him sometimes, but he never let her know it.

They were laughing over old times in graduate school when Michael rejoined them.

"We can eat now."

Michael had been testing the narrow beach for trees that were rotten and ready to fall, a common danger in the jungle. Now, for the first time, they strung their hammocks. Catherine lay awake for what seemed a long while, looking up into the gray dusk. Faint pink wisps seemed to linger on the clear gray surface of the sky. The jungle breathed about her. She could feel it on her cheek. She could almost hear it. The night crept out from its dark recesses and spread across the river. In the fading light Catherine watched flying fox bats come out to search for food, diving and fluttering erratically among the heights of the trees.

In the soaring rain forest, everything seemed out of reach: the birds; the animals; the fruit of the trees; the stars; Michael. She abruptly turned her thoughts away. Before closing her eyes, she looked at him in his nearby hammock. He was lying on his back, his arms cradling his head. In the approaching darkness she could just make out that his eyes were open and he was looking up at the sky just as she had done.

She lowered the mosquito netting and closed her eyes. No doubt it would rain again tonight, even though the sky was clear now. She had laid her light canvas cover at the foot of the hammock. She would pull it over her head when the rain came. At least her bottom would be dry tonight. In the boat she had often slept in puddles of rain which sometimes reached such depth that they would have to bail them out in the middle of the night. The comfort of the gently swinging hammock was a definite improvement, and she eventually rocked herself to sleep.

They rose to a light, drizzling rain, and ate the leftovers of their previous night's meal. After Michael divided the canned goods among them, they shouldered their backpacks. Being practical, Catherine accepted the lightest one without protest. Michael slung the rifle strap over his shoulder, and they set out toward the mountains now hidden in the mist. By midmorning they had left the plain and begun their ascent into the golden limestone of the mountain foothills. At times the growth was so thick they had to hack a path with their machetes. Catherine soon developed blisters on her hands, and Michael made her bandage them for protection. Even minor skin abrasions were dangerous in the bacteria-infested climate and environment. David soon had to follow suit. Only Michael, who had spent years in the fields, had developed protective calluses.

By four o'clock that day, after having climbed some 300 feet, they stopped to camp on a narrow rocky ledge, perched above the now swiftly moving Somneg River below. That night, for the first time, they ate some of the canned rations. No one mentioned it, but they all knew they would be trying to feed three people for who knew how long on a supply for one. There was no room to build a fire or trees to string a hammock, so they slept on the rocks.

It didn't rain that night. In that, at least, they were fortunate. It was even sunny when they got up the next morning, and they could see the green shimmer of the vast coastal plain and the ocean stretching out behind them. With a lump in her throat Catherine turned her back on that harsh but familiar landscape and once more began the climb into the mountains.

As they made their way laboriously through the narrow valley ahead, they occasionally caught glimpses of waterfalls thundering down 300-foot spills and disappearing over ledges or around rocks and bends. That day they made less than a mile, and 400 feet of it had been straight up.

Late in the afternoon of the following day it rained torrents, then quickly cleared to treat them to a spectacular sunset. They ate from their supplies for the third straight night, preparing a fire and cooking some of the rice along with tinned meat. Michael felled a small nibong palm with his ax, and again they ate the tender center leaves, boiling them first in water. He also fixed some edible ferns, but Catherine found their taste too bitter.

As they continued the next day, they saw large blue-plumed goura pigeons, but they were too far away for a clear shot. The noise, as they hacked their way through the undergrowth, frightened away what few small creatures there were in the jungle floor. As if the noise from their progress weren't enough, the jungle cockatoos set forth a racket of alarm at their approach. Fortunately this also gave any snakes a chance to escape, although Catherine did see a small three-foot tree python hanging out of reach on a limb above her head. Now and then they glimpsed a Count Raggi, a red-plumed species of the bird of paradise, winging swiftly out of sight.

The fourth night Michael managed to kill a lizard Catherine had found hiding on a branch. He cut off its head with his machete before it could flee, and they roasted it for dinner. Even in the persistent presence of the afternoon showers, Michael always managed to get a fire started.

They made their way up through a landscape pocked by chalklike craters. The jungle intruded everywhere now, even at times onto rocks where there appeared to be no soil at all. The leaves on the sago trees now reached fifty feet in length. The vegetation seemed to grow taller with the altitude. At times their progress would be completely blocked by a vertical limestone wall, and they would have to retrace their steps and find a way around it. Occasionally they would have to retrace a half day's journey. The river was usually within sight or sound, and they used it as a guide. On detours, when they were forced from the river's course by some obstacle, they used a compass, since the sun was so rarely seen that it was useless for supplying directions. Their long-sleeved shirts protected them somewhat from the thorny bushes which grew everywhere, even on barren rocks, but despite precautions, they suffered numerous scratches on their hands and bodies and tears in their clothes.

At the fifth campsite David ran across a jungle turkey's nest in a pile of foliage, with three turkey eggs in its midst. Michael had no chance to warn him that the nest also harbored the *kutimaleo*, one of man's deadliest enemies in the tropics. Tiny ticks that can hardly be seen by the human eye, they work their way under the skin and set up an inflammation which causes unbearable itching. A hard blister forms and eventually bursts, leaving a deadly suppurating wound that is vulnerable to microscopic parasites and bacteria. To his accumulation of scratches and cuts and the arrow wound which was not healing properly, David now added this dangerous infestation. However, the turkey eggs, baked in the fire, were delicious. At the time the discomfort seemed worth it to him. Later it would not.

The three travelers spoke little to one another. In their exhaustion and the increasing misery of their various injuries they developed an almost schizophrenic isolation, withdrawing more and more into themselves. David appeared to be the most affected because of either his personality or the more serious nature of his injuries. At night they were too tired even to string their hammocks and slept on the ground, rain or not. The porousness of the underlying limestone meant that at least water did not collect beneath them.

Each day they continued to climb, and they reached 1,300 feet above sea level on the seventh day. Michael always seemed to materialize with an outstretched hand at that moment when Catherine found herself too exhausted or the path too difficult. Each time she reached out and found herself looking directly into those gray eyes above her, she was deeply disturbed, and she would always quickly release his grip when it had served its purpose. Today Michael had smiled at her as he offered his hand. She blushed at the idea that he might have guessed that she withdrew her hand so quickly because she was affected by such simple contact with him.

She did not worry about it for long. She was more concerned about David. A week ago he had begun the climb in good spirits. Now he seemed brooding and morose. Catherine suspected that it was more than his injuries, that it had something to do with the unacknowledged competition he felt with Michael. Out of the need brought on by their ignorance and inexperience, Michael had assumed complete command of their situation, and Catherine felt that David's increasing depression was directly related to the degree of control that Michael now exercised over both of them. Michael's skill and knowledge were supreme here. There was no competing with him. She was not sure how much of this Michael understood, but the troubled look he took on when he had anything to do with David indicated he knew something was wrong.

Michael was always patient with them, attempting to teach them survival techniques as they went. Sensing the problem with David, he made an effort to make his instructions and directions as courteous and inoffensive as possible, but David rebuffed any attempts by Michael to be friendly or to draw him out. Once, after several warnings from Michael, David had stepped on a rocky ledge to peer at a waterfall without first testing it to see if it could take his weight. The loose stone had immediately given way under him, causing him to fall and sending rocks down on Catherine, who was climbing up below him, knocking her sprawling down the mountainside. Michael, scrambling to reach her in time to prevent serious injury, had lost his temper with David, yelling and swearing at him.

151

"God damn you, Carter! Watch what the hell you're doing. You could kill somebody. I've told you to stay away from the goddamn edge!"

Catherine had been badly bruised and shaken, but neither she nor Michael knew that it was David's ego which had suffered the greater injury.

The eighth morning they set out along the bank of the river, which was now level with them. They had not gone far when a cliff blocked their way. Rather than climb it, Michael looked for a tree tall enough to fell, in order to make a bridge across the river, where the going looked easier. David went on ahead to see if he could find a passage along the cliff wall which would not require their scaling the whole cliff. It had been raining extremely hard for the past thirty minutes, and though it had stopped now, Michael was uneasy. Such a storm, if it had also been breaking in the mountain heights above them, could release a flood upstream perhaps twenty feet high and send it rushing down the river, sweeping everything away before it. Evidence that such walls of water, or bores, were a common occurrence in this part of the river could be seen in the boulders and uprooted trees that lay strewn all around them.

Because of the danger, Michael had picked an escape route before he heard the danger coming. He felt it, really, first: a tremor along the riverbank and then a noise like a locomotive rushing down on them. With a futile shout to David out of view somewhere up ahead, he grabbed Catherine from where she had been resting against a rock. Dragging her backpack with him, he pulled her up the cliff just as the roaring water was upon them, crashing huge boulders and trees before it, snapping them like toothpicks against the rock wall. Catherine had not even had time to realize what was happening when Michael had roughly pulled her up. Now she clung to him in horror as he attempted to brace himself with his back against the cliff's smooth surface, gripping a shrub that grew from the cliff in one hand and holding Catherine with the other, all the time straining against the pull of the rising water.

The water swept by, then up around them until it reached their waists, threatening to undermine their precarious foothold. In panic, Catherine felt her grip on Michael's waist loosen in the swirling current, but he tightened his hold on her and pulled her

152

back. Finally the water level began slowly to drop as the torrent spread from the narrow canyon into the wider canyons below. With the current less forceful, Michael slowly began to edge himself up along the cliff face, one palm pressed tightly against its surface for support, pulling Catherine with him, until they stood on a narrow level ledge about three feet above the still-churning water. He dropped his backpack there on the rock and leaned back against the cliff's smooth surface, exhausted by his effort and trembling slightly from fear and exertion. She started to pull away from him, but both his arms tightened around her, holding her more closely to him as he relaxed against the rock, head back, eyes closed. She stopped struggling and rested her forehead against his chest. The blond, curly hair at his open collar tickled her nose. Perspiration had collected on his neck and throat, and she lightly tested it with her tongue, absorbing the smell and feel of his body pressing against hers.

Almost without realizing what she was doing, she began to kiss his throat at his open collar. Suddenly stunned by what was happening, Catherine started to push herself away only to realize that the only things that held her to him were her own arms, tightly wrapped about his waist. His own had dropped to his sides without her even realizing it. She saw that he was staring ahead and to the left above them where the cliff jutted out over the river. Her eyes followed his gaze until she saw what had made him drop his arms. It was David, perched on his haunches on the cliff above them with a look of intense hate.

Poor, nice David. Well, she thought resignedly, it was just as well that his jealousy was out in the open. No doubt it appeared to David that Michael had robbed him of his dignity and self-respect and now he was going to rob him of Catherine, too. Well, she would have to set him straight, she thought.

Michael was now slowly making his way to the top of the cliff, helping Catherine follow him. When they reached the top, neither of them looked at each other or at David. Michael discreetly excused himself to get firewood, giving David and Catherine a chance to talk in private. She took off her boots and set them beside her to dry out. She heard David rummaging through his backpack for something, obviously still in a rage. Catherine grew alarmed. Suppose he got the rifle and did something drastic. With relief she recalled seeing Michael take it with him.

"It really isn't what you think, David." She tried to sound reassuring. "He was just helping me get away from the water."

"How do you know what I'm thinking? Besides, I saw the look on your face when you were standing there together.".

"It was all over months ago. It doesn't matter anymore."

"First you tell me it's nothing, and now you're telling me it's all over!" His voice rose in accusation.

Catherine tried to remain calm. "I'm just telling you that what you saw were the remnants of something that was over a long time ago—before you even got here."

She regretted her words immediately. The look on his face told her at once that she had made a drastic mistake. Now she realized that she had just confirmed what he had previously felt was only a threatening possibility. He was no longer merely in danger of being made a fool. Now it was already an accomplished fact.

The tension among the three of them rose to unbearable levels in the following days. In a more civilized context David might have been able to absorb the blow. But isolated as he was emotionally and half-delirious with the infectious festering in his wound and the scratches and bites all over his body, he became a walking time bomb from which Catherine could not escape.

They had been traveling on foot for eight days and had come a total of perhaps six or seven miles. The river rejoined them as they continued their climb, but the bank was narrow and treacherous. When the water level dropped, Michael felled a tree to extend seventy feet over the river so they could cross. For a while progress was easier on the opposite side. They spent the better part of a day scaling a 200-foot limestone cliff. Upon reaching the top, they hiked an hour longer, mired in mud. The trees now crawled with leeches, and they searched for a campsite as free from them as possible, necessitating turning back and retracing part of their path.

The mud made the campsite miserable. Because of the leeches which dropped from the trees, they could not string their hammocks and were forced to improvise a platform over the mud with logs and tree trunks in a tiny partial clearing. Despite precautions, the leeches made their way into every crevice. In the morning they were discovered trapped in the mosquito net, and they had to be wiped off before the backpacks could be shouldered. The weary trio ate quickly from their supplies, not wanting to linger in that unpleasant spot.

However, the rest of the day proved no better. The leeches dropped in clouds from the branches above and worked their way up their boots and trousers. It was impossible to defend against them. Catherine was horrified to find they were so small and agile that they worked their way through the lace holes of her boots. Their favorite place to settle was in the ear. They could not be removed anywhere without tearing flesh, which rapidly became infected.

Preoccupied with physical discomfort, they were oblivious of the fact that around them the water poured in breathtaking glistening cascades over moss-covered rocks and thundered through narrow shoots to emerge in great clouds of spray. The mud, like the leeches, plagued them throughout the day, and the steady rainfall that began in the morning continued through the eleventh night of camp.

Michael declared they could not eat more of their rapidly diminishing supplies. They would now have to make do with whatever the jungle could supply them. That day, in the rain, nothing stirred. They did not stop early to make camp in spite of their exhaustion; they pushed on in hopes of finding a mud-free spot. It was not to be. Finally they stopped at a small clearing by the river. While Michael went in search of food, David and Catherine dug a cooking hole in the mud and gathered wood for a fire. They cut some palm leaves in an attempt to provide some shelter for sleeping that night. The rain gave every indication of continuing. Their rice supply was wet and fermented, and eating it was now making them ill. In addition, they all were suffering from glandular swellings. Catherine could hardly turn her neck, and the men had painfully swollen testicles.

Catherine sat numbly on a rock, staring at her boots, which were sunk two inches in mud. It hurt to swallow. It hurt even more to move. In spite of the dwindling supplies, her pack seemed to get heavier each day. She knew that she simply could not spend another night in this mud.

"I'm going to see if I can find something clear of this mud farther up the river," she said to David. He did not look up at her as he continued cutting palm leaves. He had not spoken to her or to Michael in three days. Oh, well, she thought, even if she couldn't find a smooth rocky area for sleeping, at least it would be more comfortable not to be around David.

She made her way along the mud and rocks to a place where the river formed a small waterfall, rushing over loose boulders and flowing over a small dam made by previous bores. There was no good campsite here, but she rested on a boulder, took off her muddy boots and socks, and washed them in the stream. In spite of the muddy banks, the river water was fairly clear here, for the bed itself consisted of rock and loose gravel.

She did not hear him coming. The waterfall prevented it. Still, part of her had known this moment would come. Hello, I've been expecting you, a small voice said inside her as it burst forth in panic. Suddenly she was not sure if it was his madness or hers she saw burning intensely before her, red-rimmed, penetrating.

"Oh, God," she muttered out loud.

She turned and tried to scramble over the rocks, but he grabbed her leg and pulled her back. She scraped her skin as she slipped, and her eyes brimmed with pain. She quickly forgot it as she turned to face him. He smiled. He must see my fear, she thought, and tried to hide it. He took hold of her shoulders, digging his fingers into them. She scratched and hit him. He grabbed her arms and began to push her down. She struggled with all her strength.

"Get away from me, you son of a bitch!" she gasped.

He suddenly freed one hand and grabbed the front of her shirt, ripping it open as he pinned her against a rock with the weight of his body. Deliberately he reached around her back and undid her bra. Still pressing her against the rock with his body, he began slowly to slip the straps off her shoulder, enjoying her helplessness and the sound of fear in her shallow breathing.

After he had slipped the straps down to her elbows, he pulled back enough to let the bra fall and reveal her breasts. He roughly pulled it from her along with the remnants of her shirt. The rage and fear she felt at her helplessness gave her a new surge of strength, and she lunged against him, shoving him back. When she was a few inches free of his body, she brought her knee up with all her might and struck him in the groin. He yelled as he let her go and doubled up in pain. Free of him, she started to run. He quickly grabbed a limb, and as she started past him, he hit her on the side of the head, knocking her unconscious.

When she came to a short time later, she lay naked, flat on her back in the mud. Her hands were tied above her head to a tree trunk. Her trousers and underpants lay in a muddy wad beside her. He was now using liana vine to tie one leg spread-eagle style to a stake he had stuck into the mud, unaware she had gained consciousness. She kicked at him with her free leg, sending him tumbling forward. He got to his knees and, leaning over her, struck her as hard as he could across the face. Blood spattered his shirt as the blow split her lip. The pain was terrifying. Catherine had never been assaulted physically before. She wondered what she was fighting to defend. Certainly not her virginity. Why was she struggling so hard to keep what she might have given freely to him at some other time, in some other place? Relax, part of her said. Just try to stay alive. Don't fight it. But something else screamed and overpowered reason. She could not, would not give in. Because she did not choose to give herself to him, his use of force was a violation of the deepest kind.

He had started to tie her other foot. He was working feverishly now. His fingers stumbled, and he cursed his slowness. Suddenly the scream going on silently within her found its voice.

"Michael!" she cried. "Michael!"

Now cursing her, he quickly wadded her mud-caked underpants and stuffed them into her mouth, gagging her. He knelt between her legs and lowered his pants. For a moment he stayed there before her. Her eyes avoided his erect organ; but she saw his hate, and she became frightened for her life. His eyes covered her body slowly. He reached one hand out and touched a breast. She shrank visibly from his touch and started to retch, sending the gag onto the ground. Angry at her revulsion, he struck her again and then roughly turned her face to his, pinching her cheeks and lips tightly together in his hand.

"I'm going to screw you, you bitch," he snarled, "and when I'm done, I'm going to take this nice long stick"—he held up a stick he had sharpened to a point—"and I'm going to run it from here"—he paused, sticking a finger into her vagina—"right up through you and out your mouth so you won't ever screw anybody again!"

Just then the butt of the rifle caught him fully across the back, sending him flying forward, against Catherine, knocking the breath out of her. Michael immediately grabbed David by the

157

shirt collar, pulled him from Catherine, and flung him into the mud. Then he threw back the bolt of the rifle and aimed the gun barrel at David's head. His voice shook.

"You son of a bitch! You touch her again, and I'll kill you slowly, an inch at a time."

Keeping the gun aimed at David, Michael bent down, cut Catherine free, and helped her sit up. She was still dazed. With one hand, he took off his shirt and wrapped it around her, then pulled her gently to her feet. He picked up what was left of her clothes and, holding her against him, began slowly to back away, gun still trained. When he was a safe enough distance away to keep David from successfully lunging at him, he turned his back and guided Catherine back to the campsite, leaving David sitting in the mud, staring angrily after them.

Catherine felt she was going mad. She was trembling from head to toe, and once she had to stop and empty the contents of her stomach into the mud. She was a miserable sight: Her mouth was still bleeding, and her face was beginning to swell; her hair and body were caked with mud. Michael was very gentle with her, and she allowed herself to be led by him like a trusting child. He took her to the river, and after entering it with her, clothes and all, he bathed her and cleaned her wounds with antiseptic soap. Bending her down, he washed her mud-filled hair, dried it with one of his shirts, and helped her put on some clean clothes. Then, sitting her before him, he combed out her hair. She had withdrawn into a state where neither the physical pain nor the psychic pain could intrude. She was aware of nothing, not even that it had finally stopped raining.

Alarmed that she might be slipping over some precipice he could not see, he began talking to her about inconsequential things in a warm, soothing voice: about the jungle, the river, the kinds of birds and insects. She did not respond. More frightened, he put away the comb and went down on one knee before her, anxiously searching her eyes.

"Tell me what you're feeling, Catherine. Don't keep it bottled up inside you. You can do it, Catherine," Michael urged her. "Come out of it!"

He felt like shaking her back to reality, but gazing at that poor, swollen face, he knew that it would only drive her further away. She was in a state of shock.

"You have to come back, I can't do it alone. I can't be strong for everyone. Not any longer. I'm tired and frightened, too, Catherine. For God's sake, pull yourself together and help me!" He was surprised at the desperation he heard and felt in his own voice.

Somewhere his desperation touched her, and her eyes lost their blank look and appeared to focus, confused at first, on her surroundings. Almost immediately she began to weep, deep, sobbing cries that racked her body. In his relief Michael pulled her to him and held her, comforting her until she had no more tears left and fell asleep in his arms.

To make her more comfortable, Michael built a platform of branches over the mud and constructed a tent of palm leaves to give them shelter if the rain should start again. Afraid to leave Catherine alone, he made dinner from their supplies, heartened that she ate a little. She watched him closely as he moved about the camp. Though she did not speak, he knew that she was feeling better. Finished with dinner, she suddenly put down her food.

"It's all my fault, Michael. I've really led him to—to expect more than I ever really intended to give."

Michael immediately sat down next to her and took her firmly by the shoulders.

"Don't ever say that again," he said so fiercely that it startled her. "You musn't blame yourself. David is sick. We've both seen it coming. He's dangerous, and he needs help. We have to get him to Hollandia. That much we owe him. It doesn't excuse what he did. As far as causing it, I'm as much to blame as you are."

She slept fitfully next to him. More than once he woke her from a nightmare and cradled her head on his shoulder. He slept little. David did not return to camp.

The next morning Catherine woke to find Michael gone. For the first time in more than a week the sun was shining. Her trousers and underclothes hung on the bush where Michael had put them to dry after washing them for her. She was sitting in the sun in front of the shelter when he came up from the river. Hesitantly he paused and stood looking at her, his gray eyes aloof. She read the message in them clearly.

"Don't worry, Michael," she said calmly. "Your concern for my welfare has not been misunderstood."

They looked at each other across the distance that separated them. Something had flickered briefly back there on the cliff ledge when they had almost been killed by the bore, and then it had died. Catherine turned away and finished lacing her boots.

"I can't find David anywhere," he said finally.

"What does it matter if he disappears?" she said bitterly.

"He's sick, Catherine. As another human being—and as head of whatever is left of this expedition—I feel responsible for him. We just can't leave him here. He's not capable of making it to Hollandia alone. We all need each other now."

No, Catherine thought. We need you, David and I, but you don't need us.

"I'm going to look for him," Michael said. "Perhaps I can pick up his trail at the river."

He took his rifle and started to leave; then he turned back to where she sat.

"Will you be okay if I go?"

She nodded.

"I won't go far. Signal me with this if you need me." He handed her the rifle.

She nodded again; then fear seized her. Suppose he were attacked. It wasn't safe for him to go without the rifle. And admit it, Catherine, she told herself, you don't want to be away from his reassuring presence. When he's with you, you feel you could almost make it through this hell.

"No—wait!" she called to him. "I want to come with you."

She walked over to him and handed him the gun. He shrugged.

"Suit yourself." He knew her presence would slow him down, but he had been reluctant to leave her alone in the first place.

"We might as well take these with us." He indicated their packs. He would carry Catherine's pack since she was in no condition to do so herself. He had begun to load what he could of David's pack into his own when he noticed that the supply of canned food that David had been carrying for them was gone. Michael swore violently under his breath. David must have been eating the food all along without telling them. Michael decided to keep it to himself. He didn't want Catherine, with an exhausting and discouraging day ahead of her, to know that their emergency rations were now gone.

As if in response to his mood, the sky had once again darkened, and as they set out, it began to rain. They retraced their path to the waterfall, and from tracks that were gradually being washed away by the rain they began to follow David. Throughout the day they stayed with his trail, climbing all the way. It continued to pour, though Catherine sometimes could not tell whether it was rain or leeches that steadily pelted her hat and body. Her legs were bloody and covered with sores where she had pulled the leeches from them, stopping often to do so. Her ribs began to hurt until the pain brought tears to her eyes, but she said nothing until Michael noticed and insisted on stopping to bind her ribs with one of David's shirts. It helped the pain considerably but made breathing more difficult.

The descent of darkness and their arrival at a sheer rock wall finally forced a halt for the night. Michael had pushed them hard all day, trying to catch David before his trail would be lost. They had nothing to eat but beetle larvae Michael had collected during the day from under the bark of a palm tree along the path. Catherine had already noted the lightness of David's pack and knew without being told of the disappearance of their food supply, and that David must have stolen it. The sneak, she thought bitterly, and the fact seemed to confirm every negative feeling she had ever had toward him. Michael roasted the larvae Asmat style.

"Pretend they're peanuts," he said teasingly as he served them to her. She struggled to eat them, trying desperately not to gag.

"Here I've served you the caviar of New Guinea, and you're turning up your nose. No class. This meal would cost you your best cowrie shell back in Agats."

She smiled weakly at his attempts to humor her. And though he kidded her and listened sympathetically to her protests, he made her eat.

By morning David's trail was gone. However, it was easy to surmise what he had done. With a sheer wall before them and the river cascading down it in a waterfall, there were only two ways to go. Back or up. And since he had obviously not done the former, they decided to climb after him. By five o'clock they had reached a rocky, treeless ledge some 160 feet above their last campsite. From that height, about 4,000 feet, they could still see the plain, which seemed a lifetime away, receding into the Arafura Sea. Catherine was surprised that the sight evoked no feeling in her this time.

They camped for the night. Already rain clouds were collecting around the higher mountain peaks, hidden from their view. Michael smiled his gratitude when he saw her pick up her machete and accompany him to gather the palm leaves for their separate shelters. Together they found crayfish among the rocks in the river. Boiled with wild spinach, they tasted delicious.

"Better than those maggots." Catherine smiled.

"Beetle larvae," he corrected her with a smile.

She wrinkled her nose. The next night they camped some 200 feet above the green, frothy river, churning on the rocks below. They would meet it again farther ahead where it crossed their canyon wall as a waterfall. Catherine took note of the forest for the first time since leaving the swampy lowlands. In her struggle to survive, she had looked no farther than her machete could cut. Looking around her now, she saw that the forest was beautiful. Bright parrots, cockatoos, and dozens of different species of birds of paradise sat chattering in the branches of those soaring trees. Ferns and moss covered the forest floor. White orchids grew everywhere along the forest edges and even among the rocks.

Michael had killed a lizard among the rocks during their climb. He added some red pandanus-palm fruit to the menu. Catherine did not like the taste of this cooked red fruit, but Michael told her it was nourishing.

"Funny," said Michael as they sat roasting their dinner over hot stones in the hole they had dug, "I've become obsessed with a yearning for fettucine, which I've eaten about three or four times in my life and never particularly cared for."

"Maine lobster with drawn butter," Catherine countered.

Laughingly they sat torturing themselves with their favorite meals until they ran out of menus.

"Hard-boiled eggs with chocolate sauce," Michael finally offered.

"Ugh!"

"That's exactly how we should end this discussion. With an 'ugh' and not a 'ummm.' It'll be easier," he said jokingly.

Exactly the way they had needed to end their relationship, Catherine thought. With that thought her mood changed. She suddenly became aware again of all the things that were physically wrong with her. The cut on her lip still hurt. Like all wounds in this climate, it was slow to heal. Her head still ached slightly from David's blows, and her bruised ribs still troubled her as well. She got up and walked over to the ledge to peer again at the river.

Something caught her eye, a piece of cloth among the boulders on the river below. The light was dim, and she could barely make it out.

"Michael, what's that?"

He got up and joined her, following where her finger pointed to the rag of cloth below.

"Look at that. Aren't those clothes? They must belong to David," she said.

Michael stood quietly, studying the object. The sun no longer brightened the canyon walls below, making identification difficult.

Finally he said, "It's not just a piece of clothing, Catherine, it's a body."

Catherine gave a little cry of horror.

"There's still about thirty minutes more of light. I'm going down there. I'll take the flashlight with me."

"Oh, Michael, no. What use is it? He must be dead. He must have fallen from here. Don't risk the rocks in the dark. At least wait until morning," she pleaded.

"We don't know that he fell from here," he said grimly. "He might have come along the riverbank. He might be injured but alive. If it rains tonight, the water will rise and carry him away. I can't wait until morning."

"Then I'll come with you," she said wearily, not beginning to know how she could manage it.

"No. Wait here. You'll only slow me down."

He took the flashlight and some rope and began to work his way down. It wasn't until he was gone that she realized dinner was still cooking and he hadn't eaten since morning. As it grew dark, he still had not reached the bottom. At first she could see the beam of his flashlight dance along the wall, but finally the overhang of the cliff ledge hid him from view. If he shouted to her, she would be unable to hear it over the noise of the rushing river.

Catherine huddled near the ledge, straining in the darkness to see the beam of light that would mark Michael's progress. She felt a panic at his absence that made it impossible for her to sleep. Although she had been physically dependent on him since their ordeal began, she now found herself slipping into an emotional dependence which frightened her. She did not like helplessness in anyone, least of all herself. She felt as if her very life were slipping away through the various injuries she had suffered through falls, thorns, leeches, and David. Her eyelids ached, and she knew she was filled with infections.

Dinner had finished cooking, but Michael wasn't there to persuade her to eat, so she didn't. She wanted to die. She thought that David, lifeless below, was the lucky one. She would like to follow his example, but she did not even have the energy to get up and go to the edge. She finally fell asleep on the bare rock.

It was dawn when she woke—alone. It had been raining, and she was soaked. She crawled to the ledge. The river was up. She could no longer make out the crumpled clothing that was David. Either Michael had reached him or the river had carried them both away.

Unable to bear the waiting, Catherine began the descent to the river, dragging the backpacks after her. She was halfway down when Michael found her, shouldered the packs, and helped her descend the slimy, treacherous rocks. Looking down on him as he worked his way below her, searching for a foothold, she saw the exhaustion in his eyes when he looked up at her. She knew she was a terrible burden on him, one that might destroy whatever chance he had of making it to safety. With David's death something inside her began to give up.

She had not asked, and he had not told her about David. She knew that he was dead. She did not know how she felt about it, and right now she could not afford the luxury of feeling anything except fright as she clung to the slippery surface of the canyon wall.

By midmorning they had reached the bottom. He was there, lying near the wall. Michael had pulled the body to an area high enough to escape the rising water. She stood staring, but she did not recognize the swollen, bloated shape before her. It wasn't David. David was handsome and slender. This thing was grotesque and horrible.

"Almost every bone in his body is broken," Michael said. "He must have fallen from the edge."

"Or jumped," Catherine added listlessly.

"Whatever," Michael said quietly. "Massive head and internal injuries. He died instantly."

"Then he's luckier than we are."

Michael did not answer. He stared grimly at the body. Catherine searched within herself for some regret, but found no feeling at all. Here was a man she had been close to for four years. They had talked for hours at a time, shared ideas, planned a life together.

Finally a feeling rose to the surface and surprised her.

"I'm glad he's dead," she murmured softly, and the tears came forth at last. For David. For herself. This man who had loved her was dead, and she was glad.

"Oh, God! How awful!" She sobbed. "I didn't love him. I have never loved anyone," she said sadly. "Perhaps I'm not capable of it."

"You're being too hard on yourself," Michael said softly. "Stop trying to decide who was to blame for the fact that you didn't love him. Perhaps neither of you was responsible."

They had no efficient digging tools and the ground was too stony, so they buried him by covering him with rocks. When they finished, they stood silently by the grave for a few moments; then Michael gently took Catherine's arm and led her away. She walked over to her pack.

"Can you manage that?" he asked doubtfully.

"Yes," she said, seeing his exhaustion.

She stopped to pick it up, and Michael could see in the movement the depth of her despair. He cajoled, ordered, pushed, and threatened her into continuing through the mud along the river. She could no longer use her machete but numbly followed Michael as he hacked his way through the canyon brush. They had not eaten since breakfast the previous day. They stopped at midafternoon. Michael knew he would have to find some appetizing food so that Catherine would eat. He killed a lizard and took time to dig a hole and cook it slowly with hot stones because he knew she preferred it that way. He coaxed her to eat, but when it was time to start out she refused to rise.

"Go without me, Michael—please! I don't want to go on anymore. Just leave me alone."

"Damn it, Catherine, get up!"

"No! I can't go on. I don't want to go on."

"You'll die here. You've got to keep moving." He was frightened and angry.

"I *want* to die here. Now leave me alone! Just go."

He felt like shaking her. "Damn you, you're going to get up and go on. I haven't dragged you all this way to have you give up on me. I need you! I can't make it by myself. Where the hell do you get off always assuming I'm the strong one? It makes it easier for you, doesn't it? You can just lie back and be led around. You know I can't leave you here."

She stared back at him. Somehow he seemed so far away. Still, she could see the torment on his face, so she slowly got up and, without a word, started off along the riverbank. Relieved, he followed her.

They stopped at the base of a thirty-foot waterfall. Its ledge extended out from the canyon wall about 250 feet, forming a grotto of rock and water behind the cascade where the water was deep and black and calm. He decided to camp here for several days in order to give Catherine's wounds a chance to heal. It was a pleasant spot. White orchids grew in profusion, wild and beautiful. He tested the trees around the campsite to make sure none was rotten, then climbed a wild oak and cut enough branches for several cookfires. He found crayfish in the rocks around the pool while Catherine slept restlessly on a bed he had made for her in the grotto.

Michael finally sat down nearby and watched her. He had not allowed himself such a close and undisturbed appraisal of her since Maitreya. Her hair had lost some of its silky shine. Her face was still slightly swollen from the blow she had received, giving her mouth a slightly petulant look. There were traces of dark circles around her eyes. Still, she was beautiful now in a way that touched him deeply each time he looked at her. She was unique among the women he had known, and she had complicated his life in a way that he had never thought possible. He had resented her for that, as if she were to blame for his own feelings. And he had shut her out as as a result. After Maitreya and what happened between them, he would have been greatly relieved never to have seen her again. But she had not gone away. The grace with which she had moved in and out of his life these past months never allowed him to forget her, and because she was not long from his awareness, he found that the door he had shut against her was not impregnable. Its strength had been tested by her presence and found wanting.

Now, seeing her before him like this, he could imagine her hands upon him, caressing him as they had before, soft, loving, sweetly torturing him. He tore his eyes away from her and quickly rose to pace the campsite until the turbulence inside him died. Then he lay down on the ground and fell asleep.

When he awoke, he went over to look at Catherine, asleep on one of the canvas sheets. She was even more restless than before, and the pallor that had drained her face of color had been replaced by an unmistakable flush. With alarm he realized she was seriously ill. He gave her what medication they had and for the next three days did the best he could to lower her temperature, including bathing her in the glacier-fed stream. He made broth from shellfish and frogs and forced her to eat it. She remained semiconscious and feverish. On the third day he realized that he, too, was sick.

He did not take any drugs, fearing there might not be enough for both of them, and by that evening he felt as if he were on fire. Perspiration ran down his face. His clothes were soaked. Dizzily he stood up to go over and lie in the stream. He felt panic as the jungle swung dizzily before him; then he staggered and fell helplessly, facedown. He was unconscious before he hit the ground.

For the next three days he was only dimly aware of his surroundings and then just for brief flashes. Most of the time he was delirious. When he finally regained consciousness, he found himself lying fully clothed in a pool of cool water, his head resting on Catherine's lap as she sat with him. When she realized he was conscious, she smiled at him in relief, and he was

167

surprised to see her eyes fill with tears. He said nothing but smiled at her and, reaching up, found her hand and held it in his own as he immediately drifted off into a restful, healing sleep. When he next woke, he was lying on a canvas sheet in the shelter behind the waterfall. Catherine sat nearby. When she saw that he was awake, she offered him some soup.

"It's cassowary bird," she said with satisfaction. "I shot it in the forest this morning."

"Chicken soup." He smiled. "I'll recover for sure." He was impressed and pleased.

"I found some spinach and sweet potatoes in an abandoned garden. It's in the soup."

He was weak, and the spoon shook in his hand. After taking it from him, she fed him, his head cushioned in her lap. She had braided her hair, improvising with sticks and bits of woven grass to pin it back. Her clothes had been washed. She looked fresh and recovered, but he noted that her eyes were still surrounded by dark circles and she had lost weight. His hand went up to his face and found the stubble had become a beard. He never grew a beard in the field. Besides its being uncomfortable, he considered it a sign of carelessness, an apathy that could prove fatal.

Reading his thoughts, she said, "Tomorrow I'll shave it for you." She got up and washed his spoon and bowl in the river.

"You okay?" he asked.

She nodded.

"If there's anything else in that garden, we'll stay here for a few days."

"Good," she said gratefully. "There's more in the garden. No sign of any people, nothing left of any shelter they might have built. It's impossible to guess what they might be like or what happened to them."

"We should be coming across some villages before long," he said matter-of-factly. They each sat silently contemplating what might happen in that first encounter.

"Has any explorer ever come this far into the Snow mountains?"

"Once. Some mountain climbers from New Zealand came to climb the Carstensz Glacier two years ago."

"What happened to them?"

"No one knows." He searched her eyes for a reaction. Seeing

apprehension, he added, "They were careless. They didn't have anyone with them who knew anything about New Guinea."

He was already becoming tired again. Before ending the conversation, he added, "Just think of the anthropological coup. New tribes discovered. Sure to get a dissertation with honors."

Funny, he thought as he began to drift off to sleep, they both seemed more relaxed, even though the greatest dangers of all lay ahead of them, at the hands of the unknown cultures they were about to contact. Out of their dependence had grown mutual respect and acceptance. He was grateful for the cautious cordiality that had replaced the hostility between them.

Chapter 18

When they started out again four days later, it was with strength and spirits restored. The trail Catherine had found led nowhere. Abandoned too long ago, it disappeared without a trace into the leafy canopy of trees. They began to climb steadily into the mountains. A little distance above them the clouds boiled up along the mountain ridges in a churning white wall. The second day they reached the high-altitude cloud forest. Here the ground was hollow, made of tree roots covered over with a layer of debris and moss; now and then they would break through it up to their thighs. The air became quiet and dank. Water condensed on the leaves and rocks steadily dripped onto the ground. Through the mist they could occasionally glimpse the 1,500-foot gorge that lay below them. Small mountain streams and brooks raced down the rocks. At 9,000 feet they found a pass and broke free of the mountain clouds to the clear sky beyond.

That night they camped on the roof of New Guinea. The air was crisp, dry, and cool. Fragile starlight shone above. They built a fire for warmth and woke shivering to bright sunlight. Green and purple ridges rippled in the distance before them. They began gradually to descend. The trees became tall again, and birds sang in them. Suddenly they broke from the trees into an ocean of waist-high grass, a muted world of yellow-greens and purple peaks. Forest and savanna land now interchanged and they came across their second abandoned village. This one had an unused and overgrown trail which could still be followed.

Eventually it led them back to the river, where a vine bridge in disrepair spanned the churning water. As Michael tested it with his weight, a vine cable broke, almost throwing him into the rocks and swirling waters just below. Unable to cross by way of the bridge, Michael secured a rope to a tree and began to make his way through the swift, waist-deep current on foot, holding on to what remained of the bridge to brace himself as he went. He reached the opposite bank and secured the other end of the rope. After removing his pack, he headed back for Catherine. Her heart leaped to her throat as he slipped and disappeared once before regaining his footing and continuing on to her.

"I'll give you a lift," he shouted over the roaring water.

She shook her head in refusal. She was terrified, but she was determined to be as little burden to him now as possible. He shouldered her pack and helped her get a firm grip on the rope. The current was extremely swift and cool enough that it began to chill her. It pounded around her, doing its best to lift and plunge her against the rocks. Twice she lost her footing and completely disappeared underwater. As she still frantically held on to the rope above her, the water tried to twist and turn her as if to snap her in two. Both times Michael reached down to grab her and pull her to the surface, choking and gasping for air, her mouth and nose full of sand, her eyes stinging. As she moved inch by interminable inch, she felt as if her arms would be wrenched from their sockets, but she managed to hang on. Exhausted by panic as much as by the physical exertion itself, she finally accepted the possibility she might die here in the river and, accepting it, felt an inner peace that allowed her to concentrate her energy on physical survival. She emerged, exhausted, on the other side and lay shivering and panting. The strange feeling of peace, even triumph, remained with her.

The trail beyond the river was still in use. There was little overgrowth, and they found human tracks in the mud around the river and along the path. Still, the village and gardens that they passed were abandoned, some with huts still standing and remnants of everyday life strewn about as if the occupants had left in haste. There was no clue to what had been responsible. Michael

171

picked up a sharp digging stick that had been left in an abandoned garden.

"What's happened to them?" Catherine asked him.

He thoughtfully ran his fingers over the sharpened point. "I don't know. Raids. Wars. But so many . . . I just don't know."

There were still tracks along the trail. As a precaution Michael removed the rifle from his pack and slung the strap over his shoulder within easy reach. Rounding a turn in the path, they suddenly came upon their first occupied village. It was only a few huts carved out of a tiny clearing in the woods, with no guards posted on their end of the trail. The natives appeared surprisingly listless at the sight of the two white strangers, and it became apparent, even from a distance, that they all were ill. The women wore loop skirts made of woven orchid fibers and carried large nets banded about their heads. Important possessions, including children and baby pigs, all traveled in the nets. The men, wearing long, narrow gourds over their penises, hesitantly approached the strangers who crossed the clearing through their village. Uttering, "Wa-wa-wa," they began to pull and tug at whatever interested them about the intruders. Michael gave them some shells, highly valued throughout New Guinea as a sign of wealth. They were pleased and followed Michael and Catherine to the edge of their village territory, talking with as much excitement as their poor health allowed. Their gardens were ill-kept and had little food in them. There was no point in attempting to trade, so Michael and Catherine pushed on, only to find that the same held true for the other villages they now came across. The people were sick and ill-fed; the gardens, empty. Michael and Catherine now stayed as clear of the villages as they could, trying to pass unnoticed. Clearly some mysterious disaster had struck the area, removing half the population and leaving the other half too weak and ill to carry on. The language these people spoke was unknown to Michael, so they could not be questioned.

On the fifth day of their renewed journey Catherine and Michael neared the Baliem River. Archbold's aerial map had shown it leaving the Grand Valley just northeast of the savanna land they were now crossing. Michael turned to Catherine and said quietly, "We've been followed for the last fifteen minutes. Don't fall too far behind."

Catherine looked apprehensively around her. The waist-high

savanna grass swayed in the wind, but nothing else that she could see moved. They continued for another half hour. Still, no one appeared.

"Are they still there?"

He nodded.

"Why aren't they showing themselves? Are they afraid of us?"

She did not have to wait long for an answer. Just as they neared the end of the savanna land and were about to reenter the jungle, twenty warriors armed with black palm bows and bamboo arrows stepped into the path in front of them. In appearance and manner they were different from the others they had so far encountered. Slightly taller, they were in good health and possessed an air of confidence, arrogance even. They stood quietly, making no attempt to approach but blocking the path with their presence.

Suddenly a tall figure resembling a human bird of paradise appeared in the midst of the waiting warriors, who stepped aside with obvious deference. He passed among them and stood before Michael and Catherine. He was more than six feet tall, and to this height he had added a two-foot headdress of white cockatoo feathers trimmed with cuscus fur and bird of paradise plumes. A bustle of dry grasses simulating a bird's crest and tail reached to the ground behind him. He wore a neatly trimmed skirt of grass that reached about eight inches above his knees. Two necklaces, one of shells and the other of bamboo sticks hung around his neck, and he had a white bone plug through his nose. His most incredible garment, however, was the red, ocher, white, and black paint with which he had decorated his body in striped designs. A black mask outlined in white was painted around his eyes.

"I don't think we're properly dressed for the occasion," Michael said wryly as he looked at the figure before them. "No doubt this is why they've been following us unseen for forty-five minutes—to give him and the others a chance to put on their best feathers to impress and intimidate us.

"Funny," Michael added as he listened to the dialogue around him, "I can understand what they're saying. They're speaking the language of the Kukukuku, from the Australian side of New Guinea, hundreds of miles from here."

173

Catherine was seized with fear. The Kukukuku were the most ferocious group in New Guinea, frequently sending raiding parties throughout the area west of the Baxter River, killing, taking heads. She listened and watched intently as Michael talked with the tall man who was obviously their leader. She was listening not for the words, which she didn't understand, but for clues to the sentiments that were exchanged betweeen Michael and those awesome creatures. She allowed herself to breathe a little more easily when she detected no hostility. Finally the leader turned and shouted to the surrounding warriors. Michael took her arm. They were being escorted to the village, where they would be guests at a feast.

"You're sure we're not the menu," she said with a faint smile she did not feel.

"They're cannibals all right," Michael replied grimly. "He calls himself Nomad. I wonder if he somehow took it from the English word for wanderer."

"Or from the Nomad River," Catherine added.

"Ndep John Nomad. That's the whole name. Says he led a Kukukuku trading party to the Jale beyond the Grand Valley to trade for stone axes. They liked it here and never returned. He's lying, of course."

More warriors had joined the group until plumed warriors seemed to bloom from the waist-high grass around them like exotic flowers. Like protective thorns, their long bamboo spears pierced the sky. As they neared a village at the jungle's edge, the women and children came out to greet them. Most of them were Kukukuku, supporting Michael's contention that this was not a trading party. There were as many as 100 multiple-family huts in the village, meaning a population of at least 1,000 and probably more. A man completely covered with charcoal ash stepped from among the women, children, and elders. Bright ocher stripes circled his legs, and he carried a four-foot-high narrow black drum with a head made of python skin. He began slowly to beat it, and a chant rose from the milling, splendidly arrayed crowd.

They sat down to a feast of roast pork, taro cakes, cucumbers, wild spinach, and sweet potatoes. Then Nomad and Michael began to bargain. Nomad was trading for a steel ax and beads and shells. Michael was trading for food, but in reality, he knew he was buying safe passage. When the transactions had finally been completed, Michael said to her, "He wanted to trade for you"—he smiled—"but I told him that while he had two hundred wives, I had only the one woman and he could scarcely expect me to part with you."

Catherine felt fear at being singled out. "Well, what did he say?"

"He offered to give me one of his wives and two pigs for you. You'll be glad to know that I refused. You should feel flattered by his offer. Two pigs is a high price for a woman."

He looked at her in amusement. She was furious at the laughter she saw in his eyes.

"It's fine for you to be so amused! Suppose he decides to pursue the matter without your permission?"

"He won't."

"What makes you so sure?"

"Because they don't know it yet, but we're getting out of here at sundown."

Nomad jabbed a finger toward Catherine and spoke to Michael in a boastful manner.

"And what is he saying now?" Catherine asked uneasily.

"He doesn't seem to have accepted my refusal. He says when you are his wife, he will see to it that you have no children."

"Oh?" Catherine said with a sharp laugh of relief. "I'm to be a virgin bride?"

"No," Michael replied grimly. "Quite the contrary. He means he will throw any babies you bear him into the river so that he won't have to observe the four-year taboo against having sexual relations with the mother of a young child." Nomad gripped his penis and patted his stomach. "He says he will keep your belly so full of babies that the crocodiles downriver will never be hungry."

Catherine could not suppress a shudder, but she hid it from Nomad. She knew he must not see her fear.

Later, when they were shown to the guesthouse, Michael insisted that their supplies be brought to the house immediately rather than the next morning. Several natives returned with two string baskets filled with food. The sky was turning gold with the beginning of the sunset.

"We'll leave as soon as it starts to get dark. They won't bother us as long as we have the gun, and they won't follow us at night.

175

They're afraid of ghosts. We'll be out of their territory by morning."

It was strangely quiet. Catherine sat down in the doorway, looking out at the village. Ominously she noted that the village appeared empty and that the weapons that had stood ready in the doorways of the huts were gone, too.

"Well, now we know what happened to the surrounding villages," said Michael. "The Kukukuku are hunters, not farmers. They've been taking food from the gardens, pigs from the villages, killing the people, or leaving them with little to eat. Stealing their women, too. That's how Nomad obtained all those wives."

"Why do you think he's here if it's not for trading?"

"I think John is the name of one of his white victims—possibly a missionary who took a risk he shouldn't have."

"What makes you think he's killed a missionary?"

"He's wearing a Saint Christopher's medal. It's not likely he bought it at the church bazaar. He probably fled the Australian police and is in exile here. And there are empty cartridge shells among the bamboo sticks around his neck. He probably eliminated some of the policemen who came after him as well."

"The bamboo sticks. Do they indicate the number of men killed as they do in the Asmat?"

Michael nodded. "Apparently he's killed hundreds."

The odor from the feast's firepits still lingered pleasantly in the air, and wisps of smoke threaded lazily into the sky. Michael, finished with his packing, came and knelt on one knee beside her in the doorway. The hand he put upon her shoulder felt her shudder, and he gripped her firmly.

"I'm so frightened, Michael."

"So am I. But it's not a new feeling for me. I never stop being afraid in these situations—and I must have been in dozens of them. If it's any comfort to you, I think we'll make it." He released her shoulder with a reassuring squeeze.

"Where are they?" she asked.

"Out there." He nodded toward the jungle that crowded the village on one side of the savanna. "Trying to decide what to do with us. They don't realize they won't have all evening to figure it out. We'll be out of here before they have a chance to make up their minds. They would have liked to have killed us in our sleep."

The sun had disappeared. Michael stood up.

"Let's go," he said as he shouldered his pack. He filled his pockets with ammunition and, gun in hand, stepped into the doorway and out of the hut. Catherine paused in the doorway behind him. He turned and firmly guided her close by him out into the clearing toward the trail.

Nothing else stirred as they left the village. The path was well worn and easy to follow in the darkness with the help of Michael's flashlight. Hours later they left the jungle and came out onto a vast smooth limestone plateau with no vegetation. The path was gone, but now they could guide themselves by using the stars. There was no moon yet, but the rock seemed to have its own faint gray light, making it easy to traverse. They were well out onto the plateau when the moon finally rose, reflecting brilliantly off the rock and allowing them to stop safely and rest. They would easily be able to see anyone approaching.

Except for Michael's announcement that they could stop, they didn't speak. Although they were exhausted from the emotional and physical stress of the hike, it was more the mood of the night itself that commanded silence. No jungle. No noises. Perfect, overwhelming silence. It was a setting that gave the moon an intense power. Not wanting to shake off its spell by breaking the silence, Catherine sat upon the rock staring at it until, in spite of herself, she fell asleep, huddled in a fetal position to keep warm. They had no wood for a fire, nor would they have dared build one if they had any.

When she awoke at dawn, she was covered with a canvas sheet and Michael was sitting on his heels nearby, watching the sun come up. She felt a stab of guilt as she realized he had probably not slept to allow her to sleep the whole night through. He did not look tired. The squat he had assumed was one the natives used for resting, and she had noted in the past that like them, he could hold the position for hours without tiring.

The sun was brilliant. Rising with it was a strong breeze that swept across the flat rock unimpeded.

"God, what I'd give for a hot cup of coffee right now!" Michael exclaimed, seeing her awake.

She nodded in sympathy as she sat up and turned to the view he had been watching. There, ahead and to the north of the rising sun, a large waterfall came over a 600-foot cliff. Too far away to hear, it was the only movement around them.

"How beautiful," she said softly.

"The Baliem," he replied simply.

The information filled her with renewed vigor and an eagerness to go on. Beyond the falls and the mountain was the Grand Valley. Their next goal would be to find a pass out of the valley, then on to the Idenburg River. From there they could take a raft downstream to Hollandia, the tiny coastal capital of Dutch New Guinea. They ate leftovers from the Kukukuku feast and began the easy walk to the falls. They reached it in less than an hour.

As they neared the boulder-strewn base of the falls, they saw a lone brown figure among the rocks. He wore no elaborate paint or feathers, but the bamboo sticks about his neck indicated he was Kukukuku. They could see the ambivalence on his face as they approached him, but he remained undecided whether to stay or flee until it was too late. He was armed with a bamboo spear, its base planted on the ground, and he made no effort to move it as they came up to him. Michael stopped and spoke with him for a few minutes, during which the Kukukuku gestured several times toward the falls. The conversation finally ended, and Catherine and Michael moved on, leaving him standing as before.

"He's been away from the village several days, so he knew nothing about us. Seems he's been out looking for one of his wives who ran away because she was angry. He was looking for her among the rocks. According to him, the women often come here to commit suicide. They jump over the falls, taking their babies with them. He didn't find her," he added in response to Catherine's unasked question.

She felt a surge of compassion and outrage for that unknown woman's sense of powerlessness in a culture which granted her so few avenues of expression.

As if reading her mind, Michael said, "I hope you haven't been fooled into thinking, like so many of our colleagues, that there is something especially noble about primitive cultures. Their barbarism and inhumanity aren't any different from our own—only expressed more directly. I happen to prefer the directness."

Catherine was surprised at the cynicism with which he spoke, and she guessed that it came from personal suffering in him she did not understand.

They climbed to the top of the falls. Having mounted the last limestone summit, they stood looking over the Grand Valley of the Baliem stretching out forty miles before them. Neatly terraced gardens climbed the gently rolling hills of the valley floor, and clusters of huts formed small villages as far as the eye could see. The Baliem meandered in gentle curves fed by smaller streams, and from its banks ran networks of irrigation ditches, making cross-hatched lines among the well-tended garden plots.

"It's beautiful!" Catherine exclaimed. "Shangri-la, just as Archbold said!"

"Gardens of Eden," Michael agreed. "Only there must be serpents in the garden." He pointed to the forty-foot watchtowers that rose like oil derricks beside the garden plots as far as they could see.

"Those are signs of constant warfare," said Michael. "It seems that Shangri-la is no different from the rest of New Guinea," he mused. "We'll stay as clear of them as we can."

They descended along the eastern rim of the valley wall, through trees and moss-covered rocks, across a floor of graceful ferns. By early afternoon they had reached a small uninhabited lake where they decided to camp. The water was crystal-clear and shallow, no more than waist-deep. Orchids and wild rhododendron grew around the lake and in the adjoining meadow. Catherine took a walk to a secluded spot on the other side of the lake, where she bathed and washed her hair and clothes. While she waited for her clothes to dry, she took a nap in the high grass. It was like sleeping in a basket; only the blue sky above her was visible.

When she dressed and returned to the campsite, she found that Michael had bathed and shaved. He wore his khaki trousers, but his khaki shirt hung on a nearby rhododenron bush while he chopped wood for a campfire. His back was to her, and he did not see her as she came up and sat down near him on a rock. She watched him work, noticing again those strange tattoos. The rhythmic crack of the ax biting into the wood jarred the silence.

As she sat watching the lean, hard muscles of his back rise and fall with the ax, she suddenly felt as if the ax were splitting apart her defenses, allowing the feelings she had stored so carefully away to pour out. Over these past weeks she had come to know him so well: his gentleness, tenderness, and sensitivity as well as his strength. He never gave up. He could allow himself to feel despair, but having done so, he could pick up and start again. She had seen it happen many times through the ordeal of the past weeks. She admired his courage. Her body wanted him. Needed him. She could feel it now. It would never stop tormenting her. She had loved him. Still loved him. Would always love him.

Tears filled her eyes, and she quickly wiped them away. A tightness in her chest replaced them. Just then, as if he had finally felt her presence, he stopped his swing in midair and turned to see her sitting there. He straightened, lowered his arms to his sides, and stood quietly looking at her. It was as if he were looking right into her and reading her mind. She saw the barriers in his eyes and was not surprised. She had expected them to be there.

"Let me do that for a while. You rest." She smiled, but her eyes pleaded with him. If he would not let her love him, he could at least let her help him. He did not let go of the ax. She gripped it and tugged more firmly, and still he did not release it. She looked down and saw his fingers tighten around the ax. Bewildered, she raised her eyes to his and saw the struggle going on behind them.

"Don't—please," he whispered as if it were more than the ax she was attempting to take from him. Suddenly she realized he was right. But she could no more stop herself than she could stop her longing. She stood on tiptoe and kissed his throat. He closed his eyes.

"I won't stop, Michael," she said softly. "You'll have to make me."

She reached up and lightly touched his chest. He flinched. She could see his torment in his face. He opened his eyes and looked down into hers. All she could see was that mouth bending down to cover her own softly, hesitantly. Deep inside himself, Michael realized it was too late to turn back. The ax slipped from both their hands and fell to the ground, followed shortly by their clothes.

Forgetting everything, they clung urgently to each other, sinking slowly to their knees. There was no need for preliminaries to arouse their passion. It had been intensified by months of frustrated longing. He pulled her down on top of him in the warm tall grass. The feel of his naked body touching her breasts, her belly, her thighs was a shock that quickly became exquisite pleasure. She spread her legs and lifted herself a little above him on her elbows until contact was confined to their eyes and their loins. He gently moved his hands down her back, pressing her against the firm, extended hardness of his body, pressing her swollen, tender desire tightly against his own until she yearned to open up and receive it.

"Now," she whispered fiercely. "Please." She kissed him softly.

He moved his body a little lower beneath her and began slowly to enter her. She lifted her lips from his and, looking down, let him enter her with his eyes as well as his body. There was tenderness as well as passion in those gray eyes. When he had filled her, he lay quietly, probing no more, letting her get used to that foreign presence within her. He raised his head and brushed her lips gently with his own, then returned again, longer, hungrier. As if on its own, her body began to receive him. Feeling that embrace begin within her, pulling him deeper into her, he began gently to thrust himself into it, letting his rhythm be guided by hers.

He pulled his mouth away from hers and groaned softly, "Catherine—oh, Catherine!"

He was shuddering on the brink of releasing not only his passion but his feelings, his ties with the past, even the future as he had once defined it.

The barriers were gone. Looking at him, she found herself tumbling down into his eyes as if there were nothing to break her fall. One body, one feeling. It came to them together then, that sharp, sweet, tormented release that went on and on, binding them together physically, emotionally, leaving them exhausted but fulfilled.

She lay quietly upon him, her head on his chest. Her black hair spread out over them both, a finely fringed blanket. She was completely absorbed with the feel of him, the smell of his body, the dampness of his perspiring skin against her cheek and beneath her body, the feel of that tool of his passion that remained soft and warm inside her. As they drifted off to sleep in the warm afternoon sun, the only sound was the snapping of the dragonflies as they hunted for insects on the lake.

Michael woke with her hair blowing gently against his face,

tickling his nose, tantalizing his lips. He felt her face pressed against his chest and throat and her soft breath upon his skin. It was an intoxicating sensation, and he felt happier than he had ever been until thoughts of his family crowded in to torment him. She was still asleep. He put his arms around her gently, so as not to wake her and held her close as if doing so would help drive the ghosts away. He had never felt this close to anyone. It seemed as if they had shared a lifetime together. The past, before he met her, now seemed scarcely to have existed at all. Yet it still remained real enough to haunt him.

The pressure of her body excited him, and he began to grow inside her. Though he wished to let her sleep, he could not deny his desire, and soon she stirred awake. She gave a sleepy laugh of pleasure as she felt his passion fully formed within her. She kissed his throat, his nose, his eyelids, nibbled at his ears, and ran her tongue along his throat to torment and tease him. Then she took his face between her hands and looked at him with smiling eyes.

"I love you," she said.

He looked serious, even sad. She kissed him softly. His mouth was open, yielding to her kiss, but when she drew back to look again into his eyes and still he did not reply, she felt a tiny prick of fear.

"I love you, too," he said finally, but his eyes were remote, even cool.

"Then why are you so angry?" she asked, bewildered.

"Because everything good in my life has always come too late!" His bitterness surprised her.

"Too late? Too late for what, Michael?"

"Too late to be easy or natural. Too late to be uncomplicated."

She was seized with fear. God! Was she to lose him all over again? She could not bear the thought.

"What will become of us, Michael?"

He did not answer her. Instead, he put his hand behind her head and pulled it down to his. He kissed her roughly at first and then with mounting passion as if to rid himself of both his lust and anger. His other arm around her waist, he held her firmly against him and rolled over so that now she lay beneath him. His breath came in trembling gasps, but he did not press her; he kissed her throat and breasts until he felt her body arch up against

182

his. Then, guided by the thrusts of her response, he bore deeply into her until his passion, and hers, were once again relieved. Afterward they lay still shuddering from the intensity of their feelings until their bodies totally relaxed. Then they slept, lying facing each other on their sides, their arms and legs entwined.

When she next woke, Catherine quietly disentangled herself from his embrace and sat up. Over the tall grass she could see the peaks to the northeast that contained the Idenburg pass. It seemed as distant now as the moon, and it struck her suddenly that they would never cross it. The world that lay beyond these valley walls was about to disappear from her life: her degree; Chicago; her dissertation, even Maitreya. Gone. She knew that was the price she would pay to keep him. It did not matter. Nothing mattered except right now, except Michael.

She got up to walk to the lake and was surprised at the semen that spilled from her body as she rose. God! Somebody forgot to design the damned plug, she thought, laughing to herself. She delighted in the feel of it along the inside of her thighs and wanted to prevent its escape. It was a part of him she could keep within her. Good God, she thought. How sentimental. Next I'll be wanting a baby.

They made love frequently in the next three days, as if they were hoarding against some future famine, storing love away to be brought forth as memory on some cold and lonely night. The thought frightened her, but she did not tell Michael. She wanted more than memories for her future and could only hope that he did, too.

Chapter 19

The sun had come out, but the early-morning mist still clung about the bushes like tattered remnants of dirty gray cloth. Tukum reluctantly left the dried grasses that served as his bed in the upper loft of his mother's *ebai,* or woman's house, and wandered to the cooking shed, where the *hiperi* were cooking for one of the two meals that day. The sweet potatoes were roasting over the three cookfires that glowed within the long shed, its roof and sides deliberately designed to allow the smoke's escape.

Tukum's mother crouched beside the fire, the empty nets she wore strapped around her forehead hanging loosely down her back. When she started for the gardens in a little while, they would be filled with a baby piglet in one and his baby sister in another, and when she returned that evening, she would bring back the food she had gathered in a third. Now his baby sister sat playing happily in his old grandmother's lap. Actually the baby was his half sister. Tukum's real father had been *kepu,* worthless. The only way a man became *kepu* was by being a coward in battle. A woman became *kepu* by sleeping with men other than her husband. A man who was *kepu* was not ostracized by the village, but he was unable to hold on to a wife or wealth; the other men would take these things from him since he was a coward whom none of them feared. Tukum's mother, who had been young and pretty, had been taken from his father by the great *kain,* Degewatek, when Tukum was only a baby. His real father had gone away to live among the northern members of his clan, and Tukum had never seen him again.

Only eight, not yet a man, Tukum lived with his mother in her *ebai* in Degewatek's *sili* and tended the swine herd each day. While most of the village children tended pigs, only Tukum had sole responsibility for the family herd since he had just the one infant sister and no one else to help share the burden. Though Degewatek had two other wives, neither had children who had lived.

Tukum hated pigs with a passion born of too much responsibility for a small boy of eight. With envy he would watch the other young boys play their games each day, the favorite being a war game throwing small, sharp bamboo spears. Over the years more than one child in the village had lost an eye from this preparation for the adult warrior role. Tukum, alone with the pigs, practiced on his own, occasionally taking his wrath out on the irritable and stubborn pigs by pricking their tough hides with his small spear. Tukum and his charges shared a mutual hostility. He could now hear his ill-tempered companions snorting and rooting in their house within the *sili* fence just beyond the cookhouse, and he felt his dislike rise up like a sour stomach. It quickly disappeared when his mother placed a delicious hot *hiperi* on a wad of leaves to protect his hands and he began to eat, sinking his face and teeth into its warmth, forgetting about the pigs.

Degewatek, his stepfather, emerged from the *ebai* of his third wife, Koalaro ("She who left her man"). Tukum's mother, Aku, was his second wife, and Supuk, his first. Koalaro had been the wife of a young village warrior slain in battle three years ago. She had not waited for her husband's death, but while he lay mortally wounded in the men's *pilai*, she had gone to the *sili* of Degewatek to live. It was a shocking thing to have done, and her name had been changed by the *akuni* forever to bear witness to the scandal. It had not bothered her in the least. Since Degewatek had come to live in the Homaktep village some five years before, she had yearned to be with him. He had come from the northern clans, a mysterious and brooding figure with a reputation for violence.

For all his short years (he was now only thirty) Degewatek had led a tragic life. His father had been killed in a war before Degewatek was born, and his mother had died in an enemy raid when he was three. As a child he had had no home but lived with various relatives. He had grown into an aloof, brooding young man with enough ambition and skill as a warrior to acquire the wealth to marry young. His wife had been flirtatious, outgoing, full of teasing laughter, and Degewatek had been an unusually jealous husband. When his wife claimed to have been raped by a man she did not recognize when alone in her *ebai* one night, Degewatek didn't believe her and accused her of taking a lover. She fled from him, and by the time his love overcame his impulsive anger and he followed her in order to bring her back, she had crossed the river into enemy territory—an act of suicide. He had reached the river in time to see the enemy warriors swarm down upon her. He had watched helplessly from across the river as their spears rose and fell again and again. It had seemed to go on forever, and each blow had entered his heart. At that moment he himself had wanted to die. He had thrown down his spear and taunted the enemy to come kill him, too, but they had only laughed and gone away, dancing and chanting, leaving her body behind in the grass.

He had then done a shocking thing, which had earned him a reputation as a bad and violent man. He had not gone to claim her body or burn the traces of her blood upon the grass so that her ghost would not return to the spot. Instead, he had gone back to their *sili* and destroyed the gardens and *ebai* he had made her. Then, without waiting for the funeral ceremony, he had left the village of his childhood for good. Thirteen years later, he still brooded over her death and the part he had played in it. It ached like the broken arrow tip in his shoulder which became inflamed from time to time.

His reputation had followed him to his new home in Homaktep, and he had been much feared as one of the *hunuk palin*, those given to fits of violence as well as to bravery. Still, he had been much respected as well. He was proud, fierce, and brave, and his great skills as a warrior soon made him one of the legendary *kains* of the south. In order to remember but still to soften the past, they had renamed him Degewatek ("Spear Death"). He had taken a new wife, Supuk, a widow of the village. As he quickly grew wealthier and more powerful, he took a second wife, Aku, Tukum's mother. And Koalaro had looked upon these new brides with bitter envy. Her own position as the wife of a respected young warrior put Degewatek forever beyond her grasp. He had never spoken to her, but looks that passed between them had given her hope that should she be free, he would welcome her. When the time came, he did—as eagerly and with as little thought to scandal as she herself had shown.

Now Tukum watched Koalaro as she moved about her own cookfire at the other end of the shed. She was tall for a Dani woman, almost five feet five inches. Degewatek himself was almost six feet tall, six inches above the average height for Dani men. Koalaro's skin was light brown and her eyes were deep-set, sharp black points that seemed to miss nothing. She seldom smiled. Only around Degewatek did her face soften and a kind of gentleness replace the arrogance she usually wore.

Tukum was afraid of her, and well he might have been. She didn't seem to care for children. Tukum's mother claimed she had had abortions, a common but frowned-on practice, because she didn't wish to bear a child. It was said by all the women in the village, with a hint of scandal, that Koalaro could not put up with the taboo against intercourse during pregnancy and the long period while the child is young and still nursing; she could not bear to be without Degewatek in her body for all that time, nor could she bear to think of him with someone else. Whatever the truth, she had no children and Degewatek seldom slept with his other wives, pregnant or not. Tukum's mother, with a new infant daughter, was taboo now anyhow. All of Supuk's children had died at birth, and Degewatek no longer slept with her.

Because of Koalaro's special, almost monogamous, position in what was a polygamous marital arrangement, tensions had developed within Degewatek's household that led to quarrels, especially between Supuk, his first wife, and Koalaro. Finally Degewatek had sent Supuk off to live alone in the mountains, tending a few pigs. He had built her a hut and ordered her to stay. Tukum feared that his mother might also be forced to go, and Tukum, who would go with her, would lose his few opportunities to play with other children.

Recently the danger seemed to have eased. Given the warning of Supuk's departure and exile, Tukum's mother had been on her best behavior, careful not to arouse Koalaro's wrath or cause dissension which might provoke Degewatek into sending her away, for he would never, never banish Koalaro. Even Tukum understood this without being told.

Degewatek had now joined Koalaro and sat quietly talking with her in the cooking shed while his breakfast roasted over the fire. There was a contentment between them that could not be found in most other Dani marriages that Tukum knew. Couples were never affectionate or demonstrative in public, or even in private, yet something seemed to glow between these two—in the way they looked at each other, in the sound of their voices when they spoke to each other, in the laughter each reserved only for the other—that surely conveyed as much deep passion as the most physical embrace. Tukum observed it, studied it each day, and found it beautiful to watch.

Though Tukum slept most of the time in either the men's *pilai* or his mother's *ebai* in Degewatek's *sili*, Degewatek was not considered in any way related to him. The concept of stepfather was not known to the Dani culture. In fact, natural fathers themselves were not usually very involved with the upbringing of their sons, though they often indulged their young daughters. Besides natural fathers, boys had ceremonial fathers, who were usually brothers of their natural fathers, but they provided little support either. A boy's real support came from his *nami,* or adopted father, usually a brother of his mother. Since Tukum's mother came from another village some distance from Homaktep, Tukum had no *nami,* though he got along well enough with Degewatek and the other two young warriors who slept in Degewatek's *pilai.* Because they had no wives or wealth enough yet to obtain them and build their own compounds and gardens, the young, unattached men of the village stayed in whatever *pilai* would welcome them.

Except for having to spend his days with the pigs, Tukum was content with his life, yet it seemed unlikely that he would ever become a great warrior, with all the wealth and honor which that could bestow on him. Indeed, in his deepest feelings he feared being *kepu,* cowardly like his father, when the time came to test himself in battle. It was a thought, a doubt, that lent the deepest kind of darkness to Tukum's day. So, whenever he could, he practiced with the grass spears and bows and arrows, becoming so preoccupied that his pigs would wander away and his mother would have to help him look for them, scolding him and boxing his ears for the inconvenience.

That morning he followed the warriors and women out of the fenced compound, herding the pigs before him, through the banana, and pandanus trees and tobacco plants that grew in the garden adjoining the compound, out to the gardens of sweet potatoes, cucumbers, and spinach with their neat irrigation ditches in which grew the calla lily which produced the taro root from which they made an edible paste. The warriors, carrying weapons, took the narrow path to the watchtowers where they would stand guard to prevent enemy raids on the gardens and the *silis* of the village.

The women, wooden digging spears in hand, filed off to tend the gardens, piglets and babies swinging in the nets that hung down their backs. Tukum, still munching on his breakfast *hiperi,* headed his small swine herd into the mountains, away from the gardens where they could do damage and away from the no-man's-land that bordered on enemy territory. He was headed for a spot where only he ever went, the lake where the black ducks (which were taboo to kill) swam among the reeds and the meadow grass was high.

Stick upon his shoulder, Tukum filed off onto the narrow, overgrown path that climbed toward the mountain wall. The day was still gray. The sun had not yet managed to burn through the cloud cover, and patches of fog hugged the ground. He was cold, and his nose ran with the respiratory infection that the Dani chronically endured from the damp, chill mornings. It was not polite to blow one's nose; the thin film of mucus that trailed from it now would disappear with the dryness of the midmorning air.

Tukum's thin legs and shoulders and his rounded belly were typical of a Dani boy his age. As he matured, his gangliness would be transformed into broad shoulders and strong, well-muscled legs that would carry him tirelessly over mountainous territory. He would remain lean. The only fat Dani were babies. Moisture began to collect on his dark, kinky hair, making it curl even tighter.

As he climbed higher and the sun began to open up the sky, Tukum felt his spirits lift with the surrounding mist. He had not been to the mountain lake in a week. Today he would hunt for crayfish along the stream that fed its shallow marshes, and he

189

would make spears from the reeds and practice his aim. There would be no other boys around to taunt him when he missed. The lake was almost an hour's walk from the village, and none of the children ever ventured this far away.

By the time he reached the forest of oaks, chestnuts, and conifers surrounding the lake the mist and fog had fled and the sky was brilliant blue. The birds of the grasslands, the robin chats, flew about their morning business. The scarcity of grassland birds was further evidence that the area had, until fairly recent times, been forest land.

Tukum left the pigs to forage by the lake without him and walked to the marshy area where the reeds for his spear throwing grew straight and tall. He was about to wade out to cut a few with his small stone ax when he noticed the newly built shelter of pandanus leaves and cane. That someone had come to live in this place beside the lake, far from the protection of any village, was more than Tukum could comprehend.

Tukum felt the hair stand up on the back of his neck in warning. Anything strange or different could prove dangerous in this land of perpetual war. He crouched down in the water among the reeds to watch and wait. He heard something first, before he saw anything—a woman laughing. The sound floated sweetly to him on the sunlit morning air, so free and gay it was like a song. The women of his village didn't laugh that way, yet he was sure it was laughter. Then he saw her there, near him, coming out of the lake. Her hair hung straight down her back like a nightjar falling from the sky. Her skin was so pale as to seem still wrapped in the morning mists that had left the sky. Tukum rubbed his eyes in disbelief. Surely this was a spirit or a ghost. He felt frightened.

She turned and spoke to the water, and for the first time Tukum noticed the man who swam behind her, who now rose to follow her to shore. He was tall with the same pale skin, but his hair was the yellow of the late-afternoon sun, a warm gold with red and orange lights within it. When they drew nearer to Tukum's hiding place among the reeds, he could see that the man's eyes were a strange color, that of the gray storm clouds that lived forever upon the high peaks, and they were sharp and clear like those of the hawks which circled and searched the valley floor. Tukum decided that the tall pair must have come from the high white peaks that lay beyond the valley. With their pale skins, they could not be of the earth, which was brown and dark like the *akuni*. They resembled humans, but they were clearly not.

The man caught up with the woman and took her hand. Tukum had only seen mothers with small children do such a thing. Then they did a more astounding thing. They turned to each other, bodies touching, arms tightly bound around each other, and the man's mouth came down on the woman's and took something, or perhaps gave it. Tukum wasn't sure just what had been exchanged, but it seemed to grow more urgent. As Tukum watched, wide-eyed, they sank slowly to their knees. The exchange continued; only now the man took his mouth from the woman's and began slowly and gently to touch it to her body until he reached the opening between her thighs, and then he seemed to drink from there as well. She moaned, but she wasn't in pain, Tukum could tell. It was as if whatever the man took from her felt good to give.

After what seemed to Tukum like an eternity while he squatted uncomfortably in the high water grass, the man raised himself until he covered the woman's body and then began the movements and sounds with which Tukum was already familiar. When Degewatek had visited his mother's *ebai*, Tukum had been sent to sleep in the *pilai*, but sometimes he and the other little boys would come across the adults of the village, secretly meeting to make love in the forest, and would observe them for a time, unnoticed, until their uncontrolled nervous giggles would put a sudden and often angry end to the illicit tryst.

A feeling of relief swept over Tukum. Perhaps they were not ghosts after all. Surely ghosts would not bother with the behavior he now observed before him: the woman clinging to the man, the man's body and face tense. They were obviously uncomfortable, straining, in great need. Ghosts would have no such need of each other. Suddenly the woman sighed, and the man gave a little cry. His body shuddered for a moment and then grew still, and her arms fell away from him. After pausing for that moment, the man resumed twisting his body slowly against hers as if the rhythm that had propelled their bodies to this point could only slowly be brought under control. Once again the man's mouth touched her breasts, her throat until she opened her mouth and took again whatever it was he gave her with his lips. Tukum was both curious and impressed by this mysterious exchange.

Afraid he might risk discovery if he remained longer, Tukum slipped away unnoticed and returned to his foraging pigs. Shivering from the cold water as well as the excitement of his discovery, he hurried his reluctant charges back down the mountain path toward the valley floor. When he was far enough away, he sang as he went. He had already decided to keep his discovery a secret from his family and the village for now. He would present it at some time when it would be most opportune for him. Suppose the two strangers disappeared as magically as they had come? The fear tempered his excitement but did not destroy it.

"My Tukum," his mother commented that night, "you look like the hawk that has captured the mouse."

Tukum only smiled and scrambled to his loft. He lay awake trying to remember the details of how they had looked, only to find that important points had slipped his mind or been missed. The next morning he awoke anxious to be gone. He had important questions to clear up, and only more observation could do it. His mother was amazed to find that he snatched up only a single *hiperi* before hurrying out. He didn't wait for the others but took his pigs and was gone, past the gardens into the mountains.

By the time he reached the spot he was out of breath from the rapid climb and from anxiety, but he controlled himself enough to approach soundlessly and remain well hidden. He shook with relief when the hut came into view. He had not imagined it after all. Nor had they disappeared. Wearing not so much as a penis shield or a woman's hip-hugging fiber skirt, they sat before a fire, cooking a meal.

In the days that followed, Tukum saw the mysterious touching happen often, not necessarily the final coupling with which he was already familiar but the touching of the hands and the mouths. Sometimes it was just a quick, almost careless touch when they parted, and again when they met. Often the quick touch grew

192

into that hungry touching of his mouth to hers, the one that didn't stop until the man's full organ had entered the woman's body and fed her in the way most animals, in Tukum's closely observed world, fed each other. The longer he observed them, the more convinced Tukum became that they were not ghosts but *akuni*, like himself. Perhaps, like the feared Nomad, they had come from the land far away to the south. They no longer frightened him, and he made up his mind that one day soon he would reveal himself to them. Just the thought of it sent his knees weakly colliding against one another. But the decision had been made; only the time to do it remained undecided.

Chapter 20

He loved her—without reservation. The recognition had come to him with such startling awareness that it had brought tears to his eyes and a deep feeling of release. The physical attraction had always been there, no matter how much he had resisted and resented it. But this other feeling, the one that had swept over him, overwhelming him that day they had first arrived at the lake, exhausted by their journey, that one threatened to force him to redefine his life, and he was still reluctant, or afraid, to do that. But there was no denying that he loved her.

Michael lay upon his back, deep in thought, staring at the sky in silence, amazed and a little frightened by the feelings that had swept over him the past few days. He was remembering that first day she had swum out to him on the rocks at Maitreya's pool—the fear, the shyness in her face as she had hesitantly touched him. He had been deeply moved that day by the courage it must have taken for her to overcome her fear.

He watched her come up from the lake where she had gone for water. She knelt beside him.

"I love you," he said softly but with a sense of wonder that made it seem the miracle which, for him, it was. It seemed that he had told her this a hundred times in the last few days, but each time it was a fresh revelation to him.

They had never been simply colleagues. There had always been that physical tension between them from the very beginning, since that evening in the garden when he had first seen her. She was not only his love but his companion. For the first time in his life he had someone in whom he could totally confide. He told her of his early childhood and all that he remembered of what had happened to him, things he had never told anyone before. Of Julienne, he told her everything, and when he was finished, he felt finally free of it for the first time. She heard it all and she still loved him, and that in itself had been another revelation to him.

Catherine sat next to him and lightly ran her finger down his side in a tickle that made him squirm and her smile. She loved to look at his body—so strong and lean—just as she loved to watch him move, especially that light, effortless running gait that scarcely seemed to touch the ground, yet carried him for miles across the open savannas without tiring.

He rolled over onto his stomach, and Catherine's curiosity about the tattoos was renewed.

"Where did these come from?"

"They're Iban. I got them the summer before I left for college—on a trip up the Marakam River. I usually went with my friend Ahmad, but that summer I was alone. I ran some rapids I shouldn't have, lost the boat, and hurt myself. Before I could build another raft, I was captured by Iban. Old Koh, their headman, was the most famous headhunter in Borneo. He was an old enemy of my father's. He'd lived on the Barito upriver from Maitreya and was still killing people and burning crops in spite of the Dutch. Rather than have him arrested, my father conspired with the sultan to have Koh and his village moved up the Marakam to the inland mountains, which is where he caught me and held me for ransom. They weren't in the least hard on me, though. They made me a member of the village. That's what the tattoo indicates."

"And this one?" She touched a stylized drawing of an animal.

"A panther. I killed it, and they thought it an event worthy of a tattoo."

"How convenient to know each other's history at a glance. And this one . . ." She indicated the third and smallest tattoo.

"My marital status." He rolled over on his side and looked at her.

"Oh?" She sensed a tension in his body. "Bachelor, I assume?"

195

"Married."

She looked confused. "But you hadn't married Kara yet."

"It was Minh, Koh's youngest daughter." He paused, giving her a moment to recover from her surprise. "I had no choice in the matter, but I can't honestly say I was terribly opposed to it. I escaped when I was able, at night when they wouldn't dare follow me, and I left Minh there."

"Did she know you were going?"

"No. It's not something that I'm very proud of. I considered—strongly—bringing her with me, but I knew it would never work, so I left. It wasn't easy to leave her."

His last remark caused Catherine some pain, which she tried to ignore. "What happened to her?"

"I really know very little. I heard through Ahmad that she had married the widowed chief of a neighboring village soon after I left. It didn't surprise me. Their women don't remain single for long—and Minh was very beautiful."

"And was she good in bed?" Half-teasing, half-serious.

"By what measure?" he asked, eyes twinkling with amusement.

She felt annoyed at the flush of embarrassment that showed on her face. He rolled over onto his back, laughing, and pulled her roughly to him and caught her mouth to his. Then he pulled back, eyes serious, and held her face between his hands. "If you're going to compare yourself to every woman I've ever gone to bed with, then you're going to spend a great deal of unnecessary time suffering. Forget them," he gently urged her. "I have. I love you more than I've ever loved anyone. So you see, it's not even measurable on the same scale."

Reaching up, he pressed her face tightly between his hands in helpless exasperation. "Catherine, Catherine," he chastised her. "It bewilders and frightens me at times to see how much you doubt yourself. It may yet destroy us."

She recognized the truth in what he said. Jealousy sliced through her like a hot sword at every reminder of the other women he had touched. But as jealous as the Iban girl might make her feel, it was not Minh who made her feel insecure. It was the name she dared not bring up between them which frightened her the most. Kara. What of Kara? Neither of them had mentioned her since that night at Maitreya when Michael had ended it. Catherine could tell Michael her deepest secrets and darkest fears—all but that one. She was afraid to bring it up, afraid of losing him. A sudden chill of apprehension passed through her, and she shivered. Seeing it, he drew her in his arms to comfort her, offering her his love, which was the only protection he had to give her. The unspoken fear between them was that it might not be enough.

The next day Michael found tracks along the lakeshore, small tracks belonging to a child. Searching farther, he found more, some fresher and some older, all belonging to the same child.

"It seems we've had an unseen visitor for the past week or so," he told Catherine when he returned.

She gave a little cry and reached for her khaki shirt and pants.

"Now why are you doing that?" he asked. "Whoever it is will be more shocked by those than by your bare skin. Besides, he—or she—has been looking at our bare skins and whatever we've been doing in them for the past week."

"Oh!" Catherine gulped and finished hastily putting on her clothes. She tossed Michael's pants to him. "Here. I'm not dressing for whoever it is. I'm covering up because I'll feel better. The little peeping tom. To hell with what shocks him!"

"Who said it was a he? Do I sense a latent hostility emerging from these beautiful, indignant lips?" he said, teasing her.

"Want to bet it's not a boy?" she asked sarcastically. "You're all perverts."

"Only up to the age of fourteen, at which time we become more direct." He chuckled aloud at her reaction. "I wouldn't worry about this one too much. He's not much older than eight or nine." He reached out and idly undid the top button on her shirt, letting his fingers rub against her skin as he pulled the cloth aside to reveal the gentle swell of her breasts. She snatched it firmly closed, and he laughed.

"So much for paradise," he said with only half-mocking regret. "It seems the serpent has arrived."

The next morning Michael caught the unwary Tukum hiding in the reeds. In order to keep his imposing height from frightening Tukum still further, Michael knelt before the trembling boy, giving him a reassuring smile and a pat on the head before swinging a wide-eyed Tukum up into his arms and carrying him back to Catherine. He was a rather sorry-looking sight with his fear showing so plainly in eyes too big for his face. He had a round, protruding belly, probably from the protein deficiency of the Dani diet, and spindly little arms and legs. His long gourd penis shield had slipped off its small anchor and flapped uselessly at his side just as it always seemed to do at awkward moments, forever embarrassing him. His eyes were runny with fear, and his nose ran from the cold. Michael laughed at the expression on Catherine's face. Tukum was, indeed, a sad sight, but Michael could see that Catherine had been completely won over.

It soon became clear that Tukum wanted them to return to the village with him. Now that he had been discovered, he suddenly longed for the safety of home from which to confront these strangers. It was a golden anthropological chance they could scarcely pass up, yet both were reluctant to leave their private hideaway behind. Michael read the look of regret on her face.

"We might as well go," he told her. "When they find out we're here, there will be a steady stream of sightseers, popping up at moments beyond our control."

They gathered up their few belongings and, preceded by the protesting pigs, accompanied Tukum down the mountain to the village beneath the mountain wall. As they neared it, Tukum pointed to a spot off the trail where the grass had been mashed down. He shoved the first finger of his right hand through the second and third fingers of his left and began vigorously to thrust it back and forth, graphically illustrating that this had been a recent trysting spot for some couple from his village. He pointed at Michael and Catherine and repeated the gesture, laughing as he did it, causing Catherine to flush pure red to the tips of her ears. She groaned as she suddenly remembered some of what he must have seen. Michael laughed.

"Don't worry about it. After all, he's had a much more liberal education than you've had."

She only hoped that Tukum would leave out the intimate details when he reported his discovery to the excited villagers that had already begun to gather around. Tukum's presence assured they would be welcomed. Attempting to make contact without him would have meant days, perhaps weeks of brief, suspicious encounters before trust would have been built. Now no fierce warriors would dare show fear of the strangers when Tukum did not.

After the excitement of their arrival had died down, Catherine and Michael took an *ebai* in the abandoned *sili* next to Degewatek's, and Tukum adopted Michael as his *nami*. He couldn't understand why they objected to having him move into the one-room dwelling with them. After all, what had they left to hide from him? His feelings were hurt for an entire day, but he forgave them. He visited them each morning before taking his pigs to forage in the abandoned gardens and came again after he had brought the herd home in the afternoon. From Tukum's visits, they learned to speak Dani within a few weeks, and Catherine recorded its structure and a phonetic vocabulary in her field notebook. Paper and pencils were now her most precious possessions, which she diligently conserved with her own system of shorthand and cramped but legible writing. She no longer had cameras to aid her in recording Dani life, so Michael began to sketch for her those things she wanted illustrated—beautiful drawings with such simplicity and economy of line that they went far beyond simple illustrations and became striking works of art.

It was the Dani men, not the women, who were most preoccupied with appearance, and they spent hours grooming their bodies, removing lice from each other and plucking body and facial hair off with tweezers made from a split wooden twig. Only a small fringe of beard was acceptable, and many wore none at all. Only old men cared nothing about such things.

Most food was obtained through farming. Hunting was primarily for sport since most of the game had been hunted from the valley floor and going alone into the mountains could be dangerous. Still, the men did hunt reptiles, birds, and the small and large rodents that lived in the valley, and enjoyed eating them, along with whatever insects they might find.

Dani life centered on ritual warfare which was the principal preoccupation of the men. The 50,000 Dani of the valley lived in loosely organized settlements which were divided into some twelve alliances—all potential enemies of one another. Usually each alliance warred with only one other at a time, though sometimes they might join together temporarily to fight larger wars against each other. The Wali Dani, the alliance to which Tukum's village of Homaktep belonged, traditionally fought the members of the Wittaia Dani alliance whose land bordered theirs on the south.

*   *   *

For the past four months Tukum had spent his early mornings watching Michael shave. Tukum loved looking at himself in the small mirror Michael used, and he marveled at the resemblance between that image and the sketches Michael made of him. The Dani had no art except simple ritual drawings on rocks made during initiation ceremonies or the carvings on their arrows. Tukum found Michael's drawings to be the most marvelous and magical objects these remarkable strangers were capable of creating. Michael had let Tukum use a pencil and a piece of the precious paper, and Tukum had been thrilled at the things the pencil had allowed him to make, including one drawing of Michael which Michael had solemnly declared to be a remarkable likeness.

Shaving and drawing were not the only activities that intrigued Tukum. The Dani never bathed, and Tukum found Michael and Catherine's habit of washing themselves and their clothes every day in the cold, clear spring water that flowed from the glaciers to be an impossibly dangerous ritual. They used pig fat and lye leached from wood ashes to make something they rubbed on their skin and clothes. Tukum had secretly tried it one day but had been frightened when some of his dark color ran off into the water. He concluded that the use of this soap accounted for the strangers' pale skin. They had washed away all their color, and Tukum vowed to avoid water at all costs for fear he might cease to be one of the *akuni*.

Catherine and Michael had spent these past months planting their own garden and tending two young pigs they had acquired from Degewatek. Catherine often went hunting with Michael, but sometimes he went high into the mountains where the game, ducks and doves, were more plentiful. When he traveled so far that he must spend the night, Catherine remained at home, for the cold of the mountain nights was too much for her. So much a part of her had he become that his absence made her feel incomplete. It was also a reminder that though neither of them talked about it, this could not go on forever. Eventually they would have to leave, and then what? However, only on those lonely nights without him did her fears plague her. Otherwise, she was happier than she had ever dreamed possible.

Michael was gone on an overnight trip this morning, but Tukum had kept his morning ritual, saving his still-steaming *hiperi* to eat with Catherine. The Dani had no pottery or utensils except bone and bamboo knives. They ate with their fingers and used leaves for plates. They used gourds as water containers and cups.

Tukum loved to tell Catherine about the personal history of each member of the village. He was an unreliable source, however, since he tended to make up whatever he didn't know. He was a born storyteller in a culture that had few myths and no oral history and could therefore make little use of his talent.

"I brought you something," he said to Catherine as he entered the *sili* and joined her before the fire in the open cookhouse.

"What is it, Tukum?" She smiled at him.

"Since you are not *akuni* and therefore have no *edai-egen*, then you have no seeds of singing to make you truly happy, so I brought you these." He opened up his closed fist to reveal a handful of tiny seeds.

"What are these?"

"Seeds from the white flowers of the valley floor. They can be your seeds of singing since you have none of your own." He carefully placed the seeds on a little square of tightly woven fern bracket he had made for that purpose and bound it with an orchid fiber cord that he placed around her neck. He stepped back to appraise the results critically and frowned. It hung below her rib cage.

"It should be shorter—it must hang here"—he pointed toward his heart—"where all *edai-egen* grow."

Catherine reached to the back of her neck and shortened the string until the little bundle hung near her heart.

"There," he said, satisfied. "Now you are *akuni*." His voice contained a note of relief.

"Thank you, Tukum," she said, and knelt to hug him.

He squirmed and looked around uncomfortably to see if anyone outside the *sili* had noticed the gesture. He loved being touched by her, but it embarrassed him to think that others might see it and tease him about it later.

She laughed. "No one was watching. I made sure of it first, but I won't do it again if you don't want me to."

He did not reply but smiled and reached out and took her hand. How could he tell her that his worst fear was that she and his new *nami* might go away? He was afraid even to mention it for fear he might make it happen. Now that he had made her one of the *akuni,* perhaps she might stay forever. And if she stayed, the man would stay, Tukum was sure of it. Tukum sensed that the woman was the key to it all.

The number of enemy raids against the Wali had increased in the past weeks, so Catherine and Tukum waited for the warriors near the watchtowers to light the early-morning signal fires, indicating that it was safe for the women to go to the gardens. This morning Catherine had volunteered to take Tukum's pigs to forage in the abandoned gardens so that he could play with two of the other boys. Tending the pigs was not one of Catherine's favorite pastimes, but it gave her an excuse to sit on a rock in the warm sunshine and do nothing.

By now she had become surefooted, and she performed with ease the balancing act necessary to negotiate the narrow logs that lay across the irrigation ditches, followed by the squealing pigs that swam and waded to where the bank was sloped enough that they could scramble up. She let them wander off to root content-edly among the garden's remnants. The clouds had burned off early this morning. Not far away she could see the three boys, down by the arcadian grove along the river, tossing a hoop made from a bent sapling into the air and attempting to hurl their grass spears through it. Nearby was an abandoned watchtower that had been burned in an enemy raid two weeks earlier and had not yet been rebuilt.

It would not be rebuilt this day either. The warriors not already occupied on the watchtowers were preparing a feast for the ceremony of the stones, those most sacred of Dani objects, passed from one generation to another. Once or twice a year the men would take the ancestral stones of the clan from their storage place in the *pilai,* clean them with the grease of a ceremonial pig, then rewrap them in fresh leaves before returning them to their resting place. The cleaning would renew the power of the holy stones and thus give new power and protection to the clan warriors who possessed the stones. With the increasing aggression of the neighboring Wittaia tribe, the Homaktep Wali were feeling in need of renewed and vigorous protection.

Catherine hadn't been sunning long when she caught sight of Michael returning home along the mountain trail. He must have been traveling since dawn to have made it back so early. He had taken off his khaki shirt in the warm sun and tied it around his waist. His rifle swung lightly in his hand, and the canvas bag over his shoulder contained his catch. She didn't take her eyes off of him as he approached, admiring his body and feeling a deep thrill of anticipation as he neared. He reached her and, smiling, bent down to kiss her nose. Because she was not satisfied with that, her arms encircled his neck and pulled his mouth down to hers.

"I missed you."

"So I see." He smiled again and straightened up, leaving his hand resting lightly on her shoulder. He nodded toward the boys still playing nearby. "Taking over for Tukum?" He referred to the pigs.

She nodded. "He's improving. They don't tease him anymore."

"Good," Michael said with satisfaction. He had helped Tukum practice his accuracy with the spears and had given him some exercises to strengthen his tiny arms and wrists.

As Michael watched with interest, Tukum took aim at the flying hoop and missed. Michael shrugged and smiled as Tukum disappeared into the brush to retrieve his spear. A robin chat landed on a rock and preened its feathers, eyeing the flies that buzzed over the warm, dew-drenched grass. A flock of ducks rose from the shallow ditch on the other side of the woods, and Michael suddenly stiffened. His hand tightened on her shoulder as he stood, tense and quiet, senses straining toward the river. Catherine, surveying the same scene, saw nothing amiss. The flapping ducks soared off, leaving the boys still laughing and calling to Tukum. Nothing else stirred, and still, Michael's grip did not loosen on her shoulder.

Suddenly he gave a shout of warning to the boys and swung the rifle to his shoulder just before ten Wittaia warriors burst out of the river brush near the boys, spears poised. Their appearance screamed at everything around them, although they remained completely silent. White clay circles smeared around their eyes made them seem wilder than usual. Beneath the tusks which ran through their noses, their teeth were bared. Never had Catherine seen a more terrifying sight than those feathered warriors plunging out of the brush. After a moment of frozen terror the boys screamed and began to run—all except Tukum, who had not reappeared. Michael fired as spears and arrows flew at the escaping boys. At the second shot one of the Wittaia fell. The others pulled up, startled by the sound and the sight of their fallen comrade, tentatively connecting the cracking noise with his death. They could see that he bled but saw no visible spear or arrow.

Catherine's heart caught in her throat as she watched them hesitate, their attention now on Michael. She saw the agony on his face as he waited for them to respond, praying they would withdraw. He didn't want to kill them, but he could not stand by and let Tukum and the others be killed. Now he was no longer a scientific observer, carefully removed from village life, and Michael would pay dearly for this change in status. The Wittaia warriors started toward him, screaming at him this time as they charged. He fired again, hitting the two closest to him, who fell dead. This time the rest of the warriors turned and fled, leaving the bodies and the weapons of the dead behind.

Michael ran toward the brush where Tukum had last been seen. By now Degewatek and the other warriors had reached the scene and witnessed the final confrontation. They had never seen the rifle fire, and even though Michael was their friend, they were clearly frightened by this new and deadly magic.

It was Degewatek who found Tukum. His tiny body had been pinned to the ground in the brush, and he had received some twenty spear wounds; but he was still alive. Degewatek carried him back to his *sili* and took him into the *pilai*, followed by the other warriors. Ignoring taboos, Catherine entered with them. No one seemed to notice. The light from the one entrance was dim. Inside, the *pilai* was blackened from smoke and littered with old straw bundles hanging from the rafters, unused weapons, and decrepit, molding feather headdresses. Raw meat for the stone ceremony feast hung from the rafters and dripped blood upon the floor. The smell of sweat, stale grease and the juices of fresh meat was overpowering, but Catherine scarcely noticed it. She had eyes only for the small boy who lay on his side in the dirt.

The wounds in Tukum's chest and stomach gaped open. His feet were drawn up, and his arms were wrapped around his body, as if to hold on to his life. The men gathered in the *pilai* seemed helpless. Preparations for the stone ceremony proceeded, although the chatter was now subdued. They continued with what they were doing because they knew of nothing else to do. Tukum's mother pushed her way into the *pilai* through the crowd of men and boys and stood looking at her son in silence. After a few moments she turned and left without speaking and didn't return. She took her digging stick and went back to the garden to plant sweet potatoes. She drove the stick into the earth each time with a force that suggested it was the body of an enemy, but the death of a male, even one's son, was men's business. She had no place in it except to mourn when it was over.

The older warriors of the *pilai* held a conference and concluded that Tukum must be moved outside since it would not be wise to have such misfortune present when the sacred stones were unwrapped. Degewatek gathered Tukum into his arms, and the boy gave a little cry of pain. "But I am not dead," he said feebly, thinking he was being carried away to his funeral.

"*Hakolakum!*" Degewatek replied firmly, ordering Tukum's seeds of singing to remain in place. "You will not die!"

At the sound of Tukum's pain Catherine started to protest the move, but Michael took her arm, restraining her.

"It doesn't matter," he said. "Let them do what they must."

Tukum's eyes were open now, though he looked at no one. They seemed focused on something deep within. A sob of mourning escaped the old men as Degewatek started for the door, but none followed. For the rest of the afternoon Tukum rested in Degewatek's lap before the *pilai* while the earth turned slowly dark with his blood. Little cries of pain escaped Tukum's lips from time to time, but he clung stubbornly to life while Degewatek quietly chanted over and over, "*Hakolakum.*"

An old man with the powers of a sorcerer came to crouch beside Tukum and blow in his ear in an attempt to coax the *edai-egen* back to their resting place. Tukum dozed fitfully and occasionally came suddenly awake, struggling and fighting until Degewatek and the sorcerer restrained him. He stared up at the sky and cried out in terror, "*Naijuk!*" I am afraid!

Catherine sat on her haunches, staring numbly at the fragile body. Her early tears had long since dried, and her eyes felt dry and scratchy, like her throat. Her legs were stiff and cramped, but she refused to move. Try as she might, she could not take her eyes from the terrible wounds in Tukum's chest and stomach—row upon row of small, angry mouths revealing blood and intestines. Mercifully one of the warriors from the *pilai* finally came out with wet leaves, which he gently placed over each hole, tucking back the flesh and organs as he did so. It was an act of concealment more than treatment. Nevertheless, Catherine was grateful.

Michael stood silently nearby. From time to time one of the warriors from the *pilai* would come by to look and then go away, obviously disturbed but unable to think of any act of comfort.

"Hakolakum," Degewatek chanted. *Stay.* But the look in Tukum's eyes, which opened from time to time, was growing more distant. He failed to notice that the boys with whom he had been playing at the time of the attack had gathered in the compound, standing off to one side as if fearing to draw too near. All were silent, their faces long and unhappy.

Dragonflies, on their way to hunt their prey on the sluggish surface of the water in the ditches nearby, paused to examine human death with curiosity. They darted and dipped like tiny blue helicopters before flying off toward the gardens, leaving the scene to the buzzing flies drawn by the fresh smell of blood. The mounting wind brought cooler air, and Catherine began to shiver. The sorcerer became restless, seeing a danger to his reputation in remaining too long with a lost cause. He stopped blowing in Tukum's ear and squatted morosely on the ground, wanting to leave but unable to think of a reason.

It began to rain. Like Tukum's life, the leaves which had concealed his wounds began to slip quickly away. He began to whimper with every breath, an innocent sound which contained no complaint, no demand on those who attended his death. He awoke and saw Catherine and Michael in the same spot where they had remained the whole afternoon. He smiled and attempted to talk, but his eyes refused to stay open. *"Lek, lek,"* he whispered. *No, no.* He fell silent. Only the small trembling of his narrow little chest showed he still held on to whatever life was left him.

"You will stay with us," Degewatek said, but this time it was more a plea than a command. The little chest had finally stopped its fitful twitching, and Tukum lay still. His *horim* had come loose and lay on the ground beside him, embarrassing him in death as it had stubbornly done all his short life. Catherine reached out and took one of his small hands in hers. He would have been ashamed had she done so earlier, but now his eyes, half-closed, were glazed in death, and he saw nothing. She bent her head to her knee and began to cry, and Michael put a comforting hand on her shoulder. She reached up to take it and press it against her cheek.

There had been many funerals in the village since Catherine and Michael had arrived months before, but none as large as Tukum's. More than 200 mourners from Homaktep and nearby villages where Tukum had relatives, came to the funeral feast and ceremony in Degewatek's *sili* the next day. In a culture where a warrior killed in battle was accorded the highest honors, no one's funeral had rivaled Tukum's in the number of pigs presented for the feast. There was something especially poignant about the violent death of a child, even for a people used to such deaths. After all, his body or his skill had not failed him; the *akuni* had. They had failed to protect him. The warrior who owned the abandoned watchtower felt particularly aggrieved and remained at the funeral only a short while.

The pigs were butchered and placed to cook in pits with hot stones. As Tukum's *nami* Michael had contributed a pig to the feast. The tall chair he and Degewatek had made for the funeral stood in the middle of the *sili*. It was the only piece of furniture the Dani ever constructed, and the funeral ceremony was the only time it was ever used. Degewatek carried Tukum's body from the *pilai* and placed it in the chair, and a wail of grief went up from the women who clustered around it, seated on their haunches. Tukum's legs were draped over a high crossbar, his body tied to the chair's back, while his chin was held up by a strip of leaf. The warriors rubbed him with pig grease, the first and only time his boy's body would receive that man's ointment. Gifts of woven ceremonial bands were draped over him and around the chair, along with gifts of nets from the women. They would be distributed among those attending at the end of the ceremony. Tukum's face was soft and calm, yet he looked sad, as if the meaning of all this grief had not escaped him.

While the pigs roasted, the mourning chants rose and fell. Drawn by the heat and the blood, flies buzzed about in increasing numbers. An old woman whisked them away from the body with a palm-leaf fan. Most of the tips of her fingers had been cut off when she was a child as signs of mourning for various close relatives. Many of the women present had been mutilated in this manner.

By late afternoon the feast was finished, and those who lived far away made preparations to go. The ceremonial belts and nets were removed from the body, and Degewatek, as the great *kain,* handed them out to the worthy guests. A wood pyre was lit, and a wail of anguish rose again among the women. Tukum's body was loosened from the chair. All moved quickly now, for the fire was ready. Degewatek took a bundle of grass that stood waiting and held it up for Michael, as Tukum's *nami,* to shoot an arrow in it, thus freeing the spirit from its body. Degewatek gathered up Tukum's body for the last time. The soul had fled. The seeds of singing were free. He placed it on the burning pyre. More wood was piled on, hiding Tukum as the flames leaped up to claim him.

When the ceremony was over, Catherine was struck with the fear that the Wittaia, in their need to revenge their dead clansmen, would not stop until they had killed Michael. She and he could not leave the valleys of the Snow to live in the inhospitable jungles. And if they were forced to leave this land altogether, she faced that other constant fear—that she would lose him forever.

The next morning the bodies of the three enemies slain by Michael in the attack were returned to the frontier for the Wattaia to claim. For them to remain in Wali territory would be to invite the presence of unfriendly ghosts. A hole was cut in the ventral base of the penis of each body, and magic ferns were inserted in the cut as well as in the rectum and the tiny bullet wounds. When they examined those wounds, the Homaktep warriors set up a cacophony of Dani amazement, tapping their fingernails on their *horims* and exclaiming, *"Wawawa!"* They were in awe of this man whose strange spear could kill an enemy without leaving his hands. Soon the entire valley had heard of the incident, and Michael was given a new name—*Mokatdege* ("Ghost Spear")

Chapter 21

A few days after Tukum's death Catherine went with Koalaro to the salt pools, two hours' climb into the mountains from the village. Koalaro did not want to remain in the *sili* that day, with reminders of Tukum and Degewatek's grief around her. Degewatek had been very fond of Tukum. He had three wives, yet there were no sons in his *sili*. Now that Tukum was gone, there was no child to breathe life into the compound. Degewatek's infant daughter was too small to do anything but eat and sleep. Koalaro had given him no children, and Degewatek suddenly seemed to hold it against her—along with the indifference and occasional hostility she had shown Tukum. She had always been jealous of Tukum as her only potential rival for Degewatek's affection, but now she wished he were alive.

On the way to the salt pool Koalaro was surly and refused to talk with Catherine, so they climbed in silence. The trail had been worn down to bare rock by generations of feet. People from throughout the valley gathered here to get salt, mostly strangers to each other. By custom it was neutral territory, for salt was one of the important economic bases of Dani life, too valuable to be caught up in the constant wars and quarrels. Neutral territory or not, people did not tarry here but went silently about their business and moved on.

There were some fifty other women at the pool as Catherine and Koalaro soaked banana stalks in the salty water, letting the fiber absorb as much liquid as it could before binding it up in heavy, soggy bundles for the trip back. When they returned to the *sili,* the leaves would be dried out and then burned, and the ashes mixed with water to form little balls of hard salt, which would be used as seasonings at feasts or traded. Michael had obtained the hardwood for his spear by trading the salt Catherine had made. She loved to make the trip to the salt pools. The virgin forests of oak, beech, and chestnut trees were beautiful, and a clear, rushing mountain stream kept company with the trail. Sunlight mottled the forest floor in an ever-changing pattern, and lilies, orchids, begonias and impatiens grew among the ferns and mosses in the damp earth. In their descent Catherine and Koalaro met women from a distant Wali village, brought to the edge of the forest by some of their men, who rarely went as far as the pools themselves, for that was woman's work. One of the women had been to Tukum's funeral, but Koalaro passed her without a word. Moments later Catherine glimpsed the savanna lands through the trees. With regret she realized that they would soon emerge into the heat of the afternoon sun. Ahead, some distance down the trail, she saw a Wali warrior escort relaxing on their haunches beside the trail, smoking tobacco in long, thin holders, brown bodies blending into the forest. The sound of their laughter and chatting voices carried far in the forest stillness. She could almost hear them grinding their teeth between sentences in that strange habit of the Dani men. They grew shyly silent as she and Koalaro approached, though they still smiled. No doubt Koalaro's aloof and regal manner intimidated them, Catherine thought, not without some mild annoyance.

Suddenly Koalaro, walking ahead of her on the trail, dropped her heavy bundle of water-soaked banana stalks to the ground with a cry and started to run into the forest. For a second Catherine stood stunned. By the time she came to her senses and realized that these casual strangers ten yards down the trail were neither Wali nor Wittaia but definitely enemies, it was too late. Two warriors rose quickly and brought Koalaro to the ground among the ferns just off the trail. A third, in close pursuit, caught up to them, pulled off his *horim,* and fell upon her struggling body while the other two forced her to submit. The others quickly surrounded Catherine, cutting off her escape, and were joined by further reinforcements, who materialized from the forest depths. Catherine stared at them in surprise and growing terror as she listened to the groans of the struggling Koalaro as the men took their turns with her. The rape of Dani women was a common fact of Dani life, and like rape everywhere, it had little to do with sex. For Dani men it was a natural extension of the rivalry and quarrels between men. They killed each other when they could, but the next best thing was to steal each other's pigs and rape each other's women.

Catherine suspected with sinking heart that this raid was no accident. These men were allies of the Wittaia from the area of the valley far to the south, near where the Baliem River left the valley floor, and they had risked great danger in violating the neutrality of this place. They had come after her—wherever they might find her, sanctuary or no. The Wittaia and their allies sought vengeance on Michael, but fearing his powers, they would strike through her instead. She knew she was about to be kidnapped, possibly raped, and almost certainly killed—and there was nothing she could do about it.

Their leader stepped forward. He was wearing only a *horim,* like the others, but otherwise, he had ceased to resemble anything human. His face and upper body were thickly covered with white clay so that his eyes remained his only natural features, bright black points of fierce energy which seemed to leap out from their white background. The large half-moon of a bailer shell hung from his nose, covering the lower half of his face like a mask. A Dani headdress of egret feathers swung in unhurried calm whenever he moved his head, its motion belying the violence of its wearer. He was tall, and the headdress made him taller still.

He reached for the buttons of Catherine's shirt and then, unfamiliar with their workings, impatiently tore it open and pulled it off. He did the same with her khaki pants and boots, twisting her ankle roughly. When he had finished removing her clothing and discarded it in the ferns, he studied her carefully. Binding her wrists tightly before her, he placed a noose around her neck, pulled it closed until she nearly choked, and handed it to one of his men.

The leader then turned his attention to Koalaro, who by now had grown quiet and submitted passively to whatever was done to her. He knelt over her body and put a hand roughly upon one

211

breast. His *horim* had been thrust aside by his swelling lust, but just as he seemed to make ready to enter her, he turned away and took a spear from one of his men. He rested it against her thigh and paused to look at her. Slowly he moved his hand from her breast down to the soft folds between her thighs. Spreading them open with thumb and finger, he began to ease the wooden spear shaft carefully between the opened lips, taking care not to hurt her, until it was fully within that unwilling space. He stopped again and smiled. Her eyes were opened wide in terror. He began to move the spear slowly back and forth, gently at first but gradually plunging it deeper and deeper. Koalaro began to scream, and one of the men who held her placed a hand over her mouth. Catherine felt herself get dizzy, and then the scene before her went totally dark.

When she came to moments later, she was being yanked roughly to her feet by the noose. When she looked cautiously around her, the leader of the group of warriors had disappeared. Single file, they now moved south, hugging the cover of the forest rim until safely beyond Wali territory. Throughout the following hours Catherine altered between the certainty that Michael would rescue her and the despair that he could not.

He would not realize she was missing until evening, when she and Koalaro failed to return. It was unlikely that he could make a successful search and pick up the trail until daylight. By then she and the attackers would be far ahead. Still, Michael was an expert tracker, and that gave her hope. She lagged along as much as she could, hoping to slow her captors down. She succeeded, but at the price of frequent rough tugs on the noose, accompanied by slaps and cuffs.

Michael left the stones ceremony at old Siba's *pilai* early. The late-afternoon heat was more intense than usual so that light shimmered off the unsheltered savanna land, bending the mountains into undulating shards of blue. He had stayed at the feast only a few hours. His only purpose in going had been to take notes for Catherine, who, as a woman, was excluded from such ceremonies. After a while his interest in the proceedings lagged, and he found himself distracted.

By the time he reached his own *sili* some distance away the sky had begun to soften around its edges into the warm gold of sunset. Thirsty and exhausted by the heat, he took a gourd of water and sank into the grass beside the cookshed. Catherine wasn't home yet, but then he hadn't expected her to be. Still, he was vaguely disappointed, and he wasn't sure why. Something was bothering him—a nagging uneasiness that had first begun as he had gazed through his rifle's sight at the charging Wittaia raiders on the day of Tukum's death.

He took up his sketch paper and started to finish the drawing he had begun at Siba's *pilai* but then tossed it aside. Too restless to remain at the *sili*, he decided to meet Catherine on her return from the salt pools. Halfway to the mountain forest he climbed to wait for her on the hill that overlooked the surrounding valley. He squinted into the sun, which was just about to touch the rim of the wall. Surprised, he did not see her at any point between where the trail left the forest and passed this spot. Everything else looked just as it should. He could see the warriors on their nearby watchtowers and the cookfires that were beginning to make feeble marks upon the sky. The uneasiness within him grew.

The earth still radiated the heat it had absorbed during the day, so he decided to move on toward the forest and wait for her in the cool shade. He had only just reached the shelter of the trees when he came across a piece of ginger root, wrapped in its own leaves as in the manner in which the Dani ate it, lying on the trail. Curious, he looked at it more closely. It was a favorite Dani treat, and it was unusual for someone to discard it so carelessly. Nearby, a slender pipe caught his eye. It lay broken among the rocks, its unburned contents extravagantly left to waste. Puzzled, he began to look about more closely. A dark stain remained where something had seeped across the trail and soaked into the earth. He knelt and touched his fingers to it. Blood. Alarmed, he followed the stain to where it originated behind some hillside rocks. Parting the ferns, he came upon five bodies; they were Dani warriors. He recognized none of them and concluded they belonged to some distant Wali clan, but he had no idea why the sanctuary of the salt trail had been violated. Something glinted in the ferns near one of the bodies. He reached over to pick it up, and the thing that had nagged at him the past few days became clear as he looked at the small gold medal he held in his hand. He had seen it twice before: once as a flash in his rifle sight that day of

213

Tukum's death and the first time, months ago, dangling from Nomad's ear.

Fear squeezed his gut and made his hand shake so badly that he dropped the St. Christopher medal. Nomad had entered the salt trail forest in search of Catherine; Michael was sure of it. The five dead Dani warriors beside the trail had been merely innocent victims, eliminated to prevent them from interfering. The salt trails were neutral territory for the Dani; but Nomad was not Dani, and disturbing this sanctuary would mean nothing to him. Up to this time Nomad had stayed out of the Grand Valley, content to dominate the eastern territory he had already secured, though his reputation was known throughout the valley. Now Nomad had followed Michael into the valley, forming an alliance with the Wali's enemies, the Wittaia.

Michael began to search the undergrowth on the trail ahead. He came across Catherine's khaki shirt. He had known fear before, when his own life had been endangered, but never anything like the terror that gripped him now. He roughly forced his way through the undergrowth, oblivious of the thorns that tore his hands and arms. The search turned up her khaki pants, underpants, and boots. The dread he felt now was like a physical presence, waiting beneath every fern he shoved aside. He found Koalaro's body next, and the method of her death chilled him. Honorable warriors would never kill in this manner.

As he began the gruesome search again, panic threatened to overcome him, and he forced himself to calm down. He concentrated on the tracks. Three sets of them had left the main group. He ignored those for the moment and concentrated on making sense of the others. There appeared to be ten people in the main party. It was getting dark and hard to see. Tears filled his eyes and threatened to blind him. He rubbed them angrily away.

Farther in the woods, where the tracks were less trampled but the light was even poorer, he found the first clear print of Catherine's foot. He sagged back against a tree and closed his eyes for a moment; then he clutched her clothing tightly to his chest and began to follow the trail. When he had satisfied himself on the direction and speed with which Nomad's men were moving, he turned back toward the village. The light was gone, but he had already learned enough. They were some five hours ahead of him. By the time he returned for his gun and some Dani warriors to accompany him they would be six hours ahead. During the day and a half it would take Catherine's abductors to reach the east end of the valley he could make up perhaps three hours of that. Fending off despair, he refused to let himself dwell on those three hours and what might happen after they got her where they were going. No doubt it would be a Wittaia village to the east, where she would be a war trophy, like the weapons of the dead Dani warriors which they had taken with them. Although it was hard to live with the knowledge that they had gone after Catherine for their revenge because they were afraid of him, there was a bit of hope in that knowledge, too. Perhaps he could use their fear to help him set her free.

Catherine spent that first night in an *ebai* of a Wittaia village trussed up like a pig, her back resting on the hard earth floor, her wrists and legs lashed to a horizontal pole above her. By dawn she was exhausted from the cold and the lack of sleep and so stiff it pained her to move. She could eat little of what they offered her, though she desperately wanted to keep up her strength.

The next day's walk was long and hot, and though her captors frequently drank water from gourds, they offered her none. Her feet were bruised and cut from rocks. When they stopped at dusk that night, they did so at a pretty Wittaia village set in groves of banana trees by the Baliem River. The women made menacing gestures, and little boys threw poorly aimed grass spears at her as the warriors led her to an empty *ebai* in one of the *silis*.

This time she was not trussed up but given a drink and then left to lie on her side on the hard dirt floor, wrists still bound. She was grateful to be left alone. Soon, however, some of the men of the village came to the *ebai*, curious to see the woman who belonged to the great ghost warrior. They gathered around and stared at her, young and old alike, and she became acutely aware again of her nakedness. One old man, so thin as to be a skeleton, removed his *horim* and hesitantly rubbed her thigh with the flaccid tip of his penis. It came somewhat reluctantly to life and expanded unsteadily. Thus encouraged, he became less hesitant, and she feared he might try to rape her; but he seemed content with touching her. Soon his organ softened, and he stopped. His actions encouraged some of the others to join him, including some of the preadolescent boys. As she lay on her side, they rubbed her back, her buttocks, her belly, probing the creases and folds where she kept her legs tightly closed. She shut her eyes tightly and endured it. No one tried to force her beyond this stroking, though some of them masturbated over her, spilling into the crease at the base of her tightly pressed thighs or over her breasts. Her skin crawled at the feel of the unwelcome semen. She kept her eyes closed and fervently wished she could shut her ears against the short intense pants and sustained groans of pleasure. She lay with fists and teeth clenched, prepared for her legs to be pried open at any moment. When this didn't happen, she began to realize they were afraid to enter her. She was not one of the *akuni,* and to do so might prove dangerous. It might permanently take away their sexual powers or cause great harm. After all, the Wittaia warriors on the earlier raid had been killed with invisible spears.

Suddenly the *ebai* grew quiet, and the random rubbings and probings ceased. She opened her eyes to the torchlight and saw an old man kneeling beside her, a purification feather in his hand, drawing it over her. He was a *wisum*—a man with powers of magic. He closed his eyes in concentration and chanted something she didn't understand while the men in the crowded *ebai* watched intently. He drew forth a foul-smelling bundle of tightly wrapped leaves and grasses mixed with blood and other pungent ointments. When it dawned on her what he intended to do with it, she struggled to rise, but they were already upon her, rolling her on her back, grabbing her ankles, and forcing them apart. Hands placed under her buttocks lifted her up like a ceremonial offering while the old man plunged the horrid mess into her, still chanting.

He withdrew it shortly and left. Those who had held her buttocks lowered them to the floor. Again the *ebai* grew still. No one moved to touch her, but neither did they withdraw the hold on her ankles. She felt sick with fear and disgust. The stench of sweat, semen, and stale tobacco mingled with the lingering smell of that putrid object. Dizzily she closed her eyes, and when she opened them a moment later, Nomad stood above her in the opening made by her parted legs. He carried no spear except the one that grew from his groin. If she had once entertained any hopes that her white skin might succeed in protecting her from rape, they fled now. He sank to his knees between her legs and, stretching her thighs apart, put a hand beneath her hips and began to lift the entrance of her body up to meet his sex, resting her buttocks against his thighs. His eyes already seemed to violate the only private, tender space remaining to her.

Though her wrists were still tied, her arms were free to move, and she began to hit and swing at him, struggling to free herself with all her strength. He gave a cry of outrage as her nails gashed his face. He sat up and drew back his hands and beat her severely until she lay still, and then he fell back upon her, pulled her up to him, and plunged within her as far and as roughly as he could go, straining and lunging as if to rip her apart.

"Michael!" she screamed in pain and terror, but this time he didn't come.

She seemed to float in and out of consciousness. Each time she opened her eyes she saw Nomad's face above her and felt his weight against her and the crude stab within her. It seemed to go on forever, and she could not even be sure if the face that floated above her was Nomad's or one of the many others who took his place. It didn't matter, for soon she would be dead. A spear—or many spears—would pierce her belly, like Tukum's, or be driven deep within her, like Koalaro's. Soon it would be over, and she would be glad. She no longer wished to be rescued or to live. She retched, strangled on what little rose to her throat, and lost consciousness again.

When she came to, the *ebai* contained only a small gray rectangle of morning light. She was alone, her hands still tied. Her face was so bruised and tender that it hurt to blink her eyes or move her lips. It was cold, but she did not feel it. She stared dully at the open doorway. She could see the smoke of fires from the nearby cookshed, and people had begun to stir slowly about. She did not move a muscle. Dawn had come, and she was not dead, though she fervently wished she were; she could not face more of what she had just been through.

A shadow filled the door, and Catherine was pulled roughly to her feet and hauled out of the hut. Dried blood was caked around her mouth, and her body was smeared with dirt. Her matted hair hung in her eyes so that she could barely see, but the bright morning light still blinded her. Semen, mixed with blood, ran between her thighs and down her legs, and every step she took was an agony of pain and humiliation. The warrior who held the noose grew impatient with her slowness and yanked the cord, sending her stumbling into the center of the compound.

Eyes blurred with sweat and dirt, she was only dimly aware that Michael stood in the center of the *sili*, surrounded by Degewatek and three other Wali Dani warriors. She couldn't accept the information her senses gave her; it wasn't possible that he could have reached her this quickly. She raised her bound hands and cleared the hair and sweat from her eyes, but his image did not disappear. Instead, it grew sharper. He was wearing only a *horim*, and his skin gleamed with oil; his gun was in his hand. The glance he gave her betrayed no emotion. She might have been a stranger for all it told her. He focused his attention on the village *kain*.

At any other time she would have loved the splendid sight of him wearing nothing but the *horim*, but now, revolted by what had happened to her these past few hours, she could not bear to look at him. She felt dizzy, sick. The compound began to wobble as she staggered and fell to the ground. No one moved to help her or even seemed to take notice. Michael, engaged in animated bargaining with the *kain*, never looked up. He had come to negotiate, just as any Dani might do if his pigs or wife had been stolen by anyone other than an enemy. But the Wittaia had never expected him to dare come after her into enemy territory and bargain with them as he might with an offending clansman. His approach during the early-morning hours, before the watchtowers had been manned, had angered and surprised them. More of them gathered to argue and brandish weapons.

The Wittaia had not yet agreed to return the woman, but Michael was already demanding a retribution payment of two pigs since it was the custom that the injured party in such a wife-stealing dispute be compensated in pigs. Michael could not afford to appear weak or easily appeased now. Nor did he dare to let them think that she was all he had come for. If they realized how important she was to him, it might further endanger her life. So he insisted adamantly on the pigs, and the argument grew louder.

Nomad did not appear among the warriors. He and his men had already returned to their own territory beyond the valley, having left orders that Catherine be sent to him when she recovered. It was fortunate, for Nomad would never have agreed to return Catherine. The pigs in question milled and squealed around the Wittaia *sili*, having been let out of their shed to begin the morning trek to forage and then ignored when the strangers unexpectedly arrived. Seeing that arguments were getting him nowhere and were in danger of igniting dangerous passions, Michael stepped away, lifted his gun to his shoulder, and took aim at a half-grown sow. He couldn't afford to miss without diminishing his reputation as a possessor of undefiable magic, but he had to act quickly. He fired, and the animal gave a soft grunt and fell dead in its tracks.

The sharp crack of the rifle silenced the excited debate for the moment. Cautiously the Wittaia approached the fallen pig and gingerly examined it. Clearly the weapon had not left the stranger's hands, yet it had killed. Considerably subdued, they discussed the weapon's power among themselves. After giving them a moment to absorb the implications, Michael ordered them to give him two of the pigs. To underscore his demand, he aimed the rifle at another of the *kain*'s pigs, this time a large prize breeding sow that was clearly pregnant. The threat worked. The old *kain* stepped between the gun and his threatened sow and ordered that Michael be given two younger pigs and the woman and be allowed to leave without interference from the younger war *kains*.

There were those among the Wittaia warriors present who suspected that the magic lay more in the weapon than in the man who used it and that if they could only get the weapon away from him, they would have nothing more to fear. But even those who doubted his power were hesitant to challenge it. The pigs were leashed, and the cords handed to the waiting Wali warriors. Michael crossed to where Catherine lay in the dirt. Grabbing hold of the straps which bound her wrists, he pulled her firmly to her feet. She swayed a moment but recovered enough to follow him from the *sili* with Degewatek and the other warriors just behind.

They took the narrow forested pathway that led along the river. Catherine managed the brisk pace with difficulty, but they didn't dare stop. Hands still bound, she concentrated on Michael's back as it moved ahead of her. Only the *horim* cord strapped at his waist broke the sight of its bare, well-muscled surface. He moved lightly and confidently along the trail, and she could only compare her own sorry state with his vitality. She felt ugly, inside and out. She wondered if he could ever want her again. Tears blurred her vision so that she stumbled from time to time.

It wasn't until they were some distance from the village that Michael called a halt, turning to face her for the first time. He quickly cut her bonds with his knife. She was surprised to see that he had been crying. He stood looking at her, his face contorted with something he could not express, though she could see that he was struggling to do so. Finally he reached out and drew her to him, gently at first and then fiercely, holding her tightly against him. His eyes were tightly closed, but she could feel his tears on her own cheek.

Standing amid the wild beauty of the ferns and orchids, surrounded by four feathered and clay-smeared warriors from another age, they clung to each other, drawn into that primitive world as participants against their will. The Dani warriors began to talk animatedly with each other. This was enemy territory, and they were plainly anxious to be gone. Reluctantly Michael released her. Cautiously they crossed the open grassland, gained the safety of the mountain forest, and turned north.

They stopped to rest at a small mountain stream with a waterfall. Catherine stumbled into it to let the water begin to wash away the filth, but when she tried to touch herself, she began to shake convulsively. Teeth clenched and eyes tightly closed, she struggled to control herself. Suddenly there were hands gently touching her, bathing her, rubbing her stomach and between her legs. She opened her eyes and saw Michael kneeling in the water before her, cupping his hands in the water to remove every trace of dirt and semen from her body while she stood trembling. Michael's fingers had felt like balm to her willing skin, yet now she cringed at his touch. Sensing it, he looked up, his eyes full of pain and concern.

"Do you want to talk about it?" he asked her.

She swallowed hard and turned her head away from him. Tears filled her eyes. "I can't," she replied.

He didn't ask her again. When they reached Homaktep, he gave the two Wittaia pigs to Degewatek, anxious to be rid of anything that could remind him of that Wittaia *sili*.

That afternoon, Degewatek held Koalaro's funeral. Because she was a woman and her death even less important than that of

Tukum, there was no feast or great ceremony of mourning. Her body was cremated by Degewatek and Tukum's mother who, alone, scattered her ashes and placed her bones in a ghost house.

Catherine sank into an exhausted sleep which lasted well into the next day. She woke burning with fever from infected internal injuries. When she recovered a week later, she was withdrawn and apathetic. She showed little interest in her work and was indifferent to Michael. At night she curled into a ball and whimpered in her sleep. Michael did what he could for her, but he was preoccupied with his own feelings. He was angry and hurt by her rejection and felt guilty for his anger. He also blamed himself for instigating Catherine's rape and wondered if she blamed him as well.

Even harder for him to accept was the humiliation he felt. He was revolted by what had happened to the woman he loved, and at times by her as well, and he loathed himself for this feeling. When she looked at him, she saw that he hadn't shaved in a week and his eyes were unnaturally bright.

"What is it, Michael?" she demanded of him finally, breaking the silence that had grown up between them.

He sat across from her near the door of the *ebai*. She could barely make out his features, but the haunted look came through.

"I keep torturing myself with what it must have been like. I keep imagining what happened to you, seeing it repeated a hundred different ways in my head. And I blame myself—and you—that it happened at all."

"Would you like me to tell you, Michael?" She said it in a monotone—without feeling. "Would you like to know exactly what they did to me? Then you won't have to imagine it a hundred different ways anymore. You'll *know*."

"Yes. No! No, I don't want to know. I just want to accept that it happened and get over it. I . . ." he swallowed hard and began again softly. "I saw on your body what happened to you. Maybe I just can't accept it."

"Would it make you feel any better to know that I hardly remember, that I passed out, that I don't even know all that happened."

"I don't believe you."

She turned her face away from him, toward the wall with its

rough thatched surface. "What is it that bothers you most about it, Michael?" Her voice was dry and flat.

"Your helplessness, the degradation, and you were so powerless. It's as if it had happened to me—and I can't accept it. I'm sorry." He buried his face in his hands.

"It did happen to you. It was you they wanted to hurt and humiliate, not me."

He knew that it was true. She turned back to him.

"You're going to listen to what happened, Michael. I'm going to tell you everything, and then, somehow, both of us will have to accept it."

She didn't spare the details. She told it in that same dry, flat voice, and when she was through, she looked at him dully for a moment, and then she began to cry; racking sobs shook her body, and he took her in his arms and held her close, crying with her. They slept in each other's arms for the first time since she had been kidnapped; but later, when he touched her neck with a kiss, she stiffened and pulled away from him, and he knew it was not over. Nor was it over for him. No simple act of confession and absolution would cure it. He had looked within himself, and he knew that only one thing would finish it for him: revenge. He was no longer living in a civilization where he could rely on courts and juries to redress the wrongs done him, and though that formal system might better serve justice by being impartial, here in the jungle it did not serve his human need for vengeance.

"I'm going to kill him," he announced one day to Catherine. She sat in stunned silence for a moment, contemplating him.

"But why?"

"We can't stay in the valley or anywhere near it if Nomad is alive. He'll not only come after us but seek to dominate the Wali Dani as well."

"But if we go, he may not bother with the valley. He hasn't before this."

"No. He must be killed. We're emotionally caught up in Dani life now—not just physically involved. Let's face it, Catherine, we're not an anthropology field expedition anymore. We're two human beings trying to survive in a land where the rules aren't our own, but they're rules we have to accept and live by. And if I'm not to be considered *kepu*, then I must challenge and defeat my enemies."

222

"The truth is, you want to kill him."

He didn't answer, but his silence was an affirmation.

"Please, Michael, don't do this. We can leave New Guinea. Let's go back and be married. Marry me, Michael," she added softly, and tears sprang to her eyes.

His look of utter despair gave her his answer, and she was stunned.

"Don't make marriage into some kind of test of my love for you. Try to understand," he pleaded. "You'd be giving up nothing, but those people close to me would be losing a great deal. Is the risk worth it?"

She cried out in indignation, "You love me, I know it! How can you ask if it's worth it?"

"What works so well here might be destroyed by the guilt I'd feel. It's easier this way. They think I'm dead, not that I've left them."

"Michael! They have to face it. You have to face it."

"I have obligations. I can't just selfishly dismiss them."

"If you can't do it for yourself, then do it for me. Oh, God, Michael. Why must you always put your own needs last? You're going to ruin everything for us."

"It's too soon to change things." Eyes pleading, he added, "Stay with me—here. Love me—here. Believe me when I say that the world back there will destroy us."

"Then I'll be your mistress there. I don't care. Only let's leave!"

"No!" he replied, angry and distressed. Then he calmed himself enough to soften it. "No, I won't allow it." His voice was edged with bitterness. "I've lived with what that did to my mother, and I love you too much for that."

She didn't argue. She knew he was right if for no other reason than that she could never share him with another woman. Not now. Not any more.

"So I'm to make all the sacrifices. Is that it, Michael? Give up completing my degree. Give up my career to hide here."

"Would they make you happy? Had they made you happy?" He searched her eyes, truly wanting an honest answer. "I've had those things, and a certain modest amount of fame as well." His eyes were intently serious. "It never made me happy. Nothing did, until you came along." He reached out and gently touched her shoulder, giving it a squeeze. "Have you been happy here, Catherine?"

He let his hand slide away, and she felt a little shudder pass through her. "Yes," she answered softly. "But it might not be enough forever."

"I'm not asking that it be forever. Only for a while—until they get used to life without me and find other things, other people, to take my place."

She looked at him, golden and glorious, and she knew that Kara would never find anyone to take his place. For a brief second she felt a stab of sympathy for her, but she quickly dismissed it. She couldn't afford to feel anything for Kara right now.

He rose slowly and stood silhouetted in the doorway. The sky behind him was a hard gray, cold and unbending as a sheet of steel. The way his eyes would be, she thought, if she could see them now in the hut's darkness.

"You still intend to kill him?" she asked.

"Yes," he answered softly. His voice was weary as he asked her, "What would you have me do to bury this thing between us? What do you want me to do? Be honest, Catherine!" he admonished her fiercely.

She was silent for a moment, staring at his dark shape but unable to see his expression in the dim light. "Kill him," she whispered finally, and the depths of her feeling came as a surprise. "Oh, God. I want you to kill him!" she cried. "I only wish I could kill him myself."

He turned slowly and left the *ebai*. He paused for a moment outside to listen to the sound of her bitter weeping muffled against the sleeping mat.

"Suppose he kills you instead?" she cried after him.

Without answering he reached for his spear and moved on. The Wali warriors were holding a meeting to decide if a battle challenge should be given the following morning. He wanted to make sure it was agreed.

Chapter 22

Michael stood to one side of the hill overlooking the battlefield as the Dani warriors on both sides charged down in tightly massed formations, shields before them, spears held aloft, resembling ancient galleons with oars raised, surging with inevitable momentum toward some dark collision. A chant went up among those warriors massed and watching on opposite sidelines, its rhythm carefully matched to the pounding feet. Nomad was not there, so Michael only watched.

Inflamed by the incident at the neutral salt wells, the old feud had taken on a new ferocity, and additional support was requested by both sides from Dani tribes friendly to each. By noon of the first day of battle some 1,500 Dani had gathered on each side, and more arrived hourly from distant locations at extreme ends of the valley. This battle would not be over in a day, so Michael was not disturbed by Nomad's absence. He watched the battle for a while and then left, certain that by the next day he would have his chance. In the meantime, the Wali Dani had killed two Wittaia warriors and lost none of their own.

When the 4,000 warriors from both sides gathered at the battle site at midmorning the following day, Nomad had arrived. Michael almost sensed his presence before he saw Nomad step out in front of the long line of enemy warriors on the far hill. Michael felt a strange surge of exhilaration and relief at the sight of him tall and resplendent in his dress, set apart from the other Wittaia and

Kukukuku warriors by his height and his haughty bearing. He wore a magnificent headdress of black cassowary feathers trimmed with white egret plumes and set in a headband of green viper skin. Boar's tusks pierced his nose, and he wore numerous shell bibs over his chest. Bands of brightly colored parrot feathers encircled his calves and ankles, while his skin, smeared with ash and pig grease, was almost totally black. His ferocious and imposing appearance had always struck terror in his enemies and had helped account, in no small part, for his success. He carried not one but two spears.

When he caught sight of Michael, who wore only the simple *horim* and carried no weapon but his short spear, Nomad let out an unearthly cry that was half rage and half challenge. It sent a slight shiver coursing through Michael's body. The first group of Wali warriors formed a line and began the provocative challenge ritual that was immediately taken up by a group of Wittaia. Nomad remained at the top of the hill as the ritual broke out into furious fighting that went on for some twenty minutes with numerous wounded on both sides. In a sudden surge the Wali Dani pushed the Wittaia back, chanting and shouting.

Through the swirling dust Michael could see Nomad suddenly smile, raise his spears above his head, and charge down the hill, screaming "Aiy-ee!" His action turned the tide. The 200 warriors losing ground to the Wali Dani fought with renewed vigor and were joined by several hundred fresh reserves, who had been waiting their turn to engage the enemy. Seeing Nomad's charge toward the front line, Michael lightly took up his own spear. It was shorter than the Dani spears, and better balanced. Nomad swerved to one side, away from the others, and continued his headlong charge. Michael went after him.

Nomad carried his two spears, both poised to hurl. It was Nomad's custom to throw one, and when the opposing warrior indicated which way he would jump to avoid it, Nomad would hurl the second spear, which would effectively strike his opponent just when he thought he was safe. Michael knew the danger. To overcome it, he would simply have to move quicker and farther than Nomad anticipated.

They were within thirty feet of each other when Nomad hurled his first spear with all the might his forward momentum gave him. Michael swerved to his right with every ounce of strength and speed he could muster. Out of the corner of his eye he saw Nomad release his second spear. The first thudded into the beaten earth, but the second caught Michael in the left side. He felt muscle slash and bone bruise as the spear tore into him. Because he was numbed by the shock of the blow, it was a moment before the burst of pain hit him. He dropped his own spear as he sank to his knees and pulled with both hands on the shaft that protruded from his side. It was buried deep, but he had flung himself far enough for it to miss any vital organ. Sweating profusely, pulling with all his strength, he wrenched it free just as Nomad swooped down to lift up the first spear and come at him from behind.

Sweat blinded Michael's eyes as he groped for his own spear and struggled to rise. He was only dimly aware of the red stream that poured from his side. He tried to rise from his knees, but he was too weak from shock. Desperately he swung himself around just in time to see Nomad grip his spear and raise it with both hands over his head, ready to plunge it forward. Michael grabbed his spear from the ground and slung it with all his strength at Nomad, hurling himself to the ground just as Nomad released his spear. It bit deeply into the puddle of blood where Michael had knelt just a moment before, but Michael's spear had found its mark. Flung upward and at an angle, it had entered the solar plexus at the point of the seeds of singing and traveled upward into Nomad's heart. He staggered and stood still for a moment, both hands on the spear as if to pull it out. Suddenly he threw his arms wide, and his head fell back in a cry of rage that drowned out the warriors' cries around him. He crashed forward to the earth, dead.

The Wittaia forward line had plunged past them during the battle, and Michael was now surrounded by enemy warriors. At the moment of Nomad's death the fighting around Michael stopped, and as the news spread, a strange quiet pervaded the battlefield on both sides. Arms poised high with spears were suddenly stayed in midair. Mouths opened in shouts fell silent. Only the feathers in countless headdresses fluttered restlessly in the breeze.

With great effort Michael rose slowly to his feet, hands clutched to his side to stem the bleeding. He stumbled past the dead form of Nomad. His spear had broken in two when Nomad struck the ground, but it didn't matter. He had no more use for it. He glanced around at the silent Wittaia warriors. The hill occupied by friendly Wali warriors seemed an impossible distance away. He began to take a few steps toward it, sweat pouring off his forehead and stinging his eyes. The Wittaia warriors moved aside to let him pass. He staggered through the silent enemy line, barely able to stand, clenching his teeth to keep from screaming. The earth blurred into a narrow tunnel that twisted and dipped, then threatened to disappear. No one moved to touch him, but he could feel the tension in the bodies and faces around him.

Somehow he kept on his feet and kept going. When he reached no-man's-land, a murmur began to pass through the Wali Dani ranks like the wind in the grass. He kept going, and it rose, growing louder until it erupted into a roar as he neared the Wali lines. Degewatek ran out to meet him and grabbed him while Michael hung on gratefully. Two more Wali warriors joined them, and they braced Michael between them, hurrying him to safety. Soon many strong hands stretched out to touch him. He found himself lifted up and carried along on their shoulders. The pain was excruciating, but the exhilaration of that moment almost made him forget. He was aloft in a sea of happy faces, surrounded by a forest of friendly spears. As he neared the top of the hill, he found that the world was beginning to slip away. If he lost consciousness, he would be unable to prevent the medical incisions in his midsection from draining the dark blood, incisions that would surely kill him in the condition he was in.

Women were not allowed near the battlefield but Catherine had secretly watched the battle from a nearby hill removed from the fighting. Heart pounding, she had felt the same exhilaration and pride as any Dani woman: he was a great warrior, and he was hers. She had endured the agony of watching him almost die, the pain of seeing his slow, agonized walk to safety, and, finally, his moment of victory, borne upward on that surging, tumultuous black tide. No one else would die that day—or on any other for a while. The Wittaia and Kukukuku were completely demoralized by the great Wali Dani victory. Alliances that were strained to begin with would now break. New ones would eventually form, but it would take time. Meanwhile, there would be peace. In the midst of all that turmoil the more intimate meaning of the fight had finally become clear. He had risked his life for her. Not simply to avenge her or himself but to keep her with him. He had fought in order that they might remain in New Guinea, where nothing could separate them—except death.

Fear gave Catherine strength to push her way through the flood of warriors to the litter which contained Michael, carried by four Wali Dani. The wound in his side had been covered with leaves, and she struggled to control her tears as she looked at it. He was conscious again, and he reached out to take her hand.

"It'll be all right." He reassured her softly. "Nothing vital, just muscle and ribs."

She nodded, but as she glanced at the hidden wound, she was uneasy. Already he looked warm and feverish. Even in this temperate mountain climate, infections developed and spread rapidly. When they reached the *sili*, she sent all the Dani away for fear they would make their own attempt to cure him. She boiled water and cleaned the wound, but she knew little else to do. Michael slept uneasily.

An *edai* celebration was beginning on a nearby hilltop. The warriors gathered in their finery and began a running, singing, leaping act of victory. Nearby the women held their own version of the *edai*, singing and dancing and running. Catherine got Tukum's old grandmother, Weake, to watch Michael while he slept, and she went out to join the celebration. She put on a warrior's headdress and smeared her face and arms with clay and joined the men. If Michael could not do it, she would do it for him. She felt the energy of the dancing bodies around her as she closed her eyes and became oblivious of anything but the music and the movements of her own body.

She felt, as Michael had that morning, that she was undergoing her own rites of passage, no longer merely observing but participating in primitive life. She was aware that she had joined Dani life more fully than anything that had ever come before.

Michael's eyes were still closed when she came back to the *ebai* and stirred the fire. The thin old woman who had been watching him scurried out of the corner like a spider, giving Catherine a start, and left the hut without a word. Catherine went to the creek to bathe and wash the clay from her clothes. When she returned, shivering, to sit wrapped in the robe by the fire, his eyes were open. The voices of the Dani, singing and chanting in *edai*, could still be heard in the gathering twilight.

"I danced with them," she said, looking out the door toward the sounds, "while you slept."

"I know."

She looked back at him in surprise.

"I watched you. With Weake's help I walked to the end of the *sili* where I could see."

She looked at him with alarm. "You shouldn't have gotten up. The bleeding will start again."

"It's all right."

She sat quietly for a moment, listening to the singing. "We won't leave," she said finally.

"If you want to go, we will."

"No," she replied quickly. "I don't want to go. At least not yet. Maybe never, if it means I can't have you."

Never had she looked more beautiful to him than she did at that moment, seated by the fire, face flushed, eyes bright, hair flowing loosely over the furry robe which she gripped together with one hand at her throat.

"Catherine. I—" His emotions stopped him.

"No. Don't talk." She stood up and walked over to him. "No apologies. No promises."

He reached up, took her hand, and pulled her forward to stand above him. With his other hand he pulled the robe to the floor beside him, leaving the firelight to play on her bare skin. With both hands he guided her down to straddle him gently on her knees. He had not made love to her since the kidnapping, nor had she wanted him to. What had once been natural and easy had become difficult, filled with the possibility of failure and rejection. Now they approached each other hesitantly and with a certain awkwardness.

As her body touched his, he winced. A strangled groan that was both desire and pain escaped him. Concerned, she started to rise, but he grabbed her wrists and pulled her back. "No!" he protested with such intensity that for a moment it frightened her.

She braced herself, letting her arms take most of her weight, wanting to spare his wounded body. Beads of perspiration stood out on his forehead. He pulled her forward against his chest. His mouth opened, and he softly touched his lips to hers. She gasped in horror at the discomfort she was causing him, but when she started to withdraw, he grabbed her forearms tightly with a

230

strength that amazed her and pulled her mouth back to his. His fingers tugged into her flesh as if he might ease his pain by transmitting some of it to her.

"Michael, please," she murmured against his hungry, urgent mouth. "Please. I don't want to hurt you." Tears ran down her cheeks and moistened his. She could feel his ragged breathing and knew the pressure of her body across his abdomen was excruciatingly painful, and yet his groin pressed hard against her body, which opened invitingly over it. He kissed her then, and she felt her desire for him overwhelm all her concerns, all her memories. She wanted him more than she had ever wanted anything. Eagerly she returned his kiss and responded to his demanding fingers as they explored her body. She let her own hands go where they wished, reveling in the feel of him against her flesh.

With a movement that caused him to cry out in pain, Michael shifted his weight enough to push the tip of his desire into the warm moistness of her body. He could do no more. The injured muscles of his abdomen screamed their refusal, so with her hands she guided him deeper, twisting slowly and gently until he could go no farther. The ordeal over, he opened his eyes and looked into her face.

"Catherine." There was all the love she could want in that word.

Hands on his chest, she leaned down to kiss him, acutely aware of him lying quietly within her. She trembled and pulled back to look into his eyes. Both of them struggled to keep control, to prolong the sweet agony. She caught her breath and held it for a moment, as though she were at the top of a roller coaster just before plummeting down. He caught the look on her face and felt her body change and let go. He pulled her down to him, ignoring the stabbing throb in his side, allowing himself to shut out everything but the contractions within her body, the gentle tug he felt as his seed was sucked from him. They scarcely moved at all. An onlooker would hardly have been aware of the act of love that was passing between them at that moment, the swelling intensity of the pleasure they were giving each other.

"Michael, I love you." Her voice trembled in a whisper.

The contractions peaked in sweet, sharp spasms and then went gently on, greedily draining him of all the warm, living substance he had to give. There was no sound but the sharp, trembling intake of their breaths.

As soon as it was over, she pulled herself off him, afraid that their lovemaking had made the wound worse. His breathing was ragged as he moaned and sank back into the pillows against the wall. The wound was bleeding again, its lip raw and ugly and open. This time the blood seeped and oozed rather than ran freely. He rested for a moment, his face tense with pain. When he finally spoke, it was without opening his eyes.

"You're going to have to cauterize it, Catherine."

"You'll have to tell me how," she said, controlling the trembling in her voice.

She stirred the fire until it blazed; then, following his directions, she laid the glowing knife across the open wound. He screamed once, then clenched his fists. His face drained of color. Catherine flinched but held the blade steady against his flesh, biting her lip until it bled. The sound and smell of searing flesh made her fear that she might lose consciousness, but she struggled for control. When she removed the knife from the wound, the open lip was gone, replaced by an angry red welt. Mercifully Michael had slipped into unconsciousness. She flung the knife away from her and then lowered her forehead to the earth and let the darkness slip over her.

Life slowly returned to normal. They had not made love again, Michael was still recovering, but they both knew that in good time it would happen. In the meantime, after a week of fever Michael was able to accompany Catherine to the gardens for the first time. He wasn't able to help yet, but for her it was enough that he was there. When she finished weeding the garden and gathering vegetables, she sat down next to Michael on one of the large boulders some ancient upheaval had hurled down the mountain wall. Huge thunderheads were bunched together across the valley floor to the east, moving toward them. Already the air had grown heavy with moisture and flashes of lightning lit the darkening mass.

As she watched that brooding sky, Catherine thought aloud. "When I see the sky like this, I think of David and Carl and Julienne and all the others who died back there, and I feel so guilty that all my happiness has resulted from their deaths."

She felt the comforting pressure of his fingers closing over her hand. She turned to him and smiled gratefully.

"Do you ever think of them, too?" she asked.

He nodded.

"And your family, Michael?" Her smile faded, and she searched his eyes more closely. "Do you miss them?"

His fingers squeezed hers and then withdrew, as if he could not speak of them and touch her at the same time.

"Yes. The children. My father. He always counts on me so much. I suppose I feel a little as if I've run off and let him down. And I worry about Kara. She's never been on her own before. She lived at home until she married me."

Strange, Catherine thought. Whenever he mentioned Sir Charles, she felt threatened, even more than by Kara, and she didn't know why. From the beginning, however much she had been charmed by the older man, she had instinctively recognized him as a potential enemy.

"What does your father expect from you?"

"To run Maitreya." He smiled and added, "Profitably. To be respected academically and perhaps, most of all, to take my rightful place among the English aristocracy."

Catherine looked surprised.

"Oh, yes." Michael responded to her look. "In spite of his love of the Indies, he is English to the core. He feels that his opposition to colonialism, combined with his reputation as a ladies' man, prevented a rather straitlaced King George from making him an earl." It was an honor that Sir Charles's academic achievements and his reputation as a humanitarian had earned him, but the old king was always trying to live down the scandalous excesses of Edward the Seventh, Victoria's son and successor.

"And the present King George?"

"Not likely to honor my father either, not after his brother's scandalous abdication." Michael picked up a small stone and flung it away. "So England will never give my father the title he deserves. I say to hell with England, but I know this hurts him more than he admits."

"And he wants you to achieve what he can't."

"I suppose, although he never talks about it."

"And what do you want, Michael, for yourself?" Catherine asked him.

"I've finally realized that I want to sit on mountains, not move them. I don't think my father knows that yet, let alone accepts it." He looked at her, eyes doubtful. "I wonder if you can accept it either."

"You're already well known and respected in anthropology, so it's easier for you to talk about sitting on mountaintops than it is for the rest of us." She felt annoyed with him—and criticized for her ambition.

"I know I'm asking you to give up a lot, and it hurts me deeply. But it's not forever. You can go back to all the fame and fortune you can find. As for me, I just want to run Maitreya or someplace like it. I want to keep exploring, but I don't want to write or lecture about it. I'm through with all of that. Besides, what has fame and fortune ever brought my father?"

"Your mother, for starters."

"Touché." He laughed. "But I think that was due more to his charm."

"Only partly, I'm sure. Titles and fame have a way of impressing young women."

"I think Kara was one of those young women, too, though she wouldn't admit it. I think the whole Stanford mystique had more than a little to do with her accepting me as a husband instead of the proper Dutchman her parents wanted."

Catherine failed to notice how serious his look had become.

"Would it matter to you if I gave it all up: the title, Maitreya, everything?" he asked.

She looked at him in surprise. "What is this, some kind of contest? Which one of us will truly love the real Michael, *sans* riches, *sans* career?"

He felt slightly hurt that she had not taken him seriously. "It's just that I'm afraid sometimes that I won't be enough for you, that you'll leave me."

"Oh, Michael." Her voice was tinged with remorse. "I'm sorry . . . I didn't mean to hurt you." She put her arms around him. "I'll never leave you."

His mother's words echoed in his mind. He pulled himself free of Catherine's arm and stood up, taking her hand and pulling her up, too.

"Never make a promise like that," he said brusquely. "No one should. You never know what might happen that might make you break it." His eyes softened. "You love me now. That's all I need to know."

Most of the buttons were gone from her shirt, so she had tied it in a knot at her waist. Michael ran his fingers down that deep open V to the knot.

"We'd better start looking for fig leaves," he said. "These rags haven't got much longer."

"Does it matter?"

"It will where we're going."

She pulled back and looked at him in surprise. "Going? Us?"

"We can't stay with the Dani. Not now. With Nomad gone the Kukukuku will return to the east, toward Australian Papua, but my presence here will soon jeopardize whatever peace exists, even without the Kukukuku. Degewatek tells me that every young warrior seeking glory will want to challenge the Wali Dani to battle in order to have a chance to kill me. The Dani would never ask us to leave, but for their sake, as well as ours, I think we must."

"But where?"

He nodded toward the mountain wall that rose behind them. "North, toward the Carstensz Glacier. There are forests and lakes there where no one ever goes, forbidden lands."

"Why?"

"Too cold, I expect."

She glanced at their fragile clothing. "But love can keep us only so warm without totally exhausting us," she protested wryly.

"Don't worry. I've been hunting there. The nights and early mornings are very cold, but once the sun scales the mountains, it's pleasantly warm. There's more game up there. We'll make some fur vests and boots."

"Quickly enough to keep from freezing?"

He laughed and put his arm around her, and they began to walk slowly back toward the *sili*.

"I'm going there first, to find a spot, build a shelter."

"When?"

"It should be as soon as possible. This afternoon."

"But, Michael," she protested, "you're not well enough."

Prepared for her protest, he had waited until the last minute to tell her. "I must. It will be all right. I'll take it easy, not do anything I'm not ready for."

"For how long?"

"A week. Ten days."

"I'll go with you."

"No. I want to go alone. I can't explain why, but I want to take you there with the hut built, everything ready."

"Why, Michael." She laughed. "It's your nesting instinct."

"Perhaps." He smiled.

The first sounds of thunder rumbled around them, and they paused on a knoll to watch the approaching storm. Around them stretched the neat gardens, with their maze of irrigation ditches filled with stooping women. Even in a time of peace the men still manned the watchtowers, taking no chances, though their manner was more careless and relaxed than it might otherwise have been. Michael studied the simple Stone Age scene as if for the last time, absorbing and storing every detail of it for future memory.

"Genesis country," he reflected out loud. "They still live in the early morning of the earth." He hugged Catherine close to his side. "Frightened by so much they don't understand." He watched the laboring women. "Perhaps the one thing primitive man fears most is the woman he lives with. Afraid she drains his power away when she takes the fluid he gives her when they couple . . . afraid she uses it against him later, in sorcery. And yet he still wants her. His body needs her. So he keeps giving her his precious fluid, even though it frightens him to do so and makes him angry. He feels she magically forces it from him at the time when, in ecstasy, he is most vulnerable . . . taking advantage of his weakness for her. There is little love between the sexes. Only wariness. It's a rather sad state of family affairs."

As he spoke, the rain reached the outlying gardens, scattering those villagers who had not already left, sending them running for cover beneath the trees.

"Have we really come so far in the ten thousand years of civilization that separate us from them?" Michael wondered. "Or do the same fears still exist between us, that you will take my seed from me—and use it in sorcery against me?"

His eyes were on the rapidly advancing storm, and though she had smiled at first at his remark, she could see that the look on his face was real. The wind was rising. The rain was almost on them, a solid gray wall that hid the rest of the valley. A sudden chill had arrived with it. A bolt of lightning touched a tree down by the river and destroyed it with one explosive crack. It began to rain, colder and harder than usual, and it sent them hurrying home. Michael spent the hour of the storm cleaning his rifle and preparing for his journey. He left with the retreating drops of rain, pursuing their path into the mountains.

When he returned almost two weeks later, he surprised her by standing, unexpected and grinning, in the doorway of the *ebai*, red-bearded and disheveled. He apologized for his appearance. "I was in too much of a hurry to get back, so I didn't take the time to clean up."

He bathed and shaved while she gathered up the few things they would take with them: their knives, machetes, water gourds, and fur blanket. They took seeds and cuttings to plant a garden and gave their pigs to Degewatek. They would not need them for food; the lake where they were going was full of crayfish, and they would hunt what little meat they needed. They said sad good-byes to the village. Some of the villagers, including Degewatek, accompanied them as far as the salt pools. As they passed the spot of the kidnapping, Catherine was unable to avoid a shudder. She felt Michael put his arm firmly around her shoulders at that moment, comforting her, and she was able to force the scene from her mind.

They left the last villagers behind and began to climb to the land where the Dani never went, leaving the valley. The trees changed and grew thicker. Forest birds replaced the birds of the grassland. Then the trees began to thin until only scrub brush clung to the crevices of the rocks, and a blanket of snow covered everything, making the climbing slick and treacherous. They worked their way toward two limestone portals that stood like sentinels to the Dani valley. From below the path between them appeared to drop off abruptly, as though marking an end to the earth. But when they reached the spot and stood between the portals, it proved to be a beginning, not an end. Some 1,000 feet below them lay a black lake, long and deep, fed by thin streams of glacier water running off the high rims of the canyon walls. On the far side the black waters were edged by a meadow of high grass and pink rhododendron, which, in turn, was fringed by a thick pine and oak forest that gradually climbed the mountain slope to the snowcapped summit. At its farthest point the lake narrowed and seemed to drop off the edge of the world as the melting snows and rains continuously overflowed the rim, sending a huge waterfall plunging to a river far below.

A sturdy nipa-palm hut stood cheerfully in the warm sun halfway between the forest and the lake. Above the limestone canyon rim, the purple mountains rose in jagged layers to the icy peak of the distant Carstensz Glacier, standing serene and magnificent above all New Guinea. Catherine was speechless for a moment as she stared at the beauty of that small unspoiled valley. Michael grinned as he watched her reaction, pleased with himself and what he had found for them.

"It's beautiful. . . ."

"Come on," he said, taking her hand and beginning to lead her down the boulder-strewn path toward the lake.

By the time they reached the hut and deposited their belongings the sun was about to go down over the narrow end of the lake by the waterfall. As it turned everything to a deeply burnished gold, they sat on the grass to watch, pulling the fur robe tightly around them against the gathering cold.

"All we need to make it perfect would be a few chickens, and some fish to stock the lake." Michael smiled.

"And a lemon tree to season the fish," Catherine added.

"If we hadn't given the pigs away, we could have bacon to go with the eggs."

"Don't forget grapes to make wine."

"If we have lemons, we'll have to grow tea."

"And then it's a civilized paradise."

"Only if we add a touring company of the Royal Ballet once a year."

"And the Dubuque Symphony. They'll go anywhere."

"Admiral," Michael added. "He'd love it here with nothing to slow him down. We could ride him everywhere."

They paused. "Funny," Catherine said, "how little I really miss."

Michael's hand closed over hers. The huge orange disk had touched the spill at the west end. Catherine stared at the dark body of the lake as it slowly devoured the sun.

"We should call it Lake Hathor after the Egyptian sky goddess who swallowed the sun each night and gave birth to it the next morning," she said.

Michael wasn't looking at the lake any longer. He drew the furry robe around them both and snuggled deeply into it. He leaned over and lightly touched Catherine's lips with his and then kissed her eyelids. For a moment, eyes closed, she fearfully searched for some doubt—some hesitation—in her own response. Relieved, she found none. Her arms went around his neck, and she crushed his mouth down to hers, her body arching up eagerly to meet his. She covered his face, his chest, with kisses, frustrated and yet excited by the clothing that kept him from her.

Impatiently she reached down and unfastened her khaki shorts and let him gently tug them over her hips. She pulled with trembling fingers at the hardware of his pants. For unbearable seconds it refused to cooperate, then finally gave way. With a jolt she felt his body freed and touching hers. So hungry was she for him that she found her passion sinking into the earth, running out into the lake, dissolving into the sky. She had reached climax even before he entered her body.

He encircled her tightly in his arms, reveling in her silky black hair spread beneath him over the folds of the robe, the smoothness of her skin beneath his lips, the warmth of her body, its moisture between her legs telling him how much she wanted him. He knew this was the closest he would ever come to paradise on earth. It was a sweet realization that held a surprising sadness for him which he could not explain. Then the sun was gone, his passion with it, deep into her body. Drifting down through black lake water to rest, content, and rise again.

They spent the night under the stars, blessedly alone. And they remained alone except for Degewatek, who came occasionally to visit. He had been an exile much of his life, and forbidden lands held little fear for him. His household now seemed small to him, his *sili* empty. He had begun to think of taking a new wife. Pokat, his sister's son, had come to live with him from a distant village. Degewatek had made him his heir, and he would inherit the sacred stones. Sometimes the boy came with him on his visits to Catherine and Michael. He was a quiet child of ten who stared in wide-eyed wonder at Michael's blond hair and gray eyes.

Time lost all importance for them. Nothing, including the seasons, seemed to change. It was November 1940, and neither of them had the slightest idea of what this time meant to the rest of the world.

Chapter 23
Grand Valley, November 1940

It began as a buzzing around the rim of her consciousness, no louder than the drone of the honey bees in the grass around the lake. Later she would ask herself why she had simply stood there, rooted to the spot, refusing to believe what her ears were telling her, why she had not taken her rising panic and run with it as the noise grew louder, run to find Michael, who had gone hunting that morning, run to escape into the mountain forest. But she did not run. Instead, she had stood petrified as the seaplane roared in low over the mountain wall, dipped its wings as a signal to her, then circled the far end of the lake and came down. For a moment it disappeared in the huge spray created by the pontoons striking the lake's surface, and she had a fantasy it had been swallowed by that friendly body. But then it emerged, taxiing inevitably toward her.

Civilization had come to the Snow Mountains. After more than a year they were about to be rescued from paradise. The seaplane anchored out from the shallow water near the shore and disgorged a small inflatable raft. Four figures walked along the wing and crowded gingerly into the boat, which was pitching from waves churned up by the plane's propellers. Catherine could see that one of the distant figures was a slim young woman with blond hair. Kara. Catherine was sure of it. As the boat drew near, she could also make out Sir Charles among the men. The other two she didn't recognize. One of them waved to her and shouted something, but she neither heard it nor returned the gesture. As they drew close to the shore, the reeds forced them to climb out and wade the remaining distance.

Michael emerged from the woods. He had seen the plane approach, but now he gave the boat and its occupants no more than a glance. He was staring intently at Catherine over the short distance that separated them, and she would never forget the look on his face, a look that bitterly accused her of allowing them to be too easily found.

The rescue party gathered jubilantly around him, pounding his back, hugging him, touching him in their need to prove to themselves he was really alive. Clearly they had come to this location expecting to find Michael, and just as clearly they had not expected to find Catherine, so no one knew quite yet how to deal with her presence. Right now they were ignoring her in their joy. Michael answered their questions numbly, but his eyes kept returning to Catherine, who stood alone. Once when his eyes met hers, she managed to form his name silently with her trembling lips, her own eyes pleading with his. He answered with a look of pain and anguish that fully matched her own. They were given no chance to be alone, or even to exchange a few words, before they were hastily bundled onto the plane. Michael sat in the cockpit with his father, the pilot, and one of the strangers, who was an Australian official from Port Moresby. Catherine sat in the cabin with Kara and a Dutch official from Hollandia. After brief courtesies had been exchanged, not a word passed between Catherine and the other two.

As they took off, Catherine stared intently out the window and saw the lake below grow rapidly smaller and their hut become a tiny playhouse. In less than half an hour the happiest world she had ever known had been reduced to a memory, and neither of them had protested. She listened to Kara and the Dutchman exchange news of the war in Europe, Africa, and China, accounts of a world on the verge of madness. From their conversation she also learned with a shock that Julienne had escaped the Omadesep uprising and was alive; she had not flown out with the rescue party but had remained at Maitreya. Catherine and Michael had always assumed they were the only survivors of the expedition, and Catherine had difficulty adjusting to the thought that she still shared the same planet with Julienne. Certainly the Julienne who

242

survived was no one Catherine had ever really known. Any doubts on that score had died in New Guinea with Michael's tormented confessions.

Once during the flight to Australian New Guinea Catherine felt Kara's gaze on her, cold and curious, but when Catherine turned her head to face that intense stare, Kara had averted her eyes and looked straight ahead at the cockpit door that separated the cabin from the crew.

Their destination was the Moore coffee plantation just west of Port Moresby, which was Australian Papuan territory. The Moores were friends of Sir Charles. Catherine realized, under the circumstances, it would be awkward for her to accept their hospitality even for one night, so when the Dutchman mentioned that she must be anxious to contact her family and suggested that she might wish to continue on to Port Moresby that night with him and the Australian official, she accepted.

It was dusk by the time the plane landed on the lake near the rambling one-story structures of the Moore plantation. Papuan servants materialized quickly to greet them. There was no opportunity on the crowded dock to speak with Michael alone. The plane was readying to leave as soon as it could be refueled. Kara stood beside him. Catherine couldn't see his face in the gathering darkness as she told him she was going on to Port Moresby with the others. He did not object, but his voice sounded strained when he responded.

"I can imagine that you would want to notify your family as soon as possible. I'll see you in Port Moresby."

The rest of the flight took only one half hour. To Catherine's surprise, Sir Charles had radioed the American consulate of her arrival and the vice-consul met her at the dock. He was a young man just out of college, dressed in a white dinner jacket. The consul himself couldn't get away, he explained. "A diplomatic dinner." Not wanting to engage in conversation, Catherine did not respond. The vice-consul had no car so they walked the few blocks to the hotel. He offered her a cigarette. She declined with a shake of her head.

"We don't get bashes of this sort often," he added with regret, referring to the dinner he hadn't wanted to leave. "In fact, nothing exciting ever happens here. Just defense conferences. That's all they talk about these days."

The hotel was a simple two-story frame affair surrounded by a veranda. He deposited her in the room he had arranged and promised someone from the consulate would be around in the morning to help her arrange to get home.

"I can imagine you're in a hurry to get out of here," he said sympathetically.

When he left her, she was grateful to be away from curious eyes and the need to pretend she felt anything but exhausted, afraid, and alone. She leaned back against the cool metal frame of the bed's headboard and looked up at the bare light bulb that hung from the ceiling. After a year of only the dying embers from a cookfire to light the evening, the bulb's glare seemed harsh and uninviting.

"Michael," she whispered, closing her eyes. "What will happen to us now?"

His hand on his son's shoulder, Sir Charles guided him down the hall of the sprawling house toward the Moore's library. A white-coated Papuan houseboy waited to serve the two men a late supper alone in front of the fireplace, lit to take the chill off the cool mountain night.

"I just radioed Batavia," he said, "to tell Margit and Bernard of your rescue. Margit sends her love and Bernard is going to fly in to Port Moresby tomorrow." Sir Charles caught the unmistakable look of distaste on Michael's face. "I know you don't like Bernard, but he's efficient and effective in handling the press. For Catherine's sake as well as Kara's I think it would be best to keep as much of this out of the papers as we can. The news of the search has already been much publicized. When you arrive in Port Moresby, it's going to be a circus for reporters if we're not careful. Catherine shouldn't be there."

Sir Charles sat back, scarcely touching the food on the plate beside him, savoring instead the sight of his son after a year of thinking he might be dead.

The two men looked at each other in silence. The fire furnished the only light; the rest of the room lay in shadows. Michael waited expectantly; but his father remained silent, and finally Michael took the initiative.

"I imagine you brought me in here for some kind of family chat that somehow couldn't wait until morning."

Sir Charles smiled slightly. "All right, Michael. We're both tired and want some sleep, so I'll get on with it." He paused a moment. "It seems a silly question, but I don't know how else to begin. Are you involved with Catherine Morgan?"

Michael's gray eyes were suddenly remote. "I love her, if that's what you mean." He said nothing more, waiting for his father to continue.

"And what do you intend to do about it?"

Michael sighed as he leaned back in his chair and pushed aside the small table which held his plate.

"I want to spend the rest of my life with her." He paused and took a sip of wine before he added, "I want to marry her." He could see his father's face tighten.

"You know it means giving up your children, perhaps never seeing them again."

"Kara would never do that."

"Not at first perhaps. But she will go live with her family in Batavia if you divorce her. The Van Hootens are staunch Calvinists—completely opposed to divorce. They will see that you are cut off from your daughters and forbidden to visit them. Dutch, not British, authority rules the Indies, which will favor the Van Hootens. No British court will be able to help you."

Michael slowly drained his glass of wine and sat it down. He knew Sir Charles was right. Kara would oppose a divorce. Quite aside from any vindictive feelings her family might have, Kara herself might eventually feel bitter enough to deprive him of his children. Disturbed, he stared into the fire. It was not a new thought to him. From the beginning he had realized the high price he might have to pay. What troubled him even more was the price his daughters and Kara would have to pay. He loved his children, and he didn't want to hurt Kara. He closed his eyes briefly against the pain of that thought, then opened them.

"I can't imagine spending my life without Catherine," he said simply.

Sir Charles rose and gently put his hand upon his son's shoulder and then withdrew it.

"Don't let yourself be pressured into any sudden decisions, Michael, not even by me. Take your time about resolving this thing. After all, you've been away from Kara—and the world—for a year."

Michael still stared into the fire. Without turning he said, "It didn't begin in New Guinea, Dad. I've been in love with Catherine since I met her at Maitreya. I tried to stop it then and couldn't. I don't need time to know what my feelings are."

"Then take time to sort out what you intend to do about them."

Michael closed his eyes. It was just as he had expected. His father strongly opposed a divorce. Years before, faced with the same decision himself, Sir Charles had chosen duty and loyalty over love. No doubt he expected Michael to do the same.

Sir Charles continued, "I don't think it would be fair to either Kara or Catherine for you to make any commitment to Catherine until you've had time to think the whole thing through. You owe us that, Michael," Sir Charles added. "Especially Kara."

"And what do I owe Catherine?" Michael challenged him.

"You owe it to her not to make any promises you may not want to keep. If you don't interfere, Catherine will return to the States to complete her degree. She has a bright future in anthropology." The thought crossed Sir Charles's mind that perhaps he was asking his son to give up too much. He dismissed it. What he was doing was for Michael's own good. "Let her go, Michael. For now, at least."

Michael was silent.

"I think we'd both best get some sleep," his father said gently. It had been a painful conversation for them both.

Michael made no move to leave. He drank his glass of wine and poured another. He knew there were other factors involved in his father's objections besides the ones he had mentioned. The Church of England vehemently opposed divorce. Though his father hadn't brought it up, a divorce would cost Michael the crown's support if one of his British cousins should challenge his right to his father's title because of Michael's illegitimacy. Did it matter to him? No, but it mattered greatly to his father. A lump rose in his throat which the wine couldn't wash away. His only escape from the demands of those who loved him was to hurt them deeply and irrevocably.

His father, seeing the look on his face, put a sympathetic hand on his shoulder. "I'm sorry, Michael," he said quietly. "Perhaps you wish we'd never found you."

Tears suddenly reddened Michael's eyes. He didn't care if his father saw them. He thought of the lake. It was hard to believe that only that morning he had been there, free and happy. He didn't acknowledge his father's attempt to comfort him.

Sensing Michael's rejection of him, Sir Charles reluctantly withdrew his hand. Until this moment, he had hesitated to mention the only respectable solution to such matters, taking a mistress. He had even convinced himself that an independent, career-minded woman like Catherine might even prefer the free, financially secure existence such an arrangement could provide. Kara would even accept it if she recognized the alternative.

"No one is asking you to give Catherine up entirely, Michael," Sir Charles said finally. "Only that you not marry—"

"Don't!" Michael interrupted sharply and raised his hand in a warning for his father not to go any further.

Sir Charles broke off and the two men looked at each other for a long moment without speaking. Finally Michael put down his unfinished glass.

"I think I'll turn in," he said matter-of-factly. Halfway across the room, he turned back to Sir Charles. "It doesn't really matter what I decide. I understand there's a war on. One way or another I'll soon be a part of it and who knows what will happen then." Without waiting for his father to respond, he left the room, leaving Sir Charles with the sad realization that for the first time there was an air of estrangement between them.

Chapter 24

Catherine sat alone in her Port Moresby hotel room, waiting for Bernard, the remnants of her uneaten lunch growing cold. Her eyes bore black mourning bands from lack of sleep the past two nights. The room contained no belongings of hers except the notebooks she had somehow thought to salvage in the suddenness of their rescue two days ago. The notes had been packed unceremoniously in a brown paper bag given her by the hotel proprietor. The clothes she wore were borrowed, as were her other meager belongings. She felt as if everyone were trying to impress upon her the fact that she possessed nothing here, especially not Michael. He had been on loan like all the rest.

Except for two visits to the American Consulate and dinner downstairs last night she had spent the time in Port Moresby by herself. She felt like a prisoner found guilty of high treason, waiting for the sentence to be delivered after lunch by the appointed family executioner, Bernard. She wasn't sure what her sentence would be, but it was clear to her, from her brief meeting with Bernard last night at dinner, that the Stanfords felt themselves under attack. She managed a feeble smile at the thought of herself as a formidable enemy. She felt anything but formidable right now. God, how she loved him.

Bernard, at that moment, was making his way down the narrow corridor to her room. He was impeccably dressed in white suit and white shoes and was out of breath from the steps, the heat, and the anticipation of his visit. Bernard had been a handsome man when Margit married him. Though some of his looks remained, his fine features now appeared to sag slightly. An unhealthy, ruddy hue lit his naturally fair face, giving him the air of a corpse, faintly bloated. He wasn't an alcoholic, but he drank too much gin, and it had begun to show.

When Bernard married Margit, he had thought he was simply marrying wealth and status, undeniable assets to an ambitious and promising young colonial civil servant. How was he to know he would one day be getting a political radical for a brother-in-law? Michael had been only a schoolboy at the time. Bernard wrinkled his nose in distaste at the thought of Margit's brother. Who but Michael would turn up marooned in the desolation of New Guinea with a beautiful American woman? Bernard's brow broke out in a sweat. The newspapers would have a field day if they got wind of this. My God. Just to think that a reporter from *Life* magazine had been given permission to go along with the rescue party but had canceled out at the last minute.

As he thought about his predicament, Bernard's irritation with Catherine Morgan grew, as if she had deliberately survived the Asmat massacre in order to cause him discomfort. It was a reflection of his narcissism that he thought even the forces of nature were conspiring to make him unhappy. He arrived at Catherine's room and paused at the door before knocking, to wipe his brow and prepare himself. In his brief encounter with her the night before, he found Catherine to be an uppity, even arrogant little . . . He rapped on the door, and she immediately opened it, breaking off his thoughts. Without speaking she stepped aside and allowed him to enter. He noted the circles under her eyes, then glanced around at the simply furnished room.

"I hope you slept well," he said with faintly disguised sarcasm. He didn't wait for a reply but walked to the window and turned back to face the room.

"Sir Charles has purchased a ticket for you on the Pan American China Clipper flying from Singapore to San Francisco. You can catch it when it refuels at Manila. There's a flight from Port Moresby to Manila tomorrow morning by way of Darwin."

She took a deep breath. "That's a little soon, isn't it? Besides, I can pay my own way back as soon as the American Consulate makes the arrangements."

"It must be soon. It would be unfortunate for everyone, including you, should the newspapers get the story."

"But Sir Charles said Michael would be coming back to hold a press conference."

"Those plans have been changed. I've arranged, instead, for the Dutch consul to announce the rescue and provide details which will make no mention of you. Michael's absence at the conference will be explained as exhaustion and a need for medical observation. Needless to say, we want no hint of anything that might lead to scandal."

Catherine stood up from the edge of the bed where she had been sitting and strode slowly over to Bernard. "I don't plan to leave so soon. Certainly not before I talk to Michael and learn about his plans."

"Michael will be going into military service almost immediately."

Catherine looked at Bernard in stunned surprise. She had known England was at war, but somehow she had never expected Michael to get involved in it. Until this moment the war had seemed unreal.

"Surely you didn't think otherwise, Miss Morgan. After all, England is fighting for survival, and Europe has fallen to the Nazis while you Americans are sitting on your hands." He paused and studied her. "I don't like Americans very much, Miss Morgan. To quote your own Melville, I find you 'intrepid, unprincipled, reckless, predatory, with boundless ambition, civilized in externals but savages at heart.' Tell me, Miss Morgan, do you find any of those traits to be characteristic of yourself?" Earlier he had felt her underlying contempt for him, and now he relished this opportunity to put her in her place.

"What service . . . where?" she asked.

"Well, it will hardly be the Dutch military now, will it? The British Navy, no doubt. The Stanfords have been Navy since the times of Admiral Nelson. Sir Charles himself has accepted a commission into the Royal Navy. He served as a naval officer during World War One. No doubt Michael will choose the Navy as well."

Catherine had recovered herself enough to retort, "It really doesn't matter. Michael and I have things to discuss, and I'll wait until I can talk to him."

"As a matter of fact, he'll be in Port Moresby late this afternoon, at the hotel. He asked me to tell you that he'll speak with you before you go."

"He knows I'm leaving?"

Bernard nodded.

The affirmation struck her a blow. "How come he knows when I don't?" she asked with annoyance. Then a spark of malice flashed in her eyes. "What will the Stanfords pay me, Bernard, not to talk, not to blow this whole thing? What am I supposed to get out of this?"

He remained unperturbed. "It's in your best interest as well as ours to keep this thing quiet. What you get out of it is your reputation intact."

"So I can still, for the record, call myself a virgin? How considerate of all of you."

"Your virginity or lack thereof doesn't interest me in the least, Miss Morgan."

"But you know us women, Bernard. We're not always rational. Suppose I decide that revenge is more important than my reputation?"

"You're not the type," he said coldly.

He took out the airline ticket and an exit visa, put them on the dresser, and started to walk out.

"I won't go until I've talked to Michael!" she cried. "Until I've heard it from him that he wants me to go. I don't care what I hear from you or Sir Charles or anybody else!"

He opened the door and turned back to her. "Then, my dear lady, your wish is granted. That's exactly what you will hear." He closed the door behind him.

"Damn!" Tears she had fought to keep from Bernard sprang to her eyes. "Damn!"

She sat staring at the door. So, she thought bitterly, the sentence had been delivered. The punishment was exile. But it couldn't all be over. It simply couldn't. Not something that felt so natural, so right. How could he love her and still leave her?

Bernard bought a newspaper in the lobby of the hotel, pausing to take out his cigarette holder and carefully load it with his favorite Javanese tobacco. Then he left the hotel and stepped into the chauffeured car that waited for him at the entrance. He settled back into his seat and smartly snapped the newspaper open, puffing with satisfaction. Ominous war news occupied most of the front page. Suddenly the cigarette holder dangled loosely from his slack jaw as he uttered an obscenity. There, in a little bulletin on the front page, was the headline FAMED ANTHROPOLOGIST SON OF SIR CHARLES STANFORD RESCUED FROM NEW GUINEA.

"Christ," Bernard muttered as he anxiously skimmed the article. ". . . missing one year, feared dead in the Asmat uprising. . . . Also rescued with Dr. Stanford was another member of the ill-fated expedition, Catherine Morgan, an American graduate student from Columbia University, which had cosponsored the expedition."

His hand began to shake. Well, it was out. He might as well have saved himself the trip. Who could have leaked the story? Probably one of the native secretaries in the British Consulate in Batavia. Bribable—all of them. The wire service would have the story next. The family could only refuse all interviews and pray it all died down. Meanwhile, it was absolutely imperative to get rid of the Morgan woman.

He pulled out a handkerchief and dabbed at his brow. "Jesus, what a mess," he muttered. For once he was grateful for the war. That news would continue to grab the headlines.

When Catherine read the same article later, she felt a stab of misgiving. She had shared Bernard's hope the news would not reach the papers. As soon as she had reached Port Moresby, she had cabled her parents. Wanting to spare them the shock of knowing that their only child had been found marooned alone for a year with a married man, she had mentioned nothing about Michael being with her. Her parents had reacted with a return cable expressing their joy and demanding that she return home to Chicago and a safe, respectable life which would, of course, mean marriage to a nice bachelor like David. Now there was this embarrassment of a public announcement describing the circumstances of her survival. The article appeared as a small boxed bulletin just below the news that British civilian casualties for the month of October 1940, as a result of the German bombing, were 6,334 killed and 8,695 injured. Next to it was a statement by Roosevelt, campaigning for a third term. "I've said this before, but I shall say it again and again and again: Your boys are not going to be sent into any foreign wars."

* * *

Catherine had not waited at the hotel for the Stanfords to arrive. She went for a walk along Port Moresby's deserted beaches wearing the loose, ankle-length Maori dress the wife of the hotel proprietor had obtained on a New Zealand vacation. It was the only thing that ample lady owned that would fit. She had no shoes, but in Papua's casual atmosphere, it didn't matter. She walked for hours until the sun had set and her anger was gone. No message was waiting for her at the hotel desk when she returned, though she was told that all three Stanfords had checked in several hours earlier.

She paused at the door of her room. It wasn't locked. She had nothing to steal. She wanted him to be there, waiting for her when she opened the door, but he wasn't. She felt faintly disappointed but not surprised. He would not come to spend the night with her. Not with Kara in the hotel. But she was just as certain that he would not be with Kara either. She went back to the desk and was told by the Papuan desk clerk that "young Tuan Stanford" had taken a room by himself at the end of the hall. She retraced her steps to the second floor. There was a faint bar of light beneath his door. She placed her hand on the knob, then hesitated, no longer certain that she would not find Kara there with him. New doubts assailed her. Even if he were alone he might not want to see her. In her mind, these past few days, he had become a stranger whose moods and actions she could no longer predict. She took a deep breath and opened the door. He was lying on the bed wearing just a pair of khaki pants, his hands clasped behind his head. He didn't speak as she crossed the room and stood beside the bed, but his eyes were full of pain. She knew without being told that his family had won. He reached up and quickly pulled the dress over her head then hungrily pulled her down to him, pressing her mouth and body fiercely to his.

In the next room Kara lay awake. She had gone to bed early. There was nothing else to do. At least she and Michael had a wall in common, Kara thought ruefully. She imagined she heard the door to his room open and, after a pause, snap lightly closed. He had said he would not go to Catherine, and she had believed him. Why hadn't it occurred to her that Catherine would come to him? Because she, Kara, couldn't? Had she really expected him to reject Catherine under the circumstances? Yes. She had.

She heard the slight creak of the bed as it groaned in protest at a sudden added weight. Kara's heart skipped a beat. No. She had not imagined that this would happen at all. She began to tremble and wanted to flee, but she couldn't move. Her breathing became shallow as she listened to the sounds beyond the wall. Whispers— soft, then more urgent. The sound became more rhythmical.

Kara, eyes wide open, stared at the ceiling, trapped in a waking nightmare. Why didn't she get up and go in and stop it? Create a scene as the wronged wife? The sound of gently rocking springs stopped suddenly, to be replaced by human noises muffled by pillows or a lover's body. Their meaning was so clear they made Kara's pale face blush. The sounds were followed by whispering, which finally ceased. She could imagine their bodies, entwined and sated. She lay staring at the ceiling. She wanted to cry but couldn't. Nor would she sleep.

The ride to the Port Moresby airfield had been the most painful experience of all. The American Consulate had sent a car for Catherine, a large old Packard complete with driver. Michael had joined her. She hadn't been expecting him; he had simply appeared in the hotel lobby as she was ready to leave. She was wearing a simple sun dress bought for her that morning by the wife of the American consul. To deal with the muggy heat, she had piled her long black hair carelessly up on her head in an appealing but disorganized manner. Seeing her alone in the lobby, Michael noted that the hairstyle appeared both defiant and touchingly vulnerable, like its wearer. Without a word he had taken her firmly by the elbow, guided her to the waiting car, and climbed in beside her, leaving a frustrated Bernard, who had been waiting outside as escort, to find his own transportation.

"I wanted to tell you that I'm going to join the United States Navy, and last night didn't seem the time to do it."

She stared straight ahead and didn't respond.

He continued. "I'll be sent to the West Coast for officers' training and then to Corpus Christi." Upon induction, experienced seaplane pilots like himself were being given special reserve commissions and only limited flight instruction before being assigned to a squadron. He took a folded piece of paper from his shirt pocket. "Here's where you can reach me."

She opened and read it, then refolded it without comment. It was a naval fleet address, a central posting office where mail for the naval military was sorted and routed. So, she thought bitterly, this was as personal as they were going to get. What a perfect way to dodge bill collectors and old girl friends.

As if reading her thoughts, he apologized. "I can't be more specific. I don't know where I'll be stationed, but even if I did, all military mail is handled this way for security reasons."

She still said nothing, nor did she look at him. Worried by her reaction but unsure of how much he should say about it, he turned silently to the window, staring at the passing streets but seeing nothing. The presence of the driver made talking difficult. Catherine glanced briefly at Michael, who was apparently absorbed in the passing scene. He was wearing white cotton pants, crisply creased new canvas deck shoes without shocks, and a cotton navy knit shirt. He had been to the barbershop that morning, and his hair was shorter than she liked it, but there was no denying he looked tanned and trim and handsome. Suddenly he seemed like a stranger. She wondered why he had bothered to come at all. As if to make sure he was really there, she reached out and laid a hand on his leg, running her fingers lightly down the crease in his pants. She resented that crease. Suddenly he was neat and tidy, with everything perfectly in place, including her. She flattened her palm against his leg and felt his thigh muscle tighten, but he didn't look at her. She slipped her hand to his groin and felt his body respond; there was no love in her gesture, only anger, and he knew it.

He did not attempt to remove her hand. She knew he would not stop her from doing as she pleased, but his eyes, now turned to hers, pleaded with her to stop. She moved away and turned her attention to the view outside the car.

"I wish you hadn't come," she said abruptly, still facing the window.

"I realize now I shouldn't have. I'm sorry." He sounded contrite and unhappy.

Suddenly she was afraid she was going to cry. So far she hadn't, and she didn't want to, especially now, in front of Michael. With relief she realized they had reached the airfield as the car turned into the dirt road and bounced toward the small one-room hut that served as a terminal. The American consul and his wife had come to see her off. When they saw Michael outside the hotel, they had discreetly arranged to travel in a separate car.

Bernard arrived shortly, peering nervously around for any sign of photographers or the press as he climbed out of the taxi. No one appeared to be there except other passengers and people who had come to see them off.

Relieved but still anxious, Bernard entered the small terminal to present Catherine's ticket and check her name on the passenger list. Not trusting anyone else, he had personally made all the arrangements. Finished with the ticket, he went to the door and glowered at the sight of Michael and Catherine talking outside with the American consul and his wife. Silently he cursed Michael for coming along. Bernard stood watching the two of them as the copilot crossed from the waiting plane to tell the assembled passengers they could now board. Alarmed, Bernard saw Michael start to draw Catherine aside.

Catherine looked at Michael, knowing she might never see him again. How could she give him up? How could she survive, much less enjoy life without him? Quickly she pulled herself together. She had managed without him before, and she certainly could again. He was holding her, struggling to tell her something. Suddenly he buried his face against her hair.

"I love you," he whispered, "more than anything on earth. I'll always love you. No one else. No matter what happens, please don't forget."

She pulled back and searched his eyes. Like her own, they brimmed full of tears, which he tried unsuccessfully to blink away. Finally his lips parted and slowly came down to touch hers. The touch was electrifying. Her arms encircled his neck as the world swam dizzily away and only Michael remained. She was only dimly aware that Bernard had arrived to rescue the family honor and had been shoved angrily aside by Michael. Somehow his mouth never left hers; his kiss, like hers, had only grown more urgent until finally they were clinging desperately to each other, trying to shut out the world, not just one last time, but for good.

Suddenly Michael stepped back or was pulled away from her, she wasn't sure which. She was too busy struggling to steady herself. The propellers on the plane had begun to turn. Only well-wishers and the ever-present native onlookers remained on the field; the other passengers were already on board. The door stood open, waiting for her. She wanted it to close now, quickly, and the plane to leave without her. And yet, as though in a bad dream, she found herself moving numbly toward the plane and its open door, climbing the steps, entering to take her seat by the window. With each step she expected Michael to come after her, but instead, it was the copilot behind her, slamming the door closed and bolting it.

The plane swung slowly around to taxi toward the single runway. She saw him standing with the American consul and his wife, looking drawn. She had an urge to run to the door, throw it open, and jump out. Surely this wasn't happening; surely she would wake up and be back at the lake beneath the mountains of the Snow. The plane began to gather speed, and then with a sudden lurch it left the ground. She felt the thud of the landing gears retracting beneath her. Slowly she reached up and clasped Tukum's somewhat bedraggled packet of seeds around her neck.

Michael stood on the ground watching the plane quickly disappear from view. He felt his throat constrict, but his eyes were now dry. He stood alone, staring after the plane long after it and the other bystanders had disappeared. She had not loved him enough to accept his terms. Nor could he accept hers. And on that bittersweet note it had ended.

Part Two

Wasted Hope and Sure Defeat

. . . saved for another day
Saved for hunger and wounds and heat
For slow exhaustion and grim retreat
For a wasted hope and sure defeat. . . .

Lieutenant Henry G. Lee, Philippine Division,
United States Army, Bataan, 1942

Chapter 25
Connecticut, June 1941

Catherine felt waves of pain wash over her. She thrashed about as she struggled to control it, but the pain seemed to swell, carrying her helplessly along with it. At the point where she felt she could no longer stand it, it suddenly subsided, leaving her bathed in perspiration.

"You let that one get away from you."

Through a wet blur she could see Tom, Ginny's twin brother, bending over her, his red hair slightly mussed, his pleasant freckled face full of concentration. One of his hands rested on her bare, swollen belly, his touch cool and gentle, while the other hand was held up so that he could time her contractions.

"They're getting close together now. You'll have to concentrate more to stay on top of them."

His hand detected the muscles of the uterus starting to tighten in a contraction even before Catherine felt the pain.

"Contraction's beginning."

It was her signal to clear her lungs, breathe deeply, and then pant in rapid, shallow breaths in an effort to control the pain. Catherine had trained in this method of natural childbirth, although she suspected its primary usefulness was to distract her from the pain and give her something to do so she wouldn't feel helpless. Nevertheless, it seemed to help—or at least it had for those first ten hours of labor.

"Come on, Catherine. Pant!"

As she grew more exhausted, Tom took increasing control: reminding, cajoling, and finally ordering her to respond. She seemed to float in a state of semiconsciousness between spasms of pain while her body struggled mindlessly to obey his commands. It had been a much more difficult labor than anyone had anticipated. Now she wanted only to crawl off into a corner and die, anything to be rid of the pain, but Tom's authoritative voice kept pulling her back. His will took over where hers had ceased to exist.

Now the perspiration stood out on his forehead as well. It was the only manifestation of the anxiety he felt. As her concentration weakened and he felt her consciousness slipping away, he grew increasingly alarmed. He silently cursed their isolation and her refusal to have a doctor in attendance.

It was eleven o'clock at night. It had been fourteen hours of labor now. Where the hell was Ginny anyway? he thought angrily. His twin sister should have been back from New York hours ago. She must have missed the early train. The baby hadn't been due for another two weeks, so Ginny had taken her twin boys and gone in to New York for the day to do some shopping. Tom was spending the weekend on the farm in Connecticut, as he often did, especially since Catherine had returned from New Guinea. He was in his last year of teaching at the Naval Academy in Annapolis. This summer he would return to sea duty.

He felt the knot of muscle loosen beneath his fingers. "Relax," he told her. "Contraction's over."

The hardness of that muscle at full contraction astounded him. To occupy itself, his engineer's mind attempted to estimate the pounds of force involved. It amazed him that her body could keep exerting that force for all these hours, but he began to fear something was going wrong. He had no sterile way to measure the amount of dilation of the cervix that had taken place so far, so he could not tell if things were proceeding normally. He only knew the delivery was taking much too long. He sat beside her, waiting for the next contraction to signal its beginning. He saw, rather than felt, that his hand holding the watch had begun to tremble slightly.

There was no phone, no way to call for a doctor, and he didn't dare leave Catherine. He took hope from the fact that her water had broken the hour before. The contractions, though still close together, were becoming more erratic. He could no longer anticipate them by looking at his watch and was forced to concentrate in order to feel them begin. Catherine still struggled weakly to comply with his commands, but she was giving in to the pain more each time. He struggled to control his feelings as he realized that they both were nearing the limits of their endurance.

Between contractions Catherine floated mercifully off into a state of semiconsciousness. It had been five months since she had come to live with Ginny on the farm in Connecticut. She had remained at Columbia University just long enough to form her dissertation committee and get her work under way before leaving the campus, pleading a teaching engagement in Connecticut as the reason. During her isolation she had finished her doctoral thesis, mailed it off to her committee, and had begun preparing an expanded manuscript version for publication.

When Catherine showed up on her doorstep, pregnant, Ginny had wailed in disbelief. "Certainly you aren't the first anthropologist to have an affair on a field trip but, honest to God, Catherine—pregnant? And no abortion? Have you lost your mind!"

She had been even more aghast when Catherine announced she planned to keep the baby and intended to deliver it herself—free of medical assistance—with Ginny's help. After heated discussions Ginny had finally relented, and Tom, too, had joined in learning the techniques so that he could assist, if needed. It had been a good thing. This Saturday morning, just after Ginny and the children had left for New York, he and Catherine had gone for a walk to the old covered bridge. It was then that the contractions had suddenly begun.

Tom felt a change beneath his hand. The contractions seemed even harder, and they were regular once again. He sensed the time had come. Catherine was hardly aware that he was propping her up on pillows, elevating her into a semisitting position. He bent her knees and forced her legs apart. When he told her to push, she found herself bearing down with whatever strength she could muster until his hand on her belly signaled the contraction was over.

She drifted off again until Tom's voice intruded. "Bear down, Catherine."

The order was followed by a pain that left her gasping.

"Great . . . push . . . push . . . It's coming. I can see the head. Keep pushing!" His voice was jubilant.

Catherine's attention now turned fully to the task at hand. Straining, she bore down until the blood vessels in her temples seemed in danger of bursting.

"It's coming, Catherine. The head is out."

She scarcely felt the contractions now. She pushed until the baby slid easily out onto the waiting sheet.

"It's a boy, Cat!"

She closed her eyes and relaxed for a moment against the pillows. The contractions continued, only milder, and Tom pushed firmly on her belly, helping the exhausted uterine muscles deliver the placenta into a waiting basin.

"It's over, Catherine." He looked at her anxiously as she sank back against the pillows. Her face was white, and her dark eyes seemed enormous. Tom proceeded to tie off the umbilical cord and place the baby next to her. The baby was pink and fat, but he hadn't cried at all. Yet his breathing seemed perfectly normal.

"Is he all right?" she managed to whisper anxiously.

"Perfect," Tom replied with a smile, and kissed her on the forehead. "Like his mother." She didn't hear him. She had slipped into an exhausted sleep.

Catherine named the baby Michael Charles, after his father and grandfather. The following weekend Tom came up a day early to help Catherine with the baby while Ginny was away teaching high school history. Catherine and Tom went out on the porch in the warm late-spring afternoon air while the baby slept. Tom sat on the swing, studying Catherine over his glass of beer. She sat in the rocker beside the swing, dressed in a bright print wrapper, wearing bedroom slippers. She looked serene and healthy after her ordeal. In fact, she positively glowed.

"Look, Cat," Tom said to her finally, "don't you think you ought to tell Michael about his son? It hardly seems fair not even to let him know you were pregnant."

"No!" she replied sharply. Her serenity evaporated. She left the rocker and strode to the porch railing to stare out at the woods crowded with oaks and maples. "I don't want to discuss it again. Michael has made his choice. I don't want the existence of a baby to influence his decision. I can survive without him, and so can my child."

Tom sighed. He thought she was being stubborn and foolish, but he had done all he could. He didn't know Michael Stanford, but he knew Catherine well enough not to doubt that Michael must love her as much as she loved him. It seemed such a shame. . . . He dropped the subject.

"So what are your plans, Cat?"

"I'll be moving to New York in two weeks to teach a class in introductory anthropology at Columbia during the summer session. Will you be able to help me move?"

"Of course."

"I want you and Ginny to come celebrate my final doctoral oral committee meeting to defend my dissertation. It's just a formality, but it will mean I'm finally Dr. Morgan."

"We'll be there, waiting outside the door with champagne and dinner reservations at Twenty-one."

She smiled. "You're so bourgeois."

"What else could you expect from a rising young naval officer who's sure to make admiral, provided he avoids Bolsheviks like Catherine Morgan?"

She laughed. His lack of political views had irritated her when she first met Tom several years before. It no longer did.

Michael began to cry in the bedroom next to the porch.

"I'll get him," Tom said, and rose to enter the house. He returned with the baby and stood admiring him for a moment before handing him to Catherine. Tom returned to the swing, and Michael began to cry again.

"He's hungry," Catherine said, starting toward the bedroom.

"Where are you going?"

She looked at him in surprise. "To feed him."

He laughed. "Do you really think that's necessary, Catherine, after all we've been through together recently? I've certainly seen everything there is to see of you."

She blushed slightly. "That was different." But she didn't leave. Instead, she sat down beside him on the swing and, having opened her wrapper, placed Michael at her breast, enjoying the sensation of Michael's small mouth firmly at work.

Tom watched the two of them. He knew Catherine liked him, perhaps even loved him as a friend. But there was no doubt that she meant more than that to him. When they had met four years ago, he had realized that neither of them was ready for a commitment.

But just before the baby came, he had told her, "If you decide you want a father for that little one, I'm volunteering." He had said it jokingly but they both had known he meant it. It was the closest he had come to telling her how he felt. But she was still in love with Michael, and he knew now was not the time to say more.

He put his hand on her shoulder and touched his fingers softly against her cheek. She kissed them and pressed her cheek against his hand. She grew thoughtful.

"It's been more than a year and a half since Carl's death. Ginny should be seeing other men. She's too isolated here on this farm."

"Perhaps that will change when she no longer has you and me to rely on for company."

"You?" She looked at him quizzically.

"The spring semester at the academy is almost over. My orders came through two days ago. I've been assigned to the heavy cruiser *Houston*."

"Where is it?"

"Asiatic Fleet, the Philippines."

She touched her cheek to his hand again. "I'll miss you."

He nodded without replying, watching the baby. Swollen with milk since the baby's birth, Catherine's breasts had become so transparent that light blue traces of veins showed beneath the surface. He idly took his hand from her shoulder and lightly traced the outline of one blue vein. It was not a sensuous gesture, nor did he intend it to be, but as he pulled his hand away from her breast, Michael, finally sated, released it, revealing the nipple, wet and swollen and suddenly very provocative.

Tom felt a catch in his throat and looked away from her out into the trees. It was early June, about to become summer officially, and the leaves were newly green. For the past two years of teaching at the academy he had been chafing to return to line duty at sea. Now that had changed.

"I'll miss you, too," he said softly. The ache in his throat spread to his loins, and he did not look at her.

The postman arrived in his Model T. It idled in staccato as he stuffed the mail into the big box by the road. While Tom walked out to retrieve it, Catherine took the baby inside for a nap and then returned to the swing. There was a letter from her mother.

Catherine dreaded opening it, knowing it would be full of her mother's hurt feelings and complaints. Since her return to the States, Catherine had resisted her parents' entreaties to come home, pleading the need to get to work immediately on her dissertation. Sensing in their anxious questions their inability to accept the truth about her relationship with Michael, she had succumbed to their need to be deceived. In her evasive answers they found the reassurance they needed that nothing had existed between Michael and herself. Finding the deception easier to maintain by phone than in person, she had not gone home. Then, when she found out she was pregnant, she could not face them. By now, her refusal to see them was creating a growing rift she felt powerless to stop.

"God," she said, feeling guilty and exasperated as she lowered the open letter to her lap, having only glanced through it. "I wish I had just told them everything the minute I got back." She handed the letter to Tom.

He read it in silence and then gave it to her. "Why not tell them now?" he suggested gently. "Better they know the truth than feel you're rejecting them."

She folded the letter and stared out at the garden. "I wish that were true," she said sadly. "But it isn't."

Chapter 26
New York, November 1941

Catherine never bothered reading the society page of the *Times*, but that morning she had lingered over her cup of coffee, reluctant to get to work proofreading the final draft of her book. The late-morning sun depressed her. Perhaps the pale November light reminded her that a year ago she had said good-bye to Michael. She had been a month pregnant at the time but had not realized it until her return.

She glanced briefly at the picture in the paper: military uniforms and cocktail dresses in a reception line, a common enough sight these days. She did not examine them, but the caption leaped out at her. "Sir Charles Stanford, Admiral HMRN, was the honored guest of a reception given by the British Consulate in New York. Sir Charles has been in Washington, D.C., helping coordinate British and American military efforts in the Pacific."

Without debating for a moment she went straight to the phone and called the British Consulate. Sir Charles, she was told, was still in New York but was not available at the moment. Could they have him call her? She left her number and then spent the day nervously pacing the floor, wanting the phone to ring, yet afraid that it would. It did. Several times. But it wasn't Sir Charles. Not until three o'clock.

"Catherine?" The familiar British accent cheerfully inquired. "What a pleasant surprise to hear from you. Have you finished your work?"

"Yes. Two months ago."

"Congratulations. You must send me a copy of your dissertation."

"One of the New York firms is going to publish an expanded version in book form. I'll send you a copy."

"Wonderful."

There was an awkward pause. Catherine struggled to summon her courage, then said, "I want you to come by my apartment today. I've got something to show you." She sounded surprisingly confident. "It's important."

Now he was completely mystified. He debated asking her what the surprise was but decided against it. He sensed the hidden strain in her voice and knew she was poised for flight. He strove to reassure her.

"Of course I'll come by. I have some engagements this afternoon that I can cancel. Would four o'clock be all right?"

"Fine."

"Perhaps we can go out for dinner later."

"No. I'd prefer to invite you over for dinner here."

"It's not too much trouble?"

"No trouble at all." She gave him her address. When she hung up, her hand was shaking.

"Well, Michael," she said to the baby playing on the floor, "you're about to meet your grandfather."

Sir Charles arrived promptly at four o'clock. When Catherine opened the door, he took off his gold-braided naval cap and entered, looking splendid in his blue uniform. He smiled, put his hat on the table, and took the hand she offered him between both his own.

"You're looking as beautiful as ever, Catherine. I'm delighted to see you, but puzzled, I must admit. You were rather mysterious on the phone, you know."

He glanced around the room, and his eyes fell on Michael, sitting on the floor with a wooden building block in each hand, his bright blond hair already thick and tousled around his face. His gray eyes, curious and somehow serious, were trained upon the visitor, whose clothes bore all sorts of fascinating gold objects and colorful ribbons.

The color drained from Sir Charles's tanned face. He could not tear his eyes away from the stunning image of his son that was stamped so unmistakably on those baby features. Sir Charles did not even ask for verification of what he already knew. He crossed over and bent down beside the baby. His voice was husky.

"What a fine boy you are." He held out his hand and slowly touched the top of Michael's head. "I'm your grandfather, you know."

Tears of relief came to Catherine's eyes, and she let them run, unashamed, down her cheeks.

"What's his name?" Sir Charles asked without taking his eyes from his grandson.

"Michael Charles Morgan," Catherine replied.

It was Sir Charles's turn to feel tears come to his eyes. He quickly brushed them away. He held out his arms.

"Come on, young fellow. Come to your grandfather."

Michael dropped the blocks and held his plump baby arms out in response to the impressive stranger. Sir Charles scooped him up and rose, opening his free arm to Catherine. He gathered them both close to him in a hug. Catherine closed her eyes and embraced him while Michael gurgled happily. If she still harbored any doubts about the wisdom of contacting Sir Charles, they had disappeared.

After a moment Sir Charles spoke, his voice deep with feeling. "Well, well. This has been quite a surprise you've given me, Catherine. Perhaps I should object to not being let in on this sooner, but I won't spoil this happy occasion by bringing that up now."

He sat down on the couch and pulled Catherine down next to him. They played with Michael until he grew tired. Sir Charles helped Catherine put the baby to bed. When she went to the kitchen to fix him a drink and prepare dinner, Sir Charles followed her, watching her carefully as she moved about the kitchen.

"Why didn't you tell Michael, Catherine?"

She shrugged her slim shoulders, not looking at him. "I felt he had already made his choice. I didn't want to influence him differently."

"Are you sure? Or were you angry with him?"

She glanced sharply at him. "It doesn't matter now what my motives were."

He sighed. "Forgive me, Catherine, for whatever part I played in hurting you so deeply."

She looked at him calmly. "I hold no grudge toward you. Michael is a grown man, responsible for his own choices. No one forced him."

"Perhaps . . . at least not directly."

He stood quietly for a moment, watching her work. "You must tell Michael, Catherine. I insist."

"All right!" she cried, and turned to him with tears in her eyes. "But in my own time and in my own way!"

"He's my son, Catherine. If you don't tell him, I will. He deserves to know. You should be thinking of what's best for the boy and give Michael a chance to do the same."

She turned her back to him and began to work in the sink, but Sir Charles came over and put his hands on her shoulders. "You aren't the baby's only family. Regardless of how Michael feels, the boy belongs to us as well, to the Stanfords. You need us. Especially if your own family can't accept you or the child. And they can't, can they, Catherine?" He felt her shoulders stiffen, and he knew the answer.

"It doesn't matter. I can take care of us both. Quite nicely. I don't need anything from any of you."

"The speech isn't necessary, Catherine. I never thought for a moment you couldn't manage on your own." He released her and stood back. "I want you to return to Indonesia with me for the holidays. Not to Maitreya, of course. To Batavia. You can stay with Michael's sister Margit. Michael will be on leave from the Philippines before Christmas. I'll personally see to it that he is. The two of you can discuss things then."

"No!" Catherine replied. "That's not necessary. We can discuss everything by mail."

"Michael will want to see his son."

"Then he can come here," she protested.

"He won't have leave to return to the States until his tour of duty in the Philippines is up two years from now. Some think there may be war by then, so there may not be another opportunity for a very long time."

"I have commitments here. I can't leave New York. I have a teaching job beginning in the second term," she protested.

271

"It need only be for the Christmas holidays. You can return in January if you wish."

"I have to proofread my manuscript," she countered. "I have a mid-November deadline from my publisher."

"Take two weeks to make the arrangements and finish your work. I'll delay my return by two weeks and remain here to help you. I can do some military business to justify the additional time."

She hesitated.

"Come now, Catherine. You've no excuse left, except perhaps the real one—that you're reluctant to face Michael. Isn't that it?"

She didn't answer. He pressed her. "What is it you're so afraid of?"

She wasn't sure. She only knew she felt vulnerable, and, yes, afraid to face Michael. Her Irish Catholic soul still saw her as the sinful other woman who had seduced an unwilling Michael and should now pay the price of that sin alone.

"You won't even have to see Michael while you're there if you don't wish to. I'll arrange for him to see his son without you. I'll take care of everything. You can simply view it as a nice vacation." His smile suddenly faded. "But Michael must be allowed to see his son, Catherine. When I think of those years when he was young and I didn't even know of his existence—I don't want Michael to have the same regrets I've lived with all these years."

"Maybe I don't care anymore about Michael's regrets," Catherine replied, and then gave a reluctant sigh. "All right. I'll go, but I can't promise I'll see Michael."

Sir Charles was as good as his word. He moved into the apartment with Catherine and took over the chores, freeing her to finish her book and prepare for the trip. He fed, bathed, and diapered Michael, took him for walks in his pram, did the marketing, prepared the meals, and cleaned the house, and Catherine came to adore him as the kind of father she had always longed for, which, he confessed when she told him, was what he had had in mind. He was a delightful companion as well, cheering her up with endless and often amusing stories of his adventurous explorations of other cultures.

When she wanted to use Michael's drawings of the Dani for her book but could not contact him for permission in time for publication, he counseled her, "Use them." Then he added with a twinkle, "If he objects, I'll disinherit him."

So Michael received credit for the illustrations and a fee as well. Sir Charles accepted the check from the publisher on his behalf. Catherine dedicated the book to the Dani people: Tukum, Degewatek, and all the rest. She decided on the title *War and Death in Paradise: Ritual Warfare in the Dani Culture of New Guinea*. Finally she opened the book with a prologue Degewatek had composed and sung at Tukum's funeral.

> The ghost is restless.
> It returns to torment our souls
> Until we avenge its death
> And it can rest with Nopu
> In the spirit world.
>
> We leave offerings of food
> For it to feed on,
> And offerings of love
> To ease the hungers of the heart.
>
> Leave us in peace now, ghost!
> You must begin your journey to the land of Nopu.
> But don't forget those who loved you,
> Whom you must leave behind.

> Degewatek of the Dani,
> New Guinea,
> February 25, 1940

On November 25, the evening before she was to leave for San Francisco with Sir Charles to catch a military plane to the Indies, Catherine sat down and wrote a letter to Michael. She wrote three versions of the letter before she was satisfied. The one she settled on was brief and perfunctory. It contained a photograph, a report on the existence of his son, news of her encounter with his father and her upcoming trip to Java, and a disclaimer that she wanted to put any pressure on him regarding involvement with his son. Nor was he to feel obligated to spend time in Batavia during the holidays on her account. She indicated, in so many words, that

273

she was doing fine without him. She addressed the letter to Michael via Washington D.C., to be forwarded to his unit, then sealed the letter and mailed it, satisfied she had fulfilled her promise to Sir Charles.

Chapter 27
Kuril Islands, Japan
November 26, 1941

At the same time Catherine was writing her letter, halfway around the world Kido Butai, the twenty-three-ship Japanese carrier strike force weighed anchor at the rendezvous point 1,000 miles north of Tokyo. There was a feeling of excitement aboard the ships as they plowed, single file, through the deep waters of Etorofu Island's Hitokappu Bay, out toward the open sea. The day broke crisp and clear. It was taken as a good omen. Battleships and cruisers test-fired their guns as they left the harbor, lobbing live shells into the island's snowy hillside. The deep roar of the guns and the spray of the flying snow added to the occasion.

The strike force left no evidence of its departure or its location. Crystals were removed from radios to assure silence. Garbage was stored away rather than dumped, and empty oil cans were crushed and stacked on deck. All outgoing mail from Etorofu Island had been halted, and the fishermen of Hitokappu Bay had been rounded up and detained. Submarines scouted ahead for any neutral merchant ships which might stray into the fleet's path. They were to be boarded and seized if found. The plan of action if they should come upon the United States Pacific Fleet unexpectedly was not so easily resolved, though it was endlessly debated. Rear Admiral Tamon Yamaguchi, a Princeton graduate, jokingly suggested that they "fire a salute, shout '*Sayonara*,' and return home."

The officers in the stripped-down conference room laughed, yet there was wisdom in the jest. What else could they do? They were not yet at war. They could only hope they would not be discovered in the ten days before they reached their final destination.

Chapter 28

Dutch East Indies,
November 30, 1941

Sir Charles debarked at Darwin, where the plane, full of British naval personnel on their way to Australia and Singapore had refueled. Having been temporarily diverted to help expand the system of coast watchers in New Guinea and the Solomons, he sent Catherine and her son on alone. He would join them in Batavia by December 15.

Michael's sister Margit met Catherine at dockside as the plane landed in Tanjongpriok Harbor in Batavia, Java. Margit was wearing a fashionable print, looking wildly incongruous amid the chaos of the dock crowded with military personnel and equipment. As Catherine watched, the print dress began making its way toward her, and she could now clearly see its owner. Margit wasn't pretty in the usual sense, but she was striking. There was something curiously contradictory about her even at first sight. Her makeup was glamorous, and her hair was beautifully waved; her stylish silk print dress billowed around her in the ocean breeze like an exotic flowered balloon, but she wore solid white oxfords as if to weigh her down and counterbalance any natural tendencies she might have to take off and do something foolish. She carried a large straw hat in her hand, the kind the village women wore into the rice fields, and she was clearly careless with her fine complexion.

Looking like a butterfly, this apparition finally reached Catherine and offered her a white-gloved hand. It was more than ninety-five degrees in the shade, and Catherine marveled that the hand was neither damp nor limp. She felt thoroughly wilted by comparison.

"Catherine? I'm Margit. Michael's sister." Her blue eyes, firmly fixed on Catherine's brown ones, were friendly, but she didn't smile. Margit, Catherine soon learned, seldom smiled at anything. She had a practical, no-nonsense approach to life inherited from her Dutch mother, but she tempered it with a very wry British sense of humor and fair play. Now she gave little Michael a kiss on the cheek.

"Irresistible you are, my fine blond friend. Just like your father," she said as she took Michael into her arms. "You must be exhausted," she directed at Catherine, and, without waiting for a reply, proceeded to take charge of everything, including the conversation. Catherine accepted gratefully.

Margit instructed the young officer who carried Catherine's luggage to take it to a jaunty white convertible. Margit took off her gloves and got in behind the wheel.

"I prefer this to the chauffeur and limousine the government furnishes me. It leaves me to go about my own business in case I decide to have an affair. I probably never will, but I consider it often." She glanced at Catherine beside her. "Don't take that personally, Catherine. I don't disapprove of you or what happened between you and Michael. I suppose it was inevitable under the circumstances." She said it as if, in her ordered world, she would never have let such a thing happen to her; still, she clearly chose not to judge the rest of the world by her own determined standards.

"Papa wired me that he'd been delayed. I hope he's here by the holidays. All this talk about war has become quite tiresome. Now the American firms, Goodyear, Standard Oil, and General Motors, are sending the families of their executives home—or will soon. Batavia just isn't the same. They've even painted all our beautiful white buildings a drab green and hidden big guns in the hills, but no one really seems to worry."

They passed an army truck with women volunteers conducting a medical emergency drill. The truck bore a large red cross. Margit nodded toward the group. "Bernard's forced me to join one of those women's support groups setting up combat kitchens. I hate cooking, so I drive a truck. You should hear how patriotic they all sound. There was a woman reporter here from the United States recently to write some propaganda pieces for the war effort, so we posed for her. Bernard had some island women there just so it wouldn't look as if the natives were restless and hated us—which they do. The ugly thing about it is that the Dutch have been locking up any nationalists who breathe so much as a word of opposition to the government. I sometimes think the whole war scare is simply an excuse the government invented to get rid of native troublemakers. Of course, Bernard vehemently denies it.''

Having left the harbor, they were soon surrounded by the sights of old Batavia. According to Margit, the city was founded on behalf of the Dutch East India Company in 1619 by Jan Pieterszoon Coen, the fourth governor-general of the Indies. It had been the site of an ancient Javanese fort, Jakarta, which the Dutch had destroyed, building in its place a little replica of Holland, complete with canals and small Dutch houses, both completely unsuited to the tropics. Since mosquitoes bred rapidly in the stagnant water of the canals, outbreaks of malaria had continually wiped out the early European population of Batavia. Before the cause of malaria was understood, it was not unusual for a visitor to Batavia to return after six months and find everyone he had met previously was dead. The Dutch finally abandoned their city of death and moved into the surrounding hills, where they built new and grander suburbs with an architecture more suited to the climate. The governor-general moved his seat to Buitenzorg some forty miles from Batavia, where he built a palace and began the world's most famous botanical garden.

"His wife is American, you know," Margit said as she described the current governor-general. "The daughter of missionaries. We'll drive out for tea sometime this week so you can meet her.''

They drove through the crowded canal area where its current population of poor Asians drank, bathed, washed clothes, and cooked with water from the stagnant streams. It was just before the afternoon shutdown of business, and the market areas of the city were still crowded with people and local transportation: *Dokars*, or horse-drawn carts like buses, loaded with people, carts from the country filled with produce and drawn by bullocks, and *betjaks*, or pedicabs, with their pedaling drivers in back and

279

the passengers precariously enclosed in front, careened through the streets.

The smell of spicy cooking drifted through the open convertible. Food was for sale everywhere, from coconut milk sold at the curb to restaurants slung on poles complete with charcoal stove and hot water for washing utensils. Bahasa Indonesian, the Malay-based language, filtered into the car along with the pungent smells and the heat. The crowd was colorfully dressed, especially the women, who wore *kains*, long ankle-length skirts of beautiful batik cloth. Some of the men wore *kains*, too, but most wore shorts or calf-length pants and colorful bandannas around their foreheads. The local rice brew, *tuak*, was readily available, and everywhere people chewed betel nuts, the red juices staining their lips and, eventually, turning their teeth black.

"It's a mild narcotic," Margit said of the betel nut. "Bernard says it's the reason they're all so apathetic and irresponsible. I say it's because they're depressed and don't like the Dutch, at which point Bernard always replies that I'm my father's daughter." Then she added, "He means it as an insult."

Leaving the native section behind they entered the hills and the European suburb of Weltevreden, with its wide, treelined avenues, gracious European houses, huge lawns, and lovely, well-tended gardens.

The distractions of the city behind her, Catherine said to Margit, "I'm really grateful for your hospitality—especially given the situation."

Margit eyed her frankly. "I'm very fond of Kara, but I don't hold that against you, Catherine. As I said before, I suppose what happened was inevitable under the circumstances. I must admit, I was terribly curious to meet you. It's not like my brother to get himself involved with someone else."

There was a certain possessiveness in her reference to Michael that made Catherine flush.

"I came only because Sir Charles insisted it was necessary. No other reason. Michael and I are finished. I haven't seen or heard from him since we left New Guinea, nor have I tried to make contact."

"Are you sure it's over, Catherine?"

Margit glanced ahead. They were nearing the large mansion that was her home.

"My brother has always attracted women, very beautiful women. But you're his first mistress, as far as I know, since his marriage." She turned and looked again at Catherine. "You must be very special."

Catherine found herself blushing deeply at the term "mistress," yet she knew that Margit had not meant it to insult her. "Not really special," she replied. "As you said yourself, it was the circumstances."

"No, it wasn't." Margit eyed Catherine evenly. "I can tell that already, and I've only just met you."

They turned into the large circular driveway that led up to the house.

"And how do you intend to explain my visit to your friends?" Catherine asked.

"You mean polite but gossipy Batavia society?" Margit laughed. "I shall introduce you as Dr. Morgan. That disguises your marital status rather well, doesn't it? How handy for you."

"Yes." Catherine smiled ruefully. "Quite an original motive for finishing an advanced degree, don't you think?"

"You could have had an abortion."

Catherine looked momentarily surprised. "No. I couldn't. I never even considered it."

Margit reached out and touched her hand sympathetically. "And yet you say you no longer care, that it's over?"

The car crunched to a stop in the gravel drive.

"Don't worry for my sake about what the people here will think. They'll all wonder, but no one will have the nerve to ask. No doubt Bernard will have already told them that you have an American husband in the Philippines just to tidy things up. Not that it would make any difference. The Stanfords have been scandalizing Batavia for years."

A white-coated Javanese houseboy came out to open the car door and remove the bags from the trunk. Catherine followed Margit into the house. She moved with the studied looseness of a fashion model, which reflected the charm school to which Lady Stanford had sent her awkward daughter.

"He'll be here on Christmas Eve, you know," she said to Catherine over her shoulder. She handed Michael to another servant and threw down her gloves. "Michael, I mean. Before he goes to Maitreya. It's the first time he'll have been back since he

281

left on the expedition two years ago. Does he know you'll be here?''

"I wrote to him. And Sir Charles did also." Catherine gazed longingly at the shaded tropical garden she could glimpse through the French doors in the rear of the large hallway. "I really don't want to see him."

"Now that's silly, isn't it?" Margit replied in her practical manner. "After all, the boy is Michael's son as well as yours. There are practical considerations, like what's to become of him in the future. Illegitimate or not, we Stanfords always provide for our children." She leaned over and gave Michael, drowsing in the servant's arms, a peck on the cheek.

She glanced back to Catherine and remarked offhandedly, "My husband has two illegitimate children: half brown, of course, by his Indo mistress." For the first time a note of bitterness crept into her voice. "She's very beautiful. He thinks I don't know about her, but I do—all about her, from the time it started years ago. He's a son of a bitch," she added mildly. "But then most men are."

She waved her arm toward the rooms that disappeared off through high carved doors. "Bernard can't really afford this house, but my father can, and did. So Bernard wouldn't leave me for the most beautiful woman in the world—unless she had more money. Make yourself at home, I'll be back in a moment."

She swept rather grandly out of the room, leaving behind an aura of efficiency that she seemed to have imposed on everything in the house. Margit returned shortly with her two sons and their Dutch governess.

"I want you to meet Catherine and your cousin, Michael."

The boys were fascinated by the baby, examining his tiny fingers and toes.

"If he's our cousin, then why don't we call her Aunt Catherine?" one of them asked, eyeing Catherine with curiosity.

"Never mind that now. I'll explain that someday, but right now you wouldn't understand."

"That's what you always say," he replied disgustedly, and Margit laughed.

"Run along and help give baby Michael some lemonade."

The retreating sound of chattering children echoed along the marble corridor and then died away. Alone, Margit directed

Catherine toward the cool garden. The air within it was damp and pungent.

"There's not a tulip on the place, or an English rose. I don't thrive under these conditions either. There is too much of everything here: too much heat; too much water. Nothing does well but these infernal tropical flowers with their oversize blooms, their excessive color, and their overpowering perfume. We Europeans weren't meant to be transplanted here. We should all go home, just as Michael says." She noted the high color in Catherine's cheeks. "The climate doesn't seem to disagree with you."

"No. I love the tropics. Maitreya was the most beautiful place I've ever seen, and this is beautiful also."

"It scarcely compares. Maitreya is grand and wild, and I never felt at home there."

Margit reached out and touched an orchid plant that clung to the huge banyan tree dominating the center of the garden. "Everything here is so parasitic. This banyan tree, for example; it began growing on some other tree, then sent down aerial roots which locked around the trunk of its host, eventually strangling it. Michael always said the Dutch were like banyan trees. But to the natives the trees are sacred.

"Isn't it a joke?' she mused finally. "As much as I loved Papa, I always sided with Mother against him. I hated him for all his other women, and then I married a philanderer just as she did. We apples don't fall far from the family tree, do we? Except Michael."

She caught herself for a moment and was silent. She was treating Catherine more like a confidante than a stranger, and she wasn't sure why, except that she had few friends. Then she went on. "I didn't accept Michael when Papa first brought him to the family. Not surprising. What was more unusual was that he accepted our rejection of him with that same wry humor and wisdom he brings to everything. And of course, I came to adore him. He's the best of us—by far. Certainly better than Edward, who was always arrogant and selfish. He and Michael never got along. At least Edward never got along with Michael—Edward was too busy trying to get him in trouble with Papa." She sighed. "Genetically speaking, Edward's death was probably the best thing that ever happened to the Stanford title."

Catherine felt a flood of affection for Michael's older sister sweep over her. "I think you tie him for 'best of the lot' honors."

Margit looked at Catherine in surprise, then gave her a modest but obviously pleased smile. "Thanks. God knows I've had to learn how to be a survivor, mostly of horrors of my own making like Bernard." She turned back toward the house. "I'm sure the servants have unpacked your things by now. Perhaps you'd like to go up and rest."

"Yes, I'd like that."

In the hall Catherine paused for a moment before a portrait she had noticed earlier. It was a very old painting that needed cleaning, but it was clearly the portrait of a very handsome man looking straight at her, wearing the black suit and white lace of a seventeenth-century Dutch burgomaster. It was an arrogant face with a cruelty about it that neither the subject nor the artist had bothered to conceal.

"Who's he?"

"The famous Jan Pieterszoon Coen, the founder of Batavia and an early governor-general of the Indies. He killed and tortured the British and the islanders and whoever else stood in his way. He was ruthless and very successful. He's an ancestor of Bernard's, and Bernard is very proud of that fact." As she stood with Catherine next to the portrait, a look of admiration reluctantly crossed Margit's face, and she sighed. "Bernard looked like that when we were first married. He was so handsome. And I was determined to be deflowered by the best-looking man I could find, even if I had to marry him to do it. I was always the ugly duckling."

She sighed again and began to lead the way up the stairs. "Papa was furious about my marriage at the time. He was fighting with the Dutch. I was determined to marry a Dutchman, mostly to defy Papa, but the truth is, I've always felt more Dutch than English. I've been to Holland only three times, but I loved it. Bernard promised me we would live there, but we never did. Now I suspect he never had any intention of keeping his promise. He just needed my millions to help with his career. He had fantasies of becoming governor-general of the Indies, just like dear old ancestor Jan, using similar tactics, no doubt."

A pretty, light-skinned woman dressed in a sarong and a long-sleeved, brightly printed jacket called *kebaja* met them at the top of the stairs and opened the door to Catherine's room.

"Thank you, Suji," Margit said. "And please tell Cook to send some iced tea up to our rooms. I'm wilted."

She watched Suji glide away, as graceful as a Balinese dancer. "Suji will be gone any day now, and I shall miss her. She's *Belanda Hitam*, black Dutch, but her Dutch father refused to acknowledge her, so she's worked here for the past year, saving all her money so she can pay some retired Dutch military officer to claim her legally. Then she can be reclassified as Indo or part white, enabling her to qualify for some menial office job. Frankly I'd rather work in the rice fields in some small village myself, but to her reclassification means everything. Indos are worse snobs than the Dutch, and the sad thing is they aren't accepted by either side, native or white. But they're fiercely loyal to the Dutch." Then she added, "I suppose in one way it will be good that she's gone. Bernard has been trying to get her into bed with him for a year. Poor thing. No wonder she's leaving."

Margit stood at the door of the lacy room with its huge screened windows. She didn't enter but stopped Catherine as she passed through the doorway and gave her a quick kiss on the cheek.

"Welcome to Batavia, the very Dutch and unhappy side of the English Stanfords." She gave Catherine a sad smile and was suddenly gone, leaving behind the faint smell of lavender and the distinct impression of an English rose in Catherine's mind.

Since Bernard had other plans for the evening, Margit had ordered a light Indonesian supper for herself and Catherine: *soto*, a spiced chicken soup, and *nasi kuning*, rice tinted with saffron and served with shredded coconut, along with a salad made of hearts of palm. Bernard disliked Indonesian food, preferring the blander cooking of northern Europe.

"The food is the only thing I like about the Indies," Margit commented over dinner. "It's so spicy that hours later you know you've eaten something. I like that."

In her room after dinner Catherine found a letter from Julienne, posted from Banjamarsin, propped against a lamp on the desk.

285

My dear Catherine,

Father told me you were coming to Batavia for the holidays and wanted me to come and be with you, but I made excuses because I don't feel up to seeing you or his little bastard. I'm sure you can understand, dear Catherine, since you must know everything by now. Nothing personal, you realize. So I'll stay here and keep this silly little snip he married company. She still thinks he'll come back to her, and so do I. Merry Christmas. Congratulations on completing your degree.

Julienne

Chapter 29

The score was tied as the horses came pounding down the field. The Dutch team captain took a swing at the ball, drove it expertly into the goal, then turned and galloped his horse to the sidelines and the enthusiastic applause of the Sunday morning crowd at the polo field just outside Batavia. He dismounted as the other members of the Dutch and British teams left the field. Polo was a weekly occurrence at the club, but this was a special match between old rivals, the local Dutch polo team versus a team of British officers stationed in Singapore.

A waiting attendant took the reins of the captain's well-lathered horse and handed him a drink before leading his horse away to be rubbed down. The rider's body seemed to slump slightly with fatigue as he unsnapped his chin strap and wearily removed his white riding helmet to tuck it beneath a bronzed arm. Those onlookers not familiar with the Dutch team were surprised to see dark skin emerge from beneath the shadow of the helmet, followed by dark brown hair. The Dutch team captain was not Dutch at all but Eurasian, half French and half Indonesian-Malay. And he was no ordinary Eurasian either, or he would not have been on the polo team despite his great athletic ability. He was Ahmad Açvavarman, crown prince of Matapura, Michael Stanford's oldest and closest friend. Catherine had seen him once before, two years ago at Maitreya, the first night she had arrived. This time, thanks to Margit, she knew who he was.

The prince took a towel and wiped the perspiration from his face and hair, which curled in damp brown ringlets around his face. Like most Eurasians, he was exceedingly good to look at, as if the best of both races were distilled in his features. Unusually tall for an Indonesian, he was built like his princely Javanese-Malay ancestors with a muscular form that was lean and graceful, fine-boned and well shaped. There was nothing soft about him— not his face or his body or his manner—except his laughter, which was warm and gentle.

His English, while excellent, had a slight French accent, the result of his having learned it from French tutors. His mother had been the independent-minded daughter of a wealthy French planter who had eloped with the dashing young sultan of Matapura against her family's wishes. Under her influence the prince became the first Indonesian of his royal rank to have a Western education. Although Prince Ahmad seemed equally at ease in the contrasting worlds of European society and the tradition-bound Matapuran court, he was actually in conflict with both. It was with the simple, communal people of Borneo's jungles that he felt most comfortable. He had been reared in the Spartan manner of Matapura's warrior-kings, eating and sleeping with his father's most skilled and trusted guards until he was sixteen, learning from them the ancient martial arts of karate and *pentjak* as well as the use of such weapons as the knifelike kris and the curve-bladed parang. He had not fired a gun until he was fourteen, long after he was already an accomplished warrior in the Açvavarman tradition, a tradition which viewed guns as weapons without honor.

Prince Ahmad Açvavarman tossed his towel aside and took another drink. During the rest period he did not fraternize with the other players but stood slightly apart, waiting for the game to resume. He was only partially aware of the admiring looks and open stares he received from women in the crowd of spectators. His indifference served only to pique their interest. He was wary of Western women, especially the wives and daughters of the Dutch colonial aristocracy, who, torn between their prejudices and their passion, snubbed him in public and attempted to seduce him in private. They approached him in ways properly reared Javanese girls never would: hand touching his thigh in public or brushing against his groin when no one else was looking, notes left in the pockets of his jacket or, more dangerously, sent by some messenger or servant to his hotel.

Other women were sufficiently enamored of Ahmad's wealth and title to overcome their prejudices. He had no respect for them either. Yet he remained the stuff on which to build idle daydreams on boring, hot afternoons. The perfect prince charming of female fantasies, exceedingly handsome and dark enough to be mysterious but with familiar European features which did not alienate his admirers. They gossiped about him often, but he remained an almost totally private person. There were no women in his life, since women of his own race were generally not educated enough or emancipated enough to offer him the companionship he wanted. This was especially true of the Indonesian princesses among whom he was supposed to find a bride. They had been too sheltered. Had he been more traditional, he would have married as directed by his family and found sexual fulfillment among his mistresses and companionship among his male friends. But he had not married, a fact which greatly distressed his father. As was often customary, he had been betrothed when very young to a princess slightly older than he, but she had died before they had married. By that time he had developed a will of his own which even his father had learned not to defy on some issues. There were no other engagements.

The sun momentarily disappeared behind some clouds, and the air cooled noticeably. A storm was building. It would rain within an hour, but by that time the game would be over. Ahmad turned to take his first look at the crowd around him and caught sight of Margit sitting on top of the white convertible's back seat. She smiled and waved as he started toward the car. He recognized the woman beside her, though it was more than two years since he had seen her. She was Michael's mistress, or former mistress, no one seemed to know for sure which. What he knew of Catherine had not come, oddly, from Michael himself. Margit had told him about the rescue from New Guinea and then, recently, about the baby. Ahmad knew it had taken great courage for Catherine to have the baby, and he admired courage above all traits.

Margit held out both hands to Ahmad, who gave her an affectionate kiss on the cheek.

"Ahmad, darling, that was an absolutely splendid performance. I believe you've met Dr. Morgan before."

"Yes. Some time ago. But I haven't forgotten." He smiled. "How are you, Dr. Morgan?"

Catherine extended her hand. "Fine, only please call me Catherine."

"Did you come to Java just for the game?" Margit asked him.

He nodded. "Plus a little family business."

Margit wrinkled her nose and said with a glint in her eye, "You know I'm rooting for the British. My Dutch mother will have to forgive me. We Stanfords always root for England. And you, Ahmad—of all people—trying to bring glory to the Dutch. You should be ashamed of that goal you just made."

Ahmad laughed. "It's true that I'm considered a dangerous revolutionary, but it's rather nice to find ourselves on the same side once in a while. Where's Bernard?"

"At home—sleeping off a dinner party with the governor-general and the head of Standard Oil. He wouldn't have come anyway. Just the sight of all this early-morning exercise would make him ill. Bernard believes in letting the forces of erosion run their natural course. Ahmad, you must join Catherine and me for dinner Wednesday. Bernard will be working late." She mentioned the day; airily, as if it didn't matter, but they both knew that to save a scene, Ahmad never came to visit when Bernard was home.

"I'm leaving for Borneo tomorrow."

Margit looked disappointed. "Then you must come to dinner as soon as you get back."

"Fine."

The whistle blew, signaling the resumption of the game just as Margit's two boys arrived with whoops of joy and Ahmad swung them up into his arms.

"Uncle Ahmad, you were super! Will you teach us to play polo? Uncle Michael promised us he would give us lessons, but he's away."

"Of course. You will come and stay with me at Matapura for a few weeks this summer, and I will teach you. Now I must be getting back to the field." He looked at Margit and Catherine. "Perhaps I'll see you after the game."

"We'll be leaving before the game is over," Margit said. "But we'll be at the club for dinner this evening."

"Then perhaps I'll see you there. Good-bye, Catherine. It was good to see you again."

The boys chased after him as he returned to the sidelines and mounted his horse. Margit was silent for a moment, lost in thought as she watched Ahmad gallop out onto the field.

"He's a brilliant speaker, all bright fire and fury. After hearing him address an illegal Socialist rally two years ago, even Bernard was about to take up arms for Indonesian freedom. Of course, he quickly recovered from his temporary insanity and tried to have Ahmad arrested instead. He didn't have much luck. Ahmad's father, the sultan of Matapura, is extraordinary popular—and therefore politically important." She sighed, then suddenly rose. "There! Ahmad just scored again."

She slid down onto her seat with a bounce and opened the car door. "That's quite enough sport for the day. I've had my fill of handsome young men. One more muscular thigh straining against tight riding breeches, and I shall have overdosed. I'm ready to go home to Bernard. I'll get the boys."

Catherine watched in amusement as Margit strode determinedly off, the wide brim of her finely woven straw hat flapping majestically with each step.

Chapter 30
Manila, Sunday,
December 7, 1941

Glasses clinked and voices babbled in the crowded room like a gently rushing brook. Ignoring them, Michael stood alone, staring out the big bay window of one of the reception rooms in the famous old Manila Hotel. Looking west into the sunset toward the Bataan Peninsula some twelve miles across the bay, he could see merchant and U.S. naval ships silhouetted at anchor in the harbor, their stacks and masts rising in trim profusion above the dark, tranquil water to jab at the bright orange sky.

The big passenger steamer *Empress of Japan* was moored at Pier 7, the longest pier in the world, its immaculate white surface now painted drab battleship gray, and antiaircraft guns mounted on her bow and stern. It had been redecorated almost two years ago in anticipation of a war that had not yet come but was steadily drawing near. Its makeup may have changed, but it remained the epitome of white colonial privilege it had always been. On its decks European and American passengers en route to Shanghai, Singapore, Hong Kong, Tokyo or Surabaya danced, flirted, ate, and drank in luxury. From one city to the next they would be pulled, pushed, or pedaled by native labor, passing safely through Asia's slums into international bastions of green, well-tended tranquillity the immaculate public gardens of which bore signs reading DOGS AND ORIENTALS KEEP OUT.

Manila had its own extravagant wealth contrasted with abject poverty. Michael had taken a room in the Japanese section of the

292

city, renting it from an old Japanese fisherman, Tifume, who was a distant cousin of Michael's childhood housekeeper in San Francisco. The room gave Michael a weekend retreat from the camaraderie of the officers' quarters at Cavite Naval Base. He liked its stark simplicity; sometimes he remained there the entire weekend, sitting cross-legged on the floor in his kimono, absorbed in his reading and writing, his meals served by the fisherman's tiny, smiling gray-haired wife. He often joined the two of them the for tea ceremony, and at those times he drank from a treasured family cup, properly cracked, which they kept for him in a place of honor. They spoke only Japanese, even though they had been in Manila for almost fifty years, so Michael conversed with them in that language, pleased with how quickly his fluency returned to him. It had been many years since his informal lessons in San Francisco.

Late this afternoon he had walked from the Japanese section to the luxurious Manila Hotel, an incongruous sight in his crisp, impeccably white uniform, towering over the vigorous brown mass that surged around him in the slum streets. No taxis could be found here, for the people who lived in the slums of Manila rarely left the area. Instead, the world came to them, looking for drugs, black-market goods, sex, knowing that just about anything could be found for sale here. Hordes of children and maimed beggars practiced their arts of hustling and stealing, their bloated bellies and spindly legs a testimony to how poorly they succeeded. Michael observed to himself with irony that even the flies, which swarmed everywhere, must find slender pickings here. Everything remotely edible was immediately consumed.

"Hey, American. You want to make pam-pam?" A grinning urchin wiggled her twelve-year-old body provocatively up at him. A cigarette dangled from between brightly rouged lips, and her eyelids were caked with kohl. "You're good-looking. I do it for you cheap."

He doubted it. Hunger was more real on this street than desire. For a moment his own childhood desperation on the streets of Hong Kong came flooding back to him, and his eyes filled with tears. He had seen worse poverty than this on the streets of Calcutta and Shanghai, but he still never got used to it and never stopped burning with the injustice of it all.

By the time he arrived at the luxurious reception he was to

attend honoring General Brereton, the newly arrived commander of the Army's Far East Air Force, Michael had thoroughly soured on the evening. Although he hated such large social affairs, he had agreed to meet friends here and go for dinner later, so he forced himself to stay. The reception room was high atop the hotel. Michael had checked his hat at the door, taken a whiskey sour from the bar, and then quickly found the view into which he became moodily absorbed.

He glanced around the crowded reception room but, failing to catch any sight of his friends, returned his gaze to the window. It was now dusk, and signal lights from the anchored ships blinked messages to the shore. He watched the twinkling lights of a large merchant ship as it moved with stately grace out of the harbor. It would soon pass the rock fortress of Corregidor, which guarded the entrance to Manila Bay, and reach the freedom of the open sea. He envied it. But in two weeks he himself would leave here—flying home for the Christmas holidays. At the thought the muscles in his jaws tightened. He had not heard from Kara since he had asked her for a divorce some six months ago. Things would have to be settled between them over the holidays. But her silence these past months indicated she was not going to agree to a divorce—at least not easily.

His relationship with his father was almost as strained. Their correspondence had been polite and distant since their last heated argument in Port Moresby after Catherine left. It had begun with Sir Charles's adamant opposition to Michael's plan: to join Catherine in New York.

"Let her finish her degree first," Sir Charles had once again urged.

Michael had responded angrily. "You wouldn't allow yourself to marry my mother, even though you loved her, and now you want to deny the same happiness to me. And what good did all your noble sacrifice do for anyone? You preserved your reputation, but you nearly destroyed us all!"

All the old buried anger had poured out of him that day, stunning Sir Charles into grieved silence and astonishing Michael. His adolescent rebellion, he later thought ruefully, had been late in coming. Up to that moment he had allowed himself only feelings of gratitude and love where his father was concerned. The bitterness and resentment had been carefully hidden, especially from himself.

His voice had shaken when he added, "Mother was barely eighteen. She didn't know any better, but you did."

"Don't you think I've regretted it ever since?" his father protested. "My God—I loved her. More than I ever loved anything or anyone before."

Michael had been remorseless. "Then you should have married her. Instead, you made us both suffer."

"I suffered, too."

"That doesn't make it all right. Even now you use your suffering to protect yourself from the truth. You weren't being loyal to your family reputation *or* your wife and children. You were just afraid to marry my mother. Afraid to give yourself completely to anyone."

Before Michael's eyes Sir Charles had seemed to wither as the fight went out of him. "Very well," he said, his voice defeated. "Perhaps you're right. Marry her if you must. I won't try to stop you."

But Michael had stopped himself. His own guilts, his own doubts had stopped him. Now that he had returned to civilization, his life in the jungle had begun to seem like a dream. It had been easy to start questioning everything, even his love for Catherine. He had used the impending war as an excuse to postpone making a decision. Why rush into a divorce when he and Catherine would be separated anyway? He had talked himself into agreeing to end his relationship with Catherine—at least temporarily. But as soon as he had finished his three months of flight training and was sent to the Philippines, he had written Catherine and told her he wanted to marry her as soon as he got a divorce. The memory led him to take a long sip of his drink and then another as he cast a bitter look at the Pan Am China Clipper moored to the dock, its huge wings gently rising with the thrust of the incoming tide. It had arrived today, bringing service mail.

There was a time when he had anticipated its every arrival, his stomach churning with the rest of the men. But it had been more than a year, and he had not heard from Catherine once. All his letters to her had been returned, marked "Address Unknown." Finally he had stopped writing, but it had not made him change his mind about the divorce. Whatever his relationship with Catherine was or wasn't, his marriage had never been the same after that day he and Catherine had been discovered among the Wali Dani. He now realized he couldn't expect either himself or Kara to continue with what had become a charade.

He finished his drink without tasting it and searched the room for some distraction from his painful thoughts. The conversation around him was all military talk, as people swapped stories on equipment failures and supply shortages. Supplies destined for the Philippines were piling up on the docks of San Francisco, but ships couldn't be spared from the effort to supply England. Besides, Washington and Japan were still engaged in diplomatic talks, and no one expected a war, at least not anytime soon.

Michael caught sight of his copilot, Ensign Douglas Stuart, Annapolis class of 1940, just entering the room. With him was Bud Larson, communications officer on the destroyer *Peary*, and his wife, Carol. Naval dependents in the Philippines had been ordered home the previous February over the vehement protests of the younger officers' wives, married for a short time, who wanted to remain with their husbands. Some of the more determined wives, like Carol, had gone to the extreme of obtaining a divorce so that they could be free of Navy regulations and stay in Manila.

"My parents were never very successful at telling me what to do," she had explained at the time with a defiant toss of her sleek blond pageboy. "And I'll be damned if I'm going to let a distant relative like Uncle Sam start doing it now."

Douglas Stuart's bride, however, had reacted differently. A good Catholic from a traditional military family, she had not been able to let herself defy either the church or the military. So she had gone home to live with her family, while Carol stayed and enjoyed the attention she received from all the lonely young officers left in Manila. Michael did not know Carol and Bud well. They were Douglas's good friends so he tolerated their company once in a while, more than he did with most people. Now he made his way over to the trio just as they finished paying their respects to a nearby general.

"Why go to a reception and then stand off by yourself?" Douglas asked.

"Never mind," Michael replied impatiently. "Let's get out of here and go to dinner. I'd like to get away from the military once in a while."

296

"Sure, Michael, sure," Douglas replied easily. "Just ease back on your throttle a little and we'll take off."

Outside the hotel the sidewalks were still wet from a sudden shower.

"Shall we walk?" Douglas asked.

"Let's take a cab," Michael replied, not wanting the streets to put more of a damper on his evening than they already had.

Manila certainly didn't look like a city about to go to war. Lights blazed everywhere, and the clubs and restaurants had never been busier. There were no air-raid shelters or drills to jar the public's consciousness. The shelters existed, but only in a three-inch-thick report in the United States high commissioner's office in Manila. The high commissioner himself set the example: The best solution to that threat of war was to avoid thinking about it. The populace cheerfully followed suit.

They ate at the Jai Alai Club, the favorite night spot for foreigners, Americans, and wealthy Filipinos. The orchestra played Cole Porter and George Gershwin to an audience eager to be entertained. Champagne corks popped with a regularity that seemed more appropriate to New Year's Eve than a Sunday evening. In this atmosphere of intoxicated hilarity Michael felt even more out of place. Douglas and Bud alternately danced with Carol, and then they both disappeared, momentarily leaving Michael alone with her.

"You don't dance, Michael?" Carol was wearing bright red lipstick and a white loosely crocheted hair net which neatly contained her blond pageboy. Her white strapped floor-length gown was made of chiffon. All peaches and cream, Michael mused.

"I'm not in the mood," he replied.

"Not in the mood—or is it that you don't find me attractive?" She locked challenging eyes onto his. Crap, he thought. Why was everyone in the Far East trying to start a war? She was watching him intently, keenly aware of the frozen gray eyes that were now leveled steadily at her.

"I know you sleep with Douglas and maybe most of the other officers at Cavite, which is your business. However, Bud doesn't know, and I don't want to be registered when he performs an audit on your little black book."

297

She looked neither upset nor offended, only slightly defensive. "There's nothing wrong with enjoying myself while Bud's away on cruises. Men do it all the time. You've no right to judge what I do."

"I'm not judging. Look, Carol, I don't care if you do it because you love sex or you hate men or you're lonely or you want to get back at Bud for something. I don't care if you screw bananas while Bud's away—but just leave me out of it."

Suddenly she burst out laughing. The tension that had been building between them for months was broken, and they sat for a moment in comfortable silence before Michael spoke again.

"You ought to get out of Manila, Carol, and go home."

"I know, but I can't. I just have to be here when it happens. Believe it or not, I love Bud." Her large blue eyes reddened and betrayed her fear.

"I believe it," Michael said softly, and reached out and squeezed her hand.

She sniffed and smiled through tears. "If you won't be my lover, will you at least be my friend?"

"Sure." He smiled in return. "The best dog a friend ever had. I'm famous for it."

She laughed again, and he laughed with her.

The Larsons went home after the Jai Alai Club, and a reluctant Michael accompanied Douglas to one of his favorite haunts, a geisha house in the Japanese section of Manila. At least with the Larsons gone, Michael felt more free to be himself. When they entered the premises, it was clear it was not just a geisha house but an expensive bar as well. An all-male clientele of wealthy foreigners and military personnel, seated somewhat uncomfortably on the floor before long tables, was attentively waited upon by pretty kimono-clad young Japanese women. Just by glancing at the customers, Michael guessed the bar must be a setting for intense Japanese espionage activities.

Still, the entertainment had integrity even if the proprietors probably didn't. It consisted of classic Japanese songs and dances, modified only slightly to accommodate Western tastes. Once seated, Michael soon found his attention drawn to the lovely kimono-clad young singer at the head of one of the long tables. Her face and the delicate hands with which she played the ancient lutelike instrument reminded him of Catherine so much that he found himself unabashedly staring at her. Douglas, who had never seen him show any interest in women before, was amused.

"Mikki Hatara is her name. She's off limits." He leaned closer and added in a confidential tone, "Personal property of someone very important."

"She's lovely," Michael said, and turned his attention elsewhere.

Douglas felt a small stab of disappointment when Michael didn't seem interested in who the lucky proprietor was; then he flushed with annoyance at himself. He was always trying to impress Michael with something. Michael's remoteness continually baffled Douglas, who was naturally gregarious and open. He liked Michael, perhaps "admired" was a better word, but he was damned if he could figure him out. He knew almost nothing about Michael's personal life, only that he was married, his mother was American, his father British, and he lived in Borneo. Douglas had shared a room with Michael in the officers' quarters at Cavite Naval Base since the PBY squadron had been sent to the Philippines more than eight months ago, and he knew little more about him now than he had then.

Despite this, there was an easy mutual affection between the two men. Off hours, Douglas spent most of his time with former Annapolis classmates stationed in the Philippines.

"You'll never be older than nineteen," Michael used to say, teasing him. "Not as long as you've got all your old college beer-drinking buddies to hang around with."

Douglas, in turn, would question Michael about where he went when he disappeared for the weekend, offering outrageous hypotheses of his own. Michael listened with amusement, but he never revealed the truth.

So tonight Douglas was completely floored when Michael asked Mikki-san to sing an ancient geisha song, never sung for the customers here because it was considered too Japanese for Western ears. She was pleased with the request and stayed to chat for a moment with Michael afterward in Japanese.

"Jeez!" Douglas exclaimed later in amazement after Mikki-san had been called away, "Where did you learn to speak Japanese?"

"A housekeeper," was Michael's laconic explanation.

Douglas shook his head in disbelief. "You must not have told

299

the Navy or you'd be flying some Honolulu desk job instead of a PBY.''

"That's why I didn't tell them. Couldn't stand to be buried in some office cracking codes all day." He smiled.

Outside they walked in silence. The rains had continued intermittently, and the lamplights gleamed in the wet streets. They reached the corner of a narrow street strung its entire length with paper Japanese lanterns, hundreds of glittering lights and colorful shapes dancing brightly in the breeze, undaunted by the rain. It was a street dedicated exclusively to prostitution without the rigid rules and formal arrangements that governed love in a geisha house, but considerably cleaner and livelier than the alternatives that abounded in Manila's slums.

Douglas paused at the street's entrance and cleared his throat. "I think I'll stay out for a while. Care to join me?"

Michael shook his head.

"I didn't think so. What are you, Michael? Some kind of monk in disguise?"

"No, but you're close." Michael smiled. "I'm a plant from the Vatican put here to lead an exemplary life and make all you Catholic boys feel guilty."

"Jeez, I think you're succeeding." Douglas paused, flustered.

Michael's smile faded. "Hey look, Douglas, I'm no saint. Far from it, if you really want the truth. Now go on—have a good time and stop worrying, for Christ's sake."

"Well . . ." Douglas hesitated, then added cheerfully, "See you tomorrow morning."

"Good night, Doug." Michael took a few steps and then turned and called back over his shoulder, "I'd like mine not to be the only pair of eyes in working condition tomorrow."

"Don't worry, Captain. I'll be old radar eyes himself. Not even a life raft wearing a rising sun will be able to escape these long-lashed beauties."

Michael laughed. "I just hope we see nothing bigger than a life raft out there tomorrow."

Instead of returning to the base, Michael walked to his rented room, where he quietly slid aside the doors to let himself in without waking the old couple. He carefully folded his white dress uniform, slipped into a silk robe, and lay down upon his sleeping mat. He soon fell asleep but was awakened by a disturbing dream he could not remember.

The house was quiet except for the brass wind chimes outside his room. They softly tinkled in the gentle ocean breeze that crept in from the bay, bringing with them a flood of memories that had been waiting to emerge when the busy distractions of his day had ceased: memories of Catherine and New Guinea, memories so far removed from the life he now led that they seemed unreal. Yet they produced within him an ache so intense as to be physically painful, causing his loins to throb and grow taut. He closed his eyes, and his jaw tightened as he forced the memories away.

It's over, he angrily told himself. Forget it. But it was as if her soft presence had entered the room with the sound of the chimes, and he could no longer ignore it. In spite of himself, he imagined her next to him, her face close to his, her arms around him, dark eyes shining, lips parted, her soft, sweet breath touching his mouth in a sensation as tantalizing and sensual as a kiss. He felt the excitement of brushing against her bare thigh, the tips of her bare breasts lightly grazing his chest, but he had no way to pull her to him, to bring relief to them both.

He rose and angrily slid open his door panel, as the wind chimes greeted him with a renewed burst of melody. The rains had stopped, and the sky had cleared. The moon was brilliant, shimmering off the brass surface of the chimes. He reached up and brought the chimes down with one swift tug, the jarring crash seeming to reproach him. Suddenly tears pushed their way to the surface, surprising him. He thought he was beyond being hurt by her memory. For a while, when his letters to her were returned, he had felt desperate. He had called the anthropology department at Columbia, but they wouldn't tell him where to reach her. He had tried to find Carl's widow, Ginny, but she had moved. He had finally had to accept the bitter fact that she had left him and that she wasn't coming back.

He quickly blinked back the tears, turned back to the room, and hurriedly dressed. Once out in the street, he found himself walking back to the geisha house, although it was almost 1:00 A.M., and he knew it would be closed. Once there, he knocked on the narrow wooden gate of the wall that enclosed the compound to the rear of the geisha house. When nothing happened, he rattled it harder with an insistence that surprised him. A frame slid back in the tiny window in the gate, and an eye appeared. A masculine voice spoke roughly in Japanese. "Go away. We are not open."

Michael replied in Japanese that he had come to see Mikki-san. The man with the eye sucked in his breath indignantly.

"No one sees Mikki-san. You go away."

The ensuing argument was going nowhere when suddenly a female voice intruded on the other side of the gate and a muffled conversation which Michael couldn't hear took place. The whole thing was beginning to seem ridiculous to him. He wasn't sure why he had come except that he had felt driven to go somewhere. A long-lashed eye suddenly appeared at the tiny window.

"Lieutenant Stanford!" a female voice exclaimed in surprised recognition.

He heard the latch turn and the gate swung open, revealing the young woman who had served them that evening.

"You wished something, Lieutenant?"

Michael glanced through the gate at the buildings of the compound, attractively set in a wooded parklike setting. The trees were strung with glowing paper lanterns.

"I wanted to talk with Mikki-san."

She glanced over her shoulder at a house, removed from the others, the lights of which still burned.

"I'm afraid that's impossible."

"Please." He surprised himself with the intensity of his voice.

It surprised her as well. She looked at him more closely and then stood debating with herself for a moment. Finally she stepped aside and gestured for him to enter.

"Come," she said in English.

His face broke into a smile of relief. He was inside. He glanced at the house with the burning lights that stood alone among the trees and wondered if the next hurdle would be as passable.

The young woman led him to a smaller apartment in a dormlike building nearby. It was obviously hers. She hurriedly offered him some tea and then disappeared, giving him a chance to look around. The room was cluttered with personal possessions, porcelain bottles of perfumes, plastic flowers, and photographs of American movie stars, all crowded onto two low tables. Western street clothes hung beside beautiful silk kimonos. Only the sparsity of the furnishings was Japanese in nature. The personality of the room was clearly transitional.

He heard the door open behind him. He turned to see Mikki-san enter and slide the door closed behind her. She leaned back against it for a moment, studying him. She was dressed in a floor-length yellow silk robe: her long black hair hung down around her shoulders. He stood quietly looking at her, appreciating her beauty.

"You shouldn't have come," she said finally.

"So I've already been told," he replied a bit ruefully.

For a long moment more they stood staring at each other in silence. Then she slowly came across the room and stood before him.

She loosened the tie on her robe, and it fell open, giving him a tantalizing glimpse of her slender body. She began slowly to unfasten the gold buttons down the front of his white jacket, and he let her do it, though he still wasn't sure why he had come. She loosened his belt and knelt and pressed her face into his groin, feeling the soft bulge beneath the cloth grow beneath her cheek. Dear God, he thought. How long it had been since a woman had touched him . . . since he had made love to anyone?

"What would please you, Lieutenant?" she was asking in her soft singsong voice. She raised her eyes to his, and they were bright with the attraction she felt for him. "What would you like from Mikki-san?"

"Only"—he swallowed hard before continuing—"to forget for just a little while." He closed his eyes. She had the same figure, the same long dark hair. Perhaps all he wanted was to pretend for a little while that she was Catherine. His fingertips gently touched the top of her head with its soft, silky hair and lingered there.

She slowly rose, her arms went around him, the robe opened, and her body pressed against him and her lips found his, but in that brief moment the illusion was shattered. No one touched him like Catherine or aroused the same fire in him. Regretfully he reached up and gently extracted her arms from around his neck. The hardness in his groin had already subsided.

Her face looked crushed. "You no like Mikki-san? I no please you?"

"Please. It's not your fault. Really," he said gently in Japanese. "You're very beautiful." He reached out and touched her cheek with one hand, embarrassed that she should take his failure as rejection.

She quickly turned and left the room without another word, leaving him alone to tighten his belt and button his jacket. Guiltily he left her whatever money he had with him. He shouldn't have tried to make her something she wasn't, he angrily told himself.

Just after he had let himself out the gate, a limousine pulled up to the curb. A neatly dressed enlisted man got out of the driver's seat, leaned against the car fender, and lit a cigarette, preparing for a long wait before he picked up his passenger. Michael recognized the car.

"Well, well, Mikki-san," he muttered to himself, "you travel in very high circles indeed." He ruefully thought of the money he had left for her on the table, reflecting that he would now have to walk back to the base. Shit, he thought as he started off.

It was after 2:00 A.M. by the time he got back to the base. Doug wasn't in the room. He turned on the light and took off his hat and jacket. He began to remove his white shoes when he noticed letters on the desk. Probably for Douglas, from the Clipper, he thought. One shoe in hand, he crossed to the desk.

He was right. A letter for Douglas from his wife. He idly pushed it aside, and his breath caught. Beneath it, in handwriting he immediately recognized, was a letter addressed to him. It was postmarked New York, November 26, 1941. At first he just stood staring at it dumbly. Then he sat on the bed, holding the letter before him, afraid to open it. After all this time he doubted that it could contain anything he wanted to hear. It would probably announce that she had married someone else.

His heart still pounding, he finally steeled himself, opened the envelope, and withdrew the letter. His hands were shaking so badly that he dropped it, and a photograph, enclosed in the folds of the letter itself, fell out onto the floor. He looked at the white four-inch square that lay facedown in front of him, and suddenly he knew, just as surely as if he could see through it, what it was.

He reached down and turned it over. Even his anticipation did not diminish the shock of the sight of the smiling baby in the photograph, with its pale eyes and curly blond hair. Michael's chest heaved, and a shudder passed through his body. That it could be his did not surprise him, but that it could look so much like him amazed him. He put his hand over his eyes and wept tears that were part relief, part anger, part love. He sat on the bed, elbows resting on his knees, and cried into his hands until there were no tears left.

When he finished, he gazed at the picture for a long time before he was able to put it down and attend to the letter. Its coldness stunned him. But as he read the words again and again, he began to recognize the pain and fear that lay behind them. He sat down at the desk and wrote a response. When he was done, he sealed it and left it there, slipped off his dress trousers, and fell into bed in his underwear. Catherine and his son were in Java by now. And he would be going there shortly on leave. No other man had come between them after all, except perhaps the six-month-old one in the photograph. She still loved him, in spite of the tone of the letter. He knew it now. Thank God he would see her soon. He closed his eyes, thinking that tonight, for the first time in a long while, he would be able to sleep soundly.

At that moment it was past midnight at the Hommonie Club in Batavia, but the dining room was still filled with noisy patrons reluctant to end the weekend. Five of those diners excused themselves, leaving the table's two remaining occupants to stare at the man who had just joined them with the same enthusiasm with which they might have greeted a fly in their soup. Bernard stared belligerently back and proceeded to sit himself down at the table, loudly summoning utensils from the waiters.

"You didn't tell me you were going out tonight, my dear," he said to Margit, ignoring Catherine's presence.

"I didn't expect you home, so I saw no reason to tell you," Margit replied coolly. "I can't imagine to what good fortune we owe this little surprise."

Bernard ignored the gibe and engrossed himself in ordering more wine.

"You've had too much to drink already," Margit observed mildly.

Bernard slammed his fist on the table, and the silverware responded with a startled jump. "It's none of your damned business how much I've had to drink!" He drained his glass, and

305

by the time he put it down with a thud of defiance his scowl had dissolved into a sulk.

Margit sat looking at Bernard, sunk down in his chair. For a moment she was struck by a strange sense of pity which she refused to give in to. Instead, she rose abruptly. "I'm going home," she announced.

Catherine, who had observed the scene in silent discomfort, got up to go with her. Bernard, still spoiling for a victory to make up for the fight he had lost earlier with his Indonesian mistress, followed them. Sending his chauffeur home with his own car, he climbed into the back seat of Margit's convertible.

"Brown bitch," Bernard muttered to himself. His mistress had demanded more money from him—again. When he refused, she had slammed the door and locked him out. How could he tell her it was Margit's money, not his, that paid for the way he lived? He could not ask Margit for more money without arousing her suspicions. So he had stood outside his mistress's door, overcome by humiliation and desperation, feeling himself surrounded by powerful women whom he somehow needed but could not control. In that moment he had sensed for the first time that his dependence on Margit's money had cost him far more than he had gained. That realization had moved him so close to despair that he had been immediately driven to seek out Margit at the club, not for comfort but for the familiar confrontation he knew would follow. She was always so cool, so impervious to his every attack that it was easy to rid himself of whatever guilt and remorse he felt in a cathartic argument. Besides, he sensed that she could never have been able to abide his tears and confessions of regret any more than could he. It would have changed their whole relationship beyond imagining.

They drove from the harbor to the hills in silence. When they reached home, Margit got out of the car without so much as a glance at Bernard and walked quickly into the house and up the stairs to her room. Relieved that she could now escape the two of them, Catherine followed. Bernard brought up the rear, pausing to pour himself a glass from the wine he had brought home with him. He raised it toward Catherine's retreating figure in a mock toast.

"You don't fool me." He winked as she reached the stairs. "You came here only so that you could humor the old man into leaving Michael's bastard some of his millions."

"Go to hell, Bernard," Catherine replied crisply. Without stopping to look at him, she followed Margit's path up the marble steps.

Suddenly pleased with himself again, Bernard adjourned, glass in hand, to the small library that opened its shuttered doors to the front of the house. He sank down into one of the overstuffed chintz chairs, looking like a hungry toad among the oversize print flowers. Later, he told himself, he would get even with Margit by demanding sex. He let his fingers relax, and the empty wineglass fell from his hand and shattered on the marble floor. He smiled at the sound. No sooner had the house settled back to silence than Margit screamed from her room.

"My God. No!"

Catherine froze on the stairs as Bernard, suddenly sober, came out to gape up at the second floor. Margit appeared at the top of the stairs, her face as pale as the white gown she wore. She was staring straight at Catherine.

Fear tore at Catherine's senses. "What's the matter, Margit?"

"The radio. I just turned it on. They said the Japanese have bombed Pearl Harbor!"

Catherine sank back against the railing, feeling as if the stairs beneath her had suddenly given way. After a moment of stunned disbelief she realized Michael would not be coming home on leave. And for the first time she realized how desperately she had wanted to see him again.

It was 3:30 A.M. in Manila when Michael awoke to Douglas's shaking him awake in the middle of a nightmare, shouting something incomprehensible into his face. When he came to his senses, it was to find that the nightmare was not his own at all: It was the world's.

Pearl Harbor had been attacked at 2:00 A.M. Philippine time, Douglas was telling him, the anguish of the message clearly etched on his face. Suddenly all the relief and hope Michael had felt before was gone.

Chapter 31

Six hours after the Japanese succeeded in crippling America's Pacific Fleet, they struck again. This time the newly created Far East Air Force at Clark Field in the Philippines was wiped out—caught with its flaps down during a lunch break ten hours after the attack on Pearl Harbor. The Japanese had arrived in the middle of a clear sky. Reports of the incoming enemy planes had been received by air force headquarters at Nielson Field, but it had been unable to rouse the base radio operator at Clark to issue the warning. Commercial radio station KMZH broadcast news of the approaching Japanese planes, but the announcement had been greeted with catcalls and laughter by listening crews in the Clark mess hall. Like the battleships at Pearl Harbor, the bombers and fighters were lined up in a neat, convenient row—ripe for picking. Militarily it was a disaster of the magnitude of Pearl Harbor.

As reports of additional Japanese attacks came in, each one filled Michael with a fear which was on the verge of becoming panic, not for himself, but for Catherine and his children, for Margit and Kara and Maitreya and its workers: for all those he loved. His first impulse, when the war broke out, had been to desert, to get to the Indies somehow and protect everyone dear to him, if he could, against whatever was to come. Reason had prevailed, barely, and only because he still hoped for a miracle which would enable him to get to the Indies soon, without being court-martialed.

His greatest fear was for Catherine. She didn't know he had received her letter and had learned about their son. She wasn't even aware that he had asked Kara for a divorce. He knew that every flying mission now could be his last, as the skies became dominated by the lighter, more maneuverable Japanese Zeros. Michael could accept death. What he could not accept was the realization that his death would mean Catherine would never know how much he loved her and how much he wanted their son. Unless she knew that, there could be no peace for him, not even in death.

Miracles were in short supply in the Philippines during the two weeks between Pearl Harbor and the Christmas holidays. But with each disaster the chances for Michael's own personal miracle grew. The big Cavite Naval Base had been nearly destroyed and, as a result, the Asiatic Fleet was ordered south to Java to join the combined Allied strike force made up of the Dutch, British, and Australian navies. Michael's hopes increased that the PBY squadrons might soon follow. Ginny's twin brother, Tom, was on board the flagship *Houston* when she left her moorings at Panay Island to head for Java. He had not met Michael, nor did Michael even know of his assignment to the *Houston*. Had he known, he might have attempted to get a letter to Catherine through Tom. As it was, he heard that Bud Larson's ship, the *Peary,* was leaving for Java immediately, and his hopes of contacting Catherine rose. The letter he had written her the night before Pearl Harbor had been hastily bundled up with his other possessions and moved from the officer's quarters at Cavite to the house of the old Japanese couple. There had been no opportunity to mail it. Unable to leave the secluded anchorage where his squadron had been sent to escape the Cavite air raids, Michael found a scrap of paper and wrote Catherine a hasty note, telling her that he had received her letter and that he loved her and would come to her as soon as he could. A frustrating search of his tent turned up no envelope, so he sealed it closed with tape from his first-aid kit and gave it to the supply truck driver to take to Bud, along with a note requesting that Bud deliver the note personally once he reached Java. If Catherine had already left the Indies, Michael knew Margit would somehow forward it. He had tried to cable her the day after Pearl Harbor but was told that only messages of high priority were being allowed through. He left a cable with the dispatcher in the vague hope it might get sent anyway.

The dispatcher had merely shrugged. "It's your money, wanna waste it, why not? Won't be worth much in another month anyhow."

Manila had become the Wild West of the East. Air-raid wardens armed with rifles and probably too much to drink shot out lights in houses and hotel rooms whether there was an air raid or not. The nightclubs were packed. Residents had lunch and drinks on the terrace of the Manila Hotel and watched the aerial dogfights over Manila Bay. Fights broke out later between revelers and the exhausted pilots who had risked their lives providing the entertainment.

While life had become one big party for the civilian population, the military situation on Luzon had become calamitous. On December 22 the Japanese landed a large invasion force. MacArthur had grievously overestimated the ability of his army to defend the entire island. His new recruits fell back, offering little resistance to the experienced Japanese. Without air support the situation was hopeless. MacArthur was forced to order a withdrawal to the peninsula of Bataan, where he planned to hold out, denying the Japanese access to Manila Bay until naval reinforcements could arrive. The retreat was orderly and efficient, but since supplies had been dispersed throughout the island, there was only a month's food supply left on Bataan to feed 80,000 troops. Manila was being declared an open city, and MacArthur was moving his headquarters to the fortress island of Corregidor at the entrance to Manila Bay, several miles off the shores of Bataan.

Out of the chaos and haste of that evacuation came the answer to Michael's hopes. Douglas came bearing it on the passenger side of a dusty supply truck from Manila, waving it out the window like a benediction.

"Hey, Michael, if I promise not to molest your wife or your sister, will you invite me home for Christmas dinner?"

Michael looked at the white piece of paper fluttering from Douglas's hand and felt an enormous surge of relief.

"You're going home, you lucky stiff!" Douglas shouted as he climbed out of the truck. "And takin' us orphans with you." He was pounding Michael on the back in jubilation. "We pick up the admiral and his staff tomorrow—Christmas Day—and fly him to Java. How's that for a Christmas present?''

The other Patwing 10 planes had already gone, ordered out the previous day to head for the safety of Ceram Island, in the Indies. Only Michael's plane remained. He had watched them go with a combination of regret and hope, not knowing what would be in store for his own crew. He had simply been ordered to stand by.

To celebrate Christmas Eve, the crew drank the last of the Scotch Douglas had been saving. It was not enough to keep them from rising early the next morning to strike their tents and prepare to leave. For the first time in the two weeks they had been there, Michael noticed how beautiful it was. Under any circumstances other than flying daily combat missions, he would have found it a paradise.

The palm trees came right down to the narrow strip of beach. The sand was a warm, bright gold, and the water a brilliant blue. That morning the crew took baths in the nearby natural springs, tinkered with the plane until it was in the best running order in weeks, and played cards, killing time until they were scheduled to leave. Michael had on his freshly creased khaki trousers but was still barefoot and reaching for his undershirt when one of the men called out.

"Hey, Kelly, cut out the racket.''

The mechanic rose from the sheet of metal he had been working on, wrench loose in one hand. The other men stopped what they were doing, razors poised at lathered faces, coffee cups half-raised, ears straining at the muffled vibrations, growing louder. Eyes anxiously searched the horizon, hopefully seeking the sight of one of the few U.S. planes still flying.

"Here they come!'' one of the men shouted, pointing inland over the trees.

Five fighters came suddenly in at treetop level, the sound of their approach muffled by the trees they almost touched. They approached with a purposefulness that indicated they knew just what they would find. Machine-gun fire from the planes strafed the beach as the crew went diving hastily for cover in the surrounding jungle.

Michael went immediately for the water, swimming fast and hard for the plane. The fighters banked and came in again.

311

Splashes from bullets spouted around him, forcing him to dive deep several times to escape. When he pulled himself on board the plane, he found Berchot, the aviation machinist's mate who had been standing duty, lying before the open forward door, wounded in the chest and head. Michael quickly grabbed a nearby first-aid kit and stopped Berchot's bleeding, then turned to man the waist gun as the Zeros began another pass.

The first round of fire returned from the seaplane surprised the attacking fighters. It caught the first Zero just as it leveled off for the attack. It suddenly veered to one side, trailing smoke, narrowly missing the seaplane. Michael caught a glimpse of the pilot struggling to open the canopy just before the plane hit the water and exploded. The concussion jarred the anchored Catalina, and a huge wave sent Michael sprawling against the wall, just as the bullets from the other attacking fighters ripped into the seaplane's sides, ricocheting wildly around the interior, starting two small fires.

The seaplane shuddered and settled back into the water as Michael crawled forward to fire the bow gun at the receding planes, then turned his attention to the two small fires, which he doused with an extinguisher before he climbed back to the waist gun. Silence fell as the planes disappeared to regroup for another pass. Michael took that moment to check Berchot, who was unconscious, and then returned to wait tensely beside the gun.

He heard them first before he saw them, a distant buzz like angry mosquitoes before they came storming in again over the treetops, single file. This time they concentrated their fire on the plane, ignoring the small-arms fire from the men on the beach, who had come out of hiding to watch the life-and-death struggle, helpless to offer anything but token resistance to the approaching fighters.

As he watched them line up and peel off, one by one, Michael steeled himself against the gunsights and prayed for a calm sea. He was about to commence firing at the first fighter when the Catalina was thrust suddenly upward by a sea swell, causing him momentarily to lose both his balance and his concentration on the approaching plane. The first Zero was already firing by the time he had it sighted again and opened fire. Smoke billowed from its fuselage as he scored a hit, but it continued directly at him, guns flashing blue as it passed overhead. It was still firing in furious frustration well beyond target, its bullets tearing with futile rage into the surrounding jungle. Unable to gain altitude, it disappeared over the treetops of the curving bay shoreline, trailing smoke. A few seconds later an explosion and a thick column of black smoke announced its fate.

In the meantime, Michael was already occupied with the remaining three fighters. By the time they completed their pass Michael could see sky and water through hundreds of tatters in the thin metal skin of the plane, but miraculously neither he nor Berchot had been hit. Some of the ammunition on board had ignited, and it sounded as if dozens of machine guns were firing. Gasoline, seeping from the ruptured gas tanks, had caught fire, filling the plane with smoke so thick he could no longer see to fire the guns. The fires were now too numerous to fight, and the bombs on board were in danger of going off at any moment. There was no hope left that he could save the plane. The three remaining Zeros would be back at any moment to finish off the smoking hulk of the Catalina.

Michael pulled Berchot to the hatch, strapped a life jacket around the wounded man, and lowered him into the sea, jumping in after him. The water was warm, and overhead the sky was bright and relentlessly clear. Perfect flying weather. The smoke fumes from the dying Catalina choked Michael as he locked an arm around Berchot and began to swim the fifty yards toward shore. The growing roar told him the Zeros were coming in again. Berchot came to and began to struggle against Michael's grip with surprising force. He was not fully conscious, but he was fighting both the water and Michael like a madman. Michael couldn't let go or Berchot would drown, but the effort needed to control the flailing ground crewman prevented him from swimming toward shore. Helplessly he looked up and saw the approaching planes. There were only two of them. He must have damaged the third so badly it had either crashed or given up the fight. It was little consolation. Two would be quite enough to finish the job.

Just as he braced himself for the tearing bullets, a huge explosion rocked the seaplane when one of its bombs went off, sending flying bits of metal screaming through the air. Something tore at Michael's shoulder, and he gasped in pain. Mercifully Berchot sank into unconsciousness again. Michael could no longer grip

313

with his left arm, so he switched to his right and continued to kick toward shore, but not nearly fast enough to elude the approaching planes. He heard splashes and shouts as the men from his crew started into the water to aid the floundering pair. He shouted at them to get back, fearing they would be killed.

Suddenly a breeze caught the black cloud of smoke from the burning seaplane and spread it over the water, enveloping them. Choking, Michael kept swimming until he thought his lungs would burst. Then waiting hands grabbed them, pulling them through the shallow water toward the beach. The enemy planes, their target destroyed and their enemy hidden by the drifting smoke, withdrew, nursing their wounds.

Exhausted, Michael sank down onto the sand. Blood ran down his back from the wound in his left shoulder. As he stared numbly at the burning plane, it was racked again by explosions and began to sink.

Douglas Stuart sat down beside him, his face near tears.

"I'm sorry, Michael. Not just for the boat. I know how much you wanted to get to Java."

Michael continued to stare in silence at the billowing smoke.

Douglas continued. "You'd probably get there better on your own."

Michael looked away toward the curving shoreline out toward the open sea as he struggled to control his feelings. He looked first at Douglas and then at the weary, sad faces of his dispirited crew. What would happen to them now? Fliers without planes. He knew he couldn't leave; he had already made his choice. He was in this war now, whether he liked it or not, fighting, not for the flag but for the men with whom he served. They depended on him, and he couldn't let them down.

He watched as the men hailed a passing army truck and loaded Berchot onto it. One of them climbed on board to ride with him to the hospital. Michael folded his arms on his knees and rested his head on them, wearily staring in silence at the shady spot of sand between his feet. He felt Douglas's hand rest gently upon his uninjured shoulder, comforting him.

Two days later Michael reported to naval headquarters in the Marston Building in Manila. There was nothing left of the U.S. Navy except one officer and a seaman and piles of paper strewn around the rooms. Essential material had already been moved to Corregidor. The rest had gone with the admiral when he left by submarine on Christmas Day, after the seaplane had been destroyed. Whatever was here would be burned.

The officer, a lieutenant commander, glanced at Michael's arm in a sling. "Sorry about that," he said.

Michael shrugged. "It's really nothing." He felt curiously numb. Either the medication or his efforts to ward off his bitter disappointment were threatening to engulf him. He shifted uncomfortably under the officer's scrutiny.

"I suppose you want your orders," the commander said finally.

Michael was silent, not wanting to waste the energy it would take to confirm the obvious.

"Wish we had another plane to give pilots like you, but we don't." He nodded toward the window with its venetian blinds dangling askew. "The only thing flying around here are the birds, and pretty soon, when food supplies get low, even those will be gone."

"The Japanese," Michael replied softly. "The Japanese will still be flying." His voice sounded endlessly flat.

"Yes. I suppose you're right." He looked at Michael more closely. "You okay?" he asked doubtfully.

"Look." Michael felt his irritation growing. "I just got out of sick bay. I came for my orders."

The officer nodded curtly, somewhat offended. Everyone's temper was short these days. He shuffled briefly around his desk and came up with a paper he handed over.

Michael took it almost grudgingly. "The *Canopus*!" he exclaimed when he looked at it. "I'm a pilot, not a sailor!"

The *Canopus* was an old sub tender which had been moved to Mariveles after the bombing of Cavite Naval Base. It was better known, at least to its somewhat defiant crew of 400 men, as the Old Lady. It had originally been a World War I transport, converted later to sub tender in the Navy's determination not to waste any ship that would float.

"Yes. Well," the commander replied somewhat apologetically, "all naval personnel remaining in the Philippines have been ordered to Mariveles, across the bay on Bataan. You and your crew are to report New Year's Day. It's strictly temporary," he added.

Michael eyed him wearily. "Everything here is strictly temporary, Commander. Meaning it exists until the Japanese decide to blow it up."

"No. I mean all the submarines are being ordered out of the Philippines. And the sub tender will go with them, of course."

Michael felt a rising hope he tried to suppress for fear of disappointment. "Where are they going?"

"Surabaya. Java."

Michael felt a burst of renewed belief in miracles.

"You'll be transferred back to your air squadron once you get there. With luck a new shipment of planes will be arriving in Java from Australia before you do." He glanced over and saw Michael's look of relief. "Of course, it's a dangerous trip. Japs control much of the open sea between here and Java—"

Michael didn't bother to listen. He gave the surprised officer a snappy salute and left. He was shaking as he paused just outside the door to fold his orders with one hand and stick them in his pocket. He had been given a reprieve.

"Hey, Lieutenant." The commander came to the door and called after him down the empty hall. "I didn't get a chance to offer my congratulations. The admiral recommended you for the Navy Cross before he left."

Michael didn't stop to answer. There had been nothing heroic about his actions or his motives. He had shot down those fighters because he needed his plane to get to Java. It was just that simple.

Michael stopped by the St. Louis Arms Apartments on New Year's Day to say good-bye to Carol before he left for Mariveles. The Japanese were outside Manila, preparing to enter the city within days. Carol hadn't gone to work since Bud had left her on Christmas Day to return to his ship, and she'd been drinking too much.

"Might as well drink it up before they get here and take it away. It's the patriotic thing to do. Want some?"

Michael shook his head. "You all right?" he asked doubtfully.

"About as well as could be expected for a girl who's about to be raped and murdered by little yellow monkeys."

Michael winced. Not that such prejudices were new. He'd heard them often enough, in Singapore and Batavia and Sidney and other places long before the war. The most popular story went like this: Once upon a time long ago a Chinese ship had been wrecked on the uninhabited island of Japan; lacking women, the men had mated with monkeys and so produced the Japanese race. It was a crude joke, told these days with bravado to assuage doubts and calm fears. She walked to the window and pushed aside the flimsy curtain to look at the streets below, which were remarkably quiet.

"When are you going to Mariveles?" she asked.

"Today."

She was quiet for a moment.

"In Nanking," she said softly, staring into some private space, "they supposedly killed two hundred fifty thousand civilians and raped and then murdered more than twenty thousand women. Do you think it's true or just propaganda?"

"Probably propaganda," he lied, but his own gut clutched at the thought of the women in his family. He didn't know for certain where Kara was. Margit would be in Batavia, Julienne at Maitreya, and Catherine . . . perhaps Catherine would have gone home by now; but somehow he was certain that she hadn't, and the certainty filled him with fear.

Carol assumed an alluring pose. "Surely this bod couldn't be appealing to a five-foot-three-inch shrimp."

She stretched her leggy five-foot-nine-inch California blond form to its imposing height and attempted a nonchalant smile. Visions of Catherine's diminutive form floated disturbingly into Michael's head and were pushed aside.

"Looking for something, Michael?" She looked at him a bit wistfully. "I was just wondering why you came."

"Just to see how you were and to say good-bye."

"Oh? Nobody else did. Except Bud, of course. He hated like hell to leave."

"I can imagine."

"Son of a bitch," she said, pouting. "He goes off, and I'm stuck here."

"Surely that didn't surprise you. You must have realized it could happen." He stopped himself. There was no point in berating her. It was too late to do any good.

"I . . ." Her breath caught in a little sob that she quickly washed down with her gimlet before continuing. "Never really thought it would happen, I guess. Besides, Bud could have deserted. What the hell difference could it make now? But no, he's career Navy to the end." She eyed Michael speculatively. "I bet you would have deserted it if it had been your wife. Funny. I don't even know if you're married."

He didn't answer. She finished her drink and flopped off the couch to fix another. Her shirttail was tied in a knot at her waist. She had piled her blond hair upon her head in a skewed bun. Strands of hair had come loose and trailed around her head forlornly.

"You think it will be like Nanking?" Her voice was suddenly small, like a little girl's.

"No. No, I don't." He lied as confidently as he could. He hadn't the slightest idea of what it was going to be like.

"Why did you come, Michael—really?" She said it accusingly this time.

"Just as I said, to see how you were. And to tell you there's a place in the mountains, a little village, where guerrilla activities will probably center. I could arrange for you to go there."

"Oh, God, no." She laughed. "I'm a city girl. What would I do out there alone with all those guerrillas and pigs!"

He sighed. "I thought I'd offer."

She was suddenly serious. "I appreciate your caring about what happens to me. You mean it when you say you'll be a friend, don't you?"

He smiled, though he didn't feel like it. She seemed so pathetically alone, and there was so little he could do about it.

Just past noon Michael and Douglas boarded a navy speedboat on its way to Mariveles Harbor at the tip of the Bataan Peninsula. They were the last military personnel to be evacuated from Manila. The Japanese general in charge of the Manila invasion force had paused to regroup his men. Douglas saw this as a good sign, on the theory that a rested army is a more disciplined one, less likely to loot or harm civilians. Thinking of Carol, alone in her apartment, Michael could only hope he was right.

Rather than let him be evacuated by truck to one of the field hospitals near Mariveles, Michael and Douglas had brought Berchot with them onto the boat by stretcher. His injuries from the attack on the seaplane had been serious but not critical. The huge bay was empty of all but a few local fishing boats. The merchant and military ships which had jammed its busy waters had either escaped or been sunk. Berchot, pleased to be out of the hospital, joked with everyone on board until the engines started, but then talking called for more effort than his injuries would comfortably permit.

A seaman with binoculars scanned the sky. All clear. The waterfront, too, was deserted. It was Berchot, lying on his back in the stern with no place else to look but up, who saw them first—tiny glints of light coming from the north in the direction of Clark Field. Ignoring the pain in his chest, he rose on his elbows and pointed.

"Japs! Ten of them."

The planes were making their first run on Corregidor. One of them peeled away to take in after the speedboat, spraying bullets into the water across the bow; but the maneuverable craft easily dodged them, and the plane gave up to seek bigger, less elusive targets. The boat was halfway across the bay when a thick funnel of black smoke boiled up from the direction of Mariveles. Michael's heart sank. When they reached the dock, he found the crew of the *Canopus* fighting to contain the fire and jokingly trying to salvage what they could of their New Year's turkey dinner. He climbed out of the boat and stood on the dock watching the damage control efforts of the *Canopus* crew. The executive officer came over and offered his hand.

"Lieutenant Stanford?"

Michael nodded.

"I'm Bill Oliver." He looked back at the ship, barely visible through the smoke. "I'd say welcome aboard, but I'm afraid we don't have much of a ship."

Valiant effort prevented the magazines from exploding, and hours later, when the fire was out and the heat had dissipated, the ship's quarters could be reoccupied. However, the ship had taken a direct hit from an armor-piercing Japanese bomb, heavily damaging the main propeller shaft and making the *Canopus* too slow and unseaworthy in dangerous waters. Once again Michael's hopes of reaching Java had been destroyed by the Japanese.

The Japanese attack had marked the beginning of daily new air raids. To escape, the crew of the *Canopus* moved to the army storage caves in the hills overlooking the harbor. They disguised their ship to look like an abandoned hulk, and by night they used its machine shops to repair everything from false teeth and bicycles to PT boats. Michael was ordered to set up a naval infantry unit to defend the west coast of Bataan against Japanese attempts to make a landing behind the forward line. The battalion was composed of naval leftovers, crews that had lost their planes or ships, and shore personnel from Cavite Naval Base.

The Japanese invasion force struck at the regrouped Bataan force as hard as it could, but this time the American and Filipino troops responded with confidence and determination. Although they were forced, after bitter fighting, to fall back to a second defense line, morale remained high—even on half rations necessitated by a shortage in the food supply. MacArthur made regular broadcasts from Corregidor to his men on Bataan: "Help is on the way from the United States. Thousands of troops and hundreds of planes are being dispatched. . . . No further retreat is possible . . . our supplies are ample; a determined defense will defeat the enemy's attack. . . ."

Perhaps, Michael thought cynically as he listened with the others, the general even half believes it himself.

Chapter 32
Batavia, Java,
January 1, 1942

After the Japanese attack on Pearl Harbor, no panic ensued in Batavia. There was no grand exodus of local residents, partly because it wasn't clear where sanctuary truly lay. The Atlantic was treacherous for ships, far too risky for nonmilitary passage. Now the Pacific route to America was closed, and rumors spread that an invasion of the U.S. west coast was imminent. South, to Australia, was the only route open to escape, and since the Japanese invasion of Malaya and the Philippines posed no immediate danger to that lifeline, most people decided not to give up their homes—at least not yet.

After the initial shock wore off, life went on as usual in Batavia. The Priok Yacht Club still held Sunday races, and Europeans still dined and danced at the Hotel des Indies and the Hommonie Club. December became a wait-and-see month. Most people still believed that Singapore was impregnable, that the Philippines would stand, and that, if all else failed, the combined Dutch, American, Australian, and British navies could prevent an invasion of the Indies.

Optimism managed to prevail, though it had little basis in reality. Two days after Pearl Harbor the great British battleship *Prince of Wales*, which had helped sink the German battleship *Bismarck* in the Atlantic, set out with the British battle cruiser *Repulse* to prevent a rumored Japanese invasion on the Malaya coast. The rumor proved false, but the two ships had ventured too far without air cover and were sunk by land-based Japanese bombers. It was the first time such a thing had ever happened, and in addition to destroying the naval myth that battleships could not be sunk by planes, it seriously reduced Allied naval power in the Southwest Pacific.

The Allied assumption had always been that the Japanese were capable of only one offensive operation at a time, yet by now they had landed almost simultaneous invasion forces in the Philippines, Hong Kong, the Malay Peninsula, and Guam. On December 10 Guam had surrendered. Hong Kong was captured on Christmas Day, and Manila was taken shortly afterward. In Malaya, British, Australian, and Indian troops were now retreating down the peninsula toward Singapore, all the impregnable guns of which pointed futilely toward the sea while the enemy approached through the jungle—a feat considered impossible.

On New Year's Day Catherine received a phone call.

"Catherine?" The voice crackled and faded with the poor connection. She didn't recognize it. "I've been trying to reach you for the past several days but the damn phone . . . I couldn't get through."

Her heart leaped as she recognized Tom's voice.

"We've been transferred from the Philippines. I can't say any more on the phone. Can you come to Surabaya?" The static crackled.

"What?"

"I said, can you come to Surabaya?"

"Yes. Of course. . . . As soon as I can."

"Good!"

"Tom . . ."

"Yes."

"It's so good to hear your voice."

"Same here. Come as soon as you can."

She left Michael with Margit and took the train to Surabaya. Tom met her at the station and gathered her into his arms. He held her tightly for a long moment and then released her. She was smiling, but he could not hide his concern.

"What in hell are you doing here, Cat? When Ginny wrote me you were here—before Pearl—I thought you were crazy to come. But I never expected to find you still here."

"At first there was no way I could get back to the States, so I decided to stay here until I could tell what was going to happen."

"Christ, Catherine——"

She silenced him with a finger on his lips. "Now don't scold. I plan to go to Australia on February twelfth. I have passage on a Dutch ship."

"That's more than a month away," he protested.

"It's all I could get," she said, lying.

He was wearing his navy dress white uniform, and he looked exceedingly handsome. She smiled and tucked her arm into his and began to lead him toward the door of the station. "Come on," she said cajolingly. "It may be a long war. So let's enjoy this time together."

Relenting, he grinned. "The men on the ship are never going to believe this one. Ten thousand miles from home and a war going on, and I walk into the wardroom with you on my arm."

Tom had used military connections to commandeer a hotel room for her. Like Batavia, Surabaya was jammed with European refugees from Hong Kong, Manila, and elsewhere. He made dinner reservations at the Surabaya Country Club with its wide green terraces leading down to its famed swimming pool and spouting fountains. The club was now full of allied military personnel, mostly naval officers since Surabaya was now a base for the newly created Allied fleet. Catherine and Tom sat at one of the tables on the upper terrace.

"You didn't ask me, but I'll volunteer it anyway. I didn't have a chance to get in touch with Michael. We anchored at Panay Island, and he was on Luzon. But I did find out some news that might interest you."

"Oh . . ."

"Well . . . does it?"

"Go on," she said, scowling slightly as she sipped her drink.

"One of the officers on board the submarine *Shark* told me that most of the seaplane squadrons have been ordered to the Indies. So you may see him after all."

"Can you find out for sure?"

He nodded. "If you're really interested."

She flushed slightly. "Not in the way you think."

They were interrupted by Ken Brandon, the gunnery officer who shared Tom's stateroom.

"Dr. Morgan, I presume." He grinned and sat down. "I've heard a lot about you, but Tom didn't say half enough." He waved a hello to one of the Dutch naval officers.

"Have you heard the latest?" Brandon asked.

"What is it?" Tom replied. He was feeling impatient with his congenial roommate and now realized it had been a mistake to come to the club.

"A Dutch admiral named Doorman will head the combined strike force. Jeez. Can you imagine what this is going to be like? None of us speak Dutch. We'll get into battle and have to translate our orders. Besides the language barrier, we've got three different navies with different battle procedures and tactics."

Vice Admiral W. A. Glassford, commander of the U.S. Southwest Pacific task force, a trim, distinguished-looking man, stopped to exchange pleasantries and to meet Catherine.

"Why don't you and Catherine join me for dinner in my stateroom aboard the *Houston* tomorrow night?" he asked Tom.

He found himself acquiescing when he really didn't want to. All of a sudden he was sharing Catherine's company with the whole American Navy—or so it seemed.

"Come on. Let's get out of here," he muttered at the first opportune moment.

They drove around the city in the military car he had commandeered, sight-seeing and talking. It was clear to Tom that Catherine was still in love with Michael, even though she didn't seem to realize it. It had been six months since he had last seen her. He had to admit to himself that he had been hoping things had changed. When he took her to her hotel that night, she kissed him lightly at the door to her room.

"Thanks," she said.

He looked puzzled.

"For not trying to take advantage of the situation." She smiled wryly.

He grinned. "Give me time. It's only been a day, and I'm a slow worker."

But there wasn't to be any time. He had ship's business the following day, and when he picked her up to bring her to the *Houston* that evening, his mood was subdued.

"Our orders came through. We're assigned to convoy duty,

escorting supplies from Darwin, Australia, to the British in Singapore."

"When will you be leaving?"

"Tomorrow."

She didn't hide her disappointment.

"I'm sorry, Cat. I wish there had been more time."

"So do I." Tears brightened her eyes. "Well, at least we had these few days. When will you be back?"

"I don't know, but you'll be gone by then."

"Yes. Well, perhaps you'll be coming home soon."

"Perhaps," he said softly, adding, "That is, if we fail here and the Indies fall."

"I didn't mean that I was wishing for that."

"I know."

She went to him, and he hugged her close, and she held him tightly to her. "Sometimes I'm so afraid," she whispered.

"So am I," he said softly.

He came to see her off on the early train the next morning.

He stopped and turned to face her as they neared the boarding area, his hands on her arms.

"Cat, when I checked on Michael yesterday, I learned that he won't be coming to Java—or Darwin either for that matter." He saw the fear in her eyes. "Now don't go jumping to conclusions. His plane was destroyed in a raid on Christmas Day, but he wasn't on the casualty list. I had it double-checked. It looks as if he'll be staying in the Philippines." He searched her eyes. "Are you all right?"

She nodded. The final boarding call sounded. He guided her through the crowd and onto the steps of one of the cars and handed her suitcase up to her.

"Good-bye, Cat."

"Indian giver," she admonished him with tears in her eyes.

He smiled. "Take care of yourself and the baby."

She found a seat by the window. He remained standing on the platform as the train began to pull out. She waved to him, but he did not return her wave.

A day after Catherine got back to Batavia she received a call from Admiral Glassford. He offered to arrange military evacuation for her if the need arose, hastily adding that he was certain things wouldn't come to that. As she hung up the phone, the baby crawled into the room, vigorously chewing a rubber toy. He had crankily been cutting teeth and had refused to be distracted from his pain. She picked him up, relieved when he quietly went limp, wanting to be comforted. There were times when she felt it had been a mistake to have him, that she couldn't bring him up alone. But then came moments like this when she needed him. He was all she had of Michael. All she might ever have.

Chapter 33

Point Longoskawayan, Bataan,
January 23, 1942

Berchot hadn't minded his first turn as naval lookout atop Mount Puloc. It was quiet duty, the kind which didn't put many demands on his convalescing body. He had been out of the hospital a week. He would have preferred having someone along to talk to, but the beach defense was spread so thin no one else could be spared. His perch wasn't far from the critical West Road, the supply road which ran from Mariveles Harbor north to General Wainwright's Bataan forces holding the west end of the Bataan defense line. He couldn't see the road through the jungle, but he could glimpse the Puco River and the waters of Mariveles Harbor to the east and the ocean expanse of the South China Sea to the west. It was clear. Nothing to worry about. It was nine o'clock in the evening and almost dark. He had eaten hours before and was hungry again, but these days, with rations cut in half, he was always hungry. Still, the men on the *Canopus* had it better than most on Bataan. At least they didn't have to depend for each day's rations on army trucks that often never made it to the front line.

Berchot had no wife or sweetheart back home. He always found a local girl to go to bed with when he needed it and Mariveles was no exception. That had been the only inconvenience about standing watch on Mount Puloc tonight. Some other sailor might be making it right now with his girl.

So absorbed did he become in his concern that he had almost

327

ceased to notice the terrain, but then a movement on the perimeter of the clearing at the base of the mountain's west slope caught
his eye. He grabbed his binoculars and adjusted them in the gray
light, his heart thumping as he sought to bring the area into
focus. His straining eyes saw nothing at first. There. He caught a
glimpse of a branch moving, and then, farther down, a vine
swayed. It might have been a stray caribou that had escaped the
dinner table of the hungry troops. Suddenly the jungle was
jiggling and coming to life everywhere. Berchot grabbed for his
field combat phone with one hand, binoculars still trained, and
rang up the ship.

"I think I've spotted something." His voice was excited. "I
can't make anything out, but it's possibly a landing party."

The swaying intensified, and then abruptly hundreds of Japanese
troops broke out into the clearing at the base of the mountain
and began swarming up the slope toward Berchot's position.

"Oh, shit!" he cried. "Here they come. I'm getting out of
here!"

Hanging onto the phone and his rifle, he began to plunge down
the narrow, twisted trail that had been cut only two weeks
before, heedless now of how much noise he made in his hasty
flight. By the time he reached the ship the Japanese had taken
possession of the highest vantage point in southwestern Bataan
and were poised to cut the West Road.

Aboard the *Canopus* Captain Sanders turned to Michael, who
had been present as a breathless Berchot delivered his report. The
Japanese had made an amphibious landing, behind the lines,
intending to duplicate their successful tactics in Malaya.

"Well, Lieutenant, it's up to you."

"Thanks," Michael said grimly, all too aware that his un-
trained naval infantry troops were all that stood between the
Japanese and control of western Bataan.

To Michael's mortification, while he crouched in a foxhole,
under heavy enemy fire, his sex began to swell, something he
hadn't felt in weeks. He knew it wasn't sex he wanted but love.
He wanted to feel Catherine's arms around him, holding him. He
wanted to bury his face against her breast and have her hold him
like a baby because he was so goddamned afraid. He had been in
many dangerous situations before he went to war, but none that

scared him as much as cowering helplessly beneath a daily barrage of explosives did. For a while he thought that the fear itself would kill him, so hard did his heart pound as the shelling began. But it didn't.

Another mortar shell whistled by and exploded near him, causing him to duck and hold on to his helmet. The siege let up momentarily, and as he raised his head, Douglas looked at him and said, "How do you stay so calm?"

Douglas looked incredulous as Michael began to laugh uncontrollably, the tears streaming down his cheeks.

It had been three bone-wearing days since Berchot had come running down the hill with news of the Japanese landings. By the next night Michael's ragtag naval infantry had succeeded in driving the Japanese off Mount Puloc and back toward the beach, but the Japanese force had been too strong and too well entrenched to be driven out entirely, and their presence still posed a threat to the West Road. Worse, the Japanese had made further landings a few miles north at Quinuuan Point.

Moving through dense jungle, Michael and his men had fought desperately for each bloody foot they took. They had no bayonets. Often too close to the enemy to fire their rifles, they had to resort to using machetes and knives. The artillery reinforcements Michael requested had been refused because they were needed to cover the Bataan forward defense position. So Michael's group fought on alone, inexperienced and at times outflanked. Too unfamiliar with infantry tactics to realize the seriousness of their situation, they had tenaciously fought their way out of trap after trap, earning themselves a reputation among the Japanese as an elite suicide squad.

The Americans usually stopped fighting at five o'clock, digging in at their position wherever it happened to be. The Japanese launched counteroffensives at night, screaming out of the jungle in terrifying attacks. When they didn't attack, they made noise to harass the Americans and prevent them from sleeping. Michael's men countered by digging in with equal ferocity and determination. Michael was a natural leader, functioning coolly under fire. Numerous times he risked his own life to go in after wounded men alone, carrying them out on his shoulders when they were too injured to walk. His efforts had won him the fierce loyalty of his men.

The shelling paused again while the Japanese attempted to judge whether they had successfully located the American position. Douglas sat up and let out a low whistle of relief.

"Make 'em stop, please, God," he muttered as he loosened his helmet and pushed it back on his head. Around him, in dozens of other shallow trenches and foxholes, the several hundred men of the battalion sat hunched in tense silence, waiting to see if it all would begin again. Douglas took a deep breath.

"Think they realize they've found us?" he asked, not really expecting an answer.

"We'll soon know," Michael replied.

Douglas leaned back and looked at the sky and tried to relax. It was getting late. He didn't want to have to move out and dig a new shelter. He wanted some sleep.

"Remember that girl we saw in the geisha house in Manila the night of Pearl Harbor, the one who sang?"

"Yeah, I remember," Michael replied.

"They shot her." Douglas was still staring at the sky. "The MP's did it, arrested her and shot her right after the attack. One of the air force officers told me. Said she was a spy for the Japs."

Outrage was boiling in Michael's gut, but his voice remained calm. "What made them think that?"

"I dunno. They said she was getting information about Cavite Naval Base and Clark Field from the officers at the bar."

Michael leaned back, closed his eyes, and watched a yellow silk kimono and long, silky black hair drift into view. He tried to remember Mikki-san's face, but it kept changing into Catherine's.

Unaware of the effect of his words, Douglas continued. "I heard they tortured her but couldn't get a confession, so one of the officers shot her anyway." Douglas was silent for a moment, then asked, "Did she try to ask you any questions?"

Angry tears pushed at Michael's closed eyes. "Only where I had learned to speak Japanese so well," he answered softly. He was surprised by the intensity of his own reaction.

"She was so beautiful," Douglas said wistfully. "Do you think she could have been a spy?"

"I suppose," Michael said wearily. He didn't add that he knew the reason she had been killed hadn't been for spying. She could have proved an embarrassment to someone very important. For a moment he felt sick.

A shrill whistle sounded overhead, and a mortar shell went off in the ravine, sending Michael and Douglas sprawling. Michael's helmet, its strap missing, went flying off his head. Ears ringing, he covered his head with his hands and buried his face in the dirt as the explosions began again, closer this time than before.

"They know they've got us!" Douglas yelled. "We'd better get out of here."

The mortars suddenly stopped. As the men raised their heads in disbelief, they could hear muffled blasts and see huge clouds of smoke rise in the direction of the beach. The big guns of Corregidor had opened up for the first time. The Japanese had been spotted for them by the last P-38 reconnaissance plane still flying. For fifteen minutes the guns rained 670-pound shells on the Japanese position, softening it up. When the barrage stopped, Michael stood up and gave the order for his men to move out to attack.

As Douglas stood up to follow, he felt a hand on his shoulder and looked down to see the smiling face of a Filipino scout.

"It's okay, Joe," the face was saying to him. "We help. You win now."

They did, but not for four more bloody days. The Japanese were dug in along the cliffs, and the American and Filipino troops had to fight furiously for every inch. The naval brigade suffered heavy casualties on the last day: ten wounded, two dead, and two missing. A seaman handed a weary Michael the final battle report.

"I'm sorry, sir," he said. "It's Mr. Stuart. The colonel reports that he and Seaman Berchot never returned from their patrol."

Michael's heart sank. It was more than six hours since he had last seen Douglas. Michael caught a ride from a passing jeep to Point Quinuuan, where the colonel was overseeing the final mop-up action. The Japanese had their backs to the sea. There was no escape.

In one incredible moment that left the American onlookers stunned, the trapped Japanese tossed their weapons over the high cliffs and, rather than surrender, took off their clothes and began to dive into the ocean far below. Others tried to lower themselves onto the rocks to the beach. Michael arrived at the cliff just in time to see a Filipino soldier on the point just below set up a machine gun and begin to fire into the 400 unarmed men struggling in the water below. The soldier would fire, stop to laugh so hard he almost fell over, then would commence firing again. The surf began to run red, and pink foam churned in its wake.

"My God," Michael cried. "Somebody stop him!" He shouted toward the soldiers near the gunner some fifty feet below him. "Somebody stop that son of a bitch."

An American sergeant from one of the tanks who stood near Michael gave him a quizzical look. "What's your beef? Did you see what they did to those guys in the jungle back there—and in a lot of other places in this damn war? Stop cryin' and let him kill every one of them stinkin' Japs. How the hell can we feed any prisoners anyhow? Wanna give him *your* rations?"

Michael's mouth tightened into a grim line. It no longer mattered anyhow. The water was full of bodies bobbing on the incoming tide to join the others lying on the beach. Of the 400 men who had attempted to escape, perhaps some thirty survived.

"Lieutenant Stanford?"

Michael turned. A corporal from one of the artillery units approached him, his manner respectful and slightly apologetic.

"The captain said maybe you should take a look at this." The corporal nodded over his shoulder toward the trees to one side of the road.

Michael looked at the spot he had indicated. There was nothing unusual there, just the canopied tunnel of trees stretching as far as he could see down Arsenal Alley, as his unit had dubbed the booby-trapped corridor. It was peaceful now. Mottled sunlight played on the thick carpet of leaves. Curious, Michael crossed the short distance to the spot, and the corporal followed. He hesitated for a moment and then shoved the foliage aside. Something was wrong. He sensed it first without seeing it. His eyes adjusted to the dim light, and then his mouth opened in a cry that remained silent, though it shook his body and made him gasp for air.

It was Berchot, stripped and hanging by his thumbs. His feet, if he had still had any, would have hung just off the ground. Instead, there were two bloody stumps from which the blood still oozed. He had been castrated as well. A gag, still in his mouth, had silenced his screams. Nearby, on the ground, lay two other naked bodies, both Filipino officers. One had his limbs and head hacked off. The other, hands wired behind his back, had been used for bayonet practice. Trembling violently, Michael dropped his hands, and the branches sprang back to hide the grisly scene.

"I'm sorry, sir," the corporal stammered. "But the captain thought it might be one of your men."

"Yes." Michael miraculously found a word able to bypass the lump in his throat. "Yes, it is."

He stared at the peaceful green wall before him. The trees nodded in the breeze. The sunlight danced as it had before, but this time he didn't notice. He kept seeing the scene over and over again, as if his mind were refusing to accept what it had seen. Certainly he was used to seeing mutilation in battle, but today was his first experience with deliberate cruelty.

"Hey, Lieutenant. You still wanna stop that guy from shooting these bastards?" The sergeant's mocking question came faintly up through the leafy tunnel's throat.

As he walked away, he knew the image of Berchot would always haunt him. And to think, they had given him a medal for saving Berchot's life that day the seaplane went down. The next time you save somebody from a nice clean bullet, he told himself angrily, remember there are worse ways to die.

As a pilot Douglas Stuart was used to creating mayhem from a distance. Death was rarely personal. The Battle of Bataan, with its bloody, hand-to-hand fighting, was a new experience for him. Nothing had prepared him for it: certainly not his Naval Academy training, or flight school; certainly not all those World War movies he used to love to see. The real Bataan, he thought, would be a box-office flop. Nobody would buy tickets to this war, let alone buy popcorn. Jesus, what had he been thinking of when he chose a military career? Robert Taylor in *Flight Command*? Gary Cooper in *Wings*?

He stumbled his way through the battlefield casualties. If this is victory, he wondered, what must defeat be like? It had been hours since he and Berchot had been separated after suddenly finding themselves trapped and surrounded by a unit of stealthily advancing Japanese. Now Douglas was trying to catch up with his company, which was moving up to the next battle, several miles up the road. The stench was terrible, not just from the bodies but from the wounds. Gangrene set in so rapidly that amputation was the only possible treatment. He stumbled over more bodies, alive and dead. Bones were poking through holes that shouldn't have been there. Everywhere he looked he saw repulsive, obscene sights that made him ashamed to be human, ashamed of the mess he would make when he died. No book or movie ever described how you shit your pants when you got scared enough or when you died. Nothing ever conveyed death's lack of dignity.

Douglas finally reached part of his unit camped near the intersection of the West Road and the dirt trail leading to the point.

"Hey, Mr. Stuart! You're back. What happened?"

"I was detained by a beautiful girl who forced me to eat fried chicken with her and dally in the tall grass," he said, grinning, puzzled by the surprise he saw on their faces. He glanced around, and his mood changed. "Anybody seen Berchot?" he asked anxiously.

They looked at him, at his bloody shirt, at the glaze of fatigue in his eyes that said he was near the breaking point, and they knew better than to answer. They shook their heads and stared away. They weren't exactly lying. They hadn't actually seen Berchot, but they all knew how he had died.

A medical shuttle bus stood in the road.

"What's going on?" Douglas asked a sailor who sat at the wheel of a jeep parked nearby.

"A tank crew just came back from the trail," the sailor answered, grateful to change the subject. "A Jap mortar exploded near them. It missed, but they got hurt by their own rivets popping out of the seams and flying around like bullets." He shook his head in disgust. "This damn equipment is more dangerous than the Japs. Most of the grenades I've thrown have been duds. If you use them, you just give away your position so the Japs can piss on you with those small-caliber bullets they use."

It was a familiar gripe. Douglas scarcely heard it. His exhaustion was catching up with him. He sat down on the ground and leaned back against the jeep's front tire, fumbling to retrieve the butt of a cigarette he had been saving. He lit it and shared one draw with the jeep's driver. The road looked so peaceful. The shade felt good. It had begun to drizzle. He closed his eyes. God, he was tired. Yet, now that he was back with his unit, he felt a surprising sense of comfort. Douglas had come to love these men more than he had ever loved anyone. He had never before experienced either the height of exaltation or the depths of despair he had known in the past month. He did not exactly love war, but he loved the sentiment it stirred in him. As strange and awful as it had been, there was a part of him that hated to see it end.

By February 9 the west side of Bataan had been secured, and the Japanese landing forces destroyed. There was a lull in the fighting throughout Bataan. The Japanese were no more able to carry on with the battle than their weakened opponents. They, too, had sustained heavy casualties. No one in Japan had expected their foes in Bataan to resist so furiously—or successfully. The Japanese general in charge of the invasion force had been severely reprimanded by Tokyo, and his requests for reinforcements had been twice refused. At the moment the army needed its forces in Singapore and the Indies.

So for now the men of the *Canopus* had won. And without help from anybody in Washington. They rested beneath the trees, their fatigue made bearable by the knowledge that tomorrow they were going back to Mariveles and the caves above the bay, back to the Mariveles cantino with its Filipino girls, and the hospital up the road with its American nurses, at least until the Japanese would decide the lull was over. They were in the eye of the hurricane, awaiting the second storm.

Chapter 34

"Njonja, come quick! Come quick!" One of the gardeners came running in to get Margit, who was standing in the hall, arranging a vase of fresh flowers and talking with Catherine. He tugged at Margit's hand, urging her to come faster, his eyes wide and bright with fear. "Hurry, Njonja!" Catherine put her cup down with a hasty clatter and followed them out on the front lawn.

Below them the harbor basin looked as if someone were preparing popcorn. The air was filled with little puffs of white smoke and the sounds of small muffled explosions. Air-raid sirens wailed to announce the obvious: The bombing of Batavia had finally begun. At first it was hard for those who watched from the hills to take the scene seriously. Small planes darted about, like bugs. Others droned like a child's toys. None of it seemed real until smoke began to rise from the harbor and the anchored ships, until some of the little darting bugs began to fall out of the sky and break apart.

Margit's soup-kitchen truck wasn't needed. The damage to civilian areas was slight. It was February 9, three days before Catherine was scheduled to leave for Australia. Tanjungpriok Harbor was crowded with ships seeking safety from other eastern ports under Japanese attack. Many were either sunk that day or forced to flee to Darwin. Catherine's ship was among those sunk. She arranged the earliest new passage she could get, an Australian passenger ship due out of Singapore, leaving Batavia on

February 17. Margit still refused to go. The Dutch were confident that the combined Allied fleet could successfully defend Java against an invasion. Margit vacillated between believing the authorities and being frightened, but she stayed.

The Japanese were now rapidly closing in on Java. By the end of January they had controlled both British and Dutch Borneo, putting Maitreya behind enemy lines. By early February they had taken the island of Celebes and were in bombing range of Batavia and Surabaya. As the Japanese advanced, the Allied naval task force scurried from one disaster spot to another, but without air reconaissance or protection they would arrive too late, show up at the wrong location, or be driven off by attacking enemy planes. A week after the air raids began on Batavia, news arrived which shook European confidence throughout the Indies more than any other event. Singapore, Britain's impregnable fortress, had surrendered, giving Japan the greatest land victory in its history and the British their most humiliating defeat. Margit decided to ship her two boys to Sir Charles in Australia, and Catherine gave up her next passage in order to send them and their nurse as quickly as possible. She was worried, but she still put faith in Admiral Glassford's promise to get her out on time.

Four days after the surrender of Singapore more bad news arrived. Japanese planes had destroyed the Australian port and city of Darwin, sinking many American naval ships that had escaped from the Philippines and much of the merchant fleet which had fled the bombing of Batavia ten days earlier. To the north, the island of Sumatra and its oil fields had been lost, and to the south, fabled Bali had fallen. The British decided to withdraw from Java, leaving only a few token ships behind. They didn't want valuable naval forces destroyed in a hopeless cause. The Dutch were shocked at what they perceived as betrayal.

"Damn the British!" Bernard had fumed at Margit when he heard the news. "I'll take the Germans any day."

The American forces stayed. They had made a commitment to the Dutch, and they intended to honor it until the Dutch ordered them out. Thinking of Tom's safety, Catherine fervently hoped such an order would come before it was too late. With Singapore and Darwin both gone now, Tom's ship had been ordered to join the Allied strike force in Java with all due speed.

The Allied naval force was headed for a showdown against a

337

numerically superior enemy. The Japanese invasion force now headed for Java contained seven carriers, thirteen heavy cruisers, six light cruisers, fifty-three destroyers, and ninety-seven transports, all divided into three attack and support forces. The combined Allied strike force that prepared to meet them consisted of two heavy cruisers, three light cruisers, and eleven U.S., British, and Dutch destroyers.

The *Houston* departed for Surabaya and a rendezvous with the rest of the Allied fleet. As the *Houston*'s bow cut the water of the Java Sea, Tom stood on the fantail with Ken Brandon and watched the ship's wake. Both men were exhausted but too tense to sleep. They carefully steered their conversations away from what was about to happen. Although they had been exposed to constant danger for the past two months, at this moment they felt like green recruits. The stakes had been raised. Both men were acutely aware that the small fleet they were about to join was all that stood between Java and sure defeat. Above them, lookouts strained eyes scratchy with fatigue toward the sky, searching for enemy planes from Bali. None appeared.

The silhouette of Java appeared to port side as in a series of purple ridges on the horizon, and soon the entrance of Surabaya Harbor could be seen, filled now with a good part of the Allied fleet, taking on fuel before it put out to sea.

"I'd better report to the bridge," Brandon said. "I've got the twelve to sixteen hundred watch." He started up the ladder, then paused and called down. "Hey, Tom. That woman you know in Java . . . Catherine. Is she still here?"

"I hope not," Tom replied, but the question reawakened his anxiety. He didn't want the stakes in this battle to be any higher than they already were. "She was supposed to leave for Australia."

It was now February 25, his birthday, and Ginny's. It was the first time anything had kept them from celebrating together. A year ago he, Catherine, Ginny, and her kids all had celebrated on that little farm in Connecticut. This time he had been unable to send her so much as a card or a letter.

He heard lunch piped. They would be in port only long enough to take on added fuel and ammunition. It might be a long time before he would get another hot meal, so he left the hot sun-filled deck for the wardroom.

* * *

The Battle of the Java Sea was over. The fleet had died, but he had lived, though he hadn't expected it. Tom took off his battle helmet and leaned wearily against the rail, staring at the blackened sea which had so easily swallowed the Allied fleet and half its crew. The scene of battle was heavy with acrid drifting smoke, through which the full moon stared unblinking at all that had passed. The debris of lost battles, the entrails of ships and men, floated together upon the waves. The mast of the command ship, the Dutch cruiser *De Ruyter*, could still be seen above water level. Only the *Houston*, which had been ordered to escape by Admiral Doorman just before he and his crew had gone down with their ship, and the Australian cruiser *Perth* had survived the Battle of the Java Sea. The British cruiser *Exeter*, crippled early in the battle, had been sunk later, along with its destroyer escort, while trying to escape.

The sound of pounding guns had ceased, and through the ringing in his ears Tom could hear the hum of the *Houston*'s powerful engines and the gentle rush of sea against the bow as the ship left the scene of battle. There was no talk among the men on the deck. Enemy flares still occasionally burst like frazzled nerves onto the darkened sky as Japanese planes kept track of the *Houston*'s course. There was no need. The Allied force had been beaten, and it was not going to fight again. That bitter thought was reflected in the grim, blackened faces of the men around Tom, in the fatigue which caused their bodies to slump against the hot guns, heads buried wearily in their arms.

It had been the first sea battle between capital ships since the Battle of Jutland in World War I, and it had lasted, intermittently, for seven hours. Until now war experts had predicted such a battle would be over in minutes. It had been fought without planes, one of the last true naval battles in a new age when future fleets, fighting with carriers and planes, would never even sight each other.

Without search planes the Allied fleet had never even spotted the enemy transports. Instead, it had finally come upon its protective force of four heavy cruisers. Tom had felt a surge of relief and excitement when, at the first sighting of the Japanese, the white battle ensigns had gone up and the ship had moved ahead, flank speed, leaving the hard-pressed destroyer escorts behind. The waiting was over. That first confrontation had lasted for almost an hour and lit the darkening sky like a violent storm, both beautiful and terrifying. The horizon had been a huge sheet of flashing copper accompanied by continuous deep thunder of the guns. Huge geysers of water spouted from near misses. But the Dutch admiral in command of the Allied fleet had failed to close quickly and take advantage of his initial superior strength. He had lost that superiority when the British heavy cruiser *Exeter* was hit and knocked out of action. Outnumbered then, the Allies had fought doggedly on, pursuing an enemy that successfully evaded them until the rest of the Japanese force had come suddenly over the horizon and closed in quickly, filling the sea with torpedoes. In a few big explosions the battle was over.

By one o'clock in the morning, the *Houston* had made port at Tanjungpriok Harbor at Batavia. The *Perth* arrived with it. There was no longer a navy standing between Java and defeat. There were only a few thousand Dutch and Australian troops.

When Catherine heard of the *Houston*'s arrival, she left Michael with Margit and made her way to the docks at Tanjungpriok. The loading area was bedlam. The *Houston* clearly showed the ordeal of battle. Concussions from its own eight-inch guns had wrecked most of the cabins. Furniture and clothes were strewn around, and charts and mirrors joined broken radios, and clocks, and photographs in tangled heaps on the floor. No one bothered to clean up. There was far more serious damage to be concerned about.

The heavy metal plates on the *Houston*'s decks and hulls were badly sprung from the concussions of near misses. On the bridge glass had been shattered, and the fire hoses along the passageways were leaking water underfoot. The *Houston*'s ammunition was almost gone, and there was none to be had in Batavia.

Finding Tom among the 1,000 crewmen who swarmed the decks and dock seemed hopeless. She had almost given up when she spotted him on the dock, directing the loading of supplies. She could see the fatigue in his body even from a distance.

He was surprised to see her and shouted over the confusion that he would be free in fifteen minutes, so she retreated to sit on the crates at the dock's end. Ten minutes later Tom stood before her, shaved, clean khaki uniform open at the collar, black brim hat firmly on his head, neat and military, even when exhausted.

He was smiling. The harassed look of a few minutes ago was

gone. He leaned over and kissed her on the top of the head and then pulled her into his arms, holding her tightly.

"Not that I'm not delighted to see you, Cat, but I thought I told you to get the hell out of here. You and Michael should be in Australia by now."

"Last night, when I heard you were coming into Batavia, I had to wait to see you before I left."

With a sigh he released her and leaned against the crates, pulling her beside him, his arm firmly around her shoulders. He nodded toward the frantic activity before him.

"We're leaving, Cat. The whole fleet—or what's left of it—is pulling out. The *Houston* is going home to California for rest and repairs. The *Perth* is going to Australia."

Catherine felt a flood of relief.

"You've got to get out of here, too, Catherine. They'll be evacuating diplomatic and military personnel from Tjilatjap tomorrow night and the following day. Promise me you'll go with them."

She smiled. "I promise. By the way, have I mentioned how glad I am you're safe? When you left Surabaya, I was so afraid. . . ."

He grinned. "You think I wasn't?"

Ken Brandon came up to them, shaking his head.

"How do you manage it, lady? Just when he needs you. Why don't you two run along? I'll manage alone. There's too much to do here anyway. One damned bit more not getting done won't make any difference."

"Would you mind?" Tom asked.

Brandon laughed. "Of course I would. I wish to hell I had this kind of luck, but since it can't be me, it might as well be you. Go see if you can clear it with the exec."

Tom was back in fifteen minutes, wearing a black tie with his khaki shirt. He was grinning.

"Let's get the hell out of here before they realize what they've done."

"We'll take my car." She pointed to the yellow MG roadster at the end of the dock. Noting his surprise, she added, "I got it yesterday from a British news correspondent. He was leaving the country and gave it to me in exchange for the promise that I would destroy it when I left. Said he couldn't stand the thought of its being used by the Japanese."

Tom climbed into the passenger seat on the right side. "Let's go get my godson."

While they drove through the city, they heard explosions, as the Dutch began to blow up anything that might be of value to the Japanese. They picked Michael up at Margit's and drove out into the hills behind the city to have lunch. They dined at a table surrounded by flowers and trees, far from the noise of impending disaster. As they sipped wine after their meal, Tom reached over to where Michael sat in his high chair, lids heavy, about to drop off.

"Hey, kid," he said, chiding him gently, "don't you ever forget me, hear? You may be the only son I'll ever have." Then he turned to Catherine and said lightly, "Marry me, and with that blond hair we can easily pass him off as mine." He smiled, but she knew he wasn't kidding. She changed the subject.

"Was it awful?" she asked, referring for the first time to the battle he had been through.

He nodded grimly and took a sip of wine.

"I can't help wondering if things might have been different if Glassford had been in charge of the fleet. Doorman was too cautious, too prudently Dutch. We had no air cover, but we outgunned them at close range—only we never got close enough to make it really count." He sounded bitter. "Such a waste, and what was the point? Even if we had destroyed the convoy, it wouldn't have prevented an invasion. Only delayed it. For what? Help? Reinforcements? There were none, and there won't be any. Not for a couple of years anyway." He stared out at the brilliant blue afternoon sky and idly fingered his wineglass.

"One of my men had it right. It was the all-stars going out to meet Notre Dame without so much as a practice session. No plan, no common strategy. Not even flag signals in common. Hell, we couldn't even communicate properly." He gave a weary sigh and finished his wine.

"We've been busting our butts and losing our lives for a lost cause. Do you know what it feels like to be considered expendable?" He gave a grim laugh. "Well, I'll tell you, it's lousy for morale."

"So why do you keep fighting?" she asked quietly.

"For our lives, for each other, and for the ship herself. Strange as it may seem, she begins to be real, not a machine but a living, breathing beast—gentle, ferocious, even unpredictable at times, but always alive."

"Besides," Catherine added, "I suppose they don't want us to go down like Vichy, France, without a fight."

"Yes," he said. "We're giving them lots of heroic dead they can be proud of."

She reached over and squeezed his hand. "You look exhausted. You should get some sleep."

"Would you mind?" he asked apologetically. "I am beat." He nodded toward Michael. "He looks like he could use a nap, too."

As they headed for the car, he said, "I won't have time to write Ginny before we get under way. Will you call her in case—" He broke off without finishing.

"Of course," she said. "But you'll call her yourself from California."

"Sure, sure." He smiled. "But you may get there before I do."

"I'll get in touch right away to let her know how you are."

He handed Michael to her as she got in the car. "I'd better check with the base."

He returned a few minutes later, smiling. "Still set to weigh anchor at twenty-one hundred. We've plenty of time."

As they approached Batavia through the surrounding hills, they could see the two big cruisers dominating the harbor. Slanted beams of sunlight richocheted like tracers off the hard gray metal surfaces and scattered like shrapnel upon the bright blue surface of the water.

"An impressive sight," Catherine commented, stopping the car to look at the two ships.

"Unfortunately not even one tenth as impressive as the Japanese western task force spotted two days ago, north of here, off central Sumatra. The PBY that spotted it reports it's the biggest strike force since the attack on Pearl Harbor."

"How big?"

He looked away from the harbor to where she sat next to him. "Fifty-six transports and freighters, bound for Java, no doubt, and"—he turned and looked back at the sea, pausing a moment before continuing quietly—"they're escorted by a carrier, four heavy cruisers, two light cruisers, and twenty-five destroyers plus numerous torpedo boats. Now you see why you can't waste any more time getting out of here."

Catherine felt a sudden chill of fear. "And you're escaping south, past Surabaya?"

"No, north through the Sunda Strait between Java and Sumatra. Right toward the approaching Japanese carrier force." He looked at her and saw the fear in her eyes.

"It's the only way, Cat. Our destroyers at Surabaya are going south through the Bali Strait, but those straits are too shallow for a cruiser's draft."

"So it's you and the *Perth* alone?"

"With luck the Dutch destroyer *Evertsen* will be with us, but I'm not counting on it, and neither is the captain."

"And the *Perth* will be going on to Australia?"

He nodded. "When we reach the Indian Ocean, *Perth* will turn south along the west coast of Java and head for Australia. We'll head for the Horn, then up to Panama through the Canal and home." He grinned ruefully. "One hell of a long way back to the Pacific Ocean, isn't it?"

But the lightness had gone, for both of them.

"I'm sorry, Cat. I didn't want to spoil your day."

She touched his hand lightly and forced a smile. "We won't let it be spoiled. Come on, let's find a hotel with an honest-to-goodness bed, complete with satin sheets and cool breezes, so you can get some rest."

They found a small hotel in the hills and took a suite that consisted of a small sitting room along with a bedroom and a bath. The Chinese woman who ran it cheerfully furnished a crib for Michael.

Tom opened the shutters to the veranda that faced the sea. A cooling ocean breeze immediately entered the bedroom.

"No satin sheets, but it sure to hell beats the bunk in my stateroom."

He crossed to the door of the sitting room, where Catherine was putting Michael down for his nap.

"I think I'll take a shower: not the Navy kind, a nice long one. The next one like this will be in San Diego."

"Fine. Take your time. But all they've got is the Indonesian

344

kind.'' She pantomimed pouring a dipper of water over her head. "I'll go out and buy some brandy.''

Imports of all kinds had become scarce in the past month, but she managed to find a bottle of French brandy, covered with dust and deliciously aging on the shelf of a nearby store. She bought it along with two white silk Chinese robes exported from Hong Kong before it fell. When she returned, she could hear the water splashing and Tom singing in his pleasant baritone. She smiled, poured two glasses of brandy into the drinking glasses on the dresser, then slipped off her cotton skirt and blouse and put one of the robes over her slip. She took a sip of her brandy, then crossed to the bathroom to slip the robe in for him before he finished. Just as her hand reached the knob, the singing stopped. She paused, her hand on the knob, then opened the door and stepped inside.

Tom was reaching for a towel. He was startled to see her standing there, and he stared at her before slowly raising the towel and drying his hair.

"Fancy finding you in here,'' he said, his voice unsteady behind the lightness.

"I brought you this.'' She lowered the robe to the footstool.

"Thanks. I can use it.'' He watched her, puzzled, his arms lowered to his sides.

She stood staring at him, her heart pounding, confused by the feelings that now stirred within her. She had been so happy to see him. So relieved he was alive and safe. But now she was afraid all over again that he was going to die.

She crossed to him, put her arms around his waist, and kissed his throat, feeling his wet body begin to soak her clothes. He put his arms around her.

"Hey, what's all this about?'' he asked huskily. He lifted her chin and searched her eyes for answers but saw only a confusion that matched his own. He bent down to kiss her, at first lightly and then, as his body responded, more urgently. He pulled away, and his own eyes were warm, with a touch of humor in them.

"What is this supposed to be? Your patriotic duty? Serving yourself up as last meal for a condemned man? Michael's in the Navy and you're becoming sentimental about all men in sailor suits. Oh, dear Cat, I know you too well.'' He laughed and kissed her affectionately on the nose. "But you don't have to do this, you know. God only knows I want you. Always have. And you've always known it, too. So why the offering now?"

"Because I love you." She smiled.

"Right. Like a brother, Cat. I know. Pregnant women always fall in love with their doctors. I delivered Michael, so you've suddenly come down with a postpartum neurosis."

He smiled into her eyes, but his body was still hard against hers. "I know it's because you're afraid for me, that you're fond of me and want to comfort me. Believe me, Cat, I'm sorely tempted to take you up on it, but if I let you do this I may lose you all together when you wake up from this attack of sentimentality and realize what's happened. I'm not being noble—just practical."

"You talk too much." She smiled and put her fingers on his lips to silence him as she pulled him down to her.

"Catherine," he whispered just before his lips met hers and he pressed her tightly to him, forgetting everything else.

Suddenly a loud wail came from the living room. It was Michael, and it was clear from the volume that he wasn't going to stop. Reluctantly Tom released her and said, "Smart little man. He knows. He's protecting his father's interests."

She leaned her head against his chest for a moment, collecting herself, and then looked up, her hand brushing against his cheek.

"I'll be only a minute."

She went to the sitting room and comforted Michael until he quieted. When she returned to the bedroom a few moments later, Tom was lying naked on the bed.

"Everything's okay. Must have been a bad dream."

She crossed to the bed. Tom was fast asleep. She leaned down and kissed him on the shoulder, but he did not stir. She smiled. So much for sacrifices. She lay down and studied him for a few moments. His light red hair was still damp and tousled around his deeply tanned, freckled face. Asleep, he looked younger. She rested a hand on his arm and drifted off to sleep.

She was awakened sometime later by the jangle of the phone on the table beside the bed. The room was in shadows, but the clock said only 6:10. The desk clerk put Lieutenant Brandon on the line. He sounded slightly embarrassed.

"Sorry to bother you. I need to get in touch with Tom."

"He's here. Just a minute."

346

She put the phone down and leaned over and kissed him. He stirred only slightly, so she shook him awake. "It's Brandon."

He took the receiver from her. "What is it, Ken?"

Brandon's voice carried through to Catherine. "Time's been moved up. We aren't waiting for the *Eversten*. We weigh anchor at nineteen hundred."

Tom glanced at his watch. "Jeez, that's only forty-five minutes from now."

"Yeah, I know." Brandon sounded embarrassed again. "I didn't know where to find you. I tried just about every hotel in town."

"Sorry. I should have let you know where I was, but I fell asleep."

Brandon laughed. "I understand."

"No, you don't. I can tell. But never mind."

"Better get your ass here on the double."

"Right." He hung up and smiled apologetically at Catherine. "I'm afraid we've ruined your reputation without reaping a single benefit. Sorry I fell asleep. The mind and heart were willing, but the body had been pushed too far."

He lay down on his back, pulled her to him, and kissed her.

"That's all there's time for now, but I plan to collect on the offer when we're back in the States."

"It goes only with dangerous missions."

"Then I'll have plenty of opportunity. This is going to be a long war."

They arranged for the hotel proprietor to take care of Michael and in ten minutes were on their way to Tanjungpriok. When they reached the docking area, it was so crowded they had to park a quarter of a mile from the military docks and walk. The Allied defeat in the Java Sea had created a panicky exodus. The merchant vessels which had managed to survive the air raids, their crews, and a flood of Europeans attempting to leave Java now added to the congestion already caused by the two Navy ships preparing to depart.

Tom guided Catherine to the office of the Dutch naval forces and used the phone to call Admiral Glassford in Bandung and arrange for transportation out of Tjilatjap for Michael and Catherine.

"It's taken care of," he told her as he guided her out the door toward the dock. "There are two seaplanes coming in from

347

Australia tomorrow, leaving tomorrow night. The admiral is arranging for space for you on one of them."

He stopped and took hold of her by the arm. "Promise me you'll go, Cat. I can't leave here unless I know you'll be safely out. You wouldn't want me to go AWOL and give up what promises to be a spectacular naval career." He was smiling again.

She tried to smile back. "Of course not. I promise."

Once again they were headed toward the dock. She felt fear bordering on panic as the full realization that he was leaving struck her. It was all happening so fast. They reached the gangplank without exchanging another word. It was time to say good-bye. There was no avoiding it any longer. He turned and faced her, and she could see the muscles work in his jaws as he fought to control his feelings. She could no longer control her own. Tears streamed freely down her cheeks. Unable to keep looking at her and maintain his composure, he pulled her close to him, his cheek pressed against her hair.

"In case I haven't told you," he said softly, "having had you here during these last two months of hell has meant more to me than you'll ever know."

"For me, too."

"I love you, Catherine." And then he was kissing her one long last time. He pulled away.

"Good-bye, Cat."

She had no time to respond before he took the gangplank lightly, two steps at a time, the metal clanking as he bounded up.

When he reached the top of the gangplank, he turned back to the rail and saw her still standing where he had left her. She looked so small and alone that tears came to his eyes for the first time. He brushed them quickly away and gave her a final wave, then went down to his stateroom to change into battle gear. They were about to get under way, and his was the eight to midnight watch on the bridge.

The ship pulled out ten minutes after Tom had left her on the dock. Catherine stood watching the final preparations. Gangplank raised, ropes cast off, the big ship began to move, almost imperceptibly at first, backing slowly out. She walked along the dock beside it. Sailors had begun to gather along the railing for their last glimpse of port. They were strangers to her and yet, because they were her countrymen, she felt a strong bond to them. Tears stung her eyes. By the time she reached the end of the dock the ship had made its turn. She stood watching it glide swiftly out to sea, gathering speed, taking away whatever bit of America there had been for her in Java. She lifted an arm in final farewell. The answering waves came back from the men on the fantail.

"Godspeed, *Houston*," she whispered.

Chapter 35

The watch had been a quiet one. It was 10:30 P.M. The captain had come to the bridge about fifteen minutes earlier, just prior to the course change that would take them west to the Sunda Strait. The moon was bright and full, increasing the danger of detection. The bridge was dark. From here the ship's engines were a distant hum. There was little of the customary banter among those on the bridge tonight. Officers and enlisted men alike stood with eyes fixed on the horizon, each man lost in his own thoughts.

The sea was smooth, as if doing everything it could to speed the two great ships on their way. Tom looked out on the ocean with a feeling of affection not far removed from love. This romance with the sea had been a long-standing affair for him. It had begun on the Mississippi River, in St. Louis, where his grandfather had skippered a riverboat and had known Mark Twain. Tom had made his first trip down the mighty river to New Orleans when he was five. He had been properly impressed, but when he saw the endless basin into which the river spilled, he had wanted to keep right on going to whatever lay beyond. That had been the beginning of his feeling for the sea, and it had never stopped, not even now when, fickle mistress that she was, she carried the enemy as willingly as she carried him.

It was 10:45 when the *Houston*, leading the *Perth*, passed Pontang Point at the northern tip of Java. Now only the short distance across the mouth of Banten Bay remained to be crossed before they reached Nicolas Point and turned west into the Sunda Strait. The scent of jasmine, carried out to sea by offshore breezes, reached the *Houston*, overpowering the smells of battle that still lingered on the deck. Suddenly one of the lookouts reported Japanese transports in Banten Bay, a pearly gray string of more than fifty of them lined neatly along the shoreline, off-loading troops and equipment for the invasion of Java.

"Son of a bitch . . ." breathed an ensign on the bridge watch, "we spent two days and lost five ships looking for a convoy we never found, and now we stumble right into the whole Japanese convoy."

"And no doubt the western strike force to go with it," the captain added grimly.

He nodded to Tom, who addressed the quartermaster on the intercom, "Sound general quarters."

The order came to change course, and the *Perth* and *Houston* swung south into the heart of Banten Bay. As the bells and whistles brought the ships to life, men tumbled from their beds. So conditioned were they that their feet were in their shoes and headed up ladders before they were even awake. Within seconds the phone lines and firing circuits leaped to life as, one by one, the battle stations reported themselves manned and ready.

The address system crackled to live again. "All guns, surface action port. Enemy transports. Range ten thousand."

By the guns the men waited, pulses pounding in their ears, fingers tense on firing keys, eyes strained on the crosshairs of their sights.

"All guns, commence firing."

The main batteries roared into action. The steady pom-pom-pom of the antiaircraft guns was directed at surface targets, along with the sharp crack of the five-inchers and the dull ba-room of the big eight-inch guns. The concussion tore Tom's helmet from his head and caused the *Houston* to recoil several feet starboard as it fired. Fiery tracers streaked out into the night, and star shells lobbed high into the sky to fall in firecracker bursts over the transports, illuminating the scene with an eerie white and red glow.

The *Houston* and *Perth* followed the natural contour of the shoreline the entire distance of the bay, firing as they went. As they neared the end of their run, the lone Japanese destroyer in the vicinity caught up with them and fired torpedoes, which missed the two cruisers and hit its own transports, adding to the devastation. A cheer went up from the *Houston*'s crew as they completed their run and ceased firing. The waters of the bay were full of Japanese troops and equipment, dumped into the sea from sinking transports.

Guns silent, crews jubilant, the two Allied cruisers passed out of Banten Bay between Panjang Island and Nicolas Point. After weeks of frustration and defeat this victory brought quick elation. Tom felt his body relax at the glimpse of the open sea stretching in a bright, calm sheet just ahead beyond the passage. It meant freedom. Once they were into the Indian Ocean there was little but open sea lying between the *Houston* and California. In the bright moonlight Tom could see the *Perth*, now just ahead, as it safely cleared the passage.

As the *Houston* rounded the point, Tom trained his binoculars north. The signal from the *Perth* came almost at the same time that Tom made the sighting.

"Enemy ships ahead!" he cried. "Firing range and closing fast."

They had emerged in the midst of the full Japanese strike force of ten destroyers, a light cruiser and two heavy cruisers. The aircraft carrier would not be far behind. Almost immediately planes from the enemy carrier were upon them, dropping bombs and torpedoes, strafing the Allied ships with machine-gun fire. The stern lookout reported to the bridge. Japanese torpedo and patrol boats from the landing force in the bay were now on their tail and gaining. There was no turning back.

The captain's voice was calm and firm. "We'll have to make a run for it. All engines ahead flank."

The ship surged ahead to twenty-nine knots. For a moment Tom's heart pounded in his throat, but then it settled into the steady business of war as it had done so many times before. He was glad to be on the bridge, exposed to strafing gunfire, rather than in the engine rooms. Those below could only guess at the progress of the battle.

Suddenly four torpedoes slammed into the *Perth*, which went dead in the water. Eight-inch Japanese shells quickly found their mark. At 12:05 she went down. The *Houston* continued on alone, still firing but beginning to list heavily to starboard. Tracers from its guns swarmed out into the night sky like angry hornets fighting off an elephant stampede. With the *Perth* gone, all the Japanese fire concentrated on the *Houston*. A shell slammed into its after engine rooms and exploded, bursting the steam lines and scalding the entire engine room crew to death. The ship lurched forward like a wounded beast and then crouched low in the water, trembling and shaking. Live steam poured through the breaches and cracks in the ship's structure, driving the gun crews from their mounts temporarily.

The bomb that destroyed the after engine room had knocked out the gas ejection system for the five-inch gun mounts, and they soon filled with hot, choking fumes. The guns kept on firing as the crews choked and retched. When one man passed out, he was rolled out of the mount onto the deck and someone else quickly took his place. The hot guns caused the unburned gas to burst into little wisps of dangerous flame. When a powder can split open in Mount 52, the gases erupted into a flaming flashback that enveloped the entire gun crew in an instant. In the chaos of the disintegrating ship the gun crews worked as calmly and efficiently as if it had been a drill.

A torpedo hit forward and smashed the main battery plot. The battery crew came scrambling topside for safety and were killed by a shellburst as they emerged. Turrets went to local control. Another shell hit the No. 2 turret just as the powder bags were being loaded, starting a fire. Communication circuits were overloaded with all the damage reports pouring into the bridge. Many of the phone lines were out, and repair crews were unable to rig new lines fast enough.

On the bridge the captain turned to Tom. "Get down there, Benson, and have them flood those magazines to stop that fire!" He turned to the seaman next to him.

"Signal the engine room right rudder, twenty degrees. If we're going down, we want to make sure we don't beach. I don't want those bastards to be able to salvage as much as a can of beans off this ship!"

As Tom made his way down from the bridge, a seaman manning a fire hose shouted, "Hey, Mr. Benson. If this keeps up, we'll have to leave her."

"Hell," shouted the man behind him. "This ship won't sink. The old man won't let it!"

Tom dodged the damage control and repair crews working frantically to control the fires springing up everywhere.

"Flood the magazines," he shouted to the damage control officer who was directing the attempt to put out the blaze.

"But, sir, if we do that, the eight-inch turrets will have no ammunition except what's already in the hoists."

"Do it, Chief. That's an order."

Just then a shell struck one of the forty-millimeter gun mounts and exploded, blowing the gun crew out onto the deck. One of them sat stunned near Tom. As he reached over to give him a hand to his feet, the burned flesh from the man's hand came off in his palm.

"I'm sorry, sir," the gunner mumbled apologetically and stumbled off toward sick bay.

The decks were filled with the acrid stench of burning oil and powder and the sweet smell of burned flesh. The dead and dying were everywhere, blocking passages and strewn around the deck. Twisted metal, crumpled beyond recognition, tangled with twisted, mutilated men. Tom saw a damage controlman pick up a leg and toss it overboard as casually as he tossed over bits of burning wreckage.

The chaos and havoc seemed to have reached unbearable proportions, and still the *Houston*'s guns fired furiously on.

"Load that mother faster! . . . Keep that damned ammunition coming. . . . Hurry the hell up." The gunners' tempers flared as hot as their guns, but they still kept at it.

The deck was slippery with oil and blood. Men poured up from the fire and destruction belowdecks, many of them badly burned. One stumbled out onto the deck and ran into Tom. He grabbed hold of Tom and tried to talk, but only gurgles emerged. His eyes, filled with anguish, were pleading with Tom to understand. Finally Tom realized that the man's nose and mouth had been blasted away and that torn pulp that had once been a face now blocked his breathing passages. Tom called a medical corpsman, but he had lost his scissors in a shell blast. Finally Tom obtained a shark knife from one of the crewmen, and he and the medic cleared the man's face so he could breathe.

"Get him to the side with the rest of the wounded," Tom ordered, and the faceless apparition disappeared. It wasn't until he was gone that Tom realized he had recognized the man's eyes. It was Brandon.

Suddenly three torpedoes hit the starboard side. The ship buckled and shuddered. Water began to pour into the hull, and the starboard list increased. The ship was obviously done for. Japanese destroyers swarmed in close, raking the ship with machine-gun fire, killing the twenty-millimeter gun crew in the mount near Tom. He stepped in and began firing the gun alone. It felt good to be giving something back.

At 12:22 the captain ordered abandon ship and left the bridge to go to his cabin. Just as he reached it, a shrapnel burst killed him and the crew of a nearby gun mount. His men rushed to his side, and the captain died in their arms. Buda, his cook, sat wailing outside the cabin door.

"Captain dead, *Houston* dead, Buda die, too." He refused to leave the ship.

The wounded were put aboard lifeboats; but the ship still had too much headway to be safely abandoned, and the executive officer, now in command, cancelled the order. The ship was sinking beneath them, but men went about their business coolly. The crews stood by their guns, firing until their ammunition was completely gone, at which point they even fired their flares as a last defiant gesture. Crew members forced from belowdecks, and the wounded collected on the quarterdeck, where they became targets for Japanese machine-gun fire.

Commander Roberts reissued the abandon ship order at 12:33, and the bugle sounded the signal from the fantail. Men began to jump or climb down the cargo nets lowered on the port side. The wounded were helped into lifeboats. Tom stayed on to help with the wounded.

Suddenly an explosion blew the fantail apart, and Tom found himself flung backward off the starboard side of the ship. The ship was beginning to roll over. He recovered from the shock of impact with the water and began to swim quickly away from the suction that would be created when the ship sank. His life vest slowed him down. He could see the Stars and Strips on the *Houston*'s mast and imagined that the flag gave a defiant final flutter in the breeze before it went down.

He heard a monstrous whooshing sound as the ship continued to roll. It looked as if it were going to fall right on him. The sucking noise grew louder, and he began to be pulled in. Then there was a tremendous rumbling sound, and he was flung high in the air. When he looked down, it was as if a great chasm had opened in the ocean, a liquid Grand Canyon. The ship had disappeared into its bottom far below, but the hole remained behind. As he slammed back down, he instinctively curled into a ball. By the time he stopped descending he was almost out of air. He looked up and saw a faint circle of light too far to reach. He could hold his breath no longer when another rumble sounded and he was spewed upward in a churning vortex and spit out onto the ocean's surface.

Shaken and exhausted, he looked with dazed eyes at the scene around him. The sea seemed full of the *Houston*'s bobbing survivors, although fewer than 400 of her more than 1,000 crewmen remained alive. Searchlights from Japanese destroyers illuminated the area as they directed shells and machine-gun fire at the survivors. Shock waves from the blasts slammed against the bodies of the helpless men, killing those nearby with the concussion.

A blast went off near Tom, and he could feel it rip at his body as it threw him into the air. In the light of the searchlights he saw the sea turn red around him, and he reached down to feel his legs. They had been badly mangled. Frantically he tore off strips from his shirttail and applied two tourniquets to stop the bleeding. He succeeded only a moment before he lapsed into unconsciousness, clinging desperately to a nearby hatch cover.

When Tom came to, he had drifted out of the search area. The destroyers were gone, but searchlights from the patrol and torpedo boats still lit the nearby waters. This time, however, they were picking up survivors, not shooting them. The moon was gone, and the smoke of battle had disappeared. He could see the stars overhead and smell the sweet scent of jasmine again. Bathed in the warm salt water, his wounds no longer hurt him. Still, he knew his injuries were too severe for him to survive long without help. The patrol boats were within hailing distance, but he wasn't sure he wanted to survive. He knew that he would lose his legs. With half of him gone, he would never again go to sea, nor did the prospect of a Japanese prison camp appeal to him.

Weak from loss of blood, he drifted in and out of consciousness again. When next he was fully aware of his surroundings, the gray light of dawn had developed a red border on the eastern horizon. He appeared to be alone. No ship's shadow could be seen. The sea gently held him in its caress, and he felt a deep peace. He had made his decision. He was no longer afraid. Still clinging to the hatch cover, he took off his orange life vest and let it drift away, bobbing with a kind of bright cheerfulness. Then he let go of the hatch cover, and it, too, began slowly to leave. He paddled freely for a while, watching them go. The orange border in the sky had stretched higher. He turned and floated on his back, arms outstretched, his useless legs dangling. He lay there for a moment looking at the sky, feeling the warm water pass over and around him, savoring every sensation. Then he closed his eyes, relaxed, and let the sea take him.

Chapter 36

It was almost eleven when Catherine returned to the hotel and sent away the old woman who had been watching Michael. He was still sleeping soundly. She called Bandung headquarters and spoke to one of Admiral Glassford's aides. She gave him her hotel phone number and requested that someone call her as soon as the *Houston* was through the Sunda Strait and safely into the Indian Ocean.

"We'll do that, Dr. Morgan. We should have a report by dawn."

She knew she should get to Tjilatjap as soon as possible; but it was late, and she was exhausted. The roads would be crowded with refugees. She would have to leave early in the morning if she wanted to make the seat on the plane which Admiral Glassford had arranged for her. Despite the hour, she decided to call Margit to say good-bye.

"Hello."

"Margit, it's Catherine. I won't be coming back for my things. I'm going to Tjilatjap early tomorrow morning. Sure you won't change your mind and come with me?"

"No. I've decided to stay." The gulf made by that decision opened up between them, leaving little to say.

"I just want to say thanks for everything."

"My pleasure." The awkward silence grew as the immensity of events rendered words inadequate.

"Give Papa my best when you get to Australia."

"Yes. I will. Take care of yourself, Margit."

"I will. You, too."

The phone clicked down on Margit's end. Catherine's hand trembled as she replaced the receiver. My God. Why hadn't she gotten out of here long before this?

Miles away, Margit still stood by the phone that sat on the hall table, already regretting the strain in her conversation with Catherine. The radio droned in another room, its voices keeping her company in the empty house, though she had ceased listening to its optimistic reports and patriotic messages. She had an urge to call Catherine back, but she had neglected to find out where Catherine was staying. Annoyed, she lifted the hair from the nape of her neck to cool herself and turned to go up to her room to bed. She had one foot on the first step when she noticed an Indonesian man standing quietly just inside the door, rifle in hand. She stifled a cry which would have done her little good. The servants had all fled at the first news of the naval defeat and Bernard had not been home since the day before.

"What is it?" she demanded in Bahasa, trying to keep fear from her voice.

"Message, Njonja." He smiled brightly at her, as if wanting to reassure her. He pulled a folded white sheet of paper from the cord that held up his khaki shorts and thrust it eagerly at her. Not yet convinced he was sincere, she cautiously came close enough to take it from his outstretched hand and then retreated a few feet to the hall table where she might find something to defend herself if necessary. She unfolded the note. It was addressed to Catherine and neatly typed. Feeling a little nosy but salving her conscience with the thought that the circumstances were extraordinary, she read it.

> Dr. Morgan:
>
> I promised a fellow officer I would personally deliver this letter into your hands when I reached Java but am unable to do so because our ship has been diverted to Darwin. I've entrusted it to another officer on convoy duty out of Darwin who thought he might be able to deliver it for me.
>
> Bud Larson, Lt. j.g., USN

Clipped to the note was a sealed envelope which was not addressed.

"Where did you get this?" Margit asked.

The Indonesian fumbled in a pocket of his shorts and withdrew a crumpled calling card. The engraved printing had been crossed out and her address substituted. On the back, in ink, was inscribed "William S. Armstrong, Lt., USN-USS Houston."

"I help guard the docks until all the ships leave," the Indonesian explained proudly. "American officer on the biggest ship tells me to bring a message here." He pointed with pleasure to the black naval dress oxfords he was wearing. "He gives me these and says it is very important."

Margit frowned. Whatever was she to do with it now? It was probably just a personal note from one of Catherine's American friends. Aware that the man was still standing patiently by, Margit reached into the drawer of the table for some change to give him and then realized Dutch money was no longer of use. Impulsively, she took off her gold wedding band and dropped it into his hand, telling herself it would probably be removed by the Japanese anyway. Astonished, he thanked her and hastily departed before she might change her mind.

Margit poured herself a glass of sherry from the decanter on the table. It was her third of the evening and she drank it quickly. Numbed by the wine and the bleakness of her own situation, her curiosity about the letter evaporated. She dropped it into the open drawer and closed it. Clutching the decanter and a glass to her, she headed once again for the stairs. The radio was still on. The announcer was reporting that Europeans were being ordered to evacuate the city and move to Bandung, in the interior, which could be more easily defended. Shortly after midnight she finally fell into a troubled sleep.

At dawn Catherine was jarred awake by the phone.

"Dr. Morgan?" a voice asked.

"Yes."

"This is Lieutenant Lindsey. We talked last night."

"Yes," Catherine replied, recognizing his voice and coming more fully awake.

"The admiral wishes to speak with you."

There was a brief silent interlude, and then a commanding male voice came on the line. "Catherine?"

"Yes, Admiral."

"The Japanese have landed a large troop assault on Banten Bay in the Sunda Strait some fifty miles from Batavia. They were accompanied by a large carrier strike force. With no reconnaissance planes available we didn't know they were there, of course. *Houston* and *Perth* sailed right into them."

The admiral paused, and Catherine's heart caught in her throat.

"*Houston*'s been sunk. *Perth*, too. I'm sorry, Catherine. We had a report last night from the destroyer *Evertsen*, which was trying to catch up with them. They picked up sounds of a terrific sea battle in that area, but we weren't able to get a plane out to survey the area until dawn—the last damn plane we've got, I'm afraid. They reported the Japanese are still picking up survivors from the two cruisers. They've been taken prisoner, of course, so we won't know who they are until the Japanese report them to the Red Cross."

The admiral pressed on with the urgency of a man with much to do and not enough time to do it. "You must get out of Batavia at once. The Japanese will be moving their troops any moment, and they have a clear road to Batavia. The bay is only fifty miles away. The American Navy is sending two amphibious planes from Australia to Tjilatjap to evacuate naval headquarters personnel and civilian evacuees. We haven't anything else here that will fly, so you must make those planes. I'll be on one of them, and we'll be leaving at dusk to make detection more difficult. Do you want me to send a car and driver for you?"

Catherine struggled to compose herself. "No, no. That won't be necessary. I have a car—and gas. I'll leave at once."

"Good. Don't delay. We don't know how long the roads will remain open. I'll see you this evening."

The admiral paused again. "And, Catherine, I'm sorry about Tom. From what information we've been able to gather, they put up a terrific fight. We can be proud of them. I'll see you this evening." The admiral abruptly hung up.

Catherine pushed aside the mosquito net and walked out on the terrace. It faced east, overlooking the bay. It was Sunday morning, and already it was hot. She thought of home. It would still be Saturday there, late afternoon or early evening, depending on the part of the country. Chicago would probably have the remnants of spring snow crunching underfoot. She thought of her family and friends. War would be on all their minds, but today it would

361

seem far away, as it had seemed to her until only a few weeks ago.

The bombs that had fallen on Batavia had been frightening, but that was nothing compared to the terror that gripped her now. The bombs could have killed her, but the men who were coming could take more than her life.

She felt a chill and began to tremble. In the east the sky blazed brightly. The sun had scaled the horizon's wall and seemed to pause, burning a fierce orange. It shone like a huge red rent in the perfect fabric of blue sky, a gaping hole through which she could glimpse the fires of hell.

It was just past midnight when Catherine arrived in Tjilatjap. The road had been crowded with refugees, many of whom merely clogged the road, having no destination. Most were Indo-Eurasians or Westerners. The natives sold coconut milk to the fleeing refugees while they awaited the arrival of the Japanese liberators with a pleasure they now didn't bother to conceal. The Dutch continued to deny the reality of the situation. The Navy having failed, they now believed the Army would succeed in defeating the Japanese.

Even at this late hour the streets of the small town were crowded and impassable. Catherine parked the MG and took a sleeping Michael into her arms. The area around the docks was especially crowded. She could just make out the hulking shapes of the merchant and warships now being readied for departure. With relief, she also discerned the shadow of a large seaplane at the far end of the small harbor. She made her way toward it. As she drew closer, she could make out the U.S. naval insignia on the wings, but she was refused admittance onto the pier by an armed Dutch military policeman seated in a jeep.

"I'm looking for Admiral Glassford. Could you tell me where I might find him?"

Before the young enlisted man could answer her, she heard her name called and turned to see a pleasant-faced young Dutch officer standing behind her.

"Dr. Morgan? Admiral Helfrich has ordered me to intercept you."

She looked at him questioningly. "Where is Admiral Glassford?"

"He left about half an hour ago on the other seaplane. He is expecting you to be on this one."

The fear that had clutched at her when she had heard of the admiral's departure quickly dissipated.

"Fine—"

He interrupted her. "I'm afraid I have some bad news. The admiral didn't know it at the time, but the second seaplane has developed engine trouble." Seeing the stunned look on her face, he hesitated and then continued apologetically. "I'm afraid it will be impossible for it to leave."

She felt the panic rising within her and attempted to stay calm. She looked around the harbor at the various small merchant ships preparing to leave.

"And those?"

"We had a report this afternoon that the Japanese have a second large task force which has entered the Indian Ocean south of here with the intention of preventing any ships from escaping to Australia. Most of those you see here tonight will probably be lost. I wouldn't advise escaping by ship. Besides, there are no available berths."

"And you, Lieutenant, what will you be doing?"

"I'll be leaving with Admiral Helfrich by plane for Ceylon. If I could give you my place, I would." His voice soft, he added, "My wife and two young children are here. They'll be left behind just like you. I'd give my life to keep it from happening to either of you, believe me."

She looked at him with sudden sympathy and understanding. "I know you would, Lieutenant. And don't worry about her or about us. Just do what you can to get this over with soon. We'll be all right."

Suddenly she had to get away from here, from the sight of the helpless seaplane, from her own helplessness, if possible.

"Wait!" he called after her. She turned back toward the jeep. "There's a message for you at military police headquarters. You didn't give me time to tell you. I'll take you there."

Explosions now shook the buildings around them as the Dutch began to destroy the crated American P-40's that had arrived from Australia only yesterday—too late. During the ride to headquarters the Dutch lieutenant was unable to give Catherine any news about survivors on the *Houston*. He stopped the jeep in front of a small building and took the hand she offered him. She smiled this time. "Thanks, Lieutenant. And good luck."

"I hope your news is good." He wheeled the jeep away from the curb.

Outside the military police building a uniformed man was feeding documents into a fire. Lights blazed from the one-story building, almost blinding her when she stepped inside. In the center of the room, a harassed-looking Dutch army officer sat at a desk, sorting through papers. He didn't look up as she approached. She stood before him for a moment, and when he still didn't look at her, she spoke.

"I'm Catherine Morgan. I believe you were looking for me."

He looked at her briefly; then his eyes returned to his papers.

"Not me," he said brusquely. "I'm not looking for you."

She was suddenly overwhelmed by despair.

"He is." It took her a moment to realize he was still talking to her. His head was still in his papers, but the pencil in his hand was pointing to an adjacent room marked "Commander" in Dutch.

The door stood open, so she crossed to it and looked inside. The chair behind the desk was empty. A small gooseneck lamp on top of the desk cast a yellow disk upon the cluttered surface. The rest of the room lay in shadows. She could just distinguish the figure of a man standing by the window, silhouetted by the glow of the bonfire outside. His back was toward her, but he looked familiar.

"Ahmad?"

He turned from the window and saw her standing in the doorway. Relief flooded his face.

"Catherine. Thank God they were able to find you." He crossed toward her and took Michael from her weary arms as she slumped onto a bench that stood against the wall.

"I'm so glad to see you," she whispered in relief, and then she put her hands to her face and began to cry.

Still holding Michael, Ahmad sat down on the bench beside Catherine but did not try to comfort her. He let her cry until she had finished, then he reached out and took her hand.

"You're going to Maitreya," he said gently.

"Maitreya!" Catherine gasped. "I couldn't possibly go to Maitreya. Kara is still there."

"I spoke with Kara before I left Borneo. She gave her consent."

"Then she's a far more generous and forgiving person than I could be."

"Perhaps," he said noncommittally.

"How did you know I was here?"

"Margit told me. I took a ride over here with the British consul just to make sure you'd be able to get away, and I found out the plane wasn't leaving."

She leaned her head back against the wall and closed her eyes for a moment.

"I have a boat waiting at Surabaya to take us to Matapura. We'd better get going. I'm not sure how much longer the roads will be open."

In contrast with the road which led from Batavia to Tjilatjap, the road northeast, toward Surabaya, was empty. The car's headlights threw a thin yellow ribbon onto the wide expanse of darkness. The road raced away beneath them as the warm, moist ocean breezes gave way to the cool, dry air of the mountains.

Ahmad drove in silence, concentrating on the road. A little after 1:00 A.M. Catherine drifted off to sleep. When he was fairly sure she would not be wakened, he reached over and switched on the radio. The Dutch station in Bandung was reporting enemy landings throughout Java. Troops were nearing both Bandung and Batavia, and heavy fighting was taking place. Despite this resistance, Japanese troops were advancing, and the ominous news of their progress kept on for the next two hours.

At 3:30 A.M. the Dutch newscaster announced the station was shutting down and there would be no further broadcasts. His voice cracked with emotion as he signed off. "Good-bye and good luck. Until better times. Long live the queen!"

The station went dead, static snapping and crackling in its place. Ahmad reached over and flipped the switch, searching for another station, but found only the rushing sound of empty airwaves. He switched it off. At least he had learned enough to determine which roads to Surabaya would still be safe.

It was almost dark the next day when they encountered their first signs of war, a roadblock manned by Dutch and Australian troops. Catherine watched their frightened, tense faces with sympathy while Ahmad spoke in Dutch to the young officer in charge. She and Ahmad were allowed to drive on after being warned that the Japanese had landed on the coast some seventy miles west of Surabaya but had not yet moved to take the city. If the MG held up, they would be able to make it in time.

Chapter 37

The silk pennant, with its gold background and crouching black leopard, snapped and fluttered crisply in the sudden ocean breeze. The gleaming white yacht from which it flew was the only vessel in Surabaya Harbor besides the low, lateen-rigged fishing boats making their way out to seek a day's catch. Except for the native men, wading waist-deep for clams in the bright green waters of the Java Sea, the shore lay quiet and empty in the early-morning light.

The yacht's Dyak crew, dressed smartly in white *kains* and gold jackets with white turbans bound loosely around their heads, prepared to cast off as their three passengers came on board.

"I almost forgot," Catherine said, turning back to Ahmad. "The car. It has to be destroyed. I promised."

Ahmad spoke in Dyak to one of the crewmen, who disappeared and quickly reemerged with a can of gasoline, with which he doused the car thoroughly before setting a match to it. The MG burned brightly for a moment then exploded as the flames reached its gas tank. Ahmad gave another order, and the yacht's big diesel engines roared to life. Ropes were cast off, and the last sailor jumped on board as the boat pulled rapidly away. Catherine stood by the rail, watching the blackened chassis of the car in the dying flames. As it receded in the distance, she felt an overwhelming sadness tinged with fear.

"Will we have to run a naval blockade?" she asked Ahmad anxiously.

"I don't know, but that should protect us." He nodded toward the flapping pennant which bore the emblem of the sultan of Matapura. "The Japanese respect it, at least for the time being."

Throughout the day the ship's radio crackled with Japanese voices, but they saw no Japanese ships. On the sunlit sea it became easy to believe there was no war. Ahmad sat on the cushioned bench in the boat's stern, holding Michael, who was contentedly examining his fingers and toes. He probably needs changing, Catherine thought. She was suddenly aware she must appear in need of a change herself. The full skirt of her cotton dress was hopelessly wrinkled. She was barefoot, having shed her sandals once they reached the boat. In contrast, Ahmad still looked unrumpled, though he wore the same navy knit shirt, the white duck slacks, and the tennis shoes in which he had met her at police headquarters. There was a strong sensuality beneath his elegant exterior, as if his personality contained worlds of warmth and fire. She trusted him completely, yet she had to admit that he frightened her a little. He certainly didn't frighten her son. They had taken to each other so naturally. She almost felt excluded from the strong bond which seemed already to exist between them, yet it pleased her.

From time to time Ahmad turned his gaze from the sea to her. She felt exposed, yet nothing about his expression caused her embarrassment. It was merely the fact that he was looking at her, and she realized, as she had the first time she had seen him at Maitreya, that he was not a man from whom one could easily hide things. The thought suddenly struck her that she would like him to find her beautiful. Disturbed, she closed her eyes and leaned back, letting herself be absorbed by the comfortable cushions of the lounge chair. By dawn the next day they had reached the coast of Matapura. Beyond the narrow stretch of sandy beach high green mountains could be glimpsed through the mist and clouds. Matapura had been an island which had gradually become attached to Borneo's mainland by the encroaching mangrove jungle so that it now formed one side of the bay into which flowed the Barito River. A short distance up the river was the Dutch town of Banjarmasin, and beyond it were the English plantations and Maitreya. On the east side of the bay, high atop Gunung Matapura, an extinct volcano, sat the *kraton*, ancient fortress palace of Matapura's god-kings. Its walls had repulsed foreign powers for 600 years. The modern world had not touched the palace itself. It was allowed to come no closer than the *kraton* gates, leaving everything within as it had been since the first richly carved teak columns were covered with pounded gold and set, like golden sun beams, to support the soaring pavilion roofs. Floating serene and aloof above the bay, the *kraton* seemed less a thing of the earth than a part of the universe itself, beyond time and the reach of man.

As they entered the harbor, the sound of a lone conch shell, the trumpet of royalty, floated down from the huge wooden gates of the *kraton*, announcing their arrival. It was a lonely, haunting sound, full of fragile mystery, and when it stopped, the silence left something ominous hovering in the heavy, shimmering air. It was then that Catherine caught her first sight of the enemy, as the sun glinted off the hard polished metal surface of Japanese guns mounted atop sleek launches and transports. She gave a slight shudder, and Ahmad touched her arm in reassurance.

"We will have passed them by the time we enter the river. They won't stop us. They need men for the roads they want to build through Indochina's jungles, and young women for their soldiers' brothels. My father has refused, but they still hope to gain his cooperation; they still want to appear like the saviors of Asia that they believe themselves to be."

They anchored in a secluded cove near the mouth of the Barito River and put into shore on the yacht's small launch so that they might obtain a small inconspicuous native boat for the trip upriver. Like a happy tide, the Dyak villagers near the river mouth came splashing out to meet them with friendly smiles and curious fingers, tugging and patting at Catherine's dress and hair and feet and anything else they could reach. They seldom saw a European woman.

Ahmad laughed in sympathy. "I'll stop them if you like."

She shook her head, happy at their friendliness.

In keeping with his more elevated position the village headman, the *orang-kaya*, waited on the beach to greet them officially. He wore a traditional loincloth, and the arms of an old fur coat were tied around his perspiring neck so that it hung down his back like a cape. In this area headhunting had been eliminated by the Dutch years earlier, and the Dyaks of the region were friendly and peaceful. For ornamentation they made creative use of whatever flotsam civilization happened to send their way. A broken yellow pencil stub graced the hole in the lobe of the *orang*'s right ear, and a piece of white paper fluttered like a feather from a string in his hair.

The villagers quickly set about making a celebration to honor their guests. *Tuak*, the native rice wine, was brought out in huge jars to the gallery which ran the length of the longhouse. Everyone assembled there, the men in their loincloths and the women in their colorful short sarongs. Both sexes wore many heavy gold rings through the slits in their earlobes, causing them to hang to their shoulders and below. The *orang* made a welcoming speech, which Ahmad followed with his own, and then the drinking, singing, and dancing began, accompanied by gongs and drums. Next, the *orang* gave Catherine a speech. She replied in English, which none of them understood, but they heartily applauded as if they had.

A man in hornbill headdress jumped up, producing a skull of no recent vintage, and began to dance out a headhunting tale. Catherine knew the tattoos he wore on his hands indicated he had practiced the art himself at one time. When he tired, several young women took the floor with more grace and a slower tempo. The floor ceased its ominous shaking. Catherine closed her eyes. The reality of her situation again caught up with her. The gongs began to give her a headache. The wine was making her sick.

Suddenly the women stopped and sat down. The crowd grew quiet, as if intently waiting. Startled by the silence, Catherine looked around, but nothing had changed. Then from out of one of the apartments which opened onto the gallery stepped a girl no older than fifteen, who had an unusual beauty both fragile and wild. Her long black hair spilled out of a crown of white orchids. The gold bracelets around her ankles, which were her only jewelry, brought attention to her small, slender bare feet. A short sarong reached from her waist to her knees. Like the other women, her chest was bare.

The audience sighed its approval. Simply because of her presence, the mood of the room had changed. This was Siah, the youngest daughter of the *orang-kaya*, a special child with an ability to dance that was reputedly inspired by the supernatural. Through it she magically conveyed the promise of her religion that even stones must possess a spirit and the earth itself a soul. Mountains are gods and death is not real. Within the spirit of the forest all life that has ever existed lives on. She struck a pose in the center of the room and held it without moving. Her almond eyes were fixed demurely on the floor; but her lower lip trembled slightly, and her narrow nose flared to betray an excitement which the crowd now shared. She held her arms straight out at the shoulder, one bent down at the elbow, the other up, fingers spread apart like forks of lightning. When she slowly raised her head to a proud angle, her eyes blazed. The demureness was gone.

She stood without moving as much as an eyelid until the silence in the room was complete. Then the gallery suddenly went dark. A gasp escaped the crowd, and they fell silent again, eyes adjusting to the grayness of the room, the earth. Still Siah did not move. Her body remained in the room exactly as before, but her eyes seemed aware of something far away. The deep rumble of distant thunder eerily broke the silence, and a flash of lightning illuminated the room. Siah's fingers began to move, almost imperceptibly at first, then flickering rapidly. Taking their cue, the drums and gongs began a muted beat so that they, too, seemed to come from far away. Siah broke her pose and let her body move sensuously with the rhythm of the music. So fluid were her movements she seemed part of the music itself.

The sky grew still darker. Streaks of lightning raced across the large gallery windows that opened to the porch. Someone lit a torch, and Siah began to dance close to its light, flirting with its flame. As the music's tempo increased, she began to leap and spin and touch the flame, but miraculously she was not burned. The villagers cried out in awe. Siah was at once the fire from the earth and the fire from the sky.

Suddenly a gust of wind entered the room, and the torch went out. The music stopped. When the torch was lit again, Siah was kneeling before Ahmad, her head touching the floor before him, her arms outspread in supplication. He spoke softly to her in Dyak, and she raised her face, an enigmatic smile upon it. Her eyes boldly held his for an instant; then she rose and backed away, palms pressed before her, head bowed.

The sky grew lighter as the rain began. The thunder and lightning stopped, and only the gentle sound of raindrops on the nipa-palm roof could be heard. Siah stood proudly as the crowd bestowed on her the ultimate applause of silence.

Ahmad spoke to the *orang* who sat beside him. "It doesn't seem possible, but she is even more beautiful than when I saw her two years ago. But I am surprised she has not married."

"She has refused all those who have approached her in the night for the past two years," the *orang* replied. In Dyak courting the suitor approaches the girl's pallet at night while everyone else sleeps and offers her a betel nut to chew. If she accepts his offer, then it means she will receive him in her bed and, if all goes well, marry him. If, on the other hand, she asks him to perform some chore for her, it means she has rejected him.

"I am considering giving her to your father as a gift since she will have no one."

Ahmad was silent. He did not approve of such gifts; but they had been the custom for centuries, and he was in no position to change it now.

The *orang-kaya* noted his silence and began to take offense. "You do not think he would be pleased."

"I think he, or any man, would be pleased with such beauty. Still"—he hesitated—"perhaps it would be hard for her to leave her people."

The *orang-kaya* ignored his last remark. "Good! It is good that he be pleased." Considering the matter closed, he went on to other things. It was not often that the Dyak had an opportunity to entertain the royal family, and he intended to make the most of it. Songs and dancing began again, and more *tuak* was brought out.

When Catherine and Ahmad left the village later in the afternoon, a number of villagers had passed out from the revelry, and the rest would continue until they joined their unconscious companions. Carrying Michael, Catherine followed Ahmad down the narrow path toward their boat at the mouth of the Barito River.

"Will your father accept Siah if the *orang* offers her?" she asked him.

"Of course," Ahmad replied. "Besides, he probably would never even know she is there. So many escape his attention."

Catherine felt mildly irritated. "You say that so easily. What about your mother and her feelings?"

Ahmad laughed. "My father loves being attractive to women. He must constantly reaffirm it. My mother understands and accepts it."

"I wouldn't," Catherine retorted defiantly to his retreating back. He turned and faced her so suddenly that she almost stumbled against him.

"I don't blame you." His eyes were serious; but his mouth

was smiling, and she could not tell if he sympathized or mocked her. He abruptly turned again and left her standing and staring after his retreating figure, his every move so naturally regal and commanding she was left secretly feeling a little awed by him.

Ahmad was lost in thought as he made his way down the steep, narrow trail. Catherine's remark about the harem had revived his own earlier disapproval. He didn't like the thought of Siah's going to his father's harem. He had come to this village often as a child—to hunt and fish and be free of the rigid confines of the tradition-bound court. Here no one was in awe of him or treated him as a god. As a baby Siah had ridden upon his boyish shoulders to bathe in the river, her tiny hands tightly gripping his fingers as he waded in deep water, her chubby legs hugging his neck. Though he had watched her grow up, he still thought of her as a child: one who should remain free, not locked away in a harem guarded by angry old women in a place only the sultan could enter and none could leave. He doubted that Siah was equipped to handle the many intrigues of the harem. Most of the women in it were from other civilized courts, other harems. They would have only scorn for a Dyak girl like Siah and treat her like a naked savage.

Of the thousands in the harem, only a few women ever caught the sultan's attention. Ahmad didn't know which bothered him the most: the thought of Siah neglected, left, if she was to know love at all, to learn it from the lips and hands of other women, or the image of Siah as his father's favorite, heavy with child.

When Catherine and Ahmad arrived at the boat, Siah and her cousin Mindun stood waiting for them. They had taken the path from the village to the small sandy beach. The girls approached Catherine first with a garland of flowers and placed them around her neck. Mindun knelt before Ahmad and touched her forehead to his knee in a gesture of homage, then rose and stood aside, head still bowed. But Siah, when her turn came, did no such thing. To Catherine's astonishment, Siah, with shocking familiarity, stood before Ahmad and put her small, delicate hands upon his chest. Slowly sinking to her knees, she ran her hands down his body to his thighs. Her beautiful face was turned up to his: bright and bold and open with her feelings.

"*Sang Hijang Batara Guru,*" she murmured, lips parted and inviting. "*Sang Hijang Batara Guru,*" she whispered again.

He took her firmly by the elbows and lifted her to her feet, speaking sharply to her in Dyak. Though the disapproving look on his face frightened Siah, she stood her ground, answering him as an equal. His face softened, and he released her. She broke into a smile. The conversation ended, and Ahmad sent the two girls on their way back to the village, giggling freely and talking animatedly.

"What was that all about?"

"She wanted me to persuade her father to give her to me as a gift. I told her that her father would never waste anything so valuable as such a beautiful daughter on a mere prince, though I told her I was deeply honored by her offer. It seemed to satisfy her."

He stepped lightly into the dugout and took the baby from Catherine, offering his hand to help her in. Birds, bright flashes of color glimpsed within deep shadows, took flight in noisy protest as the sound of the outboard motor suddenly broke the river's tranquillity.

So as not to be seen by the Japanese, Catherine lay down in the narrow bow, comforted by the confines of the boat's high wooden sides. The baby slept in her arms. As they neared Banjarmasin, Ahmad took off his knit shirt so that he would look more like the other boatmen on the river. He gave it to her for a pillow. It smelled faintly of soap. Royal princes seemed to be a separate species, immune from perspiration. Her own dress was annoyingly soaked.

"*Allahu ahbar.*" *Allah is great.* The call to prayer floated clearly over the water from Banjarmasin. Over the side of the boat she could just see the Buddhist temples and mosques of its Chinese and Malay inhabitants come into view. Women wearing tight-fitting batik jackets over long colorful sarongs waded in the water, carrying fishing baskets. More conservative than their city counterparts, these Moslem women wore bright scarves upon their heads which they pulled across their faces when they encountered a stranger.

Beyond the shore lay the government buildings of the Dutch civil service, now occupied by the Japanese military. The Dutch officials, held prisoners in the Dutch Resident's house, were left to run things until they could be replaced with local substitutes the Japanese could trust. Despite the sultan's disapproval, there were many Indonesians eager to cooperate with the new order.

Dutch women and children had been confined to their own homes.

As the boat passed, Catherine turned her head to stare at the houses with their deep, covered verandahs. Most homes had been looted so often there was nothing left to steal.

"Surely the Japanese will deport the civilians—at least the women and children—as soon as there are ships available," Catherine said aloud. "It's the only practical solution," she added.

Seeing the concern on her face, Ahmad agreed with her rather than tell her the truth. His father, no friend of the Dutch, had nevertheless recommended deportation for them, but he had been told by the Japanese naval authorities who administered Borneo that foreigners were to become prisoners of war.

Terns flew off from the shallow waters near the riverbanks as the boat approached. The river narrowed so that a canopy of tree branches and yellow flowers stretched across it. Their smell was sweet and soothing. Monkeys chattered noisily overhead and mated with aggressive abandon on the sandy river beaches. The current rocked the boat gently and Catherine fell mercifully asleep.

That night, as Siah slept upon her mat in the family loft, the son of a nearby kampong headman crept into the loft with a sireh leaf containing the betel nut, lime, and gambier necessary for chewing. He gently woke her and whispered his offer of the rolled sireh leaf. In the light of the dimming fire she seemed to smile at him dreamily, and his heart took a leap of hope and joy.

"Would you please stir the cookfire?" she murmured.

Crushed, he took up the sireh leaf he had placed on her pallet and crept softly away. Siah turned her head and fell back into her dream of a tall, handsome prince—the same one she had dreamed of, sleeping or awake, since childhood.

Chapter 38
Bataan, March 1942

In the caves above Mariveles the regular 10:00 A.M. newscast from San Francisco came crackling over the radio salvaged from the *Canopus*, bringing news of Java's surrender. Despite poor reception, there was no mistaking the gist of the message. The Japanese now occupied Batavia. Michael, who had been waiting tensely since the news of the disastrous Battle of the Java Sea, had listened closely along with a small gathering of the *Canopus* crew. No one spoke as Michael gave up his weary vigil and started out of the radio room.

"I'm sorry, Mr. Stanford," the on-duty radioman said as he reached the door.

Michael paused and straightened, but he did not look back. "Thanks, Phillips." His eyes were bloodshot with fatigue. Suppose he never saw her again? Suppose he never got a chance to tell her how much he loved her?

"There's a report that a convoy from the States has reached Australia and is going to start for Manila Bay soon." The information came from Corbet, the supply officer.

Michael turned and looked at Corbet and then at the other men.

"They'll have the Japs out of the Indies in no time," Phillips said hopefully.

Michael smiled as if he believed it, then looked back at Corbet. They both knew it was a lie. "I think I'll get a breath of air.'' He turned and strode briskly out to the entrance of the tunnel, swallowing hard and trying to control himself. He managed a salute to the guard at the opening.

Before him stretched another beautiful day. It was hard to believe that just beyond that peaceful-looking bay, the Japanese occupied Manila. The lull in the fighting fooled no one. Everyone knew that the Japanese had just landed fresh reinforcements, troops and supplies unused in their easy victories in Malaya and Singapore. The lull would soon be over while the Americans watched and waited for ships that would never come.

He reached into his shirt pocket and took out a note that had come for him that morning from Corregidor. It had been written two weeks before and brought in by an American sub from Australia transporting medical supplies, one of the few to make it. He reread the note for perhaps the tenth time.

Dear Michael,

    I talked with Tommy Hart on his way home to Washington from Java after resigning the ABDA fleet command. He told me your plane had been destroyed and you had been transferred to the *Canopus*. He also told me what a fine, brave job you had done for him as a flier. I wanted you to know how proud I am of you, and that, after thinking it over, I realize it was right for you to join the Yanks (although I still wish you were in a British uniform).

    As for the news at home, I'm afraid I've little to tell you, and what little I have isn't good. Catherine and little Michael have still not been able to get out of Java. I've done what I can to try to speed matters up on this end. I blame myself for bringing them there. I've been totally out of touch with Kara and Julienne in Borneo. Margit hasn't heard either. I hope to establish some kind of radio contact with Ahmad soon.

    I will be in Port Moresby, completing work on our coast watch network. I don't suppose there will be much chance for you to get a letter to me. Not much of that kind of thing going in and out of the Philippines now. I was fortunate to be in Australia at the right time to see Tommy and get this off to you. There are difficult days ahead for all of us. My thoughts and my love are with you.

Dad

The note had confirmed his worst fears. Catherine, his children, and Kara were still in the Indies. For a moment he allowed himself to feel the anguish of wondering how different things might have been if Catherine had only let him know she was pregnant. His old anger toward her returned briefly. If only she had kept in touch, let him know where she was. But then, if only he had not thought that he had all the time in the world to make his decision . . . He couldn't blame her. He shouldn't have let her go in the first place.

He thought of his son, and he felt love of such overwhelming power for both of them that it left a painful ache in his chest. Only a few days earlier Michael had learned that his letter to Catherine had never reached Java. Bud Larson's ship, the *Peary*, had been sunk in the attack on Darwin. Bud had not been on the list of survivors. Though he had not been able to get word to him directly, Michael was certain that Ahmad would know about his son by now. He would have seen Catherine and the baby at Margit's. Michael's only hope this bleak day was the knowledge he could rely on Ahmad to do everything he could to protect Michael's family and get Catherine and his son to Borneo, where they would be safe until Michael could reach them.

Bilsky, the *Canopus* seaman who stood the guard duty, decided to strike up a conversation.

"The torpedo boat crews tell me that the Japs have stepped up their patrols outside the bay," Bilsky said. "Guess they're expecting some kind of evacuation—of the brass at least."

Michael knew they were right. He was privileged to the top secret information that MacArthur and his family would be leaving Corregidor next week. Filipino President Quezon and his wife had left Corregidor by submarine weeks earlier. Before he left, Quezon, who was ill, had angrily denounced the United States for betraying the Philippines first by failing to send help and then by refusing to grant independence early so that the Philippines might have become a neutral nation.

Bilsky, who had raised his binoculars and was scanning the sea, suddenly stopped. "Boat coming, Mr. Stanford," he announced without lowering his glasses.

Michael raised his own and looked out toward Corregidor. If the placid bay had caused him to doubt a war was going on, the sight of Corregidor through the binoculars did not. The island had been pounded by bombs until every tree and building had been reduced to splinters. Only the deep tunnels and the guns remained of the fortress. At the docks on the protected side of the island he could just make out the bobbing speck of a small launch. He scanned the sky. Luckily no enemy planes had appeared. He lowered the glasses again. The boat was near enough now that he could make out the figures in it. One of them wore sunglasses and carried a walking stick. His hair was long beneath his oddly crushed cap.

"Damn," Michael muttered, then addressed Bilsky. "Go tell the captain he'd better get down to the dock."

Catherine was coming to Maitreya.

Kara closed the door to her room and leaned back against it. She felt another wave of nausea coming on, and recalled that sick, sinking feeling she had felt when the plane had touched down on the lake in the Grand Valley of New Guinea and she had seen, not Michael, as she had expected, but Catherine, standing in the clearing, suntanned in khaki cutoffs and a sleeveless shirt, her long black hair tumbling down from under a woven grass hat. Kara would never forget the look on Catherine's face. Nor could she forget Michael's grim, tight-lipped expression as he came out of the forest, because she knew it had mirrored her own. Had there ever been two more reluctant subjects for rescue?

Ten months after the massacre at Agats rumors had reached Hollandia of a blond white man living in the western highlands. The rumors had traveled the same mysterious trade routes by which the stone axes of the Jale reached the coasts. Kara had been sure the man was Michael and that he was stranded or perhaps hurt. She had never believed he had died in the massacre; she trusted his ability to survive. Since the rumors had not mentioned a woman, she and the rest of the family had assumed he was alone. Looking back now, she could see how the mistake had been made. To the New Guinea tribesmen, women were property, not individuals. No mention had been made of a woman just as there was no report of the number of pigs the white man possessed.

On that plane to Port Moresby she had found some comfort in telling herself that Michael's relationship with Catherine was strictly due to the circumstances. He would get over it once he

379

was back at Maitreya with her and the children. All she need do was be patient and understanding. Each time Michael had gone away she had prepared herself to lose him—but not like this. Never to another woman. Not Michael who was always so loyal to those he loved.

Sir Charles had suggested to her that he speak with Michael first, so she had waited alone in the dark in her room at the Moore plantation. It had been the longest hour of her life. Then suddenly the light had gone on and he was standing there by the door, his hand on the switch, his face strained. She had imagined this reunion throughout the weeks of the search. But not once, in even her most anxious version, had it ever been like this.

She had waited across the room, every muscle in her body stiffened, braced as if to protect herself from a blow.

Finally he had spoken. "I'm sorry that I've hurt you, Kara."

"So am I," she had said softly.

"I would have done anything I could to keep from hurting you."

She had believed him. He had always protected her. Too much, perhaps.

"I'm not coming back to Maitreya. At least not for a while."

She had released the breath she had been holding. He'd gone on.

"I'm leaving for the States in a few days—alone. I need to be by myself for a while."

She had wanted to go to him, throw her arms around him, beg him to stay with her. She couldn't. Wouldn't. It would have been the worst thing she could have done. She had always given him his independence without question, made no demands even though she hated that role. He had never suspected how much she hated it. She had endured it only because she had recognized, as other women in his past had not, that he needed his independence and that giving it freely was the only way she could keep him. But she had always been sure, until that moment, that he would return to her. Now she was not.

"And then?" she had asked.

"I don't know." His face had been drawn, his eyes filled with pain.

What about the children? She had wanted to ask. She had wanted then to use anything she might think of to bind him to her because she realized that he wasn't tied to her, and never had been. He was tied to their marriage, to the children, to the commitment he had made, but not to her. Her eyes had filled with tears.

"Oh, Michael," had been all she could manage to say.

He had quickly crossed the room, taken her into his arms, and buried his face in her curls.

"I love you, Kara," he had whispered, and then held her away from him and looked searchingly into her eyes. "I want you to know that."

She had nodded. "I've always known it, Michael. And I love you. With all my heart."

His eyes had filled with tears as he leaned toward her and kissed her forehead. Then he had released her and started for the door.

"I don't want you to go!" It had come out a strangled cry. She had hesitated and then cast her pride aside. "At least stay tonight. Please."

He had turned back, and the anguish on his face had been her answer. "I can't stay. I don't like doing this to you. I've never hated anything more."

He had turned and left the room and a few days later he had joined the U.S. Navy. He had said he loved her, and she had never doubted it was true. However aloof he had seemed to strangers, he had always been generous with love and affection to those close to him. In Michael's affections she had probably ranked somewhere close behind Sir Charles and Ahmad. And Catherine? She had sensed even then, perhaps before he had made up his mind, that Catherine was first in a way that no one else had ever been. But she also had known then that he could love Catherine and still come back to her. Would she want him then? Despite her pain, she knew the answer. Yes. Of course. She would want him on any terms on which she could have him.

Nine months ago Kara had received a hastily scribbled note from him written just after he had been sent to the Philippines from Hawaii. It had said he wanted a divorce. Whether he survived the war or not, he was never coming back to her. Accepting that fact, she had found a strength that surprised her. With both Sir Charles and Michael gone, she had been forced to take on the responsibility of running Maitreya, and she had done so admirably well. What's more, she had enjoyed it, so much so that she could not bear the thought of giving it up. Not to Michael. Not even to Sir Charles. Certainly not to Catherine.

Now Catherine was coming to Maitreya. Why had she ever agreed to let her come? She crossed to the dressing room and looked in the mirror. The hot, damp air caused her hair to curl into tight blond ringlets. She gazed steadily at herself. Tomorrow Catherine was arriving with Michael's child. As mistress of Maitreya Kara had given them sanctuary. She tilted her head defiantly at her own reflection. She was still mistress of Maitreya. It was a position she would now fiercely defend against all threats. Against Catherine, even against the Japanese. With surprise she noticed that her image in the mirror was smiling.

The two women standing on the dock were in striking contrast with each other: Julienne in khaki pants and laced boots, still sweating and dusty from the hard ride she had taken on Admiral that morning, Kara in a simple light green dress, cool and pale. They stood together watching the white launch approach. They didn't speak to each other. That was not unusual. They had spoken little since that first day, eight years ago, when Kara and Michael had arrived home at Maitreya from their wedding trip to Europe. They had been alone in Michael's room, Julienne sitting on Michael's bed, watching Kara unpack, Kara chattering about her trip and what they had done in Paris.

"I don't want to know about Paris," Julienne had suddenly said with annoyance. Kara had looked up at her sister-in-law in surprise. Julienne had been propped on one elbow, lying on her side on the bed dressed much as she was today.

"I want to know if you come."

"Come?" Kara had asked, puzzled by the question. "Come where?"

Julienne had shrieked with derisive laughter. "I knew you wouldn't understand." She had given Kara a look of combined amusement and distaste. "It's an expression which refers to sexual orgasms. Do you have orgasms with Michael?"

Kara had turned deep red with embarrassment and shock. When she recovered, she had eyed her sister-in-law, two years her junior, as she might eye a naughty child.

"I hardly think that's any of your business."

"You don't have them." Julienne had smiled, studying her closely. "You probably don't even know what I'm talking about."

Kara had felt defensive. "I do so know what you're talking about. I just don't care to discuss it with you."

Julienne had begun to laugh uncontrollably. Kara, reluctant to pursue the conversation further, had remained silent until she could stand it no longer.

"I hardly see anything funny. Whatever are you laughing at?"

Julienne had finally recovered enough to answer. "It's hilarious. You're married to a man every woman wants and you can't even fully appreciate him. What a joke!"

"Well," Kara had said tearfully, "the joke you're trying to make of me and my relationship to Michael is cruel, Julienne. His sister of all people! I'll never forgive you!"

Suddenly Julienne had been sober, realizing that she had gone too far. "I'm sorry, Kara. Truly I am. I don't know what got into me."

Only Kara had known she wasn't sorry. Though it was never mentioned again, the incident had put a strain on their relationship that had never been overcome. Now they stood together on Maitreya's dock, watching the boat grow closer.

Kara cast a sidelong glance at her sister-in-law. With those full, freckled cheeks and the upturned nose she looked strangely naïve and childlike. Kara wondered how Julienne must feel about Catherine's return and decided, finally, that Julienne was pleased. After all, she had voiced no opposition when Kara told her of Ahmad's request, and Catherine was her old friend and roommate. No doubt she welcomed her. Never mind that by becoming her brother's mistress, Catherine had brought scandal to the Stanfords.

Well, set the scandal aside. This was wartime. Priorities were different now. The boat docked, and Ahmad climbed out, carrying a bright blond baby who stared at the women with gray, serious eyes. Kara was surprised to feel her resentment melt away and her eyes fill with tears. There was certainly no doubt whose son this was. By the time she greeted the slender dark-haired woman close behind Ahmad, only the special bond of having loved the same man remained between them. Kara had always been a generous person, and now these feelings triumphed over the fierce competitiveness she had felt toward this woman.

Julienne spoke first. "Welcome, Catherine. And welcome to

Michael's bastard. We Stanfords collect them, it seems." She looked at the baby with curiosity.

"Strange," she mused, "how the Stanford bastards all look alike." Without further ado, she turned and strode jauntily back to the stable, her curiosity and family obligation satisfied.

Kara flushed at Julienne's rudeness. Catherine smiled. "Don't worry about Julienne, Kara. We understand each other. There's no need to apologize. Really."

Caroline and Rachel had heard the boat arrive. They now came bounding down the road from the house, expecting to be swung up into their Uncle Ahmad's arms, only to find those arms already occupied by a baby. Caroline stopped short and stared wide-eyed at the new arrival.

"Whose baby is that?" Caroline demanded to know.

"Mine." Catherine smiled. "How are you, Caroline?"

She looked down at the lovely little girl whose delicate coloring and pale golden curls might have come from an Italian Renaissance canvas were it not for the skinned knees and bare feet. "You probably don't remember me. I'm Catherine."

Caroline's toe traced a shy line in the dust before her that seemed to say, "Come no closer." She barely gave Catherine a glance before her gaze returned to Michael. Rachel arrived, puffing, her cheeks and legs still chubby. She stood next to Caroline, eyeing Michael with suspicion.

"Who's the daddy?" Rachel asked in her small, piping voice.

Catherine hesitated. "He's a man in the Navy."

"Come on, girls," Ahmad intervened. Catherine's answer seemed to satisfy Caroline, who skipped after him as he started up the road.

Rachel remained stubbornly behind. "I don't think I like this baby," she announced loudly.

"Perhaps you'll change your mind when you get to know him, darling," Kara interjected soothingly.

Looking doubtful, Rachel nevertheless abandoned her objections and ran after Ahmad and Caroline.

Inwardly Catherine breathed a sigh of relief. The tensions of that first meeting were now behind her. "I'm grateful to you, Kara, for allowing—"

Kara interrupted. "I don't want to discuss it." Her voice suddenly shook with an uncharacteristic vehemence. "And I don't want to know anything about you and Michael. If you truly are grateful, Catherine, you'll grant me that request.'' She turned away and started to walk toward the house.

Catherine called out, ''Of course'' and began to follow her. She was more shaken by Kara's outburst than she cared to show. Catherine would have preferred to discuss things, but she felt Kara was entitled to handle the situation as she wished.

They walked on in silence, neither of them realizing that in the undeclared contest for Michael's loyalty and affection, each thought the other had won.

The next morning, when Ahmad was ready to return to Matapura, Catherine walked with him to the river.

''When will we see you again?'' she asked him.

''Perhaps not for some time.'' He could not tell her that he would be leaving Matapura almost immediately to organize a guerrilla movement among the Iban and Dyak tribesmen of the mountains. ''I'll send word to you whenever I can.''

The two of them had spent the morning engaged in small talk with Kara and Julienne. Kara had become an expert at pretending things were normal. She conducted life at Maitreya as if there were no war—right down to continuing to collect and store rubber. Ahmad's earlier suggestion that she destroy the rubber trees and leave Maitreya while the opportunity still existed had gone unheeded.

Ahmad had dressed in more appropriate clothes for the river this time—rough white cotton pants tied at the waist and a loose white muslin shirt. He was barefoot. Yet despite his simple attire, he scarcely seemed an ordinary man.

''How much longer do you think we'll be safe here?'' Catherine asked, aware that as the time for him to leave drew closer, she was again afraid. His confidence and strength had bolstered her own. Now, without him . . .

''Until the summer. The Japanese will be occupied with the coastal oil fields for the next few months, repairing the damage done by the Dutch before the Japanese landed.'' He didn't add that the Japanese had made an example of those men who had destroyed the oil fields by raping and murdering their wives and daughters before their eyes, then killing them. ''They won't concern themselves with the inland rubber estates until the oil fields are operating. But you must be prepared to act quickly when the time comes to leave. I may not be able to give you much warning."

"And then?"

"By then I will have seen to it that the mountains can provide a refuge for you, Julienne, Kara and the children."

They had reached the dock. In the past few days on the river they had become good friends. Catherine reached out to offer her hand, then hesitated. Seeing her confusion, Ahmad took her hand and pulled her into his arms.

"Thanks," she whispered in amused relief, her cheek pressed against the rough cloth of his shirt, her arms encircling his waist. "I wasn't sure if it was polite to ask for a hug from a prince."

He laughed so softly that she felt more than heard it. "The French side of me has been hugging people for years," he replied.

They sought only to give comfort to each other, nothing more. But as they stood touching for the first time, a new sensation began to stir between them. Disquieted, she pulled her head away from his shoulder and relaxed her arms, but his remained securely in place. When she raised her face to look at him, she found she could not meet his eyes, afraid of what she might see there or perhaps afraid of what he might see in hers. But he was already bending down to kiss her. It was a gentle kiss, made all the more sensual by its restraint. Her hands came up to his chest, as if to push herself away, but to her surprise they lingered, like the kiss itself. Both of them needed their fragile new friendship more than they needed passion, so they parted uneasily, awkward at pretending nothing had happened between them. They could not speak of it, for that would make it too real—and too threatening. He smiled first, putting a light, careless hand upon her arm in a casual gesture of farewell. By then she was smiling, too. The boat pulled out. He waved. For a moment his dark eyes seemed to float back to her, drawing her away with him until the boat reached the spot where the shadows of the forest lay deepest on the river, and then he was gone.

Chapter 39

"My God! Is this the end of the world?" shouted one of the artillery officers on Mount Samat. No one could hear his cry. Violent explosions were coming one on top of another, blowing the carefully constructed Allied defenses to dust, demolishing telephone lines, and disrupting communications. The long lull in the battle for Bataan had ended dramatically on the morning of Good Friday, April 3, when the Japanese launched a five-hour artillery and aerial barrage against the American-Filipino line. The effects were devastating. Bamboo thickets, dried from lack of rain, burst into flame. At first the isolated fires were treated lightly, but they quickly united into an inferno which jumped clearings and swept onto the forward line with such ferocity that it cut off escape, trapping and burning hundreds of soldiers alive. Confronted by a wall of fire, soldiers in the center line were forced into a disorderly withdrawal. Showers of sparks and ashes fell as thickly as rain, and the smoke grew so dense that the U.S. artillery units on Mount Samat could not see to aim their guns.

Amid this chaos the Japanese began their ground attack. It was the beginning of the end. Only a quarter of the American-Filipino force was fit to fight. Mosquito nets and quinine were gone, and almost everyone had malaria. Rations were down to 1,000 calories a day, and the lack of proper nutrition made wounds slow to heal and infections quick to develop. The hospitals reeked of gangrene.

As soon as the attack began, Michael's naval brigade was ordered north from Mariveles to the front line to reinforce I Corps. Fed from the *Canopus*'s own supplies, they were thin but in better shape than most. When air attacks drove the trucks off the road, they walked. By the time they reached the front, the unit they had been assigned to reinforce on Mount Samat had been captured or killed. The Japanese were gone. Communications were so badly fouled that those officers in charge of planning the defense didn't know the location of the enemy.

The following days were desperate for the command on Bataan. Orders were issued and revoked because they were impossible to execute. Units failed to take up the proper positions, and even frontline commanders didn't know where their units were at a given moment. Roads were so clogged with retreating troops and deserters that reinforcements could not be moved forward. Whole units of Filipino troops threw down their weapons and disappeared into the jungle. In two days the entire army had simply disintegrated.

Michael's feelings alternated between disgust and panic. Rarely did he and his men engage the Japanese, and when they did, their support troops seemed to melt away, leaving them outflanked and forced to fight their way out. Having just escaped one such situation, his unit had been ordered to report to General Fisher on the East Road. They found him standing in front of his jeep in the midst of what had become an overwhelming flood of retreating Filipinos—his own troops.

"God damn you yellow bastards!" the general was shouting at the uncomprehending men. "Turn and fight, you damned deserters!"

He had pulled out his revolver and began firing it into the air. It had no effect on the emaciated and blankly staring soldiers who poured past him. They were beyond caring. Suddenly, in a fit of rage, the general lowered his gun and fired into the disorderly mass, killing or wounding several men. Their crumpled bodies were ignored by both their comrades and the general, who returned his gun to his holster and snapped it closed before climbing back into the jeep. Having no room to turn around, he ordered his driver to back down the road. Arms crossed, he sullenly ignored the retreating men who shuffled along beside the jeep in an ironic escort.

There was no way Michael, standing at the edge of that

continuous and tattered stream, could reach the general to report. He turned instead to his men.

"We've been ordered back to Mariveles."

It was a lie. They all knew it, but it didn't matter. It was April 9, almost one week after the Japanese attack had begun, and the battle was clearly over. Part of the Allied line still held, but the eastern section was in full rout, leaving the East Road wide open behind the retreating men. Informed of the situation, MacArthur ordered an immediate offensive, from his command post in Australia. The men were not to surrender but to fight to the death if necessary. When General King, the commander of the Luzon force, received the message, he shook his head in disbelief.

"If this continues, Bataan will be the greatest slaughter in military history." He looked at his staff, some of whom were weeping openly. It was shortly before midnight. He was silent for a long moment, then turned to his side. "Get Corregidor on the phone. I wish to speak with General Wainwright." He paused to gain his composure. "Tell them I intend to surrender."

Catherine wandered into Maitreya's library shortly before tea was to be served on the terrace, a practice that continued in this English household in spite of war and the difficulty in obtaining tea. Since she had arrived at Maitreya one month ago, she had been spending her days in the rice fields and vegetable gardens of Maitreya. Kara didn't ride, and Julienne wasn't interested, so Catherine did the work Michael used to do, riding out each day to help with the planting and harvesting of crops. Maitreya and its surrounding villages were making an attempt to become increasingly self-sufficient. Here, in the library, among the family portraits, Catherine had renewed her interest in the Stanfords. In portraits dating back to the early nineteenth century she found a sense of family she had never had in America, where her Irish family had been all too eager to leave behind reminders of an immigrant past. But at Maitreya the past was much in evidence, the links proudly maintained. Since her return to Maitreya, the family portraits were of renewed interest to her; her son was part of this history.

Marlott, the family estate in England, held the more ancient family portraits. Collected here in the Borneo chapter of the family history were more recent and flamboyant members.

Catherine was especially intrigued by the portrait of a beautiful young woman with green eyes, brown hair, and fair English skin who was portrayed in a silk sarong, surrounded by brown native women, in a Gauguin-like study that predated the work of that artist by some fifty-five years.

"It was painted by a talented ancestor."

Catherine turned at the sound of Julienne's voice behind her.

"It's a lovely piece of work, isn't it?" Julienne remarked as she crossed the room to stand beside Catherine.

"The Stanford baronets are famous for two things: beautiful wives and bastards. My mother was an exception. She wasn't the least bit beautiful. Since none of her children were either, that left my father with all the family looks, which suited his nature."

Julienne turned to one of the bookshelves and took down a small gold-framed portrait which she handed to Catherine. It was an exquisite painting of a handsome man with fine features and dark brown hair.

"That's the first Rajah Stanford, Sir James. He was something of a rogue. He never married, and his two nephews, sons of his brother William, were his only heirs. The elder, Richard, was a failure and a drunk. The work at Maitreya was handled by his younger brother, John. That's his portrait on the wall. John was a cold, disciplined, and driven man who felt more at home in native huts than with his wife and children. He had a beautiful and brilliant wife, Elizabeth, whose portrait you were admiring. Elizabeth loved Borneo and its people and wanted to share her husband's life, but he wanted her in England. She finally could no longer abide his treatment of her and sailed for home with the children. On the voyage all the children were stricken with cholera and died.

"Sir James also returned to England, content to play the country squire on his Marlott estate, having chosen John to be his heir. One day a young man turned up at Marlott and claimed to be Sir James's son, born to him of a minister's daughter he had met before he sailed to the Indies. His name was Stephen Barton, and he had remained silent about his parentage until his mother's death.

"There are no portraits here of Stephen Barton, but it is said that he was blond with intense gray eyes and very handsome. Sir James readily accepted him as his own, thought the family was skeptical, especially his brother, who saw some threat to his own son's inheritance. Sir James was adamant about the truth of the claim. He sent Stephen to Oxford. John opposed his coming to Borneo to participate in the family enterprises. During that time Stephen met Elizabeth in England, and they fell in love. Both sailed for the Indies, and Elizabeth became pregnant. She returned briefly to John until the baby was born. He didn't learn until later that it wasn't his. By that time the child was already accepted as the legitimate heir, and since John and Elizabeth were not divorced, there would clearly be no others. So the third rajah of Barito was actually the grandson of Sir James Stanford and not his grand-nephew, as the records officially show.''

Julienne smiled at Catherine. "As you can see, Michael and his son are not the first illegitimate heirs to the Stanford fortune.''

"And Stephen and Elizabeth,'' Catherine asked, "what happened to them?''

Julienne laughed. "Are you looking, perhaps a little desperately, Catherine, for happy endings? You'll never get one from me. I'll never tell you what happened.'' She turned her attention from the family portraits to Catherine.

"Just think, Catherine. Only three summers ago we were two green college girls, babes in the woods, until you got lost in the bushes with my brother and disgraced us all.'' She giggled at the thought. "Dear, perfect Catherine, a fallen woman. Who would have believed it back at the old sorority house?''

"You are a malicious monster, Julienne,'' Catherine said mildly, refusing to be baited.

"Yes,'' she replied seriously. "No doubt Michael told you all about me. Anyhow, it's a relief to have someone around again with whom I don't have to pretend. So you see, I'll enjoy having you here.''

Catherine was convinced there was no advantage to her in having Julienne free to be herself. Julienne looked at Catherine with continued amusement.

"You're much more tolerable than Kara with her eternal goodness. It had become quite boring around here.''

Julienne started for the door and then turned back.''

"I almost forgot. Damal sent me to tell you that tea was ready.''

She remained standing by the door.

"I also thought you might be interested in the news I just

heard on the radio in my room. Bataan has surrendered. I'm on my way to tell Kara. I thought you'd like to know, too."

She congratulated herself on the stunned look on Catherine's face and left.

Kara was not in her room. Julienne stopped in the doorway, taking note of all the feminine things that had gradually taken over since Michael left. Gone were his stacks of papers and books and the Oceanic carvings that Kara had always detested. Julienne frowned in disapproval. She had always hated changes. When she was a child, a book out of its proper place in her father's library would send her into anxious rage. Even then she had possessed an acute memory for detail and the servants had soon learned to keep things in their usual location. She was on her way to find Damal and ask Kara's whereabouts when he caught up with her in the hall.

"Captain Supardjo is here from Batavia," Damal said with excitement. "He has brought news of Njonja Margit!"

Julienne hurried for the river. The captain's thirty-foot boat was tied to the end of the dock and he stood beside it, wearing a long *kain* and a scarf tied about his forehead. His hands were on his hips in his usual jaunty fashion, but there was a weariness in his eyes that had never been there before. Before the war began, the captain had regularly brought supplies from Batavia and the other islands to Maitreya. This time, the sugar and rice he was carrying had been confiscated by the Japanese in Banjarmasin, but he had managed to smuggle tea and coffee upriver. He had no recent news of Margit. He had last been in Batavia two months earlier, just as the city was preparing to evacuate.

"I go to the house and beg Njonja Margit to come away with me so that I can bring her here, but she would not leave." He shook his head sadly and shrugged. "All captured by now." He leaped onto his boat and went into the cabin, reappearing quickly with a small bundle. "She sends these to you to keep safe." He handed Julienne what appeared to be a stack of photo books and mementos, tied with a string which had come loose.

Julienne took them with a feeling of annoyance. Margit was so sentimental. She might have at least sent something worth saving, like jewelry. The crew had begun to unload the supplies from the ship. Julienne followed them toward the house, shuffling through the pile of photographs, birth certificates, and children's drawings which Margit had deemed her most valuable possessions. Among them she found a letter addressed to Catherine in Margit's handwriting and felt a renewed stab of annoyance. Why would Margit write Catherine and not her? Perhaps there was one for her elsewhere. She began to go through the pile with renewed interest. Bud Larson's note turned up beneath a baby picture of her youngest nephew and she paused on the path, a sudden chill coming over her. Stuffing the note and the letter into her pocket, she walked quickly toward her room and dumped the photos on her bed without another glance. By the time she sat down at her desk to open the letter, her hands were trembling. She knew who it was from. Margit had written a note to Catherine on the back of the envelope. It was dated March second.

Catherine—This letter came for you just after you left. Ahmad called from Tjilatjap to tell me your plane had been grounded and he was going to try and find you to take you to Maitreya as he had originally planned. I hope this finds you well and safe. Fondly, Margit.

Julienne opened the letter. Inside was a folded piece of paper whose privacy had been secured with a strip of adhesive tape.

Dear Catherine,

I am still hoping to see you soon. I must get this off quickly. There is no more time for apologies or regrets or explanations about the past. Marry me. I've asked you (far more eloquently) in at least a dozen letters this past year, all of which were efficiently returned. Kara will agree to a divorce, but even if she doesn't, we'll live happily together in sin or bigamy or polygamy or whatever matrimonial state is necessary. I love you. I need you. If you remember all that existed between us as well as I do, then you know it cannot be otherwise.

Michael

Julienne stared at the letter, seeing in the hurried scrawl of Michael's handwriting all the anguish he had felt at the time he wrote it. It was unlikely there would be any other letters to Catherine from him. Not for a long time. Not until whatever love they had felt would be gone. Then Michael would come back to Kara and everything would be as before. Her hand stopped trembling. If she could help it, she would never let Catherine have Michael. She stuffed the letter calmly into the envelope and, along with Bud Larson's note, took it to the separate building which housed the kitchen and placed both papers on the fire. When she was sure they were nothing but ashes, she left.

By the time General Wainwright's reply, overruling General King's decision to surrender, reached Bataan it was too late. The messenger bearing the white flag had already gone out to the Japanese. As word spread through the scattered and disorganized Luzon forces, they began to pour south into Mariveles, hoping to escape to Corregidor. Some 2,000 of them did, taking anything that would float to get them there. By the time Michael and his men reached Mariveles on April 9 it was past midnight, and the army had begun to destroy anything that might be useful to the Japanese. Some commanders had destroyed their vehicles without awaiting orders, not stopping to realize the trucks would be needed to transport prisoners too sick or wounded to walk. One storage tunnel exploded with such force that a large earthquake which shook the peninsula at the same moment went unnoticed. Rockets and shells coursed through the night sky over the bay and burst into a spectacular fireworks display.

A skeleton crew took the *Canopus* out into the bay and sank it. It went down quickly. Some of the sailors in Michael's unit wept as they watched, and Michael found it difficult to swallow past the lump in his throat. Barges continued to move between the docks and Corregidor ferrying personnel. The 76,000 men left behind sat silently watching the evacuation, many with openly hostile eyes. Nurses from one of the two hospitals had been trapped in the traffic jam on the East Road and had missed the last barge to Corregidor. A special launch was sent for them, and they were the last evacuees. After the last barge had loaded and left, the docks themselves became the final target for demolition. Bataan had fallen. Surrounded by enemy on land and sea, Corregidor had become an island Custer preparing to make its final stand.

The men on Bataan waited throughout the blazing, sun-baked

394

day with nothing to do but anticipate the grim future. That day seemed the longest in their lives for those who spent it there, quietly waiting for the Japanese. There was fear that many of the Japanese units might not have word of the surrender and would attack the defenseless troops. At the small airfield some of the men painted large Rising Suns on white sheets, using Mercurochrome, only to have Japanese planes come in and strafe the men gathered there, killing scores. Fearing more such attacks, Michael moved his men north on the East Road, past the two hospitals, overflowing mostly with the sick, to a field where other units had gathered to wait in whatever shade they could find. The Japanese began arriving late that afternoon.

At first they came in small bands and held back from the assembled prisoners, clearly waiting until their numbers were sufficient. They wore dusty uniforms and carried light combat packs. Small woolen field caps with the gold star of the Imperial Japanese Army were perched atop their heads. Heavy wool puttees were wrapped around their legs, as if they had somehow been confused about their destination and were equipped for the Arctic. None had removed the puttees. Each man carried a rifle with fixed bayonet and wore a somewhat anxious expression. Clearly they knew as little about what to expect from the surrender as did their helpless prisoners.

Michael studied them carefully. Next to him Douglas was staring at the useless tanks lying ruined and smoking in the ditches and shaking his head.

"I dunno, Michael. Remember how we used to make fun of the Army with their canvas leggings and their riding boots and those forest ranger hats that made them look like Boy Scouts? All those horses. They didn't have many tanks, but they sure had lots of horses. At least you could eat a horse. I mean, maybe it was good planning on the Army's part after all, to be able to eat your weapons when you got through with them."

"Douglas, if they'd really planned it that way, they would have used cows, not horses."

Douglas laughed out loud, a gesture that caused hundreds of curious stares.

"Jeez," Douglas said gleefully, "couldn't you just see them on Sundays—all dressed up in their jodhpurs, riding boots, and chin straps, jumping cows?"

Michael chuckled. "Let's have a little respect. Remember that the War Department that sent us horses instead of tanks is the same War Department that decided one of the ways to eliminate waste was to order officers to stop saying hello when they answer the phone."

"And we mustn't forget the new M-3 tanks with police sirens on them"—Douglas was laughing so hard now he had grown weak—"so the enemy would pull over when they heard them coming."

Michael laughed with him, relieved to find he could still do it.

"Oh, shit," Douglas said finally, wiping the tears from his eyes. "I used to love those football games when Navy beat Army. Shit," he murmured again. "I wish I'd gone to sea. At least I'd fight and die on a full stomach."

All at once the laughter was gone, and they stared off into the dusty heat. No Japanese officers had arrived yet, but the Japanese soldiers began separating Filipino from American troops.

"Hey, look at that." Douglas nodded toward a Japanese sergeant and a group of Japanese privates. The sergeant had been instructing them, and one of them had been slow to get the point, so the sergeant had just slugged the hapless private in the face with his fist. The private fell to the ground but scrambled quickly up again to stand at attention and receive another blow. After the private had been knocked down four more times, the sergeant walked away, leaving the private flat on his back in the sun. His plight was similarly ignored by his fellow privates, who began to laugh and joke, once the sergeant was gone, as if their prone comrade weren't there.

Douglas whistled in disbelief. "Get a load of that! Five years in Leavenworth for that one."

After a time the soldiers decided to pass the time robbing prisoners, preferably taking watches, rings, pens, and lighters but settling for photographs and used toothbrushes as the pickings got slim. Those prisoners who refused to cooperate were severely beaten. One American air corps officer near Michael refused to give up his academy class ring. An argument in sign language ensued with the result that the guard who wanted the ring pulled out his bolo, slashed off the offending finger, removed the ring from the bloody trophy, handed the finger back to the shocked and bloody officer, and pushed him back into his group.

Still another search uncovered Japanese yen on one prisoner. It had been available in exchange in Manila, but the Japanese must have believed it had been removed from the body of some dead Japanese. The guard instantly threw the American officer to his knees, pulled his sword, and struck the officer's neck with a sickening thud. The head bounded into the midst of the horrified Patwing group like a foul ball. They scrambled to their feet and moved away from the spot, shrinking from the sight of the dead officer's blood gushing in rhythmic spurts from the ragged wound between his shoulders.

No one had searched Michael yet. He had only his watch and the small ring that his father had given his mother, which he wore on his little finger. He was still staring numbly at the dead officer when he became aware of the commotion much closer to home. With alarm he realized that Douglas was quarreling with a young Japanese soldier. The soldier had demanded Douglas's Naval Academy class ring, and Douglas had given it to him but not without protest. Now the soldier was insisting on taking his wedding band as well, and Douglas, who had been only loosely attached to it since Michael had known him (he had never worn it on his evenings out on the town), now suddenly seemed willing to die rather than give it up.

"Douglas, for Christ's sake," Michael hissed softly. "Give it to him. I'll buy you two dozen more just like it when this damned war is over. I'll even inscribe them any way you want, only give the damn thing up now."

"No!" Douglas retorted sharply, ignoring the angry guard. "It's not the ring; it's the principle. They aren't even observing their own Army regulations."

"Douglas, it's just a gold ring. As far as principles go, there are more worthy ones to die for." Michael's tones were measured but exasperated. "I don't want to have to dig a hole in this heat to bury your busted ass. So cut it out."

The guard was no longer interested in arguments. He had become quite excited. Suddenly he swung his rifle by the barrel with two hands, and the butt struck Douglas a full blow on the side of his head. For a moment Douglas stood wide-eyed, stunned, as a huge gash opened up just above his temple all the way to the back of his head and blood began to run down into his surprised eyes and ears. Then his eyes closed, and he slumped to the ground, knees buckling beneath him. No sooner had he hit the ground than the irate guard began to kick him as hard as he could.

Grabbing the guard and speaking firmly in Japanese, Michael ordered him to stop and demanded to speak with his superior. Startled, the guard halted and reluctantly withdrew, leaving Michael to tend to Douglas. It was difficult to tell how serious his injury might be. A concussion—or perhaps even a fracture. Michael shuddered as he recalled the sharp cracking sound of wood against skull. Douglas was out cold.

A young Japanese officer came up.

"Lieutenant?" He addressed Michael in Japanese. "I understand you speak our language?"

Michael nodded, wary and still shaking with anger at the scenes he had just witnessed.

The officer held out his hand. It contained Douglas's academy class ring. "I wish to apologize for this incident. I only just arrived. It is a violation of our regulations and our honor. You will please return this ring to your officer."

"I accept your apology. And thank you."

The officer glanced at Douglas's prone form. "I would like to offer medical assistance, but we have none. Not even for our own men."

"I appreciate your concern." Michael was trying to control his voice, but he still trembled from anger.

"I'm Lieutenant Nagasaka. You will be in my charge now, until the gathering point at Balanga fifteen miles up the road. From there you will be fed and then marched to San Fernando to take the trains to Camp O'Donnell. You will be given food and water and will be well treated. You have nothing to fear."

He spoke earnestly, and Michael had no doubt that he believed what he was saying; but Michael knew there were forces at work beyond this lieutenant's control, perhaps beyond anyone's, that could make matters far less pleasant.

The officer took his revolver from his belt and handed it to Michael, a look of sympathy on his face. "You may use it if you like."

Michael's men looked stunned and confused, but Michael

caught the meaning of the gesture at once. He shook his head and replied in Japanese, "I know that for the Japanese soldier it is a disgrace to himself and his family to be taken prisoner, but in my country it is more of a disgrace to sacrifice one's life to no purpose. My death now would serve no purpose."

For a moment they stared at each other across a cultural gap that was perhaps the widest in the world: one man representing a culture in which individualism was held sacred; the other a world where the needs of the group subordinated all others. Michael smiled, and suddenly the officer broke into a smile as well and replaced his gun.

"Where did you learn to speak Japanese?"

"In San Francisco." He hesitated. "From a woman I knew there when I was young."

"A servant?" A slight look of hostility had crept into the officer's eyes.

Michael didn't answer.

"Of course. It's hardly likely that you worked for her, or lived near her, or that she was a friend of the family."

Michael started to protest that she had been a member of the family but thought better of it. He let the matter drop, and the Japanese officer strode scornfully off. Michael heard a groan and quickly forgot him. Douglas was finally coming to.

Chapter 40

"I will repeat it again, Colonel. You are ordered to kill all prisoners and those offering to surrender."

"General Homma would never order such a thing! I demand to see a copy of the order in writing first."

"The order is from imperial headquarters," the voice replied curtly. "It is already being carried out in other divisions."

"How can I possibly do such a thing? I refuse to act without a written order from General Homma," the colonel replied indignantly, and hung up the phone. Incensed, he turned to look at the puzzled faces of his assembled commanders.

"What they ask me to do is a violation of the samurai code. You will release your prisoners at once and inform them of the best way to escape from Bataan."

His officers stared at him, dumbfounded. No one dared move.

"You heard me! Don't just stand there," he shouted.

His officers quickly dispersed toward the hundreds of prisoners. Hands clasped behind him, the colonel watched them go. No Japanese general had issued such a command. He was sure of it. It was likely the work of Colonel Tsuji, that militant troublemaker recently arrived from Shanghai, where he had ordered the execution of 5,000 Chinese civilians for collaborating with the British. Tsuji hated whites and thought General Homma too easy on prisoners. No doubt he had convinced some of Homma's staff that the prisoners should be shown no mercy. Homma was already in trouble with the Army hierarchy for taking too long to conquer the Philippines, and Tsuji was taking advantage of Homma's weakened position to make mischief. Well, Imai would have no part of it. He had covered himself and his men with honor in his victory at Bataan's Mount Limay. He was not about to stain that great victory with a dishonorable act of murder.

The men of Patwing 10 sat resting in a harvested sugarcane field near Colonel Imai's headquarters. They had spent the night near Mariveles before being moved out toward Balanga at dawn that morning. Their little group of twenty-five had fared as well as could be expected under the brutal conditions of the march. Lieutenant Nagasaka had twice given them water from the canteens carried by their guards. Not much, one half cup each, but enough, and it was not contaminated like the water from the carabao wallows that other prisoners drank. The Japanese had had no food to distribute, so the lieutenant had let the prisoners forage in the sugarcane fields along the way. There had been little there, but it had allowed them to survive in reasonably good shape.

After they reached headquarters Lieutenant Nakasaka had left them to report to Colonel Imai, his commander. When he returned, it was clear that he was upset.

"On your feet," he shouted to the scores of men he had marched this far from Mariveles.

Wary bodies slowly rose, unsure of what to expect next.

"You free to go now," he said in broken English.

The silence of disbelief greeted his announcement. A murmur finally rose as they began to question its meaning among themselves.

"You hear right," Nagasaka shouted in irritation. "Now go. To mountains, to sea—whichever. You go!"

The men hesitated for a moment, suspicious, expecting some trick. Perhaps it was an excuse to shoot them while attempting to escape. But Lieutenant Nagasaka had already turned his back and was leaving the field, his guards following him. Some prisoners began to drift away into the jungle in small groups. When nothing happened, others took courage. Soon most of the prisoners were moving out with as much speed as their physical condition allowed.

The men of Patwing 10 hesitated. It was clear that Douglas

would only slow the rest of them down. Besides, he badly needed medical attention. Having rallied briefly from his head injury, he was now feeling the effects of the fifteen-mile walk toward Balanga that morning. He was weak and dizzy.

"You men are to leave," Michael told them. "I'll stay with Mr. Stuart."

There was some protest.

"That's an order. Chief"—he addressed the warrant officer who had led the repair crews—"you're in charge from now on. Get the bloody hell out of here—fast."

They each shook Michael's hand and exchanged a few words of farewell. The men then said good-bye to Douglas, who managed a grin and handshake for each.

"I'm counting on you guys to make it out of here," Douglas drawled.

"We'll get another seaplane, Mr. Stuart."

"Yeah. We'll be back for you soon. You'll see."

"Sure." Douglas grinned. "Sure you will. And by then this damn headache of mine will be gone and I'll be ready for you."

The talk died out. There was now no further reason to delay. The decision made, the men were anxious to move on. Bilsky's eyes suddenly brimmed with tears that were quickly blinked away.

"Hey, cut it out," Douglas chided him. "You can't afford to waste the water, and neither can I."

The men laughed, embarrassed. "So let's get out of here," one of them said.

Michael sat down next to Douglas and watched them go. They didn't turn back for a last look, and he was glad.

"Closer than brothers," Douglas mumbled after them. "I've been scared shitless most of the time for the past five months, and yet, weird as this may seem, I wouldn't have missed it for the world. Does that sound crazy?"

It didn't sound crazy to Michael at all. It was a time that had resulted in incredible acts of generosity and self-sacrifice, as men directed their hate toward a common enemy. As for himself, Michael knew that there had been a hundred times in the past few months when he could have escaped—jumped a small boat down to Mindanao and then a short hop to Borneo—and yet he had postponed it again and again, until perhaps now it was too late.

"You ought to have gone with them," Douglas said softly, as if reading his thoughts. "I just want you to know I'm grateful." It was, Douglas thought, bad enough to face his own captivity. It must be much worse for Michael, who had his family to worry about. Douglas wondered what he might have done under the same circumstances.

"These past few months, did you ever think of shucking this whole war and heading home?"

"Yeah." Michael smiled and nodded. "Constantly. Did you?"

"No. But if I'd had a wife in the Indies like you do, I might have."

"It isn't just my wife," Michael said without looking at Douglas. "There's another woman." He broke off, swallowing with visible difficulty and did not go on.

Douglas watched him, puzzled. "Your sister, then?" He knew Michael had at least one sister who lived in Java.

"No." Michael hesitated a moment and then added, "Her name is Catherine. I think she's in Borneo by now, with our son. He's almost a year old now, and I've never seen him." He struggled to control his voice. "I want to marry her so that my son will bear my name, and so she won't be forced to live a lie the way my mother did." His voice trailed off. He squinted down the empty road, expecting any moment to see prisoners in columns, and, seeing none, was relieved. Their freedom would last at least a little while longer.

Douglas was visibly moved by what Michael had told him, more by Michael's revelation of his feelings than by the news itself. He knew how difficult it was for Michael to do.

"Your son and her reputation—are those the only reasons you want to marry her?"

"No. I love her more than I've ever loved anyone. I want to spend the rest of my life with her."

Silence fell between them as they recognized the difficulty of their present situation.

"You'll make it to Borneo, Michael, if anyone can," Douglas said softly. Suddenly he felt like crying for himself, for Michael, maybe even for Catherine. He wondered what she was like. He felt like asking, but the pain he saw on Michael's face held him back. The moment was finally broken by the sight of a small convoy of Japanese troops moving toward Mariveles. Clouds of dust in their wake drifted slowly across the empty field, choking them. Judging from the pain when he coughed, Douglas suspected he had a broken rib from yesterday's beating.

When the convoy passed, once again the road grew silent.

Half an hour went by. Nothing moved in the midday heat. Even the dust had settled.

"Come on, Doug, let's move it," Michael said finally, pulling Douglas to his feet. The bandage on Doug's head was soaked with dried blood. Michael tore off the end of his shirt and made a fresh one. As he applied it, he saw the cut on Douglas's head lay like an open zipper from one end of his scalp to the other. It would require stitches to close it, but Michael had nothing with which to sew.

Farther down the road the shade was occupied by a battalion of the Filipino Army Reserve, the 91st of I Corps. There was no medical officer present, but Michael and Douglas were not allowed to continue. They were shoved roughly into a ditch with Filipino officers who had been segregated from their men. A limousine approached carrying Lieutenant General Akira Nara, commander of the 65th Brigade whose troops had fought and occupied this area of Bataan. He sat alone in the back seat. The general stopped the car and held a quick conference with his officers, then drove off without so much as a glance at the hundreds of hungry, thirsty prisoners who stared intently at him as he passed.

His brief arrival on the scene spurred the Japanese into a sudden flurry of orders and activity. The noncommissioned Filipino soldiers were ordered to assemble in the road and begin the march to Balanga while the 400 officers were collected into groups of twenty-five, wrists tied behind them by telephone wire. Michael and Douglas were pulled roughly to their feet, and their hands secured behind them, though they were isolated from the other officers. After a few minutes the clustered groups were herded away from the road.

They stumbled into a ravine full of beautiful forest, untouched by war. A Japanese civilian interpreter, recruited from Manila, had already begun to address them in the Filipino Tagalog dialect. "In a predawn attack during the Good Friday offensive, Filipino troops of your division surprised and overran the Japanese Sixty-fifth Brigade bivouac area, bayoneting those soldiers who innocently slept. Now the Imperial Japanese Army is seeking justice for those crimes.'' He then pronounced the punishment.

Michael knew that, ironically, it was the Filipino 41st, not the 91st, that had committed the offense. The men present were totally innocent. One of the Filipino officers was pleading with the Japanese commander to make it quick, to use machine guns and to let the condemned prisoners face their executioners. The request was brusquely denied. Michael began to argue that the men present were innocent of the crimes of which they were accused, that any executions would be in violation of the Geneva Convention regulations on the treatment of prisoners and an act without honor, unworthy of the Imperial Japanese Army. For that, he was promptly knocked to the ground and kicked, his wrists still bound behind him.

The officers in the ravine had begun to plead for their lives. In response, some of the guards offered cigarettes to the doomed men. One even came up with a stolen crucifix which he held out to be kissed. Then the officer in charge ordered the prisoners to kneel and gave a signal. At the sound of a pistol shot swords were drawn from scabbards. At a second signal the slaughter began at both ends of the column. The Japanese weren't very efficient at the killing, often needing several blows to succeed, especially as time wore on and they became tired.

For two hours they hacked their way through the moaning, screaming columns of men, helplessly trussed before them. Finally all 400 bodies lay in a silent, mutilated pile, and only Michael and Douglas remained alive. The commanding Japanese officer crossed over to them as they sat under guard halfway up the slope of the ravine.

He forced the two men to kneel, foreheads touching the ground. Then he raised his sword above their heads and deftly swooped it down in two quick blows, neatly severing their bonds without leaving so much as a scratch on either of them. Rubbing their numbed wrists, they slowly rose, quivering with fear and relief and weak from hunger. The Japanese officer stood before them, happily leaning on his sword. Still grinning, he ordered guards to bring the two prisoners water, and when they had been allowed to drink their fill, he ordered his troops back toward the road, leaving Michael and Douglas alone in the ravine with its grisly clumps of corpses.

They climbed wearily back up the slope. Sunlight filtered pleasantly through the trees. Douglas glanced uneasily at the surrounding jungle and began to shiver uncontrollably. Michael grabbed and steadied him.

"What is it, Douglas?"

"I don't feel well," he stuttered.

"Let's go back to the road."

"What if we just stayed here in the jungle somewhere?"

"We can't, Doug. You need a doctor. There should be an aid station at Balanga."

The shivering continued unabated, and Michael grew more concerned. He helped Douglas back to the road. A ragged column of American prisoners was moving by, accompanied by guards. Most were bare-headed in the scorching sun; the Japanese had taken their helmets.

"There a doctor or a medic in this outfit?" Michael asked.

"Sure is," a voice drawled softly from among the scarecrow bodies. "But we don't dare stop to point him out. You'll just have to join us for our little stroll until we reach Balanga."

A voice spoke up sharply in Japanese, cutting off the conversation, and a guard materialized and quickly shoved Michael and Douglas into the line.

"Buck up, fellows," someone growled. "We're almost there."

The village of Balanga on the East Road at the northern end of the Bataan Peninsula was the first stop at which the Japanese had planned to feed their prisoners. But right away things began going wrong. There were twice as many prisoners as the Japanese had expected. Nor were they prepared for the poor condition of the prisoners, most of whom had eaten little or nothing in the past few days. After they had walked the seventeen miles to Balanga the meager ration they were given consisted of one soured rice ball and a piece of rock salt.

The Balanga encampment was nothing more than a series of makeshift assembly points, open fields surrounded by barbed wire, some so small and crowded that prisoners were forced to sleep sitting up. When Michael arrived at the camp, the medic in the group of prisoners examined Douglas. His head wound was rapidly becoming infected, and he had possible internal injuries in addition to a broken rib. There were no drugs available at

Balanga, so there was little the medic could do. Douglas's feet were blistered and rubbed raw by all the walking he had done since the final attack. He would not be able to walk much farther, and the blisters posed an additional danger of infection.

"He should stay here and rest a few days," the medic told Michael as he finished his examination.

"Yeah. Well, I'll try and arrange it with the desk clerk," Michael muttered.

The medic shrugged and started to walk away.

"Hey, thanks." Michael called after him.

"Don't mention it," the medic said over his shoulder.

The next morning Michael managed things rather simply. While the men from the previous day were being marched out of the enclosure, a new batch of prisoners was arriving. As the two groups passed each other in the closure, Michael and Douglas simply drifted into the line of arrivals and marched back in.

"Terrific," Douglas grumbled as they found a place to sit down again in the rapidly filling compound. "Another night at the Ritz."

"What do you think the accommodations are going to be farther up the road, Douglas? A Georgia, Sea Island, resort?"

The Japanese were serving up the day's meal. Another rice ball.

"Do you think they'll ever change the menu?" Douglas asked as he stared at his portion.

"I doubt it," Michael replied. But he managed to supplement their diet by picking a few edible plants from around the river. The Japanese forbade fires. Two Filipino soldiers who defied the order were thrown into a ditch and buried alive. So Michael and Douglas ate what Michael had gathered, raw.

Using the same ploy, they managed to stay an extra three days at Balanga, and Douglas was beginning to feel stronger. By that time the camp had turned into a fetid mess. There was only an open ditch for a latrine, and many prisoners were too sick to use it. Those with dysentery soiled themselves and their surroundings with the mucus, blood, and feces caused by the sores in their intestines. The disease began to be spread by direct contact with the infected men. Few who entered Balanga in relative health were free of disease when they left. If the camps ahead were becoming as fouled and contaminated as Balanga, it was clear that

Michael and Douglas could wait no longer. They left the next morning.

While the groups arriving at Balanga had been disorganized, the prisoners left Balanga in orderly groups of 100. Before Balanga the corpses that filled the ditches had come from Japanese planes that had strafed the crowded East Road as the men fled south. But now, north of Balanga, hunger, thirst, and illness took the heaviest toll.

As the prisoners marched north, truck convoys of Japanese soldiers moving south for the assault on Corregidor passed them. Many of these had developed the habit of swinging their rifle butts at the prisoners as they went by. Some who were struck never rose. They were simply dispatched with a bayonet to make sure they were dead.

Water dripped tantalizingly from the faucets of the artesian wells that lined the road, but no one was allowed to stop. Men became delirious and began to hallucinate. Others grew too weak to keep up but were terrified of falling behind, for it meant certain death. Their fellow prisoners offered them encouragement, cajoling, threatening, even shoving them along, but sometimes it wasn't enough. Those who collapsed attempted to crawl behind the moving column. The Japanese soldiers, trained to obey orders unquestioningly rather than think for themselves, became hysterical over the dilemma posed by the stragglers. Under orders to keep the column moving and allow no one to escape, they themselves could not stay behind, nor could they leave the stragglers unguarded. Unable to devise an alternative, they would beat those who couldn't keep up, and if this failed, they would bayonet or shoot them.

Finally Michael could bear his thirst no longer. At the next artesian well he stepped out of the column and thrust his makeshift bamboo canteen beneath the faucet and turned it on. The guard nearest him began to scream, and the prisoners halted, milling in confusion. A commotion developed between Michael and a guard who kept trying to shove him away while he just as determinedly held to his position. Finally the guard took a swing at him with the barrel of his rifle. Michael ducked instinctively, but the bayonet caught the prisoner behind him, almost severing his head. Michael stared, horrified, as the man crumpled to the ground.

"*Bakayaro!*" the guard shouted. "Stupid idiot."

Michael wasn't sure if the Japanese was referring to him or the corpse. Dazed and sickened, Michael turned away. The guard, his rage dissipated, appeared to have no need to pursue the matter. Michael felt too ill to drink the water he had risked his life to get. He gave it to Douglas, who in turn shared it with the others, passing it among them as far as it would go. It was the only water they got that day before they reached Orani.

They were unlucky this time. The day's food supply of rice balls had run out even before they arrived. Michael used Douglas's class ring to buy some fresh fruit and a bucket of water from one of the soldiers. Why the guard would barter for something he could simply have taken was beyond Michael's comprehension. He could only assume that commerce filled some basic human instinct.

The ground was too foul to lie on, though most did so. A few had blankets to protect them from the filth. Michael found a rusty can lid and climbed a bomb-scarred palm tree by the fence to saw off its remaining two fronds. He fixed them for Douglas to lie on while he sat upon his haunches and slept like an Iban warrior.

By the time it grew light again hundreds more prisoners had died. Michael woke up stiff and tired, and Douglas was feverish. They were herded out of the enclosure at dawn with nothing to eat or drink. Filipino civilians had begun to line the dusty road, searching anxiously for loved ones. Many smuggled food and water to the passing prisoners, and those who were caught were immediately shot. Dozens still made the effort and offered a surreptitious V for victory sign as well. The sympathy, the acts of kindness and courage boosted the prisoners' spirits even more than the food and water.

By the time they had completed the fifteen-mile march to Lubao almost a third of the men in their column had died in the merciless sun. The stench of Lubao was the worst of all. Those who had arrived earlier had been crammed into a warehouse to make room for the later arrivals in the surrounding compound. The building had only high tiny windows for ventilation, and the smell and the heat were unbearable. The prisoners were shut into the room without water. By morning scores more had died.

Grateful not to be forced into that writhing tangle of humanity,

Michael and Douglas found a shady spot beneath a broad tree crowded with other prisoners, but they scarcely noticed anymore. Douglas leaned back and looked up at the leafy branches. The sound of his breath was labored, and his clothes were soaked with sweat; yet he was shivering with fever.

"Green like Georgia in the summer. That's where I was born. Did I ever tell you?" Douglas's voice was barely audible, and for a moment Michael was afraid he was becoming delirious. "Where were you born, Michael? Java?"

"No." Michael watched a hawk begin a lazy loop above the branches of a tree. He was moved by its grace and freedom. The hawk glided off, abandoning the sky to the circling vultures. "I was born in Hong Kong."

"Hong Kong. Never been there. Pretty interesting place, I hear."

"I left when I was young," Michael replied, his expression grim. "And I've never been back." He rose. "I'll see if I can get you something to eat."

By the next morning it was clear that Douglas could not go much farther. There was no point anyway. There would be no medical help at Camp O'Donnell either. They would have to escape, although their chances of success were slim. This was open country swarming with enemy troops. Michael knew he could make it alone, but Douglas was too ill to travel. With luck they would find a family that would hide them until Douglas was stronger.

"Leave me," Douglas begged him. "I can't make it. You'll just get caught if I'm with you."

Michael ignored his pleas. He took off Douglas's boots. The blisters were raw again. After ripping off the bottom of each of Douglas's trouser legs, he wrapped them around Douglas's feet, then filled them with soft dried grasses from the edge of the ditch. Now Douglas could walk part of the time without assistance.

The piercing sun stabbed Michael's head, so he closed his eyes and stumbled along. Suddenly he opened his eyes and Douglas was no longer beside him. He heard shouting in Japanese at the rear of the column. The guard beside him poked a bayonet at his ribs as he started out of line, but he ignored the warning, running back to pull Douglas up from the ground while the rear guard yelled and kicked like a madman. Michael cursed himself for not keeping an eye on his friend, but when he saw the expression on Douglas's face, he knew that Douglas had deliberately fallen behind.

"God damn it, Douglas. What'd you have to go do that for? We're getting out of here at the next stop."

They got their opportunity before that. The Japanese stopped the column while two prisoners were ordered to bury one of the collapsed stragglers. However, as the dirt hit his face in the shallow ditch, the man sat up, and the prisoners balked. During the commotion that followed, Michael and Douglas crawled away into the grassy field full of cut cane stalks. Panting heavily, Douglas could make it no farther than the center of the field before he turned over and lay on his back exhausted, his eyes closed, a thin stream of blood from the recent beating trickling down his chin. Michael lay beside him, his face buried in the warm, sweet-smelling grass, ignoring the stench of the camps that still clung to his clothes. It was far from a pleasant moment. Eyes screwed tightly closed but ears straining, he waited for their absence to be discovered, bringing a swarm of guards searching the field. But after a few agonizing moments, the column moved on. Michael lay still for a long moment, waiting for his terror to subside. Then he sat up.

Douglas opened his eyes and squinted at the bright light.

"I know I'm not going to make it, Michael. I don't even want to anymore."

He closed his eyes again and was silent. Michael stared at the ground, no longer bothering to hide the stricken look on his face or avoid the heavy feeling in his gut.

"Contact my wife when you can," Douglas finally whispered so softly that Michael had to strain to hear. "You'll know what to say to her."

Silence again and then: "We met in high school. Went steady. Once I was in the relationship I didn't know how to get out of it. I felt guilty, I guess." The soft, whispered words were difficult, but he pressed on, driven perhaps by some final need for understanding or forgiveness.

"We used to make out in the back seat of my dad's car. Not all the way but as close as you could get and still technically keep her virginity intact. Somehow that seemed to allow her to preserve the illusion she was innocent, a girl Daddy could be proud of. It turned out she didn't much like sex—even after we were married and it was supposedly okay. I never loved her, but I didn't figure that out until it was too late."

He opened his eyes and caught Michael's. "That's something we have in common, isn't it, Michael? Being married to women we don't love."

Without waiting for an answer, he closed his eyes and drifted off into troubled sleep. Michael took off his own shirt and made a tent to shield Douglas's face from the sun, but there was little else he could do to cool or comfort him. Douglas visibly weakened before his eyes, his breathing becoming gradually more shallow. His eyes, when they opened, were full of pain, and he had ceased to be aware of Michael's presence.

The heat of the afternoon wore on, sapping precious moisture from every living thing. The two escaped prisoners went unnoticed until late afternoon, when one lone guard, lagging behind and thus undistracted by the need to prod the prisoners, spotted them amid the cane and came gingerly over, bayonet at the ready. Still some twenty feet away, he began to shout excitedly for Michael to rise and return to the road, but Michael refused, in Japanese, to leave Douglas or to move him.

The guard came closer to investigate, peering intently at Douglas's prone form. He gave the order again. Michael ignored him. Unsure of himself, the guard glanced uneasily around. The previous column of prisoners and guards had moved on and out of sight, leaving him alone in the field with the two prisoners. He decided it might be prudent to wait until reinforcements appeared.

The minutes wore slowly on, and the guard shifted his feet nervously some distance away. Douglas lay as still as before. The shivering and sweating had stopped; but an ominous rattle had begun deep in his chest, and every breath had become a struggle. Michael took Douglas's hand and held it in his own, idly turning the plain gold band on Douglas's third finger, the cause of all the difficulty.

Douglas was struggling into consciousness. "Michael!" His eyes opened, then focused fearfully on Michael. His hand attempted to hold Michael's more tightly, but there was little strength left in the grasp.

"It's all right, Douglas," Michael said softly, surprised at how much control his voice showed. "Just let go. . . ."

Douglas's features relaxed, and gradually his eyes glazed and lost their life, staring into a sky they no longer saw. Gently Michael reached down and closed them. He continued to sit in the field beside Douglas, holding his hand for what seemed like a long time, then he slowly got up and stood staring down at Douglas. The Japanese guard moved closer and nudged him with the butt of his rifle. Michael, who had forgotten all about him, suddenly turned and looked at the guard with a murderous rage that stunned the soldier and caused him to step back.

He recovered quickly and poked his bayonet at Michael's stomach. Michael knocked it defiantly aside but made no further move toward the guard. For a moment the Japanese hesitated, and his finger tightened on the rifle's trigger; but then he began to back slowly away, still staring at those burning gray eyes. With one brief, nervous glance over his shoulder, he walked quickly toward the road, miraculously leaving Michael standing there alone in the dust and heat and flies. Now nothing stood between him and freedom.

Without hesitating he swung away from the road and began to run, with difficulty at first. But gradually, fed by some untapped reservoir of energy, he was running lightly and swiftly, with his old endurance, in the direction of the coast.

Chapter 41
Borneo

The three women sat alone at the end of the long dining table, looking pale and fragile in the room's massive carved teak furnishings. Kara insisted that they take all their meals there together, just as the Stanfords always had. White-uniformed servants served lunch as efficiently and unobtrusively as ever. Kara sat at the head of the table in her green print dress, looking cool and unperturbed. Catherine sat on her right, wearing the jodphurs and riding boots she had borrowed from Julienne, the sleeves of her khaki shirt rolled up above the elbows. She had just come from working in the rubber tree groves, and the formality of the lunch annoyed her.

Julienne sat across from Catherine, on Kara's left. She wasn't listening to the discussion on what should be done with the harvested rubber and copra. Catherine believed they should be destroyed immediately before they could fall into Japanese hands. Kara feared that if they destroyed the rubber and copra, the villagers would panic and flee.

"Then let them," Catherine argued. "Why should they remain here anyway? To become slave labor for the Japanese?"

"We must hold things together as long as we can," Kara retorted. Keeping things just as they always had been had become her defense against encroaching disaster.

Eyes bright, lips parted, Julienne sat, oblivious of everything around her, withdrawing, as she often did, into the distant past.

In her memory she entered Michael's boyhood room. It was empty, but she could hear the water running in the shower, and she stretched out on his bed to wait for him. She was often there, yet he seemed surprised each time he found her. Guilt quickly replaced the surprise on his face, arousing Julienne's contempt. She loosened the damp towel from his waist and let it slide from his body, touching, teasing, kissing, playing with him, guiding his hands. He always resisted at first, but not later. No, not after she had aroused him. Later he would be as free as she. Both experts, trying anything and everything. Sitting afterward at the dinner table with their father, Michael would be subdued, withdrawn, his eyes averted. But not Julienne. Julienne would be flushed and laugh more than usual and her father would stare at her in puzzlement and she would look arrogantly back at him, her look defying his. "I'm in love with my brother," her dancing eyes would say, and then she would laugh gaily.

Julienne's reverie was broken by Damal, who appeared in the doorway and crossed to Catherine.

"Pardon, Nona, but there is a Chinese boat captain to see you. He says it is urgent."

Puzzled, Catherine excused herself and followed Damal to the entrance hall where a barefoot Chinese man stood wearing only a loose shirt, short pants, and an air of considerable confidence. Several gold hoops threaded his ears, and gold chains dangled around his neck beneath his shirt. They were not a vanity. In uncertain times they were his portable bank account. He wore a Javanese kris in the back of his belt, and Catherine could make out the bulge of a pistol under his shirt.

"I am Tsu Ching. The merchant Tiang has sent me with a message from Prince Ahmad. The Japanese are preparing to act on their plans to seize and occupy the rubber plantations on the Barito River. It is no longer safe for you to remain here. My boat can take you out. It has a secret smuggling hold on board."

Kara and Julienne had joined them in the entrance hall. Without hesitating, Catherine reacted.

"We can be ready at once." She turned to the others for verification.

"To where?" Julienne asked.

"Through the Makassar Straits and up river from Balikpapan

as far as the mission post. From there the prince's men will take you by foot into the mountain strongholds of the Iban.''

"On foot?" Kara asked incredulously.

"Yes," the captain replied.

"But the jungle is impenetrable!" she protested.

"Only for the Japanese. For those who know the jungle there are trails."

Kara shuddered. "I would never survive. Nor would the children."

Julienne looked at her with scorn. "You should have gone with Michael on some of his expeditions. It would have toughened you up."

"I'd rather take my chances with the Japanese than live like an animal—" Seeing the gleam of triumph in Julienne's eye, she broke off.

Catherine stepped in to interrupt before things went too far. She said to Tsu Ching, "We'll need more time. We should destroy the rubber before we go. Can you wait until tomorrow?"

"No later than tomorrow morning—early."

"All right, tomorrow morning. We'll be ready."

He nodded briskly and turned to leave, but not before his narrow eyes seemed to sum the three of them up. His conclusion was unreadable.

After he had left, Catherine turned to Damal. "Have the men destroy as many of the trees as they can and make the storage sheds ready for burning."

"If they're going to try to use Maitreya for a headquarters, perhaps we should destroy the house as well," Julienne interjected.

The three of them looked at each other in silence.

"No," Catherine said finally. "No, we'll leave the house."

Kara turned to Damal. "Send someone to bring the Sanderses and the Burtons here." There were only women and children left on the neighboring plantations; the men had joined a British regiment fighting in Singapore and were now either dead or prisoners of the Japanese.

"The boat is too small to hide so many," Julienne protested.

"It's all right," Kara said sharply. "I won't be going. They can have my place."

Catherine and Julienne looked at her in astonishment.

"Don't be a silly fool!" Julienne exclaimed. "For the girls' sake you must go." Whatever Julienne felt for Kara, she was fond of her two nieces.

"The girls will stay with me. And it's for their sake as well as my own that I refuse to go into that godforsaken jungle with its disease. Besides, the Japanese may let us stay here. They'll need someone to gather the rubber. Damal, you mustn't destroy it."

"Don't be even more of an idiot than I thought you were!" Julienne retorted. "They'll never let you stay here, and I'll never permit Maitreya to be used for collaboration just to save your cowardly skin."

"Julienne . . ." Catherine interrupted.

"You stay out of this, Catherine. Those are Michael's daughters, too, Kara. My nieces. Michael would want them to go to Ahmad. I want them to go to Ahmad."

"No!" Kara replied sharply, and for the first time anger brought a flush of color to her face and tears stung her eyes. "Michael has given up his right to interfere in my life or in the lives of my children."

"Perhaps in your life but not the lives of his children," Julienne insisted.

Kara regained her composure and replied evenly, "I am remaining here with the children. The decision is final. You and Catherine are free to do whatever you wish." She turned and started down the hall. There could be no question now of destroying the rubber without fear that the Japanese would retaliate against Kara.

By evening the Sanderses and the Burtons had arrived—two frightened women with six young children between them, none of whom was older than nine. Like Kara, both the women hesitated to escape into the wilds of Borneo, finally deciding they preferred the risks of captivity. They argued that as anthropologists, Julienne and Catherine were better prepared to endure the jungle, and Catherine failed to convince them that with her help, they could all survive. They were influenced by the hope the Japanese would allow them all to remain on the plantation since they obviously posed no political or military threat. Catherine suspected it was a vain hope. She said as much, but to no avail.

There was nothing more Catherine could do except pack a few belongings for herself and Michael and, dressed in khaki shorts and shirt, wait with Julienne at the dock the next morning. For an hour they watched the sluggish river without seeing any sign of Tsu Ching. Something had gone wrong. It was nearing midmorning, and he clearly should have been there by now. Catherine sat on the edge of the dock, holding Michael, who, frustrated by the limits his mother had set on his mobility, had finally fallen asleep. With mounting uneasiness Catherine watched the brown currents of the river pass beneath her as her ears strained for the sound of a boat amid the buzz of the insects. Suddenly she heard a faint drone. Her relief soon changed to anxiety. There was something wrong with the sound, something which she couldn't quite define. She looked at Julienne in alarm.

"I think we'd better head for cover."

Julienne, sensing the same danger, got up and headed into the nearby jungle. Catherine stood and hesitated for a moment, concentrating on the growing sound. It was harmonic. Not the sound of a single engine but two, perhaps more. She thrust a sleeping Michael into Julienne's arms and began to run down the road that led to the house.

"The Japanese are here!" she cried as she stumbled into the entrance hall. The women quickly joined her there, their faces drained of color. Only the house servants remained at Maitreya. Julienne had dismissed the others in a tearful farewell that morning, and they had faded into the jungle.

"Please, all of you. Come and hide with us in the jungle," Catherine begged. Although more confused and hesitant now, the women still refused. Catherine headed for the trees and vegetation that lined the neatly groomed road. She turned back one last time and saw Kara and other women, aided by the servants, lifting the eight children into the large banyan tree beside the entrance to the house, the older children pulling the younger ones up beside them. Slowly they made their way into the uppermost branches, joining the monkeys, which temporarily scolded the young intruders and then fell silent.

Catherine had only just made it to cover when the Japanese soldiers came down the road, jogging in loose formation, rifles at the ready with bayonets fixed. A young lieutenant led the group of some thirty soldiers. They stopped in orderly fashion before the women who stood together on the veranda before the entrance to the house. The lieutenant prepared to read a proclamation, making up for his inexperience with an air of cocky arrogance.

He read the proclamation in poorly executed Dutch. It stated Maitreya was now the property of the Japanese. At the end he rolled up the paper, and in excellent English he ordered Kara and the others to be taken to a detention camp along with "all other European imperialists."

Some of the soldiers entered the house. The lieutenant didn't stop them. Noises of crashing wood and glass indicated they had begun to rifle the contents. The servants began to flee the house, and the soldiers outside laughed at the sight as one of them fired his rifle over their heads. The soldiers next showed an interest in the jewelry the women were wearing. Kara reluctantly gave up her watch but refused to part with her gold wedding band. A tug for possession began between her and the soldier who would have it. Kara protested indignantly to the officer, but he turned his back on the proceedings, thereby giving his permission.

Grabbing a handful of Kara's golden hair, the soldier forced her against the wall and took the ring from her hand. He was joined by others and the sound of tearing cloth came out of the scuffle as one of them ripped open her dress to the waist. She screamed in protest as the other women huddled against the wall. Catherine half rose to her feet in alarm, forgetting to keep herself hidden. She had no weapon and could only watch helplessly. One of the children in the tree began to cry, frightened by what was happening.

The soldiers looked up into the tree. The Japanese lieutenant indifferently followed their pointing fingers. He gave no orders, but one of the soldiers swung his rifle up, took aim, and fired. All the children were screaming now. More shots were fired. The children clung frantically to their hiding places, but it did no good. As the shots continued, they fluttered to the ground one by one like wounded birds. Some of them were still alive as they hit.

Catherine had fully risen to her feet at the clearing's edge, but no one noticed her. She looked to the house and saw Kara's pale naked body pinned to the ground, a swarm of soldiers over it. Buttocks bare and pants around their ankles, they waited their turn, joking and laughing. The other two women were now dragged to the ground to relieve the congestion. The lieutenant did not participate, but he did not stop his men, either. He turned his back and strode slowly toward Catherine's hiding place, reaching into his jacket for a pack of cigarettes.

Catherine quickly crouched into the grass again, sickened by what she had seen. Through the foliage she saw the polished boots of the young officer pass before her, then pause as he put a cigarette into his mouth and reached for a lighter. He was so close she could see the etching of The Hague upon its cover.

Catherine closed her eyes in terror like a child, as if to make herself disappear. She forced herself to open them and stared at the lieutenant, her every muscle straining with tension as she watched him puffing upon his cigarette. She would have liked to kill him, but she had no means. So she sat, imagining her fingers around his throat, slowly squeezing until his throat began to rattle and his eyes bulge. At the moment the fantasy was all that stood between her and an impotent rage that would drive her insane.

The lieutenant turned around and moved back toward the house. She suddenly knew what she would do. It would not jeopardize Kara and the others now if she destroyed the storehouses filled with rubber and copra. She must have some kind of revenge. She would take it by destroying what the Japanese had come for.

The sheds were some distance from the house. She made her way to the stable and slipped a halter around Admiral's head. She swung up onto his back without bothering to put on a saddle. When she reached the sheds, she found that Damal and the men had done their work well. The dried brush and grasses she had ordered prepared and stored weeks earlier now lay piled high around the wooden walls of the storage buildings. Cans of gasoline stood in convenient intervals around the sprawling complex. She quickly emptied one on the waiting tinder and lit it with matches she had brought from the stable. The flames leaped up around the two large buildings, and soon the sweet smell of burning copra could not dispel the stench and heavy black smoke of the burning rubber latex. For good measure she set fire to the shed filled with bagged rice and tossed a torch into the nearby toolshed.

She rode Admiral back as far as she dared, then slipped the halter off his head and, with a slap on his rear, sent him toward freedom. She began to make her way through the forest toward the dock. She still had to pass the house. She arrived in time to

420

see the soldiers carelessly bayoneting the eight small forms that lay beneath the banyan tree. She recognized Caroline's gold curls among them. The lifeless bodies of the three women lay in puddles of blood on the veranda. Some of the soldiers had not yet bothered to hoist up their pants. They hobbled about the courtyard in front of the veranda, drinking wine and whiskey, laughing with satisfaction at jokes about the flaccid condition of their exposed sex.

Catherine felt suddenly ill and bent to the ground to retch. The noise attracted the curiosity of one of the nearby soldiers, who approached the bushes to investigate. Knees and hands pressed against the earth, she held her breath as he drew close enough to reach out with the bayonet on his rifle to probe the bushes. He was sure to find her unless she risked withdrawing farther into the jungle. Through the leaves she could see the smile on his face. He had discovered a new victim; he was sure of it. The bayonet reached within inches of her face, then wavered as he removed one hand from his gun to swat at an insect that stung the back of his neck. Then suddenly, the smile fading from his face, he slumped to the ground.

Catherine stared at him in astonishment. There was no apparent explanation for his collapse. Perhaps a heart attack. She began to pull slowly back into the jungle, intending to head for the dock, but another soldier had noticed his fallen comrade and was approaching to investigate. Suddenly he stopped short, clawed at his back, and then fell slowly forward, a glazed expression on his face.

Other soldiers began quietly to slump to the ground. Perhaps the wine had been poisoned, Catherine thought. Deciding to take advantage of the situation to obtain a weapon, she crawled forward to where the first soldier lay slumped into the bushes. Carefully she reached past the bayonet which still protruded into the bush and tugged gently at the gun. She gave a little cry of alarm as the prone soldier, the gun slipping from his fingers, convulsed and grew rigid. Frightened, she looked at his body closely for the first time and noticed the small dart protruding from his neck.

The smoke from the burning sheds had now been noticed by the Japanese. Gunfire broke out all around her as the soldiers finally realized they were under attack. Catherine flattened herself against the ground as a burst of machine-gun fire from the veranda crashed into the brush around her and swept the jungle.

"Jesus," Catherine muttered, still shaking. But she had the rifle in her hands now, and she knew how to use it. Her stomach to the ground, she pushed her way into the clearing to the shelter of the body of the second soldier. A dart protruded neatly from the back of his neck as well. She propped the gun up on his back and took aim at the soldiers, who were now concentrating their fire toward the river, which they had finally deduced was the source of the attack. Their gunfire was now being returned from that direction. Catherine took aim at the prone machine gunner and fired. The first shot missed, striking the rock wall of the veranda and ricocheting away; but the second found its mark, and he rolled away from the gun. She took aim, and another soldier fell; but she could not see whether her bullet had killed him since the gunfire was so intense.

Feathers began to appear among the jungle leaves, darting like apparitions, drifting closer to the house until they burst from the jungle as muscular Iban warriors, clad in vests of jaguar skin and bark jackets decorated with bone and shells and wearing feathered headdresses. Hair-raising battle cries rose from their throats as they charged forward, dropping their blowguns in order to wield knives and parangs made of deer horn. They bent to take swiftly the heads of those enemies who had fallen. The Japanese rose to meet them in hand-to-hand combat with bayonets drawn. The Iban were followed by coastal Malays wearing *kains* and carrying rifles and parangs. She glimpsed Ahmad, leading them, wielding a kris, and using his feet and body and hands as weapons as effectively as the others used blades.

He leaped the veranda wall as the lieutenant rushed forward to attack him with a rifle and bayonet. Ahmad stepped lightly aside and swung an elbow into the lieutenant's side, throwing him off-balance. As quick and graceful as a cat, Ahmad swung around and threw a kick which caught the lieutenant at the base of his skull, sending him sprawling forward. His knees had barely hit the flagstones before Ahmad was on him, his arms encircling him from behind. He held him tightly for a moment, and when he released him, the lieutenant fell forward, blood gushing from the open wound in his stomach made by the kris. Suddenly the battle was over, and the bodies of the Japanese lay strewn around, mingled with their earlier victims.

Catherine struggled to her feet, looking in horror at the scene around her. The Iban were busily taking heads. She felt stunned by her own part in it, for two and perhaps more of the Japanese had been killed by her. The rifle still hung loosely from her hand. She dragged it after her as she walked, dazed, through the bodies toward the veranda. Tears stung her eyes as she reached Kara and could see the purple punctures that covered the pale, delicate surface of her skin. She turned away as Ahmad came up beside her, his kris still covered with blood.

"I'm sorry, Catherine," he said softly, "for what happened here. I couldn't get here sooner."

She swallowed hard, staring at the ground, groping for words and finding none. "The Japanese officer . . ." She turned and raised her eyes to the veranda before her. "He let it happen."

"I know. I made sure he died slowly." He turned to address one of his men.

"We haven't much time. Have the men prepare a funeral bier for all the bodies."

Catherine looked surprised. He read her look. "We will bury them together—Europeans, Malays, Iban, and Japanese."

The men were already gathering wood for the bier.

"Julienne and Michael—I left them at the dock . . ." she said anxiously.

"They're all right. We found them safely hidden. Michael was still asleep." Ahmad glanced at the smoke that rose from the storage area. "Did you have that done?"

"I did it myself, after the attack began."

He nodded and smiled. "It was a brave thing to do."

Her eyes slid uneasily from his face and went to the entrance of the house. "She wouldn't come with us," Catherine whispered. "Kara wouldn't come. Julienne and I tried. We even waited a day."

"I know," he said gently. She looked at him, puzzled.

"How did you get here?" she asked him.

"Tsu Ching radioed me that one of you was reluctant and delaying the others. I guessed it would be Kara. I thought I had better come and see what I could do."

"Tsu Ching never came. What happened to him?"

"He's at the dock now. A Japanese boarding party detained him earlier, but we eliminated them."

By now the bodies had been quickly piled onto the bier and gasoline poured upon them. Ahmad ordered it lit, and soon the flames burst into life. Catherine wanted to stop them. She had not had enough time to absorb what had happened here. But it was too late. The flames leaped eagerly upward, hiding the bodies in an angry, hungry swirl and forcing the onlookers back. The acrid smell of burning rubber was replaced by the sweet stench of roasting flesh, and Catherine remembered Tukum's funeral with its grief and feasting. Here there would be no ceremony. There was no time. Catherine's eyes burned from the smoke and her tears.

"Michael's daughters are there," she said softly to Ahmad.

"I know," he replied grimly. He took her arm and led her gently away, down the road toward the dock. "Julienne and Michael are already on board the boat. It's time that you joined them."

"And you?"

"I'm taking Maitreya's amphibious plane to the mission post."

"Can't we come with you?"

"It is too dangerous for you and the baby. There is very little gasoline, so I may have to make a forced landing short of the mission. And I will have to fly dangerously low over the jungle to avoid detection by Japanese planes. Besides"—he paused as they reached the dock and faced her—"there is a chance that you may be going home."

She looked at him, puzzled. "Home? Where?"

A faint look of surprise crossed his face. "To the United States, of course." He searched her eyes. "You do want to go home. . . ."

"Yes," she answered quickly. "Yes, of course. I was just surprised. I never expected it could be possible."

He smiled. "I didn't want to raise false hopes, so Tsu Ching didn't tell you. I've been in radio contact with an American submarine for the past week. They are going to try to rendezvous with your boat in the Makassar Strait three days from now."

Tsu Ching stood by the gangplank, waiting to assist her on board. On the deck beside him, Julienne held Michael, her eyes remote, her face expressionless.

"Then perhaps I won't see you again."

"Perhaps not."

She offered her hand in farewell. He took it in both of his, and she noted that his palms were becoming hard with calluses.

"Thank you, for everything."

He smiled but said nothing as he released her hand with a final squeeze.

On board, Julienne sat huddled against the bow, numbed by Kara's death and the realization that nothing but the war and Julienne herself now stood between Michael marrying Catherine. Michael had taken from Julienne the only things that mattered to her, her father and Maitreya, and now he would have everything he wanted. She glanced over to where the baby played on the deck nearby. Seeing her watching him, he smiled and crawled toward her. Julienne had the sudden urge to throw him into the river, to avenge herself on Michael by destroying both Catherine and his son. She reached out and snatched the startled baby roughly to her, shoving him back against the rail of the boat just above her. Only her hands, digging into his sides, held him from the river.

Before she could release him, she felt a firm grip on her shoulder and she looked up to see Ahmad behind her. Michael began to cry. Ahmad took him gently from her and gave him to Catherine who, unaware of what had happened, had come up the gangplank to go belowdecks. The boat was about to get underway. When Catherine had gone, Ahmad reached down and took Julienne's chin in his hand. For a long moment they stared at each other. Julienne had no secrets from Ahmad. He had known her too well and too long; children seldom bothered to hide their wickedness from each other. Ahmad had known the truth of her relationship with Michael from the beginning, though no one had told him. And he had suspected her part in Edward's death as well.

Slowly, like a caress, Ahmad's fingers slipped from her jaw to her throat. "I know what you're thinking," he said softly. "But if anything happens to Catherine or Michael's son while you're with them, I'll kill you."

Julienne didn't try to speak, but his fingers could feel the muscles of her throat contract as she swallowed. She knew he meant it. Ahmad was the only person in the world she truly feared. He had been raised to believe it was the right of princes to dispense justice by whatever means they chose, including death. When he took his hand away, she continued to sit in silence, staring beyond him as if he weren't even there, but he knew that she had understood him.

He left the boat. Thick smoke from the burning storage sheds drifted over the river, obscuring Maitreya. In vain Julienne searched for one last glimpse of it. More than the other Stanford children, she felt bound to Maitreya. Since returning from the Asmat massacre, she had found excuses not to leave it. Even her father's urgings that she return to school and complete her degree had not budged her. She identified with the ruthless colonial principal that had built Maitreya. Take what you want from the world and destroy anything in your way. And she felt comfortable with the dark ceremonies and violence of Maitreya's ancient Iban past. Now, through Michael and Catherine or the Japanese, she was about to lose it forever. Suddenly she began to tremble. The old childhood fear returned: if she left Maitreya, she might cease to exist.

The next night they cleared the Barito River and by morning had rounded the point off Matapura and turned north into the Makassar Strait, heading for a rendezvous spot with the sub off tiny Luak Island. The strait bristled with Japanese naval forces, but Tsu Ching's forty-foot vessel was only one of many native ships that carried the commerce of the Indies. The big danger of discovery for Catherine and Julienne lay in Japanese determination to stop smugglers and pirates who had plied these waters for centuries. The Japanese Army laid claim to a moral superiority which resulted in an almost messianic need to rid the rest of Asia of crime and corruption and bring Japanese-style order and discipline to their fellow Asians.

Like most local craft, Tsu Ching's boat had a number of ingenious smuggling holds, which, on this voyage, contained bags of rice which had illegally escaped Japanese control, along with guns and supplies for Ahmad's guerrilla forces. The only quarters belowdecks housed the crew, so as soon as they reached the sea the women ate and slept on the deck. While the accommodations were far from deluxe, the food was superb freshly caught baby eels, octopus, and squid, elegantly prepared and served.

On the third day at sea they slowed their progress, not wanting to arrive early and arouse suspicion by lingering too long in one area. They reached the rendezvous point just before midnight, the appointed time, and waited for the sub to surface. The vigil was futile. By daybreak the sub had not appeared, and they were forced to leave the area, intending to return that night.

Throughout that day Tsu Ching was even more remote than usual. Julienne, who had spoken only a few words since they left Maitreya, spent the day staring at the sea's horizon and refused all of Catherine's attempts to draw her out. In leaving Maitreya for what might well be the last time, Julienne seemed to be slowly parting with reality as well. Catherine desperately wanted the sub to be there that night. She doubted that Julienne could survive whatever long ordeal would await them in the jungle.

While Catherine occasionally dozed, the boat cut a wide lazy arc in the sea. At sundown they headed on a course that would once again bring them to the rendezvouz point before midnight. It was a cloudy, moonless night with choppy water. A phosphorescent glow lit the water's surface and exploded in whitecaps. By the time they reached their destination the faint purple luminescence was gone. Catherine stared intently into the blackness, vainly searching for the tiny blinking signal light that would mark the arrival of the sub. They put out a sea anchor. With no horizon visible by which to get her bearings, Catherine began to get slightly seasick in the choppy seas. No sub emerged from the night, and they were again forced to get under way before dawn the next morning.

By now there was real danger that their presence in that same spot on two different occasions had been noted and reported by local fisherman in the employ of the Japanese. After a brief consultation with his men, Tsu Ching decided to risk a third, and final, rendezvous attempt that night. However, no sooner were they under way than two Japanese torpedo boats from Celebes caught up with them and demanded to come aboard.

Catherine and Julienne were shown a narrow hiding space between bulkhead and hull near the bow. They crawled in, and Catherine clutched Michael tightly to her. When the torpedo boat had been sighted, Catherine had given Michael a sleeping powder Tsu Ching had provided for him. Initially restless, cross, and frightened in the total blackness of the hiding space, he had fallen asleep within five minutes. Catherine wished she could do the same. She felt cramped in the tight space, her arms aching from Michael's weight; her heart jumped at every sound.

She could now hear muffled voices and the occasional clanking of metal in the cargo area near their hiding place. Her breath came in rapid, shallow gasps as her lungs struggled to find oxygen amid the stale air of the compartment. Suddenly the vibrations in the hull grew stronger, and she could hear the hum of the diesel engines in the stern. They were under way again. Moments later the compartment entry was yanked open, and fresh sea air struck her in the face. She blinked dazedly into the bright light of the sun, then staggered forward toward waiting hands that pulled and lifted her out. Another few minutes and she would have been unconscious.

"Gone. They find nothing." Tsu Ching, a man of few words, abruptly left her and Julienne to recover on their own. Catherine's initial relief at escaping almost immediately turned to despair as she realized there could be no third attempt to connect with the submarine. The attempt was far too dangerous now.

There were no further options. Catherine and Julienne stayed below as the boat passed the Japanese-fortified port of Balikpapan and headed up the Mahakam River at Samarinda. The lower river was heavily traveled by river boats, so they were safer here. Beyond the town of Samarinda the river was little used except for the weekly supply boat that journeyed the 100 miles from the river mouth to the Catholic mission post, dropping off passengers and supplies. Since the Japanese invasion that run had been stopped, and now the mission was isolated except for native praos. The three nuns and the priest who operated the mission now existed only on what food they could raise themselves or obtain from the villages around them. Like most missionaries in Borneo, they had stayed on, naïvely hoping the Japanese would allow them to continue their work and comforting themselves that if the worst happened, it would only be God's will.

As they neared the post after four days of river travel, Catherine stood alone on the bow, holding Michael and anxiously searching the river for Maitreya's small amphibious plane. Engines cut, the boat drifted slowly toward the tiny dock as the missionaries came out to greet them. They were followed by several Malays armed with rifles. Catherine knew they must be Ahmad's men, waiting to take the secret cache of guns and supplies into the jungle. There was no sign of Ahmad, and she was suddenly seized with the overwhelming dread that he was dead. Several more Malays came out of the jungle, and a flood of relief filled Catherine as she saw Ahmad, bare to the waist and clad in khaki pants, emerge behind them from that same jungle path. As he glimpsed her standing on the boat's bow, a grin broke across his handsome face and he waved. He pushed his way through the small crowd of villagers collected on the riverbank.

A laugh of delight escaped Michael as he recognized Ahmad and held out his baby arms to him. Ahmad reached out and took him in one arm, then leaned over and, with the other arm, lightly lifted Catherine over the boat's railing to stand on the dock beside him. His eyes were bright and intent on her smiling face. After a moment he released her and took her arm to guide her down the narrow dock.

"Where's the plane?" she asked him. "You gave me quite a scare when I couldn't see it."

He nodded his head over his shoulder toward the river. "We burned it. What happened to the sub?"

"It never showed. The Japanese came and boarded us. They let us go, but we couldn't stay any longer."

He nodded in agreement, the smile suddenly gone. Now there was no choice but the jungle.

"It will be a difficult journey, to a difficult life." His voice was apologetic. "I'd hoped to spare you that."

She touched his arm lightly. "It doesn't matter. We're lucky to be alive. But I'm worried about Julienne. She's been so withdrawn since we left." She looked anxiously back at the boat and saw Julienne being spirited away to the dormitory by two of the nuns. "Maybe you can help her."

"I'll talk to her later."

His men and Tsu Ching's crew had started to unload the supplies into the native praos tied to the dock.

"I thought we were going on foot."

"We are. Some of the men are going by boat with the supplies, but it is too risky for us. There are too many villages along the river between here and our destination. Someone might see you and inform the Japanese. Two weeks ago a Japanese patrol discovered a Dutch family hiding in an abandoned military outpost some twenty miles down the river from here. No doubt someone had informed on them."

"Where are we going?"

"To an Iban village called Rumah Pacou." Still holding Michael, he picked up a stick and traced an upside-down Y in the mud of the riverbank. "It's located at the point between the Mahakam River and a tributary of the Kayan River which flows east to the oil fields and the naval port of Tarakan. It's an ideal base for us."

"Rumah Pacou . . . that sounds familiar," she said. Then, startled, she realized why. "That's the village where Michael was once held hostage."

"Yes. But there's no worry. Koh, the old headman, has long since made his peace with the Stanfords and his amends to my father. He is a good warrior, as are his men."

"What happened to the Dutch family the Japanese found hiding?"

"They killed them."

Chapter 42

It took three weeks of mud slides and incessant rains to reach the mountains and temperate forests of Rumah Pacou. The village consisted of some 200 occupants in one longhouse, 1,000 feet in length, which supported its fifty apartments, full-length gallery, and open porch with considerably less grace than it had in earlier years. It was old enough that its six-foot pylons had grown unsteady and its wooden bones had begun to show beneath its dried and peeling exterior. The Iban cheerfully ignored the decay. The roof was uneven and leaky while the floor slats sagged to the point that an occasional careless pedestrian would fall through and land on the protesting pigs corralled below, an accident which would bring gales of laughter from the other Iban. In a few years, when the entire dwelling would finally collapse, the Iban would simply move to a new spot and build another.

Catherine and Julienne were each given a private *bieh* toward the end of the gallery. Catherine's was still furnished with fishing nets, carrying baskets, a blowgun, parangs, and boars' tusks, and even a wide-brimmed straw hat hung on the wall. There was a mound of earth in one corner which was used as a hearth and a primitive oil-wick lamp sat on the floor near it. Though personally clean (they bathed several times a day in the river, using lemon juice as soap), the Iban were indifferent housekeepers. Scraps of food were swept through the cracks in the floor to the hungry pigs below, and the Iban often relieved themselves in the

431

same way or out the open windows. Meat, both raw and cooked, was left to spoil in the heat. Flies swarmed over it before it was cheerfully consumed, and no one, except Catherine, seemed bothered by its rancid taste.

Physically the Iban were an attractive people: dark-skinned, short, muscular and small-boned, with delicate Asian facial features. The women wore short skirts called *sirats* which they dyed and wove themselves. On special occasions the women stacked thin brass rings around their waists, like a corselet, and wore flowers in a bun at the napes of their necks. The men dressed in loincloths and cut their thick, straight hair into the shape of an inverted bowl. Both sexes wore tattoos. The women's tended to be limited to lacy designs on their hands and arms, but the men were sometimes covered with tattoos which not only identified them in terms of their village but advertised all their accomplishments as well.

Their headman, Koh, was a Borneo legend, reputed to have taken as many as 200 heads. In old age he had assumed a respectability derived not from his virtues but rather from the human miracle of having merely survived for more than eighty years. A few of those heads which had made him famous had been collected from the shoulders of the workers of Maitreya as well as other English estates, but his raids on the English had consisted mainly of stealing pigs and burning outbuildings. Now he resembled his longhouse, being gnarled and dilapidated. But for all his faults and frailties, Koh still ruled with cunning and tyrannical authority which defied the usual democratic nature of Iban society.

It was in connection with Koh and his family that Catherine received a shock. She was attending yet another marathon Iban feast, her third since they had arrived a week earlier. It was late, but the old longhouse still swayed with the pulse of throbbing drums and the dancing feet of those sturdy celebrants who had not yet drunk themselves unconscious. Catherine had lost interest in the celebration, and was feeling lonely and homesick, when her attention was drawn to a young woman she had not seen before. She was about Catherine's age and very pretty. Behind her, in the doorway, was a young adolescent boy with dark Iban skin and beautiful black eyes and hair who did not follow the woman into the gallery but lingered instead in the shadows.

Even in that partial light there was something so familiar about his features as to cause Catherine to catch her breath in astonishment. Ahmad, who sat next to her, must have seen it also, for his drink paused midway to his lips as he stared at the boy.

"Who are they?" Ahmad asked of Koh.

"My daughter, Minh, and her son by her husband, who has just died. They have returned home to live." Old Koh's eyes narrowed with hostility.

Catherine barely heard Ahmad's translation of what Koh had told him. Her mind was trying to grope with dates. Michael had been seventeen when he was captured by the Iban fifteen years ago—time enough to have fathered a fourteen-year-old son by his thirteen-year-old bride. Michael must have escaped before knowing of Minh's pregnancy.

The discovery upset her. Because she was unsure of her own place in Michael's life, such encounters with his past, however distant, were disturbing. It didn't matter that the marriage had been forced upon him. He had been willing enough to produce a son. The boy's name was Patri, and as she studied him more closely in the following days, she noted a trace of arrogance in his expression and manner. It contained a hint of cruelty as well, enough to remind her this was old Koh's grandson.

Since she and Ahmad had arrived at Rumah Pacou there were times when Ahmad made her uncomfortable with moods she didn't understand. He would ignore her for days, only to turn up at her *bieh* unannounced and spend the evening with her, talking easily and playing with Michael. Despite the tension that had grown between them, he had remained in Rumah Pacou these past weeks to see her settled, helping her cut and burn part of the forest so that she might plant rice and start a garden. He would leave soon, returning to the coast to lead an attack on the Japanese oil installations. She would miss his occasional company, yet she would feel relief when he was gone.

As her Iban improved, she began to spend more time with Patri, who seemed drawn to her. Old Koh, fearing the contact because he believed in the bewitching power of white skin to lure his grandson away, vehemently forbade him to see her. But Patri ignored the warnings and the threats. He would join Catherine whenever she fished alone in the dam upriver, and he began regularly to take Michael to swim with him each morning. Sometimes, when she worked in her garden some distance from the village, Patri came to watch. Since male hands would offend the gods and spoil the crop, he passed the time by shooting his blowgun at tree leaves for practice.

She was working alone in her garden one afternoon, hoping to finish planting her rice before Michael awoke from his nap. She was used to Patri's sudden appearances, so she scarcely took note that day when he came scrambling up the mountain path in search of her, sending loose rocks flying down the trail. The noise caught her attention, and she looked up, irritated that he could be so careless of those farther down the path. He had begun to call her name. Even from this distance she could see the fear on his face. She dropped her digging stick and her basket of precious rice cuttings and started running toward him, scarcely noticing the rocks that cut her bare feet.

"What is it, Patri?" she cried, her own fear rising.

He stopped, panting with exhaustion and excitement, and was barely able to choke out the words. "Come quick . . . men, from Matapura . . . to see the prince . . . something terrible . . . I don't know what . . ."

She didn't wait for him to finish. She headed as fast as she dared down the steep path toward the river, leaving Patri to catch his breath alone.

"Tell me how it happened," Ahmad demanded of the group of men before him, all strangers to the Iban village. His voice was cold, but behind it, he was struggling to compose himself. The men were *kraton* guards, Sultan Açvavarman's personal soldiers. The haste and difficulty of their journey were evident in the tattered state of their clothes. Their gold conical palace hats were gone, but some still wore the rich silk pants which, like knickers, were fastened just below the knee. A few still had on the long patterned *kain*, slit up one side, which traditionally covered the pants. The Iban had gathered in the gallery to stare in wonder at these mythical figures from the most civilized part of their kingdom, a part the Iban had never seen.

When none of the men answered his demand, Ahmad's anger burst forth. "Tell me!"

His eyes searched the ragged group of refugees for one brave enough to face him. A flash of surprise crossed his face as his eyes fell upon Siah, her small form previously hidden by the men. Ahmad ordered her forward. She crossed her hands before her on the floor and touched her forehead to them in supplication. One of the guards, not realizing that Ahmad recognized the girl, attempted to intervene.

"Forgive us, but she is a woman from the harem, the sultan's favorite concubine. She escaped and hid in our boat. She said she might be pregnant with your father's child, so we brought her with us." He bent over and took Siah's arm, preparing to drag her from the royal presence, but Ahmad stopped him.

"Let her be!" If the news of Siah's special place in his father's life surprised him, he didn't show it. His expression was stern, but his voice was gentle. "You must tell me everything, Siah."

She rose to her knees but kept her head down. Her voice was strangled with horror.

"The Japanese took your father into the courtyard within the palace and demanded that he denounce you before the people as an outlaw because of your guerrilla activity against the Japanese. Your father refused and denounced the Japanese instead. They forced him to kneel on the ground and put a gold crown upon his head and poured boiling oil into it before they beheaded him. Your mother fell upon his body and demanded that they take her life as well. They executed her the same way and put their heads on poles before the walls of the *kraton*."

A shudder went through the survivors and spread to the Iban who clustered in the entrance and the hall. Even though many of them did not speak Malay, those who understood the language whispered the news to the others until a low wail of mourning filled the longhouse.

"Silence!" Ahmad shouted. His black eyes burned intently into the back of Siah's bowed head. "Go on, Siah."

"I cannot," she whispered.

"Go on," he insisted firmly.

"They raped the women of the harem, even the old ones, the sheltered ones. They raped us and forced the men to watch. The old women begged and pleaded, but it did no good." Her trembling voice was small and distant. She paused and then forced herself to continue. "They arrested and executed all the

435

Açvavarman princes, your great-uncles, your uncles, and your cousins. Their heads were impaled on poles before their palaces. Anyone with even a remote claim to the throne was killed. Babies were dragged from the wombs of wives and concubines, many while their mothers still lived.''

She fell silent, trembling with the enormity of the horror she reported and remembered. The crowd fell silent as well. Then slowly she raised her head and looked into Ahmad's face above her.

He stared down at her for a long moment. "Are you with child?" he asked her finally, his voice soft and strained.

"No," she answered truthfully, though she had misled the guards for fear they would have left her behind.

"The only Açvavarman seed left rests here, within you." She touched her hand lightly to his groin.

He drew her hand away, angry at the audacious familarity of the gesture, performed in front of witnesses and at such a time. Yet those who watched admired its boldness. Siah was not one to avoid risks.

Ahmad himself must have forgiven her the gesture, for his voice was gentle when he dismissed her. She rose and bowed, putting her hands before her face as she backed from his presence.

"Tuan Sunan," she murmured as she took her leave. The words seemed to startle Ahmad, as if the realization had only just struck him that he was now the sultan of Matapura whether he liked it or not.

Pak Anak, who had been Ahmad's teacher, stepped forward from among the guards and knelt to hand him an object wrapped in a muslin rag. From the grimy cloth Ahmad extracted the most sacred object in Matapura, a kris from the royal *pusaka* where all the family heirlooms were kept. Unlike the more valuable palace krises made of gold and precious stones, the hilt of this one was carved out of deer antler in the Dyak manner and kept in a plain wooden scabbard, but the people of Indonesia believed that it possessed great supernatural powers. Closing his eyes, Ahmad pressed the hilt to his forehead and held it tightly there for a moment, as if it might relieve his pain. When he lowered it finally, his breath escaped him in a tormented cry. Taking the kris with him, he swung over the porch railing, dropping lightly to the ground below. The pigs and chickens in the Iban barnyard erupted in protest at his sudden appearance just as Catherine arrived at the longhouse. Ignoring her, he headed for the jungle. Seeing the expression on his face, she didn't try to stop him.

As she climbed the notched log to the porch to find someone who could tell her what had happened, Siah stepped from the gallery to see where Ahmad had gone. The two women paused to stare at each other in surprise. It was Siah who recovered first, speaking to Catherine with a look that contained both triumph and a warning. Catherine didn't understand the Dyak language, but the message was clear, "He is mine now," it said.

"You're welcome to him," Catherine muttered to herself as she brushed by Siah. But she felt an odd twinge, like jealousy, sweep over her before she quickly dismissed it in annoyance.

Ahmad isolated himself for a week, taking only water. When he ended his fast, he led a village procession to the river with offerings of food to the spirits of his murdered relatives. They placed the offerings on palm-leaf boats and sent them floating down the river to meet the ocean currents which flowed through the straits toward Matapura. His self-exile ended, Ahmad remained as remote as when he had shut himself away. Only toward Michael did he show any warmth.

Nor did he go to Siah. Whether out of grief or for some other reason, he avoided her, spending most of his time with Pak Anak and his men. His indifference sent Siah into a sullen pout. She tried to hide it, but she was afraid. Officially she belonged to Ahmad now, yet she was now aware that she might still lose him. Perhaps he could not bring himself to touch what had been his father's. Catherine suffered, too. Julienne was still withdrawn and silent, and Catherine found herself missing Ahmad's companionship.

The Iban, even in mourning, could not go long without a celebration. One splendid night, when the wine had gone untouched too long, Koh found an excuse to hold a late celebration on the longhouse porch. The stars called for it, he said, and the Iban were delighted to oblige. They had already eaten, so there would be no feasting, but it was not too late for what they loved best: wine and dancing. The young Iban warriors, swords in hand, began a swirling dance in wild abandon, and when they were too exhausted to continue, Siah stepped out of the audience and, with a challenging smile, took the elaborate hornbill headdress from one of them and set the feathered crown upon her own head. She unpinned her hair, letting it fall below her waist. Slowly and deliberately she loosened the tie of the sky blue sarong at her shoulder, the one she had worn from the harem. She let it float to the ground. For a moment she stood naked in the torchlight, and a murmur of appreciation rose from the watching men in the crowd. Then she drew a short Iban *sirat* around her waist and tied it. She smiled and took up two large hornbill fans secured by threads sewn loosely through the quills. The slight smile froze mysteriously on her beautiful face. Holding her head rigid, she slowly dipped her body and swung in an elegant half twist above the waist, raising her elbows to shoulder height. Her lowered hands, at the level of her waist, began to move the fans in the way a bird flutters its wings, and suddenly, to those who watched, she ceased to belong to the earth. The musicians began a muted accompaniment on their drums, flutes, and sapihs. The onlookers began to chant a song in praise of the sacred hornbill that had come to dance for them. All were held spellbound by the magic of the performance, but Catherine, watching from the door of her *bieh*, knew there was only one member of the audience Siah wanted to enchant.

Later that night, while the villagers still danced and drank, Ahmad left the festivities early and went to the longhouse. Alone in her room, listening to the sounds of revelry outside the longhouse, Siah didn't hear him step into the entrance to her room and stand quietly watching her. When she saw him standing at the door, her heart leaped with joy. These past weeks she had prayed fervently to the spirits of the forest and made them offerings of food. And now here he was, standing before her, just as she had dreamed. She rose and flung herself into his arms with such delight and abandon that he could not help laughing as he caught her and held her tightly to him.

From that moment on Siah claimed his time at night, or after the noon meal, when he stretched out on the mat to rest and she could take off his *sirat* and lie beside him, feeling his lean, hard body beneath her fingers, against her body, between her thighs, within her arms, beneath her lips. Kissing, biting, touching, pressing, rubbing, sucking: every motion known to woman she lavished on him, day after blissful day. Siah. Bewitching child.

Enchanting beauty. Wise beyond her years. Since a tiny child, she had but one wish, and now it had come true.

Within a week Ahmad left, taking half his men and three of the women with him to help make camp. Siah was one of them. Shortly after he left, Father O'Malley, the priest from the mission downriver, came to see Catherine. He had known the Stanfords before the war. In his sixties, he was a warm man, full of humorous stories and a loneliness for which God had proved no comfort. He and Catherine needed each other's company. The Japanese had arrived at the mission at the end of May. The sisters had refused to hide with Father O'Malley in the jungle. Convinced that God would protect them, they had stoically accepted captivity and been taken away in a boat full of soldiers. Contrary as it might seem for a celibate priest, there had always been important women on whom Father O'Malley depended, whether they were his mother, the housekeepers at the rectory, the nuns at the mission, or the Virgin herself. He had felt helpless after the Japanese had taken the sisters away, so he had moved into the house of his mission cook and her son, where he continued to care as best he could for the members of his flock who had not been frightened away. As soon as he was able, he and the cook's son came to Rumah Pacou to see Catherine. She was fascinated by his Irishness, perhaps because she had always ignored her own. It had been a long and difficult journey for the priest, who suffered from a chronic heart condition that weakened him. When he left Catherine, he could not promise he would be able to return.

Chapter 43
Admiralty Islands,
July 4, 1942

The room around Michael was coming into focus for the first time. He was dimly aware of palm fronds in the roof overhead and the tanned, bearded figure of a man sitting near the bed, khaki shirt hanging open. Tobacco smoke emanated from a pipe in the man's mouth, filling the room with a sweet aroma. As Michael slowly regained consciousness, he realized that he hadn't the slightest idea where he was—or how long he had been there.

Since escaping from Bataan, he had spent six harrowing weeks making his way on foot to the southern tip of Luzon. From there he had island-hopped using native praos, slowly making his way toward the island of Mindanao, where there were still pockets of U.S. and Filipino resistance. Throughout the journey he had been hidden and fed by friendly Filipino farmers and villagers. Dozens of times he had almost been recaptured. On May 6 Corregidor had fallen. As he had listened to Wainwright's surrender speech over the radio in a village hut on Luzon, he thought of the *Canopus* crew that had taken refuge on Corregidor, and a deep sadness filled him.

By the end of June he had made his way to Surigao on the northern tip of Mindanao. From there he had managed to steal a small sailboat with the intention of sailing west to Borneo, but he was very ill with virulent malaria, which had plagued him since Bataan. He lost consciousness the first day at sea, and when a storm had come up, snapping the mast, instead of sailing west into the Sulu Sea, he was sent drifting south and east of Minda-nao, over the deep waters of the Philippine Trench toward the island of Sonsorol. He later learned that the storm had prevented his certain discovery in the heavily patrolled Sulu Sea. Instead, he had been picked up, semiconscious, by a boatload of Chinese families escaping Manila. They had no quinine on board and so could do little to treat him, but once clear of Philippine waters, they gave him over to the care of some Micronesian fishermen. The Chinese boat had been sunk a few minutes later by a Japanese patrol plane, but somehow the fishermen had escaped the strafing unharmed. It was the last thing Michael remembered.

The bearded man beside him, pleased by his return to con-sciousness, raised a brown bottle of warm beer in a salute.

"Cheers, Yank. Happy Fourth of July. Now that you're awake, we'll celebrate your independence. From the looks of you, you've had a bad time of it escaping from somewhere—the Philippines, I imagine."

He removed his pipe and tilted back the bottle of beer. "Any-how, you're the first white man I've seen for eight months, and I'm bloody glad you've finally come round, even if you don't feel like talking. You've been out of your head the four days you've been here. Started coming round about an hour ago, though. Guess the medication finally helped. You'll be all right now."

He caught the bewildered look on Michael's face and smiled. "I'm Turner, and you're in one of the most godforsaken spots on the Admiralty Islands, just off the east coast of New Guinea."

"I'm familiar with the Admiralties," Michael responded weak-ly. "I don't need a geography lesson."

His head still hurt like hell. It even hurt to blink his eyes. The fever was gone, but he was feeling far from good. He reached up a hand and gently touched his forehead and then gingerly felt his beard.

"When you're up to it, I'll take that off for you." Turner said, referring to the beard. "Unless you want to leave it, that is. It doesn't really matter much how one looks around here." He gave a wave of his hand.

Michael's eyes traveled around the poorly furnished hut and fell upon the dials, microphone, and telegraph key of the 300-pound teleradio on a table in the corner. Turner's eyes followed his glance, then he pulled out a bottle of beer, opened it, and placed it in Michael's hand.

"I'm a coast watcher," Turner replied to the silent question. "One of a hundred or so throughout these islands all the way south to the New Hebrides." He waved toward a map pinned loosely on the wall beside the radio. "But the war's passed me by. Or at least the Japs have. Came roaring through here in early January, occupying islands and then abandoning them. Headed south, they were, to take the Solomons and cut off American supplies to Australia." He stuck his pipe back in his mouth and clamped down hard. "That's where I am now. Way behind the lines, in enemy territory."

Michael's eyes traveled back to the radio. He was weak but feeling well enough to be curious. "Just what the hell do you do here anyway?"

"I'm supposed to be spotting and radioing Port Moresby about Japanese military movements. I manage a copra plantation on the big island of Manus, or at least I did until the war broke out. I volunteered for coast watching, and they sent me here. In January the Japs swept through here with a big armada, on their way to Rabaul. God, what a sight! It was my one and only sighting. They've been back a couple of times since—small patrols poking around the islands. Looting mostly. Then they always leave. I just take to the mountains when they come. I've got a hideout and a cache of supplies up there." He nodded in the direction of the screenless window where a volcano could be seen rising above the trees.

"Why did you stay on?" Michael asked him.

"Damned if I know." He gave a rueful laugh. "Except they promised me all the whiskey and beer I could drink for the duration of the war. Of course, they also promised me I wouldn't be operating behind enemy lines." He stretched and put down his pipe. "I guess I just couldn't see myself as a regular part of the Aussie Army, taking orders from some green lieutenant and living with fifty other men. I left home, in Brisbane, fifteen years ago when I was fourteen. Been on my own, mostly alone, in these islands ever since. I like it here. A man can do as he pleases and nobody asks questions.

"In March they said they were moving me south, to Vella

Lavella in the Solomons, but twice the sub that was supposed to pick me up never made it.''

"What happened?"

Turner shrugged. "I just lit the bonfires and waited all night, but they never came." He was silent for a moment and then continued. "The Japs are all south of here, down at Rabaul on New Britain. Big air and sea base there. They all fly south, too. I seldom see a plane around here. Just a patrol plane once in a long while." He tilted his rickety chair backward and balanced it on two legs. "Heard about Midway?"

Michael shook his head.

"American dive bombers sank four Japanese carriers. The Japs sent out their whole bloody fleet to take Midway, Yank, and you beat the bloody hell out of them."

"Luck," Michael commented cynically.

"Whatever the hell it was, it's something to drink to on the Fourth of July." He raised his bottle and took a long pull.

"When did it happen?"

"June fourth."

"Anything happen since?"

"Nope. But for the first time the Japs lost. They've had it easy up till now. Too easy, but now it's going to change."

"I thought the American brass was still saying Europe comes first."

"Only some of them." He let his chair come crashing down to the wooden floor. "The Yanks are going to try to take Guadalcanal. So I'll be going south to help spot those bloody bastards running down the slot from Rabaul to Guadalcanal. The Tokyo Express we call it."

"I thought you said they'd forgotten about you."

Turner grinned. "Now that I've got me a bloody VIP for a visitor, they'll be here fast enough." He reached over and lifted Michael's dog tags from his chest and held them in his hand. "About ten minutes after I reported recovering an American naval officer and gave them this information, the admiral himself calls back: against regulations, unauthorized time, the whole bit. Admiral Sir Charles Stanford himself. Excited as hell he was, too. Never occurred to me you were related, you being an American, I mean." Turner was clearly curious, but he asked no questions.

"Your orders came through while you were still unconscious." Turner grinned. "They didn't waste any time getting you a nice safe job. You've been ordered to Australia by Admiral Rockwell, to serve on General MacArthur's personal staff. Seems the general himself requested you when he heard about your escape. Wants you to advise him regarding the native populations in the Solomons and on New Guinea, planning for when they begin the campaign to recapture the islands. He wants somebody who speaks the languages and knows the customs. There are plenty of Aussies who could do it for him, but it seems the general prefers one of his own."

Michael swore to himself. He had no intention of going to Australia, but there was no point in telling Turner yet.

"They'll be sending a sub for you," Turner continued, "But there's none in the vicinity just now. You can bet I'm going to protect your valuable hide 'cause you're my ticket out of here. Me they'll let rot, but you they'll come after." Turner smiled good-naturedly. "Don't worry, old boy. I don't hold it against you."

Michael closed his eyes. He was exhausted. He admitted to himself that he wanted to escape Turner's unasked questions as well. He wasn't sure just how he felt about the man who had saved his life, but it appeared they were going to be constant companions, at least for a while.

"Your father will be on the radio tomorrow, inquiring about how you are. You can talk with him then—you'll be feeling better."

The next day there was nothing but static.

"Sorry." Turner shrugged. "It's a common occurrence, I'm afraid. We're on the fringe of the teleradio's four-hundred-mile range. Even a small tropical storm puts up a frightful interference."

Michael had assumed that Turner's isolated existence dictated a life of relative hardship, but he was wrong. The house was well stocked with whiskey, beer, and food. There was even ice from a small kerosene-run refrigerator. Ten native scouts acted as servants and cooks as well as coast-watching assistants. Fresh bread was baked each day, and the two men dined off a white tablecloth, using elegant silver cutlery.

"I stole it all from the trading company that owned the copra plantation I managed on Manus," Turner explained with satisfaction.

To Michael's astonishment, even the butter was served on ice. He hadn't eaten decently since his early days on the *Canopus*, so Turner's fare was a gourmet dream. He gained strength rapidly.

For the next two days the only thing that could be heard on the radio from Port Moresby were call letters. Static drowned out the rest.

Turner put down the headphones and folded his arms across his chest. "We may be rescued before this bloody thing works."

"Maybe the Japanese are jamming it."

"Maybe."

The next day the Japanese returned to the island, and this time they obviously planned to stay. They came with troops, supply ships, amphibious patrol planes, and fast patrol launches. They immediately began constructing docks and making a base, enlisting native help with no offer of pay, only vague promises of "citizenship on this island." The message seemed to be that if you didn't work, you'd be unwelcome.

As soon as the Japanese arrived, Turner and his scouts headed for the mountains, taking Michael with them. When they reached the hideout, Michael exclaimed, "God, Turner, you just don't quit, do you?" There, in a hut in the middle of nowhere was a second Electrolux refrigerator, stocked and awaiting their arrival.

Turner soon started a cricket match among his scouts.

"Feeling up to joining us?"

Michael shook his head.

"I could teach them baseball," Turner chided, "if that would appeal to you."

"Nope. Baseball is probably the only game in the world that's more boring than cricket."

"Perhaps it's just team sports in general you don't like, old boy." Turner's voice was cool, and Michael wondered just how much of his plans to escape this war he had revealed in his delirium.

Turner sent two of his scouts out as spies. They obtained jobs in the Japanese commissary, unloading supplies, all of which they dutifully recorded for Turner to report to Port Moresby. When the Japanese appeared to have settled on their side of the island, Turner and Michael finally returned with the scouts to their beachfront base on the opposite side. In their recent exploration of the island the Japanese had not uncovered the hut and its radio, but a storm had ripped off part of the roof so that the radio transmitter was wet and the batteries no longer charged. Once again they were unable to talk with Port Moresby.

Michael began to think in earnest about how he might escape both Turner and the rescue that could be coming his way any day. He would have to sail a great distance through waters dominated entirely by the Japanese, but at least he could find food and water as well as temporary shelter among the many islands between the Admiralties and Borneo.

Turner fiddled with the crippled radio for a while and then gave up with a shrug. "We'll just have to wait for the thing to dry out. Want to play cards? Gin?"

Michael felt irritated. Turner was lonely; but Michael was preoccupied by his own need to find a way off the island, and Turner never gave him a minute alone. "I don't play cards."

Turner got up abruptly and left the hut. Five minutes later gunshots interrupted the tranquil sound of the surf, sending Michael running toward the lagoon. There he found Turner firing his pistol at the crocodiles that inhabited the sandy banks and water.

Turner looked up and smiled congenially. "Target practice. Keeps my aim sharp."

"Shit! You're going to bring every Jap on the island storming in here."

Turner's grin widened. "Now do you want to play some gin rummy?"

Michael stared at him incredulously.

Turner chuckled aloud at his expression. "Don't worry, mate. I'm not out of my head. I'm just used to having my way."

Michael wasn't listening. His eyes were focused just to Turner's right, to a spot across the lagoon. He squinted intently, scarcely believing his eyes, but there was no mistaking it now. There, hidden beneath the palms, was a small amphibious plane.

Turner followed Michael's gaze, remarking, "I came in it. But there're no spare parts to repair the damage done when we landed. And even if there were, there's not gas enough to get farther than the nearest Japanese-occupied island." He looked at Michael evenly. "Like I said before, the sub is our only way out."

One of the scouts came running excitedly down to the lagoon. "Radio. It working. Calling from Port Moresby."

Out of breath from his run back to the hut, Turner sat down at the radio. There was still no voice transmission, but something was coming through on the telegraph. Turner began to take down the message while Michael stood in the door of the hut, intently watching him.

When Turner finished, he had a strange look on his face. He handed Michael the piece of paper. "Here. It's for you."

It was a message from his father:

M.—Regret to inform you that Kara and the children have been killed by Japanese at Maitreya. Catherine and son and Julienne safe with Ahmad in mountains. Margit and Bernard captured, but the boys were killed when their boat sank escaping Java. Would have waited to tell you personally, but you have been ordered to Australia by Admiral Rockwell to serve on MacArthur's personal staff as consultant. Sub will arrive to pick you and Turner up this night. Prepare rendezvous. Good luck. Love, Dad.

"Kara is your wife?" Turner asked.

Michael nodded, scarcely aware of the question.

"Sorry, old man—really."

Michael's heart sank. As many times as he had feared it, imagined it, expected it, nothing had really prepared him for the fact that those close to him would die in this war. He tried to concentrate on his grief and brush aside thoughts of how Kara and the children might have suffered before they died, but the images kept bursting unexpectedly into his mind. It was his fault. He should have escaped sooner. He struggled to compose himself until he could be alone. With the exception of his son, a whole generation of his family had perished.

As Michael left the hut, Turner still sat at the radio, telegraphing an acknowledgment that the message had been received. He stayed out of Michael's way the rest of the day, leaving him alone with his grief. Besides, Turner had things to do in preparation for the escape by sub that night. Humming to himself, he set about burning codes and papers.

There was no moon that night, and an overcast sky hid the

stars. Turner built the signal fire on the beach and sat alone to wait. The sub could surface safely only at night. There was no mistaking the signal fire, bright orange against the unrelenting darkness. The sub did not appear. Stubbornly Turner kept the fire going until dawn, then let it slowly die out. Michael came down to where Turner sat morosely staring at the sea. The last wisp of smoke from the fire was invisible against the gray of the early morning sky. Michael felt touched by Turner's obvious disappointment.

"Don't worry..They'll be here tonight."

"They'd better. The Japs are beginning to swarm all over the place. I had to kill and bury two of them on my last patrol." He looked up at Michael, and a faint look of amusement replaced the dejection that had been there before. "You know, up until the time you got here, I was safe."

Michael was puzzled, as much by Turner's mercurial moods as by his statement.

"A fortune-teller once told me when I was thirteen that I was going to die with another white person among the aborigines." He looked up at Michael with a cynical smile. "I'd always hoped at least it would be a woman."

Chapter 44

It was dark. The villagers had all collected in the longhouse to cook and eat their evening meal. Catherine had just put Michael to sleep on a mat in the darkest corner of the room, and now she sat quietly heating water for tea and staring at the fire as it cast oversize shadows on the rough walls. She watched the steeping tea leaves swirl around the earthen pot. Her muscles ached from the work she had done in her garden that day, but it was a satisfying ache of accomplishment. She wore her *sirat* Iban fashion, bare above the waist. In recent weeks she had overcome her Western sense of modesty and had begun to wear it that way daily. It made her less conspicuous among the villagers, and it browned her body, adding to her disguise.

Lost in thought, she didn't hear him silently enter the room and sit on his heels at the edge of the light. Finally she sensed his presence and looked around from the fire, startled to see him there, silently watching her. No longer alone among the villagers, she blushed at her nakedness.

"You surprised me, Ahmad. We had no word you were coming." It had been almost a month since he had left the village.

He said nothing but continued to stare at her with such intensity that she turned her back to him and gave her attention to the pot. Ordinarily she would have felt glad to see him, but something about his manner now made her uneasy.

"Would you like some tea?" she asked him.

He nodded, and she poured them both a cup. When she turned to face him again, she self-consciously crossed her arms over her breasts, elbows resting on her knees. Thus safely covered, she was able to return his gaze. He was wearing a *sirat* with the sacred kris tucked at the waist. A narrow piece of cloth was knotted around his forehead. His hair, never straight or truly black, had been bleached brown by the sun. It was longer than when he had left, and it curled slightly around his ears. He was barefoot, his feet toughened to the point where he needed no shoes for protection. She wondered how many men he had killed, slipping upon them unseen and silently slitting their throats. His eyes were not soft Malay eyes. They were smaller, and their size concentrated their darkness. The transformation from cultured Moslem prince to fierce Borneo warrior was now complete. She hardly recognized him. He had become a stranger. She could sense the violence in him that lay precariously close to the surface, ready to explode.

"You have become as dark as my people," he observed, finally breaking his silence. "The Japanese could arrive tomorrow and never realize we had an American in our midst."

Catherine smiled faintly, relieved that so benign an observation had come out of that intense stare. She wasn't sure what to expect from him anymore. He stared at the flame of the oil lamp she had just lit.

"I have found that I am capable of terrible things, Catherine," he said softly, not taking his eyes from the light.

She didn't want to hear about the war. Not anymore. Not since Maitreya and the killings there. She had begun to treat her stay with the Iban like an anthropology field trip, busying herself gathering data. But he wasn't about to let her escape it tonight.

"Did you know we can leave no prisoners behind? Even the wounded will be tortured and killed by the Japanese. Our last raid, on the ammunitions dumps in Balikpapan, was a trap. They were expecting us and had booby-trapped the shed. Some of my men were killed when the door blew up; some were only wounded. It was clear they had been expecting us. For the first time they followed us, keeping hard on our trail and forcing us to keep pushing on without stopping. They had expert trackers using dogs. It took us two days to lose them, and by then we were exhausted. We couldn't stop to tend to the wounded. Rather than leave those too badly hurt behind to be captured, I killed them." He broke off and looked at her, as if checking her reaction. She said nothing. "One was a boy of sixteen. He cried and begged me to let him live. I shot him anyway. The other one was older and accepted death without protest. He simply turned his face away and closed his eyes when I put the gun to his head."

She looked at Ahmad's tormented face as he stared unblinkingly into his memory.

"I found out later that we had been betrayed by a woman in Balikpapan whom the boy had met. Perhaps he had only wanted to impress her with his association with me, not knowing she was a traitor. I went back to Balikpapan to find her. She was no more than seventeen or eighteen. Very pretty. A widow who lived alone with her mother. The Japanese had given her a little house of her own because the villagers had cast her out for informing. She slept with the soldiers, worked for them, and they gave her food and money in return. She had become wealthy by village standards, with pigs and chickens of her own. I slipped into her house one afternoon while the village napped. I found her in bed with a Japanese officer, and I gagged and bound him. I raped her, and though she struggled violently against it and spit in my face, our bodies took great pleasure from it, and when it was over, we could loathe each other even more for that pleasure, and ourselves as well."

There was an edge to his voice that told Catherine he was near the breaking point. He was covered with perspiration, and he clenched his teeth tightly, as if to will himself under control. "I slit her throat while she still lay beneath me. She didn't plead for her life as the boy had done. Her face looked so young and soft, lying there with the red necklace which kept spreading across the floor. I hadn't bothered to find out why she had done the things she did to her own people. Perhaps I didn't really want to know for fear it might have stopped me. I got up and emptied my stomach out the window, hating myself, hating men, hating war, but knowing I would go on fighting. Before I left, I castrated the officer with the same kris I had used to kill her. Then I cut off her head with his sword and hung it in front of the Japanese headquarters while their soldiers slept in the afternoon heat."

Catherine wondered why he was telling her this, what he

wanted. Perhaps he was looking for forgiveness, but Catherine had none to give. The lamp flickered and suddenly went out, plunging the room momentarily into darkness before she hastily fumbled for a twist of dried grasses to throw on the embers. As the room came back to life, he leaned forward and pulled her arms away from her breasts. She tried to escape from his grasp, but he held her so tightly that his fingers dug painfully into her arms.

"Stop it—you're hurting me!" she said angrily.

"No," he replied sharply, and then his voice softened. "No, I'm not."

He lowered his eyes, and they pored down over her bare skin, violating her privacy until she was sure she could not stand the the humiliation without bursting into tears of frustration and rage. Even worse, under his gaze an ache had stirred within her, despite her embarrassment, an ache which shocked and frightened her even more than he did.

He finally raised his eyes to hers. "You have a beautiful body, Catherine. You should be proud of it, not ashamed."

He looked away from her into the dying fire, as if losing interest in what had just happened. She felt a new rush of humiliation, this time at his indifference. She started to cover herself again.

"Don't!" he said sharply, surprising her. "You need to overcome your modesty. Even around me. You will attract more attention to yourself with it than with your body. It is dangerous for you." His eyes never left the fire, and he seemed preoccupied again. "I came here for the rest of my men. We will be leaving early tomorrow morning. I won't be back for at least five months, perhaps longer."

"So long!" she protested. She felt overwhelmed.

He looked up from the fire, and she found herself staring into his eyes. Her body stirred again, and she realized suddenly that she wanted him, needed him.

"It has been so long, Ahmad, since I have felt a man's arms around me and his warmth inside me." Her voice shook, but she forced herself to go on.

"I have these dreams that torture me, of Michael's arms around me, of wanting him more than I can bear. I wake up and

I'm drowning in sweat and my body aches to have him, only he is never there. At those times I hate Michael for leaving me.''

He took a stick and angrily stirred the cookfire; then he stood up abruptly. "It's best I say good night. I'll come by to see Michael before I leave in the morning.''

She rose also but remained where she was, beside the fire. He hesitated, his feelings in turmoil. She was staring at his mouth, which she found always softer and more forgiving than his eyes. Her gaze was like a kiss. If she had come near him, he might have shoved her away, but he continued to stand quietly beyond his reach until his body trembled. He struggled to control himself. He thought he saw her lips form his name, but no sound escaped them. Unable to stop himself, he reached out and pulled her to him, his arms encircling her waist. She felt a shock at his body against her bare skin, but she did not resist.

"What do you want from me, Catherine?" he demanded. "To be a stand-in for Michael in order to relieve your frustration?" His voice was scornful. "Never! I want you to want *me*!" The softness of his voice made it no less fierce. Then his eyes closed and his arms tightened around her and his mouth found hers. He drew back and studied her upturned face. Her eyes were closed. He brushed her eyelids with his lips and whispered against them, "Tell me, Catherine, while you feel me here against you, who are you seeing with your thoughts?"

She opened her eyes and looked deeply into his proud and brooding gaze, surprised herself at the answer. "You, Ahmad," she replied truthfully. "I feel and see only you," she whispered.

He kissed her again, this time pressing her tightly to him. He reached down, unfastened their *sirats*, and pulled them away so that they might stand naked together. She moaned and clung to him, and he immediately regretted what he had done. Because of her loneliness, he knew he could have whatever he wanted from her at this moment, and the realization almost destroyed him because, under those circumstances, he could not permit himself to take advantage. Even as he recognized for the first time how much he wanted to make love to her, he was twisting an angry fist tightly into her long black hair. Although his voice was soft against her ear, it shook with the desire to drive her out of his life.

"I hate what I feel for you." He let the intensity of the words slice like a cold knife into their passion. When he felt her body tense slightly against him so that he knew he had succeeded, his voice softened into bitter weariness. "And I have enough to hate in me already without adding that." His hand slipped from her hair. She pulled her head away as if to leave him. As he looked down into her upturned face, he discovered one more terrible thing about himself.

"I love Michael Stanford as a brother," he whispered. With a grip on her arms that was tight enough to hurt, he added, "And yet at this moment I wish him out of my life—dead!" She stared up at him in disbelief.

"It's true." He answered her look fiercely. "And I hate myself for wishing it!" Once he had uttered the unforgivable, the tension drained from his face. He put his arms around her again and buried his face in the softness of her hair, relieved that she did not resist but, by some miracle, returned his embrace. The bitter honesty of his words had changed passion to the tenderness each felt for whatever was fragile and human in the other. For a long time they stood holding each other until finally the only heat between them was the sweating night.

Reluctantly he released her, bending over to pick up her *sirat* and hand it to her. Modestly she clutched at it, covering herself before he caught a glimpse of her body in the warm lamplight. Since he was not so shy, she saw how splendid he looked before he drew the *sirat* about his waist and tied it, lean and well muscled, and for a moment her desire returned. But his eyes were already full of regret. Suddenly she knew he was going to be gone a lot longer than he had planned, longer than was necessary.

"Goodnight." He leaned over and kissed her lightly on the forehead.

The next moment the room was empty. He had left so silently she began to doubt that he had ever been there. Perhaps, she thought, the isolation and the loneliness were driving her mad. Clutching the *sirat* to her chest, she sank slowly to the floor beside the cookfire, and her body began to shake with sobs. She pounded her fists against the floor in frustration. "Damn you, Michael," she cried. "Why did you leave me?"

The next morning Catherine woke to the sounds of the men preparing to leave. About 100 of them would be going, leaving a village of women, children, and old men. Since they would be traveling through the jungle on foot, they were loading supplies and ammunition into baskets and litters. The rivers were becoming too dangerous.

Catherine lit the cookfire against the early-morning chill. She put on a fresh sarong instead of a short *sirat*, modestly tying it over her shoulder. To hell with him, she thought with annoyance. The memory of the previous night suddenly made her feel acutely uncomfortable. In the cold gray drizzle of early morning she could scarcely believe it had happened. She got up from the cookfire and looked beyond the veranda, where the villagers and animals milled in cheerful confusion around the men who would be leaving. It was bedlam, and Catherine decided to wait until later to take her morning bath in the river. She saw Siah among the women who were preparing to leave with the men. She wore a belt of ammunition across her bare shoulder, and she carried a rifle with a familiarity that said she had learned to use it well. She was proud, arrogant, and very beautiful. No small part of that pride came from the fact that Ahmad slept with no other woman but her. It gave her status beyond all other women. Watching her, Catherine felt envious. Siah slept with the man Siah loved. Suddenly she realized it was more than envy. She was jealous because Siah slept with Ahmad.

Cheeks burning at the thought, Catherine turned back into her small room, put on a pot of water for tea, and fed Michael a breakfast of fruit and rice. She was absentmindedly watching him playing on the floor when she looked up to see Ahmad standing before the doorway.

"May I come in?" It was a cool, distant request, unlike the night before, she thought, when he had felt quite free to enter her room unannounced. He bent over slightly to get his tall frame through the Iban doorway. He wore white pants and a loose, white, collarless native shirt made of raw cotton.

Michael gave a squeal of delight and ran to Ahmad, who gathered him into his arms and kissed him. She noticed that Ahmad looked remarkably relaxed, and she guessed that he had taken the desire she had roused in him last night back for Siah to enjoy. Again she felt a hot stab of jealousy.

"Michael, you grow more handsome and like your father every day, but we must do something about that blond hair of

455

yours before it gets your mother and the rest of the village in trouble." He glanced at Catherine. "Dye it," he ordered. "The women will show you how. The Japanese are coming farther upriver every day on their patrols."

She said nothing. Used to giving commands and having them obeyed unquestioningly, he took her silence for acquiescence. It was not. She had no intention of dying Michael's hair or staining his skin.

Ahmad glanced disapprovingly at the way she wore her sarong, but he said nothing to her about it. She felt the satisfaction of a small victory in the struggle that had suddenly emerged between them.

"Would you like some tea?"

He nodded and squatted on his heels as he took the cup from her, still balancing Michael in one arm. Michael nestled his head against Ahmad's chest and began to suck contentedly on his thumb, something he had not done for months. Catherine noticed with annoyance that he seemed to be staring at her in defiance while he clung stubbornly to Ahmad, as if daring her to try to take him away from this warm presence he adored. Catherine realized that Michael probably blamed her for Ahmad's constant disappearances just as he held his mother responsible for everything else that happened in his life.

She watched the two of them, Michael making words and noises which Ahmad cheerfully imitated, lost in an incoherent conversation that included no one else. Ahmad taught Michael Iban words whenever he was around while Catherine stubbornly spoke to him only in English. This damned war was sure to be over someday, she told herself.

"You're so good for Michael, Ahmad," she acknowledged. "He misses you terribly when you're gone. I'm so grateful."

Ahmad looked from Michael to her, and the smile left his face. "Don't be grateful," he interrupted her. "I love Michael as much as if he were my own." He paused for a moment; then he smiled. "Perhaps we both put too much of our love into this little one."

Sensing his meaning, she frowned and poured him some more tea. "About last night . . . I think we should forget it happened."

"If you want to forget it happened, then why did you bring it

456

up?'' He laughed and then grew serious. ''If it's bothering you, Catherine, why don't we talk about it?''

He released Michael and sent him off to play by himself, giving her his full attention. Now that she had it, she didn't know quite what to do with it. She resented that he seemed not in the least perturbed.

''It was nothing,'' she said awkwardly. ''It meant nothing.''

Ahmad refused to let her off the hook. ''I don't see how we can pretend it didn't happen. It wasn't just an isolated incident; it was bound to happen sooner or later. Even if you were with Michael at Maitreya, leading a normal life, it would have happened.''

She flushed in annoyance, denying to herself what he said.

''Why it happened now doesn't matter,'' he continued. ''There are good and bad reasons why we love anyone. The reasons, whatever they are, don't change the feelings. It does no good to analyze it or deny it. Our desire pains us both. I'm struggling now to accept it, and you are struggling to destroy it. That is the difference between us.'' He put down his tea and rose to leave.

She was bothered by what he said. Even though it might be over between them, she loved Michael. She had no doubt of that. And if she were still in love with Michael, how could she love Ahmad?

As if reading her thoughts, he said, ''We are all capable of loving more than one person at a time. Only you Westerners fail to realize it and make things so difficult for yourselves.'' He smiled. ''We Eastern polygamists have known it for centuries.''

He walked over to give Michael a pat on the head. His fingers lingered affectionately on the golden hair.

''Good-bye, old fellow,'' he said softly. Then he turned to Catherine, and his expression grew serious.

''I have never competed with Michael Stanford for anything. We have always had our separate lives and separate successes. We were never after the same things, until you.'' He could not keep the regret from his voice. ''But I knew from the way I saw you look at Michael that first night at Maitreya that I had lost the race before it started. And I know now that you're still very much in love with him.''

They looked at each other in silence. There was nothing more to be said.

457

"Good-bye, Catherine," he said finally.

She could not bring herself to say anything at all.

Outside, the men were beginning to shoulder their loads and move out into the jungle. Siah, rifle slung over her beautiful shoulder, fell in behind Ahmad. She glanced briefly behind her at Catherine, who stood watching on the veranda, and a smile crossed Siah's lips before she turned back to follow Ahmad and the others into the forest.

Chapter 45
Admiralty Islands

In the faint starlight the island's silhouette was just barely visible beyond the reef. The *Swordfish*'s captain searched the beach for the signal fire. The two crewmen who would take the rubber rescue raft ashore stood below the conning tower, holding the lines to the bobbing, straining raft, ready to set out when the order came. It was 2:00 A.M., twenty-six hours past the rendez-vous time. Their arrival had been delayed by an encounter with an enemy sub and two destroyers off Rabaul.

"No sighting, sir," the seaman reported finally.

The executive officer, who stood beside the captain, lowered his binoculars. "Maybe they didn't get the message we'd been delayed. Darwin didn't indicate if its message had been acknowledged or not."

The captain swung down the metal steps that led to the deck and crossed toward the waiting raft. The rolling submarine deck was not much wider than a school bus, and its surface was still wet and glistening from the water that had recently covered it. He addressed the senior of the two crewmen.

"Richmond, I don't have to caution you. We have orders not to go in there without the agreed signal, but I'll be damned if I'm going to leave those men if there's a chance of getting them out. We don't have much time. The Japanese have built a torpedo boat base on this island, and one of their boats could be along anytime. Signal and wait for our return signal before you start back. If we should have to submerge, hide and we'll pick you up tomorrow night."

A sudden swell lifted the deck.

"From the look of this sky and the feel of this surf, there's one hell of a storm building, so get a move on. If the Japs don't get us in the next hour, the storm will."

"Yes, sir," Richmond responded as he and the other seaman jumped lightly into the rubber boat and edged slowly away, disappearing into the trough of the swells and emerging seconds later, only to plunge out of sight again.

The captain returned to the conning tower and stood beside his executive officer. "Jesus, what a night," he said with a weary sigh. "If those swells get much bigger, they'll capsize the raft."

"Well, Captain," the exec replied, "if I were the men on that island, I'd rather drown than be captured by the Japanese."

Twenty minutes later they thought they spotted the dark outline of the small boat against the churning white surf of the beach, but no one was certain. The clouds which had been rapidly building in the south now completely covered the sky, reducing visibility except for those moments when lightning flashed from the approaching storm. On the island only a narrow strip of white sand separated the dense jungle from the surf. From the sea, even on a clear night, it was impossible to see beyond the thick tangle of trees. It had been a good coast-watching spot.

Half an hour later the flash of Richmond's signal to return flashed from the shore and was acknowledged by the waiting sub. Because of deteriorating visibility, the captain ordered a periodic signal light be flashed to guide the boat. For what seemed forever the small crew on deck waited tensely for some sign of the rubber raft. The captain had come down to join them, being an impatient man for whom delegating authority had never been easy. For the past half hour he had been wishing fervently that he had gone ashore himself. Anything would have been better than this infernal waiting.

So poor was the visibility that the raft was almost upon them by the time the watch shouted down that it had been sighted. As it came alongside and tossed out lines, there appeared to be only two men on board. The captain reached for Richmond's arm and pulled him onto the deck.

"All dead, sir," Richmond said, gasping for breath and sagging in exhaustion from the ordeal of battling the heavy seas. "From the looks of it, it happened five or six hours ago. Japs must have taken them by surprise. There were five natives dead outside the hut, food still on their plates like they had just sat down to dinner. No dead Japs. Looks like the natives had no warning. Found the sentry with his throat slit. The hut had been burned to the ground, and the radio destroyed. There were two bodies inside it. One of them was wearing this."

He handed the captain the chain with Michael's dog tags on it. The captain switched on his flashlight and briefly examined the tags before slipping them into his pocket.

"Two Japanese torpedo boats to port!" the watch shouted.

The dull roar of the torpedo boats' engines was just audible against the background of the surf. In the poor visibility the boats were almost on top of the *Swordfish* before they had been sighted. Fortunately the Japanese were dealing with the same conditions and might not have spotted them yet.

"Let's get the hell out of here. Prepare to dive!"

The order was quickly relayed to the crew as the men on deck raced for the hatches. There was no time to bring the bulky raft on board. The captain hauled it in and turned the valve to release the air, in case the raft was spotted by the Japanese and betrayed their presence. As he leaned over, the dog tags slipped from his unbuttoned shirt pocket and fell into the raft. He didn't bother to risk retrieving them. He had already gotten a good look at the identification.

Seconds later the foaming water was swirling over the sub's deck. As the *Swordfish* escaped unseen, the deflated raft began to sink slowly, with all the reluctance of an abandoned hope.

Chapter 46

Julienne sat on her heels, arms wrapped tightly around her knees, staring at the longhouse wall as she had done for the past months. Her feet were becoming blue and swollen. Intrigued by madness, believing it to contain the greatest kind of supernatural power, the Iban were in awe of Julienne. They collected each day at the door of her *bieh*, watching her with the same appreciation with which they might view an exciting dance performance. It seemed to those observing her vacant eyes and her silence that she was oblivious of all that went on around her, but she was not. Like those of a blind person, her ears had become her main contact with the world.

The pain in her cramped muscles somehow did not reach her. It was a comfortable position for someone who hadn't wished to be born in the first place. In fact, she had resisted being born so effectively that it had taken twenty-one hours of difficult labor for her to be finally delivered, screaming in protest, into the world. Despite that rude beginning, Julienne had been an unusually quiet, passive, and undemanding baby. She hadn't talked or scarcely uttered a sound until she was four years old. By then everyone was certain something was wrong with her, and she had been submitted to the scrutiny of specialists, who had diagnosed her as everything from deaf to mentally retarded. The truth was she had simply not trusted the world enough to engage it in conversation, though she was perfectly capable of it. Instead, she had watched and waited. Her mother had used her silence as an excuse to ignore her, while Edward, seven years older than she, with his dirty little mind, had used it to violate her innocence before he had fled from childhood into puberty with a Bible tucked beneath his pillow and a prayer beside his bed each night. Mother's little darling. What a pious prig he had become. Julienne had mildly concluded he was more of a monster than she could ever be.

During her early period of silent observation Julienne had realized she was not like other children. At first the discovery had terrified her. She found she was often fascinated by the things they feared, such as blood, violence, and death, while the things which frightened her most didn't seem to bother them, such as a close embrace or a kiss which threatened to swallow her. But by carefully observing other children, Julienne had cleverly learned how to wear their sanity as her mask. She could not think or feel as they did, but she could behave in the same manner. As for the rest, it could be left to explode harmlessly in her brain, out of sight in dreams and fantasies. The mask had failed her only on rare occasions. One such time had been when the news reached her that Michael had been found alive in New Guinea with Catherine. The jealousy Julienne had felt at that moment was so intense as to destroy her. Instead, she had demolished every drawing of his, every photograph of him she possessed, and would have done the same to the rest of the house except Damal had stopped her, physically restraining her while she screamed and fought him. It had been the first time in a long while that she had lost control of herself in front of someone, and it had shaken her.

She had been consumed by jealousy since the day she was born. Toward Margit, Edward—even her mother. It was the strongest feeling she was capable of besides hate. The most intense jealousy of all was for Michael and Catherine. Even now she had not given up the idea that she might get even with Michael. But as long as there was the possibility that Ahmad might find out, she would not dare to harm Catherine. Not only because she feared him, but she needed him if she were to get out of here alive. She would have to be content to sit and rock and wait for her chance. She was mad, but she knew it, and the awareness, she supposed, made her less insane than others like herself.

It was almost dark now. The Iban had gone from her door, but Catherine hadn't come yet to light the evening lamp for her. Julienne sat listening to the sounds the house made. Suddenly she closed her eyes and set her teeth together and wrapped her arms closer around herself in fear. Something was definitely coming. She could feel it getting closer. Perhaps it was waiting just outside the longhouse at this moment, listening to her thoughts, testing how well prepared she was against it, waiting to see if she was afraid. A shiver passed through the longhouse and into her very bones, and she wondered if Catherine had felt it, too.

In her *bieh* a few doors down from Julienne, Catherine had finished an early meal and put Michael to bed, too tired and cross to put up with his normal childish demands any longer. She was angry at being left alone with Julienne's madness and only Patri to keep her company. The cookfire lit the room against the waning sunlight. She had just dozed off involuntarily when she suddenly awoke, startled to hear someone speak her name. The evening sky was still gray beyond the door, and flashes of sheet lightning flickered on the horizon. In the humid, still air that preceded the approaching storm, the heat of the cookfire was oppressive. A figure was silhouetted in the doorway. She sat up in surprise.

"Ahmad?" A smile of recognition crossed her face.

He stepped into the room and leaned wearily back against the wall, closing his eyes.

"What is it?" she asked, the smile fading. "What's wrong?"

In the silence that followed, the gentle patter of rain began to hit the palm-frond roof above them and trickle down to the ground below. In that moment she was gripped by a fear that was more intense than she had ever known.

"It's Michael, isn't it?"

His eyes came open, and the pain she saw there answered her fears.

"He's dead, isn't he!"

He nodded, and again the rain became the only sound. She felt as if she were visibly shrinking into the silence, bones and muscle dissolving away.

Ahmad searched her eyes as if to satisfy himself that she was strong enough to hear, and then he told her what he had learned of Michael's death from Sir Charles's radio-relayed message. For a moment she sat stunned, unable to accept the news, then deep sobs began to shake her body to its very core. Ahmad came to her and gathered her into his arms, holding her close.

"And what of your grief, Ahmad?" she whispered against the smooth skin of his shoulder, struggling to comfort his loss while giving in to her own.

"My grief is already spent," he said softly, his lips pressed into the fine softness of her hair, but even as he said it, his cheeks were wet and his hands trembled.

She cried until she was exhausted. He held her tightly until her tears were finished; then he lowered her gently to the sleeping mat and snapped his fingers. An Iban woman appeared, bearing a cup of something which she handed to Ahmad. Catherine did not even notice. She lay staring at the ceiling. She wanted to die. If it had not been for her son, she would have. Except for him, everything she had ever loved had been taken from her. She had entertained the hope that the reasons for her separation from Michael might eventually be overcome. But now she faced the irrevocable separation of death.

"Drink this," Ahmad ordered, lifting her head.

It relaxed her, made her drowsy. When she woke the next morning, he was still next to her, his head resting on his arms. But the closensss of the previous night was gone. In death, even more than in life, Michael stood between them. After breakfast Ahmad rose to leave. "Are you all right?"

She nodded. He hesitated for a moment and then went to the door.

"Good-bye, Catherine."

She merely nodded, not looking at him but at the gray morning sky beyond his shoulder. His expression troubled, he turned and left her alone, pausing to send one of the women to her before he disappeared into the jungle.

Later Catherine found Julienne crouched before the cookfire in her apartment.

"Julienne . . . Julienne. Talk to me," Catherine pleaded.

The eyes stared back, unblinking.

"Michael's dead."

The eyes did not so much as flicker, yet they seemed suddenly duller.

"Do you understand me?"

No. She didn't. Because the house was screaming all around her so loudly that she couldn't hear anything else.

"Julienne!" Catherine shouted. "Will you listen to me? I'm trying to tell you that Michael is dead!"

Satisfied that the house had finally stopped screaming, Julienne began to eat the food before her, feeding herself for the first time in weeks.

"Help me, Julienne." Catherine's voice was desperate.

Julienne's eyes glanced past her and focused on something distant. She loved him. She hated him. The part of her that loved him had screamed until it died. Only the hate remained.

Catherine began to weep helplessly as she stood looking at Julienne. Julienne went on eating as before, as if Catherine weren't even there. But something had changed. After Catherine left her, Julienne rose unsteadily and walked down the hall to Catherine's *bieh*.

"Julienne!" Catherine exclaimed, astonished to see her standing in the door.

"Don't expect any sympathy from me, Catherine," she said evenly. "I'm glad he's dead."

Catherine flinched slightly at the words.

"Has Ahmad left?" Julienne asked, glancing around the room.

"Yes," Catherine replied uneasily.

It didn't matter any longer if Ahmad were gone, Julienne thought. With Michael's death she had lost her strong desire to be rid of Catherine. Her eyes fell on the baby playing on the floor, and she smiled at him. Now he posed no threat to her. With Michael gone, one of her British cousins would inherit the title and the English estates and she and Margit would be left all that really mattered, Maitreya. Margit had never wanted it so Julienne would have it to herself.

"Things have a way of working out as they're supposed to," she said to Catherine.

The two women were silent for a long moment.

"You loved him at one time," Catherine said finally, trying to forge some link between them.

Julienne shook her head. "I wanted him—always. That's not

466

the same thing, is it?'' Not expecting an answer, she added, "In fact, I hated him."

Catherine felt a chill as she remembered the warning Ahmad had given her the first time he had left the village. He had told her Julienne could be dangerous. But by then Julienne had so withdrawn from the world that Catherine had ignored the warning. Now Julienne had suddenly resumed her life and Ahmad was far away.

"Leave me alone," Catherine told her. "Don't ever come near me again."

"I never intend to," Julienne replied calmly.

It had been almost eleven months since Ahmad had visited Catherine with the news of Michael's death, and she hadn't seen him since. Christmas 1942 had come and gone months ago, and she had scarcely noticed. Even with the men gone, news of the war occasionally reached the village, mostly as rumor but occasionally as fact obtained through a clandestine radio. The Japanese forbade Indonesians to listen to Western broadcasts, and anyone found with an overseas radio was tortured and killed.

Indonesian disillusionment with the Japanese, which Ahmad had predicted, had quickly set in when political parties, newspapers, and public assemblies had been banned shortly after the occupation. To the dismay of the Indonesians, who had hoped for saviors, the Japanese were even more oppressive than the Dutch. Indonesians now had to carry identification cards and obtain passes to travel beyond their city or village. Some had to wear armbands indicating how much they could be trusted by the Japanese. All lucrative businesses had been taken over by Japanese firms and were now being run for the benefit of Japan, just as they had been for Holland under the Dutch. Jobs were scarce; wages were even lower than under the old colonial regime, and inflation was higher. Indonesians were forced by the Japanese to serve in labor camps far from home under terrible conditions, and many of them died. In the cities there was a shortage of food and consumer goods. Hungry Batavians had stormed a warehouse filled with rice reserved for the Japanese Army, and the entire city had been called out to witness the beheading of the offenders. Pulling out fingernails was such a common form of torture that the question "Do you need a manicure?" had become the

Indonesian's wry way of threatening each another. Like the Dutch, the Japanese still refused to discuss Indonesian independence.

It was clearly going to be a long war. But if the Allied position in the Pacific had not improved much by this summer of 1943, it at least wasn't getting worse. Until a month ago the village of Rumah Pacou itself had scarcely been touched by the war, and the Japanese had seemed unaware of its existence. Then one afternoon a lone Japanese fighter plane had flown low over the longhouse, scattering dogs and children, sending eveyone running for cover. Fortunately the pilot had come upon the village unexpectedly and had not had time to fire on the first pass. By the time he made the decision to use the village for target practice, most of the villagers had taken shelter in the jungle. Only one old man, crippled by an ancient mauling by a Malaysian bear, failed to make it in time as the bullets ripped into the longhouse, thudded into the soft ground, and bit deeply into the trunks of the surrounding trees. However, his leg was only grazed. Several pigs in the pen beneath the longhouse had been slaughtered by the bullets, giving the villagens an excuse to hold a feast and gorge themselves on roast pork. They danced all night and into the next one as well. Fortunately the plane did not return, for few of them would have been sober enough to have made it to safety.

Julienne made her way slowly down the riverbank, laboriously climbing over logs in the mud, searching for crabs for her dinner. Some Iban boys had built a dam on this spot the day before, then put in poison to temporarily paralyze the fish so they would float to the surface where enough could be gathered to feed the village for several days. The dam had been hastily built with branches and mud and would not hold up for long against the river. As she drew near she could see a small boat in the middle of the river just below the dam, its bow caught in the branches. Water had poured into it, threatening to swamp it. At first she thought it was a boat from the village, abandoned when its owner could not make progress upstream. But as she climbed upon the structure of the dam for a better view, she saw two figures lying in the bottom, an Iban boy and the white-robed old priest from the mission. She thought them dead until the old man groaned and raised an arm at the elbow which immediately collapsed again across his chest.

Julienne waded out into the river. The water was only waist deep. She worked the bow free and pushed the boat ashore, wedging it against the bank until it was secure enough for her to pull the priest from it. The boy was dead, shot twice through the chest. Sandflies swarmed around the wound. She left him in the boat. A bullet had grazed the priest's head, but he seemed more exhausted and ill than seriously wounded. Julienne crouched impatiently beside the old man, unsure of what to do next. At last his eyes fluttered open. He stared at her uncomprehendingly for a long moment.

"Perhaps you were expecting St. Peter, Father." She was annoyed she had bothered to pull the boat ashore. Now she would have to interrupt her hunting and go all the way back to the village for help.

Recognition suddenly lit his face. "Miss Stanford," he cried, and reached out to clutch her arm. His voice was urgent. "The Japanese patrols are all over the river. They will be here any day." He clutched more tightly at her arm. "You must leave the village at once!"

He fell back, suddenly spent. "He was coming to save you," he said softly, his voice full of grief.

"Who was coming?" Julienne demanded, certain she would get only God and a sermon as an answer. She was tempted to leave the old fool there and forget about him.

He didn't answer her but withdrew into reverie. "The boy is dead," he said finally, referring to his cook's arm. "The Japanese shot him. He was at the stern of the boat. And then they shot the young lieutenant who had been sent to rescue you. He fell out of the boat and I couldn't reach him before he drowned. Then the Japanese patrol boat hit a log and sank, but it was too late." He was silent, lost in the memory of so many men dying and the sin of the relief he had felt. He closed his eyes and began to cry softly.

"What lieutenant?" Julienne asked, grabbing hold of him to shake him out of his lapse.

His mind focused on her again. "The one your father sent—to bring you and Dr. Morgan down the river to where a submarine would be waiting to pick you up. He was an Australian lad. Before he could reach you he was discovered and wounded by the Japanese. Some villagers from Balikpapan brought him all the way upriver to me, thinking I might help him, but the Japanese had taken my medical supplies. I hadn't even any quinine to treat his malaria. He recovered anyway, being a young, strong lad, trained for that sort of thing.''

Julienne gave a groan of frustration and released her hold on the old priest's frock. To think, she had been within a day of help in getting out of this miserable hole! ''You're sure he's dead?'' she asked.

''Yes, yes. Poor brave lad. He served with your father and volunteered for the assignment. Said he knew you.'' The priest looked confused for a moment. ''Strange, but I can't seem to remember his name. From Brisbane. His father was a professor, a friend of Sir Charles.''

Donald Oliver, Julienne thought. Eight years younger than she. The last time she had seen him he had been a skinny boy in a soccer uniform.

Seeing Julienne's frustration, the priest attempted to reassure her. ''Your father will send someone else before long, I'm sure. Now that your brother and your father's nephews are gone, he has only the little lad here to carry on the name.'' The old priest shook his head. ''So many dead,'' he murmured.

But Julienne was no longer listening. ''My cousins are dead?''

He looked confused by the urgency in her voice. She must know about her cousins. The war had come to England long before it came here. But of late he had become mixed up about dates. ''Why yes. According to the lieutenant, one of them died in the North African campaign and the other in the British bombing of Cologne.'' Was it before or after the bombing of Pearl Harbor? He could no longer remember.

Julienne stood up abruptly, her face a mixture of shock and anger. The priest was perturbed. He had not meant to upset her with more bad news than was necessary. He attempted to make it up to her.

''There is still hope.'' He struggled to pull a piece of paper, torn from the edge of his Bible, from his robe. ''The lieutenant gave me this to pass on to you if something happened to him. It contains the location where the submarine will surface three times. The dates and times are written on it. Destroy it when you know them by heart. You and Dr. Morgan still have a good chance to make it in time," he said hopefully. "But whatever you decide, you mustn't remain here."

Julienne snatched the paper from him and stuffed it in her pocket, but she wasn't listening to him. "He's nothing but a little bastard!" she shouted at the priest, fists clenched. "He'll never have the Stanford name!" But of course he would. Her father would give it to him if Catherine would let him, along with Maitreya and everything else. Just as he had done with Michael.

The priest looked up at her, stunned by the change that had come over her. It occurred to him for the first time that she might leave him there to die.

"Please," he started to implore her as he tried to raise himself up. "Just help me to the village."

But she was backing away from him, a look of cold contempt on her face.

"In the name of humanity! You cannot leave me here!"

She disliked being reminded that she never felt compassion. She paused in her retreat. In that brief moment of reprieve, Father O'Mally reached out to Julienne. She turned away and started up the river. She had taken only a step when she felt him grab her ankle. Despite a firm kick the grip didn't loosen.

"Let go of me!" she cried, appalled by the sensation of his hands squeezing her ankle. She fell down and they struggled in the mud until she shoved him away and got up. He was up on his knees and crawling. Not toward her but up the river, toward the village. It was even possible, she thought, that the old fool might make it.

She looked frantically around for a stick. There was none. All had been used to build the dam. She saw a parang in the boat beside the boy's body. She snatched it and caught up with the priest. His breath came in gasps of fear and exhaustion. Perhaps he was having a heart attack, she thought as she closed her eyes and swung the parang, taking aim, in the dark, for his neck. She felt something wet strike her face but she didn't stop. She swung until she was exhausted and then she opened her eyes and slumped to the ground, panting. He lay on his stomach, white robe covered with blood. Her own clothes were soaked with it as well. The flies came. The river was quiet. When she had caught her breath, she got up and turned the body onto its back. There was only a spatter of blood from his earlier head wound on the front of his robe. She dragged his body to the embankment and rolled it into the river. Air trapped beneath his robe caused it to billow out like a peaceful cloud upon the water, as peaceful, Julienne thought, as Edward . . . and then it sank. She ducked underwater and washed her face and hair. The blood on her clothes ebbed away. She got out of the river, threw the parang in the boat, and shoved it off into the current. She had gone a hundred yards up the river bank when she remembered she had left her basket of crabs. She returned to the spot and found them, pausing calmly to check the scene. Except for the dark stain on the muddy bank, it looked as it always did. If what the priest had said was true, the Japanese could attack the village soon. Catherine and the baby would probably die with the villagers, but Julienne couldn't take any chances that the baby might survive. She would have to get rid of him herself but make sure it seemed like an accident in case someone in the village might survive the Japanese to tell about it. She was still afraid of Ahmad.

She would meet the submarine alone. For the rest of the afternoon she feverishly planned her escape. But despite her concentration on the task at hand, an uneasiness began to permeate her thoughts, sapping her excitement and her energy. Three times she went to the river to bathe, and each time a dark stain of blood boiled up around her, darker and larger each time. Her clothes and hair seemed saturated with it. By evening the putrid smell of spoiling blood had penetrated even her *bieh*. Alarmed, she took off her clothes and burned them in her cookfire to rid herself of it, wrapping a *sirat* around her waist. It would be a better garment for her escape, she told herself. To complete the disguise, she took black Iban dye and began to trace the outlines of Iban tattoos upon her face and body, using the reflection of a shiny brass plate from some distant coastal village to guide her hand. A vine sprouted on her ankle, moved up along her thigh, crossed the mound of her small belly, curled around one bare breast before it climbed her throat and encircled her eye with several curling tendrils. Fascinated, she watched another sprout just as the first had done, until it seemed the forest itself had come to hide her. Finished, she lay down to wait until the village was asleep. But for the first time in her life she felt afraid of the dark, afraid of the forest, afraid of spirits. She rose and slipped into the galley to where old Koh had the warriors hide heads they had taken on recent raids on the Japanese. One still had its glasses and cap. She took another and tied it around her waist and went back to her *bieh* and curled herself around it, letting its powerful medicine protect her from her enemies. When she left, she would take it with her.

She slept restlessly. In her dreams she saw the nude bodies of Edward and Father O'Malley floating together beneath the surface of the river in a peaceful embrace. But as she drew closer to them, it was not Father O'Malley but her own pale limbs entangled with Edward's as they sank slowly toward the silt and mud below. Terrified of reaching that murky bottom, she woke, gasping for air as if she were drowning. Catching her breath, she listened to the longhouse, straining for any sound indicating people were still awake. Hearing none, she sat up.

Outside, the forest watched and waited for her. She could feel its moist, sweet breath and sense its mood as she sat quietly in the darkness. During the day it slept. But the night was different. At night it awoke. Nothing could tempt the Ibans into the forest at night. Julienne knew the forest was not quite sane, just as she was not. It was not merely the hunting leopard or the stealthy python that had awakened to stalk the night. The forest itself stirred. The forest itself was evil. She could feel it watching her closely tonight.

Tears of happiness suddenly stung her eyes. She had reached a decision which exhilarated her, gave her a strength she had never had before. She would not try to meet the submarine. Instead, she would return to Maitreya. Even if the Japanese now occupied it, she would wait in its forests until the war was over.

"I know that's what you want," she whispered, and she felt the forest shudder and sigh.

Quickly she tied a bright Iban cloth around her head and stuck two feathers of the hornbill into her hair. She put the slip of paper with the submarine destination on her dying cookfire. Bending over, she blew the embers to life until the paper burned. Then she got a spear and went to Catherine's *bieh*. She looked briefly at the sleeping form of Michael and then bent to kiss his forehead. The presence of the forest grew stronger. Julienne felt surprised that it had not wakened the sleeping villagers. Perhaps it touched only her, caressed only her. Bidding her to hurry, it took her by the hand, pulling her away from little Michael, the longhouse, Catherine. Catherine, she had almost forgotten Catherine. Perhaps she ought to say good-bye to her before she left, perhaps a kiss. No. She had gifts for them both. That was enough. She put the small basket she had brought for Michael beside his mat where he would find it when he woke. As she placed it, she could feel the deadly krait within it uncoil, angry and frightened at being disturbed.

Next she stood over Catherine, watching her stir in her sleep as if she had sensed someone staring at her. Julienne turned away to the pot of water which stood over the dead cooking hearth, waiting for the morning tea to bring it to life. She dropped the colorless, tasteless contents of a small clay vial she carried at her waist into the innocent pot.

She could tell the forest grew impatient with her lingerings, as if it feared she might change her mind. She laughed aloud at its fretting and followed it into the night. As she stepped with one bare foot into the undergrowth, a cobra slipped away and did not try to harm her. She laughed again. She had not felt so light-hearted in years.

Catherine slept fitfully in the longhouse. Suddenly she awoke, as if alarmed by something. She rose and bent anxiously over Michael, who appeared to be resting peacefully. Relieved, she returned to her mat and lay down. Before closing her eyes, she listened carefully to the night around her. Hearing nothing unusual, she attempted to go back to sleep.

Julienne was running through the forest now. She was using Iban hunting trails, worn free of undergrowth by constant use. Only occasional glimmers of moonlight illuminated the path. Still, she moved rapidly along it, guided by memory, deep into the body of the forest. It slowly inhaled and exhaled around her. The noise of its breathing was deafening. It grew labored, struggling, as if out of breath. Panting. From what? Fear, exhaustion, lust? She stopped and sank on one knee to the ground, her chin sagged against her chest. Her own labored breathing echoed and reverberated against the hovering forest. A familiar voice whispered ahead of her. Footsteps rustled along the path. Julienne recognized the voice.

"Mother?" she whispered "Mother?"

She rose and continued. Around her the whispers grew louder. "Michael!" she called.

She recognized her own voice among the whispers. Giggling, snickering. It was murmuring obscenities to someone. The murmur of voices grew louder, and Julienne was suddenly afraid. She rose and headed toward the river, away from the forest.

She stumbled blindly into the encamped Japanese soldiers, part of a patrol which had been attacked that morning by Iban headhunters. They were weary, hungry, and very afraid, making them even more dangerous than they might have been otherwise.

As she emerged from the forest onto the narrow sandy beach, Julienne tripped and fell over one of the reclining soldors. They were upon her quickly before she could recover. A bayonet was pressed against her throat as one of them stirred the faint embers of the dying cookfire and threw some fuel onto it until it leaped alive. When the light flared, they gave surprised exclamations at what struggled beneath their hands.

They fell upon her as if they had found the source of their earlier defeat, an enemy on whom they could reek revenge for their humiliations. Before they hacked and tore her limb from limb in a frenzy of loathing and despair, they spread her body open upon the ground and rammed their lust and hate into her one by one. Julienne, who had known only Michael's gentle touch, bled from between her legs and from her mouth as the forest screamed and shrieked around her.

It had rained earlier, as the morning dawned, and the drops from the trees still rapped the palm-frond roof of the longhouse. Catherine hadn't slept well, and it was hard for her to rise. There had been nightmares she couldn't now recall. The other residents of the longhouse had already left for the river and the morning bath, so the building was unusually quiet. There was only the hungry grunting of the pigs as they impatiently anticipated their breakfast of morning refuse.

Michael was awake, sitting on his sleeping mat, examining a small basket with great interest. She had not noticed it before. No doubt one of the villagers who occasionally tended him had given it to him earlier. He had evidently not yet discovered how to open it, for he turned it over repeatedly and then probed the lid with his chubby fingers. Once he tossed it aside in frustration, only immediately to retrieve it and try again. Catherine lay watching him for a time, amused by his determination and reluctant to budge from beneath her light cover. The morning was unusually cold, and the prospect of a bath in that chilly air did not appeal to her. Still, it had become as much a ritual for her as for the villagers, and out of habit, she stirred herself to go, taking the little basket from Michael's hands and setting it aside, not without some protest from him. She noted with some curiosity that the basket appeared to have something inside that shifted back and forth. She postponed indulging her curiosity and set it down on Michael's mat, to be examined when she returned. She picked Michael up and hurried toward the path leading to the river. Inside the basket, the furious krait refused to be mollified by the fact the jostling it had taken had come to a halt. It coiled and waited for the first object to present itself when the lid was raised.

Patri had waited for Catherine along the path as he often did, but he had grown impatient and had almost decided to go on without her when she finally appeared.

"You were lazy today," he said, chiding her, as he took Michael from her arms and hoisted him on his shoulders.

"You're right. I didn't sleep well last night," she admitted.

After bathing, she would give Patri his lessons before he went off to hunt and play with the other boys. Not only had she taught him to speak and write English, but she had developed phonetic spellings for the sounds of the Iban language as well and was teaching him to write his own language. He had been quick to learn it all, including the math and simple science she had begun to teach him. Old Koh had accepted that his grandson would spend time with Catherine and Michael, but Catherine guessed it would not be long before the jealous and suspicious old man would put an end to the lessons.

They had gone only a short distance down the path when Patri grabbed her arm and, signaling silence, pointed to an overhead tree limb where a cloud leopard leisurely finished the remains of a small deer it had dragged to its refuge. The cat looked at them disdainfully without interrupting its gnawing.

"I didn't even see him," Catherine whispered when they were past.

"But he saw you. He sees everything. My grandfather says

that when he prowls the jungle at night, he can even see into your dreams. Just then he read our thoughts and knew we would not attempt to harm him."

By now they could hear the laughter of the bathers at the river. The communal bath was a social occasion Catherine looked forward to, a time of play for both adults and children. She and Patri were almost within sight when suddenly a background noise intruded upon her awareness. The bathers had heard it, too, for the sound of their laughter and splashing had stopped, replaced by the drone of a machine. Catherine had slowed her pace and now cautiously approached the river. The attention of the bathers was directed downstream. Some of the bathers had now begun to move toward the bank, yet no one seemed alarmed. Catherine took Michael and led Patri off the path. They waited silently in the shelter of the trees, watching the river.

Slowly five canopied boats filled with Japanese soldiers rounded the wide bend of the river and made their way toward the bank where the village bathed. No panic ensued. No one ran away. The villagers came naked out of the river, dripping water, and stood frozen to the spot. Their faces wore nothing more than friendly curiosity. Run! Catherine wanted to scream at them, and yet she herself stayed rooted, unsure of what to do. Perhaps the soldiers would take food and be quickly on their way.

The five boats nudged the bank. She could see the soldiers were nervous, and it occurred to her they might be fleeing enemies farther down the river. They climbed noisily from the boats, swaggering with anxiety. The officer in charge drew closer, and Catherine gasped. He was wearing two heads, one upon his shoulder and the other suspended by the hair from the belt to his coat, bouncing against his hip like a lumpy sack of flesh. Flies already buzzed around it. Julienne! The trophy was Julienne's head. Horrified, she sank to her knees, clutching a frightened Michael, who somehow knew better than to cry.

Old Koh and the officer spoke no common language, but the officer tried to make himself understood by gestures. Koh was proving to be conveniently incapable of understanding, and the officer was becoming increasingly agitated. The Iban men had begun to withdraw slowly up the path, toward their weapons, which were fatally far away. Only a few had brought parangs with them to the river. The Japanese ordered them to halt. Some

477

refused, and suddenly shots rang out, killing the defiant warriors, and the Japanese began quickly to herd the rest of the villagers back toward the longhouse.

It had been their intention to force the villagers to prepare them something to eat and to bring out the jars of *tuak* so that they could numb their fear, but finding the skulls of Japanese soldiers hanging in the longhouse, caps and eyeglasses neatly in place, sent the soldiers into a murderous frenzy fueled by fear. They forced the Iban men to watch while they raped the women and young girls, and then they began to kill them all. Catherine could see the horror through the trunks of the trees. She was spared the sight of what was happening in the galley and apartments, but she was not spared the sounds, nor would she forget them as long as she lived. She fled, taking Patri and Michael with her.

Back in the longhouse the little krait felt its rest rudely disturbed again. Things were thumping and shaking about beyond the confines of the basket. Suddenly it was tossed through the air, causing it to thrash helplessly about in its prison. Its narrow tongue darted out and picked up the disturbing vibrations caused by human laughter and human screams. It had just recovered when gray light and a startled face appeared above it. In a split second it struck the wrist that held the basket, then found itself unceremoniously dumped to the floor, falling past the bloody, staring head tied to the basket holder's waist, to land atop polished black boots. The basket bounced nearby and rolled off to a corner of the room. A pair of knees was sinking toward the little krait and the shiny boots. It did not wait to see if the rest of its tormentor would follow to the floor. In a flash it slithered through the floor slats and dropped down in the midst of frightened, milling pigs. It gained the freedom and safety of the forest just as Catherine reached the river with Patri. They slipped a prao onto the river and headed downstream, where they hoped to find Ahmad's men.

Part Three

Weep for the Divine Land

Across the sea, corpses in the water;
Across the mountain, corpses in the field.
I shall die only for the emperor,
I shall never look back.

"Umi Yukaba," Japanese martial song

Chapter 47

The mission dock came slowly into view along the eastern riverbank, its decrepit gray wood still gamely defying the swift river current. Spunk, Catherine thought. That's what it's got, and that's what I need. Ascertaining that the current would carry her to the dock, she let the boat drift on unassisted. She was in no hurry, and besides, she was too tired to paddle anymore.

She sat staring at the trees passing over her head, almost obscuring the sky with their leaves. A breeze stirred the branches and ruffled Michael's hair where he and Patri lay sleeping in the bow. Catherine rubbed her neck. Her head ached from the tension of the past three days. Since she had fled that carnage in the Iban village, she had been traveling mainly at night to avoid any Japanese patrols. Today she had not stopped to sleep at all but had continued downstream with the current, occasionally paddling but mostly just drifting. She was weary of sleeping in the boat. And hungry. If Father O'Malley were still there, and the fact that she had seen no patrols or signs of Japanese activity for the past day encouraged her to hope he was, then she would stay there until Ahmad would find her. If not, she would find another village, farther inland, away from the river and Japanese patrols.

She was close enough now to see that it was quiet around the dock. No native children played there or around the huts, and Catherine realized that the priest was gone, probably taken prisoner long ago. Without the missionaries dispensing food and medicine along with lessons in salvation, the native population had slowly drifted away. No boats stood along the dock, which was dilapidated and in danger of collapsing into the river. Catherine ventured out onto it only after carefully testing each plank. The ruins of the small seaplane Ahmad had destroyed were now hidden completely by the river and the jungle banks. Well, she thought, at least they would have shelter tonight in case it rained. She was too numb to feel disappointment. That would come later.

She tied the prao and lifted Michael, still sleeping, onto her shoulder. She gently roused Patri and guided him toward the small group of vacant huts. She picked the old dispensary, it being the hut in best condition. Its frame door was covered with a screen made useless by the holes that now gaped in it. It creaked in protest when she opened it. The spring was worn and stretched but still sound enough to close with a thump behind her, causing monkeys to scold and screech from the surrounding trees. She passed through the front room into the tiny back room, where dusty mats still lay across the floor. Too exhausted to look for a better spot, she laid herself and the children down and immediately went to sleep.

She was awakened sometime later by the sound of the screen door, banging. Startled, she rose and cautiously peered into the front room. The room appeared empty. Realizing it must have been the wind, she lay back upon the mat. She had barely closed her eyes when she heard another sound, a soft, scraping noise, like the sound of a shoe upon the hard earth floor. Alarmed, she rolled over and stared again at the door that opened to the front room. The screen door slapped and banged in the growing breeze. A storm was coming. Huge dark monsoon clouds were building, hiding the sun and bringing an early end to the day. She guessed that the sounds had been caused by the wind. The whole hut was beginning to creak and moan.

She rose and crossed the front room to lock the rusty hook on the screen. It stopped slamming. Satisfied, she looked out at the clearing. Shafts of fallen brown palm fronds blew along the ground. The monkeys were quiet now, but it was going to be a noisy night. She reassured herself that she had tied the prao securely, and then she turned back into the room.

The three of them stood in the shadows at the back of the room, quietly observing her without moving. Her first reaction was indignation that they had surprised her. It was quickly replaced by fear. She had never seen them so close before. They wore ill-fitting uniforms, woolen caps, coarse woolen puttees wrapped around their legs, and canvas rubber-soled boots. There were bayonets, like samurai swords, on the ends of their rifles. Their surprise on seeing her come out of the back room and cross to the door had been quickly replaced by triumph.

One of them motioned her into a corner while another entered the back room. He emerged shortly, carrying a drowsy, protesting Michael and pointing excitedly at his blond hair. Patri was pulled sleepily behind him. It was clear that they had initially mistaken her for Malay or Iban, but now that they had found Michael, they were no longer sure. She might still be mistaken for a native servant. If they thought she was Malay, she would probably be raped and let go, but if they thought she was Occidental, she would probably be raped and killed. She spoke to them in Malay and hoped for the best. There was confusion because no one spoke or understood Malay. She was afraid to try Iban since the Iban were generally viewed as their enemies.

They had reached an impasse, broken finally by the arrival of the officer in charge and two more men, walking purposefully from the direction of the dock. They must have cut their engines before they came within hearing range, Catherine concluded. No doubt they had seen her boat and had come to investigate. She cursed her own carelessness in not concealing it better.

The lieutenant in charge had her stand in the light of the doorway while he circled her. She tried to talk to him in Malay, but he ordered her to be silent. Finally the fillings in her teeth gave her away.

"She is European or American!" he said triumphantly, sucking in his breath in a sharp hiss. Then he abruptly slapped her.

"Do not try to deceive us any further," he said in heavily accented English. "It is a serious crime to have avoided surrender. All foreigners were ordered to surrender to Japanese authorities a year ago."

"I have been alone and isolated. I didn't know." She was lying, and they knew she was lying, but to have admitted otherwise would have forced them to execute her.

"American?" he asked.

Catherine nodded.

"American, you come with us."

They were one week getting to the coast, but they didn't mistreat her further. One of the men had even given her his month's wages.

"Take it," he had said. "I have no family, and you can use it to buy food for the children."

On the coast they had turned her over to Japanese naval authorities. The lieutenent's last crisp words to her were: "You go to Teram Island prison camp now." It was the first time he had spoken to her since the day of her capture. The experience had helped allay her fears of what might be in store for her on Teram. She could not have been more misled.

After three days at sea Catherine was taken ashore at Cape George, capital of the southwest residency of British North Borneo. Before the war the small coastal capital of Cape George had contained eighty European men, women, and children, mostly British colonial civil servants and their families, as well as a mixture of Asians and the native Malay and Dyak populations. The Japanese had occupied Cape George on the morning of January 19, 1942, coming by launch through heavy seas some 200 miles from the Philippine island of Mindanao. During the first four months of occupation they had let many of the European men continue on in critical positions, though they were beaten and threatened, and their homes were constantly looted. In May 1942 the Europeans were abruptly ordered to Teram Island, a few miles off the coast of Cape George, where the men and women were separately interned. Inexplicably, members of the opposite sex were denied any further contact with one another. Even passing glances between men and women were severely punished.

Catherine spent the night with Michael and Patri, locked in the storage room of a Japanese launch with supplies destined for the morning trip to Teram. In the morning the fear of imprisonment finally began to overcome her. She could barely swallow the small rice cake they gave her for breakfast, so she gave it to the children, both of whom, she was relieved to note, had ravenous appetites. Well, Catherine, she admonished herself. Get yourself together. You're on your own now. So make the best of it.

Besides Catherine and the children, the tiny motor launch was carrying supplies, soldiers for the weekly rotation of the eight island guards, and Lieutenant Takahashi, the commanding officer of the Teram prison camp. The weekly guard change was practically the only time that Lieutenant Takahashi made an appearance on Teram. He preferred Cape George with its brothels. Japanese regulations strictly forbade soldiers to molest or to be otherwise sexually involved with their female prisoners, the regulation being based on the practical consideration that much-needed war supplies might be lavished away on female prisoners in exchange for sexual favors. The restrictions forced no sacrifice on Lieutenant Takahashi. He did not find Western women attractive. They were too tall and their figures too heavy or full to suit his taste.

This one today, though, almost made him reconsider. She was slender; her features were delicate. Too tall, of course, but still . . . He studied her face, wondering if she might be worth the risk. Her black hair streamed back in the sea wind, damp with the spray tossed up by the waves that occasionally surged over the bow as the tiny boat knifed its way through the stormy sea. A sudden jolt as they hit a wave abruptly took his mind off her. He hated the sea. The launch was too small for ocean journeys, even short ones, and he could not swim. Water terrified him. He grippped the side of the boat tightly as if the pressure could get both his fears and his stomach under control. The swells were getting worse, tossed up by some distant, unseen tropical storm. Once he got to shore, he would dispose of his fears and annoyance by thrashing whoever was handy. The prisoners on Teram had learned to predict Lieutenant Takahashi's disposition each week from the heaviness of the sea. He would beat the guards, who would, in turn, take their anger out by beating the prisoners, who, having nowhere else in the pecking order to go, would then take it out on each other. On a bad day Lieutenant Takahashi's anger got widely spread about.

Teram was coming into view on the choppy horizon. To Catherine it appeared to be bobbing and swaying dizzily before them. God! She hoped it was more firmly anchored than the bouncing boat. Between swells she could make out a small landing dock, sandy beaches, and palm trees. No visible buildings, or barbed wire either, for that matter. It had a deceptively pleasant appearance, seen from the ocean: When Catherine set foot upon the dock of Teram, her steps were unsteady, as if she had not left the rolling sea behind.

Chapter 48

Lieutenant Takahashi had been throughly shaken by the voyage. He had been sure they were near capsizing before they reached the dock. Once he was safely landed, he cuffed the helmsman, but that did little to alleviate his anger. The stench of the camp greeted him. Only recently he had given the prisoners permission to empty the latrine buckets in the sea a half mile from the camp. He hated the camp almost as much as he hated the sea. It not only stank, but was filled with rats, lice, and bedbugs, and the silent insolence of the prisoners. Worst of all, it was not an honorable assignment for a career military officer.

Like so many men from poor Japanese families, Lieutenant Takahashi had chosen a military career as a means of improving his prospects. In a still essentially feudal society where status was permanently defined by birth, the military was one of the few respectable means to rise above one's station. Within that proper order of things Lieutenant Takahashi was ambitious to prove himself and gain recognition and honor. The Army had become the tool of zealots who wished to rid Japanese society of corruption and reaffirm Japan's proper place in the Asian order of things. Lieutenant Takahashi was a fervent believer in that order. As a young man he had qualified for training at the Japanese military academy and had endured the physical abuse that was part of the procedure visited on lowerclassmen by upperclassmen.

It was a far more cruel and severe process than the hazing undergone in American military institutions, and he had, in his turn, readily inflicted the same beatings on those who came after him. The experience, like his childhood, had left him a volatile and potentially explosive man.

Upon graduation from the academy in 1937 Lieutenant Takahashi had been sent to China with the Japanese Army in an expedition that was supposed to have culminated in a Japanese victory within three months but that had, in fact, ended in a futile campaign which drained Japanese manpower and resources. The frustration of that effort had been vented on helpless civilians, who had been murdered by the hundreds of thousands. That humiliation had been erased by Pearl Harbor and the incredibly swift Japanese victories in the Philippines, Malaya, and Indonesia. Lieutenant Takahashi had been transferred from China to the Philippine invasion force and had distinguished himself in battle on Bataan. To his bitterness, he found himself rewarded with the command of the Teram Island civilian prison camp instead of the military post on New Guinea he wanted—all because he had spent a year of his training at Sandhurst, the British military academy, and spoke passable English as a result.

Today Catherine was the handy target for Lieutenant Takahashi's frustration. Upon reaching the camp, he mustered her to attention before his office and addressed her as if she were an assembled army, shouting himself hoarse. She felt mildly embarrassed, standing there alone before him, Michael asleep in her arms and Patri bored and yawning beside her.

"You are now a prisoner of the great Imperial Japanese Army. You are a citizen of a fourth-class country. America is a fourth-class country. You are no better than a coolie. You will be treated as such. Japan is a very benevolent country. You are lucky to be prisoner of such a country. You must rid yourself of arrogance, or we will beat you up and maybe kill you. Japan number one. America number ten!"

Arms flailing, he was clearly working himself into a frenzy. Catherine was astonished to see saliva begin to dribble from the corners of his mouth. She stared at him in fascination, no longer hearing what he was saying, totally absorbed in the sight of someone enraged enough to be actually frothing at the mouth. With the midmorning heat beating freely upon her and Michael growing increasingly heavy in her arms, she soon ceased to be aware of him at all. Her thoughts drifted instead to mountains and streams and freedom and Ahmad. She wondered if he knew or would ever know what had happened to her.

She was still standing quietly an hour later. Her arms ached from the weight of Michael, but she was grateful he was asleep. Patri had wandered off and was curled up asleep under the shade of a nearby tree. Lieutenant Takahashi's eyes were glazed, and he was in the process of shouting himself into a final catharsis. His eyes began to focus on his surroundings, and he became aware of her still standing before him, no visible signs of the heat or exhaustion reflected in her posture, though he knew she must be suffering from both. She was staring directly at him now. It was a proud stare, he thought. Unintimidated. But there was no smirk or insolence in it either. No lack of respect. She was different, this one. He did not know quite what to make of her. He stared at her silently for a few moments and then dismissed her with a wave of his arms.

Catherine was given a mat, a cup, a bowl, and some mosquito netting and escorted to the women's enclosure. It consisted of a dilapidated barracks building with a decaying palm-frond roof enclosed by wooden walls at the sides and barbed wire front and back. The stench was incredible. Teram Island, which had belonged to the Dutch, had once been the site of a Dutch prison camp for Indonesian political prisoners. It seemed poetic justice to Catherine that the prison camp now housed white colonial prisoners. It was unfit for human habitation then and now. The women's barracks now contained twenty-four women and eleven young children. Each woman was assigned a four- by six-foot living space. Despite Catherine's protests, Patri was considered too old for the women's compound and was sent to join the men.

The Ladies of Cape George, as Catherine would come to think of them, sat sullenly around the barracks floor, eating their rice lunch. No one spoke to her or offered her food. Catherine realized that to them she meant two more mouths to feed from an already inadequate food supply and another space to clear in already overcrowded conditions. She sympathized with their reluctance to accept her; it was her first and most enduring impression of the Ladies of Cape George.

She introduced herself to them as Catherine Morgan Stanford, anthropologist and wife of Michael Stanford, in the same way she had presented herself to the Japanese. It was a calculated risk on her part. The Stanfords were a famous British family, and these were British subjects. They would know the Stanfords by reputation, but she was gambling that no one would know them personally. She had decided to take this risk to protect little Michael and herself: She wanted her son to have Michael's name, and she knew Michael would have wanted that if he were still alive; she also knew that to have an illegitimate child would jeopardize her safety with the Japanese. She would be considered a woman without honor and easy prey for sexual advances, perhaps even a candidate for the Cape George brothel. So she had made herself respectable—eminently respectable, as Michael Stanford's widow. If anyone knew or remembered that Mrs. Michael Stanford was Dutch, she didn't care to say.

It was immediately clear to Catherine that the Ladies of Cape George had not been emotionally prepared for captivity. Colonial service had been exceedingly kind to them; most of them had never cooked a meal or washed clothes or changed diapers or planted flowers or cleaned anything except themselves. They had always had armies of native servants to tend them and their houses and their gardens and their children. Social leadership among the Ladies had been based upon the status of their husbands, rather than on any talents or leadership abilities of their own. In prison they had instinctively tried to hold together their old prewar social system in order to maintain some sense of identity under the stress of captivity. Grace Winfield-Holmes, the wife of the Resident, had presided adequately, even admirably, over teas, garden parties, dinner parties, etc. However, these skills were of little use in Teram. In the old order of things she was the acknowledged head of society, but she was totally unfit to organize and lead in the present circumstances.

Out of inertia or fear, no one filled the vacuum of leadership. Instead, the women quarreled and fought among themselves over food, space, and workload. What they were undergoing was not unlike the cultural shock experienced by primitive societies coming into constant contact with Western technology: It was the disintegration of a social system with nothing to replace it. The result was apathy and depression. Not since leaving her own family had Catherine been around women like these—women whose whole lives revolved around husband and children. They frightened her. In more than a year of internment the Ladies of Cape George had made no improvements in their living conditions. Indeed, their situation had deteriorated considerably. The men, however, had been quite resourceful, patching their own palm-frond roofs until they no longer leaked and smuggling various useful odds and ends past Japanese inspection each time they went out on a work crew. They had ingeniously rigged themselves a shower made of bamboo pipes, made sweep brooms from the hard spine of the palm fronds and toothbrushes from the outside fibers of coconuts. They made soap from palm oil and potash, and used urine as an acid coagulate to make latex from rubber trees, which they then used to make new shoes and repair old ones. They planted gardens and fertilized them with their own human waste, and they held classes in whatever skills and interests they had formerly possessed from Borneo flora to medieval history. Their prize accomplishment, however, was a radio they had made and hidden carefully away, which kept them in touch with the news from Perth, Australia, and sometimes San Francisco. The men shared whatever they could with their wives, but it was very little since contact between them was so strictly forbidden.

Her first night in camp Catherine learned that the barracks roof leaked profusely, especially over the spot that her obliging fellow prisoners had cleared for her. After huddling with Michael in a dry corner all night, she got up early the next morning and made her own repairs, using palm fronds from the compound and a ladder, which she crudely but effectively made by lashing together pieces of wood and tree limbs with vines that trailed along the fence. It was characteristic of her fellow prisoners that rather than repair the leaks, they had adjusted their living arrangements to avoid them instead.

Catherine quickly fell into the routine of camp life. Like the army, prison was a form of institutionalization; only there was no relief from it. They were mustered before the barracks by the guards each morning at seven. They bowed low during roll call and inspection and then stood at attention for the day's orders and propaganda pronouncements about recent Japanese victories.

Their diet, like the camp routine, was monotonous: rice and tea in buckets three times a day. The tea bucket contained cockroaches and other assorted bugs floating among the tea leaves, and the rice was no better. Catherine tried to view the bugs as a bonus of protein. The rice was what the Chinese referred to as Number Four, the sweepings from the floor after the good rice is packaged. Like all refined rice, it contained few vitamins. The Japanese sometimes added bits of salty shrimp and *kang-kong*, a locally grown cousin to spinach with the consistency of a rubber inner tube and the taste of iron.

The Geneva Convention on the treatment of prisoners forbade forced labor, but Japanese easily got around it by cutting in half the rations of those who refused to work, on the ground that they needed less. The result was effective. Everyone who was able chose to work. For the women, the morning work outside the prison compound consisted of cleaning the dock and beaches of driftwood and seaweed, cutting the weeds and tall grasses that surrounded the perimeter of the camp, and, the duty they hated the most, cleaning the guards' quarters. That unpleasant task was accompanied by pinches and lewd remarks illustrated by universally understood gestures so there was no mistaking their meaning.

The first day in camp Catherine wondered how it was that the women had managed to survive this long without apparent weight loss and vitamin deficiency. The second day she found out. After a morning of work followed by the usual lunch there was a rest period until tea at three. The heat at midday was unbearable. Catherine put Michael down for a nap and went to the water storage room to dip herself a shower. She returned to the barracks to find that the women had been joined by the guards. Provided that Lieutenant Takahashi wasn't around, it was, she learned, a daily occurence. After lunch each day the guards would lounge around the women's quarters, dressed in the small white G-string that served as underwear or wearing nothing at all. They would start by showing off before the women, performing acrobatic feats or engaging in karate and judo exercises. But the ending was always the same. Eventually they would each demand to share a mat with someone, and they were always grudgingly accommodated. The coercion was the threat of slow starvation, for the women *and* their children. The reward was the food that supplemented the guards' own rice diet, the bananas, papayas, vegetables, and fish that were dispensed to everyone in the woman's barracks as payment for either sex or silence.

It wasn't rape. It certainly wasn't love. It was sweating,

thumping, grunting bodies straining to conclusion. Like bad pornography, it wasn't even interesting to watch. If any of the women put up a struggle or protested, they were ignored by the other women, who turned their backs and went to sleep, grateful that this day, at least, it wasn't their turn. Good God, Catherine muttered, this *is* the Cape George brothel.

Michael lay sleeping peacefully under the mosquito net. Catherine decided to leave him rather than venture farther into the room. As she turned to leave, a guard not yet occupied reached up and grabbed her by the arm, indicating he would like a frontal massage. She shoved him aside as hard as she could, sending him tumbling back against the floor. As she quickly left the room, she was relieved to hear him laugh. One of the other guards consoled him.

One thing was clear. She was going to have to supplement their diet herself. She decided to spend her rest and recreation hour each day planting a garden. She obtained some sweet potato cuttings from the men's compound at the price of a rifle butt between her shoulder blades from the guard as she paused at the fence to make the request on her way to empty the latrine buckets into the sea. She smiled to herself, thinking it was a small price compared to the one paid by the other women. When she returned with the empty buckets, the cuttings were waiting in the middle of the road in front of the men's compound, wrapped in a small wet newspaper packet.

"Good luck," a cheery English voice called after her as she scooped them up and hurried down the road.

After lunch, in the heat of each day, she worked on the garden in a corner of the compound, while Michael napped in the shade of a tree or blew balloons from the pink bracelets of young rubber leaves as he had seen the older Iban children do. Lieutenant Takahashi made his weekly visit, saw the garden, nodded his silent approval, and left. A few days later the green sprouts were rapidly flourishing.

Near the end of the second week of imprisonment she returned to the barracks after lunch to discover her garden had been trampled. She was filled with rage. It had been either the women or the guards. She put Michael down and stormed inside, shaking with anger. She glared at the sight of the lounging guards and women, and seeking out Kusaka, the guard in charge, she demanded to know what had happened to her garden.

He shrugged and smiled. "Maybe elephant trample." Someone snickered.

"You destroyed it," she insisted.

"No like gardens here!" He was no longer smiling. His eyes looked sharp and dangerous, and Catherine suddenly realized how foolish she had been to come in here. She could do nothing now but see it through.

"Lieutenant Takahashi gave me permission, and you had no right to destroy it."

Kusaka rose and stood before her, his naked body shiny in the heat.

"You no have garden, now you have to stay here with us. Japanese soldiers can be very kind. You see. But if you not good, we will beat and maybe kill you!"

One of the other guards seized her from behind, pinning her arms behind her. Because he had been trained in the martial arts, his grip was strong and unbreakable. The room suddenly fell silent. Instead of turning away, as they had always done before, the women stopped whatever they were doing and stared at the scene before them. No doubt, Catherine thought bitterly, they would be glad to see her get her comeuppance.

Kusaka continued to stare at her for a moment and then reached down and slowly began to draw his hand up the inside of her thigh under her sarong. His own organ began to extend itself in anticipation, and a smile turned the corners of his mouth.

She steeled herself against the violation and spoke to him for the first time in the impeccable Japanese Michael had taught her during their months with the Wali Dani.

"Take your hand away from me. You will not touch me now or ever again."

She took the guards completely by surprise. None of the Europeans they had ever come in contact with, let alone a mere woman, could speak Japanese. Kusaka dropped his hand. She took advantage of his hesitation to slip free and back toward the door. She grabbed Michael up and retreated to the barbed-wire fence near the gate. She stood for ten minutes, staring at the door, but no one came after her. Finally she sank to her knees and began to tremble as she remembered that other time and place when she had not been so lucky. She leaned over to retch while Michael whimpered against her.

Lieutenant Takahashi arrived the next day, and the prisoners were mustered for his inspection. When he stood before Catherine, she bowed and then rose to look him in the eye.

"I have a complaint to make."

He gaped at her in astonishment.

"Yes. So?" He looked at her warily as if she had just announced she had a contagious disease. Indeed, complaints might become epidemic if he did not quickly eliminate either them or the complainer.

"One of the guards tried to rape me yesterday."

Lieutenant Takahashi was astonished, not so much by the attempted rape but by the fact she would dare complain about it.

"That is a very serious charge to make. Who was the guard?" he demanded.

"It doesn't matter. He needn't be singled out. He is one of many who sexually abuse the women here on a daily basis. He is no more guilty than the rest."

Lieutenant Takahashi was angry now and a little bit afraid. It began to dawn on him that helpless prisoners could make problems for him after all. If the complaint came to the attention of the high command, it might become aware of the fact that he spent very little time at his post, a neglect of his command that could ruin his career.

"Were there witnesses who can confirm your story?"

She nodded. "The other women. They are not only witnesses but constant victims."

He began to pace before them.

"All right. Who was witness to this act?"

No one spoke. He stared back at the rows of women and felt a wave of relief as he began to recognize that he could count on their silence.

"There!" he said with triumph. "You were lying. It is very serious offense to insult the honor of the Japanese soldier. However, you may withdraw your complaint with apologies, and nothing more will be said."

"I am not lying, and I will not withdraw my complaint."

The triumph faded from his face and was replaced with disbelief. Convinced she meant it, he glared at her for a moment, then turned and stalked away, failing to dismiss them. They stood uneasily about for a while and then began to drift back to the barracks.

"You should have kept your mouth shut!" one of them said angrily.

"You're only making trouble for everyone!" said another.

"Now we won't have any extra food to eat for the children or ourselves. I hope you're satisfied," added a third.

She was summoned to the office later that afternoon. Lieutenant Takahashi sat at his desk, a sheet of paper before him. He left her standing in front of the desk.

"I hope you have had time to think this over, Mrs. Stanford. I have drawn up a confession that the charges you made were false. Sign it, and you will not be punished for your accusations beyond this reprimand."

Catherine took the piece of paper and glanced over it. It stated that she had made the charges out of anger for extra guardhouse cleaning duty.

"This isn't true, and I refuse to sign it. Prisoners, including myself, have been sexually mistreated here in clear violation of the Geneva Convention."

"You are a long way from Geneva, Mrs. Stanford."

"Nevertheless, I will not sign this or any other confession."

Lieutenant Takahashi was clearly angry. "If these charges are true, then why haven't I heard of it before this?"

"I cannot speak for the others. Perhaps they were afraid to complain."

"Afraid? We treat you kindly. What is there to fear? You must tell me the name of the guard."

"No. I don't want to see him singled out for punishment. I only want you to stop what is going on here. I know you are a man of goodwill." A little flattery might appeal to his better instincts, she thought ruefully.

"There was no guard, and there are no complaints because there are no abuses!" He was screaming by now. "You are lying, and you will confess!"

She shook her head calmly, but inwardly she was becoming alarmed.

"You will think it over for a moment." He got up, rolled up

the paper, and strode from the room. A sergeant Catherine had never seen before stepped into the room, ordered her to stand at attention and then signaled to the guard who had accompanied her from the compound to leave. The sergeant then came over, struck her hard across the face, followed by a blow to the back of her legs with his rifle so that her knees buckled and she fell to the floor. He then began to kick her as hard as he could. She felt shame for her weakness, but she could not stop her cries of pain. She rolled into a ball and put her arms over her head in an attempt to protect herself. She felt the warm taste of blood in her mouth. He finally stopped and she heard him leave the room. She lay still for several minutes, then slowly rose and, trembling, sat in a chair. She was determined they would not find her helpless and crying on the floor. She tried to pull herself together, at least outwardly, by smoothing her hair and rearranging the folds of her sarong, aware of the acute pain that now throbbed in her ribs.

Lieutenant Takahashi reappeared, the rolled confession in his hand, touching it rhythmically to his palm.

"It is very serious matter to accuse a Japanese soldier of misconduct. Perhaps you have had time to think it over and wish to withdraw the complaint."

She looked at the floor and said calmly, "I cannot withdraw it. I told the truth. I will sign nothing."

"Very well. You will return to camp and say nothing of what has happened to you here today. Your complaint will be formally registered, but the investigation will show no witnesses corroborated your story and you are discredited. So you see, it was all for nothing, Mrs. Stanford. A pity, really." He took out a cigarette and offered her one. She shook her head. He lit his own and came to stand before her.

His face was grim, angry. She could sense that he was afraid. He reached out and touched her shoulder. It was like a caress, lingering, soft. He reached to the knot that held her sarong to her shoulder and undid it, and it slipped to her waist. His eyes went to her breasts and then slowly rose to meet hers. He smiled grimly, taking the cigarette from his mouth and holding its orange tip before her.

"You will say nothing of what has happened here to anyone or this will happen to you again." He brought the cigarette to the nipple of her breast. She gasped but managed to swallow her scream. Then he brought it to her other breast, and she could hold back no longer. When her scream had died, he said, "They are lovely. I would hate to ruin them. But if you dare to talk of this, I will." And he plunged the cigarette once more into her soft flesh, this time pressing hard enough that it was fully extinguished. She gasped and sobbed as he turned and left her, ordering the guard to return her to the barracks.

She took Michael from the guard at the gate and went gratefully to her mat. She excused herself from the work detail the next few days on the basis that she had fallen and injured herself. Guards and women alike left her alone. The pain told her her ribs were cracked, but she didn't dare ask for treatment from the European doctors and nuns who had been left in Cape George to run the hospital. They would surely protest her injuries to the military command of the area, and Takahashi's rage would know no bounds.

Still, the moment was not without triumph. Lieutenant Takahashi had all the guards severely beaten. They, in turn, took it out on the prisoners, and there was more than the usual batch of slaps and kicks and beatings, but the guards no longer came to lounge among the women after lunch. As soon as Catherine was able to get around again in spite of the pain in her ribs, she discovered a new source of fruits and vegetables; the natives from the island and Cape George who brought food to the Japanese were more than happy to barter with the prisoners through the barbed wire when the guards weren't looking. Catherine used the money she had been given by the Japanese soldier who had captured her. The other women traded clothing and other items from the suitcase each had been allowed to bring. Many of them had brought dress clothes they could not bear to part with at the time. These, along with cosmetics and jewelry, were traded for food. As soon as she was better, Catherine was determined to begin a new garden.

A week after her trip to Takahashi's office Michael woke up with a soaring fever and a case of malignant tertian malaria, which could become cerebral malaria, leading to madness and eventual death. There was no quinine available on the island. So Catherine bathed him to try to reduce his fever, but several hours later she began to get a fever herself. Evidently the malaria-

497

bearing mosquito had bitten them both. Finally Michael went into convulsions, and the guards were summoned. Catherine found herself slipping into unconsciousness, only dimly aware that they were both being put aboard a launch for the long trip to the Cape George hospital.

After they arrived at Sandakan, and when she was conscious enough to be aware of her surroundings, Catherine insisted that her supply of quinine go to meet Michael's needs first. Since quinine was in short supply, even in the hospital, the Dutch and British nuns who cared for the sick reluctantly agreed. Under their diligent care she gradually began to improve. She became aware of the kindness of the Japanese soldiers in the hospital, who carried Michael on walks once he was feeling better and brought him postcard pictures of Japan and treats to eat. Eventually she felt well enough to become interested in the hospital gossip. She learned that Lieutenant Takahashi had just been treated for his latest bout with venereal disease. Serves him right, she thought with satisfaction.

One night she was awakened by Sister Beatrice. The young nun was holding a candle and quietly pulling the white curtains around the bed for privacy. When Catherine started to question her, she put her fingers to her lips and set the candle upon the bed table. She pulled aside the mosquito net and leaned over to whisper to Catherine. Her dark eyes were warm, and she wore a smile.

"You have a visitor."

She pressed a finger lightly against Catherine's lips. Then she withdrew for several moments. When she returned and pulled the curtain aside, Ahmad stepped through it, dressed in the white pants and the white open-necked shirt of a Cape George dockworker.

He gave her hand a squeeze and leaned down to kiss her. His lips felt soft and cool upon her own. They stirred her carefully anchored feelings, and her arms reached up around his neck and pulled him to her with what little strength she had.

"Oh, Ahmad," she whispered in his ear, "I have missed you so. I was afraid you wouldn't come!" Tears ran freely down her cheeks.

Gently he encircled her with his arms to hold her close to him, but even that careful pressure caused her to wince. He lowered

498

her to the bed and, hands braced on either side of her, looked questioningly at her. Her eyes brimmed with tears of pain.

"What is it?" he asked, concern in his voice.

"I fell and bruised my ribs," she lied.

Not satisfied, he untied the string of the white hospital gown from behind her neck and gently opened it to the waist, exposing the ugly black bruises and the healing red marks of the burns upon her breasts. A slight flicker in his eyes was his only change in expression.

"Who did this?"

This time she did not hold back the truth. She knew there was no avoiding it, although she tried to emphasize how things had improved in terms of the guards' behavior. Ahmad said nothing. He slipped her gown back to her shoulders and gently tied it around her neck.

"I will have Sister Beatrice bind your ribs with elastic support to ease your pain. You can trust her not to say anything about it. Her order is from Banjarmasin, and I am well known to her." He silently studied her face in the candlelight as if trying to absorb her image in order to take it with him. Then he kissed her lightly on the forehead. He rose.

They looked at each other in silence for a moment, and then he spoke. "I had better go." His eyes were dark, unreadable. "I'll return to see you and when you're stronger, I'll take you away from here. There are no guards. It will not be difficult." And then he was gone.

Moments later Sister Beatrice entered and gave Catherine the quinine Ahmad had brought. Then she bound her ribs in a wide elastic band.

"There. That should help." Then sympathetically: "You should have told me. Poor child!"

She got up and pulled the curtains back, then removed the candle from the bedside. She looked around to make sure no evidence of the visit remained behind. The extra quinine she took with her to dispense later.

"There," she said with satisfaction. "Rest well." She hesitated and turned back, her dark eyes shining in her youthful face.

"He is a splendid man!" she said, and then flushed at the enthusiasm she had displayed.

"Yes, he is," Catherine replied, and Sister Beatrice blew the candle out, leaving them both to their private thoughts.

By noon the next day the hospital was full of excited whispers. "Lieutenant Takahashi is dead," one of the Malay nursing aides announced to the ward. "He was murdered last night." She gestured with her finger, drawing an arc from one end of her throat to another. "There were guards posted around the house where he stayed, one of the European houses on the hill overlooking the town and the harbor, yet someone killed him in his sleep. They say it might even have been the guards themselves—seeking revenge for their humiliations at his hands."

"Or maybe it was one of his bed partners," the Chinese woman volunteered.

"She already got her revenge." The young aide giggled, referring to his most recent treatment.

Catherine remained silent during the exchange, chilled by fear. There were many people with a motive, but she was certain that the man who had killed Takahashi was Ahmad. No one else would have dared.

Two days later the new Teram prison commander had appeared on the scene, Captain Kato. Like Lieutenant Takahashi, he was an army fanatic who had fought in the battle for Singapore. He had also helped run Singapore's infamous Changi prison before being transferred to Cape George. He immediately made a tour of the hospital to rid it of its prisoner patients, whether they were able to walk or not. It was evidently part of his bid to be taken seriously as a tough man who would tolerate no laziness or malingering. When he reached Catherine's ward, followed by a sergeant and corporal, he demanded to know her name.

"Catherine Stanford," she replied.

He checked the list he carried with him.

"Mrs. Michael Stanford?"

"Yes."

He looked at her closely as if suddenly interested.

"Michael Stanford, the antropologist, son of Sir Charles Stanford?"

"Yes." No inkling as to why he was interested. Perhaps the Stanfords were known to him.

"What is your illness?"

"Malaria."

"And the boy?"

"Malaria also."

He nodded and then spoke to his men in Japanese. All three left the ward. She breathed a sigh of relief. She had not been ordered to leave the hospital.

The same day, without warning, one of the Eurasian nurse's aides came into the ward and whisked Michael up to take him to what she called a special children's ward. Shocked, Catherine protested vehemently, asking why it was suddenly necessary after all this time.

"Captain Kato's orders. You'll rest better without him to care for. You'll get well faster, and then you'll have him with you."

It was true that much of Michael's care had fallen on her hands in the understaffed hospital, but she did not believe the explanation.

"I must talk with Captain Kato at once."

"Captain Kato said to tell you he is very firm about this. Protests no good." Then, sympathetically: "I will take good care of your son, Mrs. Stanford. No need to worry. When you are well, your son will go back with you to camp."

The nurse's aide placated Michael with candy and carried him off while he was too distracted to realize what was happening.

Catherine was sick with fear. She sent for Sister Beatrice, and the young nun promised to find out what she could of what had happened to Michael. A few hours later she had been able to learn only that he was no longer in the hospital. That night Catherine lay awake in the darkened ward. She had finally dropped off into a fitful sleep when Sister Beatrice arrived carrying a candle, her hand shielding it so that it cast shadows on her face. She sat it by the bedside and gently shook Catherine awake.

"He is here," she said simply, and then pulled the curtains about the bed and disappeared. Ahmad entered and crossed to her bed, gently taking her hand into his. Again the dark eyes studied her.

"You are looking better today. Stronger."

"They have taken Michael."

He nodded wearily. "I know."

"But why?"

"A number of reasons, not the least of them being that they

501

know you will make no effort to escape without him. They have few guards here. They know that there is increased guerrilla activity in the area and that the guerrilla leader is a close personal friend of the Stanfords." He gave a grim smile. "I suspect it is a precaution, as it turned out, a very wise one. He is now in protective custody until they can return you to the enclosure."

He gripped her hand harder. "There is the additional possibility that they may want to hold him hostage against me if they know how close we are."

"Oh, God. What will we do if that happens?"

"I think it's unlikely that they will realize what you and Michael mean to me. Let's hope they don't find out."

He leaned forward and kissed her lightly on the forehead.

"Michael will probably be returned to you at Teram where there is less chance for you to escape. I will come to you there, along with the local people who bring the food." He was gone before she could ask him if he had killed Takahashi.

Four days later she was sufficiently recovered to return to the camp. Michael was not returned to her before her departure, nor was he waiting for her at Teram. She asked to see Captain Kato.

"My son was to be returned to me when I was released from the hospital."

"Your son is well cared for, Mrs. Stanford. Not to worry. He will be returned to you shortly."

When she asked exactly how long that would be, she received only evasive answers. Two weeks passed, and she still had no definite word. Ahmad visited the island several times, bringing food, but he had no further news of Michael. She was also becoming alarmed for Ahmad's safety. There had been no arrest for Lieutenant Takahashi's murder, and even among the isolated prisoners rumors circulated that the list of suspects had been expanded to include possible political assassins as well.

She begged Ahmad to return to the mountains.

"Your people need you. You must go. Besides, if anything should happen to you, I couldn't bear it."

He gently touched her fingers on the barbed-wire fence that separated them and spoke to her softly in Malay.

"I cannot leave thee, Catherine." Then he added in English,

"Would you leave me if I were there and you were here and free?"

She couldn't answer him. She knew she did not love Michael any less than before. His loss was a fearsome wound that she could only barely look at and still survive. But in the year and a half since their escape from Java to Borneo she had come to care deeply for Ahmad. Now she wondered aloud, "I wonder how it might have been had it been you I met first that night at Maitreya."

He smiled at her with a tinge of regret. "We of the East rely on the concept of fate to bring us peace of mind. We tell ourselves that fate deems things to happen. By saying it was meant to be, we keep ourselves from agonizing over what might have been." He turned his attention to the business at hand, passing her the fresh eggs, fruits, and vegetables he had brought with him.

"Here, and be sure to eat your share before you distribute any to the others. I'm not risking my ass to fatten up the colonial Ladies of Cape George." She could see that he was only half-teasing.

"I'll make sure the children get it first."

"Good."

"Be careful." It was an awkward good-bye. They were always awkward, and she realized after each time he left that she had not really said what she wanted to.

He did not come again for a week. Nor was Michael returned to her. She became sick with worry for the one and was filled with a growing longing for the other. Catherine realized that she herself had begun to feel alive only in those brief moments with Ahmad at the back fence. The next day he sent word through one of the traders that he would meet her at sunset, after evening bed check. She had been waiting only briefly by the fence when he appeared. This time he had news of Michael. He was being cared for by two Japanese civilian women living in Cape George. He was under heavy guard, and Ahmad had not been able to see him; but he had news that he was well. Catherine felt relief at the news, but they both soon fell silent. The sun was setting in that rapid, spectacular way it has in the tropics. Perhaps it was the time of day that moved them to silence, a melancholy time. She sensed a sadness in him. He spoke briefly of the war news from Europe. The Italian government had overthrown Mussolini and surrendered

503

to the Allies on September 8, 1943, but the war in Italy was being furiously carried on by German troops. She hardly heard what he said, aware only of his physical presence. Before she realized it was happening, he had passed the food to her and was saying good-bye. It occurred to her that perhaps Siah was now in Cape George, and that might account for the distance she felt from him.

"I'll be gone for a while." For her own safety he would not tell her where. "I'll try to bring you food, or send it by someone, before I go. Is there anything you need?"

She clutched the barbed wire with both hands. She could not bear to have him leave her again, and yet she wished him safely away.

His handsome face was suddenly grave again, and she saw the turmoil in his eyes as he stood looking at her. He had only one thing to say, and he could not say it, though his eyes spoke it for him. Finally he whispered, "I cannot go from here. I love you."

His fingers covered hers as he lowered his mouth to kiss her, ignoring the wire that separated them. Their bodies pressed to meet each other until the barbs scratched and tore at them. Finally Ahmad pulled away, trembling, eyes closed, and rested his forehead against one of the strands of wire that tormented them.

Still clinging, white-knuckled, to the fence, Catherine sank to her knees.

"You should leave here for good. They will catch you if you stay in Cape George."

He opened his eyes, knowing that she was right. "I cannot leave you."

She knew it would do little good to argue with him. She pressed her cheek to the wire and stared dully at the road that ran around the camp's perimeter. She felt suddenly tired, the exhaustion of defeat. If they kept on like this, he would be captured and killed. She was certain of it.

"I think of nothing but when I'll see you. It isn't good for me to be this way. I'm becoming like the other women in this camp, thinking only of the man I can't have." Her voice was flat, devoid of feeling. "It would be easier for me, Ahmad, if you would go away." She looked up. His dark eyes were fixed upon her. "And it would help me to bear this if I knew that you, at least, were safe—far away from here—so that when this war is over—'' She could not finish. Tears streamed down her cheeks.

He knelt on one knee before her and, reaching through the wires, took her face in his hands and wiped away the tears.

"Very well," he said huskily, "I will go meet the submarine; but I will be back, and I will bring enough men with me that we can free both you and Michael, whether he has been returned to you or not. Now I must go. The guards will be making their patrol anytime."

He pulled her face toward him and kissed her lightly through the wire. The sky had gone from pink to purple. The light was almost gone. She could barely see him as he disappeared among the trees, heading for his small boat hidden on the shore. She continued to sit unmoving until the darkness completely settled around her, and then she rose and went to the barracks.

She lay on her mat, unable to sleep. Why, she wondered, had she let him leave without telling him she loved him?

Chapter 49

Ahmad had been gone for two weeks, and as he had promised, someone brought her food in his place. Then she was called to the office after lunch one day and presented with her son.

"As you can see, Mrs. Stanford," Captain Kato said, "he has been well cared for."

Catherine felt relieved and angry. "For that I am grateful, but I feel you owe me an explanation for the delay in returning him to Teram."

"We owe you nothing," Kato replied sharply. "You, on the other hand, owe your continued existence to the Japanese Army! The orders to detain your son came from Tokyo. Let us merely say that the presence of a member of the Stanford family in a Japanese prison camp has aroused interest in high places."

He was studying her now. "Don't you have a more suitable dress?"

"Suitable for what?" Catherine asked in exasperation.

"Suitable for a photograph."

He accompanied her back to the barracks, where he had all the women bring forth their best dresses, and he selected a white suit for Catherine to wear. It didn't seem to matter that it was much too large. She was photographed in the suit, holding Michael and a cup of tea in her hands, and was instructed to smile and "look enthusiastic" by a newspaper photographer from Tokyo. She wondered what the caption would say. Perhaps "Happy, well-

treated prisoner enjoys life under benevolent Japanese Army.''
She could only hope that no one well acquainted with the Stanford family would see the photo and recognize an impostor.

Michael clung to her for several days after his release and wouldn't let her out of his sight. He was whiny and irritable, and Catherine decided it was his way of being angry that she had ever allowed it to happen in the first place. In a few days he was his old cheerful self again, the ordeal forgotten, if not totally forgiven.

Life in the camp went on as usual, but the monsoon winds that blew across the island hit a lull, sending the heat soaring. The morning muster was considerably abbreviated. Even the guards seemed to be less interested in ritual obeisance than usual. No one was kicked or hit for failing to bow low enough; they were assembled and counted and quickly dismissed so that the guards could adjourn to the shade. That particular morning it was Catherine's turn to empty the latrine buckets into the ocean. Michael toddled happily beside her, knowing that for him, latrine duty meant a splash in the sea and a hunt for shells, provided, of course, that the guard was in a reasonable mood. They left the compound gate, followed lazily by one of the guards, who kept his distance, no more wanting company than she did.

She averted her eyes as she went by the men's compound, embarrassed by the groups of men that lined the barbed wire to watch her pass. She tried to catch a glimpse of Patri before lowering her eyes, but she did not see him that morning. She sympathized with her audience, but the stares made her uncomfortable.

She had just turned onto the road to the sea when she met a Japanese detail arriving from the launch. The men were shouting with excitement, which brought Captain Kato out onto the office porch. They had thrown some poor sarong-clad Malay to the ground and were forcing him to kneel, forehead pressed to the earth, before the captain, who came down the steps and stood, feet apart, before the prone prisoner.

It was suddenly quiet. Only the incessant flies went buzzing on about their business. Catherine stood transfixed, afraid to move for fear of attracting someone's attention and possible wrath. Her guard had stopped to watch. The captain stood quietly before the prisoner for a moment and then uttered a sharp command in

Japanese to the soldiers. A rifle butt was driven into the prisoner's ribs, and he was forced to rise.

Catherine gave a gasp and dropped one of the buckets she carried, spilling its putrid contents into the fine dirt of the road. She struggled frantically to recover it before she was noticed, but she had only just done so when she was suddenly transformed with horror as Michael, his attention finally caught by the scene, gave a delighted laugh and threw his arms out.

"See," he cried in his childish voice as he moved toward the prisoner.

Catherine had time only to swoop him up awkwardly and hurry up the road. Michael crying indignantly under her arm, the two buckets sloshing from either hand. She was quickly out of sight but not before catching a glimpse of the blood that ran down Ahmad's face and neck from an ugly wound on his head and not before Captain Kato had seen the look on her face of shock and recognition.

By the time she reached the sea her face was drained of color and she was trembling so hard she could hardly empty the buckets. The guard, sensing nothing, ambled down to the sea and sat upon his heels, his back to her, staring northeast along the coastline in the direction of his homeland. Lost in her terror, Catherine was not aware of either him or Michael, who was by now completely out of sorts. His eyes were finally caught by a lovely shell. Delighted with his new treasure, he quickly forgot the source of his unhappiness. But Catherine could not forget. She was sick with fear, for Ahmad and for herself, should anything happen to him.

She had recovered somewhat by the time she had returned to camp. The square was now empty of everything except flies. All was normal, yet she knew that Captain Kato's suspicions had been aroused. She began to rehearse what she would say when the inevitable confrontation took place.

She did not know what Ahmad had been arrested for, but he had been badly beaten, and she knew that it was serious. Nor did she know if Ahmad had seen her in the square or heard Michael call out to him. His eyes had appeared dazed . . . semiconscious. She felt fairly sure neither he nor Captain Kato had heard the little boy's cry. Her greatest fear was that Ahmad would reveal his identity in order to protect her if Captain Kato should threaten to extract information from her.

She was called to the office after lunch by one of the guards. Her stomach turned over at the briskly delivered summons, announced to the entire barracks.

"Mrs. Stanford, you will follow me please."

The other women watched with mild curiosity as she scooped Michael up. Better to take him with her, she thought frantically, as if his presence might offer some protection. After all, she reminded herself, the Japanese had sentimental feelings about mothers and children. Lieutenant Takahashi had once said so.

Captain Kato was seated behind his desk, looking stern and foreboding. She bowed low before him. This was no time to offend him.

"Mrs. Stanford." He made it a statement as he placed his forefingers and thumbs carefully together and peered at her through the triangle they formed. A few more seconds of silence, and then he suddenly rose from his chair and came around to lean one leg on the edge of the desk in front of her. She noticed that his boots were carefully polished and fitted him well, unusual from what she had seen of the Japanese Army. He was small and fastidious and gave off the pleasant aroma of scented soap.

"Mrs. Stanford," he began again, "your behavior this morning in the square when you caught sight of the Malay prisoner indicated that you knew the man. Is that so?"

Catherine felt her stomach sink, and she attempted to keep her voice calm.

"I thought at first I recognized him. He resembles one of the servants at the Stanford plantation. But then I realized I was mistaken." She could not resist adding, "He had been so badly mistreated—all the blood—I couldn't clearly see his face at first. Then I realized my mistake."

"I see." The glint in his eyes indicated that he did not, as yet, believe her. "The man you saw is accused of a very serious crime, the murder of a Japanese officer."

"Oh? What evidence do you have?" She tried to sound indifferent.

"He was picked up carrying a great deal of Japanese currency. More than a poor peasant should possibly have. It is suspected he received the money, perhaps from the Chinese, who have no courage themselves, as payment for the assassination of Lieutenant Takahashi.''

Catherine felt a small flicker of relief. She knew the evidence was circumstantial, no more than what the Japanese held against a half dozen other men they had arrested for the same crime in past weeks. Lieutenant Takahashi's murder had become a convenient excuse for arresting enemies of all sorts. The danger was that the Japanese would execute all suspects in the hope that they might actually execute the real one in the process.

"If you know anything about him, it would be best for you to inform us fully. If we find out you have withheld information concerning a serious criminal, you will be given the same treatment he receives: torture and death.''

He rose and walked slowly around the desk, his heels striking the floor in time with the swagger stick against his palm.

"I have my own theory about Lieutenant Takahashi's murder.'' He stopped striking the stick and stood quietly, studying her carefully. "I think it was committed by nationalist guerrillas as an act of political terrorism. Of course, there has been no guerrilla activity in this area, at least until now.''

He paused again. "Now. I will ask you again. What do you know of the prisoner you saw in the square this morning?''

She looked him firmly in the eye but not too firmly, lest he see the truth in her defiance.

"I have told you the truth. He resembled a former servant, and it surprised me because I would not have expected to see that servant so far from Banjarmasin.''

Michael was becoming restless in her arms. Captain Kato reached out and fingered Michael's soft hand. Michael's reaction was to cling somehat shyly to his mother, but he smiled at the captain.

"You are lying, Mrs. Stanford!'' Captain Kato raised his voice for the first time. "Your son recognized the man. He wanted to go to him; only you restrained him.''

"My son is very young. He runs to all Malays who resemble the people who have loved and cared for him on the plantation. It is natural. He misses them, especially the men.'' She no longer sounded calm. Fear had raised her voice and made her sound defensive. No matter. Kato would expect the fear to be there, whether she was lying or not.

"Perhaps we should show the man to your son again and see his reaction."

"If you insist, go right ahead. But surely the Japanese Army has better ways to determine who are its enemies than the testimony of two-year-olds. Such evidence would scarcely hold up in an American court of law." She prayed that the Japanese records were disorganized enough, and Captain Kato was new enough, that he did not know there had been another person captured with her, Patri, who could identify Ahmad if he were frightened enough.

"Huh," the captain grunted noncommittally. If she had not convinced him, she had not, at least, convicted Ahmad, and she began to feel some relief.

"There has been growing guerrilla activity near Tarakan and the mountains southwest of here, not too far from where you were captured. A coincidence no doubt. It is believed to be led by on old friend of your husband, the sultan of Matapura. Were you aware of this group?"

"I was living near the old mission station in an isolated village that had been friendly to me because of my husband's past work among them. I didn't hear of the guerrillas until I was captured and brought here. I don't know who their leader is."

"Very well. But we will not have to rely on either you or the identification of a two-year-old. Within one week Admiral Inoye will be arriving here on a supply convoy on its way to Kuching and Singapore." Catherine searched her memory. The name was familiar, and then she remembered: the Japanese trade delegation she had met that first night at Maitreya.

Captain Kato continued, "When I informed the Borneo high command of my suspicions, it sent a message suggesting Admiral Inoye could be of help since he has met Prince Ahmad, as, I believe, he has met you."

Catherine felt a stab of fear. Not only could he expose Ahmad, but he could reveal her as an impostor as well. Whatever little respect and protection she had received as Michael's wife would be taken from her.

"Your husband has a reputation among Asians that is unusual, Mrs. Stanford. He is regarded as a man without the prejudices held by other Europeans, a man with a real appreciation of Asian cultures. I have here a letter from Koji Ushiba, secretary to former Prime Minister Prince Konoye, who wrote to us when he heard of your capture. He wishes me to tell you that he knew your husband when they both were students at Harvard and that he considers him a friend to the Japanese people and all the people of Asia. He wishes that during your imprisonment you be treated with all the respect and consideration that circumstances allow and he sends to you his condolences for your missing husband."

Kato put the letter down, and Catherine felt tears sting her eyes; but she refused to break down now. Above all, she wished to show no weakness.

She said softly, "Please thank Koji Ushiba for his kind thoughts."

Kato folded the letter and put it upon his desk.

"You have friends in Japan, Mrs. Stanford. But they have no power to help you here if your behavior insults the Japanese Army. Prince Konoye is no longer prime minister; General Tojo is!" He drew himself up stiffly.

"I think you do not tell us the truth. You are disobedient. You are not respecting the authority of the Japanese Army, which asks you to speak the truth. You are a prisoner of war. You must obey!" He was shouting again. She wasn't sure, but she suspected he was angry about the letter. However much he downplayed it, the letter was stopping him from doing as he pleased with her right now.

"Take her to the square. She will stand there for the rest of the day."

Still holding Michael, she was taken to the square before the prison compounds, and while the guards lounged in the sentry box or in the nearby shade, she stood in the midday sun. The heat was unbearable, and Michael became an increasing burden, until she could hold him no longer and was forced to put him on the ground beside her. Groggy and cross at the sudden change, he began to whine and cry, clutching at her leg. His fussiness was more unbearable than the pounding sunlight, and she gritted her teeth angrily because she was unable to help him. Each whimper made her feel guilty. Finally thoroughly exasperated with both him and her tormentors, she snatched him him up and stalked over to the shade with him, ignoring the excited orders of the guards to remain where she was. She sat him in the shade,

512

crossly told the guards he needed water and a place to sleep, then returned to the square. They followed her with bayonets waving, but when they saw she was once again standing obediently in the center of the square, they returned to Michael and played with him, giving him water and a biscuit until he fell asleep in the arms of one of the guards.

Her own lips became dry, then cracked and swollen as the hours passed. As the sun got lower, it shone fully in her face, forcing her to close her eyes to protect them. Someone decided she wasn't suffering enough and gave her a heavy rock to hold in outstretched arms above her head, a favorite form of punishment in the camps. So much for friends in high places, she thought wryly. The weight of the rock combined with her need to close her eyes caused her to lose her balance and occasionally stagger as she drifted dizzily toward unconsciousness. She caught glimpses of the men's compound, and she could see them lined along the fence, watching her, but things were too blurred for her to see if Ahmad was among them. She only hoped he would not be tempted to do anything to relieve her of her torment. Surely he should know that it would doom them both.

The flies in the square bit her, but she was not free to strike at them. She tried to kick them from her legs, but a guard came out immediately and stuck a bayonet sharply into her ribs.

"Attention," he shouted at her in Japanese.

The bayonet pricks were more painful than the flies, so she complied until her knees began to buckle and she sank slowly to the ground. The stone fell from her aching arms. The guards rushed out, shouting and prodding, but she slipped away from them into unconsciousness, where she was unaware of the kick one landed in her side. Tired of the heat and exasperated with their ineffectiveness, the guards abandoned their efforts and returned to the shade, leaving her to lie, unmoving, in the sun as the day wore to an end. She slowly came to when the sun's rays no longer reached the square and long, cool shadows had covered her. Her head throbbed, and her body ached. She was weak and could barely stagger to her feet. Michael and the guards were gone. For today, at least, they appeared to have given up.

The guard at the compound gate swung it open, and Catherine went directly into the barracks. Dinner was over, and Michael was playing happily inside with the other children. She sought out her mat and lowered the netting. Gratefully she accepted a cup of water thrust beneath it. It was the first kind act that the Ladies of Cape George had shown her. She sipped it very slowly and then fell asleep. When she awoke in the middle of the night, Michael was sleeping peacefully beside her. Again she felt grateful toward those who had fed and cared for him. At least she was not totally alone.

The next day she found out that Ahmad had been removed from the men's quarters and been taken to the iron boxes built by the Dutch before the war to torture their political prisoners. Prisoners seldom survived there more than a week. Too small to stand or lie in comfortably, the cages forced prisoners to sit in their own excrement with their legs drawn up. Like ovens, they slowly baked the life from them. Most who left the cages alive did so in hallucinating, gibbering madness or total catatonic withdrawal from which few ever recovered.

Almost a week had passed and there was no indication that Admiral Inoye's convoy had put into Cape George Harbor. Catherine began to think that perhaps this had been a bluff to frighten her into a confession implicating Ahmad. Then she was prodded out of bed one morning. It was barely dawn.

"You! Come to office. Put on best clothes. Look nice. Bring son!"

The guard waited outside the hut for Catherine to get ready. She was full of apprehension. Her hands shook as she tried to dress and comb her hair. She had no other clothes except the batik sarongs made from the cloth Ahmad had smuggled to her earlier along with the food. She tied Michael's small sarong around his waist and draped her own over her shoulder. She was puzzled by the early hour. The rest of the camp had not begun to stir.

When she was led into the office, she found Captain Kato waiting for her in an agitated state.

"Admiral Inoye arrives this morning early to look at prisoner. The prisoner is my responsibility. It will not look good for me if he reveals identity of the prisoner when I cannot."

Catherine realized that it meant that none of Kato's efforts to extract a confession from Ahmad, including the cages, had worked. At least he was still alive.

"I brought you here to give you one last chance to tell the truth and identify the prisoner. Otherwise, you will die with him when the admiral comes!"

Catherine began patiently, with a calmness she did not feel.

"I told you. I never saw him before."

"Bring the prisoner in!"

Moments elapsed. Catherine's heart pounded in her chest. She was trying hard to compose herself and was terrified of how Michael would respond to the sight of Ahmad. Before leaving the hut, she had given him some motion-sickness medication she had obtained from one of the women. Catherine hoped the medication would make Michael drowsy enough to ignore Ahmad's presence. He lay against her now, his head on her shoulder, thumb in his mouth.

Footsteps sounded on the steps, and a tall sergeant, rifle in hand, filled the door. He spoke in Japanese and then stepped aside. Ahmad, hands bound behind his back, was shoved into the room by the two guards who followed. His eyes looked at her with no sign of recognition. She was relieved to see that he had survived his five-day ordeal with no outward signs of abuse. The wound on his head was not visible, and the ugly marks upon his back appeared to be healing. The vigor and good health he had brought with him into the cages had helped him survive what other men, weak from starvation and dysentery could not. He wore khaki pants, army issue, and they had obviously bathed him before bringing him into the admiral's presence. Even in her present state of anxiety she could not help noticing how extraordinarily handsome he looked.

The guards untied his hands, and each took him by an arm, holding him firmly between them. Michael, who had been resting quietly on Catherine's shoulder, roused himself, thumb still in his mouth, and Catherine's heart leaped as he lifted his head and turned to look at the commotion in the room. He gave a low chortle and reached out a hand toward Ahmad, but he did not remove his thumb or say Ahmad's name. Then he turned questioningly to Catherine and pointed at Ahmad.

"See?" he said behind his thumb, and smiled faintly.

"Yes, I see," Catherine replied softly.

Michael began to struggle weakly to get away, but she held tightly to him, confining his struggles. With relief she noted that drowsiness quickly overtook him again and he lost interest in pursuing the matter. He had not ignored Ahmad, but neither had he given firm evidence of recognition. It was the best she and Ahmad could hope for under the circumstances.

Captain Kato had watched Michael's reaction and was now more annoyed than ever. He was convinced that he had captured the guerrilla leader, but now it would be the Navy, not the Army, that would deliver the telling blow.

"You have one last chance, Mrs. Stanford, to save your life and the life of your son." He waited ominously, giving this new threat time to sink in. "You must identify the prisoner before he is identified for you!"

He was pacing back and forth. He came up and waved his finger close to her face.

"You both will be executed with this pig if you fail to obey my order. This is your last chance." He looked directly into her eyes.

"I've already told you. I do not know him."

His mouth tightened into a grimace, and he slapped her hard across the face. The blow aroused Michael, who began to whimper sleepily. Tears stung her eyes. She saw Ahmad tense and swallow hard.

Captain Kato slapped her again, this time on the other cheek. She heard a gasp from Ahmad as the blow landed. This time a tiny cut opened at the corner of her mouth and a drop of blood flew out from the blow, spraying the captain's impeccable shirt. She expected him to slap her again for staining his shirt, but he did not. Instead, he turned abruptly to Ahmad.

"You do not like to see me hit the woman. What is she to you? She is your enemy as much as mine." He spoke in English.

Ahmad answered softly in Malay, "I do not speak Japanese or English, so I do not understand your words, but if the captain is wondering why I reacted to the blow, then I will tell you that in my country it is not honorable to strike a woman unless she is your wife or daughter."

It was a remark that would ordinarily have aroused her ire, and Catherine realized that he had meant to do just that. She noted a slight gleam of amusement in his eyes that was meant for her alone. It gave her courage.

Ahmad's response sent Captain Kato into another rage. "Prisoners are not entitled to respect. They have no honor. It is a dishonor to be a prisoner. Besides, you both are lying!"

Suddenly he reached over and took the rifle from the sergeant. The bayonet was attached. He smiled, inspired. He lifted the bayonet slowly toward Ahmad and circled it slowly around his face, coming dangerously near each eye; then he stuck the point in Ahmad's nose and gave a laugh.

"Your nose is narrow, not broad and flat like a Malay nose or a Japanese nose. It is an Occidental nose. You want me to give you a Malay nose?" He laughed gleefully. "I will cut here and here"—he shifted the sharp point to the other nostril—"and you will have a flat nose like a Malay."

He withdrew the bayonet without making good on his threat and put the point near Ahmad's ear.

"Like to lose an ear maybe?" He pressed the bayonet tightly against Ahmad's face at the base of the ear. He drew it slowly back, and a thin line of blood ran down Ahmad's neck. The bayonet was placed lightly between the collarbone at Ahmad's throat and then drawn slowly down to his navel, opening a thin red spreading line reaching from his neck to his trousers. It was just a superficial wound, but it filled Catherine with such apprehension that she could control her trembling only with great effort.

Captain Kato was obviously enjoying himself. If he could not extract a confession from them, he would at least have the satisfaction of venting his rage. He turned back to Catherine with sharp, glittering eyes.

"He is a rather splendid-looking man, isn't he? Tell me, would a woman such as yourself find it attractive to engage in sex with such a man?"

Catherine's mind suddenly filled with the possibility that Captain Kato, or someone, had seen them embrace that evening by the fence. She steeled herself to respond with all the scorn she could muster.

"White women do not sleep with men with brown skins. They are not attractive to us." And she gave a shudder which she hoped would pass for revulsion. It had been a bigoted remark, the kind that would have been expected of her.

The captain gave a rapid order in Japanese which Catherine was unable to understand, though Ahmad did, and she thought she glimpsed apprehension briefly in his eyes. On the captain's orders the two guards who held his arms reached over and loosened his trousers, opening them to expose him.

"Since you have no interest in brown men, Mrs. Stanford, you certainly won't care if I make sure no woman ever enjoys this one again, will you?"

He placed the bayonet between Ahmad's legs and lifted it slowly until its sharp edge rested lightly against his testicles. He laughed and peered intently into Ahmad's face. Beads of perspiration formed upon Ahmad's forehead, and there was fear in his eyes, though he said nothing.

"Better to confess and be a dead man than not be a man at all," the captain said to him.

The muscles tightened in Ahmad's jaw. It was the only indication he gave of understanding. He stood without speaking, knowing that anything he would say might push the captain over the brink.

Catherine stared at the poised bayonet as if mesmerized, frantically trying to think of some way to postpone the slash of the bayonet until the admiral and his party arrived. She was straining so hard that she failed to hear the muffled sound of the island's only automobile, the ancient convertible that served to ferry important dignitaries from the dock to the camp and back again. The old hulk rumbled with dignity into the compound square, raising dust. Outside, the guards scrambled into inspection formation.

The captain withdrew the bayonet from Ahmad and handed the rifle to the sergeant. As the guards hoisted Ahmad's trousers, the muscles in his face relaxed in relief. For the first time he let his eyes meet and hold Catherine's. They cheered her, those fine black eyes, and gave her confidence.

She would need it. From frying pan to fire, she thought as she looked through the door and saw the admiral step from the car, then return the salute offered by the captain, who had hastily joined the official greeting party. The commanding general of Cape George was beside him as they began an inspection of the guard.

Watching the ceremony gave Catherine time to study the admiral and collect her thoughts. She realized that salvaging the present situation depended mainly on her resourcefulness. Study-

518

ing him, she clearly recognized Admiral Inoye as a member of the trade delegation that had visited Maitreya the first night she was there. She had a good memory for faces, yet she doubted she would have been able to place him had he been a face in the crowd. She realized that she was fortunate that the only time he had met the real Mrs. Stanford he had also met Catherine Morgan. Suddenly it occurred to her just how she might handle the situation. She watched the inspection come to an end and summoned her courage.

As the group entered the office, she stepped forward, smiled, and bowed very low. She was taking a serious chance in not waiting to be recognized, but she had to take the risk.

"Admiral Inoye." She raised her head from the bow.

The admiral gave a look of recognition and then appeared slightly puzzled.

"Mrs. Stanford," the captain announced to the admiral. "I understand you have met before." He watched them carefully.

Smiling pleasantly but obviously still perplexed, the admiral politely returned the bow. She was not his prisoner, so he could show her respect without losing face. With relief, she knew that he recognized her, though he was obviously confused about placing her exactly.

"Yes. My sister-in-law and I played hostesses to the admiral four years ago at Maitreya. You remember my sister-in-law, Kara? The wife of my husband's dead brother, Edward? She always presided, with Sir Charles, at the head of the table."

The confusion lifted from his face. He had, of course, remembered Catherine from that evening, though he had not placed her as Michael's wife. He did not forget exquisite faces. He noted that captivity had not robbed her of her beauty. In the vague memory of four years ago it seemed to fit perfectly into place.

"Yes. Of course. Your sister-in-law, she is here with you?"

"No. She died earlier, in the capture of Maitreya." She did not elaborate, nor did he ask. He seemed somewhat embarrassed by it all, as if it were bad manners to have waged a war on one whose hospitality he had enjoyed. It left him with an unpaid debt that was now, under the circumstances, unpayable. It was not a good feeling, and the admiral showed his discomfort.

"The war is unfortunate for all of us. It is with great regret that I hear of the death of your sister-in-law and with equal sadness that I see you now imprisoned here. Still, it is war, and it cannot be helped. And your husband and father-in-law?"

She felt a little giddy at the two charades: her masquerade as Mrs. Stanford and the ridiculously polite conversation between conqueror and conquered.

"My husband is dead. And Sir Charles is in Australia. He is the only one of us who was not captured or killed."

"Wasn't there a younger daughter?"

Catherine nodded. "Julienne. She is dead also." She shifted on her feet, wishing the conversation were over.

"And the rest of the family?" the admiral asked.

"You did not meet Margit, Michael's older sister. She and her husband were imprisoned in Batavia. Kara's two daughters died with her at Maitreya." Her voice caught, and she could not continue.

The admiral shook his head sadly. "So many dead."

The captain was getting impatient, and he motioned to the guards to bring Ahmad forward. The admiral shifted his attention from Catherine, noting Ahmad for the first time. He gave no immediate sign of recognition.

"This is the prisoner believed to be Sutton Ahmad Açvavarman, the leader of the guerrilla forces in Borneo. No one in this city can or will identify him. Since the admiral has met the prince, we have asked you to identify him."

"Yes, yes," the admiral said somewhat brusquely, and stepped forward to examine Ahmad closely.

"He is very tall. The prince is tall, too, but I do not recall him being as tall as this." Actually he was not at all sure what Ahmad looked like since it had been four years from that night at Maitreya, but the admiral would lose face if he indicated a lack of knowledge on the matter now. After all, they were counting on him to be able to identify the prince.

Catherine saw his dilemma, and she felt her first glimmer of hope. She knew that he could not admit his memory had failed him, so his examination would have to result in either a yes or a no.

Inwardly perplexed, Inoye studied Ahmad's face. He had expected some clue to jar his memory, but nothing came. Clearly this man could not be Prince Ahmad. He did not look like a prince. He did not even look Malay. He looked like a member of some wild mountain tribal group. The admiral did not remember Prince Ahmad clearly, but he did recall an impression of an elegant, well-educated man. There was no way this man before him remotely resembled the prince.

"No," he said finally, and with conviction. "This man is not Ahmad Açvavarman."

Catherine kept her jubilance well hidden. The captain appeared totally defeated. The general, though disappointed, seemed to accept the admiral's opinion readily. The general spoke to the captain, ordering him to retain the Malay, for although he was not the guerrilla leader, he was still under suspicion for the murder of Lieutenant Takahashi. However, it was clear to Catherine that this was a face-saving gesture rather than an expression of serious continued interest in the prisoner. The captain turned to the sergeant. "Take him to the compound."

Good, Catherine thought as Ahmad was led from the office. He was not going back to the cages.

The admiral was about to take his leave, and he turned his attention once again to Catherine.

"I leave you with the sincere hope that our countries can be at peace again." He bowed slightly to her, and she, in turn, bowed very low and remained bowing as he and the general left the office to return to the launch. The captain and the sergeant followed, leaving her alone with the guard who had brought her. After a moment the sergeant returned and ordered her back to the compound. As she started through the door, he placed a hand on her arm.

"Not the child. The child is to come with me. He will be returned to you soon."

Catherine was filled with a desperate need to see Ahmad. She knew he would not be kept in the civilian men's compound for long; now that he was simply another native prisoner, he would be transferred to the overcrowded jail in Cape George. Using the charcoaled end of a burned stick, she scribbled a note on a precious scrap of Japanese newspaper she had been saving, and when she went out on a work detail later that morning, she dropped the folded scrap on the road in front of the men's compound. It asked him to meet her at the beach beyond the road that evening after bed check. She had found a way out of the

521

women's compound: a narrow gap between earth and fence. She hoped he might find the same.

She could not tell if he was among the prisoners gathered outside in the men's compound as she and the other women passed by; her attempts to search the crowd for a glimpse of him were met with cuffs from the guards. She had let the note slip from her fingers and had immediately despaired that he would see it even if he were there. There was always the possibility that one of the other prisoners, or a guard, would pick it up and keep the rendezvous. She realized that she was taking a very dangerous risk.

That evening she squeezed to freedom. The narrow beach faced west with palm trees hard against the surf that frothed and pounded white upon the shallow, sloping sand. The tide was high and full. As the sun touched the ocean's edge, it seemed to dissolve into the water, spreading ribbons of bright red and gold and pink. The colors floated gently on the ocean's surface as far as her eye could see, carried toward the shore on rolling waves, tossed upon the beach by the lapping surf.

The colors seemed almost tangible . . . as if there is an enchanted moment, before it totally dissolves and disappears into the sea, when the sunset can be picked up in broken shards from the sand where it has washed ashore . . . and carried home.

When the sun was finally gone, she turned away from the sea and saw Ahmad standing quietly behind her. His expression was serious, but there was a softness about the mouth and eyes she did not often see these days. She went to him, and he put his arms around her and held her close. They stood quietly, holding each other in that gentle, comforting way. They had been friends for two years. Now they were about to become lovers as well. It was as if that new dimension they were adding to their relationship made them both hesitate for a moment, savoring the old relationship for one last moment before they let it go. There was so much to say, but there would be time for that later. He put his arm around her shoulders, and they began to walk up the beach. She slipped her arm around his waist and let her head rest against his shoulder. They strolled like lovers on a picnic outing with the future ahead of them, but they both knew they had almost no time left at all.

He chose a palm tree from among the many which lined the shore and guided her to it. He sat beneath it and leaned back, taking her hand to pull her down beside him. The ache of parting was in everything they did and felt. She gently ran her finger down the red, healing scar from his throat to his waist and felt him tense at her touch.

"What makes you so distant tonight?" she asked him softly.

It was a long moment before he spoke. "My fight is in Dutch Borneo. I cannot remain here. It has become too dangerous, and since the war is far from over, we will not see each other for a very long time. Perhaps we should keep the relationship just as it has been. It has served us well through much difficulty."

She thought of Siah, and for a moment she was filled with doubt about his love. "Is it another woman that makes you hesitate?"

"No," he answered simply.

"Then I cannot bear to leave you without something more to take with me."

She leaned forward and kissed him with all the hunger that she felt. When she pulled back to look at him, pain burned sharply in his eyes.

"This may only make the separation worse," he replied; but it was too late for doubts, and he knew it. His back braced against the tree, he roughly pulled her onto his lap and kissed her with ferocity.

When he was done, she sat up, shaken. Her breathing ragged, she touched his chest, then leaned down to kiss his hard, flat stomach; her tongue trailed upward to his throat until a shiver passed through his body into hers.

She bent forward to study his face, resting her hands upon his chest. So raw were her senses now that even the gentle pressure of his breathing became sensuous, teasing her toward fulfillment with its steady rhythm. His eyes on hers were as fierce as his kiss had been. She felt his fingers lightly touch her shoulder, and she trembled. They lingered there a moment before deftly loosening the knot of her sarong. It slipped to her waist, but his eyes did not leave hers until the moment when he had drawn the folds of cloth away from her body and it was fully revealed to him. Then, slowly and deliberately, his eyes left her face and traveled down to where her nakedness sat straddling his lap.

His hands cradled her hips in a caress, and then he raised her slightly, so that he might loosen his own clothing. When she again sat upon him, it was to the shock of his sex between her legs, demanding in its warmth and fullness. He did not enter her. Again his hands embraced her hips, only now he raised himself slightly from the sand to twist and rock himself gently against her, relaxing between each motion. She caught her breath and longed to open herself to take all of him into her womb, to carry him with her wherever she was going.

His own breath caught in a soft groan of protest that said he could endure no longer. With one swift motion he turned beneath her so that they rolled over and fell gently back in the cradle of his arms. He followed, bending over her, braced upon his elbows, and then quickly entered her. Though ready to receive him, she felt as if a fire had suddenly penetrated her, and she wept with pleasure and desire. Unable to hold back, his body began to move within her. His mouth barely touched hers as he pressed soft, trembling Malay words of love and endearment against her parted lips, her eyelids, onto the tears upon her cheeks, so that each deep thrust of his body into hers, now so much beyond his control, carried into the deepest part of her heart the softest whispers, the tenderest kisses. And when all these were finally spent with one urgent cry of release, his body relaxed. With nothing more to give her, he wept, too.

She kissed his eyes and lips and throat, surprised by the tears she felt there. Lying in his arms, she marveled at how safe she felt, even though the threat of instant death hung over them should they be discovered.

When he looked into her face, he could see the love in her eyes. He saw her lips tremble with the desire to tell him, yet she could not say it. Part of her still belonged to Michael. It chilled him to think that perhaps it always would.

For both of them, this act of love had meant more than relief from long-suppressed passion. It was a binding together of their spirits, and they felt it deeply. Catherine realized that Ahmad held none of his love back from her, while she held only the words back from him. Not the feelings. The feelings were his now. Completely.

When she finally opened her eyes and looked up at the sky, it had become a star-filled velvet blanket, drawn tightly over them, protecting them. The universe now seemed to enfold her as tenderly as did Ahmad's strong arms. Boundaries had disappeared. She felt at one forever with his body, the world, the stars. At this moment nothing frightened her. She knew that by loving him, she had accepted a future in a Moslem world where women had little freedom and no status. The only power she would ever possess in Matapura was his love for her. But as long as she held that, she had awesome power indeed.

Hand in hand, they rose and walked out into the warm sea and swam. Her own hard, steady strokes matched his. He smiled, pleased that she could keep up with him. As they came back to shore, the shallow water swirling around their waists, he pulled her toward him. The sea surged and thrust her roughly against him. He caught her tightly to him and kissed her, a kiss that didn't stop. With her arms already around his neck, Catherine hooked her legs tightly about his waist so that he could make his own connection with that tender opening in her body. He made love to her again amid the gently rocking swells, and then he carried her to shore.

Lying in the sand with her, still holding her close, his cheek pressed against her hair, he began the talk they had been postponing.

"I have Japanese currency and gold for you to take with you, as much as is safe. Save the gold," he warned her. "As the war draws to an end, the yen will be of little value, but the soldiers will be eager for gold."

"You're confident the Japanese will lose?" Without a radio to contradict Japanese propaganda she had almost begun to believe their claims that the war would last ten years and end in a Japanese victory.

"I am certain of it. In two years, no more."

Suddenly she could not bear it. "I can't survive two more years of this," she cried.

He pulled free of her and held her firmly by the shoulders. "Yes, you can!" he said fiercely, struggling to overcome his own fears for her. His fingers dug into her flesh. "Promise me you will not give up. That you will keep struggling to stay alive no matter what happens."

"I promise," she replied at last, and was surprised at the strength she felt in speaking the words aloud.

They spoke no more about it. Instead, they spent the night making love and quietly talking of other things, and when the first warning gray of the eastern sky appeared, they made love for the last time, there, in the gently rolling surf, mingling ecstasy with grief. When it was time to go, he took her to the fence and buried his face in her hair, tears filling his eyes. She was weeping openly. Slowly, reluctantly she pulled away and started to leave. He knelt beside the fence to watch her go. Suddenly she turned and cried out softly to him.

"Ahmad!" She was breathing hard. "Ahmad . . . I love you."

She turned and ran as he slowly rose to his feet. A dark shadow against the gray sky, he stood staring after her until she had disappeared.

The next morning Catherine was among a group of the women sent to clean one of the unoccupied buildings which was to be used to house an increase in the number of guards. Teram Island was about to receive two thousand British and Australian military prisoners who had been used to build roads in northern Borneo and Indo-China. As they passed the civilian men's compound, a man's voice called out softly to one of the women and a small object flew over the fence, landing in the dirt in the midst of their procession. It was quickly scooped up. Turning just at that moment to make sure the eyes of his ladies were all directed properly ahead, the guard leading the group glimpsed what had happened and called a halt to make a search.

Catherine took advantage of the diversion to anxiously scan the men's compound for Ahmad and Patri, but she didn't see them.

"What happened to the Malay man and the little Iban boy?" she whispered to a young Briton who stood behind the barbed wire just opposite her.

"Escaped is my guess," he replied softly. "They were gone this morning. Caused the guards to raise a row and beat a bit upon some of us chaps. Can't imagine how they'll get very far unless they have a boat. I'd try it myself, but I wouldn't blend in too well with the scenery." He grinned.

Catherine felt a rush of jubilation. They were free. "Thanks," she said, and smiled. He had risked a beating to answer her and she was grateful.

By then the guard had found the object of his search, a small wooden boat one of the men had carved for his son's birthday. Catherine was surprised when the guard let the woman keep it, dispensing a few slaps and cuffs for having concealed it.

With the arrival of the POWs, the atmosphere at Teram prison changed. The brutal treatment given the soldiers had a sobering effect on the civilian prisoners, a reminder that their situation could be worse. Morale in the women's compound was boosted when twenty-six nuns from a nearby Cape George convent were brought to Teram. Used to poverty and sacrifice, they were cheerful and more tolerant of prison conditions than the other women, and their optimistic outlook helped bolster everyone. But the biggest change of all came in the increased security. New fences, booby traps, and constant surveillance now made escape impossible. Besides, anyone who escaped would sooner or later be turned in by the local population for the reward.

The Japanese kept their word. On Christmas 1943, several weeks after Ahmad had left and the guerrilla activity had ceased in the area, Michael was returned to Catherine unharmed.

Part Four

Earthwind Rising

A fifteenth-century East Indies legend foretold that the Islands of the East would be ruled first by the white buffalo, followed by the yellow monkey, and then a *Ratu Atil,* a "just prince," would be born in the form of a cloud leopard within the fiery depths of the earth and come forth from the mouth of one of Indonesia's most famous volcanoes, rising on that sulfurous smoke called the earthwind to win freedom forever for the Indonesian people.

Chapter 50

When it began, there was no reason to think that August 20, 1945, would be different from any other day at Teram Prison. Certainly nothing about its beginning hinted at what was to come. It began with the same suffocating suddenness typical of the tropics. By noon the women had finished weeding the ditches assigned to them and had collapsed in the shade of the huts. The guards and camp commander had retreated to the comfort of their opium. Like food, the opium supply had become more unreliable as the war went on, causing Japanese tempers to blaze.

Catherine usually saw the lunch break as an opportunity to seek some privacy from the crowded compound and went out to tend her small garden. The money Ahmad had given her was gone, leaving her worse off than the other women. Unlike them, she had no suitcases full of prewar belongings to trade with the Japanese guards for food, so she worked harder at her garden.

Michael came with her, chattering endlessly as usual. Catherine glanced anxiously at his wiry four-year-old body as he raced past her to pounce on a large bug which he would feed to the old hen that laid the eggs which were his only source of protein. She had bought the hen with the last of her money. Michael was barefoot and wore a short sarong made from the faded bottom portion of her own. She worried about whether he was growing properly and gave him all her food she could spare. Though slender, he seemed strong and energetic. In fact, his energy often proved too much for her. Even the deprived environment of prison did not stifle his curiosity. The British Catholic sisters imprisoned in Teram had started a school for the older children. Though too young to attend, Michael had wanted to learn to read, so the sisters had accepted him. He learned quickly but was too impatient to tolerate the daily routines of school. When he did come, the sisters would envelop him in the folds of their patched and mended habits which had come to resemble colorful quilts. "Oh, Michael, we are so glad you have decided to visit us today!" And he would endure their embraces, looking up at them with wide, serious gray eyes. But he never smiled back.

While Catherine picked potato leaves from the garden to cook later, Michael stopped to listen to the jungle. All the human sounds were in the huts, too distant and quiet to interfere. As he listened, a flock of small birds rose from the bushes and grasses near the beach and flew off. He watched them go, too far away for him to see them clearly. Out of some sure sense of preservation the birds never ventured near the hungry camp.

"What's that noise the birds make, Mom?" he asked.

"Songs," she answered, grateful that the reply required only one syllable from her.

He stood quietly for a moment. Catherine was looking at the small potatoes she had just dug, annoyed with herself for digging them too soon and furious with the gnawing hunger which led her to do it every time.

"Make me a song, Mom."

"No. Not now."

"Yes. Now!" he demanded.

She ignored him, so he began to make his own song instead, a series of whistles and shrieks that became something uniquely his own. His inventiveness always astounded her. He was constantly exploring and creating, his rich imagination unfettered by reality. From mud, twigs, leaves, and anything else he could scavenge, he constructed the things he heard about but had either never seen or was too young to remember: fantastic ships of air and space and sea, trains, cities, farms. When the older children who remembered such things would ridicule his efforts, he remained undaunted. Though she still worried about the effect the long internment might have on his personality, Catherine had begun to realize that of all the people in the camp, he was perhaps the least bound by the barbed wire that confined them. Instead, she began to fear that the real world, when they were finally freed, might disappoint him by not living up to the richness of his imagination.

When they had first come to Teram, she used to tell him stories at night before they fell asleep, or teach him Bahasa Indonesian or the Dani language, partly to educate him and partly to practice and maintain her own skills. But as the food grew scarcer and the work harder, she had little energy left for anything but the garden.

She struck her digging stick into the ground and turned up another premature potato. Michael's song still filled the air. Like Degewatek, alone on his watchtower, Michael had begun to give his song words, whichever struck his fancy. Suddenly he broke off. For a moment, Catherine heard nothing except the flies that droned steadily around the garden. Gradually one of them began to stand out from the others, growing louder and holding a steady course. Crouching on her heels, her hands in the earth, she looked up at the sky, saw nothing, and went back to work, but Michael stood silently watching. Finally it was impossible for Catherine to ignore the sound. She had given up hoping long ago, but her heart pounded as she put down her digging stick, shielded her eyes, and searched the sky. Blinded by the sun, for a moment Catherine failed to notice the thousands of white pieces of paper that drifted and fluttered slowly to the ground after the plane roared by. When she realized what they were, she jumped to her feet, hands eagerly outstretched, wanting to catch one before the soldiers could come and snatch them all away. They floated down achingly slowly. Mouth open, Michael watched in wonder.

The other prisoners, stirred out of their midday lethargy by the sound of the plane, came out of the huts to take a look. Catherine was the first to read a leaflet.

August 18, 1945

To all Allied prisoners:

The Japanese have unconditionally surrendered. Because of the remoteness of your location, we will not be able to reach you immediately, but be of good cheer; we are arrang-

533

ing the implementation of the surrender, and you will be freed as soon as possible.

Major General B. Jones
Commander, Australian 9th Division

Catherine let out a cry of joy. Cheers and whoops broke out all around her as the others grabbed and read the leaflets. The guards hastily descended upon the compounds and confiscated the flyers, but they could not remove the news or the joy and hope it brought. That came later that afternoon, when the camp commandant, General Suto, assembled them all in the square outside the barbed-wire compounds and had them thoroughly searched. He was clearly in a foul mood and looking for any excuse to punish them. When the search was complete, he climbed up on the porch and began to read an announcement from Field Marshal Terauchi of the Japanese Southeast Asian Command. It stated that the prisoners were to gather their belongings together to be moved at a moment's notice to a central collection area.

"The move is for your own protection and safety!" the camp commandant shouted. "The Allies will be converging on Borneo for one last great battle! They do not care if you are killed in the process!"

None of the prisoners was fooled. Fear seized them as it hadn't in years. Rumors of Allied victories had steadily increased their confidence and hope. Now they had been shattered. They would be moved. Many of the weakest and sickest among them who had somehow clung to life would surely die in that move, but it would not matter. Those who survived would surely be exterminated in one final act of revenge, one last effort to avenge Japanese honor. Terauchi could have it no other way. In the camps at Sandakan, Ranau and Brunei the Japanese began to march the prisoners out in groups of sixty and force them to dig their own graves before shooting them. For the prisoners at Teram, the war was over, but the danger had only grown.

Catherine stared up into the palm thatch of the roof of the women's hut. There was no moon and it was pitch black inside the room, but she kept her eyes open anyway. It made her feel

534

alive. Slightly feverish, she had been unable to sleep. She lay awake, listening to the rats scurrying around. Ahmad's name sprang into her thoughts with a painful jolt. She didn't know if he was still alive. There had been recent rumors among the local people who came near the camp that he had been killed in the fighting at Pontianak. But even if he were alive, they were both different people from the two who had loved each other on that beach so long ago.

She slept uneasily, waking often. The light changed from gray to the brassy shine of morning and still the guards had not come to prod the prisoners up. Puzzled, she sat up and looked around. Michael was awake, quietly daydreaming beside her as she pulled herself up and toward the door. The other women stirred behind her, groggy with hunger and sleep. Still dizzy, she grasped the door sill to steady herself.

"My God," she whispered as she stared out at the sun-drenched compound.

"What is it?" one of the women asked anxiously, coming up behind her to see for herself.

"I don't know," Catherine replied softly.

Throughout the prison camp the gates stood open. There was no announcement. Individually and collectively the prisoners began to notice that the guards were gone. They hesitated at first, unwilling to leave the security of their predictable hell for a changed world they'd forgotten how to live in.

In the women's camp the children were the first to go through the gates. They had become bold little creatures, resourceful and independent, more at home in confinement than their mothers ever had been. Soon the children came running back with the news. The Australians were landing in boats manned by American sailors.

Suddenly hesitation vanished, and the prisoners began to pour out of the compounds, at first a trickle, and then by the thousands. All who could walk or barely walk made their way to the camp square. Many of the arriving soldiers and sailors who had come to free them wept at the sight of the emaciated, almost naked crowds which barely seemed human. Catherine searched the crowd for Michael, who had failed to come back with the other children. She was beginning to feel slightly feverish, but

535

she was determined not to miss this moment she had waited two years to see. She pressed on toward the platform, plunging into the crowd. Australian soldiers and American sailors mingled among the prisoners now, handing out food and comfort freely. They seemed so young and so healthy. They were the toughest of combat groups, fresh from heavy fighting in Borneo and Celebes, where they had taken no prisoners, even in those rare instances when the Japanese were willing to be taken. Now a love affair bloomed between the liberated and those who had come to free them. Of the tens of thousands imprisoned in Indonesia and Malaya, almost two-thirds had died. The rest were ill, many with health problems that would shorten their lives and cripple them forever.

Catherine had succeeded in making her way to the square where the Japanese officers, her former captors and tormentors, stood ill at ease, ready to turn their swords over in surrender. An American naval captain had just climbed onto the platform to address the prisoners. His voice broke as he began.

"This is my first experience at this sort of thing. I can only tell you that for the men of the American Navy it has been worth many a battle and long, hard night at sea. This is what we've been fighting for—" Unable to compose himself enough to continue, the captain turned and stepped lightly from the platform. At first there was silence, and then a cheer went up from the crowd.

A commotion developed near the headquarters building next to the platform. Through the crowd Catherine caught glimpses of Dyak and Iban warriors quarreling with a Dutch colonel, the senior ranking officer among the former Allied military prisoners at Teram Island. He and some of his junior officers were attempting to prevent the warriors from raising the red and white flag of independent Indonesia in the place of the Japanese flag. Moving to where she could catch a clearer look at the Borneo tribesmen, Catherine noted that they were wearing ammunition belts over their shoulders and carried rifles.

"Who are they?" she asked of the young American naval officer standing near her.

"Borneo guerrillas," he replied. "Seems they're all stirred up and looking for a fight."

"But why?"

"It could be the news we just got that the British sent troops to Batavia on September eighth to secure the Indies for the Dutch. Whoever spread that information should be court-martialed."

Catherine's heart sank at the news. Seeing her distress, the young officer hastened to reassure her.

"No reason it should concern you. We'll have you out of here in no time, before any trouble gets started. We intend to leave the British to handle the whole situation. It's none of our affair."

Catherine felt far from reassured, and her heart sank even further. Then it stopped altogether at the sight of the tall, splendid figure that pushed his way through the men and stepped up to the Dutch colonel. He still carried a rifle in his hand. He took the rope which held the half-raised nationalist flag from one of his men.

"Borneo was freed of the Dutch and British. Now it has been freed of the Japanese. We are part of Indonesia, and it is only fitting that the Indonesian flag should replace the Japanese."

The Dutch colonel bristled. "Teram Island is Dutch territory," he retorted.

"It *was* Dutch territory," Ahmad replied sharply.

His men let out a cheer and raised their rifles in defiance. The Australian and American officers who had led the Allied liberation force hesitated, unsure of how to handle this fracas developing among those they had come to free. The Dutch officers demanded that Ahmad be arrested and his men dispersed.

Catherine whispered to the American naval officer near her, "Better not let them arrest him. It would create a politically embarrassing incident if the sultan of Matapura had survived three years of guerrilla fighting only to be arrested by liberating Americans."

"I see what you mean," the naval commander replied with a grim smile. He dispatched a hastily whispered message to an Australian colonel who stood on the periphery of the scene. Catherine watched anxiously as the Australian colonel stepped forward to have a few private words with General Newly, leaving the two old antagonists, the Dutch and the Indonesian revolutionaries, warily sizing each other up. Catherine realized, with sadness, that the fighting had not ended for Ahmad. Only the enemy had changed. She longed to go to him. Her heart caught in her throat as she watched him standing there, barefoot in cotton

537

cutoff white pants and a loose white top open to his waist, ammunition belt hung over one shoulder, proud and confident, every inch a king.

The tension grew. Ahmad's men were armed and angry. It was already clear from the scene now in progress that the Indonesians would not willingly submit again to either Dutch presence or Dutch rule. The Australians shifted about uncomfortably. Their war was over. They were anxious to get on with the process of liberating the prisoners. General Newly finished conversing with the colonel and looked up at the armed Indonesians. He raised his hand to signal silence and stepped forward.

"Your Highness, we regret we did not recognize you. The courage of your long struggle to free your homeland from Japanese domination has been much admired by the Allies and was of invaluable assistance to us in our own efforts. It is our honor to have you here to share in this moment of liberation. We understand your desire for the independence and freedom of your country. These matters, of course, can't be settled here. They are political matters and must first be dealt with by the politicians, however distressful that may seem to us all. These matters we can leave for the United Nations to settle. I would suggest that we get on with the evacuation of the prisoners and forget the ceremonies altogether."

A cheer rose from the surrounding prisoners and troops alike. Ahmad raised his voice above the noise, and it grew quiet again.

"There are many here who have suffered greatly from their long imprisonment. I agree they should now be our first concern. For the time being we will leave the matter to the politicians and the United Nations, but if there is no independence for my country, then we will make our own freedom!" He raised his gun defiantly while his men cheered.

The Dutch officer pressed his lips tightly together, then strode angrily from the square. Surprised by her own strength, Catherine began to push her way through the crowd of soldiers and prisoners until she was near the place where Ahmad stood talking and laughing with his men. How many times she had imagined this reunion scene! Standing before him now, she suddenly felt frightened, acutely aware of the weight she had lost, the drabness of her faded and torn sarong, and the lack of luster in her hair, her eyes. She wanted to run away, and then it was too late.

The change she saw on Ahmad's face when he caught sight of her, was it shock or pity? His smile faded as he broke off the conversation and shoved his rifle into the hands of one of his surprised men. His eyes never left hers as he came to her through the crowd of people and stood before her. Neither of them spoke. He reached out and gently took her face between his hands, intently searching it. For what, she wondered, for something he might remember? The old Catherine? Tears came to her eyes, but she was unable to say anything. She saw his own fill with tears as he bent down and kissed her softly, her face still between his hands.

"Ca—" He started to say her name, but his voice broke, and he took her in his arms, alarmed by the frailness of her body against his, angered beyond words at the hunger he felt and saw in her eyes. He felt guilty at the thought of his own strong body, deprived of nothing for the past two years except an occasional night's sleep. If anything, he was stronger from the years of hardship.

"And Michael?" he finally managed to whisper against her ear.

"He's with the sisters. He's fine."

Ahmad tightly closed his eyes in relief.

"Patri?" she asked him.

"He should be in Matapura by now. I sent him back with some of my men as soon as Banjarmasin was freed."

Ahmad's first thought had been to return to Banjarmasin immediately, taking Catherine and Michael with him. He was convinced that independence had not yet come to Indonesia in spite of the declarations. It was clear to him that the Dutch planned to return, and he wanted to begin the task of organizing a fighting unit; but he was afraid now that Catherine was in no condition to make the trip.

She pulled away and looked at him, noting the concern on his face. "I'll be all right, Ahmad, really." As she said it, she was suddenly surprised to find the world grow quickly dark and slip away from her.

Chapter 51

The hospital ship was rocked soothingly by the waves of Surabaya Harbor. For weeks now Catherine had been recovering from the lingering effects of malaria. Two more weeks and she would be released from the hospital, and then what? She wasn't sure.

Six weeks ago Sir Charles had met the ship at Surabaya and had taken charge of his grandson until Catherine was well enough for all three of them to go to Maitreya. Michael was ecstatic about being with this handsome British admiral who indulged him, engaged him in long serious conversations, and took him to puppet shows and plays.

Overcoming two years of deprivation had not been easy. At first Michael stole scraps from abandoned plates at the hotel and hid them in his room. Sir Charles had said nothing, until he came across one of the food caches hidden in Michael's room.

"It must have been very hard, Michael, to have been so hungry for so long." Sir Charles had smiled and had left the cache of spoiling food untouched.

As the weeks went by, Michael's need to hoard food gradually declined as he became truly convinced that the hungry times were behind him. He then became overly generous, giving away food to those around him who looked as hungry as he had once felt. Nor was Sir Charles able to pass a beggar without giving something to him in response to Michael's pleas. Michael had yet to learn that it was not within his grandfather's power to relieve all the world's hunger and suffering as easily as he had relieved Michael's own.

For Sir Charles, who had lost so much, his grandson was the solace which helped him carry on. He took great delight in Michael's bold curiosity, his intelligence, and his resemblance to his father. Sir Charles felt as though he had been given a second chance, an opportunity to provide for his grandson all the things Sir Charles had been unable to do for his own son until it was too late. He had already set some of the legal machinery in motion to adopt young Michael and make him heir to all his estates. Margit, his only remaining child, was to be left a generous income and nothing else. Margit had survived internment but was confined to a sanitarium by a serious case of tuberculosis. With Bernard and her two boys dead, Margit was now alone.

And of course, there was now Patri as well. When Sir Charles learned about him after the war, he stopped at Matapura to meet him. At seventeen Patri was tall for an Iban. He had none of the Stanford blondness about him, but he was strikingly handsome in a dark and brooding way. Arrogant, hostile, guarded, and remote, to Sir Charles he resembled his grandfather, old Koh. But Sir Charles could also see something of Michael in the shape and set of the jaw, firm and square, and in the narrow, straight nose. Patri had black, burning eyes and beautiful slender hands, giving him a look that was at once mysterious and aristocratic.

Patri made him uneasy; nevertheless, he was Michael's son. Ahmad had said so, and Sir Charles accepted Ahmad's word as proven fact. So Sir Charles would have Patri tutored at Maitreya, and when he had progressed enough, he would send him to the best schools in England. He would give him an education and wealth, but he would never be able to give him his love—not this dark reminder of his old enemy. As for Patri, it was clear that he could scarcely imagine that this fair-skinned man, obviously an important chief, would have the same relation to Patri as had old Koh. Nor had he fully accepted yet that little Michael was his brother.

Sir Charles visited Catherine every day. He had always been fond of her, but now she had become like a daughter to him. He was with her when the news came over the ship's intercom system that Ahmad had been named prime minister of the new Republic of Indonesia. According to the news, Ahmad was still in Borneo with the liberation forces and was unavailable for comment. He would be arriving in Batavia within several days.

It had been the end of September, six weeks after the war ended, before the British liberation forces landed on Java to free Allied prisoners and accept the surrender of the Japanese troops. They arrived to find that the Indonesians had established their own independent government. The Dutch, however, were determined to return to the Indies and resume life as if nothing had changed. They refused even to negotiate the issue of independence with the newly established Indonesian government, which they regarded as not only illegitimate but composed of traitors who had no real support among the Indonesian people. The Dutch expected to be welcomed back by the Indonesians, if not with enthusiasm, at least with no more than the grudging hostility of old. But things had changed. The Indonesians were armed for the first time with weapons they had obtained from the defeated Japanese. More important, the old myth was gone: The Dutch no longer seemed invincible or even superior. And the Indonesians now had a rudimentary government around which they could rally their newborn nationalism. As the Dutch returned, the Indonesians took to the streets with riots, strikes, and acts of terrorism.

The British were caught in a no-win situation. Neither the Indonesians nor the Dutch trusted them. As civil strife increased, the beleaguered British forced the Dutch to the negotiating table by threatening to withdraw their liberating army from Indonesia, leaving the still-undermanned Dutch military forces to handle the situation alone. Recognizing their temporary weakness and their need to buy time to strengthen themselves, the reluctant Dutch had agreed to talks with the Indonesian government. However, they refused to negotiate with President Sukarno, whom they regarded as an opportunistic former puppet of the Japanese. To accommodate Dutch objections, the Indonesians reorganized their government. Sukarno remained as president, but the new post of prime minister was created to handle the matter of leading the negotiations. The post had to be filled by someone who was trusted by the Indonesians but acceptable to the Dutch as well. The sultan of Matapura was the obvious choice.

Catherine was stunned by the news. Indonesian politics had not been on her mind, so she had not expected to see it intrude dramatically into her life. Catherine had not heard from Ahmad since that day at Teram Island when she had lost consciousness and he had put her on an American plane headed for the U.S. hospital ship at Surabaya. He had sent word to her that he would come to her when he could, nothing more. Perhaps he no longer cared. Two years of separation was a long time. Now he was prime minister, and she had no idea what that would mean for her.

If she had thought about it, his appointment would not have surprised her. He was the logical choice. His credentials as a nationalist were impeccable, and his war record as a guerrilla leader meant no taint of collaboration hung over him to offend the Dutch. He had been decorated by the Allies for his part in the victory over Japan. He was both a hero to the common Indonesian people and a leader among the intellectuals.

"Well," Sir Charles remarked on hearing the news, "they couldn't have picked a better man. Damned sorry he accepted, though. Bloody dangerous business it's going to be. Negotiations imply concessions—from both sides—and neither one seems prepared to be very accommodating. The Dutch are already beginning to build an army, and the Indonesians won't be able to beat them in a conventional war. The British will see to that now, and in a few months the Dutch will be strong enough to see to it themselves. The alternative to negotiations will be a long, drawn-out guerrilla action."

Catherine lay silent, recovering from the shock. While Sir Charles thought aloud about the political implications, she could think only of herself. Sir Charles knew nothing of what had existed between her and Ahmad during the war. Catherine saw no need to tell him now since she herself was so unsure of how things stood.

"I didn't know Sukarno had it in him to pick a rival for prime minister," Sir Charles said musingly. "But I suppose he can always use the prime minister for a scapegoat should the concessions prove too unpopular. Sukarno doesn't like Ahmad, you know. The only things they possess in common are nationalist fervor and charisma. As men they are very different. Sukarno is the son of a Japanese village schoolteacher. Ahmad, on the other hand, is the epitome of the aristocratic intellectual. Ahmad will find few supporters in the rest of the Sukarno government either.

He does not come from Java, and he spent the war in guerrilla activities instead of cooperating with the occupation. They neither understand nor trust him. They are ambitious men as well and will feel threatened by the power his position can give him in future elections. Then there are the Moslem fanatics who will settle for nothing but an Islamic religious state.''

Sir Charles sighed, seemingly oblivious of Catherine's lack of response. Like an old political war-horse scenting battle, he was already formulating plans to address the British Parliament, and perhaps the fledgling United Nations, on behalf of Indonesian independence.

Two days later Catherine lay reading some of the newspapers Sir Charles had brought to her. The present cabinet had resigned and Ahmad had announced from Banjarmasin that he would appoint another with representation for all political points of view in an attempt to gain a wide base of support for the upcoming negotiations with the Dutch. In a controversial move, he had removed Foreign Minister Mohammed Husan, former head of the militia under the Japanese occupation, and dropped him from the cabinet entirely. Husan was a fervent Moslem, and his removal had already brought demonstrations and strong protests from the conservative Moslems.

There was no personal news about the new prime minister. There was one photograph of him too dark to show her anything but a dazzling smile. Damn it, she thought in frustration, and looked up to see Lieutenant Borden, the head nurse, arriving with her medication. Nurse Borden was relentlessly grim, and all the patients were intimidated by her, including Catherine, though she pretended not to be. To Catherine's surprise Nurse Borden was wearing a slightly conspiratorial smile as she pulled the side curtains around the bed.

"There's an important visitor here to see you."

Before Catherine could utter a word, he was standing there beside Lieutenant Borden. She resented him at the same time that the sight of him took her breath away and made her heart pound so hard it hurt to breathe. Why was it, she wondered, that men seemed to grow more attractive as they grew older while women did not? Perhaps because women weren't supposed to have character, only vacuous smoothness onto which men could easily project their personalities, she thought bitterly.

Lieutenant Borden was talking. Catherine could hear the words, but she could hardly believe the tone. Underneath all that professional reserve, the good nurse was gushing. Somehow Ahmad, with his strong good looks, his perfect health and vigor, had managed to charm her.

"If she feels up to it, Your Excellency, you may take her up to the deck for some fresh air. There's not much more privacy to be had up there, but at least it's more pleasant." She turned to leave, still carrying her medication tray filled with its tiny paper cups.

His black eyes revealed nothing. The silence between them grew.

"Congratulations on your appointment." Catherine smiled as cheerfully as she could as she added, "How should I address you now? Excellency? Your Royal Majesty?" And why haven't you written, you damned arrogant bastard? she added to herself.

He did not smile. When he spoke, it was in that soft familiar French accent that was itself a caress when he wished it to be. He addressed the hidden message, ignoring the spoken one.

"I'm sorry that I haven't been able to be here sooner. I wanted to come, but I've been in the oil fields trying to get production started again. We were very effective in destroying them, I'm afraid. There was no way to write."

Always a poor second, she thought, once to Kara and now to country.

"You are angry with me. Hurt, perhaps." He paused. When she did not respond, he went on. "I suppose it is no consolation to know that I wanted to come."

He sat down next to her on the bed. She was as beautiful as ever. Perhaps more so. Her dark hair, spilling across the pillow, had regained much of its old luster, and she had put on most of the weight she had lost. Her shoulders were bare above the sarong Sir Charles had brought her as a substitute for the nightgowns he had been unable to find in Surabaya. There was a new maturity about her that was hard to define but that somehow added to her beauty. She had lost the tan she had worn so elegantly two years earlier; now her face was pale, her skin almost translucent, though there was a pink flush to her cheeks and lips. He thought she had never looked more Irish, and he wondered if it was the suffering that had done it. Nor was it lost on him that she seemed to bloom at the sight of him, her eyes bright, her skin flushed with excitement. My God, how he loved her. It welled up inside him.

"Why is it, Catherine"—his face was serious, but his eyes sparkled—"that every time we've been around a bed in the past several years, you've been sick and I've had to control myself in ways I find difficult?"

She was surprised to find herself blushing, only making him laugh.

"And why is it I seem to make you blush these days?"

"You always did. Or have you forgotten?"

"I have forgotten nothing. I have relived my memories, every little detail, a million times these past two years."

His eyes, now intently on hers, were serious. "It was all I had to live for."

She reached a hand up, hesitantly, and touched the front of his shirt. He felt it tremble and brought her hand to his lips. Tears came to her eyes.

"Then take me with you," she whispered, but already she knew that he had come to say good-bye.

He felt his resolve wavering. As an American she was totally unacceptable to his more militant comrades. His involvement with her was known to only a few, but the rumors had been enough for them to oppose his appointment as prime minister. There was little doubt that his love for her could jeopardize his political future. Not that it mattered. He had taken the appointment only because there was no one else. He had no political ambitions. However, she might also jeopardize the delicate negotiations he was about to undertake with the Dutch. If his relationship with her were known, it could offend both sides; he had a chance to avert a bloody guerrilla war, and that must come before everything else.

"You can't come to Batavia. There are kidnappings and shootings daily. No white woman would be safe there, not even mine. But even if it was not too dangerous, I cannot take you with me now. My relationship with you could jeopardize the negotiations."

Her hand slipped from his shirt.

"Very well." She sounded oddly prim, like old Miss Johnson, her seventh-grade teacher, a woman trapped into living with the bitterness of lost dreams.

"It will change. I promise you," he said softly as if reading her thoughts. "I love you. You must always remember that."

She closed her eyes against his warmth.

Suddenly he was lifting her in his arms, easily, as if he were scarcely aware of her weight. The sheet with which she had covered herself slipped to the floor, leaving her in the ankle-length blue batik sarong.

At first she felt apprehensive, but as he bore her down the corridor, she relaxed against him and let her arms go around his neck.

"I can walk on my own now," she protested.

"I know." He smiled. "But that would deprive me of this pleasure."

Somehow her anger had evaporated. She rested her head against his shoulder and closed her eyes, and when they passed through an empty stretch of the narrow corridor, she even kissed him on his bare throat above his open collar and felt him catch his breath. This was her power. It comforted her to know she still had it.

"Even the Dutch can't make you a better proposition than mine," she added.

As Nurse Borden had indicated, the deck was not exactly private but was an improvement over the crowded wards. The morning sky was dull and overcast, but a pleasant breeze offset the tropical heat. As he lowered her, he caught her to him by the waist, pinning her against his hard body. The swelling between his legs pressed against her, hard and full of fire. Like a match tossed to tinder, her own passions ignited, and the torment raced between them, like wildfire, wherever their bodies touched, leaving them barely able to breathe. She stood staring into those black eyes, past their surface, into the warmer depths. If he had not been holding her firmly to him, she would have sunk to the deck. God, how she wanted him. It had been so long. They had ceased to be aware of the others on the deck, aware only of where their bodies achingly touched, down there where the fires raged.

"I love you." It came out of her in a choking sob as if he had wrenched it from her unwillingly. She moved her arms up slowly around his neck and pulled his head and mouth to hers. Too weak with desire to stand, they were in danger of sinking to their knees.

Suddenly Ahmad released her and stepped back. Sea air rushed between them in a shocking blast, as if ice water had been thrown to douse the fire. Ahmad took hold of the railing as if to steady himself. "Careful or I'll take you right here. It wouldn't do for the new prime minister to be caught copulating in public." He laughed, but there was no joy in it.

Catherine leaned against the rail next to him. "Especially on a foreign vessel, like me," she added sarcastically.

Their mood had changed. The frustration and pain that had haunted their relationship was with them still.

"Screw the goddamned ship." Catherine's breath caught in a sob. She reached out and took hold of the front of his shirt. "And screw the goddamned Indonesian government!" She leaned forward and touched her forehead against his chest, closing her eyes tightly, trying to force back the tears.

He put his hands lightly on her shoulders, not daring to let his body touch hers again.

She pulled free of his grasp and turned to look at the harbor.

"Will the negotiations be as dangerous as Sir Charles seems to think?"

"Yes," he said simply. He was surprised by the anger in Catherine's voice.

"You've done enough for Indonesia. We've both suffered enough. I have needs, too . . . and I need you to be with me. Let's go live in France, or England if you prefer."

His eyes, full of pain, reproached her. "I can't."

She eyed him defiantly. "We American women are used to having some say in the course our lives take. I just want it on the record that I'm opposed to what you're doing or to anything else that keeps us apart, whether it's my work or yours."

"You're talking about decisions to be made by normal people leading normal lives. We are not those people."

"You mean you aren't," she retorted.

He looked at her in surprise. Born to royalty, he had always been accustomed to the idea that personal needs must be subordinated to duty. He accepted this, but he should have realized that she would not. He smiled ruefully, inwardly cursing his lack of sensitivity. He should have consulted her before making his decision.

"I'm sorry, Catherine. I'm too used to acting on my own. I promise it won't happen again. Forgive me." He touched her hand, and she felt the thrill reluctantly spring to life again. She loved him. Yet fears filled her and held her back. She wondered if she was being totally honest. Did she resent his preoccupation with politics? Or was it that she resented the position itself? Equality, partnership, had always been important to her. How did one maintain equality with a king or a prime minister? She would become a mere consort to a famous man. Wasn't that what she feared more than anything else?

He stood beside her, staring at the sea as if some solution were to be found there in the green spray. He was intensely aware of her slight body next to him and the way the breeze lifted and played with her hair as if delighted by its silkiness.

"I would like you and Michael to go to Matapura as soon as you are well enough to leave the ship."

"Sir Charles has already arranged for us to go to Maitreya, at least for a while."

He frowned. He did not want her at Maitreya with its connections to Michael and a past she needed to put behind her. Still, he said nothing. He had no right, yet, to demand anything of her.

She went on. "I plan to go home to Chicago to see my parents. It's time they met their grandson. Sir Charles is coming along to help explain everything. His presence will support me and give them comfort as well." She said it lightly, as if it would be an easy thing to do, but her parents did not yet even know of her son's existence and she still feared they would not be able to accept him. "And I've been offered a teaching post at Columbia beginning with the winter semester. My book on the Dani has been a surprising success, so I'll be able to support myself quite nicely on the royalties until then."

He winced slightly and grinned. "Must you keep reminding me of how you don't really need me?"

"Oh—but I do need you." She turned her dark, serious eyes on him.

"Then come back to me," he said fiercely, and swung her up into his arms and kissed her until her head fell back against his shoulder, eyes half-closed, lips parted, giving in to him. As he

549

carried her back to her bed, the sound of other people in the corridors broke into the private place they had created between them. For a moment she clung tightly to him, closing her eyes, burying her face against the warm smoothness of his throat, resisting the intrusion.

"Is Siah with you?" Catherine asked.

He looked at her, surprised, as he gently lowered her to the bed and sat beside her.

"We Eastern men are not used to being asked such personal questions by the women in our lives. It is not considered your prerogative." His expression was serious, but there was a flicker of amusement in his eyes.

She smiled, knowing he was teasing her. "I've been jealous thinking of her for the past two years. At times it was unendurable."

The amusement went out of his eyes. "Siah is dead."

"I'm sorry," she said softly. She had expected every answer but that one.

"She died giving birth to a child conceived before you were captured. There was nothing between us after I returned from Teram, but I was with her when the child was born and, later, when she died." His voice was full of sadness, but then his expression lightened.

"I have a beautiful daughter, two years old now. I named her Kartini after the first woman leader of the nationalist movement. Kartini is in Matapura now, in the harem, but that is only temporary until I can arrange for a nurse and governess for her. Then I will bring her to Batavia."

A chill went through her at the mention of the harem. "You're keeping the concubines?"

"Of course. They're my responsibility. I've inherited them from my father. Some even from my grandfather. Even now there will be chiefs who will want to make a present of their daughters. Customs change slowly. Those recent gifts would be of use only for the times I tire of you," he said to tease her, then saw she was not mollified.

"I have already offered them all their freedom and a handsome pension. Many of the younger ones have already left." He did not add that many had also stayed in the hope of someday winning his favor.

"I love you, Catherine. No one else. There will never be anyone else for me. I know it's foolish to make promises about the future, but this is simply a statement. I slept with other women to relieve my fears and sexual needs. But much less often than you are imagining."

She looked at his buttonless shirt, which fell slightly open as he leaned forward, revealing his smooth, muscular chest, and she thought of those other women who might have shared his body, even briefly. She felt intensely jealous. After all, she had done without for the past two years, why couldn't he?

Guessing her thoughts, he said, "If it's what you want, Catherine, there will be no other women. I promise you. Is it what you want?"

"Yes."

His eyes were earnest. "In the past two years it happened only when I thought I was going to die and would never see you again."

"It's what I want," she whispered.

He bent down and then hesitated, his mouth above hers. She began to tremble and closed her eyes. For a moment more she felt his warm breath upon her lips, and then he planted a gentle kiss upon her forehead.

"Soon," he whispered, and then he was gone.

Ahmad paid his respects to the ship's captain and then joined the driver of the British military car waiting at the end of the dock to take him to the airport where the British were providing a military plane to fly him to Batavia. The Dutch bitterly resented such "conveniences" being furnished to their rivals by the British, but the truth was the British were anxious for a settlement which would allow them to extract themselves from a difficult situation as soon as possible. To them, the new prime minister was a precious political object, too valuable to entrust to anyone else.

Ahmad would have preferred to have driven himself. It had never been easy for him to trust his well-being to others. As a passenger he was a notorious backseat driver. This time he satisfied himself by riding in the front seat beside the British sergeant who was his driver. He and the sergeant chatted amicably all the way to the airfield. Neither of them spoke of the war.

551

The sergeant talked of England and his eagerness to be home after being so long away, and Ahmad described the various sights of Surabaya.

They were nearing the field when the car slowed before an overturned cart on the road. As the car stopped, Ahmad glimpsed a man with a pistol run up beside his window and take careful aim with two hands. Ahmad yelled a warning to the driver as he ducked down to throw the door open and slam it out against the would-be assassin. It deflected the gunman's aim, but he pulled the trigger as the door struck him. The gun discharged, hitting the driver in the head, killing him instantly. Ahmad rolled out and grasped the man around the legs, sending him sprawling back against the car. The gun went off again, the bullet ricocheting on the pavement as Ahmad quickly got to his feet and gripped the gunman's hand to smash it back against the hood before the man could regain his balance. The gun flew away, clattering over the metal hood, and struck the ground with a dull thud.

Ahmad relaxed, retaining a firm grip on the man he held pinned against the car. British soldiers were converging on the road around him, sirens blaring. Ahmad released the assassin and stepped back with a look of contempt. He addressed the man quietly in Bahasa Indonesian as the soldiers seized him to bundle him off.

"If we were alone, I would break your neck with my hands. You had better tell your friends they cannot afford to miss next time, for I will personally kill the next one who tries."

The soldiers dragged the man away, leaving Ahmad trembling with anger and fear beside the car. The bullet hole and the shattered glass around it seemed to mock him. Catherine. If Catherine had been with him, she would surely have been killed. He knew now she would never be safe with him, not so long as he played with such high political stakes. His own chances of surviving were slim. He had no choice now; when it was time for Catherine to go to the States, he would do nothing to stop her. If she found someone else, perhaps it would be best. She deserved freedom and happiness, and he could give her neither now. He could only let her go, to find her own.

With that decision he realized that the assassin's bullet had not missed him after all. Here, on the empty leather seat too hot to touch, behind the splintered glass flecked with someone else's blood, a part of him had died.

Chapter 52

The battle for Surabaya began in October, when the British dropped leaflets, ordering the Indonesians there to turn in their weapons. The Indonesians, not trusting the British and justifiably fearful of the Dutch, rebelled. Members of the militant Indonesian Youth Movement attacked the scattered units of the British brigade in the city, massacring soldiers and newly freed Dutch civilians alike, hacking them limb from limb. British reinforcements arrived, and soon it was the Indonesians who were being massacred, and neither the British military nor the republican government was able to effect a cease-fire until the violence had run its course.

The Dutch reacted equally forcefully. "We have been in the Indies for three hundred and fifty years," one former governor-general was quoted as saying, "and in another three hundred and fifty years, we'll begin to talk about independence." To ease the shock, shortly before her arrival home, Catherine had written her parents about the existence of her son. When she did arrive, Catherine was relieved to see that Sir Charles's good humor and enthusiasm seemed to overwhelm the room where her parents quietly received them. But when the conversation slackened, her mother seemed nervous and preoccupied, her father, polite and cold. The wit which had always disguised the forbidding, critical aspects of his personality was absent. He had little to say to Catherine. She had destroyed the illusion of perfection he had worked so hard to create in his life and he was not about to forgive her. Catherine was surprised to find that, after all those years of separation, he still had the power to hurt her. The realization left her shaken. Her mother's reaction was made explicit when she and Catherine were alone in the kitchen. It was Sunday and the servants were gone. Her mother was not used to doing things for herself. Mouth tight, she poured the steaming tea water into the preheated silver pots, one filled with steeping tea and the other with hot water to dilute it. She concentrated on making sure everything was done properly, and that the small cakes and sandwiches were attractively arranged on a silver tray, before she turned her attention to Catherine. Then her mouth began to quiver in anger. "Catherine, how could you come here like this? What will I tell people?"

"The truth, if they ask. I don't intend to advertise that I have a child out of wedlock, but I'm not ashamed of it. If you like, you can add that his father is dead and that we loved each other very much."

"How can you stand there so calmly? You've disgraced us!" her mother cried, unmollified. "And now you've come here to flaunt it before our friends." Tears came to her eyes. It was the first time Catherine had ever seen her mother cry. Catherine thought of Michael, innocently and happily chatting away in the next room. Her beautiful, glorious son. How could he possibly disgrace anyone? But appearances had always been more important than reality in her mother's life. Now she knew she had failed her mother miserably.

She was surprised at the calmness in her voice when she answered, "I came only because I wanted you to meet your grandson and for him to get to know you."

"You did it to punish me! Upset me!"

Without another word, Catherine picked up the tray and returned to the living room, where Sir Charles was in the middle of an amusing story, as if he, not her father, were the host. What had she hoped to have happen by coming here? Now she couldn't imagine. Her mother was pouring the tea, making idle conversation as if the incident in the kitchen had never taken place. Maybe it hadn't. Maybe it was all in her own mind.

"Cream and sugar, dear?" Her mother held out a cup toward her, a cool, thin smile upon her lips.

"Nothing," Catherine replied.

It was the final break.

It wasn't just the outbreak of fighting in Indonesia which brought Catherine back to the States. She had wanted to return to the university and get on with her career, and the need had become urgent. She didn't want anything more to do with wars and upheavals and sacrifices. If she could have him (and she couldn't), she didn't even want Ahmad. Ahmad meant revolution and danger and the threat of another loss.

"I'm just a war veteran looking for security and a quiet life," she told Ginny with a tight smile when Ginny met her at the train in New York.

Ginny shook her head as she gave Catherine and Michael a hug of welcome. "Catherine, you should have been a man or married an explorer like Martin Johnson. I don't believe you'll ever settle down."

Catherine felt a little stab of surprise as she returned the hug. She had always thought of the world about her, rather than herself, as being unsettled.

Ginny pulled away and affectionately studied her face a moment. "You look marvelous, Catherine. I wasn't expecting it."

Catherine smiled ruefully. "Just a little saggy around the edges."

Catherine herself had taken little notice of how she looked. Though past thirty, she was not one to search her mirror for signs of advancing age. Her self-esteem had never been defined by her looks.

"You never give up, do you, Catherine?" Ginny had observed later, when the two of them had settled Michael in the new apartment Ginny had found for Catherine near the university and had gone out to dinner. "You're tough. Tougher than I could ever be."

Catherine thought she detected a note of criticism in this last remark. "I scarcely think of myself as tough."

"You survived. New Guinea. Japanese captivity. A lot of others died, but you survived."

Carl had died. Tom had died. Ginny didn't say it, but the accusation was there. It had been Catherine, not Ginny, who had shared the last moments of their lives, and Catherine had survived.

"Michael died, too," Catherine added softly.

556

"I know. I'm sorry, Catherine. Sometimes I feel so bitter about it all. Angry with Carl for choosing such a dangerous career. Angry with Tom for joining the Navy. They should have just been good old Midwest farmers and stayed home."

"Did you ever tell Carl how you felt?" Catherine asked.

"Can you imagine me not speaking my mind?"

Catherine smiled. "He never held it against you."

Ginny laughed. "I know. We were opposites in so many ways. I was always so practical, and he was such a dreamer." She was silent for a moment and then added, "I suppose that's why it worked so well between us."

Catherine nodded but said nothing. Ginny had been remarried a few years ago to a teacher. From her description he was a practical man, like Ginny herself, never given to adventuring of any sort. Stable. Secure. One who would define risks in terms of changing teaching jobs from one small town to another. He could not be, Catherine thought with prejudice, as special as Carl.

"You ought to settle down and get married, too," Ginny said to her over coffee after they had finished dinner. "For little Michael's sake."

"Oh?" Catherine smiled. "I haven't noticed men lining up at the door with offers."

"They will be. What about the sultan?"

Catherine suddenly felt exasperated. "Really, Ginny, I don't need a man in my life to be happy."

Ginny shrugged. "No. But it helps. Especially when you're alone with a son. I know." She looked at Catherine skeptically. "But then I don't think I ever understood you very well. You wanted things more than most of us—women, I mean, or you wouldn't have gotten a Ph.D. It was such a difficult thing for a woman to do, I suppose you had to be a bit more selfish, more single-minded."

Catherine looked surprised and hurt, but Ginny went on without noticing. "Still, poor David. I suppose you never should have become engaged to him. Carl knew it was all wrong from the beginning. He said David could never handle either you or your success. David was such a spoiled little boy, really. But still, he deserved better than he got."

Catherine was stunned. This was not some jealous schoolgirl. This was Ginny talking. Ginny, who had always been her friend.

557

Ginny went on. "I wouldn't have done it, Catherine. Michael was a married man with two little children. No matter how I felt, I wouldn't have done it." She looked uneasily at Catherine and gave an embarrassed shrug.

"Why are you telling me this now, Ginny?" Catherine demanded, her voice full of hurt.

"I don't know. I haven't seen you since Tom died. I guess I'm angry. Tom loved you, too, Catherine. I was always so afraid it would spoil his life for him. You were so preoccupied with Michael." She was silent a moment. "And I guess I should be honest. I always suspected Carl was a little bit in love with you himself. I resented that. I wouldn't be honest if I didn't tell you. It's always been between us."

"You think I'm getting what I deserve? Is that it, Ginny?" Catherine asked with bitterness.

"No." Ginny looked at the expression on Catherine's face and sighed. "Look. Don't be upset. I never should have said anything."

"If I had it to do over again, I'd still do it," Catherine replied defiantly, "even knowing how it would turn out. I loved Michael. I suppose I always will. Just as you must still love Carl."

"No," Ginny said sharply. "I *loved* Carl. I don't still love him. The difference between you and me is that you never give up. You're so used to having your own way that you don't always leave things behind when you should. You haven't accepted Michael's death, or else you'd be able to let go. Michael is your Achilles' heel. He always has been." Ginny placed her hand on Catherine's arm in sympathy and sighed. "Forget what I've said. Please. You've suffered more than most."

Catherine looked out the restaurant window. It had begun to snow. The first snow she had seen in many years. She had missed it. It was one of the few things she had missed. She had never felt so much alone as she did at that moment.

Chapter 53

Catherine was surprised to find how much she missed the Indies. The decay in New York was different from the decay of the Indies, but it was no less prevalent. Here the decay was dry and brittle and cracked, gray instead of green with fungus. In the postwar boom New York flourished and it was impossible to find housing. Even the unexpected royalties from her book could not buy greater comfort than a walk-up flat with faded wallpaper and musty smells. However, it was conveniently close to the university and to the sitter who cared for Michael. He had adjusted well. Sometimes the existence of New Guinea became too unreal in the crowded grime of New York. Yet her son was living proof that it had not been a dream.

Patri had joined Sir Charles in London. He had proved an excellent student in his tutorial studies, and Sir Charles planned to send him first to English public school and then on to Oxford. But Patri had begun to develop a will of his own, so those plans were by no means certain. He wrote Catherine regularly, and she arranged for him to visit in the summer. Michael would benefit from his older brother's presence, and Catherine recognized that Patri could use a vacation from Sir Charles's efforts to turn him into an English gentleman.

Margit was released from the sanitarium but remained in England and refused to return to Maitreya or the Indies—ever again.

"I can't bear ever to see the place again," she wrote to

Catherine. "I've taken the old family cottage at Cornwall. I seldom see anyone but the servants, which is fine with me. I am becoming a recluse. In a few more years I shall have become that mysterious old woman in that mysterious old house at which all the village children shall throw tin cans and run like hell."

Catherine wrote back cheerful, optimistic letters. But there was little she could do to help Margit.

Catherine's teaching position began in February with the start of the spring semester. She was surprised to find her classes in cultural anthropology filled to overflowing. Students lined the walls and filled the aisles, many without the necessary enrollment cards. She accepted all of them and arranged for them to have credit, even though it meant extra work for her. In most circumstances veterans with wives and kids to support didn't have time to waste on something as unnecessary as anthropology, but Catherine's book was causing an increased interest in her subject.

Teaching had always been painful for Catherine. She was shy. Being the center of attention of all those eyes made her uncomfortable, but her fear never showed. She was relaxed, and joked with the students, but she had never wanted to teach with her degree. Research was what she liked. She was never so happy as when she was alone in the library immersed in words and ideas, her own or someone else's, or on field trips where she could be an observer. She was disappointed that her feelings about teaching hadn't changed, expecting to have outgrown her shyness as if it were some childish feeling. But she found that each time she entered those overheated classrooms with their clanking radiators and worn wooden floors and expectant faces, she cringed.

Old Professor Gordon, this year's rotating vice-chairman of the department, passed her in the hall. "Good morning, my dear," he muttered through teeth clenching an unlit pipe which smelled faintly foul, like the professor himself.

Catherine nodded and gritted her teeth: always "my dear" or "Miss Morgan," never "Dr. Morgan," as if his mind rebelled at the thought. The old curmudgeon lectured from yellowed notes in a rambling and disorganized manner he never seemed to notice, gleefully ridiculing his junior colleagues and heaping scorn on his students.

As she passed him in the hall, she wondered why it irritated her that his tie clashed with his rumpled shirt and his pants drooped over the tops of his shoes. He was lazy and arrogant. He never kept his office hours, and his tests were sloppily assembled and even more carelessly graded. They showed his contempt for his students. Nothing would be done about it. As a full professor he was one of the untouchables, and he knew it. Somebody should light a fire in that pipe, she muttered as she passed him—and stick it up your can. The tower chimes sounded the hour in the solemn, ponderous self-important tune that announced the beginning of class.

In April the talks between the Dutch and Indonesians taking place in Holland broke down almost as quickly as they had begun. The Dutch balked and refused to negotiate with the republican government, declaring that it did not exist and therefore they could not negotiate with it. Catherine saw Ahmad interviewed about the failure of the talks in a Movietone newsreel that preceded a movie matinee she and Ginny attended one April Saturday. She hardly recognized him in the chilly European spring air, dressed in an overcoat. He seemed so out of place, yet the unexpected sight of him made her heart leap. He had left the aborted conference to address the UN meeting in London in an impassioned plea to the world for support for Indonesian independence. He had stirred the delegates and brought renewed pressure on the Dutch.

After the movie Catherine left Ginny at the subway station and trudged home on foot. The late-afternoon air was still cold. With a shock of recognition she caught sight of a thatch of blond hair waiting in front of a store. That certain tilt of the head was so familiar, yet it belonged to a stranger. The blue eyes beneath the hair discovered her stare and quizzically returned it, suddenly interested. She dropped her glance and quickly hurried by him. She felt his eyes still on her as she lost herself in the crowd. Oh Michael, she pleaded, you've left this earth. Now leave me in peace. Leave me.

Patri arrived with summer vacation, a remarkably poised and sophisticated young man of eighteen. Michael was delighted with his company, and Patri good-naturedly took care of his younger brother much as he had helped with such chores in Rumah Pacou. He had finally accepted his English heritage, but Ameri-

561

ca's informality appealed to him. And he was glad to be with Catherine again.

In late summer the British announced they intended to withdraw all their forces from Indonesia in November, leaving the Dutch on their own. Once again the announcement had the desired effect of forcing the Dutch to agree to negotiate with the republic's representatives. In the meantime, tensions continued high, and there were scattered outbreaks of violence, although Maitreya remained out of the turmoil. Sir Charles had returned to Borneo and was anxious for Catherine and Michael to join him, but Catherine informed him she had already made up her mind to remain at the university and teach the following school year.

Sir Charles came to spend the Christmas holidays in New York, thoroughly out of sorts.

"My dear Catherine, I can't understand why you insist on remaining here when you could live at Maitreya. You're needlessly exposing yourself and the boy to all kinds of public censure."

Catherine replied hotly, "No one knows about Michael's existence except for a few people I trust. And it's nobody's business anyway."

"Catherine, I want to make Michael my heir. And when I do, the whole story will come out in the papers."

"No," Catherine protested. "Don't do it now. Wait awhile."

"Until when, Catherine? You can't hide forever. Don't expose yourself and my grandson to the kind of hurt you will experience once it's found out. Come back with me to Maitreya."

The discussion led nowhere. Catherine was adamant about remaining at the university. She had been nominated for the Peabody Chair in anthropology, a three-year research grant that went to an outstanding and promising junior faculty member. Having published her book and two highly acclaimed articles on the effect of cultural practices on aggressive behavior, she was the unquestioned front runner to receive the appointment. Granted, the fact that she was a woman could hurt her chances, but it seemed certain the selection committee of the faculty would overcome its prejudices and make her the first woman to receive the award.

Another factor held her back from accompanying Sir Charles back to Borneo as he wished. She was afraid of Maitreya. She didn't know why. A silly, irrational fear. But it existed, and it made her resist returning with him.

Catherine returned to her office one day before Christmas vacation ended. She always found the classrooms and halls a depressing place when the students were gone. The department's office staff had come to work during most of the vacation, so the mailboxes in the cramped mail cubicle were stuffed like Christmas stockings with two weeks' worth of mail and phone messages. She thrust the stack of messages aside without looking at them and sorted through her mail. One letter was from the Peabody selection committee. It had come earlier than she had expected. She opened it and read it twice, unable to believe what it contained. The appointment had gone to someone else. She walked down the hall toward the chairman's office, the open letter fluttering from her hand. His door was open. Even before she reached it, she could see the rectangle of white light on the darkened hall ahead.

"I've been expecting you."

Catherine entered without pausing and put the letter upon the desk before him. "Why?"

He was bearded and coatless with his cuffs turned up and his tie askew. He sighed, lifting a pencil which he held by each end, examining it in order not to look at her. "The child, Catherine. Your child." His voice barely concealed his exasperation. "The one you decided to have without bothering to marry someone first." He shook his head. "That little fact somehow got passed on to the committee. For that matter, it could be out to the whole world by now. Faculty wives. Shockable parents of college undergraduates. Boards of directors. Fund raisers. The donating alumni and public, not to mention an anxious administration trying to balance next year's budget." He shook his head again. "I don't know what you were thinking when you decided to keep that child and raise him by yourself. But it's not your morality that irritates me. It's your stupidity!" He was looking at her now, his eyes full of indignant disbelief. "Who did you think you were that you could flaunt your culture's values and be immune? You, of all people."

Tears of hurt stung her eyes. She wanted to be strong, but

instead, she felt weak and vulnerable. "When he was born, I couldn't give him up."

"You tried?"

"I never even considered it."

He was silent a moment. "And an abortion?"

"I couldn't." What could she tell him, that she had loved his father too much and his son was all she had? She couldn't reveal that. Not now.

He stared at her. "You're a brilliant anthropologist. If it were just me, I wouldn't give a damn. And most of the faculty wouldn't give a damn either. Many of them, like me, knew about it and kept it confidential. But it was bound to get out to the administration and people financially important to the university. The university won't fire you. Legally it can't. I wouldn't let it anyway."

She disdained giving him a look of gratitude.

"But," he continued, "you can forget about honors. And you may even have to forget about tenure as well. As the old expression goes, we make our own beds and are forced to lie in them." He tossed the pencil on the desk. "Your problem is that you let Michael Stanford into yours without getting married first."

His resentment was obvious, and Catherine understood its source. He had supervised her dissertation and hired her for the faculty. He had wanted the best for her, and now he blamed her because he couldn't give it to her. "I'm sorry," he said with finality. "I didn't say it was right or fair. That's just the way it is."

"Is this a life sentence?" she asked coldly. "I believe even the worst of criminals can get time off for good behavior."

"The academic circle is exceedingly small. It offers little room for redemption."

"Any suggestions?"

"A research institute. Or the staff of one of the museums. Something inconspicuous."

By the time she walked out of the old brick building a few minutes later Catherine felt she knew where the earth's real savages resided. When she left the campus and joined the crowded city streets, she could feel herself slipping into depression. "Oh, no, you don't," she said out loud. The busy sidewalk traffic didn't even slow down for a moment. Oh, no, you don't, she said, to herself this time, but with even more determination. She began to walk faster, and by the time she got home she was good and mad.

She slammed the door behind her and walked to the front window. She hated New York. Only the very rich lived decently here. And besides, it felt good to hate something outside herself.

"Well, city, you had your chance, and you blew it. I'm leaving."

Giving up her dreams of academic success would not be easy, and she knew it. She would have to find a new dream. She would return to Borneo, to Maitreya. And she would go back to the Dyak and Iban villages along the river, but with a different purpose this time: not simply to study them but to help them survive the influences of encroaching civilization.

"You're not going off again to play Tarzan in the jungle, are you?" Ginny wailed on hearing the news. "Be sensible! Take a museum job. What's so awful about playing with bones and dusting off artifacts? A job isn't everything. Do something creative with your leisure time."

"Oh, Ginny." Catherine laughed. "Maybe Carl didn't tell you that tribal hunters and gatherers have more leisure time than we do."

Catherine finished the term. She took daily flying lessons and found them exhilarating. She soloed in a week and had her license after two months, but she could never completely escape her depression. In early February the *National Geographic* approached her about doing an article on Matapura. Realizing the assignment would pay her expenses back to Borneo, she readily agreed, provided it would keep the author's identity a secret until after the piece was completed. The magazine made all the arrangements, seeking the sultan's permission through its political contacts in Java. The permission came back written in the sultan's own hand. If he had any idea it was Catherine who would write the article, there was no indication of it in the letter. Once she reached Banjarmasin, Borneo, she sent Michael to Maitreya to join his grandfather while she proceeded on alone to Matapura.

Chapter 54
Matapura

The red glow of the single lamp did little to illuminate the treasure house. Using her flashlight to guide her, Catherine lit the taper in the pusaka. Around her gold and gems leaped to life in their glass resting places, glowing with a special fire, as if eager to be seen. Most of the fine furniture and art objects that were in the palace before the occupation had been stolen or destroyed by the Japanese. But the sacred family treasures of the *pusaka* had been hidden safely away and rested, untouched, in the darkness of this dry crypt.

She took flash pictures of the room and its contents, which she would go over with Mr. Sujir, Ahmad's secretary, when she had developed them. With his help and knowledge of the royal family history she had been able to write the article in Ahmad's absence. Before leaving the room she returned to the one article that had most intrigued her, a gold headdress belonging to the sun goddess or to someone who had portrayed the sun goddess in some court drama or ceremony. It was covered with long, slender spikes of varying lengths, each no thicker than a matchstick, and encrusted with pearls and diamonds. She could not resist trying it on, pressing her loose black hair up beneath the snug helmet until it was hidden from sight and only the headdress framed her face. She searched among the cases and found a bejeweled hand mirror and held it to the light. Her delicate features were exquisitely encased in the cap of gold, and the jewels flashed in candlelight.

She stared at the mirror in fascination, as if she somehow recognized the stranger she saw reflected there.

Intrigued with the masquerade, she explored the chests until she found one filled with gossamer silks enbroidered with gold thread and tiny jewels. She chose one with a brilliant blue background. When she lifted it from the chest, it hung suspended around her like the sky. She slipped out of her clothes and tied the cloth around her, court style, beneath her arms, with shoulders bare. She felt as if she were transporting herself to some other time, transforming herself into some other person. She selected gold armbands and bracelets and slipped them on.

Turning her back on the candle, she struck a pose she had often seen in Javanese theatrical dance, *wayang wong,* palms pressed together above her head and tilted slightly forward, head high and turned to the side. She closed her eyes and heard the discordant notes of the gamelan begin to play within her head. Her long fingers fluttered, and she moved delicately from the hips, gliding so that her feet scarcely seemed to touch the ground. Her neck and shoulders were motionless; her breathing was invisible, her face without expression as if she were in a trance. Suddenly she kicked the trailing skirt of her *kain* aside and turned abruptly to face the candlelight. As the light struck her fully in the face, she heard the sound of a sharply indrawn breath. Her eyes flew open, and she stared in fear at the darkness that lay beyond the candles' light. No other sound followed. She slowly lowered her arms. She could see nothing, but she could sense the presence of someone in the room.

A form, dressed in white, emerged from the shadows and approached her.

"I'm sorry. I seem to have interrupted your dancing, and it was so nice that even I could hear the music. I hope I haven't frightened you." The familiar voice: slightly accented, melodious, soft.

Her mouth fell open in surprise, and she felt her face redden with embarrassment that he had observed her.

"I was able to get away for a few days, so I flew here this evening. The servants said you were working late tonight." He chatted easily, giving her time to recover while he watched her carefully.

"I save the daylight hours for outside photography."

"Very efficient. You must be in a hurry, then, to finish and be gone." He did not wait for a reply. "How are Sir Charles and Michael?"

"Fine. They're at Maitreya."

He glanced around the room. "Have you obtained all the necessary assistance you have needed for your article?"

Brisk. Formal. She might well be a journalist and nothing more, she thought with annoyance.

"Yes, thank you. I've almost completed it." She nodded toward her camera. "These are the last pictures I'll need."

"Let me take a picture of you in full costume."

"No!"

She felt awkward, silly. What had felt so natural moments ago when she was alone now seemed only ridiculous.

He sensed her distress. "The crown becomes you," he said by way of reassurance.

"I hope it was all right to have put it on—" She broke off. He had crossed to one of the cases and removed a pair of gold sandals.

"Just to complete the picture." Before she could reply, he knelt on the marble floor before her and lifted one of her feet.

"Good," he said. "The slipper fits. That means you must marry the prince, or there won't be a happy ending." He slipped the other sandal on her foot and then rose.

Her heart was pounding as she said as lightly as she could, "But the prince has already become a king."

"In that case, you're way behind schedule and had better hurry." He said it teasingly, as if she should not take him too seriously.

He crossed the room and pulled a scarf away to reveal a full-length, elaborately carved gold-leaf mirror.

"Come see if you aren't indeed a princess."

She crossed and stood before the mirror. The sight dazzled even her. He stood behind her, his hands resting lightly, almost impersonally, on her shoulders.

"This is an ancient Hindu headdress," he explained. "From the sixteenth century. Before the Dutch. Before Islam. And the *kain* should be worn thus. . . ." He loosened it and let it slip to her waist.

The candlelight trembled for a moment in the slight breeze and then steadied itself. She stood staring at her naked body in the mirror. It made her feel too vulnerable, and she wanted to hide. She didn't notice his fingers deftly secure the *kain* around her waist.

"Now it is perfect." He stepped back, and she could no longer see his face in the mirror. Without thinking, she crossed her arms over her breasts before she turned toward him.

"You are still shy with me, Catherine?"

"I scarcely know you anymore."

"But you do! I haven't changed. You put this wall of strangeness between us, not I," he said fiercely.

Her own anger flared. "What of the women I have seen you with in the newspaper photographs? Like the blond actress in Jakarta. Why is it safe for her to be there but not for me? And the redhead at the UN reception?"

"The redhead was the wife of a friend, and the blonde was a British general's mistress eager to join him in Hong Kong."

"But willing to tarry in Jakarta?"

"Yes. If I had been interested."

"Did you sleep with her?"

He looked at her sadly. "You are beginning to sound like a wronged, neglected wife, exiled to the country against her will while her husband carries on shamelessly in the city. You're an independent woman with a career of your own, but when I tell you I understand and that it is fine with me, you only resent it. You return to the United States without telling me when you'll be back, or even if you'll be back at all. You insist on your own independence, but you also resent me for giving it to you."

"Did you sleep with her!" she demanded again.

"Yes! But she was nothing to me, as I was nothing to her, except, perhaps, a challenge. Many women are like her. Wanting power and having none, they seek it vicariously through the men they choose. I much prefer a woman who, wanting power, gets it for herself, directly, so long as she will take responsibility for possessing it."

She did not respond to him. Instead, she turned her back and readjusted the *kain* to its original position, covering her breasts. It was an action as deliberate as a slap in the face. When she turned back to face him, her face was cold and expressionless.

His eyes burned angrily into hers. "You will use her as an

excuse, but it isn't an actress who comes between us. Just as some women vicariously seek power there are others who are afraid of it, who shy away from it, in themselves and others." His eyes bored intently into hers. "Why are you afraid of power, Catherine, of me?" He reached out and dug his fingers tightly into her arms. "Why?"

Again she did not answer him. He was powerless after all. A king, powerless. It was not an easy thing to feel. Yet it was true, for the solution lay within her, not within him. He knew he frightened her with his ingrained tendency to rule, his self-confidence which occasionally bordered on arrogance. Undeniably the power she feared in him was real. It was up to her to deal with it. And he could see, time and again, that she could not. She could not stand up to him when she should, or else she did so only to a point and then backed off, leaving him with a victory he neither wanted nor savored.

"Catherine," he said softly. His hands tightened on her arms, and he saw a hint of fear come into her eyes. "Don't be afraid of me. Challenge me!" he pleaded. "Stand up to me, and I will gladly capitulate. Don't surrender to my masculinity, but don't reject it either! We can be different and still be equal."

Tears rose to her eyes as she recognized the truth in much of what he said. His eyes held her tightly to him, those marvelous black eyes with their hard edge of violence whose gaze was made bearable only by their inner warmth and tenderness.

"Tell me," he whispered, "that you don't still love me, and I will leave you alone and never speak of it again."

His eyes held her in an embrace as fierce as if they stood naked and entwined. She felt her pulse pounding in her ears, and her breath came rapidly. She was aware only of those eyes and that tender mouth so irresistibly close to hers. Her own lips parted, and she began to tremble. She closed her eyes against him, and a little cry of surrender escaped her throat. He released her arms and lifted the headdress from her head. Her hair tumbled out over her shoulders as he gathered her tightly to him. Slowly he lowered his mouth and caught hers in a soft, lingering kiss that was a sublime contrast with the lust with which their loins strained and pressed together. Just when she could stand no more of such sore temptation, he swept her up into his arms. Her head fell back, and he pressed his lips against her throat. The candlelight fluttered wildly. Her arms tightened around his neck, and she buried her face against him, savoring the sweet natural fragrance of his shirt and skin.

By the time they reached the private garden the gates already stood ajar, for there was not a servant present in the *kraton* that night who didn't know the path their sultan took or the treasure that he had found in the *pusaka* and carried so gently away in his arms.

Within the bridal *pendopo*, a pavilion supported by elaborate carved columns, hundreds of slender candles lit the entrance and the high pyramided ceiling bordered by a carved wooden frieze covered with gold leaf. The carvings were beautifully rendered eleventh-century Hindu scenes of handsome men and voluptuous women in the most intimate and extraordinary postures of sensual love. Above the gleaming gold frieze the pavilion ceiling was covered with murals of a similar nature, naked men and women entwined or passionately caressing. Only the side of the pavilion next to the courtyard had a solid wall. The rest of it stood on pillars or on jutting mountain rock, open to the jungle and sea beyond except for a finely meshed, transparent curtain that surrounded the room and warded off mosquitoes. At the pavilion's far edge, surrounded by the night itself, sat the round silk-covered bridal bed. The white marble floor gleamed as untouched and pure as the virgins the room was designed to receive.

Ahmad put Catherine down and kissed her forehead. She felt intoxicated by the fragrant scent of jasmine mixed with the musky smell of incense. He loosened her *kain,* and it fell away from her, floating lightly to the floor. He caught his breath at the sight of her slender, delicately curved body. Neither his memory nor her body had betrayed him. She was exquisitely beautiful.

He reached out and brushed the back of his hand lightly against her belly, and she shivered with pleasure at his touch. His hand slid farther down, and his fingers entangled themselves in her dark triangle. His eyes slowly traveled over her. Then they returned to hers and locked. She was trembling as she reached out and unwound the wide printed belt that held his shirt together. It slipped to the floor, and his shirt fell open. She reached inside it to touch her palms against the muscles of his chest and felt him flinch. She lowered her hands until, through the cotton of his pants, she felt the hard swell that rose from his groin. Her hands shook as she loosened his pants, pulling them over his hips.

Hesitantly, shyly she let her eyes travel down his fine body as his had traveled hers. She reached out and touched the base of his straining shaft, stroking the wiry tendrils there, cupping the full-veined sacs in her hand, lifting them lightly in her palm as if weighing how much pleasure might be stored there. Then she slipped a hand between his legs to let it rest quietly, contained by the smooth hardness of his thighs. His hand sought the warm pocket between her own thighs, stroking her with his fingers until they both felt the tender opening between her legs swell and moisten with desire. All the longings she had suppressed for so long now burst forth in an unbearable ache, a desperate need.

"Ahmad," she whispered.

His arms pulled her against him. The sweet shock of his naked body against her own bare flesh was overpowering. His mouth sought hers, urgent, crushing. Her lips parted to receive his probing tongue. He twisted his body slowly against hers, and she responded eagerly, her arms around his waist, her hands on his buttocks, holding him to her, welcoming his slow, twisting thrusts that massaged her belly and left a warm sticky trail upon her skin. His mouth clung to hers a moment longer before he pulled back and examined her face in the candles' glow. It appeared so soft, so vulnerable that the passion on his face softened.

"I love you," he whispered huskily.

Her eyes, half-closed with her own desire, opened wide, and she smiled.

"I love you," she murmured softly in reply as he carried her into the shadows on the far side of the room where the bed lay bathed in star- and moonlight. Here the room was white and cool in contrast with the fire that raged in their feverish bodies. The bed, on the edge of the pavilion, seemed to soar freely out into the night, borne up only by the sea's breezes. The world dropped away 3,000 feet below them. Only the *pendopo*'s fragile mosquito curtain separated them from the universe. He gently lowered Catherine to the bed and lay down beside her, resting on an elbow so that he could study her.

"Now . . . ." she urged him. There was no need for more preliminaries.

"There is no need to be quick, this time," he answered. "Indulge my Oriental soul and have patience."

For a long moment he studied her face. Her dark hair tumbled in seductive disarray upon the cushion. In the pale light he could see her almond eyes, transformed by passion, fixed on his own. He lay beside her without touching her until they both began to tremble. Ahmad paused above her for a moment, his eyes a color darker than black, his breath a soft kiss upon her lips. She heard her name whispered before the sun dropped out of the sky and entered her. For a moment she froze, much as the night might freeze if a burst of brilliant sunlight suddenly struck open its darkest sanctuaries. But the bright flame was gentle and warmed its way deep into her very being. She heard Siah's whisper reach her from the long-ago distance of the Dyak riverbank. "God of fire." He was surely all of that and more.

He held himself back for only one agonizing moment more, covering her throat and face and hair with feverish kisses. Her arms went around his neck, and she pulled his mouth to hers. Suddenly she gave a gasp and clutched him tightly to her. Feeling her body let go, he reached up and twisted his hands into her hair, grasping tightly, as if to rein her in so that she would not too far outdistance him.

Overhead, the painted figures seemed momentarily to forgo their own pursuit of lusty pleasures to watch the struggle on the silk cushions below. It was not peaceful. Release had been denied them too long to come with anything but barely restrained violence. And then it was over. His seed burst forth, and he gave a cry as though he were dying. With his relief came hers. She sobbed and held him tightly to her until, passion spent, they collapsed together into a warm tangle of sweaty, quivering limbs and breathless endearments. He covered her face with kisses and then rolled over onto his back, pulling her close. Her head rested on his shoulder, a hand lightly upon his chest. At that moment it was not just his splendid body she wanted to hold on to but the overwhelming sensation of his deep love for her. She felt awed by the realization that he was truly hers, this fierce, somewhat frightening mixture of blazing fire and gentle warmth, warrior and lover. She felt an equal degree of wonder at the love she had for him, knowing that the greatest gift he had given her this night was her own renewed ability to love so freely and completely.

He cradled his head with one arm while he stared up at the richly detailed vines and flowers of gold. He was silent for a moment before he spoke. "Tonight was the first time I ever used this room, I mean, for the purpose for which it was intended. I never shall again. The old ways are dying, and should die."

He seemed to be speaking now more to the room and its ghosts than to her. His voice was full of emotion when he added, "I am the last sultan of Matapura."

A sea breeze made the candles flicker precariously for a moment and then glow brighter, while the curtain stirred and billowed out toward the sea.

Four days later Ahmad was called back to Java with news that the cease-fire was breaking down. Catherine felt her throat constrict as the time for parting drew near. Ahmad took her hands in his, searching her eyes while he spoke his feelings silently. When at last he pulled her into his arms and held her close, she uttered a little stifled cry of pain. She knew and accepted that he must leave and she could not go with him, but she could no longer stop the tears that came from giving him up again. His arms tightened around her.

"Good-bye, my love," he whispered, his face pressed against her hair. She put her arms around his neck and pulled his mouth down to hers in one last lingering kiss.

When she returned to her own pavilion, she found a gold tray containing a carved teak box and the traditional wedding bowl of rice. As she examined it, she gave a gasp of surprise. On top of the rice were two perfectly matched green emeralds, and inside the box was a gold chain, exactly her height—the traditional Dyak wedding gift. Only in this case, the chain was strung solid with precious gems.

There was a note: "Don't go on to Maitreya. Send for Michael, and stay at Matapura until I return and we're married. Then we'll go to Maitreya together."

The day was almost over. She stepped out into the private garden which surrounded her pavilion. Nothing in this golden scene revealed that 1,000 people had died here, slaughtered by the Japanese. The sun caught the smiling face of a bronze Buddha in a corner of the garden, looking more self-indulgent than serene. Nearby she could hear water tumbling into a wild, twisting ravine full of boulders and flowers which ran from the *kraton* wall all the way down to the sea.

Below her garden the pavilions of the court rose majestic and enchanting, their golden columns gleaming in the last embrace of sunlight. Sacred mountains. Sacred palace. What better home for a heaven-sent king than upon the shoulders of the gods? She sensed within these walls secrets that no overtures from her could ever reveal. Everywhere here were reminders of a culture far older and, in many ways, more complex than her own. Its commitment to tradition, its very age intimidated her.

The wind changed direction, and clouds of mist from the sea began to swirl across the mountain, cutting off the view. Steam and the acrid smell of sulfur drifted in from the neighboring volcanoes as though from a magician's caldron. Dusk had almost arrived. At night the *kraton* would glow with its own special splendor created by the thousands of lamps and torches and candles upon the walls.

Ahmad's daughter, Kartini, entered the small garden. She was dressed in a flowered batik sarong with a short dark jacket over it. Catherine was always astounded by her beauty: the warm brown skin, the raven hair, and the sea green eyes with flecks of sunlight in their depths and mysterious undercurrents playing beneath their shimmering surface. Kartini was a brilliant child, wise beyond her years. Catherine had grown very fond of her during the weeks she had worked on the article.

Each night after dinner Kartini danced to the soft hypnotic gongs and percussion instruments of the royal gamelan orchestra. Though Indonesian royalty was traditionally trained in dance, Ahmad had frowned on her learning it, but he had been powerless to stop it. She seemed to pick up the steps without trying or created them herself out of the movements of the trees, the sea, the trembling of the earth beneath her feet. And when she danced, this tiny sprite with the eyes from an ancient water world, it was electrifying. She danced as if in a trance, possessed by magic, no longer a child. While he was at the *kraton*, Catherine could see it had greatly disturbed Ahmad. When the dance was over, he had given a smile he didn't altogether feel and threw up his hands.

"What can I do about it?" he had asked helplessly. "She is, after all, Siah's child. More, I'm afraid, than she is mine."

"You seem very serious today," Catherine said to Kartini as she entered the garden.

"My nurse said I must behave with more dignity since I am a royal princess."

"Oh?" Catherine was amused. "And what does your father say?"

"He says that like him, I am but one of the people, but I think he does not tell me the truth."

"And what is the truth?"

"That I come from the sea." She turned and faced the ocean, watching it swell and heave against the sand. A look of quiet rapture lit her small face. "The Lady of the Sea speaks to me sometimes." She stared so intently into the sea that it disturbed Catherine. "I can hear her there—in the whispers of the surf."

"It sounds as if you feel very special, Kartini," Catherine said cautiously.

"Oh, yes. My nurse takes me to the village to help the sick. She says that only I can make them well—with my gift. Today I made a man well who was dying of a burst appendix. I touched his body, and he grew cool again beneath my fingers."

Catherine was alarmed. "Does your father know you do this thing?"

"No." She turned to face Catherine. "He would not like it. And now that you know and will surely tell him, I will not go again."

Catherine looked puzzled. "You knew that if you told me, I would tell your father and he would put a stop to it. Why didn't you tell him yourself?"

"It's a power—a gift—from the Lady of the Sea. She would not like it if I told him. She would think me ungrateful."

"I see. So you would like me to tell him instead."

"Not *like*, perhaps, but I am sometimes afraid of the gift. This morning I touched a dolphin that was dying on the shore. I felt its feelings and knew its thoughts. It made me very sad and frightened. I think, sometimes, that I can see the future, though I do not want to."

Kartini turned her gaze from the sea and put her arms around Catherine's waist. "I didn't want Papa to leave today."

"I know," Catherine said gently, holding Kartini's small body tightly to her own.

She felt Kartini shiver as a sudden updraft lifted the clouds and the *kraton* was bathed in a last brilliant flash of sunlight. Below them Kartini's French tutor was struggling up the steep stone steps cut out of the mountain. She arrived breathless and pale.

"Oh, Mademoiselle!" she cried to Catherine. "The Dutch have launched a full air and land attack against the Indonesian government. They have occupied Banjarmasin and sent notice to the palace that we are not to resist! They say there is heavy fighting between Dutch troops and the republican army in Java and Sumatra."

"And His Highness?" Catherine asked fearfully, feeling Kartini's slender arms grip her more tightly. "Did they say what has happened to him?"

"Only that all the government leaders are in Jogjakarta, and Dutch troops surround the city and can occupy it at any time."

Catherine was seized with the old dread that she had found happiness only to lose it all again. The Dutch were sure to hold Kartini hostage and under the guise of "protection" use her royal position as a puppet front for Dutch rule.

"Tell the servants to let it be known that the princess isn't here," Catherine told Ahmad's secretary. "Tell them to say she returned to Java with the sultan this morning."

Seeking to avoid the embarrassment of fighting the armed old women who guarded the *kraton* after sunset against all male intruders save the sultan himself, the Dutch posted guards outside the *kraton* gates, prepared to enter the next morning. That night Catherine smuggled Kartini out by way of the rocks beneath the bridal *pendopo,* down to a cove where a small boat waited to take Kartini to the safety of her Dyak grandfather, who would bring her in secret to Maitreya.

Catherine returned to the *kraton* to leave for Maitreya the next morning, using Ahmad's small plane. The Dutch did not try to stop her. As far as they were concerned, she was an American on a magazine assignment, nothing more.

Catherine arrived at Maitreya just before the thunderstorm. As she set the lightplane down on the runway, the sky to the west was black and huge thunderheads were threatening to take away what little remained of the day. It had been a rough flight, the roughest she had made since she had learned to fly in the States a

577

few months earlier. There had been times that afternoon, as she rode the turbulent air before the storm on the short flight from Matapura, that she had regretted her decision to fly that day. With hindsight the river, winding below her, seemed a saner way to travel. Maitreya's airfield, still in disrepair, had made the landing as rough an experience as the flight had been.

She tossed her duffel bag to the ground, and taking hold of the wing struts, she swung herself down and out of the Piper Cub. The air was very still. No bird sounds. No monkey noises. The jungle stood in silent encirclement of the field. She could not see the house, but she could feel its presence beyond the trees, and a slight chill went through her. It was as if Maitreya, with its powerful memories of the past and Michael, had been waiting for her. Hesitantly she picked up her duffel bag and concentrated on the sound of her riding boots briskly striking the pavement. Sheets of lightning had begun to flicker brightly across the sky. The clouds were moving swiftly overhead. The storm was catching up with her. Even before she crossed the field, the air began to stir, bending the huge branches of the trees, rustling the leaves. Forks of lightning momentarily flickered down to earth, and thunder rumbled after them.

Damal appeared on the road from the landing field to the house, leaning against the wind, which had grown quite strong. He had seen the plane come in and had come out to assist. He had a slight limp, a result of the bayonet wounds he had received when the Japanese first raided Maitreya.

"Nona Catherine!" he called. The wind swallowed his words, but she read the greeting on his lips and the smile on his face. It had started to rain, and he opened the large umbrella he was carrying. By the time she reached him she was soaked. He took the bag from her.

"Sir Charles and young Tuan Michael are up the river, visiting Lady Dunston at the Sanders' plantation. They weren't expecting you."

"I wasn't sure when I was coming, so I didn't let them know." Catherine was shouting to be heard.

The rain came down in solid sheets. As they rounded the bend of the road, she could barely make out the huge gray shadow of the house. During the time that the house had stood vacant, the jungle had reclaimed much of the grounds, but a major restoration was already under way. The house itself had changed little. New thatch on the roof replaced whatever had rotted away through neglect. Most of the furnishings removed by marauding Japanese had been recovered at the Japanese headquarters in Banjarmasin after the war. The most valuable pieces of art and family keepsakes had been removed from the house by the servants and hidden in the jungle and the villages. They had been returned to Maitreya at war's end and awaited Sir Charles when he arrived home. Expecting to find nothing left, he had been moved to tears to see the family portraits and photographs sitting on the floor in the empty rooms or hung upon the shabby walls. The lizards which scurried out of his path as he moved, alone, from room to room, had been the sole inhabitants of Maitreya for three and a half years. All the natives had fled the area to avoid being forced to work the plantation for the Japanese.

On her way to her room to change her wet things, Catherine stopped in the library. The old desk had been returned, but comfortable new chairs had been added to the rest of the furniture. As always, it was Michael's paintings that drew her into the room. Their vivid, swirling colors leaped out against the calm, freshly painted surface of the creamy white walls. The old magic worked its way with her as she stared at them. Alive. So alive. Uneasy now, she found her eyes being drawn to the newly framed medals and citations that hung near by. They were Michael's war decorations: the Silver Star, the Navy Cross, and, finally, the Congressional Medal of Honor, pale blue silk ribbon mounted on a dark blue velvet background. Suddenly she wanted to tear them all from the wall and destroy them, these reminders that he had always been too careless with his life when it wasn't his alone to give.

Tears began to run unchecked down her cheeks. She clenched her jaw to halt their flow but was unsuccessful. Soon her body shook with sobs, and she buried her face in her hands. When she finally looked up, her grief spent, she saw Damal standing in the doorway. He had changed into dry clothes, but his face, too, was wet with tears.

"Welcome to Maitreya, Nona Catherine," he said softly. "*Salamat datang*. We are so glad you have come home."

"*Tarima kasih*, Damal. It's good to be here." She found she really meant it. Her dread of Maitreya was gone.

Damal showed her to her room and quietly disappeared. He had already unpacked her bag. She changed her shirt and put a towel to her hair. The rain had almost stopped. Opening the shuttered doors, Catherine breathed in the smell of damp earth and clean air, sweeter than any perfume, which entered the room. Puddles had collected on the flatstones of the surrounding terrace. The newly emerging sun sent a miniature rainbow arcing across the jungle. As Catherine stood drying her hair, absorbed in the scene, a knock sounded, and she turned back to the room, bidding whoever it was to enter.

Damal came in, smiling. "I have a surprise for Nona." He crossed the room. "Please, follow me."

He led her to the front terrace where the grass sloped down to the road. One of the stableboys came toward them, leading a horse mounted with an English saddle. It was Admiral. Catherine gave a little cry of delighted surprise. Damal smiled broadly at her reaction.

"I had hoped Nona would be pleased. We found him loose and took him with us to the village in the jungle where the Japanese could never come to eat him. We took very good care of him and bring him back after the war it is over. Only now there is no one here to ride with Nona. Julienne and Tuan Michael are gone," he said sadly.

Catherine walked to the wall and sat down upon its damp stone surface. Admiral reached out to nuzzle her and gave a snort as if in recognition. She laughed and put an arm around his neck. His hide shivered delightedly beneath her touch, and she buried her face against his smooth, shiny hide. At sixteen he was in excellent health and spirits.

"Perhaps Nona would like to go for a ride before dinner," Damal urged.

Catherine hesitated. She was weary from the grueling flight, but she was still wearing the boots she had worn riding at Matapura that morning before she left. She shrugged.

"Why not?"

Damal smiled again as she jumped lightly onto the low terrace wall and swung a leg over Admiral, taking the reins and the riding crop from the boy who held him. She turned Admiral around. He wanted to run, and she let him, heading him toward the road leading through the rubber and copra groves. He took the first four-foot stone wall with room to spare, and his frisky recovery indicated he wanted more.

"Easy does it," she murmured to him. "Neither of us is up to those old risks we used to take."

But he was choosing his own way, heading toward another wall where thornbushes grew in a tangle. The wall was short of six feet, but it was higher than she felt comfortable with. She could have stopped him, but she didn't. For all she knew, more thornbushes or some other booby trap lay in wait on the other side, but Admiral seemed sure of himself. She felt his muscles bunch beneath her as he gathered himself for the leap. She rose forward in her stirrups as she felt him leave the ground. Hunched over his neck, her body tightened in anticipation of whatever lay on the other side, but Admiral had been right: The road was clear. Perhaps the stableboys had exercised him in the fields here.

He landed with a confident snort and didn't break stride as he headed down the road. She began to share his exuberance. By the time she had completed her tour of the largely untended groves and fields the sky held only a pale yellow light. Around her lay the wild evidence of how easily lost was man's toehold on this earth. Maitreya's roads and walls now abruptly ended in tangled brush and impenetrable green walls, as if they had never led anywhere, and she was forced to turn back and retrace her path. Sir Charles would soon have the fields and groves restored to their former perfection, but for now Maitreya belonged to the jungle from which it had been stolen.

The shadows were long around the pool when she arrived. She had intended to avoid it altogether, and later, looking back, she wasn't sure if she had taken the path or if Admiral had led her there. She had been tired, and the trail was invitingly clear, for it led to the underground spring beyond the pool that was Maitreya's water supply. As she neared the pool, the scene around her seemed so unchanged by the passage of time that she half expected to see him sunbathing on the rock. At first she hesitated at the jungle's edge, afraid to dismount and walk the few yards that separated her from the pool. A monkey scolded somewhere in the trees above her, and then the jungle was quiet. Reassured by the stillness, she swung off Admiral, dropping the reins to let him graze.

The rock in the pool's center lay empty and golden in the sun's last rays, the water dark and bottomless around it. Suddenly she drew in her breath sharply, and a little sob escaped her throat. She struggled to control it as tears streamed down her cheeks. "I love Ahmad!" she protested vehemently. Nothing changed, nothing moved except the soft light, which did not fade but grew deeper, brighter, richer. The rock was empty, yet something had been waiting here for her.

"Michael," she whispered. "Oh, Michael."

She closed her eyes against her tears and felt a sudden gust of air dry her cheeks, as though comforting her. Yet when she opened her eyes, the leaves were still. She had imagined it. She stood without moving, confused and shaken by the feelings stirring within her. Michael had been dead for five years, yet she had found him to be as alive within her heart as he had ever been. She realized that what had come to life here was the part of her that never wished to be free of him, that could love no one else. Was she to be forever haunted by that old unfulfilled dream? Angrily she forced the thought aside. She returned to the trail, quickly mounted Admiral, and left without looking back. She vowed never to return to the pool again.

She was scowling when she reached the house and coolly thanked a dismayed Damal when he asked about the ride. She ate dinner alone in the dining room, dressed elegantly and formally in a short green chiffon dress, successfully forcing any further thoughts of the pool or Michael from her mind.

The next day she went to the closed door of Michael's old room, the one he had shared with Kara, and, once, with her. Without hesitation she opened it and stepped inside. She was startled to see how little changed it seemed. Though the furniture was different, the arrangement was the same. It was a masculine room, as it had always been. She crossed the room and stood before the portrait of Michael's mother. She had never really looked closely at it before. She searched for some resemblance to Michael in the portrait but found none except perhaps in the bold strokes and technique of the painting itself. She too had been a talented artist. It suddenly occurred to Catherine that her son should have his father's room. She summoned Damal to arrange to have the boy's things moved from the nursery, only to hear

582

herself saying, instead, "I'll be staying here, Damal. Please have my things moved to this room."

Startled, she heard the words as if someone else had spoken them. Her pulse pounded at her temples, but she did not retract her words. Damal merely stood, expressionless, awaiting any further orders or perhaps waiting for her to change her mind and come to her senses.

"That will be all." She dismissed him, feeling annoyed, as if his silence had been an unspoken reproach, and then she realized it was her own disapproval that had angered her. She rationalized that the location of the room was better, the desk more spacious for her work, the art collection more interesting and appealing to live with, giving herself every reason for but the real one.

If Sir Charles, upon his return, thought the move to be odd or inappropriate, he said nothing.

Chapter 55

Ahmad had sensed the change in her almost as soon as she reached Maitreya. Through her letters these past months he had felt her slipping away from him, and he had been powerless to do anything about it. There was now a price on his head in Dutch-occupied territory. When the Dutch broke the treaty he had negotiated, he had resigned as prime minister, refusing to negotiate further on the grounds that the Dutch had no intention of giving Indonesia its independence. Instead, he took command of the Panji Division, the famed guerrilla unit which now functioned as an independent army in central Java and as a terrorist group within the occupied cities. The Panji were responsible for the scorched-earth policy which had led to burning European estates in central Java and to destroying the property of anyone who cooperated with the Dutch. As a result, the Dutch had offered a reward for Ahmad's capture.

There seemed little hope for peace anytime soon. The Dutch now controlled two-thirds of Java as well as Dutch Sumatra and the outer islands and were busy setting up puppet governments throughout the territory. The new Renville treaty, signed by the Sukarno government, effectively gave the Dutch control of all the land they had seized militarily since breaking the first treaty. Ahmad refused to accept the Renville agreement and vowed to fight on until the Dutch were forced out of Indonesia.

The Indonesian Republic was now confined to the mountainous central spine of Java, surrounded by the Dutch. The blockade established by the Dutch after breaking the first treaty had produced widespread starvation throughout the republic. A million refugees had fled Dutch occupation and now burdened a struggling government unable to feed and clothe even itself.

As the economic situation worsened, the internal political strife between the republic's many factions had increased. Moslem fundamentalist fanatics agitated more boldly for a religious state. The Communists were gaining power, and Tuk Malek was rumored to be returning to take charge of the Communist front after thirteen years of political exile in Moscow. Malek bore Ahmad a personal grudge tracing back to Ahmad's years in Paris when a young Frenchwoman had preferred Ahmad's company to that of his fellow student, Tuk Malek, who, unknown to Ahmad, happened to be her fiancé. In addition to Moslems and the Communists, there was always the threat that disgruntled factions of the Army would stage a coup.

Ahmad had made his headquarters in the small village of Gunungteh, away from the republic's intrigue-ridden capital of Jogjakarta. He sat now at his old battered desk in the tiny house he occupied at the edge of the village. Below it lay the terraced rice paddies, and above rose the double-humped peak of Merapi, the volcanic ash of which enriched the surrounding soil. He was rereading Catherine's last letter, which had arrived only yesterday. It contained news of Maitreya and much about Kartini, all amusing and affectionate. But Michael's name came up more often now. True, it was in impersonal references to his work and his writings; nevertheless, it was enough to tell Ahmad that Michael was increasingly on Catherine's mind.

He dropped the letter to the desk. The afternoon heat pressed against his head like hot stones, making his temples pound in protest. How could he compete with the ghost of that past love? he asked himself. He had been opposed to Catherine's returning to Maitreya from the outset. Perhaps he had sensed the danger even then.

He rose and walked to the window. Outside, the sun cast narrow stripes of shade and brilliant light across the unkempt lawn. The heat was stifling. The day itself seemed to curl closely around the house like a drowsing tiger no one dared disturb. Not even the air moved. Not long ago real tigers had slept in this forest—before Java had become too crowded for its wild, free things. He missed the untouched jungles of Borneo where man and nature were more in balance. For a long moment he stared at the sulphurous earthwind which blew up from the molten heart of Merapi, and then he turned abruptly away, his mind made up. He would ask Catherine to join him here immediately so that they could be married. There was danger to them both in having her with him, but the risk of losing her if they remained apart seemed greater.

Having reached a decision, he felt relieved. He was certain she would come; not even Michael's ghost could prevent it. Once she was away from Maitreya, she would forget Michael. As he returned to his desk, the ground suddenly lurched and then trembled. He regained his balance, scarcely noticing it. Earthquakes were common in the Indies. He accepted the violence of the earth itself as readily as he had come to accept the dark violence within his own spirit. Michael had gone to war and become a hero because it was the decent thing to do, and Michael had always had the courage to do the decent thing. Ahmad had gone to war for the same reason, but he had quickly come to like the test of will and strength and courage. He liked the physical competition of war, the life-and-death stakes. He had even developed an appreciation of the pain and discomfort, seeing them as tests of his endurance. He was honest enough to admit to himself that he might even regret peace when it finally came, though he would do everything within his power to achieve it.

The earth's trembling stopped. He sat down at his desk and wrote his letter.

Harriet Dunston let herself be assisted from the small boat that had brought her downstream to Maitreya from the Sanders plantation. The river's current was swift and high from the late November rains. It had been almost a month since she had visited Maitreya. She was arriving unannounced this time, stopping off on her way to Banjarmasin to argue with the new Dutch authorities over some of her supplies from England which they had seized. There was no sun, but it was hot. Harriet walked slowly up the road and across the wide expanse of lawn, fanning her skirt up and down to circulate air while she observed how lovingly Maitreya had been restored to its former grandeur. It was not at all like the Sanders estate, which two years after Japan's surrender still showed the ravages of war and decay.

She stopped for a few moments at the huge banyan tree beside the house, as she did each time she came. Among the ashes and bones buried beneath this tree were those of her sister-in-law and her nieces. Thanks to the war, Harriet represented the end of 150 years of Sanders history in the Indies. Her brother, Philip, had been captured in the defense of Singapore and had died later in the building of the infamous Indochina railroad. Her husband, John, had been imprisoned in Tokyo at the outbreak of the war. He had been tortured and mistreated, and although he was eventually exchanged for Japanese officials, his health had been broken, and he had died in London in 1943.

Harriet noticed that Sir Charles had placed a small marble stone beneath the tree, its white surface flush to the ground. It described the Japanese attack, gave the date, and listed the names of family, friends, and servants who had died there that day. She looked up from it and saw Patri standing on the veranda some twenty yards away, watching her. She hadn't seen him since he had returned from England, leaving school at the military academy at Sandhurst to join the Indonesian nationalist army. The move had infuriated Sir Charles, who thought that even if Patri wanted a military career, he should get an education first. But Patri had held surprisingly firm, unperturbed by his grandfather's opposition. He was used to it. He and the old man had been struggling with each other since the day Patri had arrived at Maitreya after the war and Sir Charles had tried to impose his will on an already rebellious adolescent boy and totally failed. It had been a new experience for Sir Charles. None of his family had ever previously opposed him, except for Michael, when he had joined the American Navy. An uneasy truce had finally been established when Sir Charles had backed off and let Patri go his own way. They became more like uneasy acquaintances than close relatives. Still, to Sir Charles's surprise, Patri came home to visit whenever the wartime situation allowed. Currently, as a result of the Renville negotiations, there was a new truce in effect, so even though Borneo was in Dutch hands, Patri had been able to come home.

As she started forward to join Patri on the veranda, Harriet took a good look at him. It wasn't just the fact that she hadn't expected to see him that startled her. He had grown taller, filled out. At twenty he was no longer the wild and beautiful boy he had been. He was now an extraordinarily handsome young man with dark, brooding good looks and a poise far beyond his years. In view of his background (he had virtually not set eyes on civilization until almost three years ago) it was an extraordinary change. But then Patri himself was extraordinary, an intelligent child who had quickly grasped everything his tutors had introduced to him. Much to Sir Charles's disappointment, he had rejected an admission into Oxford at eighteen. Despite all the education he had received in the past few years, he remained true to his Iban blood. Politics and the army were the things about the modern world that interested him.

Patri had one other consuming interest: women. Even as a boy he could make the women he met feel flattered by his attention. Harriet smiled to herself, remembering her own reactions to that maleness he had worn like a warrior on display. Even while she had been amused, she had been irresistibly drawn to it. As she reached the veranda and felt him lean over and kiss her cheek in greeting, she became exceedingly aware that he was now a man. She found herself feeling a familiar awkwardness she hastened to cover up, reminding herself firmly that she was old enough to be his mother.

"Aunt Harriet." He was smiling as he released her hand.

"Patri, darling," she replied. "What a marvelous surprise! No one told me you'd be here. But then I didn't tell them I was coming. Where is everyone?"

"Grandfather is away, and Catherine went for her usual early-morning ride and isn't back yet."

"Be a dear, will you? Go find Damal and have him fix me a gin and tonic. It was damned hot on that river." He returned to the veranda a moment later, carrying a tall frosty glass, and sat down.

"I hear they've promoted you. Really, Patri, aren't you a little young to be a colonel?"

"Of course." Patri smiled disarmingly.

"Well, I'm reassured that you see the absurdity of it even if those who promoted you do not."

"I see the absurdity of many things, Aunt. This is no worse

than most. The army is short of trained officers. My experience at Sandhurst, though brief, is of value.''

''And what will you do for a career when independence is won and the war is over?''

''There will be no peace. If the Dutch keep New Guinea, as they are insisting now, eventually Sukarno will go to war over it.''

''I've never understood why the Dutch want to hold on to it. It's nothing but jungle and cannibals. Or why Indonesia would insist on having it.''

''It was part of the East Indies. Let's say we just have a sentimental attachment to it.''

''Baloney. You just want to kick the Dutch out of Asia. It's nothing but pure spite.''

''Not entirely. Java is overcrowded. New Guinea is not. It can provide a new territory for emigration.''

''I see,'' Harriet said sarcastically. ''It sounds as if you'll have a brilliant future.''

Patri laughed, genuinely amused. Because of Harriet's directness, he liked her more than most people.

''To peace.'' Harriet raised her empty glass in a toast. ''A dreadful idea for an aspiring general,'' she added, gently mocking him.

''It is a political future I want. And the best way to get it in the future Indonesia will be through a military career.''

For a moment she was surprised, and then she realized that Patri would never be satisfied with military power alone when there was more around to acquire. ''I see. If you don't get elected, you can always stage a coup. A colonel at twenty, a general at thirty, and president at thirty-five.''

''Why not?'' Patri shrugged, and she could see that he was serious.

''I don't mean to be so hard on you, Patri. It's just that your association with that awful Sukarno offends me. You know there are half a dozen others better qualified to lead Indonesia, the best of whom is Ahmad.''

''Ahmad would make the most brilliant leader Indonesia could have, but he is ambivalent toward his power and has therefore made no efforts to cultivate and develop it. And he has doubts about the wisdom of permitting the old nobility to participate in

589

the new democracy. Besides, it is quite possible he will marry Catherine, and then he must give it all up.''

''Well, I hope you're right about that at least,'' Harriet muttered. Damal appeared on the veranda, and she asked for another gin.

''You must realize that Sukarno is a supremely skilled politician,'' Patri continued. ''You should see the way he holds presidential court in Jogjakarta every morning. Newsmen come to chat. Pregnant women come to have him name their unborn children. He has named himself Champion of the Women's Movement.''

Harriet gave a sharp laugh. ''The only woman's movement he ever championed was the one in bed. Politicians are supposed to kiss babies, not their mothers. He is a notorious womanizer, particularly with young women.''

''And older women are a bit sensitive on that subject,'' Patri replied sympathetically.

''I admit it,'' Harriet replied. ''Your Sukarno says that women are like rubber trees: no good after age thirty.''

''Unlike Sukarno, I find older women very attractive.''

It occurred to Harriet that Patri was about to proposition her. She decided to change the subject.

Conveniently enough, at that moment Catherine rode up on Admiral, and one of the stableboys came up to take the reins. Harriet, watching her dismount, asked Patri, ''How has she been?''

He swung his leg down from over the arm of the chair as if in preparation to rise. ''She is alone too much.''

Patri waved to Catherine and walked out to meet her. Harriet watched him speak briefly with her and then take the reins from the boy. He swung up onto Admiral's back with one smooth motion and galloped off toward the stable. Catherine walked to the veranda, smiling and wiping her forehead. She wore shorts and a halter top, and her head was bare, black hair tumbling around her shoulders.

''Harriet, what a pleasant surprise. You should have let us know.''

''I didn't want a fuss made.''

''Iced tea please, Damal.'' Catherine sat down.

"Tell me, Catherine, how do you manage to look so disgustingly fit? You never seem to grow a day older."

Catherine smiled. "For one thing, I never drink gin in the morning."

"Gin never weakens the English."

Catherine laughed. "Do you plan to stay on in Borneo?"

"Probably. Until the Indonesians run us out as they will do eventually. I have no place else to go really. London bores me, and I like the idea of getting the plantation on its feet, producing again. It was a big surprise to me to find that I'm rather attached to the place." She closed her eyes a moment. "Damn the Dutch anyway for being so stubborn. If they'd only given up gracefully and accepted some special economic relationship with the Indies in exchange for political independence. Now all this hate is going to destroy us Europeans. Even the ones who've supported independence all along." She opened her eyes to see Kartini leading her horse across the lawn toward the stable. "Charles's doing, no doubt," she said with lazy amusement, referring to the very proper riding habit Kartini was wearing, right down to her derby hat and riding gloves.

"Yes. He loves spoiling her, I'm afraid." Catherine watched the small figure of Kartini disappear toward the stable. "But don't let appearances mislead you. Kartini and Michael are more wild creatures of the forest than proper English children."

"She's an enchanting child," Harriet remarked of Kartini.

"Enchanting or enchanted, I'm not sure which," said Catherine. "The native people around here believe she has supernatural powers."

"Oh," Harriet said, one eyebrow arched skeptically. "And what leads them to conclude that?"

"They claim to have seen leopards speak to her and cobras bow at her feet." She didn't add that Kartini herself was surprisingly secure in those same beliefs. "I'm afraid she's been left alone too much in the company of her superstitious old Dyak nurse. I try to inject reality into her existence, but I sometimes feel it's a losing battle." Catherine smiled. "Instead, it's more likely she's convinced Michael that fairies and goblins are real."

"Where is my favorite child anyway?" Harriet asked, referring to Michael.

"Tomorrow is Kartini's birthday, and he has gone to the

591

village to get an orphaned baby orangutan to give her as a present.''

Damal reappeared. As if disapproving of serving Harriet a third drink, he had come to announce an early lunch for the two of them, served in the shade on the veranda.

''What have you heard from Ahmad?'' Harriet asked as they sat down to their spiced chicken and rice.

Catherine focused carefully on her plate. ''He's asked me to come to Java and marry him—right away.''

Harriet paused in surprise, fork halfway to her mouth. ''And?''

''I said yes.'' Surprised to find how shy she felt, she flushed.

Harriet dropped her fork to her plate with a look of relief. ''Thank God!'' She poked a napkin at her mouth. ''What does Charles think about it?''

''He doesn't know yet. He's been away all week, at Rabaul and Hollandia on business. But I expect him back tomorrow for Kartini's birthday.''

''I know he'll be as pleased as I am,'' Harriet remarked. ''He knows you can't stay hidden away from the world here forever. And there is no one he admires more on earth than Ahmad.''

''Strange, Sir Charles hasn't been himself lately,'' Catherine said. ''He's been moody and preoccupied. I wish you'd stay the night and be here when he arrives tomorrow. He always enjoys seeing you.''

''Can't. I have to get on to Banjarmasin and settle things before the current truce blows up in our face.''

Catherine looked away toward the forest. The scent of gardenias was suddenly strong. ''In the past, whenever I decided to leave Maitreya, something has always stopped me. Stay, it says. Just a little longer.''

''Don't listen to it.'' Harriet took an emphatic bite of food off her fork. ''As much as I loved Michael, I never regretted marrying John. We had ten good years together.'' She took a hard look at Catherine. ''Marry Ahmad and get on with your life.''

That night Kartini came to Catherine's room as she often did and stood beside the bed. Catherine put down her book. Kartini was barefoot; a short Dyak skirt about her waist was her only clothing. These days she and Catherine spoke most often in English, as Kartini's mastery of it improved.

"I've asked Papa to give me Michael for my birthday, the way the Dyak chiefs used to give Grandpapa their daughters on his birthday."

"Oh?" Catherine, aware of how much Kartini liked Michael, was amused. "And what did your papa say?"

Kartini frowned. "He said that royal princesses must possess only the hearts of the people, never their bodies or their minds." The frown gave way to hope. "Oh, Catherine, will you give me Michael's heart? I will take good care of it—always."

Catherine laughed and hugged Kartini's slender body to her. "I have no doubt you would, my darling. But Michael's heart is something only he can give away, when he is old enough to do so wisely."

"And when will that be?" Kartini asked impatiently.

"When he feels moved to do it. But that won't be for a very long time."

"Then I will wait," Kartini added confidently with chin raised imperially. She looked around the room. "I love this house," she said with a look of contentment. She reached out to touch the huge ironwood post in one corner which supported the soaring roof hidden above them by the room's ceiling. She suddenly frowned. "All but the place by Sir Charles's favorite chair in the drawing room. There's a young girl buried beneath it."

Julienne's story of the old longhouse and human sacrifice on this spot flashed through Catherine's mind. "How do you know?" she asked.

But Kartini didn't answer. She was on her way out of the room. She simply stopped at the door and looked back a moment to appraise Catherine coolly. Then, with bewitching smile, she was gone, as elusive and fleeting as sunlight in the deepest forest.

Chapter 56
Maitreya, December 1, 1948

It was early afternoon several weeks later when Sir Charles sent for Catherine to join him in the library. The request was unusual. He didn't ordinarily care to be disturbed when he had sequestered himself in the library to read or work on his history of Indonesia's struggle for independence. Today she found him seated in his large wing-backed chair, book in hand, his reading glasses on the end of his nose. Damal was also in the room, removing the remains of the small lunch Sir Charles customarily took alone every day.

She knocked, and Sir Charles looked up warmly when he saw her standing in the doorway. There was an easy camaraderie between them these days. With Margit still in England, Catherine had become his only child.

"Please come in and sit down." He gestured toward the chair opposite him.

Since he had returned from his trip, he had seemed particularly tired and preoccupied. Now she sensed something different in his eyes, something guarded. He removed his spectacles, for at seventy-one he was still vain enough to want to appeal to a beautiful woman. And indeed, he succeeded, for he was still handsome, slender, and vigorous, and looked far younger than his years. He waited for Damal to leave the room, then got to the point immediately.

"I've never discussed your relationship with Ahmad before,

Catherine, other than to say I was happy you were getting married. I felt it was essentially your business and his. I was, of course, in many ways very pleased about it. He is a fine man. Both of you are like my own children to me." He paused, and she could see that he was choosing his words cautiously.

"I love you as my own. I think you know that, although perhaps I should have said it long ago. I have come to believe you would have been an ideal wife for Michael, a true partner in his work and his life. It has been one of the great regrets of my life that I didn't realize this sooner. Things might have turned out differently. . . ." He raised his hand briefly in a gesture of dismissal and then returned it to his book. "It is that mistake that has made me hesitate to talk to you about this or to interfere in your life in any way."

Catherine felt herself tense.

"I want you to postpone your marriage to Ahmad," he told her.

She was stunned. "I don't understand. When I told you last week, you seemed happy about it." It suddenly occurred to her that she might have confused his feelings with her own. In fact, looking back on it, she couldn't recall his reaction at all.

"I'm sorry to upset you, but I think you should wait a few months. I don't feel I can go into the reasons just now. You'll have to trust me."

"No! I can't. I won't. Not without good reason."

Sir Charles sighed. "I didn't want to tell you. Not until I knew more, could be more certain."

He sat silently for a moment, his eyes sympathetic. Or were they? She wasn't sure any longer. Carefully he picked up a carved Dyak box that sat on the table next to him. When his eyes came back to rest on hers, she knew that what she had just heard had only been a preliminary. His hand, resting on the top of the box, began to tremble.

"This box belongs to Michael. After the war ended, it was turned in to American headquarters in Manila by the wife of a Japanese fisherman with whom Michael had lived. She had taken it with her into internment camp when the Japanese civilians in Manila were imprisoned after Pearl Harbor. She had wanted to protect it from looting. She last saw Michael the day after the war started when he brought her the box and other things to keep for him. He had made attempts later to have her and her husband released from internment, but the official requests were denied, and she never saw him again, though she tried to locate him in the prison camps after the fall of Bataan. Her husband was killed in the liberation of the Philippines in 1945, when their house was destroyed. She turned the box over to U.S. authorities along with a letter explaining what had happened. A little over a year after the war ended I received it in the mail, forwarded to me as Michael's next of kin by the American War Department. I said nothing to you about it at the time because I, too, believe you should not live with ghosts. I had no intention of ever giving this to you.''

He rose from his chair and set the box on the small table next to her chair. She stared at it, her feelings a confused mixture of fear and anger. If he had had no previous intention of giving it to her, then why was he telling her about it now? Sir Charles walked to his desk and turned back to her, leaning against its edge. He took a deep breath and plunged on, his voice shaking.

''I believe Michael is alive, Catherine.''

The words stunned her. Suddenly her world was turned upside down, inside out.

Sir Charles was silent for a moment, giving her time to recover. Then he spoke softly.

''I'm sorry to shock you like this, Catherine, but I knew of no way to make it easy. Perhaps I should have told you months ago about the rumors that Michael was alive. Perhaps then you would have been prepared. But I was so sure at the time that they were false. Now I'm just as certain they are true.'' He broke off, concerned by her paleness.

''Are you all right? Should I continue? Perhaps Damal should bring you something to drink.''

''No, no,'' she murmured. ''I'll be all right. Go on.''

He gave himself a moment to collect his thoughts and then resumed his story.

''About a year ago a Dutch smuggler named Brinkler came to me with a rather fantastic tale. At least I thought it farfetched at the time. Right after the war he had taken his boat and crew far up an uncharted river west of Agats, checking out rumors he had heard of gold to be found there. The stories proved false, and he turned back, but his boat was damaged in a flood, and he was forced to put in to a village to make repairs. He is very fair and thought himself to be the first white man the villagers had probably ever seen, yet his skin color did not seem to astound them as it had other primitive tribes. He later found out from the natives that another white man was living in a village located some distance away, in the mountains by a lake that fed into the river. The natives described him as a god who had come from the sky and was carried about on a portable throne. Curious, he learned enough of the language to probe further and found that the god wore khaki clothes and that his head and face were covered with blond hair.

"Brinkler was unable to persuade the villagers to take him to the lake. It was the home of their traditional enemies and was forbidden territory. But he believed the story, even though he had not seen the man himself, and he became convinced the man was possibly an American pilot downed over New Guinea during the war. When he reached Port Moresby and checked with authorities, he learned there were no missing pilots to fit the description and location, but he did hear of Michael's earlier disappearance in 1939. So he contacted me. Not out of the goodness of his heart, mind you. He wanted money, a great deal of it, to go back to search for my son or to draw maps of the location of the river and the lake. There are hundreds of them in that area, as you know.

"Well, I promptly threw him out—politely, of course—figuring he was merely the first of many parasites who would crawl out of the woodwork, now that the war was over, and try to capitalize upon my loss." Sir Charles began to walk slowly around the room, talking as he went, as if the words alone could not relieve him of the tension he felt.

"Indeed, I was right. I was contacted shortly after Brinkler by a man who claimed he had seen my son held prisoner on one of the small Solomon Islands and had even spoken with him. Michael had allegedly asked him to convey a message to me, which he would do for a price. And there was the owner of a Port Moresby bar who claimed Michael had wandered into his establishment one night, suffering from amnesia, and a psychic who claimed he had been buried alive by an avalanche on Mount Wilhelmina. I won't go on. There were others even sillier. The more reasonable ones I checked out myself or asked the American naval authorities to investigate. None proved out. However, through this colorful collection of bizarre stories there began to filter persistent rumors, drifting out of the native trade routes in south New Guinea, the same grapevine that had originally led us to you in the Grand Valley. These rumors told of a white man held prisoner in a mountain village on a lake on the south bank of the Snow Mountains. Not wanting to find hope where there was none, I did not take these rumors seriously either. If held prisoner, Michael would have escaped and made his way out of New Guinea. After all, he had escaped from the Japanese under more difficult conditions. It wasn't likely that even a determined New Guinea tribe could hold him long unless . . ." He hesitated as if his thoughts pained him. "Unless he was ill or too badly injured to escape. I remembered Brinkler's story about the throne. Perhaps it was a litter to transport a man too crippled or ill to walk on his own. I began to believe that there might well be such a white man but that of course, it could not be Michael. He had died in the Admiralties, far north of inland New Guinea. Then the American naval authorities contacted me. A small naval transport plane loaded with medical personnel had gone down in the New Guinea highlands, near the Baliem River. The survivors were there for a week until the Navy made a daring rescue by glider. It was in the magazines and newspapers. Perhaps you remember seeing it?"

Catherine nodded.

"In their report on the incident the rescued nurses and medics described trading with the natives for food and, though they didn't understand the language, being told through gestures and drawings of another plane downed on the north slopes of the Snow Mountains and a man with blond hair who was held captive in a village to the south, beyond the peaks. One of the natives had this around his neck." Sir Charles reached into the desk drawer and pulled out a pair of gold navy pilot's wings.

"The nurses traded him all their officers' pins and insignias for this. The man refused to tell them how he got it, and would only say it had come from the plane. He refused to give the plane's exact location."

He crossed over to her and dropped the wings into the palm of her hand. She stared at them for a moment and then closed her fingers until the sharp ends cut at her hand. Her heart was pounding. It was evidence, tangible evidence, not rumors, that Michael was alive.

Sir Charles went on. "After the nurses were rescued and gave their report, a careful search was made of earlier U.S. naval records, but they showed no signs of any pilot missing in that area. So the matter was closed, until just a few months ago when the American Navy received a report from the Australian government that a native named Tobi had turned up on Manus Island claiming the Australians owed him money for coast-watching activities during the war. His island had been invaded, and the station destroyed by the Japanese in 1942, and he had never been paid. He had fled the island, worked for a while on a Japanese base on another island, and had only just put in a claim for his coast watch duty because he was afraid his subsequent work for the Japanese might be held against him.

"It was his report on what had happened at the coast watch station that was of interest to the Navy." Sir Charles paused, clearly overcome by emotion. "He claims Michael escaped in a plane the afternoon before the Japanese attack. Tobi and another native coast watcher had helped him steal gasoline from the Japanese supply depot the night before. Michael had given Tobi his watch as payment. The other man had requested Michael's dog tags, and it must have been that man whose burned body was found in the hut and mistakenly identified as Michael's. Tobi himself had been out on patrol during the afternoon and returned in time to witness the Japanese attack. He waited until they were gone and then fled the island. He did not see Michael take off, but the plane was gone when he reached the station. According to Tobi, Michael had enough gas to make it to Dobu, an island off the west coast of New Guinea, where he intended to make contact with a Chinese smuggler he knew who would take him to Borneo. The plane never reached Dobu."

Sir Charles turned to the large globe next to his chair. With a trembling finger he traced a line from the tiny island west of the Admiralties across New Guinea to the island of Dobu. "It is quite possible, even probable, that the plane went down in the mountains where the reports of the white man have originated." He nodded toward her hand. "And where those wings came from."

A frown rearranged the lines on his face. "Navy investigators seem to feel that Michael may have deserted." He cleared his throat and continued. "At the time he escaped he was under orders to report to General MacArthur's staff in Australia, where his knowledge of the people of the north coast was badly needed in the New Guinea offensive MacArthur was planning. Actually Michael had been ordered to Australia just before Bataan fell, but the orders were lost in the confusion of abandoning the naval command there. However, the Navy contends he had clearly received such orders by the time he left the Solomons and ignored them by escaping before he could be picked up. Should Michael be found, there will be questions to answer. It's possible he will have to face a court of inquiry, perhaps even a court-martial, when he returns.''

Catherine looked alarmed, and Sir Charles hastened to reassure her. ''I'm told it would only be a formality. He would be cleared, I'm certain. No country likes to tarnish its heroes.''

''Do you think he deserted?'' Catherine asked.

''Given all that had happened, I think he would have done anything at the time to reach you and his son.'' The softness of his response had an edge of sadness. ''I suppose he might have decided he was through with our miserable little war and gone off to fight his own. It would have been quite like him, really.'' The last remark contained a note of pride. ''In view of its delicate position, the Navy has turned the matter entirely over to me. I have been assured it will see no reason to bring charges against Michael, provided it isn't forced to it by the newspapers or some publicity-seeking politician. We must keep the search effort limited—and discreet.''

''Does the Navy feel he is alive?'' Alive! Just the word made her heart beat faster.

''They feel me may be, but that like many deserters, he is afraid to come home for fear of being charged.''

Catherine looked incredulous. ''That's ridiculous!''

Sir Charles smiled for the first time. ''I know, but they don't know Michael as we do. Only illness, injury, or being held captive would have kept him from reaching you. The preliminary naval air searches have been halted. They turned up nothing, but that's not surprising, given the terrain. As for a ground search, it raises a delicate political situation. The New Guinea territory is disputed, and the exact authority is in question. Both the Dutch and the Indonesian governments claim possession, and the present treaty hasn't resolved it. If we attempt to get permission to

600

enter New Guinea from either of them, it could result in a public squabble over whose right it is to grant entry—just the kind of attention we want to avoid. So we should originate the search from the Australian side, from Port Moresby, where no one need know what we're up to. I'm too old to go myself. It will be difficult—perhaps even dangerous.'' He broke off, seeing the turmoil on her face, and sat down wearily. "I'm sorry, Catherine. This is all such a shock to you, and I haven't even given you a chance to say all that you must be feeling.''

He was watching her closely. She could see he could not quite bring himself to ask her to lead an expedition herself. Yet he could not doubt her answer. She knew the area better than anyone. If Michael was to be found, she stood the best chance of doing it. She picked up the box and held it, feeling the beautiful carved hornbill on its top.

"There are letters in it, written to you,'' Sir Charles remarked.

She scarcely heard him. "I think I'll go to my room now.'' She rose, clutching the box and the pilot's wings, and started for the door.

"Catherine . . .'' Sir Charles's voice turned her around. "It's true that I have selfish reasons for not wanting you to marry Ahmad. If Michael is alive, as I'm convinced he is, then I want the two of you and your son to have a life together. I feel that I helped come between you before, and I have regretted it ever since. I want to make it up to you—to both of you. But besides this selfish reason, I honestly believe that marriage to Ahmad would be a mistake for you both. Indonesia will need him to help guide the early years of independence.''

His voice was soft and full of sympathy. "I know you love them both. Only you can decide which way your own happiness should take you.''

Catherine went to her room and sat staring at the box she held on her lap. It was long and slender, like a tissue box. Her hands shook as she finally opened the lid. It contained only letters, just as Sir Charles had said, letters addressed to her at Columbia University and returned stamped "Address unknown.'' The letters were unopened. It was clear that Sir Charles had felt that whatever they contained was between her and Michael alone.

The letters were in order, oldest to most recent. She wondered who had organized them, and remembering the neat file boxes of notes and references on his desk at Maitreya and the orderly way he had kept his tools, from bone knife to steel machete, in New Guinea, she guessed it had been Michael.

The letters first expressed his feelings of loss at their separation and progressed to his decision to seek a divorce no matter what the consequences. Then the letters became full of dismay at his being unable to contact her. Finally, as his last letters came back one by one, unread, they conveyed his anger that she had deliberately cut herself off from him.

At the bottom of the box she found her letter and the picture of Michael that she had sent to him in November 1941. Beneath it she found his reply, written on the morning of December 8, before he knew of the bombing of Pearl Harbor. It was not in an envelope. No doubt there had been no opportunity to mail it. Her hands shook too badly to hold that final letter, so she paced the floor for a moment before she gathered the courage to return to it. Seven years had passed, yet nothing had changed. She still feared his reply to her letter as much now as she had on the day she had written it.

Dear Catherine (the letter began),

My God—how angry you have been with me. At first I couldn't believe you could have loved me and still kept your pregnancy a secret, letting me go off to the Philippines, letting me do the same thing to you and our baby that my father did to my mother and me. Even if I didn't know what I was doing, *you* knew. God, you must have hated me to have let that happen.

When I got your note, I was in a rage. I never wanted to see you again. I wanted to hurt you as much as you've hurt me. But now I realize how hurt you must have been in the first place. So you did the one thing that would have hurt me most—you let my son be born a bastard, just as I was. The only thing that enables me to forgive you is the fact that by contacting me, I assume you at least don't want him to be raised as one.

I've missed you, Catherine. It was if I had died more than a year ago, when we parted. I've been numb all this time . . . taking risks I probably shouldn't have. You were right. Part of me didn't want to live. That's changed now. It changed months ago when I asked Kara for a divorce. I wish you had said in your letter that you still love me and want me with you. Your feelings toward me are unclear, and that torments me. Which is perhaps what you intended.

Or is it pride—as well as anger—that makes you reluctant to tell me what you are feeling? Are you afraid I won't come to you? Well, nothing can stop me now. Not even you. You could have prevented all of this, you know. That day at the airport—or when you found you were pregnant. Perhaps you knew even then and didn't tell me. I was looking for any excuse, Catherine, to be with you. Any but my own happiness. To be with you for my own selfish reasons would have left me with too much guilt. You knew that, and still you didn't act. I can only assume you were too afraid. If only you had pleaded with me then! But then you have always given me the entire responsibility for our relationship. After Maitreya you always left everything up to me. And now you've punished me for not doing what you wanted.

Let's hope we're not too late—to make happiness for ourselves and for our son. I will see you in Batavia just before the holidays. This letter should arrive only shortly before I do.

Michael

There was a postscript hastily written a day later.

9 December

War has broken out. Everything changed. Leaves canceled. Doubt that I can even get this letter off, but I will try. Please return to States as soon as possible. I know Ahmad will help you through whatever comes. Trust him. Whatever happens, I love you. Remember. Nothing will ever change that.

I will come to you when I can. I meant it when I said nothing can stop me. Not even this war.

Catherine sat stunned and drained, staring at the sheets of paper. She was no longer sure what she had expected, but it was not this angry, bitter letter. How unhappy he had been! Suddenly she was flooded with the realization that she had blamed him all this time. She had seen herself as the injured party. She realized now that she had withheld news of her pregnancy from him not out of self-sacrifice but in anger and vindictiveness. He was right. If she had cared to face it, she would have known that what she was doing with the baby would hurt him where he was most vulnerable.

Still, he had forgiven her. She clung to those lines in the letter while, at the same time, she realized bitterly that what she had done might well have killed him. If she had told him about her pregnancy or contacted him to ask him to come to her he might have taken a desk job in Washington. His knowledge of the Japanese language would have assured it, had the Navy known. She had gotten even with him and almost destroyed them both in the process.

"Oh, Michael: Oh, God!" She lay back on the bed and wept.

It was almost dusk when she rode Admiral to the limestone pool. The sun had disappeared behind the jungle trees, leaving the pool in forbidding shadows. Yet it was curiously comforting to her. Here, of all places, with the knowledge that he might be alive, all that had passed since they had been together seemed to be swept away. This place where it had all begun between them.

She was a survivor. She usually got what she wanted, and she didn't give up easily. It had kept her alive when others, physically stronger than she, had died on Teram Island. Only the belief that he was dead had let her give him up in the first place. She loved him, had always loved him, beyond everything else in the world: her work, Ahmad, even beyond her son.

His last words came back to her; "I will come to you when I can." Not "if," but "when." If he could not come to her, then she would go to him.

She closed her eyes. The cicadas had begun their evening song. In the darkness of her mind, she felt a contact with Michael as real as if it were physical. She opened her eyes to the stars coming out and a faint yellow glow on the horizon above the trees. Admiral stood waiting patiently.

"Michael," she whispered into the night, "I love you."

And his love returned to her, strong and clear, from the surrounding darkness.

Once Catherine had made her decision, she realized she could not leave without going to meet Ahmad in Java, as they had planned. Sir Charles urged her not to go. The Dutch already occupied Jogjakarta and had imprisoned Sukarno and the members of the government, removing them to the island of Bangku. The Indonesian Army had disintegrated. Only Ahmad and his guerrilla forces still carried on the battle for independence. It was likely that the airstrip itself was under Dutch control by now or soon would be. If Catherine were captured, she would surely be imprisoned by the Dutch. Not even Sir Charles's influence could prevent it.

"There's no need for you to go," Sir Charles had protested. "Ahmad already knows about Michael. I sent the news to him through Patri before I told you. As Michael's closest friend, I thought he should know."

But Catherine was adamant. She could not go to New Guinea without first seeing Ahmad.

The landing at Gunungteh was rough. The airstrip was nothing more than a dirt clearing on the side of a mountain. It had been built and used by Dutch tea planters who occupied the area before the war. Repeated attempts by Dutch planes to render it useless had so far failed, but its surface was full of bomb craters. Catherine tensed with each lurch and bump of the taxiing plane as she thought of the ammunition her rebel pilot was carrying in the hold. Sheets of rain began to come down, blowing and whipping around the plane as Catherine swung out of the cargo door in the plane's belly and dropped to the ground.

The copilot cracked open his cockpit window and called down to her, his voice almost drowned out by the rain, "We can't stay long!"

She nodded that she understood and began to run in the direction of the buildings at the edge of the field, now obliterated by the downpour. Men in peasant garb moved quickly out of the forest toward the plane to unload it. None of them stopped her. She began to think Ahmad might not have come as she stumbled onto the porch of the first Dutch building. Somewhere beyond and below it lay the streets of tiny Gunungteh. Catching her breath, she stood in the doorway, letting her eyes adjust to the room's shadows. And then she saw him. Her heart skipped a beat. He was dressed like the others, but even in that light there was no mistaking him. Pak Anak was with him. Soaked, she stood dripping onto the floor. He made no move to welcome her, but Pak tossed her a rough cloth with which to dry herself.

"There isn't much time," Ahmad observed, no hint of emotion in his voice, as she stood, head to one side, rubbing her hair.

"I know," she replied, stung by how distant he sounded, wishing he had been angry instead, as she had expected.

Pak brushed past her to step outside. Even so, there was little privacy. They were surrounded by scores of men hurrying outside.

"It's madness, Catherine. Michael is dead!" he said suddenly. Lightning lit the room, and his words were cut off by the sound of thunder.

"No!" she replied sharply. "He is alive! I felt it even before the rumors. Since I've been back at Maitreya, I have felt it." Her tone was insistent. "He *is* alive."

"Only in your heart!" he retorted. "You have never really let go of him. And Maitreya has made it harder, that's all. But he is dead, Catherine. And you must face it instead of risking your life on this futile venture. I *know* Michael. Injured or not, he would have found his way out of hell itself by this time." His voice softened. "Stay here and marry me as we have planned. Tonight."

"I . . . cannot. Not now." She looked away, unable to face his intense gaze.

"You mean, if he is alive, it's Michael you want to marry." The room crackled with tension, as jagged and explosive as the air outside.

She did not answer. His mouth was drawn tight.

"Very well. Then do what you must. It's clear I cannot stop you."

"He needs me."

"And you think I don't? Is that it?" He shook his head sadly and bitterly. "How little you know me after all."

She watched him as he stood there so full of pain and anger. Her gaze wandered to his throat and the smooth skin of his chest that she glimpsed beneath the open front of his shirt, and she was shocked by the realization that she wanted him as passionately now as ever. It made no difference at all that she was choosing to go to Michael.

"You're wrong, Ahmad. I do love you!"

He would accept no compromise. "Then prove it. Don't go to New Guinea. Stay here."

"I can't. You love him, too. You must know I can't abandon him," she cried.

606

"I know that he is dead!"

"No!" she retorted sharply. "You only believe he is dead because you want to, because it makes it easier for you where I'm concerned. What if he were alive? What would you think then of what has existed between us for the past five years? You, his best friend, his brother!"

Some of the old fire flickered briefly in his eyes. "I would still want you for my own," he said defiantly. "Above Michael. Above all else."

"I must go and find out for myself—once and for all."

"You can't go alone. It's too dangerous. Take Pak with you—and two Dyak porters from Matapura, Pak knows which ones. They have been to the Sepik before with Michael."

"I couldn't possibly take Pak! He must stay here—to protect you. You need him more than I do."

"I insist, Catherine. Otherwise, I shall take you hostage here and now—and you will not go to New Guinea at all!" he said fiercely.

One of the plane's crew came to announce the unloading was finished.

"Go," Ahmad told her. "And take Pak with you."

But she didn't move. She couldn't leave him like this, with all this coldness still between them. He made no move toward her, so she went to him and buried her face in the softness of his shirt, seeking his forgiveness, though she was too proud to ask for it. For a moment he hesitated; then his arms tightened around her, and the familar warmth and passion which had always been between them came back. He kissed her until she felt she could never leave him, and then he put her firmly from him. An army slicker lay on the back of a chair next to the table. He reached for it and drew it gently around her shoulders, pulling the hood over her head. "Go on," he said softly, his voice strained. "They're waiting."

"I love you," she whispered.

"I know," he replied, his emotions betrayed in the tightness of his voice.

Tears mixed with rain as she hurried away toward the plane.

Pak Anak, who had witnessed part of the scene, stepped inside from the porch. "You let her go?" It was an accusation.

"I couldn't keep her from going. He is my brother. Suppose

607

he is alive? Suppose he is alive!'' he repeated, as if considering, for the first time, that it might be true.

For a moment Pak Anak was silent, his mouth set in a grim line, and then he replied, ''In the old days a sultan would have had him killed.''

''No, Pak,'' Ahmad spoke angrily. ''He was my friend. You will go with her and see that no harm will come to either of them if he lives, or you will die by my hand.''

Pak Anak's gaze was steady. He had spoken his opinion, but now had his orders, and he would obey them.

Ahmad reached out and touched him affectionately on the shoulder. ''Allah be with you, old friend.''

''And with you, my lord,'' Pak Anak replied as he bent quickly to his knees and kissed the foot of his king.

The rain had not let up by the time he reached the waiting plane, its propellers turning impatiently into the wind. He looked back once before he boarded, but he could not see the sultan. He could not even see the house. Both had vanished behind a slanting gray wall of water.

Chapter 57
Java, January 1949

Merapi was awake in the darkness. The volcano's fiery breath reflected off the low clouds and cast an eerie glow onto the surrounding world. Something had stirred it from its slumber.

"It is angry," an old Javanese peasant had told Ahmad earlier in the day as the two walked together on the road into the mountains. "It is angry that the Dutch have conquered Indonesia," the old man had added, his own sadness weeping in his voice.

It was late now and well past the Dutch-imposed curfew. For the past few hours Ahmad had had the road to himself. He had easily skirted the Dutch checkpoints throughout the day and night as he made his way back to the little mountain village of Gunungteh where he would spend the night in the house next to the abandoned airfield where he had last seen Catherine. Near dawn he would light the torches to signal the plane he had arranged to pick him up to take him to New Guinea. There was still time for him to catch Catherine before she left Port Moresby for the interior. He couldn't let her go without him. Even with Pak along, it was too dangerous.

Since she had left, the anger and hurt he had felt had faded. Only her safety concerned him now. Indonesia's revolution would continue without him. He had made sure of that by freeing some of the republic's leaders who had been captured earlier by the Dutch in Jogjakarta, though he had been forced to leave Sukarno, now imprisoned on Bangku Island, in Dutch hands. Ahmad's recent address to the United Nations, read, in his absence, by the Swedish delegate, had been a personal triumph. Through it he had succeeded in rallying world opinion to the side of Indonesian independence. Everywhere governments were demanding the complete withdrawal of Dutch forces from the Indies. Ahmad was now confident that freedom would come soon. From now on the fight would be mainly a diplomatic one that could be waged without him, despite the pleas of those who were urging him, in Sukarno's absence, to seize the presidency and make it his own. He had turned them down. For the first time in seven years, he could put his personal needs before those of Indonesia.

There were no lights as he approached the tiny house. The village itself had been abandoned in December, when the Dutch took Jogjakarta. Many of the villagers had fled to join the guerrilla forces.

Merapi now lit the sky in the east as brilliantly as the glow of a huge city. It seemed to have grown redder as the night wore on, and now the earth trembled beneath his feet from time to time. Reaching the veranda of the isolated house, he placed a foot upon the smooth stone and paused out of habit, senses tuned toward anything unusual. But the house, and the village were quiet. Only the lizards and insects of the night stirred.

Inside the house Tùk Malek heard the faint footstep on the stone beyond the door and held his breath. His hand gripped the handle of the machine gun, and his finger twitched involuntarily on the trigger. It was as if the last twenty years of his life were converging on this one moment with a kind of inevitability that both exhilarated and frightened him.

In the total darkness of the room he heard the latch lift and briefly glimpsed the pink glow beyond the door before it closed again. There was silence, then a slight noise as something brushed against the table. The scraping sound of a match being struck broke the silence again. Tuk Malek waited quietly in the shadows just beyond the glow of the match and watched tensely as it touched the lamp wick and sent a sudden burst of light into every corner of the room. He saw the startled look on the face of the man who held the dying match, and Tuk Malek relished the moment.

"It has been a long time, Ahmad, since Paris."

The surprise on Ahmad's face turned to wariness. His voice

was calm when he spoke, but his hand trembled slightly as he shook out the match and tossed it on the table. "How did you know I would come here?"

"A radio message from Jogjakarta."

There was a flicker of surprise in Ahmad's eyes, and Tuk Malek gave an amused laugh. "You did not think your nationalist friends would betray you at the first opportunity?" He laughed again and moved toward the center of the room where he could more clearly see the sultan.

"And why are you here?" Even as he asked, he already knew the answer. Silently he cursed his lack of a weapon, but he had dared not carry so much as a kris on the road for fear the Dutch might find it and arrest him.

"You are a threat to Sukarno's power."

"And you? What have you to do with it?"

"We want Sukarno to remain in power until we can seize it for ourselves, perhaps in the next few months. We can control him. Though you are a fellow Marxist, we cannot control you."

As he listened, Ahmad glanced around the room for any kind of weapon. Tuk Malek caught the look, and fearing the sultan's reputation, he started to bring the gun up to fire. Ahmad saw the movement out of the corner of his eye and sent his foot up toward the gun but too late. A burst of machine-gun fire cut the silence of the night and struck him fully. He sank to his knees, clutching at his stomach, and then slowly slumped forward to the floor, blood spurting from half a dozen wounds. Tuk Malek stood silently watching the blood soak the simple peasant garments and run onto the floor. Royal blood. "It does not differ from that of the rest of us," he whispered to the silent room. "It is no more precious."

He waited until he was sure the sultan was dead. Kneeling, he felt for a pulse, and finding none, he rose and stood over the body. "We shared more than a philosophy at one time in our lives. Now that old debt is settled." He blew out the lamp and left.

Outside, along the village street, an old man approached Tuk Malek as he passed through the village. He had been wakened by the sound of the shots but had thought it to be an explosion of Merapi. Indeed, the sky appeared almost on fire now, so deep was the red that filled it.

"Good evening, Grandfather. What keeps you up so late?"

"Is it going to explode?" the old man cried. "I thought I heard it begin." He stared in fright at the mountain, then turned back to Tuk Malek and studied the face of the stranger.

"No, Grandfather. Don't worry. Go back to bed. I will stay the night to keep watch and give warning if it erupts. Are there others in the village?"

The old man shook his head. "They all fled weeks ago when the Dutch came. I was too feeble to accompany them. Besides, what would the Dutch care about one as old as I?"

"You have no more to fear from the mountain than you do from the Dutch. Now go back to bed."

With one last glance at the mountain, the old man shook his head and reluctantly complied. As he did so, the earth gave a shudder and seemed to shift beneath his feet. He recovered his balance and turned back toward the stranger, but Tuk Malek was gone. There was only the empty road, lit by the glowing mountain.

Tuk Malek continued down the road for a short distance, then circled back to the village and quietly entered the old man's house. Guided by his heavy breathing, Tuk Malek slit the old man's throat. He wanted no one to know of his presence in the village this night. Tomorrow the Dutch would pass through the village on a mop-up operation. He wanted them to be blamed for the sultan's death.

At Maitreya, Kartini awoke screaming from a dream in which the eyes of the cloud leopard had burned before her with incredible intensity and had then gone out forever. Her nurse, who slept in the next room, went to her side and attempted to comfort her, but Kartini wept uncontrollably, refusing to be consoled. Downriver, at Matapura the mountain trembled slightly, sending the lighted candles swaying overhead, rousing the entire palace to life. No sooner were the occupants up than Gunung Matapura reacted again, this time with a sharp shudder that toppled cases filled with precious objects and sent chandeliers and glass crashing to the floor. A great crack opened in the stone of the courtyard, and smaller crevices appeared on the *kraton* walls. The mountain, which had slept peacefully for more than 1,000 years, was stirring to life. Steaming fissures opened in its base as the volcano awoke, and hot sulfur smoke poured from the mountain's wounds.

The frightened palace occupants and the villagers waited tensely throughout the night, but by morning the tremors had stopped and only the faintest hint of steam trailed from the fissures. But the villagers' fear remained.

Chapter 58
New Guinea, January 1949

The flamingos rose in unison from the marshy area where the river widened into a shallow highland lake. They exited by the hundreds, leaving the area to the noisy pontoon-footed bird that settled on the lake in a burst of spray, disrupting the mirror-smooth surface of the sluggish water.

Ian Lavery, the pilot, anchored the plane near the shoreline where it would disgorge its supplies and passengers. The flight had originated that morning in Port Moresby, bearing Catherine, Pak Anak, and the two Dyak porters from Borneo to the west flank of the Snow Mountains of Dutch New Guinea, an area completely uncharted and unexplored. The day was drawing to a close, so the group decided to camp by the lake before attempting to locate the village purported to hold the white god.

After the dinner Catherine withdrew to the edge of the campfire. Ian Lavery watched her through the firelight. At thirty-four she was an extraordinarily beautiful woman. The loveliness of her youth, with its audacity and its innocence, had been transformed into a serenity and an aloofness that was not a lack of warmth. He knew a little of what she had been through, having heard talk in Port Moresby. One thing he had heard was that both men and women who had suffered less during the war than she had had given up and died. Catherine's indomitable spirit still shone. He admired the way she had organized and taken charge of this search, firmly but naturally. He himself had been reluctant to fly into unknown territory, but he had relented because of her.

As he watched her now, the fire flickering on her skin, casting shadows on its smooth, tanned softness, he wondered what she might be thinking. He knew it was not of him, though he wished it were otherwise. Her black hair was pulled back into a neat bun at the nape of her neck. She wore a khaki shirt, unbuttoned at the collar, khaki pants, and laced walking boots. The look was purposeful—no nonsense—but it did not conceal her beauty.

Since her first sight of the magnificent Snow Mountains Catherine had felt a growing excitement. The sense of Michael's presence had been strong at Maitreya, but it grew even stronger here. She half expected him to walk into the campsite; but he did not, and by early morning she and the Dyaks were on their way to the spot where they had sighted the village from the air, leaving Lavery alone to guard the plane.

The village was located three miles away on the edge of the lake. It consisted of multiple-family dwellings built on stilts with bamboo walkways leading to the shore. Gardens floated on rafts around the huts. The villagers must have known of their arrival, for they lined the shore, wary but curious, waiting to meet them. The men were armed with what appeared to be fishing spears. There was no white man among them.

Catherine couldn't understand the language, but through gestures she succeeded in having the headman pointed out to her. She gave him the feathers and shells she had brought as gifts to be distributed among them. Taking advantage of this gesture of goodwill, Catherine indicated a desire to see any other white men who might be there.

She wasn't sure the villagers understood, but her attempts at communication caused a great deal of excitement and some emphatic negative gestures on the headman's part. Catherine wasn't sure whether it meant there were no white men or that he was refusing her request.

A commotion rose suddenly at the far end of the village. Catherine attempted to move forward for a better look, but her way was quickly blocked by instructions from the chief. She could still see the last longhouse, where some women of the village were trying to prevent someone from leaving. Finally a figure broke free of them, thrust them aside, and began to hobble across the swaying walkway that led from that dwelling to the shore. The women followed behind him, clutching at him and screaming.

Catherine's heart leaped to her throat. The figure was a white man dressed in tattered khaki with burnished golden hair and a golden beard. He used a stick to support one of his legs which had been badly injured and had not properly healed so that he could only drag it uselessly behind him. With all the strength she could summon, Catherine thrust herself free of those who restrained her and began to run down the shore toward the limping figure.

She pulled up short some ten yards away. The man was not Michael. As much as he resembled him, he was clearly not Michael. Her heart sank as she waited for him to approach.

"Who are you?" she managed to stammer.

"Turner, mum." The Australian accent came through loud and clear. "Jeffrey Turner." He could not understand her distress, so he awkwardly added, "A coast watcher off the Admiralties. I crashed near here four years ago. My legs and the villagers kept me from getting out." He hesitated, noting the stricken look that continued. "Is there something wrong?"

"I'm sorry, Turner." Catherine put her hand over her eyes for a moment. "We came because we had news of a white man here. It's just that I was hoping you were someone else who may have crashed in New Guinea during the war."

"During the war. You mean it's over."

Catherine looked at him in surprise until she realized the extent of his isolation. "The war has been over for three years, Turner." She added with a smile, "And we won."

"That's good." He grinned. They were surrounded now by the villagers. He pushed them back, speaking to them sharply. Surprisingly they complied. He turned back to Catherine and grinned. "They listen to me, sometimes."

"You're a prisoner?"

"Sort of. They think of me as a god." He laughed. "Imagine that!" He grew suddenly thoughtful. "That should change now. Since they've seen you, they know I'm not all that unique."

"I'm truly sorry. But we've come to take you out of here anyway." While she was talking to Turner, she was battling her own disappointment. She knew that somehow she had to continue to search for Michael, but she hadn't the slightest idea of where to begin. Perhaps the plane had been lost in the ocean.

"Will you be going back, too?" Turner asked her.

"No, I plan to continue the search elsewhere."

"Who is it you're looking for?"

"An American naval officer. He crashed here, too. At least we thought so. He'd escaped from the Philippines and the Admiralties."

Turner's blue eyes narrowed. "You don't mean Lieutenant Stanford by any chance?"

Catherine looked at him in surprise. "Why, yes. How did you know?"

"He was with me in the plane when it crashed."

Of course! Turner was the name of the coastwatcher who had rescued Michael. She had forgotten. She struggled to control her fears. "And what happened to him?"

Turner sighed. "I don't know."

The villagers were becoming restless and angry at the attention their special captive was showing the white visitor. They had become noisy, and sensing a rival, some of the women attempted to pull Catherine away. Turner ordered them to stop and took Catherine firmly by the arm, inviting her to sit beside him on the sand. Pak Anak fired his gun into the air, and it restored the necessary awe to give them privacy while he and the two Dyak stood protectively before Turner and Catherine.

Turner kept his hand upon her arm as he talked.

"Stanford was planning to fly to the south New Guinea coast, to Dobu Island, where he could catch a boat to Borneo. I decided at the last minute to go with him. The Japs were about to overrun the island. After we took off a Japanese plane spotted us over the north coast of New Guinea. He did some damage before we lost him in the cloud cover. We kept going but lost altitude and fuel. We couldn't make it over the Snows. Stanford wanted to land in the valley, but I was flying the plane, and I thought we could make it all the way. He was a better pilot than I. Maybe if he'd been flying, we would have made it. Visibility was poor, and the mountain wall was in front of me before I knew it. Fortunately there was a clearing, and I landed in it. Ran out of space before we stopped. Sheared off a part of the wings. When it was over, I was dazed. Stanford was unconscious. I couldn't tell if he was badly hurt or not. He didn't appear to be, but I was afraid to move him. I went off to get water; but I couldn't find a river right away, and in my confused state I couldn't find my way back to the plane. I wandered for what must have been several days before I found a river which I followed until I came across an abandoned boat. I took it down the river, but it disintegrated in the first rapids I came to, almost drowning me and leaving me with this.'' He indicated his damaged leg. ''Thought I was going to lose it. Probably should have. I became delirious on the riverbank. When next I awoke, I was in this village. When I was well, I wanted to go search for the plane. But the villagers won't cross the mountains because of the demons they believe to be on the other side, and I was too crippled to go alone.''

His story finished, he gave her arm a squeeze and removed his hand.

''Do you think he's dead?'' she asked.

''His pulse was strong and firm when I left him. He could have lived. I did.''

He studied her now, his blue eyes thoughtful as he looked at her face. ''You must be Catherine.''

''I'm sorry. I guess I forgot to introduce myself. I'm Catherine Morgan. But how did you know?''

''I didn't. Stanford didn't talk much about himself, but he did say that he had to get back to Catherine and that his war was really in Borneo.''

Catherine nodded. ''Yes. Borneo was his home.''

''There was an American sub coming to pick him up. MacArthur wanted him in Australia, but Stanford was determined to get to Borneo, even if it meant getting court-martialed for desertion. I've never seen a man so obsessed. He wouldn't even go to Darwin and see if they would give him permission to go to Borneo. He said he hadn't gone through hell in the Philippines in order to end up one of MacArthur's public relations men. He was going home, and nobody, including the U.S. Navy, was going to stop him.''

Tears came to Catherine's eyes.

''It wasn't Borneo he was struggling so hard to reach, Catherine. It was you.''

Hearing his softly spoken words, Catherine covered her face with her hands and sobbed. He had loved her. He had never stopped loving her, any more than she had stopped loving him. Knowing that made the thought of his death only more unbearable.

Finally she recovered enough to ask him, "Could you locate the crash site?"

She handed him a paper and pen on which he first drew a line to indicate the mountain summit.

"It was on the north slopes at about 10,000 feet. There was a lake and a valley Stanford recognized—here."

Catherine felt a lump in her throat as Turner sketched the oval outline of the lake that had been her last refuge with Michael. Above it and to the east, he roughed in the place where the plane had struck the mountain.

"I know the area," Catherine said in a quiet voice that betrayed no emotion.

She silently considered the situation, debating whether to move the seaplane. The lake on the map was perhaps nearer the crash site but she knew the sheer limestone cliffs above it would make an ascent to the area slow and difficult. She decided to leave Lavery and the plane with Turner and cross the mountains on foot.

None of Turner's attempts to dissuade her were of any use. She was adamant. As adamant as Stanford had been. Finally he could do nothing but accept the gun she gave him and the directions to the plane. She sent the two Dyak porters back with instructions to the pilot. She and the porters would begin their climb over the south face of the Snow Mountains early the next morning.

That night Ian Lavery struggled to stay awake, rifle in hand. He had stayed on the plane, feeling uneasy at the lack of curiosity the natives had thus far shown toward his presence.

Unable to stay awake any longer, Lavery dozed off near dawn and did not feel or hear the small thud as the first boat pulled up to the pontoons, followed by five others, each carrying five men. In a moment a faint spark became a torch which burst into flame. That torch soon gave birth to nine others while one of the intruders climbed stealthily to the door of the plane. The door was locked. A sharp blow with a stone ax broke the window, and the torches were quickly inserted, setting the plane's interior ablaze.

Moments later Lavery awoke coughing and struggling for breath.

He staggered to his feet and wrestled with the door, too late. Overcome by heat and smoke, he slumped to the floor. Burning furiously, the flames found their way quickly to the fuel tanks. The plane exploded in a huge ball of fire that rumbled like distant thunder over the sleeping village. The screams of the attackers, engulfed by the flames, went similarly unnoticed in the night that surrounded the village.

The next morning Catherine left with Pak Anak and the two Dyak porters. Turner saw her off with a parting hug borne of the affection that arises between strangers who share a common danger and isolation. Neither of them realized that their choice of returning to Port Moresby was already gone.

It took two days of steady climbing for Catherine, Pak Anak, and the two porters to reach the summit. The last day had been shrouded in clouds that made it difficult to keep their bearings. The trees grew sparse, and patches of snow covered the rocks and ground. On the last day of the climb they began to leave even the clouds behind.

When they broke into the clear blue sky, they were treated to a magnificent sight that brought tears of recognition to Catherine's eyes. Far to the east, Mount Wilhelmina thrust a snow-white breast through the veil of the clouds. Hard by Catherine's left, the soaring summit of the Carstensz Glacier loomed menacingly above, as if it might, at any minute, shake itself free of tons of rock and snow, sending them all tumbling down the mountain.

Not wanting to spend the night in that forbidding spot, Catherine began the descent down the north side of the Snow Mountains. Guided now by the familiar presence of the Carstensz, Catherine easily made her way toward the spot on Turner's crude map indicating where the plane had gone down. Often hidden by low clouds and overgrown with trees and shrubs, the area would have been almost impossible to locate without a map. As it was, after reaching the area of the crash site, it took a day of careful searching before they spotted the plane, resting among the trees at the edge of a small mountain meadow. Though one wing lay in the open, its camouflage had rendered it invisible to any aerial searchers.

Pak Anak was the first to see the plane. "Nona! Look. There!" Her eyes followed his finger, and her heart missed a beat as she saw the plane. She was suddenly filled with dread at what she might find there. Better not to see. Not to know. But the men were already running toward the wreck.

It took several minutes to clear away the vegetation that crowded the doors on either side. The men worked at it with their parangs, standing on what was left of the wing on the passenger side. The windows were badly shattered, and it was impossible to see through them, so Catherine was forced to wait for the doors to be cleared in order to get her first glimpse into the plane. It had begun to drizzle, but Catherine didn't bother to put on her rain cape.

"Damn," she muttered as she listened impatiently to the sound of the parang blades biting into the liana vines. Without thinking, she bent over and began to search for leeches that might have burrowed into their favorite spot at the top of her laced boots. Looking for leeches at every pause had become a habit.

The chopping stopped. She looked up and saw the men turned expectantly toward her. The door was free. The porters jumped off the broken wing and waited for her to come forward so that she might be the first to open it. She walked toward the plane feeling like a condemned man. She was paralyzed with fear, yet, miraculously, her legs kept moving. A surprisingly long time seemed to pass before Pak Anak's hand reached down to pull her up onto the wing.

The passenger door was slightly ajar, but not enough to see through. The hinges had rusted, and she was unable to budge it. She stepped back and let Pak Anak pry it open with a pickax.

It took only a moment for the sight inside the plane to register. It was empty! She stared at the passenger seat, then at the floor and behind the seat as if scarcely able to believe her eyes. There was no body. She could still hope he was alive. Tears of relief streamed down her cheeks. A smiling Pak who had been peering over her shoulder turned and relayed the news to the men who waited tensely on the ground. Laughter and exclamations of joy greeted the news. Revitalized by hope, they suddenly forgot the discomfort of the rain and were ready to push on.

Catherine knew that if Michael had escaped the crash, there was only one way he would have gone: down, into the Grand Valley below. They spent one more day cautiously combing the area for clues to Michael's disappearance, but found none. If he had left any, they had long since been obliterated by the climate and the jungle.

The Dani salt trail was probably no more than two days' walk from the crash site. She would find the trail, and it would take her to the valley. With the resurgence of hope, her confidence returned. She would not give up yet until she found him.

They descended the terraced limestone walls throughout one day and into the early afternoon of the next. The rains and perpetual dampness produced green algae on the yellow rock surfaces, making footing slippery and treacherous in places. They passed over forest floors of moss and lichen and liverwort, tiled in a rich mosaic of differing shades of green, from which grew a tangled carpet of ferns and bamboo and groves of pandanus palms and stately tropical chestnuts. After wading through mud and climbing over rocks and roots, they broke free of the last tropical obstacle and emerged onto the rolling savanna lands of the valley.

They stopped at noon by a swiftly moving brook and ate from their supplies. The mists had burned away, and the sun was bright and hot. Fleecy white clouds still rested atop the mountains like babes in swaddling clothes hungrily nursing at the mountain peaks. The rest of the sky was clear and brilliant blue.

Catherine relaxed, leaning back into the tall grass, enjoying its sweet smell. White rhododendron bloomed everywhere along with brilliant scarlet myrtle. Tiny robin chats bathed in the stream. The humming sound of the busy flying insects was overpowered by the screeching of a flock of parrots passing overhead.

Resting in the tall grasses, the little search party did not at first see the approaching Dani hunters. Pak Anak finally spotted them. Hunching low so as to remain unseen, he scrambled over to Catherine and directed her attention to five warriors climbing the hill single file, as yet unaware of their visitors hidden in the grass. The warriors' hunt had been a success, judging from the several large rats and birds they carried.

Catherine watched them intently, feeling no fear but rather an eagerness, for the odds were good that she knew at least some of the approaching warriors. When the dark, muscular figures drew near enough for her to make out their features, her excitement grew as she saw that Degewatek led the group, followed by

622

Wuligen and Siba. She didn't recognize the two younger warriors who followed, but they had probably been children when she had left the valley more than eight years ago.

A cry of delight escaped her throat, and the anxious Dyak, seeing her pleasure, felt reassured. She rose in full view and waved to the approaching warriors. Not wanting to alarm them before they had a chance to recognize her, she stood quietly for a moment, while they halted, startled at first, and talked excitedly among themselves.

Catherine then shouted a greeting to them in Dani and started down the hill toward them. They stared in astonishment at the sound of their names, but when she drew close enough to recognize, they shouted her Dani name in return. Catherine's three Dyak bearers, wary of the armed strangers, followed her reluctantly. Catherine felt exhilarated. She ran easily. The wind felt fresh against her cheeks. These were not just old friends but old friends who might well know of Michael. She was sure of it. She was startled as a lone white egret, roused from its feeding by her passing, rose and flapped its way into the sky. Her heart soared with it.

Degewatek, standing at the head of the waiting band of warriors, saw the egret go, and suddenly he knew what he must do. As he drew it back, sunlight glinted off the smooth polished handle of the spear. Stunned, she stopped transfixed for the instant it took to send the spear on its way with all the strength and accuracy for which Degewatek was famous. It struck her just below the heart, and she fell to her knees, her face reflecting surprise and disbelief.

Pak Anak, seeing the raised spear, had pulled his rifle up to fire, but in his haste his aim was poor, and the shot went harmlessly into the grass. Before he could fire again, a hail of arrows from the other Dani struck and killed him and his unarmed companions. Catherine placed her hands upon the protruding shaft, and with her last bit of strength she pulled it free, then fell back into the grass.

The images streamed through her mind, some from the past, some from the present, and some she didn't recognize at all.

Her parents tiptoed into her dark room and stood by the bed, looking serious. They were replaced by Ahmad, who came carrying her son. His eyes were full of love and concern.

"I've brought Michael to see you."

"Yes. I'm glad."

"Does it hurt?"

"A little," she said, lying.

"What can I do?"

She sighed and turned away. "Nothing. Only stay here with me. I don't want to be alone."

He took her hand and held it tightly. Something strange seemed to be happening. The darkness was beginning to give way to a white light which began to stab at her senses.

Ahmad looked at her sadly and released her hand. "I must go now."

"No!" she cried out. "Don't leave me."

He said nothing, but his face was full of grief. Panic pressed in upon her. Ahmad's image began to fade into the increasing brightness, and she could not stop it.

The light glowed deep and golden, like sunlight at day's end. Grass tickled the side of her face, and the earth pressed warm and soft against her cheek. She closed her eyes, and when she opened them again, she saw him coming toward her, the sun gleaming off his golden head.

"Michael!" she cried out in joy, and tried to rise but could not.

He smiled and knelt beside her. His gray eyes were tender as they searched hers.

"They told me you were here. I've been waiting for you," he whispered.

"But you're all right," she said in disbelief. "Why didn't you come home?"

He didn't answer. He was looking at her injury, and his face had become serious. Looking back into her eyes and seeing the fear there, he reassured her.

"Don't be afraid. You're safe now, I promise." Then he placed his arms beneath her. "I'm going to carry you."

"Yes, yes. Anything."

He lifted her easily into his arms. Surprisingly she didn't feel a thing. She looked closely at him. Tan and fit, he hadn't changed at all.

"Michael, I've missed you so."

"I know." He bent his mouth to hers and kissed her lingeringly.

She felt an urgent need to tell him everything that had happened, but as she struggled to speak, he stopped her.

"Don't try to talk. It doesn't matter now. Nothing matters except that you're here."

The world was beginning to grow dark again. Perhaps the sun was setting, she thought. But then panic swept over her, and she clutched Michael only to find that she could no longer feel or see him. She felt herself against the earth and didn't know how she had got there. In the last throes of sunlight she saw a blue butterfly perched upon a blade of grass nearby. Its wings slowly folded and unfolded majestically. Then even that image blurred and was gone.

The darkness seemed to grow within her, expanding until it became a universe and she felt herself flowing out to meet the stars. The panic returned, and she struggled against the dark tide.

"It's all right." Michael's voice came to her full of love and strength. Trusting him as she always had, she let herself go and felt herself dissolve into the velvet darkness, beyond even the rapidly retreating stars.

"Michael!" she called out for reassurance.

His reply came from nowhere and everywhere. "I'm here."

Chapter 59
Jakarta, Java, December 27, 1949

The gleaming launch sped north across the sea from Matapura to Jakarta, the new capital of Indonesia, known before this day as Batavia. The crewmen were dressed in matching *kains* and turbans, and the boat's silk pennants, emblazoned with leopards, snapped smartly in the wind. The boat bore its passengers, two children and an elderly man, to the celebration that would mark Indonesia's passage to freedom.

Chairol left the children on deck and went to his stateroom to make final preparations, putting on a white tunic coat and carefully wrapping a strip of patterned cloth around his head, Dyak fashion. He would not wear the black felt fez made popular by Sukarno, for as Kartini's guardian the past year he would represent Matapura, one of the only two principalities allowed to remain in the new federation of states. Chairol regretted that Sir Charles had been unable to attend the ceremonies, but illness had forced him to remain at Maitreya under a physician's care. Michael had come along because Kartini fervently wished it, and Sir Charles, like Chairol himself, had a great deal of trouble denying Kartini what she wanted. In addition, the two men knew, without saying it, that the time the two children would have together was running out. It would not be long before all foreign property, Maitreya included, would be confiscated. Not even Sir Charles's long support of Indonesian independence could hold off the flood tide of nationalist feeling and its effect on Maitreya much longer.

Kartini wore the formal finery of her rank. Her face was tightly framed by a gold crown, from which dangling precious stones sparkled every time she moved her head. She wore a patterned silk sarong edged in gold, gold armbands, gold bracelets around her wrists and ankles, and gold sandals upon her tiny feet. Michael was dressed in loosely fitting white cotton clothes and leather sandals. His only adornment was a patterned silk sash that gathered the loose open-necked shirt to his waist. He carried a kris stuck in the back of his sash, given him by Ahmad years earlier.

The two children were playing a game of chess on deck when the excited cries of the crew drew them to the railing. The boat had slowed as it neared the Java coastline, and a huge circle of glowing light, resembling an underwater searchlight, appeared to be following it, adjusting to the changing speed and direction of the boat. The experienced crewmen had never seen anything like it and were afraid.

"Look at that!" Michael cried, jumping up and down in excitement.

"I have seen it before," Kartini replied calmly. "It is the eye of the sea, and it often follows me when I swim in the sea or take out my little fishing boat."

Michael looked at her incredulously from his two-year advantage in height. "You're weird," he said. "You're really weird."

Kartini angrily stamped her foot, and her emerald eyes snapped. "I am not weird. I am a royal princess and you are my subject and you will not talk to me like that!"

Michael's indignation overcame him. "I am not your subject. I am the king of England's subject." Then he added, "At least part of me is. The rest is nobody's subject, least of all yours!"

He was prepared to be angry with her for the rest of the trip, but when he looked at her next, she was smiling that beguiling smile. And her eyes were not emeralds at all, but seawater with yellow and black flecks that played beneath its shining surface like spots of sun and shadow. Suddenly he was smiling, too, for

627

even though he was only eight, she enchanted him, and he could never be angry with her for long.

Standing side by side, they looked over the railing again, but the mysterious circle was gone.

"I wonder what it was," Michael said aloud.

"I told you," Kartini replied calmly. "It was the eye of the sea."

This time, for lack of a better explanation, he did not dispute her.

Then two dolphins suddenly appeared, one on each side of the boat, speeding alongside it and leaping simultaneously into the air.

"*Lumpa-lumpa*!" Kartini cried in delight.

"I suppose you're going to say they're your escort," Michael proclaimed rather grumpily.

"Of course they are!" she cried. "The Lady of the Sea has sent them."

As the boat drew within sight of the harbor, Kartini's heart was almost bursting with joy and expectation. She impatiently endured the trip by car from the docks to the Dutch administrative headquarters where the ceremonies would be held. There were throngs of celebrants in the square, and for a moment she felt awed and frightened by the size of the jubilant crowd. Dutch troops and members of the Indonesian Army were interspersed throughout the square to maintain order if necessary. But as she was escorted to the rear of the reviewing stand, she had eyes only for the figure that stood out so clearly from among those milling behind the platform.

"Papa," she cried as she broke free of Chairol and her army escort and ran toward him. "Oh, Papa!"

The canes on which he had balanced himself fell to the ground as he reached down for her and swung her up to him, and hugged her so tightly to him that it hurt her ribs. She didn't care. She had waited anxious weeks for this moment, ever since the news had reached Matapura that he would be released by the Dutch on Independence Day.

Ahmad had been found by Dutch troops the day after he had been shot. They had thought him dead at first, but the doctor summoned to examine the body where it lay on the

628

floor of the small room had detected the faintest signs of a pulse.

"Look at how much blood he's lost." The doctor shook his head in amazement. "I don't see how he could possibly still be alive."

Fearful of the political repercussions, the Dutch had kept their discovery a secret for several months, announcing to the world that he had been found alive only after they were sure that he would survive. His life had been spared, but recovery would be far from swift or total. Besides causing internal injuries, the bullets had damaged his spine. A series of operations had given him hope that he might eventually do without the canes, but he would never be without pain, and he would never again move with the old catlike grace and endurance. Kartini, sensitive beyond her years, saw it all in a glance, and there were tears on her cheeks as she wrapped her small arms tightly around him. He needed her, she felt it in his grip upon her tiny body, and she marveled at the realization. His need was well placed. Child of Siah's that she was, she would never fail him.

Aided by Chairol and Kartini, Ahmad moved slowly toward the platform without the aid of his canes. Each step was an agony of pain and concentration. Those in the crowd nearest him sensed the effort and fell silent, watching his struggle with faces that reflected his torment. But when he reached the front of the stand and raised one hand in salute, they cried out in jubilation at his victory and theirs, and the tumultuous shouts that rose throughout the square shook the platform.

"*Merdeka! Merdeka!*" Freedom. Freedom. Kartini stared wide-eyed at the mass of faces that began shouting her father's name with a deafening roar.

Sukarno had not joined the celebration. He had announced his intention to address the nation from the former governor-general's palace in Buitenzorg the following day, and those who knew the situation suggested that he had not wanted to compete with the sultan for the crowd's favor, knowing he might lose. Tuk Malek, who would have fought for the people's approval, had been killed by nationalist troops a few months earlier during an unsuccessful Communist effort to take over the government.

Ahmad scarcely heard the speeches made by officials of both

governments, but he was aware of the moment when the Dutch flag was lowered and the red and white Indonesian flag was raised in its place, and tears stung his eyes. The feeling of triumph was bittersweet as he realized, perhaps better than any-one present, that the chances of sustaining Indonesian unity were slim. Sukarno and other Javanese Nationalist party leaders were already determined to abolish the federation of separate states for which Ahmad had worked so hard. And Ahmad had little doubt that in the flush of unity inspired by independence, the states and territories outside Java could be persuaded to give up their inde-pendence to the central control of the republic in an emotional gesture of gratitude. It would mean complete political dominance by Java, which would sow the seeds of future strife and rebellion.

The final negotiations of the past months had left the New Guinea issue unsatisfactorily settled. The Dutch would retain New Guinea, but that prospect rankled Sukarno. As far as Ahmad could see, there was nothing at stake there except the vanity of two nations. Efforts to find oil or valuable minerals in New Guinea had so far proved futile. Even if the search had proved successful, Ahmad fervently believed that New Guinea should fall under the protection of the United Nations and be allowed to develop at its own pace, without interference.

The thought of New Guinea filled him with sadness. Its treach-erous, unexplored terrain had almost certainly cost him the lives of two people he held most dear. Neither of them had been found. That painful reminder caused him to hug Kartini to him. She looked up at him in surprise and then smiled and kissed the tears on his cheeks.

Ahmad looked around and saw Michael, looking forlorn and lost. He pulled Michael up beside him and affectionately put a hand on the blond thatch of his head. Michael responded by shyly reaching up and putting his arms around Ahmad's waist, letting himself be held close by this rather awesome man.

"I'm coming home to Matapura, Michael. And when you come from Maitreya to visit us, I shall teach you to play polo."

Kartini, jealous at the prospect, interrupted. "And me, too, Papa."

"Of course." Ahmad smiled. "You, too." And then his eyes were serious. "You are going to have to learn, Kartini, that love is not like a pitcher of water which will run dry if too many drink from it. There is always enough to go around. I can love Michael and not love you one drop less. Do you believe that?'' He kissed her on the nose.

Kartini shyly nodded, not at all convinced. With a pang Ahmad remembered that Catherine had always found that concept hard to understand as well. He looked out at the cheering brown faces before him, and he suddenly felt a flood of love and release. It had been worth it. No matter what path Indonesian freedom might take in the future, this moment had been worth all the sacrifices he had made. His love affair with Indonesian freedom had outlived all others in his life, and now there would be no more. So be it, he thought with a sense of finality that was in itself a relief. So be it. It was over now, this love affair between him and the Indonesian people, though the adoring crowd before him had no inkling of it. He would return inconspicuously to Matapura to live in semiexile. Those who had opposed him would now have the opportunity to see what they could do to shape Indonesia's destiny. In his heart he fervently wished them success.

Part Five

Waro: The Time of the Snake

We shall not cease from exploration
And the end of all our exploring
Will be to arrive where we started
And to know the place for the first time.

T.S. Eliot, *Four Quartets*

Chapter 60
Jakarta, August 1966

The military jeep pulled up to the no parking zone in front of the Jakarta New Indies Hotel. The general who was driving it got out with a smile at the hotel doorman; his rank assured him of parking wherever he pleased. He returned a careless salute from a corporal who lounged against the hotel wall, a machine gun dangling nonchalantly from the crook of his arm. The city and the countryside were filled with such soldiers. Military maneuvers took place unexpectedly on busy streets at the height of rush hour, bringing traffic to a halt while soldiers practiced defending various installations thought to be military objectives for any enemy.

The general had been delayed by one such maneuver on his way to the hotel, an army exercise aimed at recapturing the phone company. He was late now for his appointment, and he took the hotel steps two at a time. The lobby was crowded with Western businessmen setting out on their daily task of courting the new military government which had run Indonesia since the unsuccessful Communist coup ten months ago. He strode purposefully to the desk.

"Sir Michael Stanford, please," he said to the desk clerk. Then he added with a cynical smile, "Tell him his military escort has arrived and is waiting for him in the lobby."

"Yes, General, right away, sir."

The general lit a cigarette and tossed the match onto the

polished marble floor as he strode slowly to the hotel door to await Stanford's arrival. He wore a beret and paratroop boots, and his khaki fatigues bore the insignia of a paratrooper on the sleeve. His campaign ribbons indicated he had fought in Indonesia's two recent wars: against the Dutch in New Guinea and the British in Malaysia. He was fairly tall for an Indonesian—perhaps five feet eleven inches—with dark good looks which were not totally attributable to the Orient.

"Hello, Patri."

The general turned and smiled at the blond young man with the steady gray eyes who greeted him with a slight British accent.

"Michael." The general put his hand on the young man's shoulder and steered him out the door and toward the jeep.

"Well, little brother, what brings you here amidst this sweltering madness after all these years. I thought political unrest wasn't your cup of English tea."

"I came to bring your inheritance, among other things," Michael replied.

Patri looked at him in surprise. "You must be kidding. The old man wouldn't have left me anything. We haven't spoken in ages."

"He left you a rather large amount of money."

"Really?" Patri laughed. "Well then, perhaps I no longer need to indulge in vice and corruption in order to support myself in the style to which I've grown accustomed. Now I can sell my casino and whorehouse. Tell me, Michael. Is it enough to make up for that?"

It was hard to tell if he was serious.

Michael appraised him coolly as Patri started the jeep and pulled out into traffic. "I don't know how much a good whore brings in Jakarta these days but it should be enough to replace the casino, at least."

"You never blow your English cool, do you, Michael?"

"Does Ahmad know of Grandfather's death?" Michael changed the subject.

"Yes. I sent a message to him as soon as I heard it from you."

"How is Ahmad?"

"I haven't seen him. It wouldn't exactly be good for my career for me to be spending much time with him, now would it?"

"I suppose not," Michael replied mildly and then added, "It makes you feel guilty to see him; that's why you don't go."

"My conscience is clear," Patri said grimly, but an angry swerve of the jeep to avoid a hole confirmed Michael's observation. "There wasn't anything I could have done at the time," Patri added. "I wasn't exactly one of Sukarno's favorites, you know. Ahmad and I have that in common."

For almost a year Ahmad had been held under secret house arrest in Jakarta. The news of it had been the cause of Sir Charles's last stroke, from which he never recovered. Ahmad had been brought from Matapura to Jakarta at the instigation of the Communists in Sukarno's government, who were planning a coup with Sukarno's full knowledge and support. Fearing Sukarno was about to be overthrown by conservative elements of the Army, the Indonesian Communists had sought to eliminate opposition by staging their own coup first, arresting Ahmad and later kidnapping and murdering six top Army generals. The plot failed, however. They had overlooked an unknown general named Suharto, who, after the coup, had rallied the non-Communist elements of the military and staged a successful countercoup. He had arrested the plotters, disbanded the new Revolutionary Council, banned the Communist party, and stripped Sukarno of all but his presidential title. The situation was still volatile, but it seemed likely that the patient, politically astute Suharto would eventually force Sukarno to resign and would become president himself.

"Why is Ahmad still being held?" Michael asked. "Clearly those responsible for his arrest are no longer in power."

"He will be released soon," Patri assured him. "You must remember how much Indonesians revere him. Unless the new government is sure Ahmad supports them, or will at least remain neutral, they are afraid to release him. So far he has refused to commit himself. As soon as the new cabinet has consolidated power and feels secure, they will let him go."

"Politicians never feel secure," Michael countered.

The sweet-sour smell of cooking spices drifted from the pushcarts as the jeep jolted through narrow streets, dodging the bicycles and *betjaks* and stalls filled with mangoes and bananas. The canals were lined with makeshift shanties and lean-tos of cardboard, palm leaves, corrugated tin, or anything else that could be found to provide shelter for a rapidly growing population.

637

With a glance at the teeming life around him, Patri observed, "Sukarno or Suharto. What difference does it make? The average Indonesian makes less than thirty dollars a year and dies before he's thirty-two."

"And you, Patri, where do you stand in all this?"

"Wherever it's safest and most profitable for me. I don't care for causes, only opportunities. Most of my fellow officers are still filled with the fevor of revolution. And the older ones." He shrugged. "For years they've lived past glories. Me, I don't care for sentiment or political theories. Ideas or people—ultimately they all are corrupted by those who promote them." Noting the look of disapproval on his brother's face, he gave a chuckle.

"I'm no Stanford, Michael. You've always known that. I'm immune to the family idealism; to me it always had the smell of hypocrisy. I saw idealism acting as a cover for sins of exploitation which matched those of the Dutch. The Dutch just happened to be more clumsy about it."

They rode for a while in silence. Finally Michael turned and studied his brother for a moment as though considering what he was about to say.

"There's one more thing I want you to do for me, Patri."

Patri looked at him with curiosity.

"I want permission to go to New Guinea, and you can get it for me."

Patri looked at him in surprise. "That's impossible! It's off limits. There is no protection there."

"Nevertheless, I want to go, and I want you to get me the papers I'll need."

"You surprise me. You've never shown the usual family interest in primitive cultures."

Michael stared at the road ahead. "I'm going to look for Father and my mother, to find out what happened to them."

The smile left Patri's face. "Your father, Michael, not mine. He was never my father. I'm not a Stanford. I never will be."

"No one ever rejected you, Patri," Michael said evenly. "It was always the other way around. You rejected us. Grandfather's will proves you were considered part of the family."

"It proves he had a guilty conscience," Patri said angrily. "Nothing more!" He swerved the jeep off the expressway onto one of the side streets, his face grim. He pulled into a quiet

638

residential area and slammed on the brakes. Both men sat in silence for a moment. Patri was the first to speak.

"I'm sorry about the old man's death, Michael. Really."

"Yeah. Well, as you might say, Patri, we all have to go sometime." He said it coolly, without looking at his brother.

Patri stared ahead over the steering wheel. "I'll do what I can about getting you into New Guinea."

"Thanks." Michael jumped lightly out of the jeep.

"You could get yourself killed there, you know." Patri appeared to be struggling to say something affectionate.

When he recognized his brother's dilemma, Michael's expression softened. "I'll be careful. Thanks for arranging for me to see Ahmad." Michael turned and started to walk away.

"Wait!" Patri called to him.

For the first time, Patri seemed embarrassed. "I wouldn't have let them harm him, you know. He was always a good friend to me."

Noting the uncharacteristically serious look on his brother's face, Michael believed him. He nodded, then turned his attention to the hillside, which was covered with trees and dense tropical foliage.

"It doesn't look much like a prison," he observed. Only a few soldiers were in sight, casually lounging on the dusty street, their rifles leaning against the retaining wall of the hillside.

"He is comfortable here, and well cared for."

"He always hated Jakarta," Michael observed sadly. "I hate seeing him here." Villages, Ahmad had always told him, were the only harmonious places for people to live. Nothing else controlled the dark side of man's nature, he believed.

"We both know he could walk out of here anytime, and could have from the time of his arrest a year ago," Patri said. "There's not a soldier in Indonesia who would dare give him the order to halt, let alone harm so much as a hair on the sacred royal head." He suddenly laughed. "The more Sukarno tried to isolate him, the more mysterious and godlike he became to us all. It nearly drove Sukarno crazy."

Michael smiled, remembering the tumultuous adoration which had surrounded the sultan whenever he made one of his rare appearances outside Matapura. A jeep passed them and pulled over to the side of the road. Patri nodded toward the driver.

"The sergeant over there will take you back to the hotel when you're ready."

Michael nodded. "I'm going to Maitreya for a while before I leave for New Guinea. You can reach me in Banjarmasin about the papers."

"Will you see Kartini while you're in Borneo?"

Michael looked at Patri in surprise. It had not occurred to him to attempt to see her. She was a childhood memory, nothing more. "No. Why should I?"

"No reason. Just old times' sake." Patri's cynical smile reappeared. "I've asked her to marry me."

"Oh. And what did she say?" Michael smiled back.

"She hasn't said anything—yet. But she could do worse than the next chief general of the Army."

"You're being promoted?"

Patri nodded. "The Communist coup, even though unsuccessful, left certain vacancies within the Army that have provided opportunities for those of us who survived."

"Well, congratulations."

"Thanks." Patri's eyes appraised his handsome younger brother. "We haven't done badly for a couple of bastards, have we, Michael? You, the tenth Baronet of Marlott, and I, one of the military princes of Indonesia. You have the family title, and I have the power." He gave a laugh and shifted the idling jeep into gear.

"So long, little brother."

Ahmad's prison was a large villa built on a hill by a prosperous descendant of an Arab spice trader who had brought Islam to the Indies five centuries earlier. Though the walls were freshly painted, the elaborate filigree work which decorated the arches and windows of the villa was in disrepair, and the garden and trees surrounding it were overgrown, making the house almost invisible from the street. Its last owners, who were Dutch, had been imprisoned during the Japanese occupation and had never returned. In all likelihood they had died, for no one had claimed the land, and eventually it had fallen to the government. The narrow stone steps which wound up to the villa passed a small building on the way which served as headquarters for the army guards.

They had been expecting Michael. A corporal met him on the steps outside the office. Smiling, he opened the door and politely waved Michael inside, closing it behind him. The captain in command sat behind a large table which was the only piece of furniture in the small room. The table was empty except for a rubber stamp and ink pad. The captain was looking at a copy of *Playboy* magazine, which he had bought from a customs agent who had confiscated it from an American visitor. He did not look up as Michael entered the room. Instead, he kept his attention on the page until it had clearly been established just who was in control. Then he gave Michael only a brief glance, motioning impatiently for his permit papers as if it had been Michael who kept him waiting. Michael unfolded them and slid them under the captain's eyes, which were firmly fixed upon the table. A radio was blaring revolutionary messages in the background.

Listening with reluctant fascination to the stridency of the pronouncements, Michael supposed that after any revolution there inevitably were growing doubts, hidden beneath all the revolutionary rhetoric, about whether the whole thing had been such a good idea after all. Like a lot of other things in life, revolutions never quite turned out the way their supporters had hoped. In Indonesia the disappointment had until now been successfully channeled by Sukarno into anger at convenient outside villains, such as former colonial powers. But after the recent unsuccessful Communist coup Indonesians had finally turned their frustrations inward, ferociously settling them not on Sukarno himself but on their own Communist party, which they now blamed for all their woes. The result of this assignment of blame had been the murder of hundreds of thousands, perhaps as many as a million, Communists, local Chinese, and whoever else proved unpopular. Fanatical Moslems killed nonbelievers by the tens of thousands, and anybody with an old personal grudge was given a chance to even it in the name of patriotism. Even the forcibly retired headhunters of Borneo had seized on the opportunity to sever unpopular heads from Chinese bodies, and were still at it. During the height of the violence a few months ago the rivers of northern Java had run red with blood, and fishermen were forced to throw away their catches, having found that their stomachs were stuffed with the fingers, ears, and genitals of mutilated bodies. It was difficult for Michael to imagine the gentle Indonesians capable of such violence.

The captain finished shuffling through the papers. Eyes averted, he frowned and cleared his throat. Michael recognized the cue. The rich foreigner was going to have to share the wealth. While it annoyed him, Michael could not blame the captain for the extensive corruption here. The inflation rate was now 650 percent, and the middle-class civil servant had become dependent on corruption for survival. It was scarcely a new phenomenon in the Indies.

Michael took the rupiahs from his pocket and spread them on the table so the captain would not have to shuffle through them indelicately to ascertain the generosity of the amount. Seemingly satisfied, the captain opened the table drawer before him and swept the money away so that the surface again appeared clean and innocent. He had no use for Englishmen. He had been wounded by one in Borneo two years ago during the ''Crush Malaysia'' campaign, and as a result, he felt all Englishmen owed him something. After taking up the rubber stamp, the captain banged away at Michael's papers, swatting relentlessly at them as if they were the wings of some repulsive insect. When finished, he brusquely shoved them back to Michael and summoned the corporal from outside with a snap of his fingers. Michael was dismissed. The two men had not exchanged a word.

A smiling barefoot servant wearing a brilliant blue silk jacket and white pants with a gold sash was waiting for Michael at a wooden gate at the top of the steps. Bowing, he opened it, revealing a small garden surrounded by high walls and trees.

''His Highness is there, tuan.'' The servant nodded toward a collection of lawn chairs in one corner of the garden. ''He's expecting you.'' He bowed again and disappeared.

Michael turned his head in the direction indicated. For a moment the sun, low in the sky, blinded him. Against its brilliance he caught a glimpse of the outline of a man, rising slowly from one of the chairs. The sun was positioned so that it seemed to emanate from the figure in a diamond of light, white and shimmering. The sultan sunan of Borneo. Michael felt an ache in his throat. After all these years the sight of this man still powerfully affected him. He had not expected, seeing Ahmad for the first time with a man's eyes, to feel the same old childhood awe, yet here it was, rising inside him.

"Michael." The familiar voice was pleased. "How good to see you!"

Unable to swallow past the lump in his throat, Michael could say nothing. As he reached Ahmad and they embraced, he saw the two canes in Ahmad's hands. When Michael drew back, it was to see a man still imposing in his appearance. Nothing about his smooth dark skin or his hair revealed he was now fifty-seven, but neither could his youthful appearance hide the fact that he had become increasingly crippled by his old injuries. Michael had heard that it was difficult for Ahmad to walk and that he was constantly in pain.

Michael sat down and was served lemonade by one of the servants.

"I was sorry to hear about your grandfather," Ahmad said. "I wish I could have seen him before he died."

"He wanted to return, to die at Maitreya. But of course, that wasn't possible."

When Sir Charles had left the Indies in 1952, Sukarno was quarreling with the Dutch over the future of New Guinea, the last Dutch possession in the Indies. It was clear to Sir Charles that Sukarno would eventually confiscate all Dutch property in retaliation for Dutch refusal to relinquish New Guinea, and the property of other Europeans was likely to follow. Sukarno hadn't forgiven the British for their occupation of 1945, and he was suspicious, even then, of the British presence in Malaya and North Borneo. Sir Charles had decided to dispose of his land before the government seized it so that he might deed it to the villagers who had worked it for the Stanfords for one and one-half centuries.

The lemonade was warm. Michael put it down, faintly disappointed. He had forgotten the warm drinks of the Indies. He had been thinking of the last time he had seen Ahmad, at Maitreya, the day he and his grandfather had left the Indies. Michael had never seen his grandfather cry before, but Sir Charles had wept in Ahmad's arms like a small, weak child. Michael didn't want to remember that day. He turned his eyes away from Ahmad, toward the blooms of bougainvillea which hid much of the garden wall. One thought takes the place of another. His mother had taught him that at Teram Prison at night when the sound of

643

British soldiers being tortured kept them both awake. The Japanese soldiers were always kind to children. The next day they would offer him candy or fruit, and he would take it, all the while wondering if they were the ones who hurt the prisoners. He didn't hate them the way the women did, and each time the British soldiers cried he felt guilty, as if he had participated in their torture because he took the candy and did not hate the Japanese.

"Patri brought me here today. He wouldn't come to England to see Grandfather before he died."

"I know," Ahmad replied. "But don't be too hard on Patri, Michael. He isn't the cold, hard cynic he wants to appear. Quite the contrary. He has always wanted to believe we are better than he thinks we are, but it is difficult to be a political idealist in Indonesia these days. Perhaps everywhere."

"I try to stay away from politics," Michael interjected with a coldness that surprised even himself. "I've been on a dig in the desert for the last three years. We didn't get much news about politics there."

The remark caught Ahmad by surprise. The Stanfords had always been embroiled in politics. It seemed part of their nature. "Your grandfather kept me up-to-date on your studies until his stroke last year. The dig was Luxor, wasn't it? Ancient Egypt. A doctoral degree in archaeology. Congratulations. Your grandfather was very proud."

If that were true, Michael thought, then why was he feeling as if he should apologize for breaking yet another Stanford tradition by concerning himself with the ancient past instead of the primitive present? But Ahmad had changed the subject before Michael rallied to defend himself.

"Patri has asked Kartini to marry him. Did he tell you?"

"Yes," Michael replied, carefully venturing no opinion since the matter hardly concerned him.

Ahmad frowned. "I'm fond of Patri, but I don't like the idea of such a marriage. Perhaps I'm simply a meddlesome father." He sighed. "My opinion is something I keep to myself. Kartini is a very independent young woman who will do as she pleases." He smiled, as if the thought pleased rather than offended him. "I would like you to see her. You'll be going to Maitreya?" The question implied that of course he was going to Maitreya; anything else would be unthinkable. "She's in Banjarmasin, staying at the palace there with her aunt. You visited it as a child. Perhaps you remember?"

He did, vaguely: a palace with long stone steps leading directly down to the river where he and Kartini used to launch the small boats they made of wood and grass. "I'll be staying at Maitreya only briefly. Grandfather's will left some money in trust for the villagers. He wanted me to tell them about it. I'll stop by to see Kartini on the way." He couldn't refuse, although he didn't want to go any more than he wanted to visit Maitreya. It was part of what seemed a distant past. He decided it was time to reveal to Ahmad his real motive for returning to Indonesia.

"I came to tell you that I'm going to New Guinea to find out what happened to my mother and father." Why, Michael wondered, was it always so difficult to say those words? Mother. Father. True, they didn't elicit in him memories of a lifetime of love and confrontation. They represented shadowy, unreal figures. Yet these words were as laden with emotion for him as they were for anyone else: perhaps more so.

Ahmad was silent for a moment, trying to accept a statement he had always anticipated but had never wanted to hear. It was as if Catherine had come back to tell him again that she was going to New Guinea and nothing he could say would stop her. Ahmad blamed himself for Catherine's disappearance, for not stopping her from going or for not going with her.

Now it appeared that history would repeat itself.

"I couldn't go until Grandfather died," Michael said. "He was totally opposed to it."

"And Patri will arrange all this for you—the necessary papers to get in to New Guinea?" Ahmad asked.

Michael nodded. It would not be easy. Since they had emerged in control of New Guinea after the "war of liberation" waged against the Dutch in New Guinea in 1962, the Indonesians had been reluctant to admit foreigners into the New Guinea territory.

"Patri is a good arranger," Ahmad remarked with a sigh. "He has a bright future here, in politics."

"So he has told me." Michael smiled.

"They both are dead, Michael," Ahmad said, returning abruptly to their previous topic. "Too many people have already died searching for them. Why not leave the past alone?"

"No." Michael's eyes were leveled at Ahmad with defiance. He had expected disapproval, but he had not come for Ahmad's permission.

"And what do you want from me in all this?" Ahmad asked.

"Only the promise that you won't blame yourself if something should happen, as I know you have for whatever happened to my mother."

"I'm sorry, Michael," he said sadly. "That promise I cannot give you."

There was nothing more to say about it. They were silent for a moment, and then Ahmad said, "Tell me about your aunt Harriet and Margit. How are they?" They began to talk, cautiously at first, of whatever was safe to remember about the past. There had been a time in Michael's life when Ahmad had been like a father to him. It was not difficult for either of them to go back to that time and to those feelings. When the appointed hour came for Michael to leave, Ahmad walked him slowly to the garden entrance, and Michael saw that he was thinner than he had seemed at first and his face was more drawn and tired. They paused at the gate.

"Forgive them, Michael," Ahmad softly urged him. "If this journey to Borneo helps you find forgiveness, then it is worth the risk. I know you have blamed both your parents for leaving you."

"There's nothing to forgive," Michael said, and, by his dishonesty, revealed to both of them how much he had at stake in this journey. Michael had never lacked for people, Ahmad among them, who had tried to make up for the loss of his parents. And to a great extent they had succeeded. But a loss of such magnitude, particularly in one so young, could never be totally compensated for. By finding out what had happened to his parents, Michael hoped to lay that unfulfillable longing to rest forever.

They reached the gate and faced each other. Ahmad concentrated on Michael's face, memorizing it, not a difficult task since Michael bore such an astonishing resemblance to his father. Ahmad had last seen Michael's father twenty-seven years ago at Maitreya, on the night of Julienne's homecoming. Ahmad had left immediately after dinner that night because of political business in Banjarmasin which could not wait. Michael had walked with him to the airfield. "Julienne's friend from America," Ahmad had said to him as he stepped on the wing and prepared to enter his small plane, "do you know much about her?" It was dark, but Ahmad could see Michael's face clearly in the light of the torches which had been lit around the field. "No," Michael had replied; but Ahmad could always read Michael's thoughts as easily as his own, and something in his face had given Ahmad a sense of what would follow. It had seemed such an innocent and ordinary evening at the time, yet it had contained so much they all would look back on. Certainly he and Michael could never have imagined it would be the last time they would see each other. It had not been like this parting, now, with Michael's son. This good-bye already had a sense of permanence about it which each man recognized but neither mentioned.

"Is there something you'd like me to tell Kartini when I see her?" Michael asked.

"No. Nothing. I'll write to her this evening. She is going within a few days to see her Dyak grandfather. He has moved his village to a tributary north of Banjarmasin to escape the Javanese immigrants the government has attempted to resettle on the coast. He says they have spoiled the hunting."

"After New Guinea I'll be going straight back to England."

"I know. I hope you find what you are seeking."

The two men embraced in farewell, and Ahmad said to Michael, "May the spirits of the forest be with you." He smiled and his hand lifted the cane to touch Michael's arm in a last affectionate gesture. "You might make them an offering. Where you are going, they will be of far more use to you than a civilized god."

The gate, swollen with age and humidity, scraped noisily closed behind Michael, leaving him alone at the top of the stone steps leading down through a tangle of tropical greenery to the street. Tears blurred his eyes so that he stood still for a moment, staring down through the trees to where the sergeant waited patiently for him in the jeep. The captain, hearing the gate shut, came out of his office halfway down the path. He took out a cigarette and stuck it in his mouth.

"Want a woman tonight?" he asked as Michael passed him on the steps.

"No," Michael snapped over his shoulder, angry at the intrusion.

"You English eat too much meat!" the captain called after him, more defensive than offended. "It makes you angry."

Inside the garden Ahmad heard the captain's last effort to extract a few rupiahs from his prosperous visitor. He could guess, on the basis of experience, just how much Michael must have paid to be allowed in. Over the past year Ahmad had come to admire the captain's audacity and energy, although he wished they would be put to more constructive use. He turned wearily away from the wall, the street, the outside world. The sun had now finished its sojourn across the garden, leaving it in the cool shadows of the trees. Pots of impatiens had wilted in the day's heat, but the gardener would soon come to revive them with a can of water. Ahmad decided to stay in the garden awhile longer before returning to his office to conduct whatever part of Matapura's business he could manage from exile.

At the moment he was regretting not having told Michael the truth—that he was dying. He had already lived well beyond the two years his doctors had given him and far beyond what the Dutch doctors had told him years ago when they had repaired the damage from Tuk Malek's bullets. He had kept his condition from Kartini, knowing she would insist on coming to Jakarta to be with him. But Jakarta was not a safe place these days for political progressives of any kind, especially one as outspoken and well known as Kartini. University faculties had recently been purged of those with politically liberal views. The ones who had simply lost their jobs had been lucky. Many had been exiled, imprisoned, or executed, the sultan's old friends and political colleagues among them.

Because he did not want Kartini to know, he had kept the truth from Michael just now. He did not want Michael, seeing Kartini for the first time after many years, to be burdened with that secret. Unspoken, it would surely come between them.

Pain fought for his attention with each step he took to cross the garden, but he had learned to ignore it. Death did not frighten him, yet he had clung tenaciously to life beyond even his own expectations. Why, he wondered, when it would have brought him relief from the relentless pain he had endured so long? He had asked the question before and had no answer except that his life still felt unfinished, incomplete. Why he could not say. After all, hadn't he seen his greatest dream come true? He had helped conceive and bring to life the Indonesian nation. Yet it was not enough. Never religious, he had begun to slip into what he conceived to be his ancient Hindu past: a longing, vague and illogical, for some kind of unity with the universe. The thought of it left him annoyed with himself.

He reached the lounge chair and carefully lowered himself into it, hanging his canes on the back. A hoop of mosquito netting hung from a tree above the chair, waiting to be lowered and drawn around him so that he might nap in the cool of the garden each evening before dinner. Overhead, the sky had given up its hard brilliance to surround the approaching evening in translucent light of a fire opal with its hot streaks of orange and pink and blue. He pulled the cord, and the mosquito net descended like a thin veil around him. In the nearby mosque the call came for evening prayers, and he felt the servants silently withdraw to observe it. Only the Dyak remained, those members of his staff who were the closest to him in his exile. They still clung stubbornly to their pagan forest spirits, unimpressed with desert prophets. He envied them their certainty.

Above him, through the branches, the opal sky surrounded him like a womb. The mosquito net wrapped him like a cocoon. He imagined himself a newborn, with a lifetime still ahead of him, but another behind, not yet forgotten. Impatient with the ridiculous nature of the thought, he closed his eyes in hope of sleep.

A child. The word emerged as a revelation, forcing his eyes open in surprise. Not the troubled infant of Indonesia's future. Kartini and Michael's child. A child who, by the simple act of existing, would bring together finally, in the rhythm of that one fragile heartbeat, all those whom he had loved and lost. Catherine, Michael, Siah, his parents, Sir Charles. Yes, that was the reason for all these years of waiting. Yet nothing seemed less likely. He had become aware of his dream only to realize, at the same instant, its absurdity. He closed his eyes again, wearily.

Chapter 61

Michael had not seen Kartini in the thirteen years since the Stanfords had left Borneo. He remembered her as he had last seen her, a child of the forest, as he had been, playing with brown Dyak babies, naked in warm river waters. He was not prepared for what she had become when she received him in the reception room of her uncle's palace in Banjarmasin, dressed in a batik *kain* and a dark muslin *kebaja*, her black hair pulled straight back and bound up with small white flowers. He was surprised by the serious, self-assured young woman who stood before him, offering her hand and inviting him to be seated in the comfortable grandeur of a gold silk-and-gilt chair.

Her eyes. He had forgotten about her eyes. Kartini had been a strikingly beautiful child, and now she was a similarly beautiful woman. In her features she most resembled her French grandmother although her skin was dark like her Dyak mother and she was tall, like the Açvavarmans. It was her father she called most to mind, not in her appearance, but in the aloofness of her manner and her slightly imperial air. Kartini had almost completed her medical studies at Bandung when her father had been arrested. Then, when the violence of the counter-coup erupted, she had left Java for the safer haven of Borneo, interrupting her studies until the political situation stabilized. As her father had admonished her, two Açvavarmans under arrest would benefit no one except their enemies.

"It's good to see you, Michael," she said as she took a seat opposite him. "I was sorry to hear of Sir Charles's death. He was very dear to me and to my family."

"He would have liked to have returned for a last visit, but his health didn't permit it."

"It's just as well. It would only have distressed him to see Maitreya now. It has many happy memories for me, but the jungle is at home there now, and increasingly it resents intruders."

Seeing Michael fall silent, Kartini became increasingly puzzled about why he had come. He had asked to see her, yet he seemed almost reluctant to be there. Wearing jeans and boots and a denim shirt with the sleeves rolled up, he looked out of place in the slightly decaying formality of the room. Since the Japanese had killed her husband and her sons, the sultan's aunt by marriage had retreated into purdah with her women, neither seeing nor caring that mildew dusted the rich teak carvings of the pillars and furniture and spotted the plaster of the walls.

"I saw your father when I was in Jakarta two days ago. Patri arranged it for me."

So that was it, she thought. This was a polite duty call, a favor to her worried father. The thought annoyed her. "How is he?" she asked.

"He seemed well," he lied.

Kartini broke in. "The *dukums* in Matapura are saying he will soon die, and the servants and guards have deserted the *kraton*, believing the old prophecies will come true. It is said that when the dynasty ends, Gunung Matapura will erupt to destroy itself and the entire peninsula."

"*Dukums* have been wrong before—many times as I recall," he countered, reminding himself that in many ways the cultural gap which separated this generation of Stanfords and Açvavarmans was greater than had ever existed between the two families. Kartini's experience, after independence, had been essentially Indonesian. She had little of her father's exposure to Western culture, nor did she share his tolerance for foreigners. Revolutionary in spirit and outlook, proud of her country, she had chosen to be educated in Indonesia's new schools and universities.

For her part, Kartini viewed Michael with many of the same suspicions with which most Indonesians viewed Westerners. He seemed so English to her now, so foreign. He carried some of the

651

chill of the Cornish countryside in his cool gray eyes, something of its harshness and wild beauty, as she imagined it. He seemed a man used to being alone. She remembered him as a good-looking boy of twelve. Youthful gangliness had given way to lean muscle. His blond hair had darkened only slightly, but the freckles on his face were gone, replaced by a dark, even tan from the Egyptian sun. Why had he reappeared unexpectedly in her life just to be quickly off again? It would have been better if he had not come at all, she thought. She felt annoyed with him and with herself.

"Where will you go, Michael? What will you do now that your grandfather is dead?"

"I'm going to Maitreya for a short time, to take care of some matters for my grandfather's estate, and then to New Guinea to find out what happened to my parents if I can."

"And then?"

"Back to England."

"I see. To lead the life of a titled English gentlemen."

"No. To teach."

"Of course. Oxford and England are no doubt in desperate need of another archaeologist." She smiled condescendingly.

He was stung by the unexpected criticism. He didn't understand it. Why should she care where he went or what he did? "It's my need," he said quietly, "Not England's. I've never pretended otherwise."

"Most of Indonesia's own historic treasures and ruins lie unattended or undiscovered. Time and the jungle will soon destroy them. The Dutch never took any interest in preserving Indonesia's past," Kartini remarked. "Western archaelogists have rarely been interested in restoring Eastern ruins." For a brief moment, her eyes challenged him.

"Indonesians scarcely seem in the mood lately to accept assistance from Americans or Europeans, archaeological or otherwise," he said mildly.

"But you're right, of course. The English are especially unwelcome now. Sir Charles was wise to leave when he did."

"It wasn't just the political situation that caused him to leave. He needed constant medical attention."

"Yes. I remember," she replied coolly.

Somehow they had gotten off to a bad start, and he regretted it but felt helpless to change it. She seemed to have taken immediate offense to him, and he was beginning to wish he had not come. He had done it out of affection for her father. He had expected, he now realized, a more sheltered princess, not this proud, sensitive, and strong-willed woman.

At his suggestion, they left the palace to walk in the garden. Once away from the formality of the reception room, he hoped some of the tension between them might ease. The physical neglect inside the palace seemed even more obvious in the sunlight outside. The unused fountains were full of crumbling stone and marble. Water weeds choked the lily pads in the black water of the reflecting pools. Paint hung in strips from the pillars and ceilings of the pavilions and from the doors and walls of the enclosed buildings. There seemed no excuse for much of the decay since there were plenty of idle hands among the hundreds of servants supported by the palace.

"Do you remember this garden?" Kartini asked him. As children they had sat here to be entertained, far into the night, with tales from the Hindu *Ramayana* and *Mahabharata* performed by shadow puppets or live, brilliantly costumed actors and dancers.

"I remember very little about the past, I'm afraid," he replied. It was one of the reasons he had decided to come back to Maitreya: to try to recapture some of the past before he set out for New Guinea and his search for his mother and father.

"Even your mother?"

"She doesn't exist for me except as a faint memory."

"Strange. Because I remember her clearly and I was younger than you."

"Then you remember a fantasy."

"Maybe so. But I cherish it. If you do not remember her, then why are you going?"

"It is something I have to do. I have to know what happened."

"Which do you fear most, Michael; that they are dead or that they are alive and have turned their back on the world and on you?"

"I'm sure that they are dead."

"If you are so sure, then why must you go find out what you already know?"

"I must finish it."

She looked at him sadly. "I feel sorry for you, Michael. You have lost so much, not just what the world had taken from you but what you have given up in your heart.''

By the time they reached the wide stairs leading down to the river it was time for him to go. His boat, tied at the bottom, had risen several steps with the water; floods and the sea's tides drastically affected the height of the river here. Standing on the landing, looking down, Michael had a flash of Kartini long ago, dancing on these steps to the motion of the rising wind stirring the surrounding jungle trees. It quickly vanished. He could not connect that image with the young woman now beside him.

"What will you do when the political situation settles down?" he asked her.

"Finish medical school and come back here. We have few doctors in Borneo, especially in the remote Dyak villages. They will accept modern medical practices from me which they might reject from a stranger.''

They were silent for a moment, staring together at the brown river in which they had once launched toy fleets.

"I won't be coming back," he said finally.

"I know," she replied quietly without taking her eyes from the river. It was *musim kemarau*, the dry season, and although it might still shower daily in the higher elevations near Maitreya, it had not rained in Banjarmasin for weeks, and some of the jungle foliage, even along the river, had turned brown. Despite the lack of rain, the humidity was still high, and the heat, higher than any other time of the year, was intense.

Michael stepped from the landing to the first step and squinted at the sun. "It's getting late. I'd better be going."

She nodded. Maitreya was two days' journey up the river. He turned and descended the steps into the small boat he had rented for the trip. The first time he jerked the starting rope the motor sputtered and died. For an instant the aloof mask on Kartini's face slipped, and her lips parted slightly, as if she were about to say something. He looked up and caught a fleeting glimpse of emotion in her eyes before it was quickly hidden. He paused a moment before he tried the motor again, but her expression didn't change. The motor caught on the second try. He looked up at her one last time as he backed the boat slowly away from the steps. Kartini remained on the landing above him, surrounded by the ancient water palace. He had never seen a sight lovelier or more harmonious.

As the boat swung its bow upstream, Kartini stood motionless, glad, she thought, that she had remained silent. She had almost asked him, at that last moment, just why he had turned his back on her all those years ago, why she had never heard from him after he left the Indies. As the silence had stretched into months and then years, she had become certain that once he had reached Marlott, he must have found the white English girls more appealing. While she stood watching the boat disappear, a fretful wind came up, perhaps signaling an early arrival of the monsoon rains. The boy whom she had resented all those years was gone forever. It seemed childish to her now to hold old grudges against the man he had become: a stranger.

Despite Kartini's warning, Michael was shocked to find Maitreya empty and in total disrepair. All the furnishings and possessions had been moved to England when the family had left Maitreya. Now much of the frame of the huge roof lay exposed, its thatch gone. The gardens were overgrown, and the jungle pressed against Maitreya's walls. It would not be many years before it would bring down the house, as it had already destroyed the stable and the other outer buildings. Only the statue of Maitreya, god of paradise to come, remained unchanged. It still stood at the foot of the terrace steps. No one had tended it, yet no vines encircled its limbs or clogged its base. Even its bronze surface was free of corrosion, its smile still hinting mysteriously of a knowledge man did not yet possess.

Upon hearing of Michael's arrival, Damal had come immediately from the village, wishing to serve him, but Michael gently declined. He broke the news of Sir Charles's death to Damal and others who had loved and served the Stanfords over the years, dispensing the mementos Sir Charles had requested they receive along with a considerable amount of money.

Michael asked Damal to provide him with a sleeping mat and some mosquito netting. Damal was greatly distressed that the head of the Stanford family would live in such dismal conditions, but Michael was adamant. He spent his day hiking across the plantation and through the villages, reacquainting himself with the people and the places of his childhood. To all who beseeched him to return to Indonesia, he made it clear that this was simply a holiday on his way to New Guinea and that he planned to return to England.

Everywhere that Michael went he listened to the villagers' problems, and there were many. He was startled by their poverty. When the Stanfords ran Maitreya, the villagers had prospered, sharing in the profits of the plantation and participating fully in day-to-day decisions. Since the war rubber was not so profitable, and the oil fields had been confiscated by the government. The government stripped the forests of timber and mineral resources, removing the profits to Java or to the pockets of corrupt officials. The kampongs had little say over their own lives. Civil and military control was everywhere.

When Michael listened to their problems but did not respond, they came to realize he truly meant what he said. He would not be back. He fished in the river, cooked over an open fire, and ate whatever fruits and vegetables he could find growing among the shambles of the gardens. In the morning and late afternoon he bathed at the limestone pool that had furnished Maitreya's water. He felt most at home there. Of all the landmarks from his childhood memories, it alone seemed unchanged.

Michael had now been at Maitreya one week. In two days this pleasant interlude would come to an end. The poverty of the people disturbed him, but he could do nothing about it. Today was especially hot, so he had gone for his afternoon swim immediately after lunch instead of later. He shed his clothes and dived deep into the limits of the sunlight that shimmered green and yellow along the limestone sides of the pool. When he rose to the surface, he was startled to see Kartini seated on the sloping bank of limestone, watching him. In jeans and boots, squatting on her heels by the water's edge, waiting for him to finish his swim, she looked completely different from when he had seen her before. Her hair hung loose and straight around her shoulders.

He came reluctantly out of the water, surprised to find that he was embarrassed by his nudity.

"Sorry. I wasn't expecting company."

"I'm spending a few days with my grandfather. His village was relocated about an hour downriver from here." Seeing his discomfort, she laughed. "You needn't apologize. I used to see

656

you like this all the time when we were children." She grinned impishly.

He smiled uneasily. "That was scarcely the same thing."

"Oh, I don't know." She eyed him critically. "It's been remodeled a little, but the basic architecture is the same."

Her eyes boldly traveled down his fine body. He was as much embarrassed by the admiration he saw reflected in her eyes as by their boldness. He leaned over to pick up his clothes, and when he looked up, he was startled by the change on her face. The teasing was no longer to be seen in her eyes; the bemused smile was gone.

"There is something I must tell you, something I was unable to say back at the palace. I have loved you and wanted you since I was old enough to know about such things. I promised myself that someday I would let you know; only you moved away before I could."

He was too surprised to react at first. Before he could manage a reply, she was gone. He hurriedly dressed and ran after her, but he did not know the overgrown trail as well as she and could not catch her. By the time he reached the dock it was empty. Only his own boat lay rocking quietly by the water's edge, and he noticed for the first time that the warm, brown, sunlit water of the river resembled the color of her skin while the dancing tender young leaves were the color of her eyes.

Leaving Maitreya when he was twelve for the cold climate and the structured discipline of the British public school had been a shock so severe as to make Michael close the door on his past forever. In time he had even come to hate the memory of Maitreya. Now he was seeing it with a man's eyes for the first time, suddenly aware of all it had once meant to him. Remembering, he had a sudden urge to go after Kartini and ask her if she still danced with dolphins by the sea and spoke with the leopards of the forest. Or had she, like him, lost all that she once had been? For a moment a deep sadness threatened to overcome him.

Despite the promise of the smiling god at the foot of the terrace steps, there was no future here for him or any other Stanford. Not anymore.

Chapter 62

Michael landed his plane in the small untended airstrip at Wamena in the south end of the Baliem Valley. The Wamena outpost had been built by the Dutch in 1956. Since Indonesian independence in 1949 the Dutch and Indonesians had quarreled over control of New Guinea, which, according to The Hague Round Table Conference that granted Indonesian independence, was to remain under Dutch control. The quarrel had erupted into open warfare in 1961, when the Indonesians invaded New Guinea.

The New Guinea issue was resolved in August 1962, when the United Nations took over western New Guinea, intending to transfer temporary control to Indonesia in May 1963 and to hold an election under its auspices no later than 1969 to determine the island's ultimate status. The Dutch had abandoned the Wamena outpost, and only a few missionaries remained, now perilously isolated. Left to themselves, the Dani had resisted the influence of missionaries and had revived the old war-like ways outlawed by the Dutch. But the world would not leave them alone for long. As soon as the territory was theirs, the Indonesians planned to bring immigrants from their overcrowded islands to settle and pacify the valley.

Using the map from his mother's notebooks, Michael traveled north for three days along the Baliem Valley floor, skirting villages in order to avoid contact with the inhabitants. Dutch government accounts of his mother's disappearance indicated that

Turner had reported his father's plane in the mountains beyond the north rim of the valley. Turner had not been contacted until 1961, when a Dutch patrol from Wamena had entered the area. It had been unable—or unwilling—to find the plane or search for his mother because of the hostility of the people of that area. The only clue Michael had to his mother's whereabouts was Turner's belief that she recognized the area he had described as the site of the crash. Michael hoped that the Wali Dani might have some knowledge of what had happened to her. They had remained isolated and had never been contacted by white men since his parents were rescued from their original trip in 1940. Expeditions into the area as late as 1962 had never returned.

Though he was too young to remember it, Michael's mother's disappearance had created an international stir at the time. She was a successful author, young and beautiful, and the Stanfords were a titled, famous family. The story had stirred the world's romantic imagination, but aerial searches had turned up nothing. Romance had turned to tragedy when one search party was killed by tribesmen, and the world, wearied by years of tragedies, had forgotten.

As Michael approached the area designated on the map as Wali Dani, he searched the sky for telltale signs of smoke from cooking fires, but the morning fog was still thick enough to disguise it. He could not be sure the village still existed. Villages moved as alliances changed, the land gave out, or wars destroyed them. His straining eyes caught no signs of the village and he was plunged into sudden despair. On his right a rain forest of casuarina trees grew along the Aike tributary. On his left were the curving limestone cliffs of the valley rim. Before him, a grassy slope climbed rapidly upward and became a giant rocky plateau reaching toward the Mountains of the Snow. The savanna ended in a cloud forest of great oaks and giant araucaria trees.

Nearby a black robin chat and a yellow whistler sang from the trees, but no human voices reached his ears. He stopped and looked more carefully at the distant river forest, familiarizing himself with it until he could finally make out the slender watch-towers rising against the thick green background of trees still laced with fog. He was flooded with relief as he started out again, quickening his pace. Thirty minutes later the sun had burned off the last remnants of fog, and on the rolling grassland before him, exposed white quartz sand gleamed like snow where grass and soil had been worn away by Dani feet.

Suddenly on the ridge of the hill before him there stood the lone figure of a warrior, standing on one foot, the other foot resting on his knee, balanced by the tall spear before him in a typical Dani pose. He was some five and a half feet tall, powerfully built with lean, narrow hips, muscular legs, and an indolent grace apparent even in repose. A *horim* rose from his loins, its tip decorated with a piece of cuscus fur. He wore braided armlets of bracken fern.

Michael had learned Dani from the extensive notes in his mother's journal. Still, there were subtleties of sound that could not be fully described, and he was not sure he would either understand the language or be able to make himself understood. He raised his hand toward the figure and called out a Dani greeting.

"Ye-we-yo."

There was no reply, and the figure did not move. Michael decided to approach him anyway. As he drew nearer, he could guess the man was perhaps ten years older than he. The warrior was staring at Michael with great curiosity and what appeared to be an undercurrent of excited recognition. Without moving or speaking he waited as Michael paused some ten feet away and spoke again.

"I am a friend, and I come seeking information about someone who once lived here."

"I am Amoli," the man replied. And then, as if to clarify it, he added, "Once called Pokat." He searched Michael's face as if he had expected some sign of recognition but found none, so he withdrew again to his noncommittal stance.

"These people." Michael fumbled for the photographs and realized his hands were now shaking. "I'm looking for information about these people," he repeated, and approached Amoli with the pictures.

He saw Amoli's eyes widen as he looked at the photos, and Michael's heart began to pound heavily within his chest.

"Do you know what has happened to them?"

Amoli handed him the photos and stared intently into his face as if debating something.

"Come," he said finally, and Michael realized, to his relief, that he had been able to make himself understood.

Balancing his spear, the warrior set out toward the village at a light run, never once looking back to see if Michael followed. When they arrived, Amoli crossed to the men's house and gestured for Michael to remain outside while he disappeared within. After what seemed like a long time he emerged followed by a thin old man, long past the vanity of the plucked body hair of youth.

"This is my *nami*, my mother's brother, Degewatek, and it is he alone who can tell you of the people you ask about."

The old man approached Michael, squinting his eyes to confirm what he had been told. He felt startled, even frightened, by what he saw before him, but then who was he, a mere man, to be surprised at the mysteries of life? So shrunken had his skin become that it was pulled back tightly around his skull, baring his teeth.

"I will take you to them," Degewatek said. His voice was high but strong.

"What do you mean by that?" Michael demanded. "Are they here? Alive?"

If the old man understood, he did not answer. Instead, taking Amoli's arm, he beckoned Michael to follow. The blood pounded in Michael's ears, and his throat constricted to the point of choking him. He had considered every possibility except one: that they were still alive. Stunned, he numbly followed the two men, scarcely noting that they had left the valley and begun to climb toward the Mountains of the Snow.

They climbed steadily for two hours. Here there were no signs of human life, but the number of birds and animals increased dramatically. Degewatek stopped often to regain his strength, but in spite of his feebleness, he appeared as driven as Michael to push on. Here and there patches of snow that had fallen in the night began to appear where the sun had not yet warmed the earth, and forests of conifer and oak fought for foothold in the thin, rocky soil. When they stopped to rest, the vista of the valley spread below them; even Wamena could be seen at the far end of the valley some forty miles away.

Ahead of the climbers stood two huge limestone domes, like sentinels, or portals, and Michael realized, without needing to consult his map, that they were approaching the lake. His excitement mounted as they entered a short strip of trees and emerged to see the lake stretching before them, a narrow, irregular band of blue surrounded by grassland and forest on one side and a sheer limestone wall on the other.

"There." Degewatek pointed to a hut some 100 yards away at the edge of the trees. It stood in the deep shade of the forest, resting on the grassland, just as his mother had described it, and his heart was in his throat. He tried to speak but could not. Yet even from this distance, as he studied it, he realized that the hut was small, too small to be a dwelling, and his newborn hopes sank within his heart. It was a Dani ghost house.

In a high singsong voice Degewatek began to tell a story, much as he would recite a myth, with gestures and no pauses for questions or interruptions. Flapping his arms over his head, Degewatek told of a great noisy bird that had come into the valley many years ago. It had been followed sometime later by the visit of the white man Mokatdege and his woman, Eken. They had made their home with the Dani, and those had been good times. Old enemies were defeated. Important wars were won, and Degewatek became the great *kain* of the Wali Dani.

Then Mokatdege and Eken had gone to live in the mountains, here, by this lake. And again the great bird came. It found them, and when Degewatek next visited the lake, they were gone. The hut was empty. Time again went by; only now there were bad omens. The sky to the east and north was filled at times with a red glow and strange distant thunder that didn't stop for days. From time to time the noisy giant birds returned, but the man did not. Mokatdege had told him that they were not birds at all but strange huts with wings called airplanes.

One day, when Degewatek was going alone into the mountains for salt, he saw one come down and crash into the mountain. Degewatek described how afraid he was, but conquering his fear, he journeyed a day and a half into the mountains to the place where the airplane went down. He found Mokatdege in it, unconscious. He took him from the plane. He was bleeding from a cut on his head and arm. Degewatek attempted to stop the flow of blood with leaves. Mokatdege did not wake, and the blood seeped slowly from the wounds. His life grew fainter. Degewatek demonstrated how he had then opened small wounds in the stomach in order to drain the bad blood that began to fester on the wounds. He had stayed there three days without leaving Mokatdege's side. He chanted, *"Hat nahalok loguluk!"* You are not going to die! He breathed into Mokatdege's ear, *oo-Phuh, oo-Phuh*, over and over, to persuade the *edai-egen* to stay with the body. But it did not. It left on the morning of the fourth day without Mokatdege's opening his eyes or speaking.

Degewatek paused in the telling of his story. A deep wail of grief escaped him, overcome with the memory, and he covered his head with his arms. When he recovered, he continued. He had carried the body of Mokatdege down the mountain to the lake. Remembering what Mokatdege had told him of the white man's customs, he buried him beneath the soil in a shallow grave and erected a ghost house to please the spirit.

But things had gone poorly for Degewatek from that time on. He had become ill; his third wife had died. He had failed to kill enemies in battle, and his leadership had been eroded by rivals. Others had freely stolen his pigs. He had been convinced the ghost of Mokatdege was unhappy and had brought this all about, possibly because his death could not be avenged. However, Mokatdege had told Degewatek that deaths were not avenged in the village where he had come from.

One day, out hunting with several other warriors, he had found the woman, Eken, with two porters from beyond the mountains. Degewatek now smiled at the memory of that meeting. She had been as glad to see him as he was to see her and had run toward him down the grassy slope. A lone white egret flew in the sky above her, its neck outstretched like an arrow, and suddenly Degewatek had known why the ghost was unhappy and punished him. It had wanted the woman with it, and she had been sent for that purpose. Degewatek demonstrated how he had raised his spear and sent it toward her. It had hit her here—he pointed toward his stomach—and she had fallen. One of the porters had drawn a stick and fired it, wounding one of the warriors who had raised his spear. The warriors with Degewatek had quickly drawn their bows and fired an arrow just as the porter fired a second shot. The arrow had struck him in the neck, and he had fallen. The other porters had had no sticks and turned to flee, but arrows had stopped them as well. The three Dani warriors had then fled in case the noise of the stick would bring others.

Degewatek had returned later for the body of the woman. He had taken it secretly to the lake and buried it beside Mokatdege with their hands touching so—Degewatek placed one of his hands over the other in illustration—just as he had often seen them touch each other. He found the gesture a strange one, but it had seemed always to give them pleasure, so he had done it that way.

Degewatek's story had come to an end, and his voice seemed to drift off with his thoughts. He stood staring into the lake, lost in his memories and his ghosts.

Michael, shaken by the truth he had sought so diligently, fought back the tears of frustration and rage at the waste, the ignorance, that had cost him his mother and perhaps his father as well. His father might have survived the crash with proper medical care instead of chants and prayers and the letting of blood. But it would do no good to vent his rage on this hapless, ignorant old man who had murdered his mother without being aware of his crime.

Michael started toward the ghost house. When he reached it and looked back, he found that Amoli and Degewatek had disappeared into the woods, leaving him alone to take out his rage on the ghost house. He destroyed it with his parang and strewed its remnants around the forest floor. Then he took the small pick and shovel from his backpack and began to overturn the earth, his anger now directed at what lay beneath him, at his father, whose torment and guilt had, in part, caused his son to be born illegitimate and his mother, whose pride had done the same. He felt the old bitterness burn within him . . . toward them both.

He worked feverishly but carefully, digging and scraping the soil away from the shallow grave until they lay before him just as Degewatek had described. The fury of his digging spent, he stood staring down at the fragile remains until the anger drained out of him, to be replaced by an overwhelming sense of loss. There was no room left for doubt. There was the ivory ring his father had worn on his little finger and the chain of gold with two pearls that had been around his mother's neck.

When they died, they had not been much older than he was now. They were forever young in his thoughts of them: not parents but peers.

Sobs shook within him, and he sank to his knees, touching his forehead to the ground between them, tears streaming down his face, until his tears, like his anger, had been purged from him.

He worked gently to remove the ivory ring from his father's finger. The wind was rising as a sudden storm came up, and he hastened to finish. He stood and was about to replace the earth when something stopped him. Whispers seemed to stir around him, though he knew it was only the rustling of the leaves and grass in the rising wind. Still, the sounds held him spellbound.

Ritual voices murmured around him.

"Who giveth this woman to this man?"

He was surprised to hear himself reply, "I do."

The wind carried the words off. The grasses sighed and were quiet. The rustling stopped. Then, with trembling fingers he knelt and began to slip the ivory ring onto his mother's left hand, the hand that touched his father's. The earth's whispers rose again around him.

"Do you, Catherine . . ."

"I do. . . ."

It came again more urgently. "Do you, Michael . . ."

"Yes . . . yes. . . ."

"Till death do thee part. . . ."

The storm was very near now. A heavy gray curtain completely hid the mountains. The air stirred around him as he came out of his reverie. He took up his shovel and began to work rapidly to replace the earth. The first shovelful fell into place, and his breath left him in a gasp of pain. It seemed so final, this burying the past.

He transplanted a small white orchid onto the bare earth that now covered the grave and spread leaves upon it to hide the scars. The grass and flowers would soon overrun the spot, and within a week not even he would be able to find it ever again.

With a final wrench he spoke softly to the earth before him.

"Good-bye."

New tears blinded his eyes. With fists tightly clenched he flung a final defiant challenge at the earth and sky that stirred around him.

"Let no god put asunder what man hath joined together."

Thunder rumbled on the mountain. He turned and headed toward the spot in the forest where Amoli and Degewatek had vanished. He did not look back.

He found Amoli waiting at the forest entrance. Degewatek sat alone on a rocky ledge beyond, crouched like a spider, looking out over his beloved valley. He was lost in his old man's thoughts and took no notice of Michael's return.

Michael offered his hand to Amoli in the Dani handshake of farewell. Amoli ventured a small smile which grew wide with relief as he took Michael's hand. Whatever the *waro* had come for was finished.

''Tell your uncle''—Michael nodded toward Degewatek on the rocks—''the ghosts will trouble him no more.''

The grin spread across Amoli's brown face. Michael broke away and started down the savanna's rolling hills. His feet, his spirit felt suddenly light. The warm brown earth smelled moist and musky, and the tall grass rippled sensuously before him. He thought of Kartini, and suddenly he knew he would return to Maitreya. Perhaps to teach at the new university in Banjarmasin. Perhaps to plant Maitreya again, on a communal basis with the village. The government would not be pleased to have him there, but by God, he would make it let him stay. However reluctantly, Patri would help him. At Maitreya he would be near Kartini, near enough to help her, near enough, perhaps, to love her as he knew he could.

He felt a surge of joy born of a newfound freedom, like the rolling grassland that stretched before him from here to the far southern mountain wall. He broke into a run, a long, easy stride.

Above him, on the limestone ridge that floated out over the valley, Degewatek watched him go and thought how he had seen that stride before, so long ago, when Degewatek himself was a young man not much older than the one who ran below him. He congratulated himself on how wise he had been not to burn the body in the Dani manner but to bury it instead. The man had returned to claim his ghost, just as Degewatek had hoped. Now his luck would change.

A cluster of bees came and sat upon the blue flowers that had taken root throughout the valley. Degewatek listened to their buzzing. The Dani had no name for either the insect or the blue flower. They did not belong in the valley. They had come with the *waro*. It was said that most of the *waro* who had come to the far end of the valley had now gone. Perhaps so, but the bees and the flowers remained. Degewatek knew, as surely as the bee stayed, the *waro* would return—like the bee, in numbers too large to kill, and the old ways would be gone forever.

But that would be long after he was gone. He would soon die, but the thought did not disturb him. He had already lived longer than most. For the time left to him, life would be good. There would be feasts and ceremonies, and there would be raids to avenge the spirits, just as there had always been since the time of Nopu. He would live and die without the world's knowing he had existed. Like Nopu, he would leave no words behind to tell of his deeds, his feats, his history. After all, death was part of life. Every moon, every year, every day, every wind comes and is gone. All blood, too, reaches its place of quietness. Only the spirit lives on.

He began to sing. Though his limbs had grown weak, his voice remained strong and clear, so he sent his song to fly in the wind and race along beside the retreating figure.

> Shall I depart as the gardens that withered?
> Will anything remain of my name?
> Nothing of my name on earth!
> At least my seed, at least my songs!

As he sang, the rain began to fall, like tears of mourning, cleansing the air and bringing forth life from dormant seeds, renewing the earth.

AUTHOR'S NOTE

The books and periodicals listed below were important historical and anthropological sources in the following areas:

I. The Grand Valley of New Guinea

Archbold, Richard. "Unknown New Guinea." *National Geographic,* 79.3:315–44, 1941.

———, A. L. Rand and L. J. Brass. Results of the Archbold Expeditions. No. 41. Summary of the 1938–1939 New Guinea Expedition. *Bulletin of the American Museum of Natural History,* 89.3: 197–288, 1942.

Gardner, Robert, and Karl G. Heider. *Gardens of War: Life and Death in the New Guinea Stone Age.* Random House, 1969.

Heider, Karl G. *The Dugum Dani: A Papuan Culture in the Highlands of West New Guinea.* Aldine Publishing, 1970.

Matthiessen, Peter. *Under the Mountain Wall.* Viking, 1962.

Temple, Philip. *Nawok!: The New Zealand Expedition to New Guinea's Highest Mountains.* J. M. Dent and Sons, 1962.

II. Indonesian Culture and History

Hughes, J. *Indonesian Upheaval.* McKay, 1967.

Kosut, Hal. *Indonesia: The Sukarno Years.* Facts on File, Interim History Series, 1967.

Neill, Wilfred. *Twentieth-Century Indonesia.* Columbia University Press, 1973.

Sjahrir, Sutan W. *Out of Exile.* John Day Co., 1949.

Vandenbosch, A. *The Dutch East Indies: Its Government, Problems, and Politics*. University of California Press, 1942.

Vlekke, B.H.M. *Nusantara: A History of Indonesia*. Rev. ed., Quadrangle Press, 1960.

Williams, Masylyn. *Five Journeys from Djaharta: Inside Sukarno's Indonesia*. Morrow, 1965.

III. World War II in the Pacific

Falks, Stanley L. *Bataan: The March of Death*. Norton, 1962.

Keith, Agnes. *Three Came Home*. Little, Brown and Company, 1947.

Lord, Walter. *Lonely Vigil: Coastwatchers of the Solomons*. Viking Press, 1977.

Morison, Samuel Eliot. History of the United States Naval Operations in World War II. Vol. III, *The Rising Sun in the Pacific*, 1948; Vol. XVI, *Victory in the Pacific*, 1960. Little, Brown and Company.

Morton, Louis. *The Fall of the Philippines*. Department of the Army, 1973.

Romulo, Carlos. *I Saw the Fall of the Philippines*. Doubleday, 1943.

Toland, John. *The Rising Sun: The Decline and Fall of the Japanese Empire, 1936–1945*. Random House, 1971.

Wainwright, Jonathan. *General Wainwright's Story*. Doubleday, 1946.

The EXPLORERS

WILLIAM STUART LONG

The romance and adventure that characterized the
settling and civilization of the Australian frontier continues in THE EXPLORERS, the fourth volume in "The
Australians" series. Against this colorful, sweeping
background of a nation yet untamed, the legacy of
beautiful Jenny Taggart prevails as Justin carries out
her vision to discover new and bountiful lands and the
promise of a new era.

"An exemplary historical saga." —*Publishers Weekly*

A Dell Book   12391-7 $3.50

Bestsellers

- ☐ **ELIZABETH TAYLOR:** The Last Star
  by Kitty Kelley.................................$3.95 (12410-7)
- ☐ **THE LEGACY** by Howard Fast....................$3.95 (14719-0)
- ☐ **LUCIANO'S LUCK** by Jack Higgins...........$3.50 (14321-7)
- ☐ **MAZES AND MONSTERS** by Rona Jaffe...$3.50 (15699-8)
- ☐ **TRIPLETS** by Joyce Rebeta-Burditt...........$3.95 (18943-8)
- ☐ **BABY** by Robert Lieberman.........................$3.50 (10432-7)
- ☐ **CIRCLES OF TIME** by Phillip Rock............$3.50 (11320-2)
- ☐ **SWEET WILD WIND** by Joyce Verrette......$3.95 (17634-4)
- ☐ **BREAD UPON THE WATERS**
  by Irwin Shaw..................................$3.95 (10845-4)
- ☐ **STILL MISSING** by Beth Gutcheon...........$3.50 (17864-9)
- ☐ **NOBLE HOUSE** by James Clavell..............$5.95 (16483-4)
- ☐ **THE BLUE AND THE GRAY**
  by John Leekley.................................$3.50 (10631-1)